[JYZE IN LOVE]

Annals of The Jyze Age

Jyzeburst

Jyzemelt

Jyze and Jyze Alone

Jyze in Love

Deep Jyze

The Jyze Millennium

Jyze of the Heavenly Year

Scat Jyze

Jyze in Love

G.P. Sandefjord

Annal Four of The Jyze Age

Cover art by GPS
Published by House of Jyze
ISBN 978-0-9964173-5-8
Library of Congress CIP pending
www.HouseOfJyze.com

For Ticiang

Jyzere est agere. (To jyze is to act.)

                        -- Seneca (apologies to)

BOOK I

[JAMR Jyze]

1

Comes crawling out of dreamland into a new year.
Five pips from the alarm. Of course to be thinking
straight at a time like this isn't even thinkable. So
how about crooked then?

Still in bed. Up in the loft. The little wall-
mounted lamp gives most of the light. The bruisingly
familiar tight quarters. One moment I'm lying prone
(wearing just a heavy red long-sleeve henley), the next,
as now, on my side, on the ancient orange sheet with
white pinstripes, head propped up on left forearm (still
dressed the same, though). The urge to yawn. The true
grog. (Here's the yawn.)

In dreams something about postponing publication of
the first issue of a new underground paper. We're stuck
way out in the Mentoka badlands and miss the last ferry
(on a river that must be the Mentoka itself). Karen A.
is present. Something sexy, mostly lost now, with her
splendid breasts.

Woke up in the middle of the night with an acid
gulp. I'm blaming it on the nightcap intended to
welcome in the Year of the Recluse. In general, though,
I think I'm doing dinner too close to bedtime.

Rain's still tapping lightly on the windows. It
was pretty much the promised stormy opening night, with
roaring winds and vines lashing sadistically on glass.

A new year, oh boy. One for jyzing around the
room: the nine jyzones of unit B-2. Also a matched pair
of Glennarian milestones. A deep strangeness bubbling
up, I do hope. I'll do my best. Or maybe it's just a
pipe dream. But whatever it may be, let 'er fly. My

5

hunch is I'll be able to squeeze in closer to the true
jyze.

A welter of five pillows. Mother's old white
electric blanket (unplugged) and my old scope-office
sleeping bag (unzipped to act as a second blanket). The
ceiling looming about twenty inches above the top of the
futon and, at this moment, maybe half an inch above my
scalp. By Pavlovian process I've learned to maneuver up
here without bumping the ceiling but it still does
happen occasionally. The usual culprit is an elbow and
the bang usually comes when I'm trying to readjust the
position of the slippery sleeping bag while half asleep.

It's not easy to find a comfortable jyzing posture
up here. Every minute or two, as already noted, I have
to shift positions and the tolerance for any one of them
keeps dwindling, that is, the physical strain is partly
cumulative. But so it goes -- and who can say, maybe
it's much the same out there in the real world, meaning
the portion of it (very large) outside the jyzones.

This loft is snugged into the northwest corner of
the room. I usually sleep at a diagonal with my head
near the corner itself (where the dark is darkest but
also the air is worst). Tan walls and ceiling, all
lightly stuccoed with a goose-pimply look and feel. A
bare two-by-four rail running lengthwise on the outer
(south) side of the loft-top platform guards against
falls (the drop is six feet) but whether this rail would
actually stop an energetic nightmare-powered flip or
thrash, for instance, I have my doubts. Fortunately
nightmares don't normally work that way on me, at least
not so far as I know. Or perhaps I should say at least
they haven't yet.

A cubical bookstand, about a foot on all sides,
also made of heavy-bore unfinished lumber, rises from
the southwest corner of the platform like a small
blockhouse. Directly above it hangs the reading lamp,
the upper rim of its shade flush against the ceiling. A
small black digital clock radio perches on the cube
itself. Half a dozen books nest within, including the
big black volume of "Lofty Essays" (my title for it)

which I've been chipping away at for months as bedtime
reading. Arrayed on the bare wood surface between the
edge of the futon and the edge of the platform, and
almost beneath the rail, are more books, a small faux-
antique "colonial" battery clock (which once stood
proudly on Mother's nightstand: this is the one that
emits the five pips), a quote notebook, a stack of
miscellaneous periodicals, flashlight, roll of paper
towels, and my still virginal jyze dreambook.

But I'm moving into dreams now, yes I am. Last
night I neglected to wear my nightshirt inside-out (as
advised by the Heian court ladies for anyone courting
dreams) and I still caught me a pretty good one. Nor do
I intend to censor anything. On the contrary, I expect
most if not all -- okay, all -- of the bawdy action I'll
be seeing this year will come from dreams and thus I'll
want to make as much of them as I possibly can.

Could be tedious too. The whole schmear. If so,
though, I'll be content anyway. I'm going right ahead
with it. Jyze likes to be entertaining if it can be.
If it can't be, or if it can but it doesn't come
naturally at any particular moment, well, to heck with
it. Just bore away. (And how about that for a jyzey
New Year's resolution!)

All jyze sessions will attempt to be like this one,
going down in a real place here in unit B-2 or at the
hideaway office or the storage unit or, once the job
starts up again, the scope office. We're talking JIRT,
jyze in real time. A toilet flushing on the other side
of the wall and like that, as for instance right now
pressure-induced pain is mounting in the small of my
back and the side of my neck and also in my general
bladder area (and I haven't even tried to describe the
pillowcases yet, not to mention Karen's breasts in the
dream -- if only I could have them back briefly for
modeling purposes) (of course I could go by memory of
the real-life flesh, but this is not, after all, the
memory palace; maybe next year for that).

-- That's right, I'm still steering clear of the
memory palace. Instead -- well, I've said it already.

[Jyze in Love]

*   *

Recluse. Isolato. "Artyr." It won't be a year
for a lot of socializing, no. However, I do have a
dinner engagement lined up for tonight. Will it be the
last until next year? Quite possibly.

I'll have to begin dressing for this engagement
even while jyzing away. Just over an hour until the bus
pulls out. And here I sit in green terrycloth robe and
ancient fleece-lined moosehide moccasins, my hair still
wet. A combination of aspirin and pounding hot water
seems to have driven away the headache generated by the
cumulative strains of the recumbent loft jyze session.

This at the rectangular redwood worktable standing
diagonally across the room from the loft. The walls
above and to the side still bear the same array of jyze
posters painted up during last fall's high period of
jyzo eruptions. Today I'm not one whit less pleased
with them. "The Things Jyze Makes Me Do." (You go,
jyzer!) And I'm hoping the new year will see some new
activity in this same realm, and again not only as a way
to counter the social void but -- of course! -- for its
own fine sake. "For Jyze You Know You Must." (That's
one of those high-period jyzos that's already made it
onto a poster and also become a J-book title -- for No.
8, the previous one -- and even so it still grabs me.)

One slight correction regarding this morning's
entry. For jyze venues I won't be limiting myself
strictly to the four sites listed there, I've decided,
but rather will also include the buildings in which
those sites are located and the courtyards outside.
Thus the hallways, staircase landings, lobbies,
bathrooms, conference rooms, laundry room, so-called
workout room, along with any lesser nooks and crannies
presently known or yet to be discovered (by me): all are
hereby certified eligible.

Any other revisions in the ground rules that might
be necessary as the year proceeds I'll try to remember
to mention in these pages. Probably won't be many, if
any. Otherwise all the standard jyze conventions from
previous years will remain in force. Keep it real

simple, that's what it's all about. When in doubt, KIRS. An acronym to build a jyze oath on. KIRSes!

Today's engagement: a delayed holiday get-together at brother Rob's place serving also as a kind of going-away party for cousin Kar and his wife, the newly name-changed Kerani, nee Elaine.

Five-ten. Now a towel's draped around my hips (robe's off) so as not to offend or traumatize anyone out in the alley tall enough to see in the west windows. (The blinds on both of those windows stay permanently one-third raised so the Santa Claus hardy fuchsia perched on the inside windowsill -- and now blooming again -- will receive as much light as possible.)

And so having thoroughly embarrassed myself and the art/act of jyze I prepare to clomp off to the bus stop.

*   *

Surprisingly it's a day later. Mixing too much wine and whiskey at Rob's place whirled me into a stupor by the time I arrived home last night. So now I get to try my luck in one of the other rooms of the "my room" I'll be jyzing around this year: the office of Jyzer Ink, also known as "suite 225" and "the hideaway." This is down in the historic quarter near the southern end of the same two-mile-long "bipolar zone" (or more accurately it's tripolar, a very shallow isosceles triangle) whose borders I rarely ventured outside of last year and expect to cross even less this year.

-- Pause to slip off sweatshirt.

A few minutes ago I finished drawing up a schedule calling for completion of the "Jyzer" raw draft by the end of this month. During the same period I'll be fleshing out the working outline for the second volume of the Mentoka series, "Mentoka Dreams," which I hope to be jumping into immediately after "Jyzer" -- the very next day, if possible. My aim here is at least to go down swinging on the whole damn trilogy.

The party was enjoyable. In our winter coats Kar and I babbled out on the garage-roof deck, drinks tinkling in our hands, as he barbecued the salmon. Rob showed me a personal photo album I'd never seen before.

[Jyze in Love]

(I was impressed by his labeling, which resembles what I
keep intending to do for my own albums but never get
around to.) All seven of us, including, to my surprise,
both of Kar's sons, bellied up to the kitchen table for
the feast. I liked Aaron better this time, especially
his tale about roasting a religiously didactic play in a
review he wrote for his high-school newspaper. Kerani
explained why she'd changed her name and I was truly
touched; even invited her out for dinner sometime before
she leaves town so she can tell me about her travels in
India and the ashram from which her new name, which
means "Sacred Bells," derives. (Her massage school, it
turns out, is well within the tripolar zone, about a
ten-minute walk from B-2. And although Kar has already
started the new job, she won't be joining him until
early February and maybe she'll be lonely. Thus my
social life might flare up one more time, feebly, before
guttering out completely.)
     -- So for about the cost of a fast-food burger meal
a day I'm granted use of this hideaway office here.
Much as I love the place, I'm less and less pleased to
be laying out the bucks for it. In other words, nerves.
Crunch time directly ahead. In early February I'll be
starting up the Jyzer Ink nightscoping work again after
a four-month layoff; and not long after that, or maybe
even before, the funds set aside for the layoff will be
running out. By the end of March I'll need to come up
with an amount about six times that of the rent here
just to meet monthly expenses. I'll also need to
rebuild a cushion for the inevitable slow scoping
months. Almost certainly I'll be raiding the deep
reserves for some of this. The only question, really,
is: For how much? And exactly when to do it? Ideally,
wait until I know what my taxes will be for this past
year. But that may be cutting it too close.
     Uneasy financial times ahead. It might be mid
April or even later before I get a good feel for what
the rest of the year will hold in that respect.
     The new Jyzer Ink business license is up already, I
want to report -- proudly! -- the words "Post

conspicuously" again winking conspiratorially as the paper flutters above the small fan by the door.

(The weather is still unseasonably warm and this is making the building interior unusually warm too. The urge is upon me to strip down further. But also upon me is the urge to resist that urge. Why bother to unbutton the outer shirt when I'll just have to button it back up again in a few minutes?)

All the above leading nowhere. Fine. How it is.

(On the office carpet I found a belated Christmas card from my old high-school sports semi-buddy Grady W. Several times over the past decade he's sent me one, apparently as some sort of church project. What's interesting this year, he says he obtained my new address from our high-school alumni directory -- just out -- and the address is a little off; the suite number is 3225 instead of 225. This time the mailman caught it, but other times maybe he hasn't or won't. Thus any former classmate trying to reach me by mail might fail. And I need all the social hope I can lash into existence. So -- dang!)

But no, to repeat, I won't be looking for a social life this year. Nor do I really need one, except in a craven, neurotic, truly pitiable way. Nor do I need one in that way either, damn it. "Get a life." "Don't want one, thank you very much." -- Or if I'm to have one, or even a small part of one, it would be well advised to seek me out and catch me at a vulnerable moment (of which, to be sure, plenty have been bubbling up in the past few years, and likely will continue doing so).

(This good news must be mentioned: the potato crop just coming in is said to be a "double bumper." Bakers could be going for fifteen, even ten cents a pound. Already I've seen them selling for two bits a pound at the public market. And these are grade A spuds, top of the crop.)

Meanwhile I need to work off some unexpected holiday pounds I've put on, a full belt notch's worth. Yesterday's twin feast -- Rob's salmon spread, plus I did an orange Danish pig-out for a special New Year's

[Jyze in Love]

Day breakfast -- clinched it. -- Of this pastry I
bought an extra can (it's the pop-out type) since I'd
made a special trip to the backup supermarket at the far
northern extreme of the tripolar zone to fetch the first
one, and if the sell-by date is to be taken seriously,
this second can will last until about February 19. So
I'm setting it aside for the holiday closest to that
date: Valentine's Day. Between now and then I'll be
locked down in a severe no-frills chow regimen.

     (And I see the "library-quality" black bookbinder
tape with which I patched up several deteriorating
binders is itself bleeding a sticky substance where the
tape presses against the vinyl. A scary reminder of
jyze mortality and all other kinds as well.)

     Down with the old newsstand calendars! (In fact
the new ones have already been up for weeks, right
behind the old.) Be gone, damn year! (The new year
won't be taking any more notice of the old. Not if jyze
can help it. All those sad stories: dead. Even if no
new stories come along. Instead, new anti-stories.
Ghost stories. Dream stories. Which is to say, or at
least I hope so: jyze plenty jyzey enough.)

                          2

     Jyzin' in the play zone. Seems I couldn't wait --
J-day's not until tomorrow. Though at two-twenty a.m.
we're technically there already -- and so officially as
well -- and I can say this because when it comes to jyze
I'm Da Man.

     First thought was to start out in the dressing
jyzone. Even went so far as to snap on the lamp in the
nook there (and it remains on now, directly at my back,

making for shifty J-book shadows). Then noticed how hot
that nook was with the heater on. Yet didn't want to
turn the heater off since it's the only one for the
whole room and mama it's cold outside.

So now: stretched out on the carpet in the middle
of the open floor. Lying prone, in a north/south
alignment, feet planted almost directly beneath the
nerfhoop (seven feet beneath, or say somewhere between
six and seven depending on which part of the actual
flesh-and-blood foot), J-book resting a few inches from
the south wall's baseboard (atop which squiggles a brown
speaker wire, stapled there by me). To the left, the
bottom shelves of a foldable wooden bookcase; straight
ahead and above, the wall itself, kept bare in this area
for wallball caroms during my workout sessions; to the
right, the lower reaches of the foldable wooden end
table next to the couch (a/k/a "loveseat"). Tucked
between the long legs of the end table, a stereo speaker
which looms about fifteen inches away and seems to be
glaring down at me, the three circular forms pressing
from inside against the oval of black fabric composing
the eyes and much-larger mouth of a ghostly "The Scream"
face. Dolorous piano jazz issuing quietly therefrom.

Why this? Why now? Maybe just a bold move to
carve out something a little different. In any case,
I'm pleased to yield to the urge -- and even more
pleased such an urge should arise.

Hot news: the hardcover version of "Memorials" is
here and it looks much better than expected. Other hot
news, not so good: the week's been almost entirely a
bust for my own work, and not solely because of the need
to shift time to "Memorials"-related tasks (of which
there have been, however, many). In short, more crisis
over exactly what it is I'm trying to do with the
Mentoka trilogy and specifically with "Jyzer." And the
good side of this bad news, the crisis seems to have
passed after sparking some alterations in the grand
scheme which will permit yet another new beginning -- or
rather new continuation, since except for a couple of
gimmicks things will be picking up pretty much from

where they left off a week ago.

Pushing on. Hoping against hope I can stick it out all the way to the end. But forced to acknowledge I'm quickly running out of wiggle room.

(And tempted by the old stuff, the protojyze: how I'd love to go back and tighten it up a bit, which is to say: make it more jyzelike. On the other hand, how I'd love to latch onto another desktop computer so I could do some of the revisions ("layerings") on "Jyzer" and its Mentoka successors -- and maybe do some of the scoping too -- right here in unit B-2.)

Already I've checked the lobby once tonight for the arrival of the new J-day's first outside-world news hit. Hadn't come yet. Now, an hour after that initial run, I can't hold back any longer on the next one.

*

Yup, it's here. "The night paper." Still the same stinky blue plastic wrapper. Latest wrinkles on a prominent national right-wing politico's shady maneuverings to elude seemingly airtight ethics charges. In my apple-juice bottle, a new batch of guava juice ensorceled into being from the very last remaining package of the old pink powder, a kind of detritus from the end-time with the once, the now, the forevermore Lady U, also known to me on occasion as Madam Ex. Floorboard creakings of my overhead neighbor "Claire Voyant." His buzzer sounds frequently and at most hours of the day and night and so do lots of sharp footfalls. Can't help wondering: just what is it he's pushing up there? But I've never met him and for that matter a good many others around here. Happily or not, I can now say the residents of this building keep to themselves at least as much as I hoped they would from the start.

J-book still laid out flat on carpet. An overall light brown, this rug, with individual fibers spanning the spectrum from creamy tan to dark brown. Short fibers. Deep plush this is not. But the stuff wears well: that's what's best about it. Being up close to it like this puts me in mind of other carpets I've come to know intimately, especially while catnapping in downtown

offices during the era of long-distance commuting.
Surprisingly, this one seems free of the chemical
bouquet most of those others gave off.

(I'm just noticing the shims still faithfully
propping up the legs of the bookcase and end table --
the legs farthest from the wall, of course, since the
bunching of the ill-fitting carpet next to the baseboard
otherwise causes the furniture to tilt slightly toward
the center of the room, making for an eerie drainfield
effect. -- Today, by the way, being the first day of
Ramadan, the new moon having been officially sighted: a
better time than most to ratchet up one's belt-
tightening semifast another notch.)

So "Memorials." The printer, it turns out, is
located deep in the heartland, a long way from the
publisher on the far coast, and thus the shipping delays
become a bit more understandable. Thirty-two books in
the box, each individually wrapped in cellophane. No
obvious flaws. I think the author would be pleased.
Also his oldest daughter. I know I am as his oldest
grandchild. And more than that, relieved. At times it
seemed the odds against anyone's actually seeing this
book in print had soared to near infinite.

Now I've had to cough up another forty bucks for
mailer boxes, which no one in town has on hand in the
proper size, so more waiting awaits. And more expenses
for postage. And more time loss. But none of this is
all that troubling. Far outweighing it is the pleasure
of being able to fulfill ol' Mom's dying wish. (Not
just dying wish. A lifelong wish, or half lifelong
rather, from the time her father died and she took
charge of completing his unfinished manuscript.)

Letters off to aunts, uncles, cousins, Mom's exes,
others. (And I did finally hear from her final ex, Jim
Q., who's gone south to their old winter digs for six
weeks or so. He even enclosed a delayed Christmas check
for fifty bucks -- down fifty, alas, from last year.
Says maybe he'll be swinging back up this way to see Rob
and Gail and me this summer. If he does, that would max
out my social calendar for the year and then some.)

[Jyze in Love]

-- Every now and then the small of my back starts
twingeing. Unlike up in the loft, here I can relieve
the ache by rising to my hands and knees, and just did.
Jyze on in a kneeling posture. On all fours, I was
about to say, and actually that's not wrong: two knees
and not two hands but two elbows, with the left elbow
bearing most of the upper-body weight and the left
forearm and hand propping up my head at the chin. Like
a toppled statue of The Thinker, I'm thinking -- but
then by the jyze rules themselves jyzers shouldn't be
thinking too much. Worshipping the jyze deities on
elbows and knees, though, as now, is to be encouraged.

Heavy green long-sleeve henley, black sweats, the
horrible white cheapo rubber jumping shoes. These shoes
I always change out of before I leave the room, even if
only to make a two a.m. lobby run. I bought them
because they were the last pair of any color of this
particular sturdy imported brand available anywhere in
Jyze City as far as I could tell and word had it that no
more would be allowed into the country. But in the year
since then I've seen plenty of them for sale, in many
colors and even cheaper.

Later today I'll be visiting brother Rob in the
Yuke (university quarter) during his dinner break to
deliver his copies of "Memorials." He's too busy with a
January clearance sale to be able to stop by here and I
know how eager (and anxious) he is to see the completed
book, so I figure I might as well take a jaunt out that
way. Anything to bring into my daily life a little
variety (however limited -- this being just one more in
the long-running jyze series of returns to various old
stomping grounds) and a little human contact as well.

Today's also the day Kerani ordinarily stays in
town to teach an evening class. If she'd really wanted
to get together I expect she would've called. Or maybe
something came up and forced her to put it off until her
next evening class a week from now. Or could be it's
payback time for my many delays in contacting her and
Kar over the past year or so. In truth I was looking

forward to a little female companionship -- strictly
conversational, to be sure -- and I'm disappointed.
But not really surprised, no. Fits right in with my
extended streak of social botches and contretemps.

   Again, enough for this deviant all-fours posture.
-- Any final observations, though? Last call!
-- Noticing now the long row of numbered volumes
standing on the bottom shelf of the bookcase just to my
left and the seventeenth-century English protojyze
grandmaster's painted portrait on the cover of the
volume at the end gazing out from between the supports.
Usually I meet up with this face in the bathroom --
numerous times per day, in fact, since the volume I'm
currently gnawing away at in there rests with the cover
peering upward atop the toilet tank -- so to encounter
it down here is odd, sort of like running into an old
friend in an unexpected part of town.

*   *

   Lofty thoughts again. The lamp on. Seemingly very
early a rampaging vacuum cleaner awakened ---

*

   Right there I learned something. The phone rang
and for some reason -- first time ever while up in the
loft -- I decided to answer it. A strange impulse. And
I made it down just before the answering machine clicked
on. Dismounting via that steep and narrow loft
staircase wearing just the usual red henley nightshirt,
still half-asleep, a little stiff and sore and bloated
and tumefied in the usual wake-up ways -- I could easily
have taken a nasty spill. (And even without doing so
would've made quite a comical sight, I suspect, had a
passerby been glancing in my courtyard window at just
the right moment and from just the right angle.)
   Possibly I was thinking the caller might be Kerani.
Yes. For lunch. Because yesterday at the same hour I
was thinking the same thought. -- But it was Rob,
letting me know about a change in his work schedule.
He'd be closing the store, he said, and so he couldn't
meet me until two hours later than previously agreed.
Would that be okay? My groggy replies -- but fine,

17

sure, seven o'clock, I'd be there. Then the alarm went
off up in the loft and wouldn't stop its five-pip bursts
on its own and I clambered back up in a hurry almost as
awkwardly as I'd come down.

     And I've stayed here. The warm bed. Double tick
of the two clocks, always right in sync (so different
from those crazy manual alarm clocks in potato-chip cans
that provided "red noise" for daytime sleeping back in
my former life). "On all fours" again now, like down on
the carpet -- discovering I can too, after all, do it up
here. Just enough room overhead, like a crawl space,
literally. (But this time half-naked -- the lower half
-- and now with free-swinging heat-drooping genitals,
so the feeling's quite different. And I can brace my
bare posterior against the ceiling for firmer full-body
jyzestick control, and am so doing. And the futon's a
lot easier than the carpet was on the knees and elbows.)

     Also I see a new black stain on the orange sheet.
Interestingly it's an almost perfect four-sided diamond,
size of, say, a large mascara-stained teardrop. -- From
tossing the pen down with the cap off when I scrambled
to answer the phone. "Jyze spilled in the sheets."
Literally. A lifetime first for me I'm all but certain.

     Dreams. Reading old protojyze with Lady V, hers
and mine. Unk Erik telling me about the proudest
moments of his post-divorce stay in his garret apartment
as he helped me move into the one down the hall --
something puzzling about fire hazards reduced. Must've
been prompted by psychic pressure from the fire station
standing right across the street from his bedroom.

     I had some other dream material and hoped to
salvage still more but then the call scattered the
remnants and blocked all return wormholes. Lady S was
in there too -- I was trying to remember in just what
way when the call came. A shame, because how often does
one's waking dream come true that an old love will
reappear in one's sleeping dream, to say nothing of two
old loves at once? But of course in truly deep
dreamland it might happen all the time with no one ever
the wiser.

[JAMR Jyze]

     So anyway: it turned out the vacuuming didn't wake
me up "very early" after all. Three or four minutes
early at most. It just seemed early because I was so
tired, and I don't know why that was. I clicked off the
lamp at four-twenty a.m. (after being able to plow ahead
only a single paragraph in the sixteenth-century French
essay grandmaster's magisterial treatise on women, one
of his best and the sexiest by far -- actually titled,
for camouflage purposes, as if it were about classical
poetry), so I slept seven and a quarter hours, which
usually is plenty. Tired eyes. But I'm fine now.
     Have I explained yet about the flashlight? (I
think not!) I have to turn off all the room lights
before climbing up here at night, but the loft reading
lamp can be reached from floor level only by clambering
atop the back of the armchair, which is a cumbersome
process by itself and also risky: the armchair's shaky
and injury-prone; and if it should collapse, so am I.
So I use the flashlight to ascend the loft stairs in the
dark, sort of like a spelunker trying to scrabble up to
a high hidden rock platform in a cave, the light beam
lurching crazily about with each shift of handholds.
(It's the shortage of handholds that makes climbing up
to the loft, and down too -- more -- so tricky. I've
hit on a fairly good way to do it but even when I'm not
in a hurry it's still awkward and a bit perilous,
something like going up or down a rickety stepladder
planted on soft ground with your back to the ladder.)
     A foot to the left of my left foot and only inches
above eye level as I write now, the nozzle of the main
B-2 fire sprinkler juts out from the ceiling like the
outer phalange of a metallic middle finger. If it ever
went off while I was up here, I might drown or be hurled
against the wall and pinned there like, say, a fire-
hosed protester. Nor do I know for sure what would set
it off. Is a heat detector built into it? Would torrid
mating behavior do it? Or since it's highly, even
laughably unlikely that mating behavior of any type or
intensity will ever take place up here, how about the
mere thought of mating behavior? Mere dreams of it?

19

[Jyze in Love]

    Mere dreams is right. -- But I've again exceeded
the loft discomfort level for jyzing. (Yet must add
this final thought: did the presence of the sprinkler
maybe set off, in a sense, the dream about Unk Erik and
the fire hazards?)

                        *   *

    Odd place to feel I've hit bottom. Or finally
reached ground zero, as for some reason I seem to want
to think of it. But it's the B-2 bathtub, filled almost
to brimming with hot water, my pinkly and hairily naked
body simmering almost amniotically herein. Doing the
jyze thing at last on my proudly self-customized
bathboard, beneath the extender-arm lamp swiveled out
across the bathmat from the jerry-rigged sink-side cedar
shelves. A towel rests under my jyzing hand -- slides
along beneath it, back and forth, margin to margin -- to
act as a kind of sweatband in hopes of keeping this J-
book dry.
    So what's my new beef? But -- correction -- it's
not new. Same old. I'm up against it. Period. I
realized this shortly after handing Rob his copies of
"Memorials." The release. Though distribution tasks
remain, they're minor. The main obligation has been
met. No longer will it serve as either a psychic drain
or an excuse for not plunging ahead on the real work.
    Says it as well as anything: I've run out of
excuses. Time to put up or shut up on "Jyzer." (All
the same old pep-talky cliches. Of course! But whereas
before an at least slightly anticipatory angle existed
for invoking them, now the authentic end of the line
looms. Do it or else it won't happen.)
    Entirely appropriate to be pink and naked and hairy
and simmering at this moment. Likewise to be pausing
every few lines to mop my brow. (And being careful not
to lean forward too far, because if I do, the brow, even
if freshly mopped, might drip on the page.)
    Twenty-five days until scoping starts up again.
Sabbatical (so-called) ends. A major component of the
old life clicks back into place and the walls of the new
life start closing in again.

[JAMR Jyze]

Can willpower do the work of the "Jyzer"
imagination? I'm all inspired out. So why not go back
to sheer grinding? Once again defer until later any
worries about rhythm, beauty, sense. Once again observe
wistfully that those qualities just might decide to pop
up on their own no matter how grim I feel. -- But if
they don't, they don't: repeat that grim tautological
fact too. And by all means remind myself not even to
hope for anything.

     -- Twisting and squirming, trying not to make
splashes or waves or swells or seiches. The most
physically comfortable bathtub jyzing posture, I'm
discovering, is an odd one: torso listing about thirty
degrees to port, left arm resting against the top of the
tub side wall (gunwale?), with forearm and hand raised
to prop up head. Meanwhile the J-book rides atop the
board crosswise and directly above the same side wall
and the jyzing arm (elbow and forearm) rests on the
board and works across my chest and only inches in front
of it. (Is this clear enough for some future
instruction manual, the chapter on bathtub jyzing?
Maybe not quite.) Legs meanwhile stretched out straight
underwater and crossed at the ankles, feet propped
against the side of the narrow far tub wall just beneath
the faucet and on either side of the overflow drain, all
ten toes sticking out. Count 'em -- yes, ten. And in
spite of everything they're wriggling contentedly just
the way the sages of idleness say they should be.

     Could describe more parts of this apparitional pink
hairy body (never before witnessed entirely naked in the
jyzing state, if memory serves -- not even by the jyzer
himself). Could rhapsodize about all this gleaming
sanitized bathroom whiteness. Or could wrench myself
out of it before I'm permanently heat-bent into this
ludicrous contorted posture.

                   *   *

     To finish up I'm calling myself back on the carpet.
The wiry short-haired brown carpet. But this time my
body (here it is again, always hanging around, always
demanding to be part of the jyze action) -- this time

21

this newly cleansed and still heat-glowing body is
stretched out at a different angle with respect to the
end-table lamp. In this position the shadow moves along
directly beneath the J-stick instead of dragging behind
it in the very spot a jyzer most needs to see. A big
improvement. Wish I'd thought of this last night.

No other new insights. No new keys. So instead
I'll mention a few of the week's triumphs. Oddly enough
there were some. Minor, yes -- extremely minor -- but
still, maybe a sign of better times ahead. (Or at least
pretty to think so, yeah.)

First, for months I've been needing a larger
breadboard and a cake pan but dreading to spend the
money. Then late one night during a lobby newspaper run
I came upon a pile of domestic items dumped on the mail
counter beneath a "Free Stuff" sign. Among them: a
large breadboard and a cake pan. Now all I have to do
is scrub or chip the gunk off them both and sterilize
them with boiling water and they're good to go.

Second, ever since moving in I've been thinking
about putting up shelves in B-2's bizarre interior
entrance hallway (almost ten feet long!). The day after
finding the kitchen items, I noticed something odd while
bending to put clothes into the dryer in the building
laundry room: the wall underneath the permanent "Free"
table there seemed to have moved in closer. Then I
realized what I was seeing was a stack of designer
cinder bricks. Sixteen of them! A perfect fit for the
shelving boards packed away in my storage unit! And all
mine for the taking, or so I presumed (and very
reasonably, I'd say). Thus the big new triple stack of
designer cinder bricks now shoved up against my
interior hallway wall.

And third, a different kind of triumph -- a
conceptual one, I guess. After bugging me for years, it
finally dawned on me what the loft reminds me of. As
seen from outside, with the lamp glowing on the counter
inside, it's like the "forts" I built as a kid with
Dad's hand-me-down set of wooden blocks. I would set up
a small flashlight inside the blocky finished structure

and then, with my head down at floor level (as now), peer in, and from that perspective the creation looked wondrously lifelike and life-size -- just as the loft does now. And in fact is. And: those wooden blocks of Dad's were made from two-by-fours and four-by-fours just as most of the support structure of the loft is, except the blocks were of course much shorter and sanded better and shellacked.

(Week of mudslides, potholes, sinkholes, a massive cleanup in the aftermath of the giant storms of the "Twelve Days of Christmas" period. All regional intercity passenger-train runs have been canceled until February.)

And just to mention: I had to fight off a nostalgia attack during the hour with Rob. Because his former favorite cafes have all banned smoking, he now takes his breaks at outdoor sites, choosing among eight or ten on the basis of wind direction, rain access, sun angle, grodiness of other occupants, whether students are lined up nearby for a movie, and so on. This time we sat on the sheltered outdoor benches at the very bank branch where I opened my first account in this town. And still standing right across the street, still drawing a good crowd, was the movie theater where Lady U and I nearly wore out a row of seats all by ourselves (in those days it was a rerun repertory house, with new double features showing daily). The flashing marquee over there seemed to create an eerie feeling of something like infinite regress, as if Rob and I were now sitting in a slightly larger theater watching a movie of those days in which Lady U and I were sitting in the theater across the street watching a movie of an earlier theater where.... (And Rob patiently lighting his pipe before cracking open "Memorials": how he reminded me of Dad prepping for "a serious talk about your future" in his study.)

But no more visits with Rob for a while. No more nostalgia either. I'm out here all alone and up against it. A crucial time. Pussyfooting's banned. Sink or swim. Throw together a complete raw draft of "Jyzer" (and then light it up inside!) or drop the idea forever.

3

Grim week. Now grim Friday night. Cold and rainy;
I just traversed the portion of it between here and the
only real bookstore. "Here" -- the hideaway. Suite
225. Brown armchair. Jangly live rock music throbbing
up through the floor as usual on weekend nights.

What's my gripe this time? First, another "Jyzer"
crisis, though again I seem to have weathered it, my
resolve undiminished to push on to the end (but with
little to show for real progress so far). Second, and
much more damaging in the long run -- I'm all but
certain -- another nasty letter came in from sister
Barb. It threw me into a tailspin for two full days
while I tried to stomp down the urge to break off with
her once and for all. Succeeded, I think, but I also
know things will never be the same with us.

Her poison-dart notes. Indignant accusations. A
single mildly irreverent line in my Christmas card to
her was enough to set off a tirade. The offending
phrase this time was "spiritual stuff."

I wrote back -- appended a couple of sentences to a
brief letter about "Memorials," though she's already
said she has no interest in seeing the book which Mother
and I (not to mention the genealogist himself) put so
much work into -- and said her note raised vast issues
which I don't want to be battling over with her or with
anyone. Suggested she go back and read the offending
phrase in the way it was intended, that is, as friendly
and mildly irreverent. But in truth it no longer
matters how she reads it, because I'm finished. I just
don't want to state it flat-out and (A) cause

unnecessary pain, and (B) (probably more to the point) violate my death-bed promise to Mother not to "abandon" Barb no matter how outrageous her provocations.

I won't abandon her. I'll simply abandon hope we can maintain even a marginally decent brother-sister relationship.

It's really too painful to write about. I don't have the heart to spell out the details.

Such a fury I was in. Somehow -- just barely -- I'd kept the door open to her for these past fourteen months despite all that happened before. Turned out it was the negative version of a grace period.

There won't be another. I absolutely cannot bear any more of this.

*

And what about this jyze right here? I'm thinking it might not survive the rigors of the "Jyze Around My Room" scheme -- a/k/a JAMR -- and therefore the scheme needs modifying. Best to loosen it up a bit. Say just part of each entry, not the whole thing, must go down in unit B-2 (or here in 225, or at the scope office or the storage unit, or elsewhere in the buildings containing these four sites).

Seems jyze, just like the jyzer himself, still needs to be able to look forward to getting out some.

Now trying to think of things to say about this past week. Other things.

There's this. Kerani didn't call.

And this. The annual tax forms finally arrived, forwarded by the post office from the old backwoods address. After doing some rough computations I'm satisfied the quarterly prepayments I've been sending in for Jyzer Ink will cover everything, even including a fairly hefty (for me) last-minute "surprise gouge" from the accountant who's helping Barb with Mother's estate (I'm figuring such a gouge is all but certain, just like last year). Fortunately it appears I'll be able to get away with deducting the rent I pay on this office right here as a business expense -- and in fact this deduction is the key to my staying within the prepaid amount.

[Jyze in Love]

        And -- an article appeared in yesterday's paper
about gentrification of my current home hood. In the
foreground of one photo stands my puny little five-story
U-shaped apartment building. Right behind it, sketched
in by computer magic, looms the much larger structure
(ten stories) that will soon be going up there -- with
its south wall rising about twelve feet north of my
apartment's door, that is, B-2's. This is not really
news. But to see the size of the thing in black and
white is -- graphic, yeah. Although no groundbreaking
date is given, it's clear that when the first bulldozer
arrives I'll be needing a major upgrade of my "red
noise" device for daytime sleeping.
        And -- many of the sidewalk-overhang roofs around
town are still leaking from damage caused by the Boxing
Day storm (the weight of waterladen snow having buckled
many of the metal panels). This is true often enough
that you're generally better off walking in the rain
than under the roofs.

                    *   *

        -- So now, some six hours later, slouched down on
the jyze throne itself: the one and only funky green
armchair. Not that this will be going anywhere, this
second segment of the entry. Just so I can say I've
complied with the "two attempts" clause in the jyze
rules and therefore can claim the first exemption of the
year.
        Stacks of printed matter in various forms mounting
ever higher on the couch just beyond my feet. The
fuchsia nuzzling in close to my right shoulder and once
again profusely abloom with miniature red-and-white
Santas -- it's an all-out "Miracle in Unit B-2" arriving
just a few weeks late. Lean my head rearwards until
it's resting atop the chair back, parallel with the
floor, and sight straight up the clifflike loft bookcase
to the big wood-framed wall clock and, staight above
that, the loft reading lamp and, a few feet to my left
up there, the sprinkler spigot. Waggle my head for a
while, it all seems to be underwater, myself included.
Little twin convoys of breath bubbles appear to be

floating upwards from my nostrils.
     -- And that had better be it. All I can do anyway.
Jyze's most feeble performance yet over what will soon
be a full three-year run. But I'm hoping to storm back
next time and make up a big chunk of lost ground.

4

     What must be one of the landmark nights of my life.
For: tonight I'm giving up on "Jyzer." Throwing in the
towel. More than that even: I'm quitting on myself as a
maker of fictions.
     True, it's only tentative. I'm putting the Mentoka
material aside "for a while." I'm hoping to be able to
come back to it someday. I'm also hoping to hit on
ideas for new fictions inspiring enough to start things
up again regardless of what happens to the Mentoka
trilogy already planned. But both of these are stances
I've taken at times in the past, maybe even both at the
same time, as now. What's different about tonight is
this: for the first time I'm conceding it's possible --
it's even likely -- neither will work out.
     (This from the hideaway at 7:51 on a Saturday
evening. The desk. Same place where I've churned out
all the pages of "Jyzer" which in the end have served
only to convince me it's time to be doing something
else. Or rather: have convinced me it's jyze itself I
ought to be concentrating on and not mere fiction about
it, that is, jyze in real time instead of jyze in
fictive time, JIRT rather than JIFT. And this even
though it's the cause of making fiction that begat the
idea of jyze in the first place.)
     It's been a long run. I figure the fiction project

came into being the summer I was nineteen with the short story that ran in my college lit mag that fall and later became a chapter in the ill-fated novel "Hot Stuff." Over the years the larger project generated a whole lot of words arranged in "works of prose fiction of a certain length," the few surviving volumes of which now sit on the shelf labeled "Fiction" right here on my desk. But not one of those remaining works is anywhere close to ready to go before the reading public, to the extent such a public for this kind of writing still even exists or for that matter ever existed. I suspect I'll wind up burning every last page.

What brought about the disaster? Nothing particularly unexpected. I tired of the struggle, that's all. The passion guttered out.

Or better perhaps to see it the reverse way: the jyze grass looked greener. The jyze passion broke through its fictive eggshell and left me no alternative but to tend to its raucous real-time demands.

Probably I won't be announcing this change of focus to the world. Better to keep going as before, simply saying to anyone who's interested enough to ask that I haven't come up with anything I really like just yet but I'm still scribbling away as always in hopes a breakthrough will be arriving someday not too far off.

Indeed I'll be doing exactly that: keeping on keeping on. Jyze and the protojyze. I'll work like hell at it -- push the jyze as far as I can, jack the protojyze as high as I can. I still believe in all of it. I still think it can make for a "bright book of life" I'd be proud to call my legacy, fictive or not.

For the protojyze it's really just a huge editing job I face. I always enjoy revising my own stuff and I even get a kind of physical kick out of pounding in the changes on the computer -- like wallball or nerfjump but not as sweaty. So why the hell not just get on with it. And the same goes, only more so, for the three existing jyze annals.

And then there's the new jyze annal, and that's the real key. It moves up to where it's been agitating to

be for several years: to number one. Cutting edge.
It's right here, right now, scratching along at the tip
of the J-stick in the jyzer's right hand, squeezed
between his first two fingers and thumb (all three
aptly, and blackly, ink-mottled at this moment).

It's painful to admit failure. It's also a relief.
I'm hoping some exciting new paths might start opening
up, and not just in my work. But I recognize that the
deeper consequences of leaving the old path -- the old
universe really -- may take some time to make themselves
known.

Ten days from now, roughly, Jyzer Ink will be
cranking up again. My four-month "sabbatical" will be
over. And from this point of retrospection so abruptly
reached here today it seems that in at least one very
important way I've used these months well, for I've
found out what I wanted to know. Tentatively, I'm
saying, right, but still: I think this is it.

The big talent for fiction. Just can't wait
forever for it to blossom. Isn't half an adult human
lifetime long enough? I could come up with lots of
excuses and subterfuges -- fiction itself is dying,
the form is exhausted, the age is wrong for it -- but
even though any or all of them may be true, I don't
really believe any of them and certainly not all of
them at once. I grew up believing fiction mattered
greatly and in an emotional sense I simply can't
discard that belief. Nor do I want to. I'll just have
to accept that I'm a flop at creating that culturally
valuable kind of fiction myself. And meanwhile I'll do
everything I can to make something good out of jyze --
not in the sense of banging a drum for it, but in
exploring its possibilities. It may not pan out to the
extent I'm hoping, but for now at least I think I can
believe in it with the same passion I've always felt for
fiction. Or maybe even more passion. Fiction, after
all, is somebody else's baby, or many people's. Jyze is
mine. Mine and mine alone as far as I know.

So: I'll say mission botched as far as the fiction
goes, accept the sorry fact and push on with the new and

even grander jyze mission (which in point of fact I've
been engaged in on the side in a rudimentary way for
just about the same period I've been rasslin' with
fiction; I just didn't know it for most of that time).

(And as so often in the past several years I'll say
this entry is a disgrace to the name of jyze and I'll
vow to do better in the future. And now maybe more than
before I can believe I might actually succeed at doing
better since I won't have anything much else to distract
me. Pure jyze focus it is. Period. Over and out.)

*   *

Now the very same spot but almost twenty-four hours
later. And I'm happy to report the decision seems to be
holding so far. Oddly enough I'm feeling the best I've
felt in quite a while. Meaning: eager to get on with
the jyze in real time, the JIRT, which is to say: this
right here. Noticing things around me in ways I wasn't
noticing them before. Even brimming once in a while
with a kind of pure writerly exuberance. I was grinding
away so hard I'd almost forgotten how it feels.

Nose still frigid from the hike down. Possibly a
little red too. (And actively snuffling for sure.)
We're in the midst of a cold wave. "Brr, wind's off the
lake" -- words overheard while I was trudging northward
on a late provisioning run, last night, and for the
first time this year I wore a pair of heavy gloves for
carrying the grocery bags. Plowing through the Sunday
paper this afternoon I had the green-and-white-checked
blanket pulled up to my neck and tucked in bib-like.
(It's not the room temperature that's the problem or I'd
turn up the thermostat, which I keep at sixty degrees
F.; rather it's cold radiating from the nearby
windowpanes. Fiddling with the blanket is preferable to
moving the armchair, especially since there's no place
to move it to where it won't seriously obstruct
something else I don't want to be obstructing.)

It'll take me a full week to dismantle my "Jyzer"
fiction setup here in 225. Arrayed around me right now,
for instance, are maps, character lists, reminder
sheets, inspirational slogans, and much else, all of it

30

attached to the shelves on the desk, creating a triptych of sorts like one of those three-sided reflector boxes for sunbathers. My head's been roasting inside this box for most of the past year (and metaphorically for much longer than that). Now the box is coming down. But I'm throwing nothing away. Don't want to burn any bridges -- or boxes -- just yet. Tentative is still the word.

My life. what else is doing?

First the ongoing major concerns. A glance at the list. The impasse with sister Barb. Nothing's changed there. Mainly I'm waiting to see how she replies to my note. This will determine whether I spell out my decision to her -- no more personal communications -- or simply put it into effect and let her draw the conclusion herself. A showdown seems inevitable, but I'm in no hurry for it. My mind is firmly made up. I'd relent on this only if she apologized in a major way, and did so without my having to ask her to. And the chances of this happening look atomic-slice thin. Because I requested that she send me some info from Mother's address book, I expect to have soon, and I hope by next J-day, a good sense of exactly how all this will play out.

On distributing copies of "Memorials," no progress. The mailers still haven't come in. I'm putting off the chore of writing the individual cover letters until the mailers arrive.

On the proposed dinner date with Kerani: nothing.

And that's about it for matters of ongoing concern. Other such matters exist, to be sure, but they fall into a different category since I wasn't expecting changes in them this week -- the money crunch with taxes, for example, or the restart of the "day job" (though the job will still be performed at night, of course, as always, or at least it seems always even if it's been merely a little more than a decade and a half).

-- I did notice a new kind of awkwardness in the way I read the book-review sections in today's Sunday papers. It appears I'm suddenly seeing fictionizers of the literary variety from a different perspective.

slightly more hostile. "Why are these folks wasting
their time like this?" Unsettling. But I suppose I'll
get used to it. -- Or maybe start compensating by
fantasizing about a triumphant return to "Jyzer" or a
successor to it at some future time. Indeed it's hard
not to do that. Habit, I guess. Maybe ineradicable.

      If my adult life span -- meaning exactly that, my
years as an adult -- turns out to be of average length
according to current actuarial tables, it's just about
exactly half over. In fact this year's twin lifetime
milestones, briefly mentioned earlier, together mark the
midlife peak as I projected it long ago on the basis of
two different calendrical systems: the Gregorian and
(ahem) the Glennarian. And for some reason morbid
thoughts about these milestones are suddenly popping up
these days like fields of bizarre post-deluge mushrooms.
And so I'm giving myself a kind of halftime pep talk to
make such thoughts go away. "We may be down a few
points, boys, but this game's not over. Take it one
play at a time and don't even think about the score.
Now get out there and MAKE SOMETHING HAPPEN."
                  *   *
      So I'm an "out" midlifer again. This morph (or
transmog) occurs when I push back my hood upon entering
the digi-cafe. Or hoods rather, since both my
sweatshirt and my jacket are hooded. In our hood of
many hoods I'm apparently one of the few doubly hooded.
      "The usual" for an evening drink here: schooner of
root beer. A small table back in a shadowy corner, a
convenient shaft of light falling on this very page.
Intrepid internet explorers feverishly tapping away on
three sides (each atop a high dunce's stool). Mildly
bizarro music playing on the sound system.
      It's funny, but with a hood up, or even more with
two hoods up, I truly am just another street punk or
derelict or anything in between. Push back the hood(s)
and I'm suddenly a nark or something worse. "People,
this is not your father's face!"
      More pep talk. Or call it not-pop talk.
      Truth is I think if I worked at it I could still be

a player. I could shake and bake again, I'm all but
certain of it.

So am I about to do it? Tart myself up?

Hell no! -- Happy to be just like I am! (Just
wish others could be happy for the same reason -- be
happy I am just like I am, that is.) (My sister, for
one.)

A first tonight: I walked straight up the street
all the way here from the hideaway. "The middle road."
Slightly uphill the whole distance, and against the one-
way vehicular traffic (though of course I was on the
sidewalk and the vehicular traffic was in the street),
trying to jolt myself into taking notice of the usual
points of interest which I've trained myself so well not
to take too much notice of. Decided to put such things
off for at least a little while longer. You can't rip
your blinders off in a single day -- you might go blind.

Instead I'm giving myself a treat stopping in here.
Once again a new era in my life is getting underway and
so why not celebrate? -- Because it's been a damn tough
couple of weeks. And that's not even to consider the
damn tough couple of years preceding those weeks. (I
was asking myself what's been truly new in my life since
I moved back into the city. Celibacy, in a way. Beyond
that I could come up with only corn toaster muffins and
jyzos. And I suppose I should add preparing all my own
meals seven days a week. Other than that, not much.)

And now some music of the spheres.

Health sphere first. A nasty cold came on,
starting in the usual way with a rough patch of throat
which I failed to recognize for what it was until it had
raged out of control. The second night I didn't sleep
at all (and in another first, heard the morning paper
thump down outside my door a little before seven a.m.
and got up and read it, hoping to induce irresistible
sleepiness but failing). The invalid period might've
been much worse but hot baths, gallons of fruit juice,
extra sleep, megadoses of vitamins, and immobilization
(moping around B-2 for two days straight without going
out at all) -- all these kept the bug from moving down

into my chest, and now it seems to be retreating.

Shopping sphere. My favorite breakfast cereal finally went back on sale, half price for the giant "family size" boxes and just when I was down to my last two boxes. Three long marches up to the main "north pole" supermarket and back and now I'm fifteen boxes to the good.

Clothing. Because all the "new" workshirts from six or seven years ago have worn out, I'm once again wearing my ancient plaid flannel shirts. They're admirably worn-looking themselves yet not quite threadbare like the workshirts. This was the week of the red-and-black plaid, but as of today I'm again going with the blue-and-black plaid. Also I've shifted from black jeans to blue. And I'm back to using the normal belt notch. If sweating out the cold didn't do it, hauling all the cereal boxes did. (And for shoes, still the brown soccer lowcuts with black trim, though one -- the right -- is leaking at the big toe.)

Which is enough of the spheres for now. For a few minutes. It's time to head myself on home.

*   *

Did that. Made it. Nowhere in evidence during the trek of a block and a half was a moving vehicle. This on three of the busier local streets. All of which is to say (as I meant to do earlier): it's Super Bowl day. Tonight this country is not out making things happen.

I'm hunkered down in the green armchair. The green-and-white-checked blanket is pulled over my lap quasi Betsy Ross style. My feet are braced against the wooden footstool, which itself is braced against the couch, which in turn is braced against the wall. All this converts my thighs into a sturdy jyzing platform.

During the walk home I thought of a few more items worth a mention.

For one, this was inaugural week back in the national capital. What week more apt to inaugurate this umpteenth new life for me?

For another, I came up with an additional item for the list of elements new to my life since returning to

the city: the answering machine. I resisted the things
as long as I could; now I'm glad to have one. (But what
I really need, I've been thinking, is some sort of life
monitor. One day this week while tottering about with
the head cold I again nearly took a spill from the loft
stairs. I started thinking how easily I could become
trapped in this room, paralyzed by a fall, say, helpless
to reach the outside world. Obviously you don't have to
be an ancient for such a thing to happen. -- And if I
croaked, my body might not be discovered for weeks,
depending upon the season, I suppose, and whether the
heater was on or off and the consequent sniff factor.)

     For a third, Aunt Shar sent a note saying she was
"thrilled" with "Memorials." This mattered a great
deal to me.

     And here's a whole neglected sphere: reading. At
the downtown library I happened upon a book with "Around
My Room" in its title. The first word is not "Jyze" but
"Voyage," as in "make them, attempt them, that's all
there is." This book is said to have been very
influential a couple of centuries ago. Best of all, a
second, shorter work by the same author appears at the
back of the volume and this time the "Around My Room" in
its title is preceded by "Nocturnal Expedition." A
sequel for those of us who live by NUT time, meaning
nightscoper upside-down time. What a delight!

     I ordered a copy of this superb little book just so
I'll have its cover to gaze at for the rest of the year.
As a JAMR I may be needing frequent recharges and I
think the "Voyage" cover could provide at least a few of
them all by itself. JAMR: that, of course, as I first
realized last fall, is the acronym for "Jyze Around My
Room." As in culture jammer, yes. Or at least I can
always hope that will apply. -- And for those same
recharging purposes I've pinned the JAMR acronym on the
loft above my head in big red letters with an
exclamation point. (I checked out all the usual
bookstores trying to find a copy of "Voyage." Nobody'd
ever heard of it or of the author. Yet this new
translation was published just two years ago.)

[Jyze in Love]

    Also I picked up an item on contemporary Western
philosophy as viewed through the lens of critical theory
and wasted a lot of time reading it all the way to the
end. (And note this: the author of this tome has the
same fairly unusual last name as last fall's briefly
revived romantic hope, Lady K, now does, but as far as I
can determine is not related to her through marriage or
otherwise.)
    With no work to do on "Jyzer" I suddenly had plenty
of time for reading; that was the trouble. But I guess
I should be grateful for the distractions.
    Is there a thread here somewhere? A point? Or is
this all just more static of the spheres?
    -- And for the past couple of pages I've been
hearing the call of the reheat. Yesterday's hamburger
helper, with surrogate soy beef. And hunger now decrees
that this entry end right here. ("Obey your hunger!")

5

    Sad time. I was wrong, it's turned out, in
thinking I could avoid openly breaking with sister Barb.
As of last night I've done it, shoving a letter into the
streetside box at the main post office (after making a
special eleven p.m. trip down there in the rain) -- not
actually saying or even thinking "good riddance," but
that's basically how I was viewing it. And still am.
As I sit here at the desk in the hideaway and glance up
at a picture of the mother of us both. To apologize for
failing to live up to my vow to her.
    No doubt Mother would be crushed. But I also think
she'd understand. I do know this: I've done my absolute
best. This is true not just for the past fourteen

months since her death but for many years before that, and the whole time it's been mainly for her sake, not Barb's. Had it not been for Mother's pleas I would've taken this same step considerably earlier, maybe even as much as two decades back during the summer Dad died.

Early this week Barb's reply to my note came in (the note asking her to regard my impugned "spiritual stuff" remark as intended to be friendly and mildly irreverent and nothing more). Instead of accepting this olive branch she angrily swatted it down. She'll have me know she's in no mood for "irreverence" (which she puts in quotes) and "I doubt I ever will be." In essence she dares me to sever relations with her. She shows not even a hint of willingness to negotiate, conciliate, find a peaceful/loving way to agree to disagree. Capitulate or be swept aside, insect: that pretty much sums it up. My own sister!

So I'm ending it. For four days straight I did nothing but agonize over this. Was I sure I wanted to do it? What would be the best way of doing it? I wound up sending her a short, almost legalistic letter, just two paragraphs, saying I'm "withdrawing from any further personal relations" with her (and also saying, to paraphrase, I trust we can deal civilly with each other concerning any business matters that might arise). I didn't even attempt to reply to any of her accusations and avoided making any of my own.

How will she react? I may be wrong, but I suspect she'll be relieved (just as I am). That will predominate. She'll probably go silent, and indeed I hope she does. She might lash out one last time, and if she does, I'll do my best to shake it off without responding in kind. I doubt she'll make any effort to change my mind -- more likely she'll try to confirm it -- but if she does, I'll listen. Before, however, I'd reverse myself, she'd have to show a degree of understanding and acceptance I haven't seen from her in ages (if ever -- and truly, probably not ever).

My note could also affect her badly -- throw her into a depression or something. I could even imagine

her killing herself. Not as a result of this alone, but
if it came on top of a number of other blows; and I
can't deny it might. I hope it won't. The chances are
extremely small. But still it's a risk I'm obviously
willing to take at this point. Am taking. Of course
she takes similar risks in launching her attacks on me
and she doesn't hesitate -- she does it over and over
and over. In light of this sorry truth it's a little
easier for me to live with my own harshness now.

The most likely outcome, I'd say, is that we'll
simply never speak or meet again. Estranged siblings --
I hate to see myself falling into the category, but of
course many do. Isn't there something almost flagrantly
Scandinavian about it? The years will go by and
eventually one of us will fall critically ill, or one of
our siblings will (or die suddenly), and maybe under
that kind of pressure a reconciliation, almost certainly
partial at best, could occur. Other than that I see no
real possibilities.

What ghoulishness. What absurdity and pettiness (I
suppose). But this is what it's come down to.

A farewell to my only sister. Wish I could work up
more sorrow over this. Think of some good things to
say. -- Would if I could. -- Can't.

Pain, yes. But even this isn't as bad as it was at
the time of her shocking "you're a liability" ultimatum
just days after Mother's death. In my view that was the
primary act of estrangement. This now is more a delayed
confirmation of the effects of that -- fourteen months
delayed. And still it hurts plenty.

It's done now. End of the family as I've known it
and loved it (to cite only one, but the chief, among a
whole lot of conflicting emotions; and ignoring several
earlier cataclysms which very nearly blew us apart).

*   *

-- Now four days later. Time to get back to jyze.
To hell with Barb. (By now she's surely received my
letter. She might've called if she wanted to be
conciliatory. She hasn't.)

I'm moving on. Tonight's task is to describe (or

rather, try to figure out) just where I stand so at
least I'll have an idea what I'm moving on from.

But in one way I've already made a move, and this
just tonight. Flipping through the personal ads in the
two local weekly papers -- this while taking a break at
the ORB cafe (only real bookstore) -- I came across one
that sounded pretty good. At least I fell within the
qualifying age range. So on the spot I dashed off a
page of personal info and quickly sealed it in an
envelope and dropped that into a mailbox before I lost
my nerve (and almost did anyway at the last moment).

My thinking went like this. I'm no longer trying
to do fiction -- tentatively. I no longer need to bear
down quite so hard. I've had enough time to rally past
the main part, anyway, of the shocks of two autumns ago.
I'm about to return to my regular job and resume my
"normal" life. Valentine's Day is coming up and I
don't have a single Valentine's candidate (or rather
thought I didn't until I hit on the idea of enclosing my
most recent note to Aunt Shar in an old unused Valentine
card I happened across in my scrap box). I need some
distractions. Years of various types of isolation have
left me without romantic prospects. I dislike hanging
around meat markets or joining social clubs. So why not
take a flyer on a personal ad? What difference does it
make if it leads nowhere?

Oddly enough, this one's exactly the same age Lady
U was when we split up. A man of my vintage (and quite
a bit older, actually) is acceptable to her as long as
he's "mature and highly educated" and stands five-seven
or taller. She describes herself as "petite" and "very
attractive," a "professional writer." What she's after,
she says, is a "quiet, traditional lifestyle." Granted
she might be looking for someone very different from me,
I still think it's possible I might, with a nip here and
a tuck there, fill her bill. A crazy hunch nudged me
into doing it.

What if she writes and says I've made the callbacks
and now she wants a photo? My most recent one in which
Lady U doesn't appear is more than a decade old. -- But

why worry about it now.   Just an outside chance she'll respond. Maybe, though, she'll at least be kind enough to send a rejection note rather than do nothing at all, like, for instance, the recipient of my one other venture in this realm, the literary-review personals candidate of last fall (but then that one lived in a city 140 miles away and so had a better excuse).

Truly I'm expecting nothing. At this stage a failure by her to reply wouldn't even rise to the level of a perceived rejection.

*

This is the night Jyzer Ink was supposed to roar back into action. A bad omen: grand jury canceled today. But it's still on for tomorrow, an all-day session, and that means I'll be restarting on the night the Chinese lunar Year of the Ox lumbers in: surely a good omen.

Here's another angle on the inspiration behind the reply to "Boxholder" (no name was given). One day last week as I sat working at the loft desk I heard a loud pop and then an odd muted metallic tinkle. It seemed to come from the direction of the kitchen, but for a full day I couldn't figure out what had caused it. Then as I was reaching for something in the fridge a bizarre sight caught my eye. A huge albino slug, it appeared, had keeled over and died while trying to escape from the meat tray. -- What had actually happened, it turned out, was that the metal top had popped off the can of orange Danish rolls I'd been saving for my special Valentine's Day treat. Obviously Cupid had something else in mind for me. And maybe this "petite" one in the personals is it? (The dough for the rolls had badly dried up but I threw it in the toaster oven anyway; the results, though somewhat cardboardlike, and even wooden in places (and I mean hardwood), were still edible.)

And a fine little surprise: a manila envelope arrived containing a genealogy chart brother Rob drew up with meticulous care (never telling me a word about it while doing so). The chart came in both a large foldout paper version and a reduced-size laminated card intended

to be inserted in "Memorials." Accompanying it was an
amusing but also touching cover letter addressed to
"Aunts, Uncles, Cousins, and Siblings." Vintage Rob
and ya gotta love him for it. (Posterity, don't fail to
notice what a splendid fellow this brother is! -- And
also please forgive my own petty grumbling over that
important Mentoka research book he neglected to return
to me for so long, the rascal. In the end I haven't
really needed it anyway and now probably never will.)

This week I've been devoting a lot of time to
wrapping books (the mailers did finally arrive) and
writing cover letters and mailing same. It's costing me
a bundle too. (If I had any doubt before now about the
necessity of raiding the deep reserves, it's expired.)

Where's this going down? Redwood worktable.
Coming up on one a.m.

The plants have all been trimmed and repotted and
the starters transplanted. A massive four-washer load
of laundry is out of the way. I've beaten back the
general B-2 clutter for the first time in months. I've
discovered, or rather confirmed, a new staple for my
cycle of cheapo meals (microwaved store-brand chicken
pot pie swaddled in half a cereal bowl of microwaved
frozen green peas). I've completed the transfer of all
Mentoka-related materials back down to the hideaway.
I'm all set up and ready to get cracking on a serious
edit of the fifteen annals of protojyze. I've also
typed up a couple more entries from jyze annal three.
I've changed the sheets up in the loft. I'm pretty well
caught up on periodical reading.

In short, I'm about as prepared to move on as I
know how to be. And so then: move on where?

-- But is this really such a puzzle? I'm committed
to working fiercely on the protojyze for at least the
next few years. I'm also committed to working fiercely
on the jyze itself -- whatever the project is -- for the
rest of this year and then for as many years thereafter
as I can keep it going, and preferably for as long as I
can keep myself going. Therefore, given these two long-
term -- lifetime! -- commitments, I can authorize myself

to kick back a bit and maybe try to stir up a few
swirls of jyzable action, so to say, in my daily life,
and preferably at least some of it will be of the
romantic kind. And I do mean the real thing, flesh and
blood and other crucial body fluids, and not, like last
year, just ghosts, demons, phantasms.

If I can't do it, fine. I'm not planning to
devote a lot of time or care to the stirring. Most
likely I'll embark on authentic interpersonal action
only if I think I'm being strongly responded to (as
seemed to be happening once at the ORB cafe last week,
by the way, but unfortunately I was caught totally off
guard and let the chance slip away). Still: at least I
can say I'm theoretically open to new developments in
just the way I vowed not to be before.

Anything else crucially in need of jyze annotation?
We've had the groundhog predicting an early spring.
We've had the newly reinaugurated president urging a
"national spirit of reconciliation," I think is how he
put it (in any case, nothing new or real or feasible).
We've had the letter K go dark -- in honor of the end of
things with Lady K? -- on the big pink neon sign at the
public market. We've had a none-too-friendly lawyer
move into the empty office around the corner from the
hideaway, an Asiusan of probable Chinese extraction (and
yes, I'm planning to go with the "Jyzer" argot on race
and culture again this year: Eurusan, Afrusan, Asiusan,
USAn, Cawk, and so on). (And Walt A., the three-dot
columnist I knew slightly in one of my former lives, has
died of lung cancer, his death coming only nine months
after first diagnosis, compared with Mother's eleven
months.)

-- I've written Jeff and Rob, I should note, and
explained why I've broken with Barb. Unfortunately my
decision affects them too, if only in the sense that
full family reunions will become impossible and their
own relations with Barb thornier, most likely, just in
case they weren't already thorny enough. I apologized
and assured them it was a step I'd not taken lightly.

6

J-day again so soon?

Four more days gone by, yup. I ended that last
entry four days after starting it. The eighth day of
"On the Eighth Day He Jyzed" is today.

At the hideaway. Back in the old brown armchair
this time, with the floor lamp glowing (just above my
left shoulder) and the small portable fan whizzing (atop
the three-drawer wooden filing cabinet over by the door,
which is cracked open six inches so the fan can blow out
a day's worth of stuffiness, and therefore the Jyzer Ink
business license mounted on the door frame above the fan
can once again be smartly fluttering).

Back into last summer's lifestyle too. In many
respects things are the same now as they were then, just
before the "sabbatical" began with its fierce focus on
the late (almost certainly) and much lamented "Jyzer."
I'm back to coming down here earlier in the afternoon,
usually around three unless errands need to be run, so I
can put in a solid five or six hours on the protojyze.
Then I march up to the scope office to work on the
machines there, taking on either a scoping job or
corrections on a scoping job or data-entry or printing
tasks related to my own work, or some combination of any
or all of the above (and many nights I don't know what
the mix will be until I get there). I return home
sometime between one and two a.m. or occasionally an
hour or two or at most three later than that.

For this first month reporter Naomi will be working
only one or two days a week and the scoping jobs will be
relatively few. Next month she'll go to three days a

week, which should roughly double my work hours, to
between fifteen and twenty a week, and that will
probably be the norm for the rest of the year.

Meanwhile the cold I thought I'd thrown off has
come roaring back and this time it's just about totally
shut down my lungs. As nasty a cold as I've been up
against in, I'd say, my entire adult life. Or ever?
And to have it hit just as I'm trying to reaccustom my
eyes to the computer screen causes an extra dose of
misery. So yeah, say ever.

-- And thinking I ought to do some fine-tuning on
that declaration last J-day concerning possible rebirth
of my social life. A bit of backing down. I may or may
not be ready to start living full throttle again. A toe
in the water here and there may be all I can stand.
Last week's letter to "Boxholder," for example, may've
constituted exposure enough to send me shivering back to
my reclusive regimen. Could be I'll wind up plenty
pleased enough just to be scribbling away on my own
under the JAMR banner for the rest of this year.

No reply yet from "Boxholder." Having now had a
little more time to digest the contents of her ad -- all
those conservative terms -- as well as the nature of my
perhaps overly unguarded reply -- which didn't fail to
mention my dissident politics, my lack of wheels, my
generally casual approach to most things -- given all
this, I must say it'll be a downright miracle if she
cuts me from the herd for further inspection. (From the
zip code for her P.O. box I figured it must be located
in the downtown post office just around the corner from
the scope office, and indeed I found it there. The
notion of staking out that box and waiting for her to
show up did occur to me. A fool's game, I decided, and
promptly rejected it. But considering the number of
hours I've spent in and around the post office over the
years it's quite possible she and I would recognize each
other if we ever did officially meet in person.) (I've
also considered, but firmly nixed, the idea of sending
her a second letter spelling out some of my less
controversial qualities. Better to have her decide

what's next on the basis of the info she already has.
The odds are high I'd be wasting even more time -- good
money chasing bad, or rather bad money chasing bad. Who
knows what her real agenda might be.)

Hack hack, snuffle snuffle. Reach into my backpack
for another extra-strength cough drop. I've gone
through so many now they have scarcely any effect.

No word from sister Barb either. It's beginning to
look as though she'll indeed reciprocate -- possibly
even with relish -- my "abandonment" of her. I've gone
through some rough times over it myself (including an
ugly dream last night) but by and large I remain
convinced it was the right thing to do. At times an
almost euphoric sense of release sweeps over me. For a
few days I was trying to prepare myself for a phone call
from her, conceivably quite nasty, or maybe from Keith
(assuming she's still with him), or possibly from
brother Jeff trying to broker a reconciliation. Nothing
like any of these outcomes has occurred. The only words
I've had about the whole sorry situation were from
brother Rob on the phone, and those were brief and
sympathetic (he pointed out that Barb's "intemperate"
letter about Gail's pet ferret -- which letter seems to
have permanently alienated him as well, along with Gail
to be sure, though he said neither of them plans to make
it official with Barb -- that letter also came at
Christmas).

Now with my solitude ratcheted up another notch I'm
back to thinking morbid thoughts. Death coming up
sooner or later anyway, of course, and always sooner
than the last time you thought about it, but what if
this or that or the other body part wore out or went bad
ahead of schedule? And me with no medical insurance,
living alone and in a dangerous part of town, having a
scary family history of early demise among males,
lacking even a warm and fuzzy pet to ease the stress.
The unnerving truth is I could be living on borrowed
time right now.

Anything I can do about this? Realistically?
Beyond what I'm already doing (eating more or less

healthy, getting plenty of exercise, taking my vites and supps)? No. Wrangle my papers into order, I guess. But that in itself would be a lifetime project (and I mean a full actuarially probable lifetime, not merely what I may have left in reality).

        -- And meanwhile: intimations of spring. I hadn't really noticed, but one day while cutting through a parking lot across from the arena on my weekly grocery run I overheard a mother telling her kid, "Look how the cherry trees are starting to bloom already!" I lifted my eyes and sure enough, a whole row of them suddenly quivered before me as if they'd just that moment popped up from the ground, all fetchingly smudged with pink. After that I started seeing cherry blossoms everywhere. And also primroses and winter pansies freshly planted in street boxes. A new season coming, it's undeniable, and as it rolls in I'll be starting a new seasonal cycle of my own, having officially completed my move into the city at the end of March last year.

        And here at Jyzer Ink all is well. I figured it out the other day: the number of linear feet of bookshelves I've packed into this room exceeds the number of square feet of floor space by a factor of one half. Yet it really doesn't feel all that claustrophobic. Quite spacious and comfortable, I'd say, in a cozy way. The unusual height of the ceiling -- fourteen feet -- helps a lot. And I'm still pleased with what's hanging on the walls. All but a couple of the paintings are the work of brother Rob or Ladies U, S, or V. Sketches of admired writers and thinkers up there and also the original Kenneth P. picture-poem "Words Gettin' People Crazier All the Time." Large framed photo of young Mom in a tweed suit, age twenty-five or so, kneeling to hold the imbecilically grinning three-year-old Jyzer G (that's me, folks!). A shelf-ful of memorabilia. Rotating antique bookcase with a large canted dictionary spread open on top. Wooden coat tree. Two large old-fashioned windows and a windowed door, all three sporting tan blinds permanently closed.

        And lots more.

[JAMR Jyze]

    Imagine if I should have to dismantle all this!
(Yet being realistic, it's not a question of if, it's
only when. Barring some financial miracle. -- So love
it while you've got it.)
                        *   *

    -- Jyze on down to the inner sanctum. Being just
another tag, this, for the enclosed work space beneath
the loft sleeping platform. Stolen, to be sure, the
tag, from, among other places (for example, that old
radio show), our name, Lady U's and mine, for a hallway
in our second rental abode in this city. But never mind
that. (Does it even make sense, that sentence right
there with all the commas in it? Eight of 'em!)

    This little inner sanctum here, almost everything
about it is basically the same as when this loft stood
in its previous locations. Exceptions: the staircase
used to be on the other end and less steep. And when I
look around I see only loft framework and built-in
bookshelves and cream-colored wall, not windows giving
on deep dark woods or a neighbor's moss-covered garage.
Definitely no deer or bear wandering by. No question
it's a whole different kind of wilderness out there now.
    To the right of the jyzebook the telephone rides
atop its faithful answering machine with the usual
double zeroes showing in its message-indicator window.
To the left stands the old desk lamp with the shade I
painted myself in a kaleidoscopic color pattern to
soften the light in the shed in its earliest days. This
lamp still provides a warm stained-glass-like glow I
hate to shut off and rarely do, other than at bedtime.
    The hot news here: I again have an in-box and an
out-box. That is, no longer are they both in-boxes, all
but buried under a huge mound of papers. Which is to
say: yes, I've already begun putting my papers in order.
After ten months of procrastination I finally went
through everything in that mound, salvaging maybe a
third of it, and neatly filing most of that. Now I just
have possibly a hundred times that much stuff to go
through at the hideaway and a thousand times that much
in the storage unit. And that's not counting Mother's

two overstuffed four-drawer filing cabinets.

Someday in the not-too-distant future I may station a computer in here. What's more it may be a very familiar computer. Reporter Una happened to drop by the scope office Friday night -- sheer serendipity, she being the very person I needed to talk with about resuscitating the laptop after the lamentable dayscoper Amy ignored my note seeking help -- and we got to talking about the possibility of the firm's selling to Jyzer Ink the old desktop computer on which I'm now doing most of the nongovernment scoping (and much of the government work too -- though this latter is against regulations and strictly hush-hush). Una seemed delighted with the idea. She'd also be happy to sell me the laptop once a new system for doing government work is in place. Because of these machines' near-obsolescence the prices would be low -- maybe a hundred bucks apiece.

Will it actually happen? Will Una move on this? I think she will. But it might take months. The first thing she must do is consult with reporter Fran, who's technically the owner of both machines and as a rule poorly disposed in advance toward any plan I propose.

And so. What else while I'm at it? -- Maybe nothing. Maybe eat something first and go at it again later.

*   *

-- And now just a kwikjyze nightcap from above. From the upper sanctum, as it were. Top of the loft. Lying prone and warm, red nightshirt on, tucked beneath purple sheet and white blanket and green unzipped sleeping bag as the ceiling looms inches above. The two clocks tick and the third glows green beneath the tan-shaded bedside lamp and an empty truck thunkety-thunks by outside on the viaduct and then total silence. Except, that is, those ticks so excellently in sync. (Haven't coughed for at least three, four minutes.)

Wanted to mention the postage stamp I affixed to my plea to "Boxholder": it was "Mighty Casey," the mythical baseball stud who in the end, of course, strikes out.

Would she be the type to appreciate such a "lick" of
self-deprecating humor? (First coughs now, here in
Upper Mudville.)
     My most resonating thought of the week concerning
my literary career, such as it is, being this: why be
ashamed? It's just taken me a little longer than
expected to learn my trade, that's all. And I should
give myself some credit: in my extended apprentice years
I've churned out a whole lot of stuff, and some of it's
not half bad. Depends on how you look at it: half bad
or half good. Toss out the half-bad part, what's more,
and you can say the remainder's all good. So now, this
year, finally, I'm ready to figure out which half is the
bad one and toss it. Therefore I believe I can also
cast aside the apprentice role and take my place as a
master. Jyzemaster G! (I've been rehearsing the new
role for several years, true. But now: it's live, it's
real, it's happening. -- Just how it is.)

7

     Jyze pays a courtesy visit to the downtown train
station. On a dismal rainy late-winter night. As lite-
music radio plays over the P.A. and a seemingly endless
freight rumbles by just outside. A kind of bus-terminal
desolation about the place, as almost always, except at
this moment it's far less populated than the average
urban bus terminal. (The board says three of the four
long-distance passenger trains -- "continentals" -- due
in later this evening are running on time, which may be
a record; and so the room might start filling up before
long. But then again travelers are wary of trains these
days -- even more so than usual -- because of this

winter's many weather-related shutdowns and so the
numbers probably won't be all that big.)

Just over a year ago I was sitting in here on a
night much like this one. A different roll of the dice
at that time might've had me living a block up the
street in one of the big artist co-ops. With Maxine, a
recent art-school grad: fun-loving twenty-something
Eurusan leaseholder of an authentic industrial loft
studio with adjoining metal beds separated by a flimsy
curtain up on the loft itself, one of which beds
would've been mine. -- And just this week the owners of
that very building announced an "upgrade" to condos and
fancy offices, with all the artists to be evicted. In
fact they've put together a plan to redevelop the whole
quarter if the city will pony up a mere fifty million
dollars to bankroll the first stage. Or was it a
hundred and fifty million? (This is the same pinchpenny
outfit that owns most of the block around my hideaway
office, but not the building itself, just a third of a
mile north of here.)

Is all still well with me otherwise? I guess maybe
so. Could be the freedom created by the scuttling of
"Jyzer" is causing me to fly off the handle a bit.
Intellectual excitement. This past week I've blown a
hundred bucks I don't really have on books I don't
really need (but am dying to read). Also romantic
excitement (pathetic as it is): I've answered two more
of those personal ads. The suspense and all the raging
ideas, together they're just about killing me.

And this: the number of the next check I write will
match the Gregorian number of the year. A whole
lifetime it's taken me to reach this milestone. Never
to be repeated, almost certainly.

(A passenger train, a continental, is rolling in.
The place just barely stirs to life. "End of the line,
folks.")

-- And brother Jeff, as I figured he would, did
call. "Yo bro!" We talked an hour and a half, my every
second or third sentence punctuated with a cough (and
roughly the same's true of these written sentences here:

I'm still battling this damn cold!). I told him the sad
story of the latest clash with Barb (who still hasn't
replied to my note and so I'd say it's confirmed she
won't -- though she's surprised me many times before).
In Jeff's view we siblings are breaking apart without
Mother here to hold us together and we're pretty much
helpless to prevent this. And her death seems to have
left him just as mortality-conscious as it has me.
Suddenly we're both talking about how short life is, how
we all really ought to get cracking on the things we've
always dreamt of doing, meaning our various "immortality
projects" (his term). No point in wasting time and
energy on family feuds, he pointed out. And I say: amen
to that. (His own immortality project is reconstructing
the "farmette" into an ideal home for his retirement
years. He's not sure what Barb's is, but he's sure she
has one. He knows I do, of course, though I gave him no
clue about its recent makeover. He thinks Rob may need
another one -- maybe tracing family roots on Dad's side
-- but I think Rob, with his painting and protojyzing
and his huge collection of classical music, is at least
as well set as the rest of us and probably better so.)

     The usual talk about visits. Will we ever see each
other again? Always a place for me at the farmette, he
assured me. I do fantasize at times about moving back
to the old Mentoka zone (as I continue to think of it),
especially when things here aren't going so well. I'd
love to hang around the ancestral turf for a year or two
and try to salvage something from all my Mentoka-series
research -- a JIRT annal, say, maybe "Jyze Goes Mentoka"
or some such title. Perhaps actually live at the center
of the zone in my old fictive grad-school town Mentoka
Falls, with frequent trips to Wachute (Dad's fictive
birthplace) and Lahontan (my own fictive birthplace and
Mother's fictive home during her high-school and college
years). But I doubt I'll ever be able to afford any of
those. The chances of Jeff and Angie popping out here
for a visit seem somewhat better, but still slim.

     Jeff, in a sense, now replaces Mother as the family
nerve center. As he pointed out himself, he can get

along with Barb only because he has no interest at all
in her various intellectual and religious passions (not
to say dogmas -- and I didn't use that word with Jeff).
Also he has enough diplomatic talent to pull it off.
And to an extent he and she are natural allies simply by
virtue of birth order: the beleaguered middle two. I
offered him all the support I could; said I was well
aware Barb might maneuver him into a position where he'd
have to "tilt" toward her and he should go right ahead
and do so and I'd fully understand. He's got his work
cut out for him with Barb and he knows it.

    (Another train's backing in, a regional this time.
The baggage carousel again kicks into action with a
horrific groan. A few visitors from the hinterlands
wander in looking sleepy and puzzled. Could this
possibly be the place?)

    -- And back to romance. Last Tuesday I flip-
flopped again, having decided a few days earlier to
revert to reclusion for a while if I didn't hear within
a day or two from "Boxholder," the personal-ad-placer
I'd impulsively written to the week before. Then,
completely without premeditation, I again found myself
glancing through the personals in the new editions of
the weeklies (they both hit the streets on Tuesdays
now). A couple of ads caught my eye. Then a couple
more. Then another. And another. Six possibles! But
I still didn't expect to do anything about them.

    Then during a walk to the supermarket I found
myself composing a letter in my head to one of the six,
"Adventuress," divorced, Jewish, five years my junior,
a former public radio reporter with "enormous
intellectual curiosity" who's seeking a Francophone man
interested in Freud. When I got home I rattled off a
three-page handwritten letter to her, surprisingly bold
-- especially considering I'm neither Francophone nor
Freudophile -- and then hustled downtown to mail it
before, again, I lost my nerve.

    This put me on such a high I soon found myself
writing in my head to "Feisty," another of the six, a
"half-Filipina" two years my senior, originally from my

home city (fictive Centropolis), possessor of a self-declared "nice body," a lover of books and progressive politics and "healthy stuff" who's seeking a man "with smarts" who shares these interests and also is "working class" -- so she could "do more than" read the paper (the indispensable one from the far coast) with him on Sunday mornings. Back in B-2 I dashed off a one-page letter to her and rushed right out and mailed that.

Four eligibles still remained, but I decided two "auditions" in one night was plenty, especially since at that point "Boxholder" remained, I thought, a live option.

And today I'm still waiting. "Boxholder" is no longer so live, I'm afraid, but if I understand the way the system works, the other two would just now be receiving my letters (and yesterday was a holiday, Presidents Day, possibly delaying matters further). I'll be surprised if I don't hear from at least one of them in the next few days. (And if I don't, it's back to solitude for sure this time. And I'll be well prepared because I've just begun reading what looks like a pretty good book about that very topic -- solitude -- just in case. The author is a fellow Mentokan about my age, it turns out, and possibly for these reasons he seems to be speaking personally to me in a way few other philosophy types, whether solitudinous or not, ever have.)

-- This depot scene's getting to be too much. Usually it treats me with total indifference, but tonight it's actively hostile. The janitor, I'm talking about, who seems new. A meaner breed for sure. ---

*   *

Thinking during the soggy walk home it's B-2 I like best now. Quite possibly "Jyze Around My Room" was a good choice of theme after all. I know this: here's where I'm most inspired as a jyzist. And here's the place I like best to be coming to. The hideaway, though still a fine spot, has lost some of its allure for me, and surely not through any fault of its own but rather just because I go there to work. (But also: here I have

53

more space, more comfort, better music, walls festooned
with my own hand-painted jyze posters, windows open to
the outdoors as opposed to just the hallway, a well-
stocked fridge, a bathtub set up for reading, a loft bed
for naps, a phone which at any moment might ring.)

In any case here I am. Reminding myself of the
"Nocturnal Expedition" man himself as I ride a wooden
chair I've placed at the head of the entrance hallway
for purposes of tonight's jyze session. That other guy
liked to jyze, after his fashion, while straddling his
windowsill as if it were a hobbyhorse and occasionally
baying at the moon. I too might go for doing something
along those lines, but a stormy winter night like this
is probably not the best time for it.

(Also I wanted to note my breakdown last week --
scribbling the pleas to "Adventuress" and "Feisty" --
must've been caused, at least in part, by the ubiquitous
commercial drumbeat leading up to Valentine's Day, which
was Friday. And I, having been forced to consume my
Valentine's Day treat prematurely -- the albino slug --
was thus facing a bleak and murky day.)

-- So now my back's to the door (maple, it looks
like, or at least the color's right) and my scalp rises
to just beneath the level of the little brass peephole
(which in my entire time living here I've never had
occasion to use or even thought of doing so). My feet
are propped on one of the three stacks of designer
cinder bricks claimed from beneath the "free" table in
the laundry room and now lined up along the wall to my
left. A standard brass-and-rubber doorstop is affixed
to the wall to my right at doorknob level, a foot or so
beneath a gray fuse box which I've never opened. Since
all the power for unit B-2 runs through this fuse box it
could conceivably be seen as a key for deconstructing
this J-book's "JAMR" theme (a hint for any lit-crit
types out there searching for a truly obscure project).

On the other side of this same wall would be, come
to think of it -- for the first time from this angle --
part of Kevin's unit. It's his bathroom. Because it
abuts mine, we share the same pipes and sometimes

perform noisy parallel toiletries.

Same storm-trooper-tough brown carpet here as elsewhere in B-2.

(From my bathroom reading I'm stealing a phrase or two to use for the personals ladies: this week I've found myself "sporting in fancy" with them, just as the author of the bathroom reading himself once famously did with the Queen of England after spotting her from afar. -- I also like his verb "towse," which seems to mean something like "play with her [or his?] genital parts." Today's language of love offers an empty evolutionary niche, so to speak, which "towse" could fill nicely.)

-- Along the wall to my left, above and beyond the cinder bricks, stand big stacks of cardboard storage boxes, a supermarket-size display of cornflakes boxes, and the green plastic recycling bins. Exciting! Beyond all that, the kitchen -- or kitchen nook really (don't want to be too grandiose here). And leaning against the wall to my right, a large cork bulletin board for which I've still found no use (building rules decree, it turns out, that it can't be attached to a wall). Cream colored, these hallway walls, and goose-pimply here as elsewhere. Round two-bulb ceiling light fixture, otherwise utterly nondescript, glowing steadily.

Aesthetically it's not a rouser, the B-2 entryway. But one day I may try to spruce it up a bit. If I shut down the hideaway, the portable bookcases from there will line this hall. Otherwise I'll go with the cinder-brick shelving. Possibly I'll even get ambitious and build in some shelves crossing the hall above head level; a lot of space is going to waste up there. Eventually the whole of B-2 could become a kind of bilevel, with the loft gradually expanding to cover everything in the main room, sort of like a crawlspace attic (but at no point being attached to the walls, which, again, is forbidden).

(-- And which of the three ladies would I prefer to be with given what I know right now? Probably "Feisty," just because I figure our chances of hitting it off would be a little better, owing partly to our age

and background similarities and partly, as I judge from
the scanty evidence of the ads, to the likelihood that
her expectations for a man would be less idealistically
extreme. But then again would she be expecting anywhere
near as little as I'd be able to offer? -- Or maybe
I'm wrong, maybe I'm ready to love again. Rather than
renounce love, that is, and in its place start trying to
cozy up with the next life or with just plain
nothingness, Buddhist-style. -- But would any woman
willingly climb up into that loft? And would not the
low ceiling there make copulation utterly ridiculous?)

Oh the anxieties. I'm eager but it's obvious I
still have much to overcome.

As dinner hour approacheth. And I need to step
around the corner and jump around for a spell.

*   *

-- Wotta coupla fine two-bit-a-pound bakers!

And now picking it up again here at the redwood
table for the stretch run. After first sweeping aside
some clutter, which for B-2 as a whole is the worst it's
ever been. A good thing brother Rob's coming over for
dinner this week: I'll be shamed into doing some early
spring cleaning -- maybe even some vacuuming. And if
this turns out to set the scene for a surprise visit by
"Feisty" or "Adventuress" or even the dilatory
"Boxholder," so much the better.

About the hallway, I neglected to mention the small
freestanding wooden doorstop, wedge-shaped and unpainted
and well worn, which rests on the carpet in the corner
beneath the door hinges. This doorstop came with the
place, and it's worth mentioning because it's the only
unattached item that did.

So you open the door to B-2 (it swings inward) and
follow the rug straight ahead about ten feet between the
aforementioned items stacked or leaning against the
hallway walls. At that point you hang a hard right (as
does the carpet) and go about five feet more, passing
the kitchen nook to your left and a map-plastered wall
up close on your right. Then slip through a narrow gap
between, on your left, a stack of three cedar boxes

abutting the end of the kitchen-nook partition with its built-in cabinets and sink, and on your right, the door to the bathroom. You emerge into the main part of the room. At the redwood table to the immediate left you see, if you happen to be entering at this very moment, the jyzemaster himself, happily at work in his black sweats and jumping slip-ons. A table lamp stands just beyond his J-book, its glow illuminating the fabulous triple-tiered, double-walled gallery of jyze posters.

Tonight the fridge, which is full size, is gurgling dyspeptically, or so it seems. Some nights it sounds even angrier, especially if the freezer's recently been restocked (supermarket sales time).

A meager week for personal news:

** Saturday afternoon, which was unseasonably warm and sunny, a theater company rehearsed a play in the courtyard patio ("jyzeyard") right outside my window. I have no idea who they were or what the play was, but the performers numbered a dozen or so, a racially diverse group of mostly twenty-somethings, I'd say. They seemed to be enjoying themselves, and I certainly liked having them there (peeking out several times through my half-closed blinds, a kind of reverse voyeur, looking out instead of in -- and from little stirrings of the blinds across the way I know I wasn't the only one).

** Yesterday on an impulse I took a walk through the old fairgrounds for the first time since moving back into town. This included visits to the arcade which gave birth to "Hot Stuff" and the theater where Lady U often performed and also where she and I played out some of our most dramatic personal scenes ever during her escapade with Marco of the "Indigenes" cast, and also to the carnival where I worked as a barker for a summer at age nineteen (and met Kristi K. who was herself barking in the next stall). Nostalgia bubbles floated up at times but after brief moments of indulgence I resolutely popped them all and moved on.

** A few days ago the murderers of the young Cawk guy whose memorial marker stands just a block from the hideaway building -- who died almost exactly a year ago

-- were finally caught, and they turned out to be a
couple of drifters -- indigenes themselves -- who'd been
hanging out in the triangle and nearby streets for most
of the intervening year. The chief villain is an
extremely nasty dude named Sheldon E. who several times
has personally cursed me out when I've spurned his
brusque demands for smokes and/or money.

     And that's about it, jyze fans, for another lost J-
week. Or no, I want to note I've also read the bulk of
two fine books and an excellent quarterly. And these
all by themselves went a long way toward making this a
good J-week to be lost in.

8

     Sprawled atop the loft again. "Upper sanctum." A
drizzly gray morning, twenty minutes before noon, wall
clock laboriously ticking (I changed its battery
yesterday, first time ever, but it still seems to be
dragging). And for once I do have a dream to report.
     Clearly it was inspired by my typing several
entries from last year's jyze at the scope office last
night. Incest and self-reflexivity! Those entries
covered the period when Lady U and I were divvying up
the community property. This is what we were doing in
the dream too, but somehow I had come by train to visit
her to do it. Bizarrely, she was now living with a
certain famous politician of Scandi descent, a former
vice-president of the USA and more recently ambassador
to her ancestral homeland. He came in with a video he
wanted her to see, and he genially invited me to watch
it with them. It turned out to be soft-core porn
featuring a slinky Asian/Cawk lesbian duo. Pretty tame

stuff, I thought in the dream. For some reason I was
holding on my lap, as we watched the video, the ancient
electric typewriter which I bought during my stay in
that same homeland of hers. I knew I wouldn't be able
to carry such a clunky machine back to the city and
offered it to the lady as a gift. She was delighted;
said she'd use it to practice her keyboarding and thus
avoid putting wear and tear on her shiny new computer.
(Was the veep delighted too? Can't recall. Like most
dreams it was very postmod in its refusal to offer any
kind of ending at all, beyond an abrupt cutoff.)

*   *

   -- On an impulse I've moved down to the couch/
loveseat. First time for me here in many months.
Six months at least. But last week I cleared off this
seat for brother Rob's visit Saturday night. It's the
inner one, closest to the center of the room, next to
the end table supporting the white fan, the stacks of
old papers, the ancient portable radio (itself unused
for even longer than six months), and the black tobacco-
company-logoed ashtray liberated from the "north pole"
retro bar (Rob having given this ashtray its first
workout on Saturday). The outer seat, closest to the
west windows and the windowsill row of potted flowers,
is still crammed with books, journals, magazines -- even
more so, because I shifted most of the stuff from this
seat to the stacks over there.

   So now it's almost four hours post wake-up. The
Lady U/veep dream is a distant memory -- and as with
most of my recorded dreams, I remember writing about it
far better than I remember dreaming it. In the meantime
a shower and the usual lengthy breakfast while reading
the papers. The good life. I'm still wearing my
bathrobe, the same green terrycloth one with its right-
side belt loop hanging by a thread. Because the robe
falls open so easily -- and because at times I sprawl on
the green armchair in positions which even with the robe
closed would look indecent, I suspect, from certain
angles -- I've kept the blinds closed on the south
window that's now at my back. If they're open, the

occupants of half a dozen rooms in higher stories across
the courtyard can look straight in at me when I'm
sitting here or in the green armchair. (More and more
I'm keeping those blinds closed all day, opening just
the ones on the west windows.)

     And it better be the good life. Because it appears
I'll be sticking with it a while longer and maybe
permanently. Almost certainly for the rest of this
year. Because: I was wrong again. Neither "Feisty" nor
"Adventuress" has responded. With these silences coming
atop the ongoing one of "Boxholder," I think it's time
to call off the romantic quest. Looks like the jyzeman
has indeed struck out.

     Of course a slim chance remains I'll hear from at
least one of these three. I rate it as something like
one in twenty and shrinking fast. (It was two weeks ago
yesterday I sent off the last two letters. Even
allowing for creaky mechanics at the weekly's personals
department, the letters should've been in the women's
hands by the end of last week. If my words had made any
impression at all, either woman could've called; I
included my phone number in both letters. A reply
written over the weekend and mailed on Monday should've
arrived by now. -- But then I still haven't checked
today's mail, since I don't like to go up to the lobby
in this shabby robe and in fact never have. So maybe
the odds are slightly better than I've been thinking.
Say they're still one in fifteen. If nothing's up there
today they'll shrink to one in thirty.)

     But the good life. I'm preparing to embrace it.
I'm working on some new angles. If I really go hard at
it I think I can overcome the absence of a love interest
for at least the rest of the "JAMR" era. It won't
happen in a day, though, this vanquishing.

     Still, it's hard to beat rising shortly before noon
and then the deliciously stretched-out breakfast. The
meal itself I prepare more or less by rote now: coffee,
cornflakes with a sliced banana and thawed-out frozen
fruit (I've added peach slices and blueberries to the
mix), three pieces of wheat toast with butter and jelly

or (on alternate days) two corn toaster muffins with butter and honey. Too much butter, I know, but I've decided to indulge the craving for a while and hope Scandi evolution has provided me with an efficient way to process the stuff. I am cutting back on coffee, though, from twenty-four ounces daily to sixteen. Twenty-four at one sitting was an experiment and several times nearly floated me right out of my chair.

Breakfast in silence. Always. No radio. Cars flitting by outside at eye level on the elevated viaduct roadway but I scarcely notice them now (and am not necessarily displeased they're there when I do). If Kevin starts up his music next door he usually waits until about three to let it rip. The stuff he plays is mostly disco/techno, the same maddeningly insipid cuts over and over, and sometimes I try to mask it with the radio, but to succeed the volume must be unbearably high. (So I'll face a problem if I ever do decide to give up the hideaway. Either find a place to work outside B-2 -- the downtown library, say -- or take up earplugs. Then again Kevin could be moving out before too long. Once not long ago I heard him cry out, "Whoooeee, I'm gonna be a proud papa!" -- And with such innocent elation it just had to be for real.)

Most afternoons I try to pack up and leave by two-thirty or so. But this is one of the things that makes the good life good: I'm free, I can arrive at the hideaway late or skip it entirely and nobody will give a damn. If I get hooked on reading something here or at a newsstand or a bookstore I can stick with it, and sometimes I do. Or I can just sit here, or anywhere, cogitating, and sometimes I do that too. Or if not sit to do it, stand. Pace. Jump, even, as in nerfing (usually a good way to jar some ideas loose).

Today, though, I need to make my weekly public-market run. If I postpone it much longer this afternoon my chances of finding decent bananas and tomatoes will plummet (because in just a few minutes the after-work crowd will begin snapping up what's left of the good stuff). -- So now this cranky ol' jyzer goes to market.

[Jyze in Love]

                    *   *

     -- Back an hour later with the bananas, the
potatoes, the tomatoes, the bread, and -- a card from
"Feisty"! Also known as (or so she signs the card)
"Zoelie B." (yes, with just the initial, not a full
surname). Says she'll be calling me in March when she's
back in town.
     So it seems the jyzeman hasn't struck out after
all. What looked like a third strike was a foul tip and
the catcher dropped it. The grizzled vet's still got
life. He's hangin' in there.
     whoooeee!
     Not that I should be doing too much celebrating.
But for a few minutes I can't help myself. And I know
for at least a few days -- say until Saturday, which is
when March starts, and perhaps even until four weeks
from next Monday when March ends -- life will be a lot
livelier than it would otherwise have been, and that's
even after allowing for all the attendant anxieties.
     Was the business about a "slim chance" a setup?
Not at all! But maybe I was sensing something when I
improved the odds from one in twenty to one in fifteen.
(And I note the card is postmarked Monday, February 24,
fitting right in with my odds-improving scenario.)
     No doubt I'd be celebrating even more except the
mail brought in something else: a letter from sister
Barb. I haven't opened it yet, but its minimal heft
only increases my foreboding. Like maybe it'll be a
four-word message: "Good riddance for sure!"
     Which would be fine with me, come to think of it
(but I do have to remind myself of this; the thought
doesn't arise spontaneously). In any event I'm not
about to open it now. Save it for later. Maybe even
another day. For now I want to savor this rare romantic
triumph. (Limited though it may be, sure. It's still
the one and only of the new regime and in fact the first
in eons in which I've been -- if only in a manner of
speaking -- the aggressor. I mean, she placed the ad,
true, but it wasn't aimed specifically at me. It was a
general call for suitors. My letter was not general but

particular, addressed to her alone, and therefore I see myself as being the one who went after her and not the other way around. -- As if it matters a helluva lot.)

"Zoelie." Doesn't sound Filipina or even half Filipina to me, but I suppose it could be. Her postcard is quite large, five by seven, but her handwriting is also large (in purple ink!) and so, intentionally maybe, she can't fit much in. "Egad," she writes, "got a kick out of your letter." The "egad" is playing off my use of the term (a favorite of Mother's) in my letter to her, and I like that. (I wrote something like "Egad, is it possible you wouldn't be interested?") Then the line about calling in March. Then her signature. And after that, in parens, "Don't actually subscribe to" -- and here she mentions the newspaper referred to in her ad, the same one I pick up in the lobby every night at two a.m. Truth in packaging, I guess.

And that's it. Comely free-flowing calligraphy, though, and an amusing choice of cards, the picture side showing an idyllic "resort and conference center" with the mountain it's named after rising behind it in the shape of an (eponymous) woman sleeping on her back. The card is postmarked from a presumably nearby town somewhere out in the wilds of the northeast quadrant of the state. This could mean a lot of things or nothing at all. Is Zoelie B. attending a conference? Does she work for the resort or some other nearby outfit or in a job which keeps her on the move? Does she have family in that area? Given her interest in finding a working-class man (as expressed in the ad) I'd be inclined to think she'd be working class herself and thus not too likely to be attending a conference at a resort for an extended period, unless maybe she works in social services or something similar. Therefore I'd guess she does a lot of traveling, whether as part of a job or for other reasons, and probably lives here in the city or nearby but might often be away from town for extended periods. Good or bad for a relationship with someone the likes of me? I'm not sure. Depends, I guess. How serious a relationship? How trusting?

Rank speculation. But why not?

A breath of fresh air for jyze!

-- This from the same couch seat as earlier. Dusk has deepened into darkness. From here, I'd almost forgotten, a portion of a glowing orange neon hotel sign is visible down on the waterfront, with the traffic on the viaduct seeming to whiz right through it, or in front of it rather, like speeded-up clouds streaking in front of a gawdy cartoon moon. And this is one of those days when reporter Naomi's available for work, meaning I need to check in at the scope office around nine -- carrying some of my own typing to do there in case the drawer and the safe are empty -- and before then I want to put in at least a couple of hours on editing protojyze at the hideaway, that being the bare daily minimum I've pledged myself to these days. And so: time to shove off.

(But things sure do look different now. With newly bolstered confidence I even find myself thinking it's a little likelier "Adventuress" will be coming through as well. I put a lot more time and effort into the letter for her. Of course that could be just why the one to "Feisty" worked and the one to "Adventuress" didn't, if it turns out that way. The latter missive may have made me sound too eager and/or desperate -- which lord only knows I was, and am. The one to "Feisty" I dashed off quickly and spontaneously, almost as a kind of afterthought, and thus I may have accidentally come across as devil-may-care. Or something. As if there were any way to know what might or might not draw a response in any particular case.)

*   *

-- And now back home and the same lucky couch seat one more time. Jazz on the radio (the big one) and the end-table lamp shining a little more brightly than before on these pages (I moved it closer a moment ago) but otherwise all's the same.

Some work did await me at the scope office tonight. A good sign, I hope, though there's no particular reason to think so. February brought in only about half what I

64

need to average per month for bare subsistence.
Probably it won't be until June, I'm thinking now, that
I'll have a good idea whether I'll be able to get by
without taking a second job (horrible thought).

   -- No, all's not the same. "Feisty"'s card is
tacked to the side of the loft doorjamb in a spot where
I can almost hear it whispering in my ear. Zoelie B.
Fantasize away, me lad, while ye may. And at the same
time, in theater B as it were, be preparing for
disappointment. For one thing, she might've gotten a
bigger kick out of another or several or even many other
replies; she might've sent this card just to keep me in
play as a remote fallback option. And who knows what
kind of person she really is. Everything in her ad
sounds good, but how true is any of it? And what if
it's all true but the chemistry's bad regardless? Or
what if she lives way out in the boonies somewhere? A
great many things could go wrong here. And though it's
true March starts on Saturday, she didn't say, as she
might've, she'd call "this weekend" or "next week" or
"in early March." Just "in March." I could be
squirming on this hook for five weeks!

   But I'll take it, yes I will. Bless you Zoelie.
(Which is a name I've never come across before. It's
not even listed in my fine-print, 363-page character-
naming manual. Nor do I have a sure sense of how it's
pronounced. And I'm thinking it's a little odd that a
Fil/Eurusan (as it were) of her age raised in my home
city, as the ad said she was, would stick with her
Filipina name, if that's what it is. Maybe it ties in
with her declared "prog. politics," and if that's the
case, of course I applaud it. But then I wonder how
flexible she'll be. But then again there's her declared
sense of humor, which seems to be displayed (maybe) by
her choice of the card showing the shapely sleeping
mountain woman. Still -- will I be expected to love
Filipino food? Take up Tagalog? Entertain unending
entourages of relatives from the old country, say as I
used to have to do with Lady U and also Lady S?)

   Barb's letter, meanwhile, I'm planning to let sit

unopened for a while longer. Until I'm good and ready
to face it.

     -- And this past J-week, what else about it? week
of a supreme leader's death overseas and a fine writer's
death here (one of his books being among the most
influential for me during my early apprentice period, if
I can call it that). week of dipping into a big batch
of philosophy-related tomes, including one specifically
intended to prep me for "Adventuress" -- just in case --
not to mention a magisterial recent reevaluation of the
life work of my college-days philosophy hero, who's
suddenly starting to look good again to at least one
vociferous faction of the arbiters of intellectual
fashion. (All this dipping and sampling because I'm
pondering a "philosophical turn" as a way of bolstering
my move beyond fiction. Maybe philosophy, of all
things, is what will give me a life again -- literary
and perhaps even otherwise.)

     Best of all, on Saturday night brother Rob's visit.
Fish sticks and tater tots, cheapo burgundy, a bout with
jyzos. Lots of talk about Barb too, and just as
expected Rob confirmed that his current relations with
her are much like mine and he's virtually without hope
they'll improve. Nonetheless he won't take the final
step of breaking off with her unless she pushes him into
it, and I fully support him on this. (Oddly enough he
seems to be even more bitter toward her than I am. In
the end we decided this is because I'm more congenitally
optimistic than he is -- or if not congenitally, say
temperamentally -- although temperament must be at least
in part (large part!) congenital too. In any case: even
after severing relations I'm the more hopeful of
effecting a rapprochement with her.)

     Also, in a sense paralleling my reborn interest in
philosophy, Rob's thinking of getting back into
painting. (And we bantered a lot about all the time
he's losing to house upkeep. How lucky I am to be in an
apartment again and what's more a very small one. And
truly I fail to sound this note often enough in here.
The thousand and one ways I'm pleased to be away from

the houses and yards of the Lady U era and the endless
headaches involved in their maintenance.)
    -- If not for Zoelie B.'s postcard tacked up here
and what it represents (its picture side showing the
resort buildings clustered beneath the eponymous rock
formation, which looks to be a section of ridgeline,
actually, in the shape of an improbably busty supine
indigenous "maiden," as the caption on the reverse side
states) -- if not for this card, I say, I'm sure I'd be
describing the evening with Rob in much greater detail.
His adventures at the thrift shops. His battles with
his new store manager. The ways our age gap affects our
worldviews and also our views on family and hometown.
    Reminding me: day after tomorrow is Mother's
birthday. And two days ago a box arrived from the
"Memorials" publisher returning all the items Mother and
I sent them, including the photos used in the book.
Although I expect to have more dealings with this
publisher (hopefully including some monetary ones
involving checks for purchased books), the return of the
material in this box effectively marks the end of the
project. A great relief, yes, but with a sorrowful
dimension to it. Working on "Memorials" was one way of
keeping in touch with ol' Mom and now that's over. On
this ever-spinning globe we do keep whirling right
along, oh yes we do. (I think of all her papers
moldering away over in my storage unit. It's extremely
unlikely anyone will ever want them for anything. And
is this not how memory itself comes to an end?
-- Though I can't resist adding: no, it absolutely is
not, or at least not if Jyze has any say in it.)
    Also this week the world's been set agog by a new
advance in cloning. Before long the streets could be
crawling with sets of identical twins, triplets,
quadruplets...all the way up to millituplets and beyond.
Maybe even long-dead ancestors will be replicable if
some part of the body, even if only a single strand of
hair, is still lying around somewhere. Maybe even far-
longer-dead dinosaurs will be resurrectable, some think.
Meaning if you nurse the delusion that genetic

replication is the same thing as immortality and you
want to walk the earth forever you'd better not be
cremated. (Me, more than ever I want to be cremated.)
     -- But not cremated just yet if I can help it, no.
Especially not now when I'm on the verge of being
romantically resuscitated, quite possibly, as a kind of
creaky instant clone of my old courting self.
     Saved at the brink? Could it be?
     -- At least we've got a potentially interesting
story line here to keep jyze hopping for another few
weeks if not longer. (But I was ready to embrace all-
out reclusivity and I don't think I want to stop being
ready to do that. Lately I've been talking out loud to
myself more than ever, I mean lengthy dialogues at
times. I even did this while Rob was here --
unconsciously got to muttering to myself out in the
kitchen as he sat by the window smoking his pipe -- and
he came up with a good line about it: "Sounds like
you're getting to be almost as bad as I was after Marcia
and I split up: sort of like a one-man odd couple."
-- Which is to say: could be I'm halfway to certifiable
already. And: I'm ready to launch into the equivalent
of a convict's obsessive exercise regime just as a way
of battling to stay sane here in my JAMR cell.)

9

     A moment ago rain was pelting against the window,
which remains beaded with it, and then the sun lit up
all those beads for a dazzling moment (and the walls
too, deep into the room), and now everything's gray
again and a noisy new splatter is starting up.
     All week it's been like this. And I've done a lot

of extra walking out in it, hoping to melt off a few
more pounds and make myself as presentable as possible
-- just in case. Much of the time I've been twirling a
folded-up umbrella, reviving memories of the spinning
baseball bats of adolescence. And thinking
(fantasizing) the umbrella might conceal a pepper-spray
device inside the handle. The street hostiles do
occasionally take notice of that twirling umbrella, but
most likely because in its tightly folded and sheathed
state it resembles a short black billy club.

Not that I'm obsessing on bad guys or gals, crime,
any of that. Far from it. The streets are actually
looking pretty good these days, relatively speaking.
Even if they weren't, who wants to squander time and
energy worrying about such matters? At all times be
alert and ready to practice avoidance and that's it.
(Wood here somewhere? Knock until it splinters!)

In today's mail, retrieved moments ago, not much.
A note from cousin Lars providing sibling addresses for
"Memorials" mailings, and an improbable notice from my
favorite secondhand bookstore of bygone days (it's since
moved from downtown to up north somewhere): they've
located a book "something like" one I asked them to find
for me five years ago (Mentoka research). Thirty bucks.
Back then I would've gone for it but now I can't. Nor
do I need it. I may even have it already, and I know I
have the actual one I asked them to find as well as
several others dealing with the same topic. Of info I
have plenty; of research I've already done far more than
enough; of ability and/or inspiration to complete the
project for which all this spadework was intended it
seems I've fallen short.

Meanwhile not a peep from "Feisty," my preposterous
romantic hope. She still may come through but even so
this long delay can't bode well. Is not my expression
of interest, however fatuous, being further trivialized?
Am I not being left to twist slowly in the wind?

For the past couple of days I've been thinking it's
probably time for this dangling feeder strip right here
(me) to make itself available to some other bird. Which

means: yes, I've hit on another prospect. I vowed no
more, true, but again this week I found myself glancing
through those damn personals. (Last week I did manage
to ignore them, but I guess the first thrill of success
in drawing a response has emboldened me.) The new one
is "Professor/Artist." She's seeking an "intense" man
"fanatically devoted" to his work. She's interested in
"art, literature, dance and not much else." Sounds a
little coldblooded but -- maybe worth a try.

    But not for a few more days. I know it's utterly
absurd, but I'm trying hard to stay loyal to Zoelie B.,
lady of putatively shapely albeit sleeping provenance.
She's my first real personals infatuation.

    (Rain pelting again now. And here in my upper
right peripheral visual field dangle the red-and-white
Santa Claus fuchsias, a miniature parachute invasion
frozen in time and what's more one hundred percent bug-
free for the sixth straight week. And over on the
couch, where the inside seat still remains litter-free,
rests a new stack of philosophy tomes from the library.
Realistically speaking, that might be the best augury
yet of my future for the JAMR era.)

    -- This being the heaviest day of what's turning
into an unusually demanding Jyzer Ink workweek. We're
into March now and the shakedown period is over. And:
if I can average one week like this per month while the
other three weeks combined add up to roughly its
equivalent, I should be able to stay in the black
indefinitely, meaning pay all my bills without eating
away at the deep reserves. (But this week I did send a
note to Lynn, the guardian of those reserves, requesting
a one-time draw equivalent to three months' living
expenses. This will replenish the nearly empty savings
account I use as a cushion. Even after the withdrawal
the deep reserves will remain slightly larger than they
were at the start nine months ago. In short, a great
year for the financial markets has just about
compensated for the scoping income I lost out on during
my "sabbatical." Over the long run I'll be delighted if
I can support myself through the Jyzer Ink contract work

while the deep reserves merely keep pace with inflation.
The very early returns are suggesting I may not have
hoped for too much on this score and so, yes, I'm
delighted already, even if only provisionally.)

    And then sister Barb's letter. I waited two days
to open it. What I found inside did nothing to change
my mind about anything. Her attitude is -- not
friendly, let's say. Nothing even faintly warm about
it. Yes, be gone, sinner, it says in essence, but if
you want to crawl back someday and perform extensive
penance, I'll think about letting you back in.

    It's my hunch Barb doesn't understand yet how
serious I am about this matter. I'm done with her,
period. (She declares my "behavior" in the past couple
of years to be "utterly inexplicable." But I haven't
noticed her seeking any explanations or trying to reach
any understandings or accommodations, and I have seen
her contemptuously shrugging off my efforts to do these
very things. In a nutshell it's been abide by her
extremely severe rules and interpretations or else.)

    -- And I must be moving on. Probably I won't be
able to return to these pages (you must jyze your low-
end quota!) until tomorrow. Eight or nine hours in
front of the screen tonight will drain me to the marrow,
maybe even of the marrow. And the lousy working
conditions at the scope office won't help any. Bad
ambient light, at once too glary for the screen and yet
too dim for the printed material I need to consult at
times. A horrible low-backed chair. Pathetic keyboard
ergonomics. -- But for pay at three to four times
minimum wage, freedom to wear what I want and come and
go as I please (during nighttime hours), and the
priceless perk of using the machinery for my own stuff:
still well worth it. (The contortions I've gone through
to hang on to this job -- in fact keep the job itself
alive, when scopers have become an endangered species in
this city and in-office nightscopers quite possibly
extinct, except for me -- I just shake my head in
amazement that it's all worked out as well as it has.)

                    *   *

     -- And here's tomorrow. Scope-office conference
room. I just checked for surprises in the safe and the
reporter drawers. None. Only the seven hours of
Thursday's -- yesterday's -- grand jury to scope. And I
know they'll be fairly tough pages because I've already
scan-scoped them. In the worst of the witnesses I came
across a nasty three-page patch not just margin-to-
margin but also entirely lacking in punctuation; and for
most of this bramble the witness is quoting an overheard
dialogue between drug dealers who are themselves quoting
other drug dealers, many in Spanish or Spanglish. I'm
guessing I'll be out of here about four a.m.
     First this.
     At the big oval table. Windows reflecting inward,
an image on offer of my own scruffy nightscoper self in
green hooded sweatshirt hunched hood down over the J-
book. Thinking maybe this jyze has been getting a
little too chichi lately. (In fact was already thinking
this as I rode the elevator up. And speaking of chichi:
first choice for this evening's jyze venue was the
artiest bar in town, but the joint was jam-packed and
charging at the door for something called the Kirts
Show, "well-hung boys in skirts.")
     Also rattling around in my head: a rail-thin seven-
foot-tall black dude in a "Crew" shirt who strode by on
the sidewalk looking like a Masai warrior loping across
veldt. A newspaper article on the leveling a century or
so back of my current home turf, the sluicing away of
the first big hump and the belt-lining away of the
second big hump. A woman who looked a whole lot like
last year's unrequited crush Sofie ("Our Lady of the
Clocks"): saw her emerging from our local market and
heading my way so I quickly angled across the street.
Like all other women of the past, including Lady U,
including Mother, including Lady K after her brief
resurrection last fall, including now sister Barb as
well: Sofie's history.
     But "Boxholder" may not be. She finally did write.
A letter from her came in this afternoon. True, it's a
form letter, personalized only in the salutation, and it

does say she's met a guy and they're "progressing" in
their effort to get to know each other better. But it
also says if this new romance falls through she might
want to meet me for a cup of coffee. And she does sign
it by hand in blue ink with her first name: Debbie.
(No initial for the last name, though, if that means
anything.) And the canned text does attempt to salve
any wounds her long silence may have caused; it says my
letter is one in a stack she'd lost track of and this is
why she's been so long in replying. In the meantime,
however, she's picked this other guy. But if she hadn't
misplaced my letter, she seems to be kindly implying,
the lucky guy could've been me, and so the silence was
simply a matter of bad luck and not the result of any
personal shortcomings on my part.

This was heartening and so I immediately wrote back
and said by all means she should call me (supplying my
phone number) if her new romance hits a bumpy patch.

-- So now all of a sudden I'm batting .667.
"Feisty" Zoelie and "Boxholder" Debbie. Only
"Adventuress" has failed to reply. (And the distant-
city prospect from last fall, but that one doesn't count
anymore. This is a whole new personals season.)

Two more days for Zoelie because I've got this soft
spot for her. Then I come up with a pitch for "Prof/
Artist."

With extreme shame I have to admit all this
personals stuff can be wildly exciting at times. I
imagine it's something like fantasy baseball, except
here you could actually meet the object of your fantasy
and maybe even wind up doing whatever it is you
fantasize doing with her/him. At the same time the
whole business can be ridiculously depressing. So it's
come down to personal ads, has it? (But this afternoon
after receiving "Boxholder" Debbie's form letter I was
striding the streets feeling pretty goddamn slick.
Absurd, I know, but there it is.)

-- Also in the same mail another kind of form
letter from sister Barb addressed to her three brothers
informing us we still have to pay some taxes on Mother's

estate. It was something I'd been expecting (and had
warned Rob about) but in recent days I'd allowed myself
to think maybe I'd figured wrong, so now the news feels
even worse than it otherwise would've. Yet I won't have
any problem coming up with the money. In fact I'm in a
minibinge mood right now knowing the supplemental cash
infusion from the deep reserves (that is, my portion of
Mother's estate) will soon be arriving. I've bought
several magazines and books and I'm thinking if only
this Zoelie B. would come through I could show her a
good time and win her heart for sure -- maybe even take
her to a movie or something. (I've also thought of
giving her the still-unboxed color TV with built-in VCR.
Seriously. And if that wouldn't do the trick she could
have her choice of anything in the storage unit. How
about a full table setting of antique silverware? How
about a large Chinese vase? How about the massive
console built by the company that employed my father for
the better part of his adult life? -- Feisty Zoelie,
you don't know what you're missing out on here!)

Meanwhile my horrible cold has finally cleared up.
Aunt Shar has written again (more profuse thanks for
"Memorials"). Newspaper articles have persuaded me
that selennium and ginseng supplements may improve the
odds of my health holding up over the long haul and so
I've added them to the mix, meaning I'm now up to eight
pills a day. I've pulled two different muscles in my
back, the second while overcompensating to protect the
aching first (but nothing too serious, I hope; and I
know the underlying cause -- the godawful chair I have
to use at the scope office -- and so I also hope I can
avoid further injury by frequently changing the way I
sit there: posture, angles, cushions, and so on).

And: I've discovered sales prices are twenty
percent lower at the big chain drugstore near the
northern border of my normal tripolar domain (near the
supermarket) than at either of the downtown outlets and
I've accordingly altered my provisioning route and in
fact expanded my household hoarding facility to include
one of the three cedar chests stacked at the end of the

kitchen counter (and that chest is now filled with large cans of vegetable juice scored from the drugstore sale).

I have a strange hunch things will be looking much different by next J-day. A breakthrough. Zoelie B. will be the one, or at least I sure do hope so. If I'm wrong and fail to hear from her, well, just say I'll be dejected and ornery as hell. And even then March will be less than half over and therefore I won't have to give up the last shred of hope on this woman for another seventeen days. And meanwhile by that point I'll have a letter out to the latest troller-for-suitors I've taken a shine to, "Prof/Artist," meaning the number of at least slightly live prospects will increase to three, or four if I count "Adventuress" (she too may come a cropper with her first choice and therefore stumble across a stack of "lost" letters, mine among them).

A year ago I was warning myself not to get caught up again in the old love hunt. Never in my worst nightmares of that time did I picture myself entangled in this form of it. And so entangled! -- But I'm enjoying it, at least at times, just as I said. For me love's much too important to give it up without a very good reason -- and corny though it must sound, less so the being loved than the loving. The crazy loving. Trying to make someone's life a joy. Sometimes I miss it so much I'd chew through drywall to have another go at it (and often feel I'm already doing some of that crunchy/chalky kind of chewing). But in other respects all's well -- except for the fiction realm, of course, where all remains lost -- and since resolve to devote myself completely to working on fiction was a very large part of my reason for giving up on love in the first place, why not go for love now?

So keep pushing it a while longer, yes. Yet also try to stick with the JAMR scheme. This week I've let it go, the chance has slipped away, it's too late, I'm done, need to shoo myself back into the computer room and tend to Jyzer Ink business. Next week, then, look for some new way to get off on once again -- probably just the first of many more times -- jyzing around B-2.

[Jyze in Love]

10

    Friday afternoon, that flashy time when the B-2
walls pulsate with shards of sunlight reflected from
cars creeping along the viaduct. Almost like a fierce
summer electrical storm, I'm thinking, but with the
wrong soundtrack. And flashy too because at any moment
"Prof/Artist" could call. In theory. My letter said
I'm most easily reached between one and four, p.m. or
a.m., and she probably received it yesterday or today.
It's now quarter to four. Still a fifteen-minute window
for her.
    But it's not "Prof/Artist" who's got me tearing my
hair out. (It's wet, by the way, the hair; I'm fresh
from the shower, wrapped in the funky green bathrobe, a
towel riding the top of my head like a prayer cloth.
Sprawled in the green armchair, right leg once again
propped against footstool to shore up right thigh as
platform for perping major jyze action.)
    Zoelie. Zoelie B. I waited all last weekend for
her to call. Late Sunday night I finally broke down and
wrote a brief letter in response to "Prof/Artist"'s ad
and then Monday afternoon dropped it off at the
newspaper office (only my second appearance there on
this kind of mission, but I felt almost like a regular;
and this may've made things even more painful when the
receptionist's eyes, as I handed her the envelope, met
mine with a look of what I took to be mingled
recognition, disdain, and pity). Next to the hideaway
where I discovered I was utterly incapable of working.
So onward to the ORB (still the only real full-service
bookstore in this town) for a long empty-headed browsing

session. And then, because I avoid the scope office on
Monday nights (since I have no legitimate reason to be
there and fear being caught in flagrante churning out my
own work on their equipment), home. No sooner did I
settle into the armchair than the phone rang. Zoelie.
(It's two syllables, I can now report, emphasis on the
first and with a long O: ZOH-lee.)

     What followed had to be one of the most awkward,
uncomfortable, excruciating -- yet exhilarating --
ninety-minute periods of my entire life. (Was it really
ninety minutes? Two hours? One? I lost all track of
time. But I think we might've kept going all night if
she hadn't suddenly announced, "I'm fading fast." And
within maybe thirty seconds was gone.)

     I don't know why it was so awkward. Surely the
cause went well beyond mutual nervousness and
embarrassment to be meeting in such a way, on the phone,
via the personals. Maybe I'm just a total klutz at this
sort of thing. Maybe she is too. Or maybe, as I
suspect, our emotional styles are a perfect hundred and
eighty degrees out of whack, thus accounting for not
just the strangeness but also the powerful sense of
familiarity, as if we were mirror opposites running into
each other in the street for the first time. And what
opposites! I'm wet, she's dry; I'm warm, she's cool;
I'm hang-loose, she's guarded. A list that could go on
and on.

     Worse yet, she responds to my attempts at humor in
strange and discombobulating ways. Sometimes it's with
a hearty laugh (a terrific hearty laugh!) but just as
often it's with a prolonged silence. Dead air. And my
efforts to draw her out are likely as not to draw only
more of same. To fill that emptiness I start talking
too much, saying even goofier things -- desperate
things, let's face it -- and I know I'm turning her off
and she's thinking I'm pretty weird and I start to
panic. Bizarre shifts of subject. Odd chuckles.
Sudden off-kilter questions.

     Horrible, horrible, horrible.

     Yet we pencil out as a great match. If we filled

in computer matchmaker forms the machine would disgorge
us onto the "sure thing" pile. (I say this knowing
nothing about how she looks other than she's five-seven
and "people usually guess I'm Native American" and she
has, according to her ad -- I wasn't about to inquire
further on the phone -- a "nice body.")

It turns out we grew up less than ten miles apart
(she in the city proper, as her ad implied:
"Centropolis"). She and my father have a degree from
the same university and so do she and my mother, but
this second university of course is a different one and
my father has a degree from that one too -- which is to
say Zoelie attended grad school (in social work!) in the
same city ("Lahontan") where my parents met and I was
born. She served as a social worker for a year with the
same tribe on which the "Mentoka" of the Mentoka trilogy
are based. She writes -- poetry even! She reads --
widely! She rides -- a bike! She dances! She paints!
She sings! (Jazz at one time, with a band; and has a
marvelous sexy-jazzy phone voice, vibrant and throaty.)
And: she shops at a co-op! She's into all the righteous
political causes and in active ways! The building where
she works is just a few blocks from the hideaway!

But...is it that she fears intimacy? (She's never
been married. Was engaged twice, the second time
fifteen years ago.)

She calls herself a mestiza -- father a Filipino
immigrant, mother the daughter of Polish immigrants.
Right away I sensed some internal Eurasian and Asi/
Eurusan (as it were) tensions familiar from the Lady V
era (probably there are similar religious ones too) and
also was reminded of some passionate but fiercely self-
protective women I've known -- especially the one who
was a mestiza herself, though in that instance the
ethnic mix was different on both sides. And also as
with that one this Zoelie's close to three years my
senior. In fact her birthday is this week. Tomorrow!
The ides of March! Beware! -- But if she's throwing a
party for, say, selected ad repliers, my invitation
hasn't arrived yet.

She's plenty busy these days. Works full-time
for the city's combined utilities as editor of the
newsletter that goes out with all the bills and thus
has, as she proudly noted, by far the highest
circulation of any "news publication" in the state. So,
yeah, a substantial kind of person we're talking about
here. (I confessed to her that through an apparent
oversight my B-2 household has never received one of
those utility bills and thus no newsletter either. Now
when she and I fail to hit it off, watch her feel
morally obliged to turn me in: "This reprobate's been
getting a free ride at the ratepayers' expense!") She's
also studying close to full-time at a local leadership
institute to score a second master's degree in something
called "systems management." This is why her postcard
came from the mountain resort: it's the site of the
institute's weeklong intensive schooling sessions.
While there she caught a bad cold and this kept her from
calling me during her first week back in town. And she
hadn't meant to convey anything at all, she said, with
the "sleeping maiden" mountain imagery on the card;
"They were free and I just grabbed a handful in the
lobby and never noticed what the caption said. That so-
called legend is apocryphal anyway."

But she's even busier than all the above would
imply. Toward the end of the call I sputtered out
something about, "Well, should we get together sometime
then?" She: "I have a date for you." It turned out to
be, after much thumbing of her datebook, Monday the
24th. Two weeks away! (My reply was an aghast and
supremely uncool "Two weeks?! You gotta be kidding!"
She laughed heartily. I: "It's just that I'm, you know,
sort of a spur-of-the-moment kind of guy." She: "I
can't be spontaneous until after June 21st," which is
the date she completes her studies. And June 21st, as
it happened, was a hundred and four days from that day,
Monday, which makes it exactly a hundred days from
today. -- So I ruefully accepted Monday the 24th.

I did manage to persuade her to change the hour on
the proposed meeting day from lunch to dinner. For the

location she suggested right off, with no prompting from
me, the very spot where I'd first come across her ad:
the ORB cafe. When I expressed a preference for keeping
the dress casual she came back with one of her funnier
lines of the call: "Like black leather and chains?" My
reply I forget, but it was lame. Or just say
forgettable. (A lot more of my replies I wish I could
forget but can't.)

When I first protested "Two weeks?!" she said,
after more irksome datebook riffling, she could squeeze
me in on the 17th, but she'd be very tired that day
after rising early to attend some sort of breakfast
meeting at a downtown hotel before work. So I nixed the
17th. Then, after still more datebook thumbing, she
proposed a "late lunch" in the second week of April as
her next available opening after March 24th. This new
date would've been more than a month from now. So we
were back to the 24th.

Then she chaffed me a little: would I need to be
reminded about the 24th as the date approached since it
was so far beyond my usual time horizon? "No no," I
grumbled, "I don't think I could forget any of this in a
hundred years."

Finally when I asked for her last name and phone
number so I could reach her if necessary, she gave me
the name -- which the jyze rules of course forbid my
mentioning here -- but I can say it ends with a Scandi-
sounding syllable that, she informed me, traces back
many generations to a Norwegian sailor who jumped ship
in the Philippines and "went native" -- meaning she's a
tiny part Norski herself! But in sidetracking ourselves
on this odd bit of genealogy we both spaced out the
crucial matter of the phone number, and then she hit me
with "fading fast," so I never did get the number; and
then afterwards I discovered it's unlisted.

So now I'm wondering why this lack of urgency on
her part. How many other replies to her ad came in and
how many made her callback list? What am I up against
here? Will I even be granted a full-fledged chance to
present my case? Has she lined up a different candidate

for lunch or dinner every day for those two weeks? Or
say only two or three others have made the semifinals,
or one or even none; then I'd have to wonder just how
interested she is in romance if she can put off a
meeting for so long.

And why hasn't she called back to give me her
number? -- True, I could look her up through the city's
departmental listings, but I don't think she'd
appreciate that. When I suggested holding our first
meeting outside her office building during lunch hour
she sounded horrified: "They'd [her coworkers] all be
out there watching!" -- But really now. Is she fearing
I'm Dracula or what?

And shouldn't she be at least a little worried I
might meet someone else in the meantime? If she is,
she's shown no sign of it.

I wish I'd thought to ask her to call if an earlier
slot opened up in her schedule. Or better, if she just
felt like talking some more on the phone. But I wasn't
that swift. And besides, it was plain she'd already
heard enough of my fumbly spiel. Clearly I ought to be
grateful simply that she's willing to give me another
shot, and what's more this time in person. And I am, I
am! (Another of her quick hearty laughs came when I
said I couldn't recall exactly what I'd written in my
letter to her and she said, "Well, you say here you're
six-two, one-ninety, in good shape" -- and I replied
with a horrible chortle, "Oh yeah, that's me all right."
But it is! -- or it's close anyway. And one of the
first things she commented on, sounding dubious, was the
age gap: "So it'll be like I'm a high-school senior and
you're a freshman?")

What else can I recall of our conversation?
Suddenly I'm blank. No matter, though; other snatches
of it will no doubt be popping back up as I tramp my
usual paths (I've been replaying the damn phone call in
my head all week, but more in the form of sound bitesI
can't turn off, like hard-sell political ads in the days
before an election, and with the order of the replays
totally jumbled, just as in this account here).

[Jyze in Love]

    She lives in the city, I should mention, on the top
floor of a four-story apartment building four or five
miles north of my usual tripolar turf. Her view there
-- she was looking out at it as we talked (maybe
becoming absorbed in it during those long silences?) --
is "spectacular." So her salary must be pretty good.
But presumably from conscience she drives the same make
and model of car I did until a year ago, and hers is ten
years older. And she commended me for having chosen to
go carless in the city. And she's very big on recycling
and energy conservation and environmental justice.
Moved to this region several years before I did. Made
an around-the-world-in-eighty-days trip shortly before
going off to grad school in Lahontan at roughly the time
of her 10K Day/Glennarian Rollover. (Hey, I'm on a roll
here!) Hopes to get back to doing watercolors at some
point soon. Visited Mentoka for an alum-fest a few
years back (hung out in some joints whose names I
recognized). Wants to check out the Afrusan artists'
show which I'd just viewed myself a few nights before, a
block from the hideaway. Is a member of a book club
(and when I told her about my tastes in books she asked
if I'd read a certain novel, a copy of which happened to
be sitting on the shelf at my side, so in one of my
better moves of the call I flipped it open and read a
few sentences aloud, pretending to have them by memory;
and when I confessed my trick she laughed uproariously
and admitted she'd been totally taken in by it). -- She
eats organic whenever possible and doesn't do dairy.
Her first engagement failed because the guy didn't want
her to go to grad school. The second failed because --
"It was horrible! A disaster! I don't want to talk
about it!" -- and she reacted poorly to further
questions about this and about her recent social life,
so I steered elsewhere.
    That's all I can think of right now.
    -- For a full day I tried to come up with a way of
framing all this. "Framing"? Yes. How to get a handle
on it. How to keep all the strangenesses and longings
and contradictions -- not to mention the imaginings and

frustrations and euphorias and discombobulations and unknowns -- from consuming me. (Being the kneejerk romantic I am, how could I not?)

Decided this. Unless she called back, I wouldn't make a play for her (of my traditional crazy all-out kind -- that is, assuming I'm even still capable of launching such a blitz) before the meeting at the ORB cafe. In ---

*

(The phone just rang and I leapt up to answer it, heart pounding. Zoelie, her mind changed, wanting me to come see her tonight? "Prof/Artist" maybe, a little late for today's afternoon window but seeking intensity right now? Picked up the phone, "Hi" -- it's a woman's voice, and not Zoelie's -- "I'm with Arden Marketing...." Arrrgh!)

As I was saying:

On further thought I decided Zoelie, in setting our meeting date so far in the future -- and well on the far side of her birthday -- was telling me I shouldn't become too involved too fast or let my hopes rise too high. She would almost certainly be using this two-week delay, I figured, to check out any other candidates who made her callback list, with the earliest meeting dates likely accorded to the best prospects (so we laggards could simply be canceled if one of the front-runners seemed to be working out). Therefore I shouldn't feel too bad about the possibility of my being contacted by "Prof/Artist." In a way I could even look upon the delay with Zoelie as a lucky break. Otherwise I might always have wondered if "Prof/Artist" could've turned out to be the one. (For if Zoelie had called me earlier or agreed to an earlier meeting date I would've said to hell with "Prof/Artist" or anyone else.)

How ludicrous all this is. Absolutely, I know it! I'm never for a moment unaware of it! Yet I'm affected deeply regardless. I can think of little else. My own work has ground to a halt. I talk out loud (to myself and also to Zoelie; but not, so far anyway, to "Prof/ Artist" or any of the others). I snort derisively, I

kick brick walls. I make ironclad eternal vows and
abandon them twenty minutes later. Madness!

   -- As of now I don't know how I'll hold out for
another ten days. Nor can I imagine surviving an entire
sit-down dinner with this Zoelie if it turned out to be
anything like the phone call. Will she duck under the
table every time I lift a knife or fork? My tentative
plan is to try to lure her up to my office in hopes she
might form a better idea there of what I'm all about.
Most likely, though, she'll decline. Visit the lair of
a virtual stranger and possible maniac? In a big empty
building at night? In our scary quarter?

   So then the fallback plan. If dinner on the 24th
appears to be nearing its conclusion with no sign of a
breakthrough, ask her if she too finds things a bit
awkward between us. Assuming the answer's yes, point
out that her congested schedule makes it all but
impossible for us to overcome this barrier. Therefore,
propose postponing any further meetings until after
June 21st, the "hundred days" date when she said she
could "start being spontaneous." And in the meantime:
no obligations, promises, expectations.

   Is this unfair or cruel? I don't think so. She
basically proposed it herself with her remark about not
being spontaneous until after that date. (I should say
that of course I'm the one who actually counted the
days, and that wasn't until today.) -- But if she
dislikes the proposal now, she can say so and come up
with something better. Just about anything would do.
-- And if it happens "Prof/Artist" does call at some
point, slender though the chances may be, by all means
I should check out what she has to offer. This is what
USAn courtship's all about. Yes, even this grotesque
form of it. Maybe Zoelie's excessive caution or her
yen to play it coy or her resolve to vet all comers
before deciding on one -- or simply her dubious
decision to run her ad at a time when she's far too busy
to act on its implied promises (truth in advertising!)
-- maybe this will be what turns out to open the way
to an entirely different kind of life for me, and

conceivably for her too. Who knows!
     -- Or more likely it won't open the way to
anything. More likely I'll soon be right back into the
same old utterly solitudinous life I was leading before
I took the plunge on these ads. Impulse shopping! Nor
will I embarrass myself again by saying such binges are
sure to come to an end with my (probable) strike-out
with Zoelie. But I do think a vow of no more personal
ads is the likely outcome. Not forever, maybe, but
unquestionably for a good long recovery period. Three
months? Six? A year? It'll be a while before the old
ticker can take another uproar like this.
                    *   *
     -- It's one day later and so now only nine days to
go until the 24th. And this being Zoelie's birthday,
maybe she'll call and invite me over for the party (not
that I know she's having a party; I'm just spozin).
"You said you were a spur-of-the-moment kind of guy, so
you wanna spur yourself over here right now and help me
blow the candles out? Then maybe we could guzzle some
bubbly in my hot tub. I mean, you know, if you're
willing to take your spurs off first. Or would you
rather leave them on to go with the black leather and
chains?"
     Speaking of blows and wetness, it's a stormy day.
All day and right now too. I've stayed home so far, and
for a similar kind of reason: stormy mood. This
would've been the most likely afternoon for "Prof/
Artist" to call if she'd been wowed by my note, so I'm
presuming she wasn't. The odds on her, low to start
with, drop almost out of sight, just like those for
"Boxholder" and, even more, "Adventuress." Looks like
it's Zoelie or nuttin'.
     A few more things I've recalled about her. For
one, her given name's only part Filipino (the "Z-o"
part) (that's what she said!). And she's embarrassed,
she told me, by how little she knows about the
Philippines, although her world trip did include a brief
stop there. And back in her college days she and my
sister attended summer classes at the same art institute

in Centropolis, maybe even at the same time. And when I
said I like a certain jazz musician, she mentioned she'd
once seen him perform live and I said, "Not at" -- and
mentioned the club, also in Centropolis. "Yes!" "Me
too!" (When I first asked about her taste in music she
said "eclectic" and then started to rephrase in simpler
language. "'Eclectic' says it just fine," I objected.
She seemed relieved. Not until that moment did I feel I
might be passing her entry-level "smarts" test.)

    Meanwhile I'm thinking maybe I'll ask her to come
up to my office right away when we meet at the cafe on
the 24th (when and if) rather than waiting until after
dinner. Best way I've hit on so far to break the ice.
It would give her something to do -- look around, ask
questions -- and give me a less self-conscious means to
reveal myself. If she'd do it. Since the hour would be
fairly early I could honestly assure her that at least a
few people of more or less good repute would still be
lingering in the building.

    The obsession. Already I'm sporting with her in
fancy. Will she ever look this good to me again after
we actually meet? (But I suspect she will, at least in
terms of physical appearance. She's been around, it's
obvious. Not just around; swarmed after. A certain
blase' confidence she exudes, a verbal swagger, diva
type almost. And all that exercising and "healthy
stuff" suggest she hasn't lost much, if anything, of
what drew the swarms in. Half a step at most, that's my
prediction.) (And on the age gap it's my thought things
nicely balance out. She's two and a half years older,
true, but actuarially I'll still predecease her by two
or three years. I'm even thinking we could have us a
real good carnal run here at the start if we could just
actually get started.)

    But I'm also ready to turn up the heat on her if it
appears things aren't clicking. Get to the bottom of
why they're not. Ask the tough questions. Be ready to
withdraw and stay withdrawn until June 21st --
"Spontaneous Day" -- if that looks advisable. Or to
take a flat-out rejection. But I'm involved now; I'm

not pretending otherwise. If she drops me it'll hurt
plenty.

     -- In other realms this past eighter, scarcely
anything. If there had been something, I wouldn't've
noticed anyway. Well, no, brother Jeff called again
from Lahontan; on the side he's now become a part-time
salesman for a long-distance phone service and he wanted
me to switch over if I wasn't already with that service,
which I wasn't. So I did. Of Jyzer Ink work this week,
none, and I learned the crucial week of the 24th will
also be light because some key office players, reporter
Naomi among them, will be decamping with their spouses
to southern climes to take in a week of baseball spring
training; so it's a good thing week before last was
heavy and in addition the check from the deep reserves
will soon be arriving to repad the cushion a bit.

     And a few more items that pop up. Two fire alarms
sounded one day, the first catching me in bed asleep and
the second on the throne (porcelain kind) a-gruntin'. I
began a new campaign to keep my left Achilles tendon
from unraveling again, this time trying something
counterintuitive (at first glance): alternating thirty-
minute daily sessions of wallball and nerfhoop. For the
first time ever I spotted a news story datelined the
city of my second and third "exile years" overseas.
And: also for the first time ever I plucked a gray hair
-- from an eyebrow! (It was sticking straight out
almost like a cat whisker. Seemingly sprouted
overnight.)

     I discovered I don't, after all, have the book that
the used-book store found for me and thus I have a good
excuse to visit Zoelie's turf this weekend, since the
bookstore is serendipitously located in the same general
area.

     And realized: it was just about exactly a year ago
today that I put down a deposit reserving a studio
apartment which turned out to be, after a certain amount
of jockeying, the very unit B-2 I'm so irresponsibly
failing to restrict my jyzing around to right now.

[Jyze in Love]

11

    Jyze for the first time ever touches down in the
Zoelie zone. Oh with tired legs. Hiked all the way out
here, I did, about four miles, up and over the big north
hill, and then tromped methodically up and down local
streets searching for a four-story apartment house with
lake-view windows and Zoelie's name on the buzzer list
or mailbox labels. -- Just for the hell of it I did
this. To see if I could gain a little extra insight on
the woman. But found nothing. Or found lots, rather,
but no sign of her.
    Sure I'm crazy. And rightfully so. There have
been developments.
    -- As right now with her it's crashing and burning.
Most likely. It appears we're into the endgame without
ever having visited the mid- or any other part of the
in-the-flesh game. In fact without ever having set eyes
on each other. Or at least not that I know of.
    Classical guitar on the P.A. Neighborhood cafe.
Dusk. A quiet Saturday evening. Half the tables empty,
most of the others hosting studious twenty-something
singletons or pairs, everyone but me nursing exotic teas
and organic crumpets (I've got a peanut-butter sandwich
I brought with me and a glass of cherry cider). Sunny
again most of the day, as was yesterday, after a week of
torrential rains bringing on a new round of weather-
related emergencies. "Worst Winter Ever" groans a
railroad official in a front-page headline quote. As of
yesterday the mainline north-south tracks were buried
under mud avalanches in a dozen different spots.
    Zoelie. Such a week of obsession. Total self-

indulgence on my part, no question. I'm an emotional
wreck. A big chunk of it without doubt has little to do
with her and much to do with my own long-running self-
chosen introversion. "Recluse." "Isolato." My every
move is warped by big-time neediness and I know it. Not
that knowing it helps a whole lot.

Two key setbacks. First, not only did she fail to
call back to give me her number after our long telephone
talk, but she remained totally silent for eight days.
Second, when she did finally break the silence, she did
it to cancel our date for the 24th. By voicemail!

Three or four separate times this week I've
resolved that I'm through with her but then recanted.
Now, after yet another setback -- still in force at this
moment, as for that matter so are all the others -- I've
flip-flopped and decided to wait her out. Might as
well. If I were to tell her I'm dropping out of the
chase I'd still be waiting her out regardless, because
when it ends with her it ends with romance. For a while
anyway. This year, say. And maybe next year too. (Why
not up the ante? Live dangerously!)

The Zoelie zone, her hood, is doing better than
expected. I paid my respects to various familiar
landmarks. Visited the co-op market where she told me
she shops (whose bananas cost almost twice what I
normally pay, as does just about everything else they
carry -- though of course most of what I eat they would
never allow on their shelves). Also hit the magazine
shop, part of a chain owned by a guy I used to know
slightly a decade or so back (he's sold it since then).
The hood here is gentrifying, funkifying, technifying,
artifying all at once, so it appears, and yet the scale
is still fairly small-townish. It remains a likable
place, although a huge new office complex for a software
company is in the early stages of construction. When
that's up and running, look out. Of course! But for
the immediate future I'm still fantasizing about putting
in lots of time out here and enjoying it.

(During the Lady U years I visited this area a few
times on foot by myself and drove through it many more.

Dined ceremonially with Lady U, Mother, Unk Erik and
cousin Leif and several others at the Greek restaurant
which is still packing 'em in on the corner across from
the drawbridge. Strolled the summer-solstice street
fair most years. But never really bonded with the place
because it was a bit too arduous to hike over here on a
regular basis, just as it is now when I'm coming at it
from a whole different direction. And it had fewer
cafes then. It was quite possible to trudge the three
miles to get here only to find no table available for an
extended stay. And without one of those what good is a
hood, then or now or anytime? -- For a jyzeslinger,
this is, I'm thinking, but conceivably for quite a few
other types as well. Not least, of course, students.)
        But back to Zoelie.
        Tuesday evening, after the eight endless days of
silence, she finally called while I was out and left the
message coolly breaking our date. She'd just learned
her master's orals would be held the morning of the
25th, she explained, and so she'd need the night of the
24th to "settle in with the books." But she'd like to
reschedule to -- and here again, even as the answering-
machine tape whirred, a lengthy and distinctly audible
riffling of her datebook pages -- she'd like to
reschedule to either the following weekend of the 29th/
30th or (more riffling) not the next week or weekend
after that but (more riffling!) how about the week of
April 7th, maybe a late lunch on Thursday the 10th? And
that was it, except, at the end, a flip little
afterthought: "Oh -- sorry!" Click. Perfect timing
too: just as the tape ran out.
        Infuriating.
        After a few hours of stewing I pulled myself
together and replied in writing, which was the only
option, of course, since I had no phone number for her.
Glad to reschedule, I wrote, but guess what: such
lengthy timelines as she operates under just don't work
for me. If a late cancellation should open up a slot in
her jam-packed schedule, I'd be happy to meet her at any
time and under any conditions -- but no longer than,

say, three days after she'd conveyed the news to me. A
longer wait than that would be intolerable. I pointedly
wondered if she was simply too busy to be starting up a
new relationship right now and her entire way of life
perhaps too structured for the likes of me. Said I
didn't want to talk about any of this on the phone. (If
she wasn't making herself available by phone, why should
I? -- But didn't say that.) Said the best way to get
in touch would be to shove a note under my hideaway
door. Even attached a hand-drawn map showing how to
find it (actually just two and a fraction blocks from
her building, not four or five as I was thinking).

Also said it appeared to me she and I were -- by a
crazy stroke of personal-ad luck -- practically meant
for each other in terms of background and interests but
to me the real question was one of heart. In the realm
of man/woman relations I was the hang-loose, intuitive,
all-in type. What type was she? Said I'd like to know
but from her long silence and breaking of the date and
failure to supply her home phone number or address I had
a hunch I never would know. Hoped I was wrong about
that. Told her I didn't feel I was "in the tent," as
she'd assured me I was during that long first call; said
in fact I felt I wasn't within two weeks' camel ride of
the tent and it seemed to be moving ever farther away,
mirage-like, at well over top dromedary speed.

Then: stuffed into the envelope a hangable kiri
ribbon with a big black "G" hand-inked on each of its
six square gold-ball panels and said I was doing this to
remind her that as the days and weeks went by with no
word from her and no meeting between us I was out here
slowly and grumpily twisting in, yes, the Zoelie zephyr.

Next morning I rose four hours early -- unheard of!
-- the exact middle of my night! -- and hoofed the
letter seven blocks for immediate delivery by bicycle
messenger. (First I obtained Zoelie's office address
from the city listings. To my surprise it's the
utility's engineering department she works for. Can it
be? I'm obsessed with an engineering type? Okay then,
if she's not one, what the heck is she doing there?

Isn't it eating away at her innards?)

That night when I returned home from work at one a.m. I found another voicemail from Zoelie. It was dawning on her, she said, that evenings were not a good time to reach me. But she'd received my letter with the ribbon in it and she didn't see why (contrary to what the letter said) we couldn't talk about it on the phone. So she'd wait half an hour and try again. (This message had come in sometime between seven and ten p.m. but because the recorder on my answering machine was on the blink -- and still is, and in a way only an engineering type might know how to repair -- I couldn't tell exactly when.) Nothing to suggest she'd be going along with my proposal to put a limit on lag time between her calling and our meeting or any hint of softening her other rigorous conditions or any suggestion of respect for my notions about how we should proceed after she'd broken our first date. So I decided immediately I wouldn't return her call.

At eight the next morning she tried again (possibly twice; an earlier call came in around six or seven a.m. -- I heard it from above in the loft bed -- but it was a hang-up after an unusually long period of silence, with no message left). The voicemail message for the eight o'clock call was something puzzling about not wanting to infringe on my sleep time but "turnabout is fair play" (was it because I'd kept her up until her bedtime with that very first call? -- As if she'd had nothing to do with it!) -- and that was all.

That was Thursday morning. Since then, nothing. No call, no letter in the mail, no note shoved under my office door. Nor have I caved in and attempted to return her call. Nor will I. It's crunch time. Must everything be done Zoelie's way? Best to find out right now just how flexible she is. And how interested too. Two birds, one stone. (Ultra lightweight, crumbly, disintegrating, true, but still: the only stone around.)

A key passage in my kiri letter said if I didn't hear from her proposing a short-lag-time meeting it would "eventually" dawn on me she was just too busy for

such a loose-hanger as I. -- And in the days since then
I've written several drafts of a note saying this
dawning has already occurred. I've fantasized
delivering this note to her in person at her office next
week along with a big bouquet of flowers and a cluster
of party balloons. "Hello, Zoelie B., glad to meet you,
and goodbye forever!" But no, I haven't sent the note.
I'm waiting her out. I swear I can do it.

(A whole different kind of notion: let her stew for
a week or so and then send her a completely neutral
letter -- one not even acknowledging we're locked into
this showdown before we've even met -- telling her
what's happening in my life. Goofy little feel-good
missive.)

-- Also in the kiri letter I suggested maybe we'd
be better off if she were to wait to reply until after
finishing up her studies in late June, when she can
again "start being spontaneous." But late June was so
far beyond my normal time horizons, I went on, I
couldn't really be sure how I'd react at that point.
-- Could perish of a slowly metastasizing heartbreak
long before then. Her too. As I said! "You too,
mama."

-- So why a showdown now? To me it's utterly
obvious why. Can't let her keep jerking me around like
this! No way! -- Once again, though, at this point I
probably lack the emotional leverage to pull it off.
And just generally I suspect I've moved beyond the stage
in life where I can get away with - that is, succeed
with -- a brash, edge-walking, take-it-or-leave-it
courtship style.

Nonetheless: I'm sticking with it. No caving, no
slippage, no "goofy little feel-good missive." We'd
have this fight later anyway, I tell myself, so better
to have it now when any damage done would be relatively
minor. (Trouble is, she seems to have "systems
management" on the brain, perhaps because of her current
school focus but perhaps also as a deep-seated character
trait. In either case, from her perspective it seems
I'm just one more dubious outlier phenomenon popping up

in a system to be managed. -- But doggone I do like her
feisty (as advertised!) spirit. Her strength of will
too. Her "smarts." Her wit. But I want her to know
she's met her match in spirit power, I'll call it (just
for the sheer woo-wooness of it; I mean, why should
engineering lingo rule?). -- And if she's unable or
unwilling to accept this, I want to know that too.)

     Maybe she'll try to reach me by phone after her
orals on the 25th. But if she doesn't come up with a
concrete proposal I'll try to ignore that call as well,
whether she leaves a voicemail or not.

     -- It's dark now in the Zoelie zone. Three or four
out of the scores of women I've seen out here might
possibly be her. How bizarre it is to be looking for
someone whose looks are entirely unknown to you except
in the most general sense ("most people guess I'm Native
American"). And even more bizarre, or perverse even, to
be obsessing on that same person.

     One thing, in spite of everything I'm feeling much
better physically these days. I may be going mad but at
least I'm not looking and feeling half-dead as I was for
the previous couple of months. Yet I've also decided
the time has come: I must start working out in earnest.
This is not to lash myself into truly "good shape," a
state which my letter to Zoelie foolishly boasted I was
already in; I know that's an impossible task. I'd have
to devote countless hours to it, and even then it might
be beyond reach. No, this is merely to try to slow down
deterioration. For years I've felt the day of reckoning
was creeping up on me; now all of a sudden I realize
it's here. Zoelie or no Zoelie. I mean, with my two
big self-proclaimed transitional lifetime milestones
coming up, this is the year for it. And I'm hoping
disciplined observation of a health-and-workout regime
will assist on sanity too. But such a regime will also
mean lots of pain and suffering, no question. Yet maybe
even that will provide distraction from whatever
emotional upheavals, positive or negative, lie ahead.
Or worse yet, by far, the absence of such upheavals.

     -- And now the long walk home in the dark. This

time I'll go around the big hill instead of over the
top. Follow the curvy avenue that starts on the far
side of the bridge, that's all I know to do. But I'll
be back out here at least once more no matter what
happens with Zoelie, because the used-book store is
still holding that book for me. I meant to pick it up
today but the ridiculous mailbox search took much longer
than expected. And I'm pleased to have an excuse to
return. Even if we never meet, Zoelie B. is clearly the
story of this volume and probably of the whole year.
Could be lifetime too if I get real lucky. And she does
too, absolutely. (Brash statement? No doubt!
-- Signifying nothing but more desperation to be sure.)
                    *   *
    What a sweet shocker if something from her were
awaiting me here at the hideaway -- especially
considering the building is locked up all day on
Saturdays (and with not just a new code but a whole new
code machine on the side-door entrance; just now it took
me several minutes to figure out how to get in). But
I've given her my address here as well as the map laying
out the path to my door; and if she didn't want to risk
making a personal appearance she could've written
something that would've arrived in today's mail.
    Could've but didn't. Nothing is what there is.
Same as what was on my answering machine and in my
mailbox back at B-2 a short while ago.
    This some five miles and roughly two hours after
leaving her turf, including half an hour with my feet
propped aching on the footstool in B-2 (blisters forming
on all three middle toes of right foot) -- glaring
across the jyzeyard at a stretch of solid brick wall.
The lethal glare.
    Not a bad walk though. Lake shoreline much of the
way, mostly maritime enterprises with empty parking lots
and switched-off lights, but a few scattered bars and
restaurants doing brisk business. This shamelessly
prosperous city. I'm striding along at a rapid clip,
the big hill looming darkly across the avenue to my
right with all the fancy vehicles hurtling by, a misty

full moon floating overhead (and a "new" comet blazing away up there somewhere too, streaking by planet Earth for the first time in thousands of years, officially confirmed now as the brightest comet of the century -- though not yet visible here because of generally poor viewing conditions).

This being the second full day of spring. Is, then, this Zoelie obsession just another instance of spring fever? A seasonal spiking of hormonal foolishness merely to be survived, like the similar but perhaps somewhat lesser flap over Sofie E. exactly a year ago? And in that case, I should note, we'd met in the standard in-person way, not via an ad, and so things weren't so maddenly abstract, removed, and hypothetical -- not to mention utterly blind.

Whooom-whooom of the usual Saturday-night double-rock-band dissonance, but louder than normal: its vibrations are massaging my sore feet through the floor. (Good to see, though, that the quarter's jumping tonight. It's been dead enough lately to worry me and many others that those nasty developers might try to do away with the local nightlife scene entirely and throw up a cluster of fancy highrises. Then it would be bye-bye cheap rents and thus bye-bye hideaway.)

Also should mention: a glancing contact with Lady U this week. Tax forms she forwarded, the "No Longer at This Address" printed on the envelope in her familiar hand. No other message inside or anywhere else. Seems to confirm my strong impression we'll have no more direct contact, ever.

-- One other Zoelie note (she to whom I was addressing fiery words off and on for all five miles of the walk, many of them muttered out loud and a few bellowed up toward the looming hill -- which was too sodden, I guess, to deliver an echo): in the voicemail she left after receiving the kiri letter she said she had reactions to that letter -- "what should I say...a panoply, how's that, a panoply of reactions." A nice reach, to come up with that splendid six-bit term spontaneously as she certainly seemed to do; but she

pronounced it with four syllables instead of three,
"panopoly," as if it rhymed with "monopoly." No big
deal, but it was amusing anyway, mainly because of the
almost sadistic pleasure with which she stretched out
the pronunciation, "pan-ahhhhh-po-ly," as if mock-
warning me to gird up for a severe tongue-lashing.

But...the odd truth is even though I'm no more
masochistic than the next guy (that I know of) I really
liked the spiritedness of that message. I like the way
she's ready to get down and grapple. A real soft spot
I have already for this Zoelie -- as noted before, but
now even bigger -- and probably for lots of kinky
psychosexual reasons I don't even suspect yet. By
uncanny instinct she seems to know how to knock me off
balance and out of ruts and for that matter clear out of
my senses. For this talent of hers all by itself I
should thank my lucky stars. Or the new comet might be
better for thanking purposes since my lucky stars, come
to think of it, may be pretty well played out by now.
New comet, I thank you! (And I know if given the chance
in the flesh I could melt down this Zoelie's guardedness
and cure her of her apparent intimacy phobia, I just
know it.)

Oh such fine intensity. Of course I'm digging this
too. For whatever underlying reasons (not to exclude
extreme neediness and all that) I've been brought
burningly alive. The pain when it hits pierces right to
the heart.

June 21st, by the way, Zoelie's "Spontaneous Day,"
falls exactly three months from yesterday. So at least
I've found an easier way of counting the days. But
something like ninety-one, must be.

(Meanwhile. Financial reinforcements arrive from
the deep reserves and I'm high on those for at least
twenty-four hours. Reporter Una at the scope office,
citing reporter Fran's dubious opinions, names a price
for the two rehabbed computers I'm hoping to buy for use
in B-2 and here in the hideaway, and this price strikes
me as way too high; I've told her I'm thinking on it.)

-- A new crazy idea popped up on the way down here.

[Jyze in Love]

Monday the 24th, which is day after tomorrow, why not
show up at the ORB cafe to meet Zoelie? Five-thirty
sharp, just as originally agreed. And despite her
cancellation she'll be there too: in spectral form.
Just as Sofie E. was supposed to be present "in spirit"
at a certain coffee bar a year ago (and then ruined the
plan by coincidentally showing up in the flesh -- but no
danger Zoelie will do anything like that with her exams
looming, or at least so she says, the next morning).
     Then: with the spectral Zoelie serving as witness
at the cafe table I'll scrawl out a crazed letter for
the real one. I'll send it too if it turns out offbeat
enough. (Will all this deviant behavior of mine appeal
to her buried social-worker side? That's another angle
I might want to explore further in coming days.) (And
at some level as all this jyze pours out I'm hoping
she'll read it one day in the not-too-distant future and
be touched and thrilled to recognize herein the early
thrashings of something -- big. Deep. Sublime. -- Ha,
dream on, king of fools!)

                    *   *

     Kwikjyze postscript next morning.
     No, I won't show up at the ORB cafe to write to
Zoelie as her ghost looks on. I've been losing sight of
my main mission here. I don't want to interact with the
world any more than the absolute minimum necessary. I
want to stay in my cell, as it were, and do my work and
then only afterwards and on the side, to the extent
possible, deal with whatever else life hands out to me
or requires of me. I hunger for a woman and for love,
yes, and in answering these ads I've already made the
requisite minimal moves to appease the hunger. Now
here's Zoelie -- maybe. In some sense we're both
damaged goods -- scarred, used, far enough along in life
to be limited in major ways by the choices we've already
made. The real question now ought to be this: given
these scars and limits, are the missions we're on even
faintly compatible?
     My letter has me positioned to find out what I want
to know about this very matter. She probably feels the

same about her calls which I've failed to return. But I
still see the next move as being hers, so I'll just
continue waiting her out. If things fall apart with
her, they fall apart. They are whatever they are -- or
aren't. (Huh? What's that again?)
     -- In the meantime I've hung a kiri ribbon from the
fire-sprinkler nozzle overhead and a couple of feet to
my left -- this jyze is going down in B-2, the green
armchair -- and it's supposed to represent the spirit of
Zoelie. It has "Z"s where the almost identical ribbon I
sent her has "G"s. Because of the heater drafts in here
this Z-ribbon is in constant gentle twisting and
undulating motion up there, sort of like the fins of a
giant hovering Siamese fighter tropical fish. Spirit of
Feisty! I'll keep it there as long as I still feel
there's any hope at all with her.

- - - - - - - - ·

12

- - - - - - - ·

     Another week of tremendous ups and downs and now it
appears it's really happening. I mean the miraculous
thing. And we still haven't met. But tomorrow's the
appointed day.
     Am I wrong again? Never have I gone through such
wild emotional swings coming so rapidly one on top of
another. Not even in Lady V times. Which I thought
could never be topped. And also wanted never again to
be even remotely approached. (But more and more the
comparison looks apt.)
     -- This is jyze on the short week. Tomorrow night
or Sunday the jyzeman returneth to report on how the
meeting went, good or bad (but surely not indifferent:
that's been resoundingly ruled out). Meet-up time is

four o'clock tomorrow afternoon, by the front door of
the magazine shop just around the corner from the cafe
where jyze touched down last week -- out in the Zoelie
zone.

Up until six hours ago I thought this crazy quest
was about to end. For the previous two days I'd been
zeroing in on just how best to close it out. Then in
this afternoon's mail an envelope from her: a letter, a
page photocopied from her master's thesis, and a short
poem. They bowled me over; everything flipped; "the
world changed on a certain Friday afternoon in the year
jyze four." Shame shame such hyperbole! But maybe not.

(This at the hideaway again. The other day
something of hers showed up here also, a short note
scrawled in big letters on a large swatch of butcher
paper; and it seemed the world changed that day too.
For exactly twenty-four hours I was the man than whom
none could be more euphoric. Then she called and I was
devastated, shocked, stunned, killed. And that demise
lasted until today.)

Going back to last J-week, the "damaged goods"
anti-epiphany at the end of that entry did serve to set
me back on solid ground after two straight weeks up in
the clouds cavorting in imagination with a fantasy
Zoelie B. Relief! I was ready to accept losing her if
she didn't respond to my earlier kiri letter (the one
asking her to call to set up a meeting if a slot in her
busy schedule opened up through a late cancellation).

But then where did I find myself at five-thirty
p.m. on Monday afternoon the 24th? Of course: the ORB
cafe, our original agreed rendezvous spot. The very
same table where I'd first encountered her spirit, as it
were, in the personal ad. And soon I was conversing
with her ghost, also as it were -- but it felt spookily
real -- and writing the woman herself a postcard to let
her know about the "shady lady" I was hanging out with
at that moment (herself, that is, albeit in spook form)
and where and when and why.

Next day, even before she could've received that
postcard, she struck. Another of her mountain-resort

cards arrived in the mail, this one posing four possible
explanations for my silence and asking me to check off
the correct one. Clever posings too. Among them: Was
my "camel" sick? Was I trying to make her, like the
kiri ribbon, "twist in the wind"? Even better, later
the same day I found the butcher-paper note shoved under
the door here with this message (and not a word more):
"Cosmic inference -- your phone machine is on strike."
    It wasn't anything like what I'd asked for but it
was enough. It showed some interest. Maybe I'd gotten
to her a bit after all.
    So I went wild. On old Christmas "Happy Holidays"
stationery I blazed out a ten-page letter saying, in
essence, I was still upset but also delighted and the
camel was now prepared to stick its nose in her tent,
and I proposed we meet at her neighborhood magazine shop
at four on Saturday. ("By a happy coincidence I'll be
out in your part of town this weekend.") Also did a
quick sketch for her using some new markers: a weirded-
out version of myself asking a cartoon-bubble question:
"Was it something I said?" Also put together a "gift
package" containing all the stuff I'd been planning to
give her at our canceled Monday meeting, including a
book on the Mentoka (that is, the tribe she worked with
after her first spell in grad school) and a stack of
clipped articles with attached comments, most of them
touching on matters we'd talked about on the phone. All
this had been intended to be a birthday present, I
wrote, but since she'd been a schmuck and failed to
invite me to her party, now it was an early graduation
present instead. The next day, Wednesday, I messengered
the box and letter over to her city office at noon.
    At two she called. This time I was there to
answer. "Oh, you're a real person!" she declared. Then
she announced testily that she'd just received the box
and letter and wanted to talk right now, but first she
would close her office door. A pause, a surprisingly
loud slam, a distant "Oops," another pause. "So...what
the heck's going on? You're overwhelming me!" She
couldn't figure me out, she grumped, and was not happy I

was running these, quote, "mind games" on her. Not only
that but she had a bone to pick about a "classist/
colonialist" remark in my letter. And this had to do
with, wouldn't you know it, my chaffing her about her
sadistically gleeful mispronunciation of "panoply."

She did agree to meet me at four Saturday afternoon
(as suggested in my letter), but she sounded very
dubious about it and hinted she had other plans for
later in the evening. She also told me straight out
she's seeing other guys (respondees to her ad). When I
asked where I stood compared with the others, she said,
"On a bell curve, both very high and very low." She
also flat-out refused to give me her home address. "I'm
a woman," she pointed out, "and" -- in a category switch
I wasn't quick enough to object to -- "you're a male."
Instead I immediately deepened my plight by revealing
that I'd trespassed on her turf last week specifically
to hunt for her place. So now I morphed from the high-
low guy on the bell curve to the stalker. Will she show
up tomorrow with a couple of armed bodyguards?

After hanging up I sat motionless in the armchair
for three hours. Cataleptic fit. Heart pain like I
didn't know I could still feel it.

Finally I began stirring, but only to prepare
everything needed for withdrawing from the competition
on Saturday. Withdrawing with panache! A memorial card
with a sketch of the heavens, white ink on black paper:
"Comet Zoelie...blazing thru celestial quadrant G on
the night of the full eclipse of the moon." (Next day
sensational news: thirty-nine "cultists" die in a mass
suicide intended to release their souls to catch a ride
on a spaceship they believed to be zipping along in the
wake of the spectacular new comet. Today an
illustration appears in the newspaper showing a photo of
the comet zooming past a towering letter "G" --
standing, as it happens, for the name of the cult (the
image was taken from the cult's website) -- and by a
remarkable coincidence this illustration looks almost
like a mock-up of the "quadrant G" card I made yesterday
for Zoelie.)

[JAMR Jyze]

    I also started putting together another "gift box"
for her, one which I hoped would, as my parting gesture,
"overwhelm" her even more than the previous one did.
And for the past forty-eight hours I've been working
fiendishly on its contents. They include:
        ** several custom-made "Waiting 4
        Zoelie" buttons (just like the one I now
        plan to be wearing when we meet);
        ** an "Under a G Spell" pendant with a
        chain necklace, and on the back of the
        pendant a hand-painted message: "Memo to
        Zoelie: Be Heartful";
        ** for her Sunday-morning reading
        pleasure (and maybe that of the ad respondee
        she'd be seeing Saturday night?) a batch of
        annotated newspaper clips along with a
        giftwrapped package of corn toaster muffins;
        ** a copy of my urban politics tome --
        because she seemed to disbelieve me when I
        said I'd written a book that touches on
        certain aspects of the very topic she's
        addressing in her master's thesis;
        ** a fresh-cut rose (a late addition, to
        be inserted at the last moment);
        ** and then the piece de resistance: In
        connection with refusing to give out her
        address she'd joked, "How do I know you
        don't have mold growing between your toes?"
        So I crumbled up a slice of bread and
        painted the crumbs green and placed them in
        a plastic baggy and stapled this to an
        official-looking document (composed last
        night at two a.m. at the scope office)
        certifying my intertoe area to be "mold-
        free following surgical removal of toxic
        organic matter (see enclosed baggy)."
                         *
    I still plan to take the box along to the meeting.
But now more just for laughs. Because in her letter
today she in effect apologizes for any unintended

103

slights and admits she's as caught up as I am in the
craziness of this unfolding melodrama. And the poem in
which she admits this is dated 3/22 -- the same day I
was out "stalking" her.

Or am I again misjudging? The apology doesn't
touch on specifics (with one exception) and isn't
exactly sweeping. And the poem, though skillfully
written, is a shade, I'll say, ambiguous. It talks
about her dormant emotional patterns reviving, her
awareness that she's doing awkward things while caught
up in "the minuet," "the hormonal thrust and parry"; her
wish to go to the depths rather than play games or skate
on surfaces; and offers these final two lines: "Sooner
or later I shall / just look at you and breathe."

What I'm wondering: is that "you" meant to be me
or is it just the eventual winner, whoever it may be,
of the Zoelie B. Personal Ad Sweepstakes? Or is it an
even more general "you," a kind of disembodied romantic
hope? The poem offers no clues. Did she perhaps
distribute copies to all the sweepstakes semifinalists?

In any event: I'd sure like to be that "you." And
the good news is that now things have changed -- changed
enough -- and I believe I can hang in there and show her
why she should make me that "you." And I have a strong
hunch that at some level she's already convinced I am
that "you," even though at other levels she's clearly
still fighting it.

In just one page the thesis excerpt shows she's
socially and politically aware in a way I can definitely
relate to and admire. (It turns out that the type of
"systems management" she's studying focuses on
personality/psychology in the workplace personnel
"system," not on engineering processes or hydraulics or
anything similarly technowonkish.) The excerpt cites
the emotional "patterns" she picked up from being

> the 'middle' between my father and mother
> and between my biracial family and the
> white community of my childhood [and also]
> my 'rebel' position toward authority -- my
> very traditional Filipino, authoritarian

father and the patriarchal, race, class
and gender hierarchy we lived in.
And it describes the prejudice she faced in college as
a result of her mixed-race, working-class background.
Most of her classmates at the elite U of Centropolis
(where my father received his MBA just a few years
before she enrolled as a freshman scholarship student)
were white, rich and from private prep
schools.... Only in hindsight did I realize
that I wasn't stupid and inferior, but that
my 'smarts,' skills and strengths belonged
to a different world -- one that the faculty
and students were blind to. It is very easy
for me to slip into those old feelings [at
her current grad school] surrounded by
white, middle-class faculty and students.
Long quotes, but she sent that page over
specifically as part of her apology (the one exception
referred to earlier) for having accused me of "classism/
colonialism." At first glance my "right on!" reaction
to it may seem odd -- considering I'm a product of the
very world that was "blind" to her (and no doubt in many
ways still is) -- but then what else have I been
rebelling against my entire adult life? Her fight is
the reverse image -- but with many of the same goals --
of my fight! And: I believe sooner or later she'll come
to realize this.
So I immediately called her at her office. She
answered with a rushed, breathless, energetic, hard-at-
work voice, "Hi, this is Zoelie!" That marvelous jazzy
phone voice! And when I said, "Hi, it's Glen, can you
talk for just a minute or two?" -- a long stunned
silence. And then a lower, more composed voice, or
rather an excited voice trying to sound more composed.
And in the change of registers she was already saying
what I'd hoped to hear.
-- Or is all this preposterous? Well of course it
is! But will I someday be shaking my head in dismay
over it? Say in about two weeks? (Not to be doubly
preposterous but right now it seems more likely we'll

be together the rest of our days. Just like that.
Luckiest strike of my life -- and maybe of hers too.)
     Told her I was calling to say her letter and poem
and thesis excerpt had just arrived in the mail and I
wanted her to know right away how much I liked them all.
Thanked her. Said I hoped we could talk about them in
depth tomorrow. And asked a favor: could she bring
along a copy of the master's paper so I could read the
whole thing? She was just that moment binding it, she
said, still seeming somewhat nonplussed. But yes, she'd
bring it. And then another call came in for her on a
different line, she had to go. "Four o'clock then?"
"Four o'clock."
     Emotional power and richness. Oooeee, she's got it
all right! Hours later I'm still agog over it.
     Now I can be much more natural with her. Won't
fear so much I'll blow it. Won't have to worry about a
bunch of superficialities and pretending to be a less
complicated person than I am. Can let it all hang out.
     Issues remain. Probably she still won't move
anywhere near as fast as I'd like. "Time to lose the
other camels," I'll say -- but she may not be
immediately obliging (especially if she's scheduled to
meet one right after she sees me). Therefore I should
simply say I'll hang back until she does lose them; I'm
not going anywhere; as far as I'm concerned this is a
lock. "Let's head for the depths just like your poem
says." And I believe within a week or two (at most!)
we'll be doing so.
     That's the rosy prediction. Now to see what new
surprises she has in store for me.
     (Other life items from this J-week can be
dispatched in a paragraph. I talked reporters Una and
Fran down by almost half on the two used computers; the
deal's done. Mother's long-lost college boyfriend Eddie
wrote from deep in Mentokaland with thanks for receiving
his copy of "Memorials." The president of the U.S.A.
and thus de facto ruler of the world is limping around
on crutches after injuring his knee. And to my great
good fortune in this week of unrelieved Zoelie

obsession, the scope office has virtually relocated to the baseball spring-training realm, as previously announced, and Jyzer Ink has had little work to do.)

-- Yes, she'll be different. Yes, I'll have to change my life again and in truly major ways. Yes, I'm willing to do this for her. Yes, my own work will suffer -- quantity-wise for sure -- but maybe also improve, sharpen, deepen. Yes, I believe it can all happen with her in a way it never has with anyone else. Yes, I realize this is a colossal freaking miracle.

*   *

-- Now Easter Sunday (the previous section went down on Good Friday). Trying to sober up. Big windstorm thrashing frail budded branches against B-2 windows. An hour ago Zoelie told me on the phone she'd unplugged her computer as a precaution against the rising storm. And we've talked again since then (just a quick question: would I happen to know the actual source -- not the author, but the specific book -- of the famous quote about using the master's tools to tear down the master's house?).

No, it won't be everything I was fantasizing. But it will surely be something. And maybe once it gets going it will be even more than I was fantasizing.

On my way over to Zoelie territory yesterday, starting atop the big north hill and then as I hiked down the far side, and right after that while killing half an hour standing at the south end of the drawbridge as it opened and closed like, as I was thinking at that surreal time, the mouth of a huge salmon rising again and again in ponderous slow motion to pluck puffy low clouds from the sky like fishfood on the surface of a gargantuan tank -- lasting through all that, a deliriously extended epiphanic moment. Suddenly I saw everything clearly, the dynamic underlying my wild excitement about this Zoelie B. whom I was finally about to meet. It was fantastically complex, a lifelong arc of interweaving threads both mythical/fictional and real, yet also ridiculously simple: the arc completing itself like a rainbow right there on the far side of the

bridge. Bringing it home! Inevitability! The final
and best act of my life about to begin!
     Ain't kidding. Just how it was. Major
bedazzlement. And then the curtains of the heavens
parted and I marched zombielike across the unpuckered
lips of the great salmon. Celestial trombones blared.
     So -- Zoelie. A blue raincoat just outside the
open front door at the magazine shop as I stood waiting
just inside. A strikingly attractive "mestiza" face,
yes, round and high-cheekboned, with full lips and warm,
curious, intelligent, laughing eyes. She: "Are you...?"
I (nodding gravely and pulling back my left jacket panel
to reveal the "Waiting 4 Zoelie" button pinned to my
shirt): "I'm the one." She: a quick glance at the
button and no further reaction, almost as if to say:
what else you got, bub?
     "So," I asked, "would you mind walking a few
blocks with me first? I need to pick up a book."
     "Pick up a book? Now?"
     "Remember I said there was something bringing me
out to your part of town today? This is what I was
talking about. Besides which, I'm thinking maybe a
little walk would be as good an icebreaker as any."
     So we started walking.
     On the way (several more blocks than I'd thought) I
gave her the mock health certificate with the attached
packet of toxic intertoe mold. Not much reaction.
Maybe she wasn't too happy to have to fumble in her bag
for her reading glasses and don them to check it out.
     Most of the early going, sorry to say, is lost in
high daze. Small talk, jitters, awkwardness. One vivid
memory: her sexy amble as she wandered off into the
stacks while I talked with the bookstore clerk. Black
tights, fitness-club shapeliness. "Nice body." No lie.
     Then the hike back to the commercial zone and a
search for a place with smoke-free outdoor seating.
Much to-and-fro but we could find no such place.
Settled on indoor seats at the same neighborhood cafe
I'd visited last week and in fact I ended up in the very
same chair.

Just lots of nervous get-acquainted questions.
From the start she seemed strange. Hard to explain how.
Ditsy almost. (She apologized for unintentionally
misinforming me about her age: she's only a year and a
half older, not two and a half. She got her own age
wrong, and in the unflattering direction! In other
words, if she were a high-school senior, I'd be not a
freshman or a sophomore, as we'd been thinking, but a
junior, just as I was when my very first serious
girlfriend was a senior; and in fact Zoelie was one
class ahead of me in high school and then on through
college.) -- Wandering off, mentally and physically.
Long delays or freezes in the face of questions she
disliked. (She confessed she's often criticized for
being "oblivious.") Bristling with sass and attitude,
often not at all hidden, regarding race, class, gender,
colonialism; and it just so happens I fall into every
one of the categories she's bristling toward. And she's
contentious, disputing sharply a large number of things
I said. Suspicious. Controlling. Prickly. "Feisty"
-- again, no lie.

Worse, she showed no obvious physical or romantic
interest in me. Didn't flirt, wasn't seductive, wasn't
suggestive, wasn't encouraging, wasn't flattering. The
one comment she made that might remotely be construed as
complimentary was "You have a very good memory," and
even that one sounded resentful (I'd reminded her of a
statement she'd made during our first phone conversation
flatly contradicting something she'd just said). Nor
was she sensual or warm, despite the warm eyes and sexy
appearance; in fact, she noticeably recoiled when I
touched her arm in the course of conversation, to the
point where I felt obliged to apologize for, as I said
to her, my southern-style touching habits which came
straight from my mother. (After that I strenuously
avoided touching her at all.)

Yet do I like her? I like her! True, while with
her I was frequently thinking it could never work,
especially during the blowup at the end (on which more
anon, to be sure), but walking home afterward I found

the doubts quickly dissipating. Don't know why. (There
is the fact she's the only hope anyway.) -- Mainly it's
her stimulating and challenging mind, I think. And then
-- no, more -- feeling for her, the way she's embattled
and hurting inside her bristling defenses. And of
course looks and shape could have something to do with
it too. That striking face. More Native American than
Eurasiusan, I'd say, just as many others have told her
and in fact she had told me herself on the phone, but
also with a touch of what might be Jewish or Mideastern.
Short salt-and-pepper hair, mostly black. Long neck,
almost Modigliani proportions. Sexy circles under those
beautiful clear brown eyes (we squabbled over whose were
the darker brown). Luscious full lips. (Do I repeat
myself? Very well then, once more: luscious full lips!)
     And there's her voice. It's even better in person.
(For a while she was into jazz singing -- and for this
all by itself I might adore her forever.) And though
she might dispute this, we're pretty much politically
attuned, I think, and she does read widely and speak
vividly and once even dropped out of the rat race
(namely, her position at that time as director of
minority affairs for a local community college) to try
her hand at writing a novel while living off early
withdrawals from her state pension fund ("but I
discovered I wasn't disciplined enough").
     And not to be minimized in its importance for a man
on a jyze mission, there's another kind of "literary"
attraction: her aptness as a character in my story. (As
it happened, she arrived in the real-life version of
Lahontan for social-worker grad school on the very day
of the notorious antiwar bombing -- that is, the birth
date there of my fictional alter ego, the narrator of
the entire Mentoka series. For this reason as well I
ought to love her eternally.) (And not for one but two
years she "worked social" with the Mentoka in fictive
Coutawa, just forty miles from Mentoka Falls -- although
that was a good five years after I'd left the area.)
     She's also the proud possessor of what appears to
be a fairly strong New Age streak. "I make a

distinction between spiritual stuff and spiritualism."
To her, "spiritualism" is bad (as an example, she cited
the comet cult now the talk of the land) but "spiritual
stuff" is good, like, for instance, the Sufi meditation
she does each morning and also, apparently, at least to
a degree, Western astrology (right away "what's your
sign?" and the drearily predictable groan at Virgo --
and then lots of chaffing comments about my being
detail-obsessed and overly rational -- she being a
Pisces, as were Lady C and Briana T., if memory serves).
(Oddly enough she came up with the very phrase sister
Barb condemned me for using, "spiritual stuff," and yet
for Zoelie its connotations are positive.)

    In some ways we're so different we meet coming
around the back side. She's a morning person, for
instance: gets up at five every day, weekends included.
And in effect she's an only child (has a half-sister
seventeen years older but they never lived in the same
house). "I was very much a daddy's girl." (Here's Lady
U all over again, looks like.)

    She does like to dance. (Even brought this up
herself.) Does often have a mischievous twinkle in her
eyes. Does wear clogs. Doesn't use much makeup, if
any. Does insist (and I mean insist) on paying half the
check. Does sometimes show she's been taking in
everything even when appearing not to. Does have that
beautiful face and alluring shape and beguiling voice
and sexy gait. Does surprise me conversationally in
delightful ways with offbeat observations, sudden
twists, quick jabs, unexpected challenges, felicitous
phrasings, exuberant bursts, sassy digs, hearty laughter
at wholly unexpected moments and a terrific toothsome
smile to go with the laughter. (One time as I expounded
about something else entirely she cut in with, "I'll bet
you don't have a television either!" -- She seems to
relish making sly little "gotcha!" remarks.)

    She was free, as I'd been forewarned, only until
seven. Along about six-fifteen she suddenly stood up
and announced she'd start walking me home, go with me
partway. "You mind if I finish my drink first?" "Oh.

okay." Oblivious. (Sometimes it does come off as
rudeness, though, or lack of consideration, almost as if
she'd be embarrassed to be seen by the gods to be polite
to a colonial-settler Cawk raised in the burbs -- or at
least she'd like to have me, and maybe others nearby as
well, think she is.)

So we started walking again. Crossed the
drawbridge.

"Well, time to start summing it up," I said.
"where do we go from here?"

"I'll walk with you a little farther," she said.

"Double meaning there?"

Hearty laughter -- but no direct reply.

I'd already invited her to have lunch with me at
the hideaway (she: "You mean you'd get up early for
me?"). Now as we kept walking we tried to fix a date
(she: "What's your least grouchy morning?"). This went
on, with nothing decided, until we'd gone a block or two
farther along the semicircular avenue skirting the base
of the hill. Then I nobly pointed out she wouldn't be
able to make it home (the exact location of which she
was still refusing to disclose) by her deadline unless
she turned back soon. I asked if she'd mind if I walked
her back as far as the drawbridge if I promised to stop
there. This was okay by her.

Only now as we reversed directions did I bring up
the issue of "the other camels." Told her I'd been
thinking before her letter with the poem came in that
maybe we should forget the romance stuff and see if we
could just be friends for a while, but then I'd dropped
the idea -- but now I was wondering again if that might
be the best way to go, and what did she think? No
direct reply. Instead she started talking about our
"dynamics." She'd noticed that when I didn't get my
way I "pushed back," and then she "pushed back," and off
we went. -- As we did now. The fight.

No point in trying to recount it blow by blow.
Basically I was trying to let her know I wouldn't be
rolling over for her on everything. Ninety percent
maybe, as up to then, but not a hundred. I questioned

her willingness to negotiate (after she'd used the term); she said for her lots of things were simply not negotiable; I said she should at least get her nonnegotiables out on the table so we could try to arrive at clear trade-offs on them, hers and mine. She did admit she'd consulted a friend about my objections to her lengthy timelines and the friend had advised her to "speed it up a little" in choosing among the camels.

     And then this jaw-dropping exchange: "Once you asked," she said, "why I would run the ad at a time when I was so busy, and I never gave you an answer. Do you want the answer now?"

     "Yeah."

     "Because my mind needed some diversion." (Or did she say "distraction"?)

     The flip way she came out with this bothered me. I told her I thought she was being cruel -- used that word -- in stringing along a bunch of guys merely for her own "diversion," especially over such a lengthy period, and explained why.

     "I disagree with you emphatically!" she exclaimed.

     "And I disagree with you emphatically!"

     It wasn't long after this that she observed, "I think we're having our first fight."

     Surprisingly, the parting wasn't all that bad. By this time we were standing at the south end of the drawbridge, in fact at the very spot where, three hours earlier, I'd experienced the epiphanic moment with the great salmon. Now I launched into a little impromptu speech about my being a one-on-one kind of guy, about how I hoped she'd soon be losing those other camels or otherwise this camel's nose right here might freeze up out in the cold, about how even though it might seem I was running "mind games" on her, as she'd said on the phone, a lot more than just gaming was involved -- even a colonial-settler Cawk dude from the burbs can feel real feelings, including real pain -- and if we're talking romance here I'd sure like to see those outside hindrances eased out of the way. Or if we're not talking romance, then maybe we should just do the friends thing for a while.

No direct reply from her on any of this. She held out her hand. "Very nice meeting you, sir." Sir! And she'd be calling to let me know which day would be good for lunch. (And earlier she had let me know -- she'd brought this up herself -- she'd be busy this coming weekend, Friday through Sunday, purportedly for school-related reasons.)

*

Wotta trip. I never even got around to giving her most of the stuff I hauled out there. Within the first five minutes I'd abandoned the corny idea of buying her a rose. She did present me with a package which I opened later in B-2; it contained recent copies of two of the same alum magazines my parents received in the mail when I was a kid (which I did appreciate) and a clip from yesterday morning's Jyze City paper about the perils of midlife crisis, although the clip wasn't even minimally annotated. And besides I'd read the story when it first ran in a much longer version in the "night paper," which, by the way, she blithely admitted she rarely reads even though her ad implied otherwise.

At the cafe, when she opened the "Comet Zoelie" card I was crushed by her utter lack of reaction to it. "Thanks," she said, after a quick glance at it, sliding it back into the envelope.

Couldn't help myself; I asked, "Well, what do you think of it? Aren't you going to say anything at all?"

"I already said thanks."

"Well, yeah, but you could respond to it, you know, at least a little, so next time maybe I could try to do something a bit more up your alley if this isn't it."

"Actually I didn't look at it that closely. I'll check it out again later."

End of discussion. Also end of any notion of my giving her the "Under a G Spell" necklace, and as for the high-schoolish "trust me" approach to doing so -- "May I put it on you?" -- definitely scrap that. Just scrap the whole thing. And even though matters improved after that, this little episode still stings.

[JAMR Jyze]

     In-your-face insensitivity and/or provocation. Can
I stand so much of it? Even with her full attention
would things improve very much?
     -- It was a long day, emotionally exhausting.
Bruising even. And I'd slept little the night before.
So at three a.m. last night I went to bed, an hour
early, after seven straight hours of mulling over the
meaning of this first meeting and watching with utter
fascination as my feelings for her quickly returned to
and even exceeded their former level, though now perhaps
they were less distorted by the incandescence of
outright fantasy. Now more grounded and realistic, I'd
like to think. Now suitably chastened, humbled,
restrained, forewarned. Maybe it would work and maybe
it wouldn't. Snorts of disbelief at sudden flashes of
memory of the evening. So sleep on it and see what
happens tomorrow.
     Forty minutes later the phone rings. From up in
the loft I listen to that marvelous jazzy voice speaking
to the tape below: "Hey, I thought you said you stayed
up until four! Guess this must be an off night for
you." I thought about calling her back immediately to
ask how the other semifinalist's audition went, or was
going so far if he was still there, perhaps lying next
to her naked and chortling, but dropped the idea. To
hell with all that. (But if she'd said, "Come on down
from your goddamn loft and talk with me," I would've.)
     This afternoon at one I did call her. We set
next Tuesday for our lunch meeting. She said she'd
worked up a "class-based" answer to my "cruelty
accusation about the other camels" and she'd be
giving it to me then. Also, she'd checked my first
letter and it said I was six-two, "but I'm five-seven
and you're only an inch or two taller than me, so how
come you said six-two?" I said I might've shrunk a
bit in the last few weeks since writing that letter
but I'd probably still be a couple of inches over six
feet come Tuesday -- "Wanna bet?" "Yeah, I'll buy you
lunch if you are. Can I bring a measuring tape?" And
before I could react to that: "Can't talk any more,

I've got company. See ya Tuesday."
     Wish I'd been quick enough to slip in something
along the lines of, "Well, your ad said 'nice body,' so
can I bring a measuring tape too?" (In fact a few
moments ago I tried to call her to say just this. But
she had her answering service on and I hung up without
leaving a message. And I'm glad I did. It's quite
possible she'd've taken such a remark the wrong way.
-- But I'll hold it in reserve, just in case. Use it
with a light touch on Tuesday, maybe. Or maybe not.
-- Possibly give her the "Be Heartful" necklace then
too. Just for the helluvit. Or again maybe not.)
     -- And when she called again with the question
about the "master's house" quote, I said (this time I
did manage to ad-lib something) I'd just gotten back
from a search of local thrift shops for used platform
shoes to wear on Tuesday. "Hah!" she said and was gone.
     Hope it can keep going like this. Hope I can take
the grief. Hang in there. See if a little romance
might start creeping in on her side. Try not to give up
on her despite all the taunts and provocations. (But
don't fail to keep pushing back -- no matter what.)
                              *
(By the way, during her first call this afternoon
she also pointed out, again with an almost sadistic
relish, that Tuesday, day of our next scheduled meeting,
happens to be April Fool's Day. -- So be prepared, my
lad. -- And I'm recalling it was exactly one year ago
today that I began moving into this place, unit B-2.
Which I've been neglecting so shamelessly and doing so
little JAMR-ing of the past few weeks. But then again I
think I could bear the frustration if I had to stretch
out this neglect just a bit longer.)

[JAMR Jyze]

13

     Well, I've tried to bow out with grace and style,
leaving the door open a crack -- just in case. Mailed
the farewell package earlier today. Or didn't mail it
(that I tried to do Saturday and failed because of its
size); messengered it instead. Ever since I've felt
sick at heart. (Nine p.m. now, the hideaway.) Didn't
think I'd be able to do the jyze thing even though it's
J-day. But will give it a shot now out of the same
sheer masochism that got me into this mess in the first
place.
     Yet another tumultuous eighter. Actually it all
comes down to one hour (and a ten-minute spillover) on
Tuesday, April Fool's Day: preparing for it, suffering
through it, reacting to it. Our "second date."
     The key moments took place right here. We both
arrived on the dot, half past twelve. My jokes about
our bet on my height fell flat. (First, the one, which
in the end I couldn't resist using, about measuring key
dimensions to see if her body really was "nice"; second,
rather than buy me lunch if she lost, would she sight-
read a song of my choice? The song being "This Could Be
The Start of Something Big." -- Didn't matter anyway;
despite conducting a lengthy search at various downtown
sites, I couldn't come up with the sheet music.)
     We measured our heights. She lost. In fact she
turned out to be the one guilty of false advertising:
she was only five-six (though she refused to believe it;
insisted the tapes must be wrong, both hers on the first
round and then mine from my desk when we remeasured).
She also seemed quite perplexed about how she could've

117

been so far off on my height. I tried to tease her:
"You might ask yourself, 'Why am I trying to shrink
this man?'" This too fell on stony ground.

Serious blow number one came when she handed me a
box containing all the contents of the box I'd sent
her, including the box itself (as if she thought it
might be contaminated and couldn't bear to touch it).
"I wouldn't have time to get to any of this until
summer." "But I gave it to you. I don't want it back."
"Well, you keep it anyway."

Serious blow number two, when I invited her to
step into the hideaway (this room right here) so I
could give her "a better idea what I'm all about," she
announced "I'm feeling very shy" and refused to come
in. Only by opening all three sets of blinds to the
hallway and foyer -- which I had never done before --
could I entice her to take a step or two beyond the
threshold, and then she stood in a slightly crouched,
hyper-alert state, looking frightened enough to bolt at
any second. She asked no questions, showed no interest
in anything except for a brief glance at the two framed
pages of family pictures from my photo album. "Which
one's you?" (Her one question.) And when I pointed at
myself, she declared: "That can't be you." (Matter
settled.) I explained I have those particular pages on
display because my family's pretty much broken apart now
and they show the last time we were all together. She
said she still couldn't understand my motivation.
Shrugged; "I just don't see why you would do that."
Then when I tried to explain about the protojyze and
pulled out a volume at random to show her a few pages,
she commented, "Boy, are you ever a Virgo." Meanwhile
she kept glancing anxiously at the door as if suspecting
it might be rigged to swing closed behind her at the
touch of a hidden lever. My rows of books about Mentoka
and the three "cities of the interior" where she and I
grew up and went to school ("the cities we're homeys
of"), about the tribe she worked with for two years --
none of this or anything else in the room drew even a
flicker of interest.

     So, lunch. To the ORB cafe. On the way she
blithely hit me with serious blow number three: a
comment to the effect that "what we're doing today is
we're seeing if we want to be friends or not." My
dumbfounded reply: "So...you mean...you're saying the
whole love/romance business is kaput?" She didn't
reply. So then I provisionally took her to mean we were
back to square one; we'd have to go through the
"friends" testing before love/romance would be allowed
back on the table. I also had the impression she might
be retaliating for my having mentioned the "friends"
option on Saturday, but I really wasn't sure what she
was up to. I decided to let it go.
     Since she'd lost the bet about my height, she paid
for lunch. It didn't cost her much; I'd just eaten
breakfast and so I ordered only a dish of apple cobbler
and my usual bottle of root beer. We sat in the back
area where we'd originally agreed to meet for our first
date on March 24th (before she broke it), but on the
opposite side of the room from the table where I'd
initially come across her ad and later conversed with
her ghost and then wrote her the "shady lady" postcard.
I pointed out that table (it was occupied) and ran down
my personal history with it over the past six or seven
weeks. No detectable reaction.
     What did we talk about? She wanted to know who my
friends were, "what circles you go around in." It was
more testing: was I reliable or not? At times she
sounded so suspicious and hostile I could scarcely even
think. I mumbled and fumbled and no doubt confirmed her
worst fears about me. For her next observation was
this: "The second guy I was engaged to could also be
charming and he turned out to be a sociopath." I: "You
mean you think I can be charming? I don't believe it!
Wait until my circles of scuzzy friends hear about
this!" This reply seemed to totally discomboble her;
she actually blushed.
     Next topic, psychological testing. She was
wondering where I thought I belonged on certain test
scales based on choosing which of a pair of antonyms

better describes oneself (I forget the pairs she
actually cited -- she had a long list ready! -- but an
example would be "sensate-abstract").   I asked her at
what time? In what mood? Under what kind of moon? Was
I in love at the moment? Constipated?   -- And went on
to dispute the value of that sort of testing even in the
realm of job applications, let alone vetting for romance.
Admittedly I was becoming a bit irked by now. But I did
my best to remain civil. Still, we were clearly
fighting again.

     Meanwhile it was already time to go, she let me
know. "Let's walk back to your office," she said. (I'd
somehow convinced her she could safely leave her heavy
bag there while we did lunch.) Again my drink was only
about a third finished, just like Saturday. Again I
chugged most of the remainder; we left.

     On the way back she asked -- since I'd said
something about preferring quick intuitive judgments to
elaborate assessments reflecting someone else's dubious
psychological categories -- she asked what my quick
intuitive judgment was of her. "I guess I just can't
help myself," I said, trying to squirm off the hook, "I
like you a lot." Her reply: "But who do you think I am?
What does that great intuition tell you?" Again,
blatant hostility.

     So I equivocated. Informed her -- after a good
block and a half of hemming and hawing -- I couldn't
offer a quick intuitive judgment about her in a few
sentences; I could say lots of things about her and tell
lots of stories about her and about us, but I didn't
want to reduce her to a few simplistic formulas and that
was the whole point I'd been trying to make in the first
place about the psych testing. Even to my own ears it
sounded evasive. Feeble, in fact.

     By now we were back here, No. 225, standing outside
the door. Again I invited her to come in and sit down
for a few minutes. She said she had to be getting back
to work and pointedly refrained from stepping across the
threshold. Before handing over her bag I asked for the
claim ticket. "You're very funny," she said

sardonically. Then I gave her a few clips culled from
the big stack I'd intended to leave with her last
Saturday. Sitting on the desk chair were copies of
"Memorials" and my politics book; I told her I'd planned
to give her those to look through but I guessed that
now, since she'd returned the first package, she
wouldn't be interested in them until summer either.
"You got that one right," she said.
    "So what's next?" I asked.
    "I'll be out of town this weekend. I'll call you
next week."
    "Okay." -- No doubt looking crestfallen. She was
already edging away. "So, Zoelie, I guess all I can say
is -- see ya."
    "See ya."
    That's it. -- Except earlier at the cafe I did
give her the necklace I made for her. She did not seem
pleased, either by the necklace itself or the fact that
I was giving her a fairly serious gift. She was also
suspicious about just what I meant by the phrase written
on the front: "Under a G Spell." And she clearly
disliked the inscription on the other side: "Memo to
Zoelie: Be Heartful." Why would I think she needed
reminding? Who did I think I was to be hectoring her
about such things?

*

    Sad afternoon. Wasn't everything extremely clear?
But I still couldn't quite believe it. Despite all the
warning signs, my own heart (incorrigibly heartful!) was
still going out to her. I was desperately thrashing
around, seeing the futility but not wanting to give up.
    For some reason I couldn't stop obsessing about the
sheet music for "This Could Be The Start Of Something
(Big)" (that's the real title, I found out, with the
"Big" in parentheses, as if to say: fill in with
whatever term fits your needs, for example, "Tiny" or
"Hopeless"). Finally found it in a collection of jazz
standards at one of the chain bookstores. Bought the
book, made a photocopy of the three pertinent pages,
scribbled a note. "Maybe in some other life we'll be

121

singing this tune in each other's ears and you'd like to
have the chart now to start rehearsing just in case."
Something horrible like that. Folded it all into an
envelope adorned with "Mighty Casey" stamps -- what
else? -- and mailed it off.

Next day, more mulling. Happened upon a critique
of psychological testing in an academic journal; a
number of the points it made resembled the ones I'd been
trying to get across to her. It also availed itself of
the term "Z score," which according to the dictionary
refers to "units of deviation from the mean" -- or as my
note to Z herself said, "Maybe it's like a kind of
sociopathology score?" And best of all, by sheer
coincidence, the article included a nifty deployment of
the camel/tent metaphor. At the top I scribbled a note,
"Sorry to keep bugging you but...," and mailed it off.

By now I was thinking if I didn't hear from her
again before she left town for the weekend I'd retire my
camel for good. I hit on the idea of giving her a copy
of my favorite crypto-neoprag/Taoist East/West
philosophy tome as a going-away present, since it nicely
explains why I'd live as I do and lays out any number of
things I've been trying to say to her but does it in a
truly inspiring and graceful way. So I bought her a
brand-new copy (discovering to my surprise that the
book's recently been reissued in a hardcover classic
edition) and started writing out some notes to accompany
it. Turned these into a long tangled letter with little
sketches crayoned in. Put together yet another package
for her. Stuck in some photos, including one of the
great Osage/Eurusan ballerina from an earlier era whom
Zoelie strikingly resembles from certain angles (she'd
never been told this before), and the goofy one of
myself (taken through a Japanese coffee-shop window on
which is written "Persistent Pursuit of Dainty") that
I'd intended to give her before she left my office so
abruptly. Stuck in a mola-like bookmark. Cited her to
apropos passages in the book. Tried to make everything
cheery, bright, and unpushbacky.

In the letter I said the time had come for me to

drop out of the chase. That was point one. Point two,
I was issuing a standing invitation for her to visit me
on some Saturday evening in July or August after she's
finally done with her coursework and her "spontaneous
season" is underway. Good talk, good music, and no
sociopathology: that was a promise. Point three, if she
chose not to accept the invitation, I wanted to thank
her anyway for giving me a helluva whirl the past
several weeks and hoped she'd remember me by this book
(a/k/a "wise idleness") which I love.

Friday night I decided to go ahead and mail the
package the next day instead of waiting until Monday as
I'd been intending. I hadn't heard from her again
since our lunch meeting; she hadn't responded to either
of the items I'd sent earlier in the week (the sheet
music, the psych article). Better to start putting this
instant flop of a romance behind me as quickly as
possible.

I thought the post office stayed open until two on
Saturdays and so I arrived there at one-thirty. It had
closed at one. Then I discovered that stamped packages
weighing more than a pound can't be put in a curb
mailbox, and I felt sure mine was well over a pound.

Back home, and I find a package from Zoelie on the
lobby mail shelf. Inside are two very handsome blank
journals -- banana paper, no less -- and a letter. She
says she "really enjoys" our conversations, and she
underlines that. She does have two questions she'd like
me to address. One is the same one about why don't I
have a circle of friends. The other is, what happened
to my teeth? (She noticed they're not perfect, the rat!
And then she dared to ask!) In any event, if we can
keep meeting at a pace that's acceptable to both of us
instead of getting into "either/or" ultimatums, she'd
like that, and I should call.

Oblivious is the word for her, yes. I could see no
reason to reopen my package and change anything. But I
did want to thank her for the blank journals and also to
let her know my letter inside the box was not a response
to this letter I'd just received, so I wrote another

letter that went a step further than the one in the
box, saying I'd concluded she was looking for a safe
relationship and found my directness too threatening
and so I wouldn't be expecting to hear from her again.
But if she wanted to surprise me, by all means I hoped
she would do so. Or better yet, ASTONISH me. (And did
the "surprise" in medium-size glittery paste-on letters
and the "ASTONISH" in large ones.)
     And that's it.
     No immediate response from her. Probably won't be
a response, period. If there is, it'll take a helluva
plea on her part -- or an ASTONISHING surprise -- to
persuade me to see her again before this summer. And
by then, of course, all this current turmoil will be as
remote as some absurd junior-high crush (not that I
think I'll be forgetting her anytime soon -- but then I
haven't forgotten the junior-high ones either). I
think I've learned a lot here. Maybe I haven't
disgraced myself quite so thoroughly as might at first
appear. Certainly I shouldn't consider the time
wasted. Just as I told her, it really has been one
helluva ride. And at times it still hurts in the same
way the real loves have in the past -- so maybe in a
sense (a post-romantic-prime sense, say) it is a real
love.
     As for the lessons, I'll try to go into those some
other time. Should have plenty of opportunity.
     -- The hot new comet, by the way, I still haven't
seen. Could it already have passed out of celestrial
quadrant G? I've made several special trips to scan the
skies but my timing on cloud cover's always been bad.
     And a great Eurusan poet died. An important figure
in my life, though I never knew him personally and
probably wouldn't have wanted to. A memorial reading
this week. -- And now we're into Daylight Savings Time,
and I'm into, therefore, the Nightscoper Upside-down
Time (NUT) version of that, or NUDST, I guess.
(Pronounced "nudist"?)

[JAMR Jyze]

14

     Tax day. I'm right where I was last J-day and the
one before that as well, sunk into the brown armchair at
the hideaway. Half past eight p.m. Twenty minutes ago
I was bucking the long lines of procrastinators outside
the downtown post office to mail a couple of important
items, neither of which was a tax return. That pesky
distraction I actually sent off "early" this year --
some four hours ago. No, these were both postcards for
Zoelie. And they weren't even the first mailings of the
day to her. A letter preceded them, dashed off
impulsively from a perch atop a stack of bark-mulch bags
outside the drugstore at the northern tip of my standard
tripolar turf (under the glass arcade roof because a
hard rain was falling). And before that we'd talked an
hour on the phone and she'd agreed to come over to my
place B-2 for a visit Sunday afternoon.
     So it's still going on, yeah. Wild times.
Torments! Agonies! Three-hour calls! Shocking
revelations! And we haven't even seen each other again.
Nine weeks out of the starting gate -- which I see as
the day I read her ad and mailed off my reply to it --
and our face hours still stand at three and a fraction.
     (Harking back to our last meeting, the lunch at the
ORB cafe two weeks ago -- and my last sighting of her,
by the way, was as she edged nervously away from my
foyer here on that day -- I've recalled one other
serious blow she delivered at that time. This would be,
if I'm right, serious blow number four. Or was it
number five? Anyway, she blithely confirmed my hunch
that the poem she'd sent -- which played such a big part

125

in my deciding to keep my hat in her ring -- hadn't been written specifically for me. The "you" was indeed generic. -- Also at that lunch she'd observed, "You know, you move a lot faster than I do." "You mean romantically?" "Yeah." But really now: how could she possibly believe my wanting to see her for more than three and a fraction hours in nine weeks -- or seven weeks at that point -- is moving fast?)

    -- So the next day after I sent her my farewell package (the one containing the "wise idleness" tome and the letter inviting her to visit B-2 this summer) she called and left a message. I called back. After a few amenities she had the supreme gall to ask if I'd agree to wear my "choppers" to our next meeting (a bridge, I guess she thought, since my letter had joked about using one). I said, "Why don't we wait until this summer to talk about things like that." "Oooo-kay," she said, with a rising inflection across the first syllable peaking on "kay" before falling abruptly, conveying "That's it for you, buster; you had your chance and you blew it" -- and then a clipped "Bye" and she hung up.

    Outrageous! That was the end for me. Down came the "Z" kiri ribbon. Down came all her cards and letters tacked to the loft bookcase. Everything associated with her I flung into a box which I banished to the storage stacks in B-2's internal hallway. Fury. -- But quickly transmuting into sorrow and despondency.

    Next day a phone message from her: apology. She had "nine-one'd" me, she said, this being psych jargon for who knows what (but I think maybe meaning she'd demanded to have things all her own way). Also a hand-delivered manila envelope arrived at the hideaway containing a full chapter from her master's thesis, further apologies, a proposal we go on a "long ferry ride" sometime after her last day of school on May 12 (apparently she'd advanced the previously sacrosanct "Spontaneous Day" of June 21 by six weeks or so), and a challenge to a remark I'd made about "working-class aesthetics" (and I thought I'd carefully phrased that remark to avoid any possibility of just the misreading she was giving it -- this in the letter accompanying the book), and containing one condition: the first topic of conversation on the ferry ride would be "social class."

Zoelie zeroing in. The J-master vacillating. Finally I couldn't resist; I blazed out a reply to her challenge on the "working-class aesthetics" remark, stamped it, addressed it -- then sat there staring at it for two days. (Her "long ferry ride" card had also said she was "sad and mystified" about my sudden withdrawal from the chase.)

I held out until Friday. At one p.m. that day she called again and left a message saying she had three "brilliant ideas" she wanted to talk about and asked me to call her back. I sat frozen in place in the green armchair listening to her speaking to the answering machine. For the next couple of hours after she hung up I stayed right there, motionless, debating with myself whether to reply. Eventually I convinced myself I faced a stark all-or-nothing choice. If I did reply, it would mean I'd be with Zoelie the rest of my life and be forced to endure lots of painful sanitizing and prettifying of my ways and person. If I didn't reply, it would mean I'd be living the rest of my life in reclusion right where I was, in unit B-2, lonely but also churning out lots of work. And probably not with a whole lot of excitement.

I called.

A transformed Zoelie answered. Her "brilliant ideas" weren't too impressive -- I can't even recall what they were -- but for the first time she at least seemed to be showing some real interest. She told a story about her officemate commiserating with her -- "You look so sad; it must mean that guy still hasn't called." This seems to be about as direct as Zoelie ever gets on expressing emotional involvement with a man. She'd also finally decided to give me her home address -- if I promised not to "surprise" her by showing up there uninvited. And to drive the point home she warned me that her neighbor is very protective toward her and has a "double black belt" in karate.

But she still wouldn't let me off the hook. She
wanted to talk in depth about those two matters
mentioned in her letter -- circle of friends, choppers
-- as well as social class, and now she raised a fourth,
patterns of breakups with former lovers.

Her wonderful musical voice. I was elated. I
agreed to call again Sunday night -- when we could have
a good long talk -- and take up all these matters. By
god, if she really wanted to hear my thoughts about
them, I'd have plenty to tell her.

-- But did I really want to do it? All weekend I
equivocated on this. In my farewell letter I'd asked
her to ASTONISH me. Had she done that? She had not.
Maybe if she'd called again on one of those weekend
nights -- when, from things she let slip during our
jockeying to find a good time to talk, I knew she'd be
out, both nights, and I presumed she'd be with another
"camel," or "camels," since she didn't indicate
otherwise -- but if she'd called or contacted me some
other way, yes, I'd've felt much better. Instead as her
silence continued, a major gloom descended on me
Saturday night and deepened all the way to zero hour
Sunday night. Again the stark "lifetime" questions
arose. Back and forth I went. Out I tore my (thinning)
hair. Grindingly I gnashed my (less than perfect)
teeth.

And did call her at seven Sunday night. A two-and-
a-half-hour talk ensued. I bared my soul. The
childhood traumas, the failed loves, the son I scarcely
know, the gritty trade-offs and sacrifices of lifelong
"artyrdom." The whole horrific boyhood smash-mouth
tale of the teeth: grinding wheels, dental-school guinea
pig, symbolizations, mortifications -- all of it. (I'd
almost forgotten what a poignant story it can be -- a
couple of times nearly started bawling myself.)

Learned a lot about her too. Astoundingly enough,
she went through an ordeal similar to my smash-mouth
torment except far worse. She was born with six toes on
both feet! Had to undergo all kinds of operations
starting as an infant and continuing until she was

eleven; and because these were all performed in a
charity hospital, she had to come back every year well
into her teens to walk for the assembled charity doctors
(sounds a lot like the squads of dental residents
peering into my mouth twice annually from my ninth or
tenth year into my early twenties) (and also may explain
why her walk is so distinctive and sexy in what might be
called a somewhat learned or self-conscious, but also
very proud and even defiant and so still sexier, way).
-- And heard her weep as she told me about a friend who
died last year, for whose adopted kid she's now serving
as a surrogate mother (or an extra mother, rather, since
the friend who died was a man, Zoelie's "blood brother,"
but the adoptive mother who's also the friend's widow
lives on and has become Zoelie's good buddy and the
adopted kid is now Z's godchild).

Then truly was ASTONISHED: she suddenly volunteered
-- I wasn't trying to persuade her (though I had been at
other times; just not at that moment) -- volunteered to
stop seeing the other "camels." And not only them but
also any other human being, "male or female or you name
it," who happened to hit on her, whether an ad respondee
or not.

Yes, I was plenty happy. After she ran out of
steam again (abruptly too, just like our very first
telephone talk) I more or less danced my way around the
usual circuit: down to the hideaway, up to the scope
office, back home. I was even in a state of sexual
semi-tumescence much of that time (as for that matter I
had been during the call; her voice all by itself can
affect me that way).

Shortly after I'd gone to bed the phone rang.
Those same marvelous warbler's cords summoning me
through the answering machine: "Can you come down and
talk just a minute?" I shakily descended the stairs
naked in the dark, called her back. She said she'd just
awakened and realized she'd better tell me something
else about herself: she has herpes. I said I know
nothing about herpes but it doesn't matter, couldn't
possibly make any difference. I said she'd made me very

happy during our earlier talk. She reminded me she goes
slow; it would take her months to feel truly at ease
with me. Fine, I said; no need to rush now.

A sudden seizure of conscience on her part? I
guess. It must've been difficult for her to keep quiet
about the herpes thing during our earlier long phone
talk while I was all but opening my veins for her. And
I was deeply moved. Stayed up and made her a special
card commemorating this night on which she had indeed
ASTONISHED me and I even wrote flat out "and now I'll
surely love you forever." And meant it! Then attached
a note with an arrow pointing to that line: "This may
seem a bit premature but just wait, you'll see." And
tossed in some goofy aluminum Mardi Gras coins I'd come
across at our local costume shop a few days earlier.

So a day of wild delight (and the requisite
trepidatious fears mixed in too, oh yes).

As before, this lasted one day. Then another
reversal.

I'd arranged to call her last night (Monday) at
half past eight. This would be the start of the new
relationship (just sixteen hours after the herpes call).
She assured me she'd turn off her answering service so I
could get through. -- But she hadn't done that. For an
hour I tried (from one of the antique wooden booths at
the ORB cafe, recalling similar maddening attempts of
long ago to reach Lady V from an even more ancient
wooden booth in another cafe and city and state). No
Zoelie. Left her a message. A sense of foreboding:
could she be backing out again?

She was. When I got home from the scope office, a
message from her, please call, she wanted to "revisit"
our talk of the night before. The lack of the slightest
trace of warmth in this message was the real message. I
knew. Felt like an utter fool too, for having sent her
the "love you forever" card (on which my pal at our
local branch post office, Seb, after spotting the
telltale Valentine's stickers on the envelope, gleefully
slapped a "Love" stamp) and having endured such
humiliation, having reopened my wounded heart to her --

and now WHAAAP. Again. I was seething over this all
night. Half mad. More catatonia! More howling furies!
     Blazed out a letter saying this was it, I was out,
we were done, I'd eat those words I'd sent her. Sealed
it. Stamped it. Set it atop the stack of books on the
couch and stared at it for hours.
     And again after a thrashing night in bed was back
to staring at it this afternoon when she called. Just
as I feared, second thoughts on her part. But not quite
as bad as I'd been assuming. Mainly she was feeling I'd
pulled the wool over her eyes. "You're just amazingly
articulate. Only later did I realize what I'd done."
Which was what? She'd agreed to be "monogamous" without
extracting anything in return! And so what about my
choppers, she asked. Would I be willing to call in a
dentist this week or next as a quid pro quo?
     -- Took me aback, this did. Finally I pointed out
-- managed to recall -- the quo we'd actually agreed to
in exchange for the quid of her "monogamy" agreement was
that we'd go slowly, at the pace she preferred; I
wouldn't expect her to become emotionally involved with
me in any significant way anytime soon, or at least not
until we knew each other a whole lot better. (We'd
talked about this at length.)
     My reminding her of all the above did the trick,
but only momentarily. She wouldn't drop the matter
about the quid pro quo. Now she insisted my original
quo hadn't been big enough for her quid (ha!) and we'd
have to reopen the negotiations. -- She's a bulldog. I
like this about her. I like it a lot. I also know
it'll be causing me a helluva lot of grief before she
and I are done (if we ever are).
     And she consented to come over Sunday afternoon.
"I can't believe I'm agreeing to do this." Before then
she has no free time at all. Not even ten minutes
during an afternoon break for a look-in at a coffee shop
near her office. (She won't even say she likes me.
"Let's say I'm warily fascinated." Well, doesn't she
have any fantasies at all about this guy she may be
about to hitch her star to? (Of course I've already

admitted to having all kinds of same about her.) "Just
one," she says. "What's that?" "I imagine us reading
a book together. I think that would be lots of fun.")
     So it stands. With five days still to go before
her very first visit to B-2. Anything could happen.
     (The herpes part looks bad. I read up on it at a
downtown bookstore. Essentially you have to give up all
unprotected sex, including oral. And she wants to play
hardball on minor physical shortcomings? Feisty, yeah.
Volatile too. Massively attitudinous. And the really
galling part is she'll win. That is, if she doesn't
walk first.)
     One other little oddity. What a coincidence this
is. Back a few days, at one of the times when it seemed
she'd kissed me off for good, a letter arrived in a city
envelope and for a moment I thought it was from her.
Then I realized what it was: my long-delayed utility
bill. The one whose appearance I'd been dreading for
most of the past year. The one I made her swear not to
be a snitch on. -- But I don't think she was. And the
bill itself is not staggeringly high. About two hundred
bucks. And since my taxes were roughly two hundred less
than expected, I'm scarcely even feeling the pain. And
the enclosed utility newsletter, edited, laid out, and
mostly composed by Zoelie herself, she tells me, is
colorful, bright, lively, witty, well written -- an
impressive and very winning production of which she
should be proud indeed.
     (By the way, the two postcards and the letter I
mailed to her earlier today, they were just lovey-dovey
little things but also carrying on various disputes
we're caught up in. She's stimulating me in a thousand
ways and it's terrific.)
     (And she says she's not a reforming lesbian or
bisexual, as certain remarks of hers had led me to think
she might be. Many of her friends are lesbians, she
said, because she supported their cause starting back
when it was risky to do so and she found she "really,
really liked them as people and 'fellow' feminist rebels
and outsiders" and they liked her in the same ways and

maybe some other ways too, yes, but this didn't bother
her at all. She did go out on a date with a woman --
once, years ago, to try it -- but it didn't work out.
What went wrong I didn't ask. Another time for that.)

15

    Day after Earth Day. Afternoon. Back in the green
armchair this time, unit B-2, and slowly and sassily
twisting in the air overhead is the "Z" kiri ribbon.
It's back up, as are all the old cards and letters and
some new ones as well. We're cooking right along.
Courtship turbulence to the max. Head over heels here
we come. (Or am I there already? Is she?)
    Wotta quantum Z-shift. Every now and then I pull
back and wonder how this year's jyze annal can possibly
hold together. On faith alone I say it will. Or maybe
just lop off everything before Z bursts upon the scene?
Because unlike that morbid earlier stuff this Z-story's
got legs and all the other key parts. Everything's
shakin'. Everything's aglow. Boogieing to beat any
mere fictive concoction that ever could be. So take
that, ye non-J novelizing grandmasters of yore!
    How's it break down then? Just one more meeting,
our third, in which she sat on the couch across from
where I sit now (she looking so fine in a long black
polished-cotton skirt with a slit up the front and a
soft white jersey) and then, as part of an exchange of
agreed-in-advance "double-blind requests," a visit to
her apartment (followed by dinner at a nearby Chinese
place -- a favorite eating-out spot for Lady U and me,
as it happens, "back in the day," and the Z-woman was
the one who suggested it). On both sides of this

meeting, major crises resolved in surprising ways. And
lots of voicemail, long phone talks, letters and
postcards -- two, three, four contacts every day,
sometimes more or even many more.

Last night one of the resolutions. Scoping work
kept me downtown until two a.m. Arriving here I found
three phone messages from her. Until earlier in the
evening I'd been downhearted over a couple of outright
humiliations she'd laid on me, new ones (on which, to be
sure, more later), but then I found a long "Happy Earth
Night" letter from her at the hideaway -- first time
she's written me at such length. Suddenly a tone much
less bristling and suspicious. She's wanting to
"understand" me. She's apologizing. She's even making
with the strokes. (Openly admits to liking something
about me. What is it? My phone voice!)

So I call to leave a message saying I'm okay (she's
worried I'm "lying injured in the street somewhere" and
I'm planning to say, "No, I'm sitting injured on my old
wooden desk chair" -- here a couple of stagy creaks --
"beaten to a pulp by a swarm of your crazed and cruel
voicemails!") -- but she answers the phone herself.
Live. At two a.m. She's been reading a book I gave her
on evolving postmod forms of intimacy (serious sociology
stuff). We schmooze until past three-thirty. She's
told me our phone talk turns her on erotically. I've
told her it does the same for me. (She doesn't tell me
directly, though, as I tell her. At best she tells me
what she's told her friends or, in this case, her
"counselor." I don't know much about this "counselor"
yet but I do know Zoelie's been seeing "counselors" of
one sort or another "at times of need" all her adult
life. And this, it clearly follows, is one of those
times of need.) -- So then we talk sex. First times
and such. How I like to do it. (She's not quite ready
to reciprocate on this last -- but I can sense she's
heating up as we talk. And this of course I like too.)

Right now I have no other life. Zoelie is it.
"Wholly Zoelie." "Holy Moly Zoelie!" When I'm not
mulling my next move with her, I'm reading something

she's suggested or something I might want to foist on
her. (We're exchanging stacks and stacks of stuff.)
I'm reading her master's thesis all the way through (and
it touches me deeply because of the fighting spirit and
penetrating intelligence and also the surprisingly high
degree of social hope it shows -- and just like the
utility newsletter only even more so, it's exceedingly
well written). A few hours go by and I'm missing her
and yearning to hear her voice again. (Next time for
that will be at eight-thirty tonight. It's the regular
calling hour these days. Every night, except the last
two -- the exceptions. On which more coming up.)

Adorning the worktable across the room, a bouquet
of red flowers she left tied to my hideaway foyer
doorknob last Friday, helping put an end to another
crisis. Don't know what they're called (and neither
does she) but -- colorful. Shapely. I like. (And the
day before that, unbeknownst to her, I'd bought a
bouquet of a different kind of red flowers to spruce up
unit B-2 for her visit. They're also here now, gazing
across at hers from a vase on the chest of drawers.
Neither of us has a name for these either. -- Nor, it
must be admitted, for a whole lot of other things going
on with us and around us.)

That crisis, it boiled down to monogamy/choppers.
It ended when she called to say she'd just informed one
of the other "camels" she'd been going out with that, as
per her promise to me, she wouldn't be seeing him
anymore. "I'm calling to whine and complain...I didn't
like one bit how I felt doing it!" She acknowledged
"you've caught me on your hook." Then reversed herself
to say she wasn't agreeing to "go steady" (as I'd dared
to suggest we call it) just because I wanted to; she
wanted to also.

However, she still tried to extract a concession
for it. Would I agree in advance to do something
without knowing what it was if she agreed to do the same
for me? (This was the "double-blind exchange of
requests," as we later dubbed it.) I would have to
think about that one, I said. Next call I accepted her

proposal but with the proviso that we each have one veto, the precise nature of which we'd write down beforehand, as we'd do with the request itself, and then we'd seal both in separate envelopes. The veto would remain secret unless it was used. "Ooh, sounds like fun!" she said. (If nothing else, I'm getting better at playing this drama-loving woman's kind of games.)

Sunday she came prepared with a couple of fancy red-ribboned envelopes, one containing her request and the other her veto. (And bearing shopping bags full of new shoes. -- And I spiffed up the place pretty good beforehand and broke out my favorite blue canvas shirt and "dress" black jeans for the occasion. -- And she presented me with a numbered list of topics for discussion during her visit. The large yellow postcard on which she wrote them -- in her usual purple ink and large, rounded, slightly back-slanted lefty handwriting -- is propped on my chairside tray right now. And the tray itself is a new development arising from a thrift-shop run made while prepping for her visit.)

Long story short: her request had nothing to do with choppers or doctors (that was my veto position: she would defer to me on all my own medical/dental affairs, thank you very much) but to "change/cut your hair into a contemporary style." Ouch. Oof. That hurt bad (and still does). (But this upcoming Saturday I'm heading out to her place and I'll be letting her chop away at my locks however she likes. She wants me to have it done at a salon but I'm refusing, which I can do because her request didn't specify how I should get the "change/ cut." That is: only if she agreed to play a hands-on Delilah would I consent to be Samson.)

My request was to see her apartment immediately. To my total surprise, she complied with no apparent reluctance or hesitation, driving us there that same afternoon at four-thirty. Her building, it turns out, is located about two blocks farther up the hillside than I managed to ascend during my reconnaissance mission last month. It's a four-story, L-shaped, motel-like structure with an outdoor pool on the ground level and

nothing but balconies on the downhill, view side --
which runs east and west -- and outdoor hallways and
staircases on the uphill side (and the balconies painted
a hideous pink), and the view from her top-floor one-
bedroom apartment is spectacular just as she said,
featuring trees and hills and urban lake and downtown
skyline off in the distance. And inside the place is an
almost equally spectacular mess. I was delighted to
discover this: not only because it told me she wasn't
domestically uptight or a neatnik, as I'd been fearing
(because of her planning mania), but also because it
suggested she might be equally willing to open up about
other kinds of intimate matters -- and this proved to be
true, at least in some areas.

Most intriguing of these areas, I spotted a couple
of books on sex addiction on one of the built-in shelves
above the head of her beckoningly unmade queen-size (but
of course!) bed. "You a sex addict?" I boldly asked.
"Maybe," she said. "Suddenly I think I'm starting to
understand something," I said. (Her resolutely antisexy
stance up to that point (despite her sexy good looks and
body and clothes and walk and, at times, vibes), her
failure in the early going to say anything flattering or
seductive or remotely encouraging, her recoiling from my
touch during our first meeting: could it be these were
all concealing a craving, like an alcoholic-gone-AA's
shrinking warily from a bottle of prime hooch?)

And: a wonderful photo of her with her parents at
her college graduation in Centropolis. No surprise at
all but back in her high-gloss days this woman was an
over-the-top Hollywood-class glamourpuss. More things
falling into place. (Later: lots of tales of men hotly
in pursuit. Swarms, yes, just as I'd intuited during
that first phone call. Reputation in college as "the
sex goddess," which she first learned about from a
school "counselor" -- a shrink, I presume -- who told
her he'd heard it from several different sources, all
counselees of his who were madly infatuated with her.
Of course he then tried to put the moves on her himself.
But got nowhere, she says, although another one in later

years did much better. But not for long on that second
one -- "I couldn't take the nonstop analysis." So
better watch yourself, Jyzer G, for sure, in this and a
whole lotta other ways.)

And: a dozen mysterious acronyms taped to her
bedside wall to remind her of various tasks and vows
(just like my "JAMR!" poster). An authentic working
antique zoetrope labeled "Zoelie Trope" rehabbed as a
gift for her by the deceased "blood brother" mentioned
earlier, Manny, with a photo of him standing next to it
and, on the moving belt inside (she fired up the machine
to show me), shots of him and his family and Zoelie
capering amusingly at a picnic. Also a framed album
cover hanging in the hall: "Wild Women Don't Get the
Blues." A closetful of ancient picket signs for various
causes which in every single instance I had strongly
supported myself. A gorgeous soulful acrylic portrait
of the Z-woman herself mounted on the bedside wall, done
by a well-known local artist who took a fancy to her
when she performed a "home energy audit" at his house
and begged her to pose for him. A large printed poster
proclaiming "Asian Americans Against Homophobia" with Z
among those pictured.

And: huge stacks of unwashed dishes in the kitchen,
counters piled high with bottles and boxes, the cupboard
doors all wide open and the cupboards themselves
entirely bare ("If I can't see it," she explained, "I
don't know it's there; and if the doors are closed, I
can't be sure the cupboards are empty"). Fridge door
covered with photos (mostly of impossibly cute "kids of
color"), a couple of which fell off, along with the
magnets holding them up, when the door stuck as I was
trying to look inside and I yanked it open a little too
vigorously. Also a wooden zebra, size of an eohippus
crossed with a small pony, that collapsed -- a leg
detaching itself, no less -- when I brushed against it
while trying to thread my way through the clutter near
her bed ("Not to worry -- it happens all the time" --
which she'd also said about the fridge photos). ("Just
in case you're wondering," she assured me, "I know

exactly where everything is in this whole apartment.
And it's all clean except the dishes.")

A brief period of holding hands as we walked to the
restaurant. But it was awkward, as was the dinner
itself. After I escorted her back home she wouldn't let
me come in; somewhat coolly said she had other plans for
the evening. A long puzzled southward hike by the usual
hill-skirting route. I walk in the door at B-2 and the
phone rings: Zoelie. Good talk clarifying some minor
misunderstandings. Then at five a.m. another call and I
listen to the message coming in as the machine records
it. She can't keep it to herself, she says, her "FOO"
(family of origin) upbringing leads her to expect a man
to act a certain way in courtship and to want to "look
his best" and she doesn't get it with me, the choppers
and the hair and, especially galling now, "that awful
blue shirt with your belly hanging out" -- and she
starts wailing uncontrollably.

Later she left another voicemail apologizing for
this "meltdown," as she called it herself. Then a card
under my hideaway door, also apologetic. But I wasn't
so easily mollified. I saw new complications arising.
The gap we'd have to close suddenly looked much wider.
And I realized this gap wasn't just of her making. It
was also a creation of my cumulative life decisions,
I'll call them, and especially the ones made over the
past several years. In effect I was being stretched out
over an abyss produced by my own increasingly conflicted
needs.

Or to view it from a different angle: it was
gradually dawning on me that as long as we might stay
together, Zoelie and I, my very way of being in the
world would remain, at least to an extent, a source of
irritation or resentment to her. In some crucial sense
I was flipping the bird at the very society she had
grown up aching to join as a fully fledged member and
was now holding a grudge against because of the many
ways it had unjustly excluded her and her family over
her entire lifetime. To her, of course, such behavior
on my part looks like privilege squared.

But still I can't let her be constantly insulting
me like this. She'd never respect such wussiness.
(Later she admitted as much: in all these incidents
she's in some sense testing me, pushing to see what I'll
do and how far I'll let her go. She did this with her
father too. -- And her father was a flashy macho
Filipino man, very handsome (I saw several photos), very
dignified, very sweet, she told me, but also very
morally upright and authoritarian. He didn't let her
date in high school. When they watched TV at home he
massaged her feet. Saturday she can't meet me until
five p.m. because before that she'll be going in for a
three-hour sauna and pedicure. -- And yes, she appears
to be fully cognizant of the various erotic/
psychological undercurrents here. The pain associated
with those "polydactylic" extra toes, the delicious
masochism. A bit of foot fetishism maybe? What new
kinks ahead?)

Sunday when I asked if she felt any physical
rapport at all with me she said, "I don't know yet." At
the time this sounded like another way of saying no.
It stung just as badly as the haircut request and the
shirt/belly meltdown (admittedly the shirt fits less
than perfectly and my posture isn't always the best, but
she went way over the top on that one). Last night,
though, she admitted this was all part of her standard
courtship M.O. (show absolutely no early interest and
plenty of disdain) -- which I'm not totally sure I
believe -- but more important, irrespective of what she
was saying, she was actually letting some rapport
develop.

She's beautiful. She's sexy. She's very smart.
She's vivacious. She's funny. She's imaginative.
She's inquisitive. She's artistic. She's hopeful.
She's caring. She's passionate. She's politically
active. She's taking no shit from anyone. She's got
sass and swagger. She's got great style. She's
continually surprising me and finding ways around the
obstacles we run into (including the ones she herself
puts in place). I respond strongly to her. I'm

deeply impressed by the way she's handled all the shit life's thrown at her. I delight in her exuberance and her vivid presence and her unexpected moves. I want to reciprocate everything and give her all she can handle (and then some, if possible). I see a strong chance for connections at every level, including, I have little doubt, two or three -- or more! -- or many more! -- I don't even know about yet.

     -- And so this is how jyze stands at the end of the first book of the fourth annal: wildly infatuated and obsessed with Zoelie B. (and sure, with the idea of being wildly infatuated and obsessed with Zoelie B. -- is there even a difference?). All else gets tossed to the winds. I'm hanging way out there. I'm taking some nasty beatings. I'm riding some boggling elations. I'm "going steady." In short: it don't hardly get any better than this.

     (But will it work? Will my funds hold out? Can I still rock'n'roll? And with a herpes girl? -- All this and much, much more in the jyze ahead, next book, I do oh so fervently believe. Ain't just jiving here. Yes, BELIEVE.)

BOOK II

[20K Jyze]

16

Just a little to start out with. So this J-day
won't pass without (J-ing -- yeah).
     Half past one a.m. Unit B-2, and the worktable,
and the jazz station's on, and I've changed into sweats
and listened to voicemail from Zoelie and left some for
her. Hers was wondering if I'm maybe a bit irked at her
over something, she knows not what. Mine said no way
and rambled on about this and that.
     Gaga over the girl. (Or better, "grrrl."
Otherwise she'd raise a stink just as she did this past
weekend when I unthinkingly used the term "girlfriend,"
even though she had used it first herself, not that it
matters.) Or simply: wild about the woman. (This be
okay, Z-duck?)
     -- So here starts a new volume. In this one,
barring some calamity, we'll become lovers. It's
already agreed. Or if not, it sure does seem to be.
No, I think it actually is. And regardless I know it'll
happen.
     Today I talked with her on the phone twice, left
her two messages, received one letter from her in the
regular mail here and three "special delivery" at the
hideaway (shoved under the door when I wasn't around,
presumably by her), wrote her a letter and worked on a
sheet-music version of "Teach Me Tonight" with altered
lyrics (titled "Teach Me Zoelie B.") which I'm planning
to give her next time we meet, Saturday at her place.
     It'll be our fifth meeting.
     On the agenda this time: "lots of kissy-face."
     So far: one kiss. At the end of get-together

number four last Saturday. In her wagon (cream colored
and lightly Dalmationed with painted-over rust spots)
across the street from the entrance to the upstairs
lobby here, a few minutes past midnight, rain tapping on
the windshield and roof. Ever since I've had the
zazzles for her. Double or triple zazzles really,
considering how far gone I already was.

Every day two, three, four, five contacts. Zoelie
with her barrages of questions and comments. Her
marvelous melodious laughing voice. We're learning so
much about each other -- "going deep" -- I can only
sample it in here. My fine focus is completely out of
whack. Jyze boggles. But boggles with delight.

And this the time of her most serious book-
cracking. What's in store for us after she's shattered
her last tome? (The orals take place next week at the
same mountain resort from which she first contacted me
by postcard.) Whatever it is, I'm ready and eager.
Absurdly, no doubt, I'm certain we can ride right over
any glitches that may pop up.

I'm saying it again: this is for life. Anything
short of that, I'll be shocked and crushed.

Delirium. I'm dancing with it.

(It's spring. Some splendid warm days. Vines
budding again outside B-2 windows. Fruit flies back.
Swatting at them is just about the most serious activity
I'm capable of that's not to do with Zoelie B., except I
somehow manage to grind out my Jyzer Ink scoping work.
In a stupor.)

-- Oh, and I'm almost a bald guy now. Zoelie
chopped off about ninety percent of my hair. No pattern
to it; it's as if she hacked away at random, blind-
folded, leaving just an isolated tuft quivering here and
there. She goes for the "straightforwardness" of this
look. Fine, great, as long as it works for her (just
ignore the gapes of passersby and avoid all mirrors).

-- And now it's time to bake a potato. Must eat --
remind myself. (She's just terrifically wonderful --
did I say? Speaks directly to my soul and does it by
hot wire. Can reach where no one else has even thought

to try. And stir it all up. And make me love the
stirring. -- And this is new. This is only once in a
lifetime. Quantum leap beyond old loves. Twelfth-
string dimension. So -- miracle. Simple. Truth beyond
possibility of self-delusion, or my name ain't J-slinger
G, G-slinger J, whatever.)

*   *

    Next afternoon, now at the newly semi-retro (nights
only) bar toward the northern end of my tripolar turf,
and I suppose I should try to sober up a little. Even a
lot. But surely will fail.

    Streetside window booth, jyze going down (hack
hack) in a patch of dazzling sun.

    At two a "hit and run" call from Z. "To tell you I
got a massage at noon in hopes it would cure me but it
didn't." The gull lunges: cure her of what? "Of
thinking about you all the time!" (This being, I
suspect, part of a new campaign to show me she can too
flatter -- even in words and even directly.)

    At four I mailed her the sheet music for "Teach Me
Zoelie B." (in a black envelope with the address slashed
in white, and on this envelope Seb at the post office
gleefully slapped another "Love" stamp, as he regularly
does now, even on my bill payments). I also mailed her
a "Positivity Breeds Content" card, the message inside
saying the maxim was aimed at her frequently expressed
fear that we'll fail just as her other loves did, and
then adding "Cuz our odds are EXTREMELY HIGH -- which I
can say BOLDLY because I'm a BELIEVER -- and will do
WHATEVER IT TAKES to KEEP THEM JUST THAT WAY" -- the
caps here indicating medium-size sparkly paste-on
letters (not enough room for large ones).

    "Hey Jude" now. A Thursday afternoon. Away from
the windows the standard tawdry daytime barroom
darkness. Empty seats, empty dancefloor, stale air,
glowing neon beer signs. Female bartender slicing
lemons while chattering away with a dude slouched on a
stool, the only other customer, a pathetic long-faced
longhair in denim overalls. Last time I was in here
that guy was me.

[Jyze in Love]

    -- Saturday then. Another hike over the big hill
and across the drawbridge on another glorious spring
afternoon. I'm in black short-sleeve henley and black
jeans, shades, zipping right along on strong and spunky
spirits. Up the long incline, up the stairs, the
vivacious Zoelie B. greets me at the door (in sexy
little blue-denim cutoffs and red utility T-shirt, the
gold lightning bolt zigzagging between "Public" and
"Power" looking like a flashy tilted "Z"). As agreed,
I've brought haircutting implements along with gifts,
clips, books. She plies me with stuff too: books,
articles (one a published panegyric to the Z-woman
herself, written by "blood brother" Manny, he who gave
her the fabulous Zoelie Trope and also a magnificent
handmade -- by Manny himself -- mahogany lap writing
desk (he died during an attempted liver transplant, I
learned, Christmas Eve before last). She also presents
her usual written list of topics she wants to discuss.
Seats me in the chair with a view, herself on a nearby
hassock.
    What sort of topics? All sorts, but typically it's
something I've said or written which stirs up her
suspicions: is this revealing a worrisome strain of
sexism in me? Classism? Colonialism? (Invader type?
Settler?) Some other form of typical suburban Cawkazoid
benightedness? Pink-skin privilege or supremacy maybe?
Usually I don't have much trouble wriggling off the
hook, because usually she's misread or misheard me or
jumped to an unwarranted conclusion. Once in a while
she makes me squirm a bit (and I think this is good).
-- And as time goes by she's questioning me less and
less in this way. But her curiosity hasn't abated at
all. (So I'm thrilled. If I told her this she'd
probably ask why. What are the deep childhood sources
of this thrill? Or is it that some former lover of mine
was perhaps a curious type too, maybe even more so? If
not prettier, sexier, smarter?)
    She's hungry. This time it's her turn to pick the
restaurant. Thai it is, and a walk of ten blocks or so
back to the commercial area near the drawbridge, holding

hands all the way. She: "I'm getting used to being with you." While waiting for a table we stand outside the entrance on the busy sidewalk -- right across the street from the magazine shop of our first in-the-flesh meeting, a/k/a "Meet Day" -- leaning against each other back to back, swaying this way and that in surprisingly rhythmic "davening sync," as she calls it. (Later she cites this as proof she was being "physically responsive" all night -- but aside from the hand-holding it was the only real contact until the very end.)

After dinner a stop at the co-op market for dessert (she spurns refined sugar) and then a stroll back to her place in a light rain that was just starting up. There, as I head for the armchair facing the windows, she says she'd be more comfortable sitting on the loveseat-size red couch next to her bed, so we go there. All evening we're joking about my upcoming haircut. I invoke "don't change a hair for me" from "My Funny Valentine"; she swats it down. Eventually she takes pity and says we don't have to go through with the shearing; I insist we do. To the kitchen then, where a dinette chair already awaits me at the center of the room along with a white sheet to pin around my neck like a barber's cloth and newspapers spread on the floor. I'm under the impression she'll just trim a bit here and there but she keeps lopping away and I'm too distracted by the shapely up-close circling body parts to realize fully what's happening. At the end I immediately put on my Batman cap which I've brought along in my bag for laughs, but moments later when I pull it off in front of the bathroom mirror I'm shocked. Am I a shorn collaborator from a World War II movie? Is Zoelie punishing me for having slept with the enemy, which is to say: any and all former lovers? In any event I vow to wear my disgrace with dignity and pride.

Back to the red couch. Awkward moments. The couch itself is inherently awkward; it's armless, with unusually soft futon-foam cushions that cause me to slide slowly forward and floorward no matter where or how I sit. Her tone changes and I can tell she'd like

me to bust a move. I'm not about to, though, until she
calls or raises the hand-in-her-lap move I've already
busted. This isn't for a game-playing reason (not
primarily anyway) but because I've previously agreed to
"go slow" with her and let her set the tempo: the quid
pro quo for her agreeing to "monogamy." And she never
does call or raise. On the contrary: she pulls her bet
from the pot by abruptly moving farther away from me
with a display of in-your-face nonchalance.

Suddenly it's the bewitching hour. She's decreed I
must not stay past midnight; I've promised to respect
her need to get lots of studying done these last few
weeks before orals. Because the rain has intensified I
accept her offer of a ride home. On the way she brings
up the matter of smooching on the red couch -- hadn't I
wanted to? We laugh a lot about how we're misreading
each other's signals. "The dance." "John and Martha."
If only she'd leaned in, I say, or responded in some
other upping-the-ante fashion. And so, parked across
the street from my place, she says, "I'm leaning in
now." (She claimed she had lifted her lips toward me
earlier, on the couch, as a signal. I must've missed
it, I said, probably because it was one of those moments
when I was sliding out of sight. Or maybe she'd already
moved away from me by then.)

A short kiss. I pull away quickly and leave her
awkwardly positioned, a cute little pink tongue still
sticking out and waggling. "Is that all?" she asks. So
then a longer one, very sexy. (As soon as she got home
she called and wanted to talk about the kiss. "Was it
good for you?" Joke joke. Then it's time to unpack the
meanings.)

On the red couch she'd said (for the first time,
other than a hint in her reference to my phone voice
being sexy): "I am attracted to you." (And later she
said in explaining why she "held back" on the couch --
in fact acted utterly indifferent as far as I could see
-- "I was waiting for you to start breathing hard."
From just holding her hand!)

-- Well, it's fun. Contrary to early signs she'll

be a hot lover, I'm convinced now. The kiss said so and
many other things did too, including the mention in an
autobiographical sketch (written for her master's
program) of having undergone a twelve-step treatment
program for the aforementioned sex addiction -- and
similar programs, incidentally, for two other
addictions: work and money. Also she's had lots and
lots of lovers. At age eighteen "I suddenly became
aware I had this tremendous power over men and it didn't
start fading until I was in my late thirties." "So
obviously it was only a brief fade," I teased her,
"before it surged all the way back up again." And she
did seem to appreciate this even though her left eyebrow
arched skeptically and her eyes rolled up to about
ninety percent white.

 For a stretch of a decade or so in the middle of
her self-declared maximum-power period with men she was
trying to prove she could be "as free and aggressive as
any man about sex." Lots of pickups, one-night stands,
lovers in every port, boat-rocking yacht trips, "popcorn
sex" and "filet-mignon sex" and on and on and on. What
finally caused her to seek treatment was a messy three-
way entanglement followed not much later by the crack-up
with "the sociopath," Arvin, the man she became engaged
to on the rebound from the three-way. (She also got it
on with various celebrities, including a Centropolis pro
hockey player whose name I recognized and a folksinger I
once met myself: Jack E. -- the ramblin' man.) (She's
very open about this sex-history stuff and sometimes in
an almost taunting way. Tends to chortle a lot as she
relates the tales. In this as in so many things she
shows some real good swagger oh yes she does.)

 And: she left me a note about pressing her bare
breasts against her futon and thinking of me. So I
immediately wrote back describing certain X-rated
engagements I've had with my own futon since meeting her
and suggested we might do better now to cut straight to
flesh-on-flesh and bypass "those stuffy surrogates."

 Her own explanation for the recoil when I touched
her arm on our "Meet Day": she falls prey to "shy

attacks." The S-word topic itself (meaning SEX) can
cause them. So then is my breathing hard the best way
to help her get over these attacks? I'm still waiting
for more clarification on this matter.

The herpes booklet she ordered for me came in. I
read it and told her I still think it might be best if I
get the Big H too -- "share" it with her -- so she won't
have to worry about infecting me. This way of seeing
things, she said, with tears welling up, just blows her
away. (Earlier at her place on Saturday she'd announced
two conditions for our becoming sexual: we must go in
first for STD testing, and we must always practice safe
sex. No problem on the testing, I said; but the safe
sex, I hoped we could soon reach a trusting state and
dispense with all rubber goods.)

-- Been rompin' in the jyzefield long enough. Got
work to do. Before that, got shopping to do. Turkey
ham on deep markdown this week.

*   *

And now. Another day later. (Quick before I
forget, yesterday was May Day.) Stopping by the digi-
cafe for the first time in weeks, a table in the new
riser section with its street view refracted through the
same old two large industrial windows divided into
multiple small panes: the fly's-eye perspective. As the
same guy (tuner?) I saw in here once before blazes out
scales in odd truncated bursts on the baby grand back in
the corner. Or it could be a quirky New Music opus.

I've been putting together Zoelie's daily postcard
fix. The picture side on this new one shows a
reproduction of a produce label featuring a Tinkerbell-
like fairy perched atop a cartload of giant carrots, the
fairy clearly in charge. It's an image, I'm telling her
-- "a visual trope for Zoelie B." -- of how to think
about those flops with previous carrot-bearers (because
she's said she's worried about what her "history of
failure to have a lasting relationship with a man"
portends for us). "Own your past!" declares the fairy
via cartoon voice bubble. A woman does need to keep her
skill set honed, after all, while awaiting the arrival

of the carrot-bearer of her dreams.

   Reminding me: the next night after our first kiss I
opened a call to her by crooning some slightly altered
lines from "A Kiss To Build A Dream On." For days those
lyrics were haunting me. Corniness running rampant!
Rampancy running corny! -- And today the second of her
messages started out with a sweet-voiced rendition of
"You Send Me," but only the first few lines, to "honest
you do, honest you do" -- and then she cracked up.

   A couple of hours ago she called again. She'd been
wandering around in the triangle outside my hideaway
building. Such a fine happy mood she was in. (In the
first message this morning, a frowsy-voiced one phoned
in from bed just after her alarm went off, she said
she'd been fantasizing about our sleeping spoon-style
and so she wanted to know: "Do you have zits on your
back?" -- So I invited her to check it out for herself
tomorrow and maybe while she's at it we could also gauge
the fit on the spoons. -- Already I can feel naked Z-
breasts pressing in. Every day the woman finds half a
dozen new ways to zazzle me up still further.)

   Other things I learned about her this week: her
birth name was Louise (from being born on St. Louise's
feast day); in a Gatsby-like move several decades later
she legally changed it to Zoelie (a combo of the last
syllable of her father's first name, Vincenzo -- his
friends all called him Zo -- and the first syllable of
her mother's, Elsa, plus "ie"). She did this as a
tribute to them both shortly after her father's death
and because "I never liked Louise or Lou or Lulu; and
Zoelie -- because I'd actually come across it a year or
two earlier in a detective story and really liked it --
Zoelie reminded me of my father, and then I realized my
mother's name was in it too." She contracted herpes
around that same time but hasn't had an outbreak in a
couple of years (but thinks sexual activity will likely
trigger some). She speaks only a few words of Tagalog
or Visayan (her father spoke both) and even fewer of
Polish (her mother spoke it at home growing up in
various mostly rural places on the far U.S. coast,

northern states), and regretfully admits knowing little
about either country, but still delights in calling
herself a Polapina (as well as a mestiza).
    Also: she's bored with her job and thinking about
launching a search for a new one this summer. The ad
which I answered received about a dozen "serious"
replies and scores of lesser ones. From pubic bone to
belly she has a nasty scar, she told me, left by a
fibroid-removal operation a few years back (she refused
to let them do the standard ovary removal).
    And: she works out two or three days a week,
usually during lunch hour, at a fitness club located a
block north of her office and so about three blocks from
the hideaway. (And these workouts likely have something
to do with why she looks so good in those skimpy little
denim cutoffs with the bottom of the front pockets
hanging out.) And: the unidentified red flowers she
gave me are still blooming. She refers to B-2 as "the
hermitage." She reminds me, maybe not entirely in jest,
to keep the lid down on the toilet "so the feng shuis
won't escape." She didn't start driving until age
thirty "because I always had guys fighting to drive me
wherever I wanted to go." (Ooh can she do diva!)
    And: last month someone crawled across her roof and
broke into her apartment via an open window on the
balcony, making off with her backpack. Her suspicions
focus on the manager's son, with whom she's been feuding
ever since she moved in (and who else would have access
to the roof, the door to which is kept locked?).
    And: one of her postcards said she'd used the term
"lovesick" in diagnosing her current state to a friend.
"Wild Thing" has always been one of her favorite rock
songs. She sees her counselor, Anita (an Afrusan about
her age), every Friday afternoon at five (which is to
say: she's likely seeing her even as this jyze is going
down) and lately they've been focused on psyching out
Z's new venture into romance and especially what kind of
person this "jyzer/nightscoper/hermit fellow" might be.
    Other news? Cousin Kar and wife Kerani sent a form
letter: they're now well settled into their new home

five hours south of here by car. Reporter Fran from the
scope office visited unit B-2 to help me figure out why
the used desktop computer she sold me wasn't working
(turned out the keyboard plug was defective). And for
the first time since moving in I locked myself out of my
room. (The new building manager, Carolyn, let me in.
She's a tall, skinny, friendly twenty-something Cawk
with a kid about two years old. Just yesterday they
moved into the unit directly across the courtyard and
one story up. I already know she likes to perch on her
window ledge, where she can look down on me as I sprawl
in my green armchair, which means I have to be extra
careful about what I'm wearing or not wearing and how
I'm sitting if the blinds are open. -- At this point
we're still waving a lot, with the kid taking the lead.)

17

     For the first time trying it on a writing board in
the green armchair. It: jyze. The writing board
fashioned from -- or rather consisting of -- a hinged
lid removed from one of my old cedar chests (the ones
stacked atop each other facing sideways along the south
wall to form the album-holding stand for the ancient
stereo). This on a sunny afternoon with a light breeze
tickling the newly leafed fence-clinging vine into
shimmery paroxysms of delight. And in ten minutes I'll
need to be fetching my clothes from the laundry room.
     So anyway, it's love. Zoelie and me. Proof is I'm
wearing her ring around my neck (as per a certain anthem
from our teen years) and she's wearing mine. "To tell
the world / you're mine by heck." Hers is a bloodstone
she bought during social-worker days. Mine is one of

the cheapo enamels I salted away on sheer speculation
during roughly the same period, the impressionistic --
though that can't be the right word -- Chinese character
for "love." (I sewed it onto a leather thong whose
length she changed several times so she could dangle the
ring just right cleavage-wise.) (And she does have some
admirable cleavage on her, I can now say for certain.)
(And "shapely," come to think of it, might be a better
word for the Chinese character.)
     Yesterday she returned to the mountain resort and
she'll be up there until Sunday afternoon. Sunday night
we'll be sleeping at her place. Six days from now we're
scheduled for STD tests at her doctor's office. The
first line of the message on a postcard which came in
from her today: "I **** you beginning ****" (asterisks
hers). (The rest of the message shows worrisome signs
of backsliding, however, on which more later.) Poised
ready for mailing atop a stack of books on the couch, a
letter for her I scrawled out in blood last night. (Not
literally. But might as well've been.)
     -- And now the laundry calls.
                    *   *
     A mound of rags rises at carpet central. Hot rags
once but cold now, some seven hours after I dumped them
there. Because when I returned to the room I found a
fresh voicemail from Z. It warned of a "hiccup" letter
headed my way and finished off with "but I do love you."
Uh-oh. More backsliding for sure. So I wrote her
another four pages. Impassioned stuff. Not at all
Buddhalike. Then charged downtown to fire off both
letters in a single Express Mail package that set me
back eleven bucks. On the way home bought her a jazz
CD. Half an hour later, at the small "north pole"
bookstore, bought her another jazz CD. Same sax man
supreme featured on both: the one she and I heard live
in a Centropolis club on the same night, it would
appear, or at the very least the same weekend, way, way
back, even before the dreamtime.
     So now what? I'm downhearted again. Almost surely
without reason. Lately I've been moody as a thirteen-

year-old. (But not usually openly so with Z. -- And so
now she's poking me in various tender spots, trying to
stir up trouble. Things are going too smoothly for her
taste. She's a complicated woman. I'm in love.)
(Jyze is in love too.) (Which of course is almost to
say the same thing but not quite.)

      Last Saturday we didn't stop at kissy-face. An
awkward beginning (again) on her confounded red loveseat
but things changed quickly when she agreed to hit the
bed instead. Turns out she's not only deliciously
sensual but possesses a tremendous sexual gift. Comes
often and extremely easily. Nipple tweaking, clothed
body rubbing, kissing, even just thinking sexy thoughts
can do it for her. I've never seen its like before.
Not even close. You're smooching and suddenly it's as
if an electric jolt passes through her and she roars
into overdrive. Squeezes her legs together or rubs her
crotch against you, I mean hard and fast. Ooh-ooh-ooh.
It's for real. A dozen or more comes for her in a few
hours and by ironclad pre-agreement -- of course
instigated by her -- we both stayed dressed "below the
waist" the whole time. Sexy as hell. Unbelievable.
(And for her, bad whisker burns causing big clown lips.)

      A hike up to a Japanese restaurant between frottage
sessions. I was checking out a mixed couple at the next
table -- young and pretty Asiusan woman, old and homely
Eurusan man -- and this led Z to ask later, as we walked
back to her place, about how I look upon "younger
women." This was one of the few times she's shown any
reluctance or embarrassment in asking a hard question.
It wound up with me taking her face in my hands, leaning
in close, and proclaiming in an intense low voice as
forcefully as I knew how (as she stood on the curb and I
in the gutter facing her), "I find you tremendously
attractive -- how can you not know that?"

      Next day on the phone she said she was dropping the
"almost" from her earlier statement about "almost like
falling in love." (And noted in passing: "You were just
really way cool last night.") Two days later in a phone
message she said, "I was going to wait until I left for

the mountains to tell you but I want to say it now: I
love you." As it happened, this was the morning of her
theory orals; it seemed possible she was not fully in
possession of her senses. But then after finishing up
the orals she called (from the test site somewhere out
in the burbs) and proposed getting together for dinner.
Forty minutes later she arrived, we chowed down at the
pub across the street, came back here, wound up making
out like horny teenagers on the carpet and then up in
the loft -- another scorchingly hot session -- and I
told her I wanted to hear her say those same three
words, up close, while we were pressed together, eyes
locked. And she said them. (But I still don't think
she really means them. Not yet. Not with soul-deep
fierceness. But I believe it'll be happening soon.)

    Again we both kept our pants on. And both times as
she came again and again, at her place and mine, she
eventually asked what about me, didn't I want to come
too? Yet she'd already told me, and I mean adamantly,
that she didn't want to move into direct sexual touching
-- oral/genital especially -- until after the tests
came back. So I told her I didn't think frottage
through denim would work for me as it did for her and
I'm a total dud at nipple comes and I was fine with
waiting. And that's where it still stands now.

    She's so bogglingly, breathtakingly responsive.
Truly she has now ASTONISHED me. And she also relishes
our loving: "I can't believe how you turn me on." (One
of her phone messages the next morning: "My nipples are
whining for you.")

    For each step forward half a step back. She
decided I was overdoing my reaction to her stunning
sexuality. (I hadn't tried to play down my delight --
euphoria really.) Was I splitting off her sexuality and
failing to appreciate her whole being? Oh lord. Out
she hauled the hoary psych categories. Letters, calls.
(Again all eighter these exchanges continued, on this
and a dozen other topics.) Self-defense. Walking the
tightrope. FOOs up the wazoelie. (And then yesterday,
as she said herself, came her turn on the tightrope as

she tried to explain what it is she tells her friends
about me. I'm nurturing, I'm supportive, I'm funny....
I look sort of like that goofy French actor with the big
nose, what's his name? Movie about an illegal green
card -- um, oh, you know! (Wait until she meets brother
Rob!) -- And by the way, I've now told her it's okay
with me if she wants to talk about our sex life with her
friends. Earlier I'd asked her to keep at least that
much private. But several times she grumped about the
hardships this supposedly imposes. Aw, go ahead and
tell everybody then, said I oh so magnanimously.)

She gave me a recent photo of herself with her
eighty-two-year-old mother. Said she likes my arms --
arms are important to her -- and is glad I'm "sorta big
down there" ("your whatzis") and also that I don't have
"white-boy lips." For days we explored the possible
causes of the frequent stomach upsets she's suddenly
been suffering just as she did back in her twenties but
hadn't since then, except during the short period of
turmoil with her second fiance, the sociopath. She told
me about her deceased friend Manny's daughter who
finally met a wonderful man after enduring years of
messy romantic troubles with others, married him, and
almost immediately dropped dead, literally -- this is
the daughter, not him -- from an undiagnosed heart
problem as it turned out. She spoke of the fear her own
mother drilled into her regarding success: "Don't make
God jealous." (Her "smothering" mother with whom she
slept in the same bed until age eleven.)

Sex addiction -- now it's easy to see why. Her
"tremendous power over men" -- not just a matter of
looks or shape or charm or canny moves, though she's got
all those too and in abundance. Men always hanging
around breathing hard, banging on her door, taking her
fancy places, plying her with gifts, ready to do
anything for her. (Now she laughed in recalling my
initial puzzlement, my haplessly earnest questions
prompted by her recoiling from my touch early on: "Do
you like sex?" etc. She loves sex! The catch is it
makes her so vulnerable. When the pleasure comes so

easily it's devilishly hard not to go for more and
more, to the point of seriously disrupting her life.)
     Now I become the caretaker of her gift. (No doubt
she'd disapprove of my saying it this way.) Sometimes
it'll be a trial too, I'm sure of it. But I'm ready.
And eager!
     -- Also she did another number on me regarding
medical/dental stuff. Her total shock: I haven't seen a
doctor in how long? And she's disturbed by my
"cringing" if I think she's staring into my mouth as I
talk (which she does like to do, at length and in depth,
as if she's counting the teeth). But she's said she'll
stand by me regardless. She figures we ought to make
it to at least age ninety together. (I confessed that
my sealed "veto envelope" from a couple of weeks ago
asked her to defer to my judgment on my own medical/
dental matters. Now without my saying anything more she
agreed to do this for a full year, no strings attached.)
     Her last master's "module." When she returns from
it Sunday she'll be moving into a new post-study
"spontaneity realm" and I'll be moving into it with
her. Time to have some fun. Time to explore the ways
of getting down with a herpes lady. Condoms! Could be
I'll need an adjustment period. (After her fifth or
sixth bed-shaking come on Saturday night she groaned,
"Yeah, let's hurry up with those tests." And yesterday
up in the loft: "I can't stop thinking about what it's
going to be like with you inside me." And I'd said I
wanted to see her eyes sometime when she came, so she
let me do that. This after her warning, "You have to
let me be me.")
     -- She joked a lot about the low ceiling above the
loft bed but seemed to adjust to it easily once we were
up there. And the feet tromping just inches directly
overhead appeared not to bother her. What did upset
her, I think, was the difficulty we both had in stopping
once we'd begun. Our projected "long neighborhood walk"
had to be cut back drastically to a quick scamper down
to the new pier and back. "The trouble with sex," she
confided, "is it makes everything else seem unexciting."

-- She said she'd been thinking this while visiting her
friend Jessica on Sunday. And here it was happening
again. -- And in one of yesterday's letters she
confides her eagerness to get acquainted with "the skin
beneath your belt" on Sunday.)
     Oh it's gonna be so so so fine....
                         *

     -- And much else is happening with us. Whole
realms I can scarcely touch on. The psych talk.
Politics. Music. What we'll read. A dozen or maybe
more like a dozen dozen ongoing disputes. Questions
about "spirituality." Projects ahead. Concerns. (What
will I wear to her graduation ceremony? How about next
week's "vetting dinner" with her friends Wei and Alison,
and maybe also one with her best friend, Aida?) At
least a close shave right before she arrived on Tuesday
-- a close chin-scraping razor shave by me, that is --
succeeded in preventing a second episode of "clown lips"
for her. (She made a special call to report this and
thank me.) (And confessed that her spontaneous call
from the burbs proposing we meet immediately for dinner
was highly unusual for her; among her friends she's long
been known for her perpetually crammed calendar and the
consequent barriers against acting spontaneously.)
     -- Such pleasure to me, catching a glimpse of my
ring dangling right where we both want it between her
breasts. (She in a khaki shirt-dress with open collar.)
-- And such fine firm breasts too. Large nipples, not
Filipina but rather (like her fairly large nose) a
direct inheritance from buxom blond Polish Mama (and
breast size -- not that I'm obsessing here -- maybe
halfway between average Filipina and that same mama).
The splendid jolt I got upon leaning into the crotch of
her black jeans after we'd been going at it for hours,
my nose grazing, the strong sex whiff. Yo, Zoelie!
(Love this name she's chosen for herself.) During our
scamper to the pier her arm snaked around my waist and
she even patted my ass (acting as if the pat were
inadvertent: therefore I liked it even better).
     -- Meanwhile warm days. Such pleasure to be going

about in them! Thanks to Zoelie everything's
marvelously enhanced right now just the way bezazzlement
spoze to be. (What's more, Team USA seems to be coming
out of its decades-long funk at least a bit. "The best
of times" economically. Could be I'm meeting Zoelie
just as the era of the Asian wars is finally petering
out. -- But not if the jingos and reactionaries have
their way. They're already pounding the drums about the
biggest and baddest Wild Far East tribe of them all,
"the coming civilizational clash." Disgusting. I want
to believe no one's listening to these neocon crazies.)
    More now? Nah. Sort and fold that laundry. Do
some serious wallballing. (I'm determined to shape
myself up for this woman.) Eat, but not too much. (And
I'm already weak from hunger!) -- Her first (and just
about only, so far) flattering words about my chops as a
lover: "I do really like the way you kiss." (Her friend
Mark, an economics postdoc, proclaimed I must be "an
important guy" after she'd told him about my newspaper
days. This seemed to raise my stock with her quite a
bit, as if she'd still been fearing I was just another
inner-city weirdo ("sociopath") with sadly outdated
hairstyle and clothes and pickup patter. This same Mark
also had the nerve to ask her if we'd reached "FFD" yet,
"First Fuck Day." Zoelie: "I'm not a prude; I didn't
mind. I told him we're waiting for the tests but we've
already had 'FHLD,' First Hot Loving Day." -- And for
a few minutes we acted out her voicemail fantasy about
sleeping spoon style with her nipples pressed against my
back. And yeah, it was good. It was real good. So now
our plan is to go for a whole night of it this weekend.)
    -- Alas, it grosses her out that I don't
necessarily wash my hands after taking a whiz in my own
bathroom. Not to mention drinking milk from the carton,
wearing no underwear, sucking on plastic bottles, etc.
etc. My sorry conventional corporate supermarket grub.
My strange "survivalist-like" hoarding of just about
every kind of nonperishable food and household item.
    Meanwhile she, the supposedly healthy-living one,
eats out often and loves big juicy burgers with all the

trimmings, including greasy fries. A TV perches on a
chair by her bed. She consumes schlock detective novels
by the truckload. Her apartment's far more cluttered
than any I've ever lived in. She wrinkles her nose in
disdain. Has lots of freckles and moles on her body
(and can raise either eyebrow singly and wiggle either
ear singly or both in tandem). Drives a bit recklessly,
sometimes seemingly verging on road rage. Carries so
many pills with her you can hear her rattling half a
block away. Fills up all her pockets, and sometimes
mine too, with co-op goodies rather than accept a
plastic bag at the checkout, but burns enough gas while
driving the easily walkable eight blocks from her place
to the co-op to make a dozen bags. (Her "veto envelope"
said she would not grow her hair longer or dye it --
neither of which I'd ever dream of asking her to do.)

Her friends tell her she's "glowing" these days.
She confides to me: "It's code for 'You're fucking
again!'" (And by the way, she has firmly muscled arms
and well-developed pecs and deliciously shapely and
velvety-smooth glutes to go along with the excellent
legs and the talented eyebrows and ears and various
other impressive parts.)

*

O jyze, how your focus has changed. Think of a
year ago. No time to dally over little daily details
anymore -- from the mopey quotidian we've leapt into the
roaring sublime. (But this coming Saturday a trip over
to my storage unit. Just me, by ferry. Not to fetch
anything, though, and certainly not to wallow in
nostalgia. Week after next Z will be going over there
with me and I want to spruce up the place a bit first.
Also I'll look through my bags of old clothes and see if
they contain anything that might pass for "contemporary
style." Anything there to appeal to her desire to be
chivalrically courted the way they supposedly do it in
the working-class world or anyway did back when she was
forming her expectations of men and romance?)

The jyzer in love. This is something else. This
is how it oughta be.

[Jyze in Love]

18

    Jyze for the eve of Norwegian Constitution Day.
We'll be attending the parade out in the Scandi quarter.
First time for me. The papers tell of Norski media
descending en masse to beam the festivities back to the
old country.
    "We" being Z & me, by mutual decree. But also it's
Kathryn, "Kat," Z's seven-year-old godchild, adopted
Guatemala-born daughter of Z's deceased "blood brother"
Manny and his wife Betty, a nurse from the deep upper
heartland outback who's, to repeat, become Z's good
friend since Manny's death. This trio, along with Z,
being the ones flapping their arms like birds in one of
the photo belts on the Zoelie Trope by Z's bed.
    No turning back now. We've weathered our make-or-
break crisis. It's real love, both sides. And hot
love. Super-sexy love. Arrayed here on the floor of
unit B-2 in what's normally the nerf play zone (viewed
from, no surprise, the funky green armchair) is my futon
from atop the loft, now wrapped for the first time ever
in ol' Mom's electric-blue silk sheets -- but with
pillows encased in clashing orange cotton because in the
matching blue silk cases they become slippery like
hockey pucks on ice, it turns out, silk on silk offering
no stay-put bracing friction for the loveplayers.
    We slept there last night. First time in B-2.
Little sleep, though. Can't get enough of each other's
stuff. And: we're down to just shorts now and hands may
sneak inside them and eyeballs scope out all contents.
"Whole lotta towsin' goin' on." She comes and comes and
comes. I stiffen up again and again and again (but so

far don't come since she's so quick at it and the shorts
make things so strange and awkward -- but I expect I'll
soon be coming lots too) (but she worries I'll be like
her last lover, Jerry, five years her senior, who didn't
come lots, blaming it on age). She sings in my ear in
her smokiest low voice and this all by itself turns me
on, and not just genitally: I mean every cell from scalp
to toes, fingertips to fingertips.

   At six-fifteen the alarm goes off. Some languid
morning-breath smooching and banter and up she eases, to
meditate, sitting cross-legged on the couch just above
me, having asked me not to watch. Then she showers as I
doze on coverless in the extremely warm room (the
tropical half of her heritage, she says, demands the
heat be turned up high, and so it is), she dresses in
the nook in jeans and red "Trash Team" T (Fridays being
dress-down day at her office), she sits on the carpet
next to me and with one hand nibbles on a power bar,
sips at rice milk, pages through the morning paper while
with the other hand fondling "the endowment" (her
flattering term) inside the shorts. Then she lays the
paper to one side and leans in for a goodbye kiss which
turns into something more, and she stretches out, I slip
her jeans down, "Ooh-ooh-ooh" -- twice. Her astounding
gift. I'll be in its thrall merely for the rest of my
days. Haven't even a shade of doubt about this.

   -- And pulls jeans back up, zips backpack closed,
leaves me sprawled adaze as off she clomps in clogs. An
extra set of keys for my place in her pocket, just as I
now have a set for hers. (Yesterday we submitted
ourselves to her doctor for STD testing. We also talked
about my joining her health plan under the city's
domestic-partners provision, and most likely I'll do it.
She also let me know the exact status of her finances
(appalling) and her obligations to her aged mother
(extensive) which she asked me to honor once our
property becomes community under state law, assuming it
does (as we're both doing). Of course! I told her, to
all of it. "The whole nine yards and all the open
country beyond.") (Yes, this thing we've got going is

going the distance. She's telling her friends -- even
her counselor -- we're "born soul mates" -- which is how
it sounds when she says it, but how she writes it, on
one occasion at least, is "Zole Mates.")
     The vines outside the window now richly green,
impenetrable, sunlight-dappled. So fine it is to be so
besotted. Big bunch of mixed flowers thrusting up and
out from a vase on the table, actually two bunches for
the price of one bought at closing hour at the public
market yesterday as I rushed about purchasing items for
this first of Z's overnight visits (we've already
agreed, what's more, she'll be staying here regularly on
Thursday nights and maybe Tuesday nights too, and I at
her place on Saturday nights and maybe one other
weeknight). Readied the place, then hurried down to
fetch her (from a drunken after-work promotion party for
a longtime "Trash Team" friend), walked her back along
the waterfront beneath magnificently sun-streaked
cumulo-cloudy skies (she coughing almost uncontrollably
at times in reaction to a powdery anti-hangover pill
she'd just gulped down), then here prepared our dinner
(reducing her to tears from being reminded of her father
at work in the kitchen) (she's extremely labile!), read
with her on the couch opposite, took a hike while she
talked long-distance on my phone with her mama, as she
usually calls her, who's been "disorientating" lately
(whole vast webs of gulp-inducing complexity concerning
their relationship I know about already, with much more
yet to come, she's warned me), and then at ten to bed.
Vowing, both of us, she'd get plenty of sleep so as to
be able to function passably at work today. She,
however, in wickedly sexy loose-fitting red PJ shorts
and no top. Could we possibly hold to the vow for more
than ten or fifteen minutes at a stretch all night long?
Not a chance! Except for maybe thirty or forty minutes
somewhere between three and five. Her face so lovely by
alleylight, I gazing hypnotically. Besorceled. Awash
in tenderness waves. "Do you know what it means to ache
for Z.B. / to yearn for her all night long?"
     -- But. The crisis. Back a full week now. Her

"hiccup" letter from the resort was much worse than anticipated, aburst with anxieties, doubts, backsliding, second thoughts, soul-shredding insults (yes!). It condemned me to a sleepless night and a robotic following day and was doubly infuriating because it crossed with my love letter "written in blood." Betrayal! I fired off another long letter, eight pages of rage. On Friday she'd left me a single voicemail, saying her response to my letter was "Yes. Yes. Yes." -- but framing this in a way that made it seem intentionally equivocal ("yes" to which parts, the crazed loving parts or the parts asking if she was pulling back? Or maybe to both parts at once?).

On Sunday she returned to the city and swung by here at four p.m., parking in the alley right beneath my window and giving a toot on her horn, and as I came out the courtyard door she was standing at the gate (looking stunningly gorgeous, and thus ratcheting my resolve up even higher) and her first words were, "Are you mad at me?" "You know I am." She wanted to hash it out right away in my room, I said not there, we settled on the little pocket park two blocks to the east. Walked over. In a low fury-shaking voice I started to lay out my grievances and the changes I was now demanding (no more nookie until she was ready to quell her self-proclaimed "anxieties" about it, no more submitting myself for approval to her ever-growing "vetting squad," no more deferring to her idea of what our pace should be -- but I'd go even slower than she wanted, not faster, etc. etc.). She replied that she couldn't get a handle on what I was saying because the park was too distracting (it was crowded with the usual gritty bunch) and again insisted we take our dispute to B-2. This time I caved.

Sitting on the carpet in B-2. "Scary talk." She wept. Owned up to a "tendency to act self-destructively." Refused to cede on nookie and going slower. A showdown. Big gamble on my part -- but I couldn't have her treating my hanging-way-out-there avowals so cavalierly. And to her great credit she stuck to her guns (relying on her grad-school-taught

negotiating principles, she later confessed) and battled
with me and with herself, didn't yield to the urge to
storm out, struggled to grasp why I'd found certain
things she'd written so hurtful or damaging, apologized
for those things yet didn't simply run up a white flag
-- rassled with me on several of my "changes" -- and in
the end I agreed to drop all but one: I'd no longer be
submitting to the systematic "vettings" by her friends.
On this, hallelujah, she was the one who caved.

"That," she said, "was really, really scary." But
we recovered fast. Back to our earlier plan, just a
couple of hours behind schedule. To her place, with
tales told on the way of her many school intrigues and
triumphs (she'll be a graduation speaker) and a stop at
the usual co-op market to pick up dinner-to-go and wine.
A wonderful alcohol-vivified repast at her table looking
out from well up the hill on the dusky postcard-pretty
urban-lake view, Z suddenly becoming actively amorous,
moving her chair up close, wrapping her arms around my
neck, showering me with kisses, licks, bites, exploring
with her hands, laughing, loving, giddy with it all,
delighted, wanting me, wanting us -- and of course I'm
reciprocating it all and then some, turning on to her to
a degree I can still scarcely believe -- ecstatically
afloat in what I kept dumbstruckly thinking must be a
supreme lifetime moment (nor was I wrong in this euphoric
view, I say now in relatively sober recollection).

-- This moment lasting for the next twenty hours or
so, all of which we passed in her bed, entirely
sleepless except for catnaps here and there, making love
of the noncopulatory kind again and again and again,
literally dozens of times -- was it thirty? forty? --
ten or twenty or thirty minutes apart, in all sorts of
positions and postures and ways, she coming once or
twice or three times each round (laughing about her
self-proclaimed insatiability, "how amazingly responsive
I am to you"). The enforced abstinence of all this
serving mainly, it seemed, to heighten and prolong all
pleasures. She revealing as never before (at least with
me) her kinky needy funky sensual sexual soul (or Zole).

[20K Jyze]

Frequently talking aloud as we loved. Singing.
Murmuring. Hanging out between my legs and pulling the
top of my shorts down and rolling my stiff or semi-stiff
"whatzis" against her face, neck, breasts (astounding
me by coming numerous times from this alone) (and yet
owing to the same STD restraint never taking me in her
mouth, though declaring she wanted to). "Do you know
how much I love you, Jyzeman G? Tell me you know."
-- She entoning "I love you" hundreds of times mantra-
fashion in quick succession like the "ooh"s as pleasure
builds and then surges to climax (you can literally feel
it with her, like strong current in a writhing wire).
Other mantras too: "I want you in me so bad." "Do you
know now?" "I'm so hot for you." "You're so good."
"Ooh I love your hands so much." "Oh you're fucking me,
I'm fucking you, we're fucking fucking fucking."
        Stupid guy to suggest any comparisons. But I'll
take it over any other night of loving ever.
        Our separation while she was out of town, the fears
and anguish, the fight (the gamble), then the loving --
this sequence bonded us for life. I'm saying so. But
what really matters: so's she.
        -- Wheeeeeewww. Hots me up something fierce just
to think about all this. Jyze, such hots ye never knew!
And here on a glorious sunny Friday afternoon, late,
"Happy Hour." Taped to the wall opposite is a poster
she made, in imitation of the ones she saw here, on
want-ad newsprint (though not from the personals); and
it says this: "JYZE, ZYZE LOVZ GYZE..." Exact meaning I
couldn't suss out for sure but its jyst is plenty clear.
        The couch swept clean of all books, binders, etc.
A shelf in the medicine chest set aside for her
toiletries. Her clothes hanging in the closet, her
vittles crammed into the fridge. My daily schedule
shifting, sleep hours moving earlier so as to put us in
better sync. Gonna be lots of changes. And this is
okay by me. I'll find ways to do my work/jyze things
within the new framework. I foresee no major glitches.
Maybe a few minor ones, but none to shudder over.
        She wept remembering her first lover ("cherry

man"), a law student roughly four years her senior, coldly critiquing her performance on their first night together -- she'd never told anyone about this trauma before. Her neuroses and kinkinesses. Once in a while she still shows an abrasive rigidity resulting, she says, from the mental/emotional troubles she went through in her twenties (as my mother did also), and this draws me to her even more (rigidity which quickly dissolves in intimacy and usually isn't evident at all but shows up at unexpected moments and helps to keep me on my toes in loving her). She's struggled hard to overcome shynesses, resentments, class differences, mixed-culture confusions, racial putdowns, "erotic exotic" manipulations, hospital trauma and outright "freak treatment" (for the extra toes, the clompy shoes of her grade-school years, and also for "sex mania" later) -- all without giving up a shred of pride. ("Story of O" was a turn-on for her; she sought help from a feminist counseling group in dealing with this politically incorrect psychosexual fact about herself.)

     She fills me in on all these things. She openly wonders if I can jerk off with her lying there watching. (So far I've been strangely reluctant to make even a perfunctory attempt.) She likes to sniff my armpits and crotch for "pheromone hits." She stands naked in front of me and says, "Part of me still wishes I could wow you with my nineteen-year-old body" -- knowing very well she's wowing me just as she is. She catches me gazing at her vulvar zone and says, "Well, is my muff up to snuff?" (It sure is! Very comely, I'll say, pinkish clit and dark brown clamshell lips bordered by an oval of handsome black brushstrokes like chevrons almost.)

     And: she's trying to coax me into eating more organically and seeing doctors "so we can still be fucking like crazy at a hundred and five" (at ninety she'd said earlier, but that will no longer suffice). She tells me all her friends, including even the Afrusan lesbians, are siding with me on the "vetting" issue. Rare is the day when I don't wake up to find three or four voicemails awaiting me from her ("Hi, you!" and

"Yo, jyzer-person!" among many other salutations). And
then find three or four more when I come home later, and
this after calling her at nine or so from the booth at
the ORB cafe or the reception desk at the scope office
and gabbing for half an hour or more.

Miraculous. Iz true. She's thinking so too. And
trumpeting the news for all to hear. ("And you know
what they all say? They say, 'Oh, we already knew you
were in love. It's so obvious!'")

Yesterday we met at her doctor's office downtown.
(Both of my elbow hollows today feature gruesome black-
and-blue marks because I got a jitter or two at blood-
drawing time and the nurse kept missing the vein on one
arm and then almost as badly on the other one.)
Afterwards I tagged along on a trek through big downtown
department stores and watched with awe (happy kind, like
young marrieds) as she accomplished the gnarly feat of
exchanging a pair of shoes (owing to her childhood foot
operations she's extremely hard to fit). Then we hiked
up into my home turf for dinner at an upscale yuppie
noodle shop, the sidewalk-cafe section. The chicken was
overcooked; she complained rather crossly to the server;
they didn't charge us for it; I was impressed. I walked
her back to the Z-mobile at a downtown garage and in
embracing her turned on enormously and could barely
force myself to let her go -- so she could attend the
monthly meeting of her longtime book group for the first
time this year, so busy has school kept her even before
she and I met -- and then I couldn't turn myself off and
finally had to resort to some wanky-panky, to adopt a
bawdy yuk-it-up term of hers -- she who doesn't hesitate
to say she jerks off frequently, often with a vibrator
-- I paddled my pickle, yup, in the scope-office
bathroom just so I could tend to the night's GJ job.
(Jyze blushes to say -- and that's a fact.)

She's insisting I attend her graduation ceremony
even if I have to wear a paper bag over my head (to
avoid the scrutiny of the decommissioned "vet squad"
assembled en masse). Funny thing is I'd already been
planning to sneak in if need be.

[Jyze in Love]

        Zoelie B. Wow. Could go on like this about her
forever if not for the jyze rules which say no no no.
        I shoo-goo'd eight pairs of old sneakers, how 'bout
that. (And with good results.) Brought my big tabletop
fan out from storage for its second annual high-summer
B-2 spin. Rearranged items on shelves in the loft inner
(under) sanctum so as to provide better ventilation for
horseplay activities up above. Snooped around for more
cards to send the Z-woman (we're both keeping those
cards and letters flying, along with everything else).
        What in addition? Concluded Z may well be the
sexiest woman alive. Failed, despite extended efforts,
to get the scoping program up and working on the new
(rehabbed) desktop computer (but the laptop's fine).
Went into shock when Z's scale reported I'm ten pounds
above the weight I've been going by since bicycling days
(and the doctor's scale confirmed this). Learned Z has
a Sufi name, Daena, from the goddess of the sunrise (and
thus for nightscopers the goddess of bedtime). Took up
reading the hip horoscopes in the two major Jyze City
weeklies because she does ("just for kicks"). Tacked up
on the loft a batch of loving notes she folded into
paper airplanes and sailed my way. Bought a bunch of
junk at thrift stores, mostly as potential art supplies
with which to make goofy gifts for her.
        I'm spending money like crazy but I know there'll
never be a better time for it -- because I know there'll
never again be such a heady period at the start of
loving such a fantastic woman -- because I know this
love will only be going deeper and deeper and there'll
never be another love, period. (She says all this too,
and just as mushily: "I love you so much but I'm going
to love you even more, more and more and more" -- this a
quote from one of the airplane wings now handily
fluttering on the doorjamb by my left ear.)
        Ferried across to the storage unit (on Saturday
while grimly pondering the crisis with the absent Z) and
fetched some old clothes. My furious "changes" letter
insisted we not even see each other again until June 1,
during which period of separation I'd be trying my best

to adjust to the new reality of a severely circumscribed
relationship. She bought a horrid country-and-western
CD just so she could play me "You're One in a Million"
over the phone (and I could hear her cracking up with
laughter in the background as she did so). (Lots and
lots of laughs with her, yes indeed and how...and howl!)
She credits her current graduate program with teaching
her how to handle complex "diversity issues" even to the
point she can deal with a burb-warped Cawkamamie like
me. "I paid thirty-five K so I could snag you." "I got
you now," she whispers in first one ear, then the other,
her hand meanwhile reaching inside the blue shorts to
rev up my "gen set" (on the phone earlier she said she'd
never heard the term before I used it -- like who's she
trying to kid? Didn't she tell me her most serious
recent lover, Jerry, was a big-time yachtsman?).

     Mad, mad, mad about this Zoelie. In lo-o-o-o-ve.
It's the best of times. They just keep on a-rollin'.

-------·

19

-------·

     Brain-fried. Jyze cycle messed up. Even crazier
in love than before. "Endowment," alas, not functioning
right. STD test negative. Full tilt Zoelie. (Week of
composing more zany songs for her, among them "Tooling
Along With Zoelie," "Zounds It's Zoelie!," and "It's
Zoelicious. It's Zoelrageous. It's Zoelmongous."

     Now a time squeeze. It's two a.m. Friday night,
B-2 windows tapping with the first rain in a week.
Tomorrow's supposed to be J-day -- that is, Saturday is,
but we're also in the opening hours of Memorial Day
weekend and the Z-woman and I have big plans. Three
days of decadence at Jess and Gwen's house (tending the

doggies while the pretty mamas go rafting) with
introductions to various Z-friends mixed in. Errands
starting at noon. She's vowed she's gonna get me --
drive me wild -- suck me off nonstop -- fuck my brains
out. Just might happen too, the good prick willing.
(Am I in a protracted adjustment period or what? Trying
not to be anxious about it. Agog over her sexuality and
her marvelous and, yeah, to me somewhat strange, not to
mention unprecedented, yet still no less Zoelicious way
of loving.)

Meanwhile a tough scoping job blows in out of
nowhere, close to three hundred pages, destroying
tonight. Eyes burning holes blurring jyze scratchings.
Grittin' it out here.

The doc's call came shortly after the last jyze
entry wrapped. Negative, that is, we're a go. Actually
I hadn't figured on knowing so soon. Zoelie, with her
usual quick insight in such realms, spotted my unease
and offered a swap. She'd drop the safe-sex requirement
if I'd cancel my refusal to submit to any more vettings
by her friends. She promised the next round would take
place "in a more natural way" (vetting round, she meant,
but the words applied to sex rounds too). Agreed.

Saturday, a rollicking afternoon with seven-year-
old Kathryn, the adoptee. The Scandi parade. Kat and I
pals from the first moment. She drew decorations with a
black marker on my canvas sneakers (at my urging) and
tickled my ribs with her heels while riding my shoulders.
Then the three of us moved on to a nearby park for
swimming (Kat only) and roller-blading (again Kat only,
though I trotted alongside at times to serve as a kind of
catapult or booster rocket, sending her zooming ahead),
then to Zoelie's for bubble-blowing as our feet dangled
off the balcony edge (all together floating out enough
bubbles to make the city look carbonated).

Zoelie and I, at her place that night we
technically became lovers, I guess, intercoursers, twice
in fact but probably less than five minutes for the two
combined. A first fuck for the ages it was not. For
her both times were painful. Both times I quickly

wilted. The rest of the night we loved each other up
just as fiercely as before but for a third round of
fucking my timing was way off. She comes and comes and
I have trouble finding my natural rhythm. Performance
anxiety too, I suspect. Simple fact is I'm going head
to head and gen set to gen set with a prodigy.

It's all so odd. Another simple fact is I'm
sexually hyped up and blissified as never before, and
I'm talking lifetime. She too, she says, and I believe
her. We just can't stop feasting on each other, never
mind the glitches. Kisses so sweet and impassioned,
just unbelievable. You have no idea what a truly hot
kiss is until you've kissed someone (on the lips, the
facial lips, and otherwise not touching) to orgasm.
I've already done it three times. With her, I'm saying.
And only her -- ever.

Tuesday night and last night she stayed here. Last
night nearly sleepless up in the loft. We're trying to
find ways to bring this nonstop "horseplay" under better
control so she won't be a zombie at work. "Mama's got a
squeeze box / Daddy can't sleep at night" -- but it's
Mama that matters right now, since Daddy's mostly a day-
sleeper anyway.

How I walk talk eat sleep slurp gobble Zoelie. All
circuits blazing. Letters, cards, telegrams, visits,
calls at all hours, plans, books, magazines, notes,
lists of questions, gifts, vows, songs, flowers, pet
names -- "limerence." It's the state we're both in, so
dubbed by Anita, Z's counselor. When all is wondrous in
a blooming new love. A "flow" state of the heart -- or
rather of two hearts, together, amen. (Gave her, Z, a
letter from my long-ago-dismantled high-school sweater,
the green-and-gold sophomore Gatefield "G," I did: a
lifetime first for both of us.) (The varsity "G" I'm
saving for later when it will signify a real varsity
conjugal feat -- by me, I'm saying.)

She's so sensually/sexually gifted and runs so hot
she's had men creaming over her and on her and in her
all her post-age-eighteen life (and truly was herself
sexually addicted) and so, oddly, she's never had to

learn much about getting a man off. Spoiled. She's had
it easy. She says this herself. And her own passion
sweeps up so often and so intensely she loses any focus
she may've attained on stoking up the dude's. Gonna
have to coach her. Hoping this weekend to work up a
come or two for, yeah, myself. (Haven't had a single
one so far! Yet bizarrely enough I'm not all that
bothered by this except it's making her feel she's a
sexual dud. "The resume of my failure / is written up
in your groin" -- she wrote that.)

Her poems. Half a dozen of them this week. She
wants to spend "mondo time" with my babybook (which she
glanced through during a brief hideaway visit). She's
angling for a way to cover me immediately on her city
health insurance. She's beating the drums about eating
organically since she thinks maybe it's my bad diet (or
hormones leaching from plastic) that's costing me my
pop. We're breaking into something wholly new: postconfluent love. "I want to drive you wild! As wild as
you drive me! I'm determined!" -- As if she can't see
she's been doing it all along. (Well, maybe sometimes
she can't. Her anxiety attacks. Sez I'm already her
"quintessent" lover, though, after having previously
used the term (in talking with me!) for a certain
college-era main squeeze she took up with again for a
while years later. -- But for six years immediately
prior to my arrival on the scene she went without sex
-- "cold turkey, yup" -- except for the solitary kind,
which is to say: wanky-panky. Stocked up on dildos and
cucumbers. Sprang for lots of massages. Mastered in
sublimation. Hung out with the girls, and many were
lesbians. She'd had it "forever" with men.)

(By the way, it may be true she knows only a few
words of Tagalog and Visayan, as noted before, but she
sure can speak a lot of syllables of same. Issues them
in bursts, mostly when she's bored or frustrated but
also just for the helluvit. Has no idea what they mean.
Started doing this as a kid when her father's Filipino
friends visited and spoke their native languages and she
felt left out. Imitated them as best she could and drew

applause from the menfolk. Tagawocky, I call it: a kind of happy-smoke gibberish. -- But true, to fluent Tagalog/Visayan speakers the nonsense might be much less pure. In her view this is possible but "not likely.")

Massive changes in my life. For a couple of days it appeared I might be moving in with her right away, or we might become official "Deeps," as they're called among city employees, for domestic partners or D.P.'s (just like Gramps's old nickname for me, "Jeep," from my first two initials, G.P., same as those for the "general purpose" vehicle or jeep, as jyze has mentioned numerous times before, though maybe not yet this year). I let her know -- frequently -- I'm in this for good and forever and that's settled, period. If marriage is what she wants, marriage it'll be. No unseemly haste is called for, but I don't want her to think I'm limiting things to mere shacking or Deeping. And she keeps telling me she's letting all her friends know we're "Zole Mates" and she's "crazy in limerence not to mention love -- but okay, that too" and they're saying they just can't believe she's talking like this, their post-romantic firebrand-feminist buddy Zoelie B., now driving the "eew factor" readings right off the chart.

I finally visited her office. Just a single diagonal block from the hideaway, it turns out, fifth floor, a good-size room maybe four times the square footage of the hideaway but partitioned in the middle, with a colossal amount of clutter on her side much like her apartment but even more like certain newspaper city rooms I've known. The two of us then schlepped bags tourist-style on a crosstown trek to B-2, she preparing to stay overnight. (And how I delight in gazing down at her surreptitiously from the loft as she wanders around in her sexy underwear at seven a.m. while readying herself for work. But -- did I say? -- she's asked me not to do this while she's meditating or stretching.)

Best of all I love the way she can't get enough nookie. Says so and confirms it over and over in the trenches. Keeps starting things up again. Talk about libido! "Put your finger back in?" "G-man wanna visit

G-spot?" "One more for the road?" For her getting off
is -- well. She wants at least a couple this weekend
with no touching at all. But -- by lips, by breast, by
ass (that is, lightly caressing her sweet smooth firm
little buns with my fingertips and palms), even by scalp
(running fingers through her hair). Astonishing. Has
she ever ASTONISHED me! This may be my number-one
ASTONISHMENT of all time. I'm her willing slave. And
it goes on and on, week after week, only getting better
and better -- erratic whatzis behavior to one side or to
the dunce seat in the corner for the moment. -- Or more
to my liking, to that dunce seat forever. Begone,
erratic whatzis behavior! And soon, goddamn it!

     (What else? Sister Barb wrote. It seems it's
finally dawning on her that I meant what I said. Now
she's upset about the "tone" of my last letter in which
I broke off with her! Yet she offers no apologies. The
best she can do is grudgingly concede Mother's death may
have contributed to our difficulties. But that's
nowhere near enough for me. -- I'm mulling this one.
Taking my time. Talking it over with Zoelie too. How
fine it is to have someone who's willing, even eager, to
converse in depth about such thorny personal matters!)
(She counseled students for several years while serving
as director of minority affairs at the college.)

     Z's previous lover, Jerry, was, I learned, "hard
all the time" though he often didn't come. As she'd
already told me, he blamed this on age. She fears I'll
also often fail to come, like Jerry, or worse, fail even
to be hard, unlike Jerry, or will be hard only rarely,
unlike Jerry, or hard only briefly, unlike Jerry, or
hard only when it doesn't matter, unlike Jerry. Says
she'll love me anyway. No matter what. Says how Jerry
was has nothing to do with it (but only after filling me
in on all the glorious intimate details, including the
length of his yacht and the impressive heft of its, and
his anatomical, gen set) (he was a fireman who retired
young after making a killing in the stock market -- had
lots of big muscles too; one time, as Z cheered him on,
he beat up a guy who'd somehow mildly insulted her).

True, we'd have enough -- plenty -- even without
the great (though bizarre, as of now) sex. But without
great sex we're not gonna be. Not if I can help it.
And I mean (also!) great sex of the mutual,
reciprocating, ever-building, and wholly or at least
preponderantly unbizarre -- even vanilla! -- kind.

Last night I arrived at B-2 late. She'd attended a
women's political convention held nearby and beat me
here by several hours. Starting just inside the door I
found a row of little folded-cardboard pup tents pitched
on the carpet leading all the way to, and then up, the
loft staircase, with each tent containing a word or two
of a majorly mushy message. Notes were everywhere. Her
luscious material self was bundled up in the white
comforter (also hers) in the loft, sound asleep. For a
while I just sat down here naked in the dim light
filtering in from the alley and basked in my blessings.

Of course it's true I'm losing many of the best
features of my previous solitudinous life. My regimen
is shattered. I'm getting little done on the protojyze
or the jyze typing or any other work of my own except
the new JIRT in all its shabby glory right here. I'm
not exercising, or only a little (coming up with a new
wallball variation to enliven running in place). My
long-term reading campaign has foundered. The stacks of
unread periodicals and books keep building -- lately
reaching monumental proportions not seen since, again,
newspaper city-room days. Says Z: "I never thought I'd
meet anyone with PMS worse than my own, but you're it."
PMS -- printed-material syndrome. A term of near
derision these days, sorry to say, as we all careen ever
deeper into the digi-dystopian age.

Can't squeeze out much more right now. But maybe
while we're together this weekend, Z and I, a gap will
open in which I can push this entry a little further.
Next time, next J-day, is the long-awaited, but recently
totally neglected, 20K Day: first of this year's dual
set of official adult-midlife milestones. The Z-woman
will be part of that too -- of both, I do believe,
including the Glennarian Rollover in the fall. (She

puts a hand in one of my back pockets as we walk along.
She leaves me flowers and chocolates and gooey letters
-- all at the hideaway, among other places. She writes
a poem about Karen A. after my revelation about being
her first and only lover before her motorcycle-crash
death at age twenty-three. Z's own first time at
nineteen with the law student was a "political act"
inspired by reading -- and I invoke a jyze-rules
exception here -- the fabled Emma G. Her poem, Z's,
wishes we could've been each other's first lover.)
     Got to stop now. Got to.
                    *   *
     -- Don't know if I can pull this off. Blank mind.
Day of daze. But here it is Sunday afternoon, and this
is Jess and Gwen's house, and Z's napping upstairs and
I'm slouched sideways on the couch in the living room
determined to give it a shot. Jyze for the sake of jyze
and for the love of Zoelie B. (As from now on all
things will be for -- ta-da! -- the love of Zoelie B.)
     Just back from trotting a block to her apartment to
fetch the Sunday paper. Overcast skies. A familiar
feel to the southward view because it's only slightly
aslant from the one I lived with daily for almost six
years roughly two and a half miles due east of here.
Also similar demographic makeup in the two hoods: nearly
all Cawk, students and artists in pockets but mostly
working families -- call it a broadly midscale Eurusan
colonial settler zone.
     Flurries of castanets rise from the basement as
J&G's dryer whirls my metal-button shirts round and
round. (In fact I should go down there right now and
smooth out the previous load before the shirts get too
wrinkled. Whack-whack side of head: this is turning
into negligence weekend. But lots of fun and lots of
loving even though I'm still a failed cocksman with this
woman who's to be -- already is -- my last and best and
for sure baaadest love. And this failure of mine is
causing her pain too -- maybe even worse than my own --
and I'm feeling plenty disconsolate about that as well.
Wish I could just press a button and the creaky old

appendage would obediently rise, just like, say, the
ancient cloud-eating drawbridge eight or ten blocks down
the hill. If it can get up there, why can't the
appendage? I'm pressing all the buttons I know of but
it's still not doing it, or at least not when and for as
long as I want -- and need! And so does she!)

*

Back from folding laundry.
And here I sprawl. Dumbfounded. The change in my
life. I'm shooting the white-water rapids, hanging on
with equally white knuckles but also I'm euphoric down
to the last cell, excepting, it would appear, a few
crucial ones located in a certain tubular hank of
flesh. (Surely the refractory hank will one day start
working right. How could it not? How could it resist
her?)

Such a splendid full-body massage she bestowed on
me this morning, Zoelie did. I'm still vibrating from
it, stumbling around in the fragrant aura of a special
lotion she came up with somewhere, a type advertised --
falsely, it turns out -- to possess can't-miss tumefying
powers.

(I should be taking a nap myself. But if I were to
go up there and try, neither of us would sleep a wink.
This is becoming a big problem and we're both determined
-- still -- to wrestle it into submission. Of course I
could try stretching out the rest of the way here on the
couch. I'm not even sure why I don't. Maybe I will.
But later.)

Two small dogs and a cat. Small house, recently
remodeled, with all the planning and carpentry done by
Jess herself. Cathedral-ceilinged living room with
white walls and polished wooden floor, a semi-austere
feel to it. Scrawny leafless tree limbs and gaunt black
metal sculptures for decor. (Now she must've shifted
positions up there because I can hear her breathing.
The garret bedroom opens out onto a small Romeo-and-
Juliet-type balcony overlooking the living room. Superb
acoustics here because of the abundant bareness.)

Jessica P. Z's good friend and work colleague
(currently the city's anti-graffiti czar) and one of the

most kick-ass lesbians around. Also the "double black
belt" in karate Z warned me about in the early days when
she suspected I was a stalker (but weighing in, Jess, at
maybe 105 pounds tops). On my first visit to Z's place
she, Z, called ahead and we stopped by here so Jess
could check me out -- she peering sternly into the open
car window, passenger side (my side), and asking several
tough questions before waving us on. And I owe her for
even more than that: turns out she was the one who, with
help from Gwen, her partner of four or five years, drew
up the rough draft of Z's ad -- the one I answered.
Except for a couple of last-minute edits Z herself had
nothing to do with it -- other than, that is, the minor
matter of providing the raw life content.

    -- Last night Aida, Z's best buddy. She and I
clicked pretty well, or at least I thought so. Did
smoked salmon at a cozy restaurant two blocks from the
drawbridge, then dessert at the same cafe Z and I
visited on our "Meet Day." Aida a live wire, a full-
blooded Filusan whose family moved to the States when
she was fourteen. She's recently divorced, has one kid.
Though I haven't told Z this and probably won't, at
least not for a while, in vivacity, looks, size, even in
some mannerisms Aida reminds me a lot of Lady U. A
similar impish high-energy theatricality and drama-
department background, and only a year apart in age.
Warm and funny, smart, well spoken, admirably prog in
politics. For her Z's not just a friend and a mentor
but a member of the family, a kind of older sister, even
a mother figure in some ways. If things work out right
maybe I'll become a kind of older brother to her myself
(as Aida's boldly predicting). And I'm pleased as punch
about this, just as I am about my "subunclehood," as I'm
calling it, with the beguiling little Kat (whom we'll be
seeing again tomorrow; Z reports the card I sent to
thank Kat for decorating my shoes scored big). ---

                 *   *

    I'm sorry to report the bad dick lolli is still
short on -- pop, yeah. Not worth a lick. In a major
funk. Yet we're laving in limerence regardless, Z and

I. She confirmed this in a phone call at noon today
(two hours ago -- and it's now two days since the
previous portion of this super-stretch entry went down).
     I'm back at B-2. The cockpit. Slept twelve hours
straight last night and today. Now, belted into the
green armchair, I'm trying to get serious about
launching yet another new regime. Up at nine a.m., to
bed as soon as the night paper arrives. Gonna try it.
     Sunday night and Monday morning were not so good.
Z melted down over the no-fuck issue. "When are you
going to? How long do I have to wait?" Ulp. The
looming face in Jess's bed (whose spongy mattress is way
too soft for good fucking anyway). What can I tell her?
But she cooled off and wised up and before much longer
we were back into the realm of gangbusters no-fuck
fucking. (Which got so good the night before, it twice
wrung from me tears of joy/love. This was a virginal
event for me, something in its way better than even the
most supreme yes-fuck fucking imaginable -- unless the
yes-fuck fucking could also produce a pair of tear-duct
joy/love ejacs. -- Eep! And yet: what a visual!)
     One hypothesis we're going under -- and going at it
under as well, the no-fuck fucking -- is that the newly
prominent imminence of death, although most likely to be
preceded by a long doddery downward course, is what's
making the loving between us as midlife-primers the best
loving there could possiby be (except for...yeah).
     Breakfast at a motorcycle cafe with Nurse Betty and
the mischievous Katgrrrl, she and I working so hard to
fill in the polka-dots on her table-crayon drawing of
Ilk the Blue Dino that our waffles went cold. Cleaning
up J&G's house (we never did take the doggies for a
third walk and later Jess, noticing their restlessness,
nailed us on this). Hauling Z's vast store of recycling
-- it occupied most of her balcony -- down to the local
recycling center (whose signs she helped design years
ago as part of her job). A failed attempt to goose the
never-before-used TV I've now given her into unlimited
operational status (we lacked batteries for the remote).
A hyper-greasy dinner at the local burger-chain drive-in

near her place (in her twenty-two years in this town
she'd never once eaten at any of the chain's outlets).
Then a couple of hours of "horsing around" in her bed,
aiming to restoke our sexual limerence to what it was
before the meltdown. And we did manage to do that.

(Her amazing orgasms. Still can't get over them
and maybe never will. Just from lip brushes. But I
said that already. Okay, just from biceps squeezes.
Just from gazing into my "hazels," as she's dubbed them.
My favorites so far: one in which I was diddling a
"displaced clit" on the sole of her right foot, another
in which my arm was reaching through her crotch and my
hand pressing against her midback as my biceps massaged
her true clit zone.) (She does go for biceps. At our
vetting dinner she told Aida I have "pretty good ones"
and then squawked when Aida impishly gave the nearest
one a squeeze. She also thinks I have "good" legs and
"not bad" glutes. During the full-body massage she
pulled back for a moment to observe, with mock chin-
rubbing seriousness, I was "looking sorta hunky today.")
Oh how she writhes when she comes. The arching.
The hard breathing. The mouth wide open, taut, almost
Muncheanly O-ish. The "hai-hai-hai" as if she were
Japanese. The time she startled me by suddenly diddling
herself to a quick one. (How many comes for her overall
this weekend? At least fifty or sixty, and that's just
counting -- not that I was actually counting -- the
distinct, unmistakable ones. Unbelievable. But real.)
And a romantic bath, candles and wine, in J&G's
antique bearclaw tub. Goofy singing from the fakebook.
My dozens of ill-timed, unbold, on-again-off-again hard-
ons and rubbery-ons. The spasmodicity of sleep. The
tale of her antireligious vision at age twelve and her
vile sexual experience at thirteen (when, as she cheered
the horses at a race track with her father, a creepy
rat-faced Cawk man ejacked all over her brand-new many-
petticoated skirt; and even at that tender age she had
the presence of mind to get rid of the evidence before
her father was any the wiser, for fear he would kill the
guy). The scores of new tidbits of Zoelie history

surfacing. Her unexpected ongoing fascination with the
sophomore "G" from my old letter sweater. Her proposal
that our slogan regarding the refractory penis should be
"We're gonna lick this thing" (tongue in cheek?). Her
statement, very serious, that one quality of mine she
really appreciates is that I'm "emotionally always right
there." Her amusing way of offering third-person
observations about the progress of our relationship,
something like the P.A. commentator at a fashion show:
"They're really into coupledom now...for this kinky duo
we can foresee nothing but major, major mush." -- All
these as we revise and integrate personal slants on the
first three months, putting together a workable mutual
romantic "myth of origins" which we then try out on Z's
friends as I meekly sit for the never-ending vettings.
"And whoa, you shoulda seen the look on his face after
he checked out his punky new 'do in the mirror...."

     (Of course once again a few other things happened
this eighter. Sister Barb's letter from last week still
goes unanswered. A photo of Lady U's former lover
appears in the night paper. Yes, "Broadway Marco." For
years I expected he might at any moment jump out of the
theater reviews from the far coast and now he finally
does so, and in a starring role too. I thought of
clipping it and sending it over to her -- or did I
already note this? What confusion! -- Did clip it,
didn't send it. Won't. That era's over. Forever.)

20

     So it's 20K Day. Sunday. Rainy. And jyze is on
live with Zoelie B. Her place. Dinette table.
Famously spectacular view. Big lake and big trees and

big far-off skyscrapers and also big black clouds.
Jazzy radio playing. Standard blank mind of these days
of overwhelming new love hookup.

Took me 20K days to get here. She running half a K
ahead. Me in pursuit all these days but didn't know it
until a tenth of a K, a/k/a a C, as in C-note, back.

Oh yeah. A sigh. Big big sigh.

She's sitting maybe eight feet to my right on the
red couch -- or no, on the floor now with her back
resting against the front of the red couch. She's
protojyzing. She's the fifth person anywhere on the
planet to be in on the secret of jyze. And here on the
table her terrific 20K Day present for me, a bound
collection of twenty original marker-drawn posters
featuring jyzos of her own conceiving (and a loving
handmade card). "Going Out Of My Jyze Over You." "Jyze
Lover I Don't Want To Jyze Alone." -- Two of my faves.

In a whole lifetime never a gift to compare with
this. And from her it's been one gift after another,
all kinds, many many, a fabulous cavalcade -- how she
takes my breath away. (As I've said. But must repeat.
And -- repeat.)

Words like words. (Scratch of her pen. Her
whisker-inflamed cheeks this time. But ooh how she
whizzes along and lefty too, just like Mom.) Homey
cluttery chaos of her apartment and of our lives right
now (in response to which remark, uttered in much the
same form earlier, she chirped clutter and chaos she
likes, just as I would, and do, especially this kind
here, rapture kind, madly proliferant).

Little else we can do other than loveplay and
lovetalk in between, and the occasional basic
subsistence act. Eat mostly. Sleep scarcely at all.
So no surprise this jyze right here is also subsistence
level. (She may be looking to catch a few winks right
now, finally given a chance. She's shifted over to her
bed in the corner just past the red couch, but out of
sight from here, and "might zee out a little," she says
now, in Z-speak, aloud but to the spirits and not
directly to me, as she's respecting jyze etiquette.)

-- So far no movies, no plays, no dancing except last
night a little wobbly naked two-stepping in the kitchen
in front of all the cluttered counters and the empty
cabinets with the open doors. No reading aloud either.
Just can't get to any of these good things. The list of
fun stuff to do in the weeks ahead lengthens ever more.
But nookie almost always trumps.

The one exception of note, yesterday we traveled by
the usual route, two ferries and then foot, to the
storage unit. The usual route except -- not. Made
wholly new by the galvanic presence of Zoelie B. She
picked out a couple of my retired jackets she likes --
"classic retro," she declares -- and now they're
flapping away, partly visible from here, pinned on the
clothesline out on her covered balcony. Scarecrows.
Ghosts of former Jyzer G's. She tells me she
encountered bliss aboard the eighty-year-old wooden foot
ferry, top deck, outdoors, seated on the covered prow
just in front of the pilothouse, as we plowed across the
inlet toward the last remaining outpost of my former
life to which I still have a key or any remaining reason
to visit.

Thinking now to introduce her formally to these
pages I call out, "You still awake?" Silence. So maybe
I'll go smooch her awake instead (never any jyze a tenth
so smoochy and schmaltzy and smarmy as what's going down
these days) -- and this way she'll open her eyes on a
new reality. Come on in, Zoelie. Welcome to jyzeworld!
(So get in there and osculate, fool!)

٭

So did. A Z-illion of 'em. Or one very long
one with occasional breath-catching pauses.

So then how is it we're still not consummated
lovers? Yes, it's frustrating. It hurts her and so
doubly hurts me. Yes, so it goes. But no attempts at
deep explanation or explaining away. Just what is.

Last night for a while it seemed she might be
unable to remain so sexually open (being miffed,
naturally enough, by my flesh's failure to respond
properly to her ministrations and, as it must appear to

187

her, to her very being, even though the rest of me be
turned on and roused up beyond all imagination (yeah,
and I know I've wailed this tune before)) -- but we
recovered.

Just before starting this entry (big 20K Day bash)
we drove over to B-2 to fetch the two J-sticks, first-
stringer and backup, No. 5 and No. 6 respectively, which
I neglected to slip into my pocket in our rush to catch
a bus last night. Along the way a stop at the co-op
market to load up on her craved-for organic waffles and
other compensatorily nutritious items, then breakfast in
my room, then a tandem reading of the paper -- a brief
one, swapping sections like snatches of newsroom
tickertape -- and then we're at it again, she's kneeling
on the floor between my legs, I'm hand-guiding old
whatzis into her mouth and painting her lips with its
clear "precome" juices (and even though this is a
powerfully erotic sight the punky thing's still only
half tumefied, even when she's coming in colors simply
from rubbing her crotch against my thigh, or her nipples
against my groin) (frottage!) -- and then collapsing to
the floor we tumble, for more loving and more and more
and more. (And a mutually tearful interlude when she
thought of the grim fortune that's prematurely cut down
three of her closest friends in the past several years
and worried aloud that I'd be next. Her tears bringing
on mine. In every way but the one most physiologically
fundamental -- meaning the dumbest -- I'm so responsive
to her I'm stunned again and again.)

Lots and lotsa laffs too but most of them slipping
away unjyzed. Shameful. (And to think one day Z will
read this -- as I expect she will, and probably when I'm
gone in just the way those friends of hers are. Sorry,
sorry, sorry Zoelie I'm not up to jyzifying all this the
way it oughta be. Not so far anyway. Someday maybe.
Or closer to it at least. Or not. But sitting here at
your table right now in this apartment 401 to which
you've given me a key, this jyzer, as is, is. You
curled up beneath your navy blue comforter, you Zoelie
B., also as is, are. ZOWIE ZOELIE! Even your snore's

irresistible! Z's zees, that's what. Z-speak is all-
speak. Yeek! Talk about decay, jyze, me!)

     Still think the yes-fuck fucking will be dynamite.
But worries mount. Rise ye obstreperous pecker, damn
ye, and stay risen! Not necessarily forever but at
least long enough!

     Distant hilltop radio towers blinking. Next-yard
treetops thrashing. Barrelhouse piano spilling (from
the radio). Tuck comforter closer around precious one's
shoulders and legs.

     So I ought to be mulling the 20K days. At least a
little. Yet so caught up am I right here in this
twenty-thousandth -- the primest of all! -- that the
other 19,999 are like scattered ashen dream fragments,
with all but a few wholly embered out (and this in the
resonant dark, lights off now, the other ones, but not
this dazzle of a love lamp a foot to my left).

     "Breathe deep." Yeah. Just want to go over there
and dive in. Restless shifting sounds trickling around
the corner. Little whimpery murmurs. She twist left, I
twist left. She moan, I moan. So...go dive! (True, I
could use some winks myself. If it comes to that.)

                    *   *

     Bringing it back home. B-2, the unit. Unit for
jyzing around. JAMR unit, it says so right here on the
wall -- and with an exclamation point. But forget
that. Forget JAMR too. For now and I'd wager forever.
Except of course, I'd like to hope, the culture-JAMR
kind.)

     Tail end of life day 20K. How grand is it? I get
it -- twenty! Twenty grand! But after the long
homeward trek, then a full night's scoping, I'm in even
worse shape than when the day began. And yet determined
to press on. Or my name ain't -- Prime Time Jyzer G?
Shall I say? Because that's just how it (newly) is.

     Within minutes the nap with Z turned into a
canoodlefest. Very fine except -- another wanger flop.
Wouldn't you know. I even gave wanking off in her
presence a vigorous go. Got nowhere. Some dispirit
ensued, both parties. Not the best way to end a weekend

together. But I believe we're still solid. (I'm
recalling yesterday's hot walk up here from the ferry
dock with "sailor/hooker" stops in doorways every twenty
or thirty paces. Truly lovely. Then rolling together
on the carpet, bodies torridly asquirm, at times right
where, or just below where, my feet now calmly ride the
wooden footstool.)

A rush job tonight. Fortunately scoping work's
been abundant lately: enough so to keep me a step ahead
of the game financially despite the crazed buying sprees
of the past several weeks (mostly wacky stuff for Z).

So how about some perspective then. Balance.

10K days back? Hmm. True adult life getting
underway. Promotional film-making and speech-writing
day job. Major fictionizing effort "Symphony No. 5" at
home. Counterculture busting out all over. Brother
Jeff visiting from AWOL stockade. Lady S and I just
weeks away from our primary crack-up.

No, not where I want to go right now. Not bad in
their callow way, those days, but far, far, far from
prime. Ten K days far! (In the back of my mind, and in
a big chunk of the front too, I'm mulling how to phrase
the upcoming wake-up voicemail message for Z.)

First day of a new month. Big big day it's been.
Here a celebratory bunch of wee willies, red and white
and maroon, blooming atop the chairside newspaper-stack
"table" -- but bought originally, these blooms, to
brighten up the place for Thursday night's Z visit.
("One last come for the road," she whispers, as she
often does. Love this loving! -- And it turns into
three last comes, including a triple-digit, at her
request, finger fuck, "to stretch me out more." Not
since high-school nights have fingers fucked so much in
this whack-offy old life.)

So...here's where day 20K finds me. Tomorrow, 20K
plus one, who knows. A whole lotta flagstone steps down
the winding path and it'll be 30K. Tripping merrily
along, me & Z, stone by stone, let's hope. Then 40K,
why not. Ten K bonus for good behavior. Long odds but
juicy payoff. Or dry and creaky by then most likely,

but still far better than -- the alternative, yeah.

(Maybe next J-day I'll try to say something about the snooty letter sister Barb sent brother Rob. He forwarded a copy to me with a dismayed cover note.)

On this long-awaited day quite possibly the lamest J-sling ever. And I'm too enthralled to care. Life in the Z-lane. Imbecile! Doesn't matter though. Wildly crazily daffily it's all Z all the time. Solely wholly Zoelie! (And maybe developing a 'roid or two, me, I no doubt shouldn't even mention. Bloody kind. Yike. But worry some other time. For now, "sit on it.")

21

Fine, fine afternoon. Pure blue sky, a frisky breeze, the big courtyard tree shakin' out a loose-limbs shimmy. Laundry done yet one more time, though only a small load (including Z's gray custom-made "Mestizas Rule" nightshirt, which four or five times now I've had the pleasure of slipping off her in the noirish reflected alley light -- or watching her slip it off herself -- and now the more domestic pleasure of washing and drying and folding it for her, laying it oh so gently in its niche in her half of my newly bisected top bureau drawer in the dressing-nook jyzone).

G-man still a-sweat from a twenty-minute workout. It's the new wallball regime, running in place while whacking a nerfball off the wall, hands for paddles, first left then right, aiming for four different marked areas sequentially, keeping volleys alive as long as possible (and sometimes reaching three or four minutes). Then later when I return home at night another workout, but only for ten minutes.

[Jyze in Love]

In the meantime (while tending to laundry) pushing
ahead on a quick reread of the book on postmod intimacy
-- the one bearing thickets of Z's stickies -- and also
my first crack at an academic journal exploring changes
in various disciplinary domains over the past half
century. Will Z find any of the contributions to this
journal enticing? Will we "dialogue"? As we did
yesterday afternoon: reading aloud the first chapter of
something called "A Year to Live." Doing this on her
bed for forty-five minutes before a preset "horsing
around" period, also of forty-five minutes. "A more
structured life." An experiment. By setting some
limits can we prevent ourselves from being wholly
consumed by the rampaging hedonic urge?

So much schtupping, so little sleep. Her amazing
talent. My intractable appendage. Another astounding
eighter, in particulars much different from previous
ones (as has been true every eighter of the Z era so
far) but in essence much alike (also the ongoing thing).

So here I sit for the first jyze of my post-20K
prime. Green armchair. White fan whirling. Except for
the profusion of Z's letters and poems and notes pinned
to the loft bookcase and now gently aflutter in the
backwash (for the fan's pointed in an unusual direction,
toward the two worktable chairs on whose backs ride two
incompletely dried pairs of pants, each briefly breaking
into a crazy-legs jig as the fan's beam passes by,
almost as if they're getting down with the shimmying
tree outside) -- except for these various flapping
items, I say, this room looks exactly as it did at the
start of the year or even last fall. And yet -- wotta
change!

*

So how about the new regime then? It's like this.
Up at half past nine, out at noon or one, work on my own
stuff at the hideaway until five, hustle back to B-2 for
dinner (and a workout M/W/F), head back down to the
hideaway or the scope office to do scoping or editing as
the occasion demands or permits, try to be home by
midnight, hit the loft by two a.m. (by which time the

192

newspaper's arrived most nights).

I've cut way back on walks up to the old "north pole," from daily to just once or twice a week. Thursday night Z comes down to the hideaway after work and we hike up here for dinner -- I prepare it -- and she stays on for the whole night, though I have to head off to the scope office when she hits the sack at ten or so, and then I slip back in and join her up in the loft at one or two a.m. Saturdays I go out to her place midafternoon and stay until dinnertime on Sunday. Every evening when not with her I call between eight-thirty and nine. (This week I changed my phone service from measured to flat rate since I'm now making so many more local calls, almost all to her.)

New regime, but already I'm comfortable with it. The toughest part is not seeing her between Sunday and Thursday. Last Tuesday we met at her fitness club during her noon-hour workout and I expect we'll continue trying to find ways to get together at least once, if only briefly, during the long four-day stretch. (Yup, cuz we're both hung up right now -- aching for physical presence -- and I expect will be for a long time to come. "Forever." She's saying the same.)

I've never known any love like this. It's working at all levels except the genitosexual and even there it's terrific anyway. And the sexual aspect as a whole is (not to repeat) amazing. Latest theory: my wanger is refusing to perform out of not just discombobulation but also something like envy of the rest of my physical parts, which are now frequently in a state of high arousal for hours on end (whereas the wanger is used to being in charge, focus nonpareil of erotic excitation).

She does this, has this effect. Her rhythms are new and different, unprecedented for me, tremendously stimulating and thus bewildering in a strangely dramatic way. She moves fast and she can go and go and go. Tremendous sexual resources. She expresses herself through sex to a degree far beyond anyone I've ever encountered or even heard of. She's in a whole new dimension. Six weeks of this with her now and I'm still

gasping in a state of blissified disbelief. "Erotomania."
And a big part of this is the way her physical/emotional
responsiveness lifts me into that new dimension with
her, sexually and otherwise. I'm meeting a new self of
my own here. If it weren't happening I wouldn't believe
it possible.

The irony of this. I'd already lived the ultimate
sexual/loving life -- so I thought. Nothing new to
experience there -- so I told myself. Truly I'm glassy-
eyed over the fantastic new reality. A babbling idiot.

Yes, my sexuality is special to her too. But for
her I'm not the creature from a whole new dimension.
This is just a fact I have to accept. For her what's
best is that this love is working on so many different
levels. She says she's suddenly come to realize why she
rejected all those other guys and could never sustain a
relationship beyond two or three years: she was refusing
to settle for less than what she's finding now ("at the
conscious level I didn't think it could exist, but
unconsciously I knew"). Repeat: this is what she says!

It can be confusing, her special gift. How to
handle it. She wants to be loved for herself, of
course, not for a mere sexual talent (and says so flat
out); yet everything about her is strongly influenced by
this talent, and not always in ways that are easy to pin
down or deal with. Her strange combination of extreme
confidence and fear of inadequacy, of being seen as
"abnormal" or "freakish" or of being loved for the
"wrong reason." The battles she must wage with her own
amorous impulses for fear of starting up the sexual
engine and being taken advantage of or simply losing
self-control. The difficulty for others, myself
included, of reading her moods and sexual intentions.

Bizarre. Wondrous. Hard to get a grasp on.
Exhausting. Confusing. Wildly exciting.

The other loves I've known were nothing like this.
They seem long ago, far away, and (suddenly) massively
incomplete. I can't fathom this but so it is. Severely
limited, those others. This is just so shocking I can't
get past the simple fact of it to consider anything

else. (What's it like? Sort of like -- I'm struggling here -- sort of like jumping overnight from the era of daydreamy innocent preadolescent yearning in which sex exists only as something vaguely abstract and rumored, to the fully voluptuous "adult" sexual love. In any case: a quantum leap for sure.)

Gulp. Gulp. How is this possible? I feel colossally blessed, almost as if I've been chosen to participate in a select experiment in which a prototype ordinary human (a healthy-enough specimen but still representative of the average and normal) will be observed interacting with a newly evolved (that is, mutated) fabulous new kind of being. Preposterous. Yet true! (If Zoelie were telepathic/clairvoyant and could prove it I don't think I'd be any more surprised or amazed than I am by her sexuality.)

Are there others in the world with this same gift? Evidently so. "Multiorgasmic" -- it seems this is what the term means, but out at the edge. I'd been thinking a woman (men I won't even consider) who could come several times within a short period (say a few minutes) was multiorgasmic -- defined the term. And as a statistical norm this may be correct. Eight or ten times in a night maybe. Possibly an ability to come from nongenital touching. But Z apparently represents an extreme "outlier" case (think astronomically high "Z score" -- deviations from the mean). For her, as I keep marveling, just thought can do it. Touch anywhere on her body can do it (she just needs to focus on it and think sexual). She can come several times in a row within minutes or less than minutes, yes, but then she can recharge her batteries for a moment or two and do it again, and then again, and can keep repeating these cycles indefinitely, pretty much as long as she wants to. She can come dozens of times in a few hours, scores overnight -- has never felt she's reached a limit. And these aren't little twitching comes either; her body arches, her jaw locks open, she cries out, loses herself. How does she do it? How can it be she's not utterly exhausted after just the first few? (She does

snack a lot in the interstices while we're going at it
-- constant munching and hunger pangs, roaring stomach,
urge to refuel.)

She worries I'll be bored by the repetitiousness of
all this. Maybe I will -- someday -- but, no, I don't
think so. I love it too much for that. For me the
pleasure is not orgasmic (so far) but rather it's an
enhanced state which in a way is better than or beyond
orgasmic, like being elevated to a newly discovered
higher level of preorgasmic "plateau" for magically
prolonged periods. Or maybe simply call it a magically
prolonged state of orgasm itself but one lacking the
accompanying spasms of ejaculation. (I always thought
those Taoist manuals must be exaggerating about the
power of "semen retention." Now here I am doing the
retaining myself, involuntarily, true, but nonetheless
discovering, again, a whole new world -- for when you're
"trapped" on that new plateau for a long period, hours
on end, it starts taking on bogglingly otherworldly
qualities. -- Zoelie too experiences something like
this in a mirror-reversed form and has done so since her
teen years. She likens it to, among other things, being
stoned on incredibly fine weed. Thus the sex addiction,
exacerbated by her inability to keep a relationship with
a man going for very long: thus her need to be
constantly on the hunt for new men during her peak
hormonal years. "The Libido Kid rides again...and again
and again." Yet for the past six years prior to our
meeting she succeeded in fully "sublimating" it, in
part, she thinks, owing to the sex-addiction therapy.
For her, going without entirely is much easier than
trying to regulate her sexuality when there's no one
person to focus it on.)

Am I making any of this up? I must be. Can't be
true. Gotta be subpulp fiction. "The man's lost his
grip. He's blown all his circuits." I'd say so too.
I'd bet against this. The odds it could be real --
infinitesimal.

Would we have zoomed off to this new planet (in
some ways it's new even to her) if I'd been immediately

and reliably stiff-pricked with her? Perhaps not. So
I'm thinking my prick maybe isn't recalcitrant or
discombobulated after all, but rather farsighted and
intuitively wise. It knew something I didn't. Prick's
a blinkin' genius! (If only Z weren't feeling she's
failing me by being unable to get the thing up or keep
it up when she wants and especially to make me come.
Admittedly I'd love to be coming too but not at the
price of giving up what I'm now getting from her. But
I've not been successful in convincing her of this in a
way that holds. I'm just grateful she hasn't closed
down on me sexually as a result. She understands in
flashes, sporadically, or at least seems to, and that's
proving enough, at least so far.)
     Well. How it is. I mean -- wow. I mean -- I mean
-- I mean, I'd be crazy in love with her even if she
lacked this astounding sexual talent, or at least I
believe I would. But how can I really know since (not,
again, to repeat) it influences her at all levels and
surely she'd be a profoundly different person without
it. But then presumably without it she'd be to me a
lot like I am to her now: we'd be connecting on all
these different levels and in all these different
realms, I wouldn't even know about this particular
extraordinary one and therefore wouldn't miss it and
would think myself -- and indeed would be -- extremely
fortunate. So in this sense I ought to try to regard
the sexuality as a bonus, a kind of super-lagniappe.
Try. But know I'll fail because it's so much more than
that. It ramifies everywhere and on everything.
     La-la-land it is. I'm gaga to the Zth. (Crazy
ecstasy, I think of a toboggan chute, rider tumbles off
the toboggan, is wildly careening down, arms and legs
ragdoll akimbo and most of the bumps and bruises are
pleasure instead of pain, the sled's somewhere around
too but who knows where, flying down, the beautifully
terrifying slide -- like for example the one when I was
eight years old during which my mouth got smashed.)
     -- So how jyze on even one word farther? Can't do
it. Go run some errands instead. Come back sobered up

if possible.

*   *

As the "Meet Day" button says: "Waiting 4 Zoelie."
Am doing so now. It's a day later, quarter past seven
in the p.m., and I've just arrived at the hideaway after
walking the Z-woman downtown from my place. She's
attending a focus group exploring obstacles to ratepayer
equity. At quarter to nine I'll be meeting her at the
main library and walking her back to B-2. Unless, that
is, I have too much scoping work to do, in which case I
won't show up at the library and she'll walk to B-2 by
herself. That's our arrangement. As it turns out,
though, tonight's rush job canceled -- as I learned a
short while ago at the ORB by phone -- and I have no
work at all. But even if the rush job were on I'd still
show up to walk her home, because, as her friend Jess
the double black belt warned her, the streets of my home
hood are dangerous for women at night. (And I agree.
Not as dangerous as a few years back but still
dangerous.)

And then what? Probably not much. The new deal is
she sleeps eight hours when she stays at my place or
otherwise she picks up a demerit, and when she hits five
demerits I'm permitted to ask her to do whatever I want
and she must comply. (She dreamed this up to balance
out my own demerit plan, first proposed as a joke,
whereby I pick up one demerit for each time an erection
deflates inside her, a total of five meaning I have to
comply with a request of hers, anything, no questions
asked. On this plan I already have three demerits.)

Enh, why not. Better a lighthearted approach to
such truly tough issues. For the nonce anyway, long as
it holds.

Today a foldout brown-paper poster, two feet by
three, arrived in the mail. Written thereon with a wide
purple marker: "Grok this, beloved / I am WAY HAPPY /
loving with you." It's already mounted on the wall
above the loveseat in B-2, right next to her original
jyze poster. Ninety minutes ago she was sitting in
front of those same posters reminding me I've promised

to remove all this compromising stuff from the walls and loft before letting anyone else enter the room.

(Just now a roaring vacuum cleaner burst into the room right here. The janitor hadn't realized I was curled up back in the corner. Lately I've been leaving the lights on while away so the plant will get more -- lumens! Yes! -- This being one of the new janitors, a Ukrainian, I believe, female, who speaks little English but has a hearty laugh somewhat like Z's and let loose with a fine specimen of same when she spotted me as the big gray machine dragged her into the room like a frantically sniffing bloodhound on a short leash.)

Zoelie. Today in the front-slit black skirt and soft white top I like so much, her face still bearing traces of makeup applied for a utility PR video she appeared in this afternoon. Feeling feisty after a couple of run-ins with antediluvian male Cawkazoids at work, one of them being her boss (against whom she's long nursed a grudge for his highhanded treatment of her, going back to the days when they were coworkers in another utility department -- Z then serving as an inspector who went around qualifying homes for the city's free insulation program). Worrying things, such as her shifting relationship with her officemate Leola -- Z wants to be sure I'll take her, Z's, side when we see Leola at the charity dance on Saturday night -- and our alleged inability to talk about personal torments the way she and her best bud Aida do -- the main problem here being an imbalance, an apparent failure of reciprocity, she believes, because I, just another typical repressed U.S. Cawk male don't you know, rarely bring up matters I'm worrying about and so the problems we're talking about are usually hers. (And not much can be done about this, in my view, since I don't have large overlapping circles of friends supplying me with endless fodder for agonizing over; I work at my Jyzer Ink night job and have neither boss nor coworkers since I am Jyzer Ink and Jyzer Ink is me; and my concerns about my real work -- the protojyze, say -- are far too abstruse for discussion with anyone, often including even myself.)

[Jyze in Love]

    She arrived when I was in the shower. I liked
toweling off with the bathroom door open, flashing
patches of steaming pink hairy nakedness at her from
time to time as she sat on the couch. Then as I was
shaving, still naked, still with the door open, she
passed by on the way to the kitchen and stole a
lingering down-and-up-and-down-again glance. She didn't
think I was looking but I saw it in the mirror. Finally
on her way back she came right in. "Mmm, you be my
naked hunk." Said it with her eyes too, unmistakably --
even blushed this time when she saw me see them saying
it. (For sure I love being lusted after by her.)

    The plan had been to go out to a place of my choice
for a cheapo dinner, but at work someone tipped her off
that both of the joints I proposed are smoky. She hates
smoky joints. I went down the list of what I could cook
up at home and she rejected everything except a toaster
waffle with butter, maple syrup, and fancy vanilla soy
ice cream. Our Lady of Perpetual Healthy Stuff!

    What I especially liked, I was sitting in the green
armchair and she on the couch and I glanced up at the
clock and she said, "We still have five minutes for
hanky-panky," and patted the cushion next to her. So we
took five, all five, necking and petting away as if
there were no tonight, as it were (recalling that under
the new sleep plan there really will be no tonight as
far as hanky-panky goes, at least in theory).

    -- But time's just about up. 8:28. Don't want to
cut it too close. (She did present, as usual, a written
list of topics for discussion, four items, and we
covered them all, including numerous unlisted subpoints.
She also had several articles for me to read, and I a
like number for her. And she zipped through the
afternoon paper. And we were both nibbling on red
flames throughout. Me in my red shorts and sleeveless
khaki henley -- that one because she goes for arms. Ooh
the vanity. Not that she's short on it herself. Three
different instances showed this in just the past day,
regarding (1) reading glasses, (2) breasts looking
better if she's lying down, she thinks (wrongly, I'd

200

say), (3) moles and "cherry spots.")
    -- But no time to elaborate. Later.
                    *   *

    How much later? Twenty hours or so. Now back
home, wearing just the same red shorts, ready to
wallball up a storm after topping off this entry. Five
p.m. Gray and intermittently drizzly/mizzly day. Hard
scoping work ahead. No Zoelie until Saturday.

    Last night I wanted to jyze so bad but was in far
too languorous a state. Z was asleep up in the loft and
I'd just come down after an hour of loving, the
chairside alley window was open as far as the screen
would let it go, the fan was spinning, I was again
wearing only these same shorts, just the one table lamp
was turned on (next to the couch), and I was so achingly
aburst with love for the Z-woman I could scarcely
breathe. (Our lengthy lovemaking sessions usually leave
me feeling this way, and the longer they go on, the
deeper the ache and the more pervasive the daze.)

    Her words coming back to me now (one sentence from
scores like it): "Do you know how completely I'm yours?"

    This time she didn't once bump her head or an elbow
or knee against the ceiling. Nor did I. We're becoming
adept at the mechanics of loft loving.

    -- Then this morning. She'd let me know she was
budgeting time for "horsing around" both before and
after sleeping. I joined her up there around one a.m.
and we actually did desist from any real loving --
mostly did authentically sleep -- until five-thirty,
which was half an hour earlier than she'd planned on and
had set the alarm for. But she woke me up and -- again.
What a turn-on! This time a hard whatzis for the whole
shebang. (But no actual bang of the she, no. Poking it
through her crotch as we lay on our sides was as close
as we got. Such a juicy and moanful time, though,
delicious far beyond anything merely copulatory.)

    For all this she racked up one demerit. But we
also amended the agreement so that from now on the
demerits kick in at seven hours, not eight.

    Earlier I'd licked her clit to climax for the first

time, herp or no herp (and maybe in part because she'd
said she's now pretty well convinced my psychosexual
discombobulation can be ascribed to the herp factor) (a
week earlier she'd been stunned when I mentioned that
the impossibility of impregnating her -- since of course
at 20.5 K days she's postmenopausal -- might be a factor
too, given the idiot animal mind of the beast; she swore
she hadn't thought of that one before).

This time her "one for the road" was a request for
some serious nipple-sucking -- turned into five separate
O's (right nipple, left nipple, clit, vagina, both
nipples at once (but one by tweak)) and so she, Wizard
of O's, began her meditation fifteen minutes late.

Earlier, again, she'd given me some detail on her
mother's "inappropriate touching" -- only the second
time she's mentioned it. Evidently it was extensive
when Z (Louise then, though to some Lou or Lulu or, to
her seventeen-years-older half-sister Camilla, Weezie)
-- when she was around six or seven. For a while it
happened when her mother was bathing her and then, or
maybe all along, as they were sleeping together. For Z
there was no pleasure in it; it was nonorgasmic. Not
until decades later did she realize all this was a form
of incestuous abuse (and she briefly joined an incest
survivors group). The major lasting effect, she thinks,
is the uneasiness she feels when women try to be
physically close with her. (I suspect it had a larger
impact on her sexuality than she recognizes, but this is
really just a psychobabblish hunch. Truly, though, this
aspect of her sexual history mainly serves to deepen her
emotional/sexual mystique for me.)

*

And the previous week. So much happening. Every
day some seemingly huge new twist. We're roaring around
a bend, unexpected panoramas are opening up and then
momentarily flipping upside down as we loop the loop and
come sailing out into a short ground-level straightaway
headed in a whole different direction before angling
skyward into the next boggling new twist.

Try to hit a few highlights here, I think, quick as

I can; no way to do more than that.

Monday the focus was on the delinquent appendage. I found a long letter from her under the hideaway door. At first it was dispiriting (she was referring to the possibility of letting me go should I become too frustrated by our sexual conundrum) but it forced me to clarify the issue for myself, just where I stood thanks to my male member's hopefully temporary reluctance itself to go priapic -- to stand up and stay standing and "be counted" or even more be "counted in" when and where it counts; and in the slightly longer run I came out feeling at least somewhat better (after going over the letter with her on the phone, sentence by wince-inducing sentence).

(The previous Friday, I want to mention, she'd run into her ex-fiance at the co-op -- yes, the "charming sociopath" himself, Arvin; first time she'd seem him in ten or twelve years -- and so we were also still dealing with the after-tremors from this. They didn't talk; she wasn't even sure he'd noticed her. "He definitely was not looking good." Nonetheless she was all shook up and lots of intimate stuff related to their time together was surfacing in our talks and some of it was stirring up my jealousy, envy, fears -- all that good stuff.)

(What really turned her around concerning her worries about my rascally dick, she said, was an I Ching reading which advised her to look inward for causes of pain and to foster an innocent view of the world. Later in the week I was stunned by revelations of the extent to which she was once, and in some ways still is, caught up in various faddish New Age notions. Just about the only ones she hasn't explored extensively are those featuring swamis. I teased her about this, very gently, and regardless of my caution she was still fearful I was putting her down. "Equifinality" was the buzzword savior: acceptance of the many means to an end. (And what, may I ask, is the "end"? Anything other than the cessation of the means? Or better maybe: anything other than the noncessation of the means?))

*

[Jyze in Love]

And now to crunch events even more ruthlessly.

Tuesday at lunch hour we chatted as I stood in street clothes and she strode smartly along in short black shorts, red "Public Power" T, and black headband and wristbands, on a treadmill at her fitness club. At the same time she introduced me to her officemate Leola (Afrusan from the high plains U.S. interior, very sociable, likable, physically fetching, less vehemently political and also less New Agey and "New Edgy" than Z); she was chugging along on the next treadmill.

Wednesday, the usual evening call, Z had accidentally cut a finger with her scissors and taken this as a warning that she was trying too hard to keep up with me in the wooing department (letters, cards and the like) and announced the time had come to slow down the pace. I suspected this might herald the end of the initial "limerence" period, and maybe it did, but so far the preponderance of the evidence suggests otherwise.

Thursday, open house at the fitness club, meeting more of her friends (goofing with Jess, the foxy "queer grrrl," as she likes to call herself, in her skintight biking gear), then the long-awaited artwalk with Aida. During dinner at the old cafe just across from the side entrance to my hideaway building Z snapped at Aida (probably because, as Z admitted later, Aida and I were getting along, as it appeared to her, a little too well and this stirred up an old fear of losing a boyfriend to a rival -- as happened once to Z's half-sister Camilla with Z as a witness in the infamous "tight white shorts incident," way back in Z's early teen years -- and the rival then was Camilla's own younger half-sister on her mother's side, Merry, who later became a Hollywood B-movie starlet and married a rich reactionary corporado). Aida snapped right back, about Z's missing meetings with her, and soon the sparks were flying as I studied the woodwork and took a lengthy restroom break -- became fascinated with a shelf of free postcards on offer there and grabbed me a pocketful. After that, ostensibly because Aida was worn out from a hard day, we canceled the rest of the walk. Z's blithe comment on all this:

"Nothing to worry about -- we fight all the time!" (A
funny moment earlier as the three of us strolled by the
local stationery shop across the street from Z's fitness
club and the clerk there spotted me and came running out
yelling "Sir! Sir!" to let me know a batch of editing
pens I'd ordered had come in. Thereafter whenever Z
wanted my attention or just to get a laugh, she'd call
out, "Sir! Sir!") -- And all this leading to a nearly
sleepless night, lots of talk and lots of loving.

     Friday I found a big bunch of flowers dangling from
the outside knob of my hideaway door (they're still
gracing the redwood worktable in B-2 right now, shedding
blue blooms) and also two love poems she'd written in
her dazed and exhausted state. During our call that
night she said she'd been perusing the copy of "C-H
Memorials" I'd left with her and had concluded I might
have some African blood. Could be, said I, and if so,
I'd be more than fine with it -- and jyze would too --
but I doubt it's so. More likely I'd have a lot of
distant Afrusan (by racist U.S. one-drop definition)
relatives with Chandler or Hutcheson slave-owner blood.

     Saturday she picked me up here at two p.m., handing
me another new poem (later she regretted having done
this just as we were going out, because the poem had
meant a lot to her -- she asked me to keep it under the
futon "right below where your heart is" when I slept --
and apparently I hadn't seemed to appreciate it enough;
and so later, after some fierce cramming in the
bathroom, I surprised her and recited it by heart).

     Then to a men's consignment shop because she'd
offered to split the cost of a dress shirt for me to
wear to her graduation ceremony and, probably more
important, to the big party Aida will be throwing for
her afterward. We found two. Sexy moments as I
stripped to the waist to try on shirts which she brought
into the booth -- she biting my shoulders and arms and
chest, getting me gargantuanly turned on, including
priapically, as wouldn't you know would happen in such
an inopportune setting, and herself turned on the same
way as she later admitted. Her "kept man." "Boy toy."

    Then grocery shopping -- I was driving the Z-
mobile, as I'm doing more and more now -- at an
unfamiliar (to me) branch of the co-op market where we
ran into the last of Z's major Jyze City friends I
hadn't met yet, Olwen -- thin and refined-looking Cawk,
blond, a widely published poet, New Agey like Z only
more so, city worker by day, victim of multiple chemical
sensitivity, onetime co-member in Z's radical-therapy
group -- and then to Z's place for a quick round of
loving -- during which I was every bit as aroused as I'd
been in the changing booth, except, unlike then, the old
wanger was refusing to join in -- maddening! -- but all
I can do now is try to be lightheartedly stoic about
such things (as per Z's "innocence" hexagram) -- and an
eight-block walk to a yuppie-ish restaurant for our
double date with "the other Jessica," a classmate of Z's
at the leadership institute, and her boyfriend Neil; and
then a serendipitous stop with them at a nearby coffee
shop where a dynamite young jazz trio was playing -- led
by a very fine Japusan pianist whose sister Z's known
for years -- and we were almost the only audience and
had a terrific time, keeping up a bantering conversation
with the musicians until we closed the place down.
    Then home, more loving. (A brief squabble when she
thought my being caught up in reading a long op-ed piece
meant I didn't want to join her in bed. Easily worked
out, though, as most of our brambly moments have been so
far. She lets me know her objections immediately,
that's the key. But she's amazed we get along so
relatively frictionlessly and wonders if we shouldn't be
fighting more often for the sake of long-term
relationship health -- "That way no big explosions
happen." "Oh no, not the old hydraulic theory." "So,
are you saying the hydraulic theory holds no water? You
think I'm all wet?" -- Her incorrigible punny streak,
even worse than mine.)
    And then: another night of incredible fuckless
fucking. And a good part of Sunday too. And sitting
out on her balcony reading in the sun (she reaches back
to tap me on the leg, turns, melts her eyes into mine

and says: "Bliss." And it was for me too. All of it!
And not least our rampaging sappiness!). -- Then a
knock on the door, it's her landlord whose son is the
alleged roof-creeping thief, he's announcing a hundred-
bucks-a-month rent increase. And then the reading
session in bed, out loud, "One Year to Live." Not my
kind of thing, it turns out, that particular book, and
happily not hers either.

*

Jyze sketches. Should I be going for more detail?
Maybe so. But can't. Must hold to jyze form. As
always I'm hoping -- strictly on faith -- any truly
important missed stuff will turn up later on its own.
But let's face it: much won't. Just, at best, hints of
same. Traces. Or otherwise jyze would become something
else. So I swallow the frustration. Move on. -- But
do still enjoy trying to touch on all I can in the
allotted space, of which this entry here, by the way,
has now reached the absolute extended limit and even a
bit more. So -- flat-out contradiction? -- Well, okay!
(Here too faith abides.)

22

Is trouble brewing? Right now I'm on the run from
Zoelie. Serves her right for taking me so much for
granted. For being so cranky. For a whole bunch of
reasons, none of which I'm convinced are all that good.
What's going on here? Damned if I know. I'm
telling myself let's see how she likes it. Likes what?
Likes my being indifferent to her. If that's it.
This is her graduation week. Day after tomorrow is
the ceremony (almost certainly not by coincidence it

falls on the solstice). B-2's decked out with "Hats Off
to the Grad!" pennants and elaborate crepe-paper
foofaraw but she's too busy to see me for even a minute.
I squawked about this; she just laughed. -- But ha ha
ha, ho ho ho, who's got the last last last last --
      Ha. If only it fell out so neatly. Truth is I'm
cranky myself. What's more, I can come up with lots of
legitimate reasons for being this way which have nothing
to do with the Z-woman. (No Jyzer Ink work this week,
hair falling out, protojyze looking bad, money running
low -- and that's just for starters.) Nonetheless I
think it does have to do with the Z-woman.
      Simple: we're still not "consummated" lovers.
Still! And I'm becoming paranoid about this. I suspect
she's starting to think I just won't do. She's too
good-hearted to admit it -- to herself even, maybe --
but I believe it's happening.
      Or do I? Sometimes yes, sometimes no. But at all
times I fear it.
      (All times? No. But enough times. More than
enough. It's getting to me.)
      Holed up at the hideaway. Right about now she's
meeting a group of friends for dinner at that same
noodle house we agreed was the pits last week. It's
Thursday, her usual night for staying over in B-2, but
that's off for tonight, even though she's dining less
than two blocks away. Being the ace planner she is, she
canceled tonight's sleepover weeks ago. But now she's
stewing a bit, suspecting my "feelings are hurted." So
I wouldn't be surprised if she showed up after all.
      All day she's been leaving me messages, their tone
increasingly worried. She's admitting she was wrong to
insist we be separated for so long. She's wondering if
I'm in the hospital. She left me a letter here
(containing a hand-drawn heart inscribed with remorseful
words) and then returned a few hours later to add a
sticky to it: "Pining." But mixed in with all this was
more crankiness...enough to make my ears smoke.
      Yet as long as I remain impotent (there's that ugly
word -- I said it) with her in the sack I feel

increasingly impotent and the less I can respond as I actually feel. Or rather: I simply can't feel anything but impotent (again) and so respond exactly that way: impotently (yeah).

This time the big deflation came after she'd climbed aboard with a straddle move and shoved it in. A splendid hard-on it was too, no sign of a flaw or a second thought -- then poof. Early Sunday morning this was. Just...embarrassing. Sad. Humiliating. Mortifying. And another demerit. Four now.

Saturday night was fine, the charity dance shindig at the main downtown convention hall, seventeen hundred attendees, Z and I stepping out (that is, boogieing) for the first time in public. Fun. We were the vintage, relatively, heart and soul of the utility's dance team. Up on the stage a celebrated soul queen belted out her big hit of twenty years ago; out on the floor the jyzer twinkle-hoofed it in his first new pair of dress shoes in twenty years ("courtin' shoes"). A potluck dinner beforehand at the home of Z's openly gay workmate Craig A. (whose fridge is plastered with beefcake photos -- and commendably he felt no need to sequester them from the gaze of this mostly hetero crowd) (Craig being close to my age, I'd guess, but in overall lifestyle he's from a whole different earlier era). A bottle of organic wine at Z's place afterwards. Lots of necking and rolling in the hay and cascading O's but again not even one of those O's was a G-man O.

Next morning our first shower together. Then our first movie, seen at my urging, a three-hour clunker, it turned out, for much of which a barge bearing a huge recumbent statue of a fallen Commie icon drifted down an extended system of sluggish Eastern European rivers at real-time speed (call it BIRT: barge in real time). Then another chain drive-in burger dinner, then "parallel play" at Z's place and I wound up staying over Sunday night too and then the next morning drove over to the Scandi quarter with her to drop off her wagon for servicing, then rode all the way downtown with her on the bus before hoofing it home (more firsts). And a fine time was had by all, but -- but but but.

A new humiliation too: she asked me to cease-and desist all wanking in private -- "no playing with willy." So I agreed. Not that I was doing much of that anyway, except a few times out of extreme frustration and a couple of others to make sure the equipment was still capable of performing as per warranty (and in both instances -- for that matter all those instances -- it was). Then yesterday she withdrew this request -- decided she had imposed it unilaterally and against the counsel of her I Ching "innocence" hexagram of a few weeks ago. Great -- so I'm free to jerk off again.

This is perhaps making her sound fatuous. She's not. Nor is she unempathetic or unsympathetic. The reverse in both cases (if there's even a real difference between the "em" and the "sym" there). And she's trying her best. And while in pain over this herself. Nor does she fail to let me know about the pain.

I'm still hoping I'll be all right. Nature will take its course. I see no reason why it shouldn't. But -- maybe it won't. Maybe it's got some other course in mind. Or maybe before it can take the course I want it to take, and hopefully it wants to take as well, the repercussions will prove too great for Z and/or me to bear.

Meanwhile she's about to shift into frugality mode, Z is. Right after graduation her massive school loan will start biting back. Full repayment will take a decade or more, with each monthly chunk equaling about half my entire estimated income for the same period, "deep reserves" interest included. Frugality, what's more, does not please her. Nor do I please her when I offer frugality tips. (Her father used to tell her she was as good as any millionaire's daughter and did all he could to make her feel so, which is to say he spoiled her to the max. At times in prior eras she's been even more addicted to money than to sex -- and lately she's been "joking" about reupping for more treatment programs on both, "post-doc level this time." To her the money addiction is a class/colonial thing. Obviously it

conflicts wildly with her politics. The woman is
riddled with contradictions. -- And usually knows how
to laugh about them, thank god.)
     She warns me she'll be "spiraling" about this
frugality business during the coming days just as she
already is about a number of other matters, including
the amount of time we should be spending together.
(It's dawning on her she can't stay tight with every
last member of her extensive preexisting friendship
circles while also installing me in a prominent place in
her life. She's trying to figure out what to do about
this, where to cut back. Some of her closest friends
-- chiefly Leola but now also Aida and one or two
others I haven't even met -- are up in arms over her
choices. Of course one of the reasons she let herself
get so deeply entangled in these networks in the first
place was to protect herself from any temptation to
start seeing men again after the breakup with Jerry II.)
     Earlier this week she told me limerence had come
to an end for her. Now, she said, she was going over
to "loverence." A calmer state. Again I suspected a
reaction against -- yeah. That. The bloom was off the
unrisen rose. It hurt me. But what right do I have to
protest? The "loverence" bit was a last-second improv
aimed at salving the wound. I think. So it seemed to
me.
     She would achieve the calmer state of loverence,
she said, by slowing down the pace. And slow it down is
what she's done. Now I've reacted against this by
unilaterally slowing it down a little more, and thus
more than she'd like, at least for the moment. This in
turn seems to be causing her to panic a bit and show
some renewed limerence-like interest (today's flurry of
calls and notes).
     I do wish I could view all this with more
equanimity -- this whole process. "Ordinary shakedown
cruise, that's all we're talking about here." But I
can't, and it's not so ordinary. To start out with,
she's different. Romance has never worked for her for
long. And I'm different too, for her, for myself. And

there's this damn -- yeah. That. (Also her bouts of
"lovesickness." Antiromantic backlashes hailing from
her extreme feminist period. Her "hippie-dippy streak"
and her "wild-woman streak" (both terms she applies to
herself quite often). Her nonstop therapy. Her
control-freakiness. Her diva-grrrl and "high
maintenance" and "Zoelipsistic" aspects. Her sex
addiction to be sure -- all those conjugators of hers.)

One startling incident: she showed me an anthology
in which four of her poems appeared. Called "12-P/AQ,"
it came out the same year I first hit town (with Lady U,
of course) and it featured, just as the acronymic title
suggests, a dozen "Poets from the Asian Quarter." I
bought a copy of it back then (she could scarcely
believe this and I'd like to have shown her my copy as
proof, but it's buried somewhere in the storage unit)
and even all these years later I still recall being
struck by the beauty of one of the women in the group
photo of contributors. That woman, it turns out, was,
and is, yes, Zoelie B. (though then still Louise B.).
Amazing -- but true! And this means that long before
our first telephone talk three months ago I did, after
all, know, if only from afar, who she was and how she
looked and how she thought (poetic version). At some
level I may even have been dimly aware of this. Why
else would I have felt so sure about her physical
attractiveness before we'd met face to face? And we
talked about her poetry-writing and her ties to the AQ
during that very first phone call. (And the punny
acronymic title of the anthology? I said I'd wager a
bundle that was her concoction and she admitted it was.)

If we'd met at any earlier stage of our lives
I'd've been just as crazy about her. I felt all but
certain about this before. Now with the revelation
about this photo and sheaf of published poems I know it.
I can even say it's something like a verified fact.

So is it because of some sort of cosmic payback
that my cranky old joystick refuses to deliver for her?
Nope, I just can't believe it is. (And how many times
will I ask myself this ridiculous question? How many

times have I already?)

    Some sort of breakthrough must occur. What might
bring it about I have no clue. Main thing is not to let
myself freak over this. (One fear: freaking would
itself be the breakthrough, the only one with a real
chance of working. My primary sexual part would finally
start functioning but I'd be gone round the bend, a
raving, drooling lunatic feverishly humping anything
that moves.)

    -- Stopping right here. Tired of obsessing. The
repetitiveness is giving me the willies all by itself --
as if I didn't already have willies enough (and not even
talking about the willy willies).

    One line left in which to mention this is as bad as
jyze gets but -- yeah, it's still jyze. Must be. Or if
not, will have to pass for it until the real stuff shows
up.

23

    The hours surging by. All eighter they've been
doing this. Now on Friday afternoon I'm realizing too
many have swirled down the drain and the eighter's
become a niner and panic's about to set in. Jyze will
not be happy with itself today. Therefore this vow:
J-day shall return. Not immediately, but after the
weekend. For as long as is necessary. (Nor is this a
novel solution. But it's rescuing me right now.)

    So much going on. Scoping work up to my elbows
all week. Zoelie coming by tonight (she vows to let me
sleep not a wink, thereby avenging my most recent
alleged sleep theft from her), then tomorrow afternoon a
venture by auto to a far-northern burb along with Z's

friend D'Arcy, Sunday afternoon a get-together with
little Kat and her mother, Sunday night a live blues
show, on and on and on. Jim Q. has confirmed he'll be
hitting town in less than three weeks; cleaning and
planning tasks abound on that. Full life. (Just what
I was always hoping for!)

   Mutual husband/wife fantasies. Talk of living
together ("but there's no rush"). This morning nine
messages were backed up on my machine, all from her, and
as I was listening to them the phone rang: a tenth. (It
flustered me. I didn't know how to stop the tape. What
if this were Jim Q. calling and the tape were audible to
him as it rambled on? Embarrassing personal stuff on
there such as references to Willy's ongoing debacles.
-- Though Tuesday night, the first I've bused out to
spend with Z at her place under our latest new regime,
tumescence set in to an unprecedented, almost grotesque
degree and a solution looked imminent.)

   Z's graduation ceremony. Aida's "Tea Party for
Z.B." (Photos already in! Some taken by me! -- Or
actually just one that came out well.) A splendid live
theater production of "Lady Chatterley's Lover." A
street-fair stroll at the hugely thronged solstice
festival out in Z's home hood. First dips into her big
"lifetime" box of photos. Lunch at one of my favorite
"south pole" restaurants with its chugging model choo-
choos delivering the grub. Spectacular clouds framed in
ever-shifting parallax by the arches of the drawbridge
and the high bridge during a stroll after the festival.
Brewing troubles of the previous entry successfully
decanted (keeping them out of bed). Post-grad lunch,
just the two of us, a fine "south pole" blues bar,
sidewalk-cafe table. Lots and lots of loving, best of
all the middle-of-the-night half-dream stuff (and best
of the best -- such a stunner I'm still in erotic shock
over it -- in her bed just hours before the ceremony).

   Afternoon traffic. It's not quite loud enough to
drown out the ticking up in the loft. Z's stuff's still
plastered all over the bookcases and walls but most will
have to come down soon (Jim Q. will likely be staying

here and I'll be crashing at her place). Graduation
decorations dangling. The hardy fuchsias of last year
again blooming prolifically but now in virtual anonymity
(mainly I worry they'll expire in the desiccating heat
of the closed-up B-2 during my long absences).

      Z's climax glamour period back in her twenties.
Sensational! Wild passion too: several of the surviving
couples photos taped together, salvaged from shreddings
during battles with various hotheaded and hot-bodied
lovers. (And one night in bed we enacted a fantasy
meeting, student union, Lahontan, because we discovered
we were both present there within days of each other way
back during my grad-student era at Mezzu. This coming
to light after she'd stabbed me in the heart by saying,
while viewing some of my own photos from that time, that
we'd never have gotten along back then. Putdown!
Vicious! Later she pleaded that she'd said this out of
"jealousy," but the plea itself appeared mainly gestural.
-- This being one of the aforementioned troubles
banished from bed. As we agreed we'll always aim to do
with any looming nasty stuff. For sleeping with her is
just unspeakably fine. Nothing better ever than the way
she awakens for loving. The tongue. The warm body
pressing. The roaming hands. The moans, twitches,
jolts, hot breathing. "My nipples are burning for you."
The arching. The juicily overbrimming cleft de
jouissance.)

      I buy a book for Jess P., she who wrote the first
draft of Z's ad that brought us together (and now Z's
interim boss at the utility). Jess's lover Gwen feels
neglected because she too played a role in our meeting
(including taking my side when Jess was urging extreme
caution because I might be a stalker). So now I'll
either write a song or do a watercolor for Gwen. And
week after next we'll again be house-sitting for J&G and
sleeping in their damnably soft garret bed. (And this
Sunday is the Gay Pride parade but we won't be attending
since J&G are themselves passing it up to go rafting.
And tomorrow, Z reminded me on the phone this morning,
is our three-month Meet Day anniversary. And last

Sunday we retraced our steps from that initial day,
focusing on the walk at the end across the drawbridge
and a block or so farther, "our first fight," and she
fessed up that she hadn't really had another date at
seven o'clock that night. Instead after returning home
she got right on the horn with various "buds" to discuss
the pros and cons of the new prospect. "Wotta easy mark
I was!" cried I. -- Not that I'm really complaining.)

(And what was Z wearing as she reeled off this
tale? My glittery Lady V "art jacket." Would its maker
be jealous, Z had asked, or angry? Maybe both, I said,
but for that very reason I liked her, Z's, wearing it
even more. And truly it was so. Could be that in some
strange way only now is the Lady V era ending. Yet I
often flash on her these days because the way Z loves is
similar in a number of respects. "Fellow" fiery
Eurasiusan and lapsed Catholic. Fortunately the deep-
down nastiness and violence aren't there with Z even
though the passion is and so she's like an answered
prayer. The poetry, the intensity, the political zeal,
the physical beauty, the reserves of ferocity, the
emotional richness, the mystical/spiritual streak, the
strong and quirky radical intelligence -- all there with
both, though of course differently inflected to say the
least. And on top of all these the supreme sexual gift
that's Z's alone. Yup, I'm still boggled. Am I ever!)

Trying to be everything I can for her. She likes
my body? -- Must preserve it insofar as I'm able. Time
to get really serious about wallball, forty minutes a
day. Thirty just won't "cut" it, meaning the body, as
in buff it up. Rivers of sweat. The wild lunges bring
back kidhood games of "spectacular catch" at the beach
and elsewhere. Ironic how, thanks to years of manual
weed-whacking, my arms may indeed have become my best
physical feature (as any other former contenders slowly
deteriorate or flatly fail to function). Hair like a
spiky gangbanger, yike. Who's this post-20K punk I see
in the photos these days? Even the shape of the face
appears to be turning Nazi. -- Well, she loves me, I'm
convinced of it (usually). Thinks I look good enough, I

guess, or at least says so -- says "passable" -- but
then, alas, acts surprised if someone else tells her I'm
"not bad-looking," as Leola and apparently some other
work friend did -- but who the hell cares. As long as I
stay away from mirrors I can live with however I may
look to her or even to myself. ("Sort of like Marlon
Brando in his forties before he got too fat," Z said the
other day when commenting on some photos of me, but
impishly, most likely trying to soften the earlier
"passable" diss after I squawked about it.) (She whom
professional photographers likened to a certain
bombshell Italian movie star -- and as soon as I heard
this I could see it myself, in a finer-boned Asianesque
or indigenous USAn version, especially from a left
profile.) (Big jyze-rules exception back there on
Brando even though it's a quote.)

    Bizarre midlife-prime folks cavorting like
lovestruck teens. Is this okay? We interrogate
ourselves and shake our heads over the spectacle we make
and then go right on making it. Probably couldn't do
otherwise if we tried.

    -- Okay, time. Blast open jyze escape hatch.

*   *

    Resuming Monday afternoon, three days later. Last
day of June. Our three-month anniversary plus a day.
I'm back, same place. Green armchair in which on Friday
evening I left a book-review-cover painting of a faintly
"The Wild One"-looking gent reading a book while
sprawled in a green armchair (same painting that hung on
the wall above my old brown armchair, itself now
stationed in the hideaway, during those harrowing final
months of my former life, the Lady U phase of it) --
left it with a cartoon speech bubble drawn in, words of
welcome for Z whom I expected to arrive shortly after I
departed for work -- but then she surprised me by
showing up early. (And later set up on the carpet
another line of pup-tent notes to greet the returning
nightscoper.) (Yes, we're still doing antic stuff like
this and lots of it, still digging it big-time, even as
a less frenzied normality also appears to be setting in.

217

-- Last night she said she's starting to realize living
together really would be easier. -- "But there's no
rush." I too still tack on qualifiers like this. See,
no pressure! Or maybe really just for laughs, as I
insist to her.)

   Except for the live blues show, the weekend came
off without a hitch. Trash art in a far-northern
satellite city (not really a burb), first at a museum
and then at a row of "antique" shops featuring acres of
schlock from roughly 12K to 17K days back, Z wearing the
other jacket Lady V made for me in the 10K long-ago, the
fringed horsehide classic. (And a trio of female
midlifer collectible hunters came upon Z and me nuzzling
in a back aisle and one said, "It's good to see folks
who are still loving." For a moment it seemed they
might try to carry us off like a couple of the beat-up
used life-size cardboard cutouts of Hollywood stars for
movie-theater-lobby display standing nearby. -- We late
bloomers (not boomers!). -- Every single one of those
stars now long dead (but not extinguished!).) And:
salmon dinner at Nurse Betty's (endless horsie rides for
the Katgrrrl and then a charades session in which Z
shone -- she wearing the new "WildKat" earrings I gave
her for graduation -- and everyone else guttered out
from exhaustion, first of all me -- but not the
indefatigable Kat herself, no way).

                        *

   The previous weekend, I never did get around to
jyzing up its big doings. On the way to the graduation
ceremony downtown I bumped into D'Arcy (same one we were
with this weekend; she lives in a condo highrise a few
blocks from B-2). We wound up sitting together in the
balcony (of a huge old church) for the ceremony. Talked
about the news game mostly -- she's a flack for the city
and from what I hear a very good one -- and the real
story behind my shiny new courtin' shoes. Listened to a
fiery address urging the mainstreaming of alternative
medicine. When the time came for Z to march across the
stage (she didn't give a speech after all; the institute
changed its plans, with all sorts of sturm & drang

involved, much too complex to go into here) I was crouched nearby to snap photos and she gave the camera her most fabulous thousand-watt smile. A reception followed downstairs -- drinks, handshakes, faces finally attaching to names I'd been hearing for months.

Then out to Aida's for the "tea party." Impressive, this. Eighty or ninety people showed up, maybe more. For me it was something like the supreme vetting, not to mention a tough memory test as I tried to recall names of previous vetters I was now seeing again. A highly diverse and lively crowd, the proceedings themselves more structured and old-country (Philippines) than I would've expected. A "Congrats to the Grad!!" sweatshirt was spread on a panel for all to autograph with colored fabric pens. The food was terrific; Aida a sparkplug; her parents ("the D's") a warm and friendly pair who referred to Z as being "like another daughter to us" (they have three real ones, plus two sons and ten grandkids).

The high point of the party was a kind of roast in which everyone crowded into the living room and adjoining areas and the spotlight moved around an inner circle of some two dozen of Z's longtime friends and coworkers, each in turn offering a favorite Z story. Many of these were amusingly revealing, often zeroing in on her "eccentric" side (later she professed surprise, itself surprising to me, at the frequent use of that term and others like it -- seemed a bit hurt), and several mentioned her new boyfriend. When the spotlight got to him, the B.F. (or "Beef"?) stammered out something like, "My name's Glen and I'm pretty sure -- but I guess I'd better confirm this with the graduate here -- pretty sure I'm the one who's been referred to a number of times as 'the new boyfriend.'" Got a few audible chuckles, it did. And then near the end: "So I just want to say I'm learning a lot today from all your stories and if you're wondering why she keeps whispering in my ear all the time while you're telling them, you're right, she's saying 'Don't believe that one either!'"

Well, all right, maybe it wasn't quite that slick.

[Jyze in Love]

At the very least a few mumbles and stumbles in there.
But still, something like that. And then Z gave a funny
and spirited talk to wrap it up (she's an excellent
public speaker -- charismatic even -- as I already knew
from several videos she'd shown me earlier) and that was
about it for the party -- except to mention how terrific
it was to see her like that, in her element, so excited,
so proud (and me too, of her!). (Among the things I
learned, she was a co-founder of both APWA, the Asian
Pacific Women's Association, and JCEJ, the city's first
environmental-justice group.) (And later that night she
told me a moving story -- tears streaming -- about her
junior-high graduation and its virtually all-white
crowd, for which her father, so that he wouldn't stand
out too much, powdered his face with talcum.)
                             *
     Whew, B-2 heating up. I just flipped on the fan.
The next couple of nights Z will be staying here after
attending nearby evening focus-group sessions (job-
related). Friday she brought over a couple of large
bags of clothes and assorted toiletry and kitchen items.
It seems we self-declared wannabe postcolonials are
cross-colonizing. The new regime being five days
together, two apart: a reversal of the previous one.
"Because now," she said, "you feel like home to me."
     Last night was the first we've stayed together
without even a moment's canoodling. Reasons: her
extreme need for sleep and panic about today's heavy
work schedule and lateness in getting out thank-you
cards for the graduation gifts. And also, as she'd
attested earlier, exhaustion from over-'gasming.
(Saturday night there must've been close to -- well no,
maybe not a hundred. Surely more than fifty. Seventy-
five?) (But then later she changed the diagnosis to
protein deprivation, a/k/a "hypoglycemia.") As we lay
talking in bed she declared the moment to be another
all-time supremely blissful one and within seconds was
softly snoring. And earlier said she appreciated my
"flexibility" in being willing to cancel the dance
plans and the live blues show -- in fact, in general.

"It's one of the things I really like about you."
     And willy? Still the same. Too much flexibility
there, I suppose I could say. Another brief bad period
over this -- Z's fears that I see her as an incompetent
lover -- but no hysteria this time, as she proudly
pointed out herself. She's still convinced that dread
of "the herp" is causing it (or at least sometimes she
is) and admits she goes to pieces herself now and then
over having an STD, seeing it as divine punishment for
having been "so sexually active." At those times it
seems to her just about the worst penalty imaginable.
(And probably because I'd done some overenthusiastic
towsing, rubbing her raw in the vulvar zone, she feared
for a few days that the resulting sore spot might signal
a new outbreak of the Big H. But nope, not this time.)
     It turned out she'd never heard of Taoist semen
retention. I dug up several old books on Taoist and
tantric approaches to sexuality. At first she resisted
looking at them out of suspicion they were "hand-me-
downs from a previous carnal era." Eventually I managed
to persuade her otherwise, and without any kneading of
the truth, because as far as I know Lady U never took
the slightest interest in those books, and Lady S, who
surely would've scarfed them up, was long gone from my
life before such books became widely available. -- But
Taoist semen retention, unconscious type, may become my
new shtick. For a while anyway. At least it beats the
"erectile dysfunction" paradigm now coming into medical
vogue.
     Meanwhile I'm genuinely retaining all semen when
I'm not with Z, hoping the extreme buildup will pressure
a breakthrough. A gusher. It'll look just like the
picture on the card I've laid aside for her in
anticipation of the happy occasion: a color photo
showing two schoolkids, a boy and a girl, holding hands
and staring in awe at an eruption of Old Faithful. But
then again neither do I want the apparatus to fall into
disuse for so long it can no longer function at all. So
this semen-retention scheme too is an experiment and
could be scrapped at any time. And most likely the

scrapping will come about unconsciously, if it comes
about at all, as in a teen-style wet dream. -- Which,
now that I think about it, was exactly the kind of
eroto-sexual life I was hoping for (the very best option
realistically available) when the year started out.
     -- Reminding me that when we saw "Lady Chatterley"
the guy who played the horny isolato gardener Mellors
(often fully frontally nude in the play) put Z in mind
of me in terms of his most prominent frontal feature
("john thomas"), or so she said, as he also did somewhat
in his Scandi looks and his (fictional) reclusive
backwoods way of life. In her high-school days "Lady C"
-- Chatterley, this is; not that other Lady C of my own
long-ago days -- "Lady Chatterley" was a very important
book to her, she let me know, because she more or less
discovered sexuality through it (by wanking off to it,
and at first without even touching herself). And back
then when she owned up to all this ("more or less") at
confession, the priest told her she'd have to stop
reading that kind of book; and that's what clinched her
dawning awareness that her days with the church were
numbered and the number was very small. (She told me
her toes curl when she comes. Did I mention this yet?
It's an image that sticks with me. The teenage Z lying
in bed reading "Lady C" with her thighs rubbing together
and toes slowly curling and uncurling like pumping cat's
paws, oh yeah...and those phantom sixth toes a key part
of the action for sure.... -- And she said the first
come is usually the most explosive, those that follow
tending to be "relatively calmer," though with plenty of
exceptions and at totally unpredictable times. -- And
curiously enough, just as with "Taoist semen retention,"
the high-energy Polapina had also never before heard the
quasi-racist term "hybrid vigor.") ---
                    *   *
     -- And another day later. The hours slip, slip,
slip (by, by, by).
     How so? Well, just so.
     Today I'm working on a tight schedule, not quite in
the six-minute billable increments favored by

contemporary law firms but almost (except for the billable part). Want to do that card for Gwen. Want to put together a postcard for Z herself (she being displeased by my failure to mail her even a single mushy missive last week, although this failure was itself a perhaps slightly excessive response to her plea to slow down the pace and move deeper into the calms of "loverence"). Want to make up for last night's canceled wallball workout (Z arriving here an hour early just as I was about to launch into it). Want to hit the hideaway (which is no longer quite so hidden away as it was, incidentally, because Z now has a key for it, as I have a set for her wagon). Also want to squeeze in a shower since she'll be coming over again tonight.

One of her numerous self-professedly "dangerous queries" last night: "So, do you think all the men who told me I was a great lover were deceiving me or didn't know what they were talking about?" Ha! They saw the same thing I do! But I still think she didn't need to learn much about how to "pleasure" a man -- the physiological techniques and all that -- simply because her responsiveness itself was so arousing. -- So then why isn't it equally arousing for me? Well, it is -- but then the moment passes because she's off and coming again and demands full attention for her own moment. Or just say her responsiveness stuns me so much I somehow can't get myself unstunned. So say I'm overresponsive to her in an unusual way. Or say this: I'm not one who likes to plunge right in sexually (as opposed to romantically). Nor have I ever been. Always a slow-hander and a ratcheter and an easer and a teaser and a bender and an edge-hanger and a stretch-it-outer. And yet...no. None of this really nails it. It's a mystery is what it is. I love her, I lust for her, I'm tremendously turned on by her; loving her is a wild pleasure even without "penetration" and "ejaculation" and all that other run-of-the-mill textbook stuff, including even sometimes (crucial times) plain old stiffies.

Frustration. So jyze keeps scratching at that bad

itch. Too much. And as a consequence so much else goes
unjyzed. And not only would I like to jyze it all up,
or as much as format permits, but protocol demands I do
so. Thus it is I'll be tacking on a kwikjyze session
tomorrow (circumstances allowing) even though the next
scheduled J-day rolls around only three days after that
(which happens to be a Saturday, meaning Z and I will
likely be spending the whole day together -- for we'll
be starting a new spell of house-sitting at J&G's that
same day after hosting Z's annual fireworks-watching
party on her balcony the evening before, the Fourth).
                    *   *
    (Well, no. No kwikjyze. Other than this little
squib right here, that is, and this coming two days
later, not one, and therefore the next J-day is day
after tomorrow so I might as well hold off until then on
anything major, not to mention minor, and will.)

24

    Jyze jump-cut to Tuesday afternoon next and still
crazy in love. Gonna live with this woman. Gonna marry
her. And yet sexually we're still just about where we
were -- but then isn't this how it was in the olden
days, you waited until after you were married to get it
on? So I hear. (And so I believe was widely true, at
least in certain precincts of certain strictly regulated
classworlds, in one of which I myself happened to grow
up and then rebelled against and am still rebelling
against and surely will always be rebelling against.)
-- And who knows, I might even be developing my very own
first "herp" outbreak. And in an awkward spot: right
across from what I'm assuming is my first-ever 'roid

(which has now shrunk to snow pea size).

So there! At twenty past three, hair (if you can call it that) still wet from the shower, cedar jyzeboard spread across naked lap, blinds canted to deter any voyeuristic activity, however unlikely, from across the courtyard, rain tapping lightly on the windows, and in ninety minutes I'm due to meet Zoelie and the Katgrrrl at Z's office. We'll ride home on the bus -- home, by the way, this week again being Jess and Gwen's house. Then we'll go out for dinner. Nurse Betty, the mom, will pick up "the child" (as the mom often calls her) about nine. And I just talked with Z, and she's okayed my proposal that I stay over with her, Z, tonight even though she's facing a difficult morning: she'll be self-administering two enemas before going in for her "fort-yearly" sigmoidoscopy.

This proposal reverses my prior plan, to stay here in B-2 tonight for the first time since last Thursday. The rationale I presented to Z for the change is what I confirmed a short while ago by calling the scope office: no Jyzer Ink work tonight. But the real reason (and actually I told Z this too) is I don't want to appear to be avoiding her merely because she'll be scampering off to the bathroom all morning and maybe sometimes not making it. I want to be there for this -- for all difficult things and especially for the funky difficult things. And it's good practice for the third 10K of our days, I reckon, not to mention the third Glennarian stage, which after all is due to begin in less than six months. Not to mention the fourth stage of both as well as any succeeding stages (not too likely, those more distant projections, no, my previous speculative remarks to the contrary notwithstanding) (and that's a quadruple or even quintuple negative right there, so what could it possibly mean anyway?).

Her bold words the other afternoon: "I do want to marry you someday." Mine to her a little later in bed: "I want to marry you right now." She: "I want to hear you say that when you're not drunk -- in the morning." Me (for though I was a little drunk on wine at that

point -- she too -- and we'd left a trail of clothes
from the B-2 door all the way up the loft stairs as we
stripped each other -- I was much more drunk on loving
her and I don't even mean just metaphorically): -- but
never mind. (And I did say it again in the morning.)
     Loving morning noon and night. Last week she put
together a "horse-o-meter" -- complete with a working
spinner arrow! -- to show what time we'll need to go to
bed on weeknights to fit in a couple of nookie sessions,
"horsing around," one at bedtime and one in the a.m.
before she leaves for work, each up to an hour long.
weekends we can go for a third session in the middle of
her night (to my mind the best kind, whereas she prefers
morning) or any other time that the 'mones may so decree
(as yesterday on J&G's couch and then later on their
furry black bathroom throw rug after a joint shower --
and that one led to a real quick shower do-over).
     Some other signal events of recent days (and never
mind that J-day's falling three days late, I'd better
say; just how it is):
     ** Our walk home Friday afternoon (from my place
to hers, over the big hill this time, about four miles
in all, retracing my footsteps from our Meet Day);
     ** Her fireworks-watching party on Friday evening
(a score of vet-squaders new and old showing up -- Betty
and Kat among them, and also the boisterous Aida and her
nine-year-old, Charles -- to gain an excellent view from
z's balcony of the big show above the inner-city lake
whose northern shore lies some seven or eight blocks
down the hill);
     ** A vetting lunch with her grad-school buddy Lee
M. and his wife Carol on Saturday in the Asian quarter
(he an amusing fellow, around our age, with prominent
Adam's apple and academic/preacherly demeanor, but
twinkly-eyed, somewhat squeaky-voiced, interrogating me
and concluding "I think you must be a very special guy"
-- even grilling us about when we'll be tying the knot)
(this the very man who some six weeks ago counseled Z
that I must be up to no good, thus inspiring her "green
letter" sent from the mountain resort and our subsequent

make-or-break fight starting at the pocket park) (his
job presumably fitting him for such counseling: he
arbitrates disputes between nuclear contractors);
    ** Taking in another bad movie, it turned out,
with Z's Chiusan friend June (with whom I talked
enjoyably at some length at Z's party) and her
Eurusan boyfriend Wade, this on Saturday night at the
bargain theater way up north;
    ** Meeting Z's friends Wei and Alison (likewise a
mixed couple present at the party and also, like June,
very likable; reminiscent of Andy and Tera from my
former life) -- meeting them again at noon Sunday for a
shopping spree at a huge bulk discount store, during
which we hit on the idea of developing an "Ecobigboxical
Corps" (Z's term) -- an activist outfit that would
patrol checkout lines at such emporia to warn people of
environmental hazards associated with various products
they were about to buy -- as Z and Wei, longtime work
chums from the utility, actually did do with an amused
customer standing behind us in line hugging a giant box
of slug poison (which alas he still purchased).

    And a couple of minor quarrels. -- But save those
for later. Time to roll along. Almost four. Hair
still wet -- but now this B-2 unit boasts a much more
powerful and yet also more energy-efficient hair dryer,
brand new, bought by Z during the shopping spree. It
replaces my trusty old blower, twenty-some-odd years
ancient, and I had no idea at all just how relatively
weak and wasteful and inadequate ("blown out") this old
appliance of mine was. A fitting emblem for the times,
yes. -- To the junkheap with it! (But not just any old
junkheap. State-of-the-art ecojunkheap.)
                *   *
    Next day. Green armchair. Red shorts. And good
news: Z's colon is "beautifully clean." She called to
let me know.
    Also passed along a story from her friend June
about our double date. June had informed her boyfriend
Wade (a social-services administrator she met last fall
through a personal ad of her own) -- informed him that

Zoelie's ad had sought a "working-class" man. Wade's
impression of me (as Z reported with a cackle): "Well,
he certainly does look the part -- the hair especially."
     June was born in mainland China, raised in Taiwan,
worked as a reporter there, came here in her mid
twenties (and now is roughly double that), and still
speaks USAnese with a strong accent and seems to live
mostly by old-country values -- in some ways reminds me
of Lady S just as Z's friend Aida reminds me of Lady U
(and for that matter Kat with her Mayan beauty recalls
Lady V). Hearing about my stint as a "professor"
overseas seemed to boost June's opinion of me quite a
bit (though her first reaction was unabashed disbelief).
     Was it June's ad that sparked Z's decision to run
one of her own? Z says no; she says people she knows
have been using them for years. Possibly she placed one
herself, or more than one, in earlier years; I don't
think I've ever asked her. Or if I did, she failed to
answer. (Add that to my list of questions for her.
Every time I see her or talk with her on the phone she
has a list for me and I've come to feel I'd better have
one of my own for her. -- But her lists seem to be
shrinking lately as we spend more and more time together
and before too much longer they may vanish entirely.
Though I doubt it. Yet our mail exchanges appear to be
doing just that already: for two straight weeks, nothing
on either side. -- And I keep thinking I don't want the
die-out to happen, but then my search for good new card
ideas comes up empty. Surprising and yet -- not.)
(She's frequently telling me how annoying she finds it
when some friend inquires knowingly about what stage
our romance is in -- "Is the honeymoon over yet?" and so
forth -- as if ours is like all others, scripted from a
standard playbook. Yet it also bugs her when we start
thinking of our "G&Z Story" as being exceptional, that
is, more "miraculous" than anyone else's.)
     Most notable about last night, for only the second
time we stayed together an entire night without doing
the deed, which is to say, the fuckless-fuck deed. She
wasn't interested -- didn't respond any of the several

times I tried to stir something up. Only this morning
did she ascribe this reluctance to anxiety about the
medical procedure (belatedly agreeing, rather, with this
diagnosis which I'd first advanced in the middle of the
night and she at that point had scoffingly rejected).
She had also warned me a "hypoglycemic fit" might ensue
from protein deprivation caused by her pre-procedure
regimen (clear liquids the only permitted food for
twenty-four hours, I think it was, or maybe only
twelve). The observation about this being our second
no-loving night was mine, by the way; she thought it was
the first.

Lots of joking on this stressful night but also
some edge to the jokes now and again as I expect will
often be the case with us, stressful times or not.
She's notorious for being difficult and "'tudinous" at
fairly frequent yet highly unpredictable intervals (and
this time said she's proud of the rep -- also for being
"feisty" and "provocative" and "outrageous"). Often at
unexpected moments I find myself doing some serious
scrambling to climb back into her good graces. On
balance I think this is itself good. Keeps me on my
toes, that's for sure, if I may repeat myself yet again.
Boredom is not an option around Zoelie B.

She tells me I top her list of priorities for the
summer. Several times she's objected that I'm not
appreciating this fact enough. Because of me she's
making lots of changes in her life. Of course I'm doing
the same for her in mine, but most of my changes don't
involve other people, and most of hers do. As noted
before, in a sense she's having to cut back with just
about everyone in her various friendship circles, and it
continues to be the case that some of the friends are
not pleased about this, and what's more the circles as a
whole are starting to tsk-tsk her about it. Also she's
much more deeply attached to the way of life she's
making adjustments to than I am to mine, since she's
been living pretty much as she is now for much longer --
in essence since college days (except for a brief spell,
called by her "the fugue period," of cohabiting with

"the charming sociopath" Arvin before their engagement
blew up). And before college days she was basically an
only child whose parents both worked. In short, living
alone is her accustomed way, with friendship circles
always, and not merely for the past six years, serving
as an extended support network. Even during her most
impassioned romances this has been true. (The FOO for
these circles, she tells me, and very seriously, being
the need for protection against the gangs of white boys
who made fun of her clompy way of walking as a kid --
caused by her ongoing foot operations and wearing of
orthopedic shoes -- and also they sometimes chased her
home while calling her nasty racist names: "Jap,"
"chink," "gook," among others -- and "crip" too.)
     All of which is to say: she has little familiarity
with the kind of day-to-day "coupled-up" living which
was my generally happy lot for almost two decades with
Lady U and with others for much shorter periods before
that. What I think of as the ordinary give and take of
everyday domestic life Z can sometimes experience as a
series of affronts to her dignity and integrity.
-- Thus a goodly portion of the frictions leading to our
minor quarrels. Or anyway this is my view, and at times
she appears to share it. Other times, no. Seems to
think this view blames her for our failures, as if I'm
claiming to know how intimate living is done and
suggesting she's ignorant about it. Better we should
find our own way starting from scratch, she insists.
And how can I disagree? (But how can we actually work
this out in practice?)

                         *

     -- Breathing hard. Did twenty minutes of wallball.
Ol' jock jyzerman. Came up with a new twist on the one-
bounce variation. Wallball solitaire might be the right
name for the whole set of no-brain games.
     Last night the Katgrrrl and I played some wallball
doubles in J&G's basement room. Lots of fun. Great
kid. Fine to look at too, as already reported, and as
seductive as they come in a kid way (not that I'm
feeling any pedophiliac urges). Energetic and funny.

Vain. Sly. Deeply dimpled. Flirtatious. Physically
affectionate. (Z is taken aback to see how much so.
-- And feels sorry for me, not to have had more than a
short period of such fun with my own kid.)
     Last night's crisis, a bee sting on Kat's cheek
half an inch below her left eye. While tossing a ball
for the dogs to fetch in J&G's fenced-in backyard she
misfired and the ball wound up lodged deep in a large
hydrangea bush; then in trying to retrieve it we stirred
up a hive. Off to the drugstore we raced, the kid never
crying -- poised as hell -- but Z and I perhaps a bit
frantic. All turned out well, though, and after an hour
or so of our applying store-bought remedies the swelling
had nearly disappeared. (Nurse Betty, Kat's mother,
pronounced our medical care "flawless." Earlier she'd
dropped Kat off at Z's office before attending a nursing
continuing-ed class. Z and Kat and I then rode the bus
out to J&G's, playing hand-slap games all the way. Z
again found me "great with kids" and I was beaming over
this. But later in bed we sparred briefly when she
asked about just why it is I'm "great with kids" and I
spoke of various kids I've known in previous lives, most
prominently Lady V's Danny. We're still a long way from
being able to talk with the requisite empathy/compassion
about those parts of our pasts involving former lovers.
A similar tussle arose Saturday night after I mentioned
something about Lady U's dance career in response to a
question from June and Z overheard the exchange.)
     -- Touching on the quarrels just as a way to
"balance" the general euphoric tone. In reality,
though, balance is not in the cards; euphoria wins hands
down. (But Z was quite nastily cool to me during the
show at the bargain theater after overhearing my remark
to June about Lady U and for hours wouldn't explain why.
Stalked off to her apartment when we pulled up at J&G's.
Finally upon her return I confronted her about all this
and that led to reemphasis of our standing policy of
dealing with frictions immediately when they occur
rather than risk growing them to menacing proportions
simply because their cause is unknown. I thought until

recently we'd done pretty well at this but it turned out
she'd been thinking otherwise and in particular that I
wasn't doing as well at it as she was.)

These days. A rainy summer so far, with the Fourth
a well-timed exception. Top of the news, a small
robotic vehicle (size of a kid's wagon) is crawling
about on the surface of Mars and sending back the first
up-close info about what's there. (And what's there?
Surprisingly Earthlike rocks in a scrabbly desolate
environment which at least superficially resembles,
we're told, certain desert landscapes a few hundred
miles southeast of here.) Congressional hearings open
in the far-off U.S. capital targeting Asian fundraising
for U.S. politicians -- one more sign we may be in the
early stages of a new Cold War, with Asiusans
increasingly at risk of facing a neo Yellow Peril
campaign (the struggle against which would become a top
political priority for me and of course for Z --
something she and I could get involved in together).

Meanwhile this eighter for us. J&G's bed with the
groaning springs (having removed the overly soft foam
mattress, we now sleep directly on the lightly padded
springs) and the sheets frequently coming loose because
they're shaped for the mattress, not the springs. Long
walks through grassy gravel alleys to the park near the
zoo with mutts Cy and Kiba, scooping up their warm poop
with plastic "glove baggies." Cy humping everything in
sight, my legs often included, almost as if Z's secretly
tasked him with showing me how it's done. For meals,
mostly my usual cinnamon-raisin toast and lots of
bananas and red-flame grapes. Z's happy because during
sexual romps in J&G's detached house she can scream and
groan and moan to her heart's (and parts') content (and
does she ever!). -- One early morning I awoke with Z
surfacing between my legs like a sea otter with a
flopping fish caught crosswise in its mouth. (At the
utility office Edie comes up to introduce herself -- one
of the last of Z's work-unit colleagues I haven't met --
and says, beaming, "I've heard everybody really, really
likes you." A jyze must-mention for sure!)

     -- But talk about sexually heightened states. How
bizarre this is! I'm still waiting for a breakthrough
on the semen-retention campaign. Meanwhile I'm horny
all day every day. And I'm stiff or semi-stiff with Z
for hours at a time -- but still the "right moment"
(when I feel sure I won't humiliate myself and draw my
fifth demerit by deflating inside her yet again) -- the
right moment doesn't present itself. We're supersensual
with each other, totally in erotic sync, her orgasms are
exploding like strings of cherry bombs, and yet for some
inexplicable reason our rhythms are as out of whack for
intercourse as it's possible for rhythms to be. I'm the
tortoise, she's the hare; every time I come lumbering up
with outstretched obscene tortoise-neck-of-the-groin (if
I'm lucky) she scampers off to the next 'gasming way
station, simply because it gets her hot to see me
getting hot. It's boggling. Yet in a way it's gorgeous
too. I don't even really feel frustrated, I swear it,
except at being perceived as a lousy lover (on the fuck
level) and causing her to perceive herself as a lousy
lover (at the tortoise-tending level).
     Strange. And marvelous. I wonder how this
conundrum will resolve itself. It'll be fascinating to
see. And what will happen after it does? Will we find
ourselves canoodling much less often and/or for much
shorter periods? Be able to come up with new ways to
prolong the engagements? My weight's roughly half again
hers -- or maybe even half again that half -- but she's
strong and she comes powerfully and at times with almost
violent body motion. What will happen when she's doing
this while I'm invaginated? Will it become a kind of
wrestling match at times? Will I too be singing "she's
got a whole new way of loving...when she gets through
loving me / from my elbow down is sore"?
     And who would've thought this could be happening
now. Me at the 20K stage and counting (but again: who's
counting?). Crazy in love and all's new, mystifying,
wildly exciting, sometimes frightening in its intensity.
Ooh mama, this is good beyond all dreams....

[Jyze in Love]

25

    Fresh out of a solid two-hour nap. Oblique rays of
late midsummer sun slicing all the way across unit B-2
to inflame a parallelogram of worktable wall. Blues
show rollicking on the radio. Saturday night in Jyze
City. And it finds me alone. Surprise! First time on
a Saturday night in I don't know how long, but surely
since the Zoelie era began (last and best era of my
life, I'd stake my life itself on it).
    J-day officially not due to start until midnight,
but I say got to get with the program while the
getting's good.
    The occasion, Z's friend Aida asked for help in
throwing another tea party this afternoon, this one for
her sister Serafina (in town from Indonesia with her
family for a three-week visit with the grandparents) and
then a pajama party for various kids tonight. And
tomorrow night we'll be joining the clan, "the D's,"
grandparents and all five available grandkids included
(the other five reside on or near U.S. military bases in
Germany and the Philippines), for a birthday dinner at a
waterfront spaghetti house. Sera, eldest, "the Bantam,"
tiny and famously bossy and a former housemate of Z's
during the wild times. She kidded Z after we bumped
into her at another restaurant last week: "You've just
got the hots for him." To hear about that, boy was I
flattered. (Even though she was opposing hots to love.)
I'm feeling so damn physically unconfident these days.
Hair and teeth falling out and sexual apparatus
dysfunctioning will do this to you even in an era of the
highest-possible hots and love too, yeah, meaning my own

234

-- and I say they're not even slightly opposed! -- my
own hots and love for Z, we're talking. And how!
     Last night could've spawned another crisis.
Probably did. Two meltdowns in one night, Z bawling on
the couch and later up in the loft. Her heart's
breaking because she can't get me off. It's so fucking
humiliating I want to hang myself, to cause her such
pain. Yet otherwise I'm blithely, stupidly, sappily
happy, I'm even ecstatic, and even purely physically so,
not to mention a whole bunch of other ways. And she is
too, usually, I'm just about certain. (Though as she
points out, what irony. In her view it's all punishment
for having lived such an active sexual life. The second
major punishment for her involving this issue, the first
of course being the Big H.)
     These major meltdowns over sex seem to be coming
every couple of weeks or so. She's promised to try to
stretch out the intervals between them, but gradually.
Next one, she vows, won't be for at least three weeks --
and then "only if viscerally and amygdally necessary."
     This was to be the weekend in which I turned
passive and she aggressive. This at her request, or
rather more like decree. "Thus spake Zoeliethustra," as
she joked, but still holding firm. After thinking the
matter over for a few hours I modified my assent: one
session a day she be the aggressor, one I be, and which
would she prefer for hers? Definitely morning, she
exclaimed. So I'm bedtime. And anything in the middle
of the night or any other time is up for grabs.
     In the breach, "Nunh-unh," as she might say. Overt
physical aggressiveness to the degree she was intending
doesn't come naturally to her in the openly sexual
realm. (Though she did surprise me with a calendula-oil
gen-set massage as a morning wake-up. And I was turned
on too, "morning wood" at the start slowly modulating to
authentic handjob hard-on. But no ejac. And when after
a while I started to deflate she gave up too quickly.
This happens often now: she even shies from touching my
erections or partial erections for fear of making them
wilt or vanish. Ouch. Oof. The shame of this! -- And

so, meltdown.)

     The first of the two came at the dinner table,
ostensibly over my failure to engage her in serious
mealtime talk. This surprised me because I was playing
some old blues albums for her and thought we were raptly
listening as we munched. She weeping to the couch. My
dumbfoundedness. "C'mon, that's Memphis Minnie!" (Jyze
exception there.) She blaming the outburst, eventually,
on the odd circumstance that this was a Friday evening
and she's always cranky on Friday evenings. Under our
current schedule she's usually off from me Friday nights
(as Monday nights I'm off from her) but this time she
insisted on coming over in the evening to make up for
the last-minute change in our plans for tonight
regarding the pajama party. And for sure I was pleased
to have her here. Then later she decided the tension
over the erectile-dysfunction (hereafter e-dys) issue
was the real cause of this incident too.

     (That "Thus spake Zoeliethustra," I meant to note,
was a phrase "blood brother" Manny used in response to
her diktats. -- He who made her the Zoelie Trope.
They actually called each other "Bro" and "Sis." She
swears they were never lovers. "We both knew it
couldn't possibly work." I believe her. -- Oh, and he
reminded her of her beloved half-brother-in-law and
childhood-years arts mentor Ben, half-sister Camilla's
husband, a designer/artist himself and also a writer on
the side and Jewish and very funny and good-looking.
All just like Manny. And this is the source, she says,
of her lifelong attraction to Jewish men.)

     -- So between, say, seven and ten, when she went to
bed and I went off to work, loving on the carpet. Atop
the threefold blue gym mat. My jeans on the whole time
and my whatzis hard or semi-hard for most of it. Oh the
psychosexual weirdness. Then when I returned home and
mounted the loft stairs by alley light, two more hours
of loving. And almost that much again in the morning
after the second meltdown. In all, close to seven
hours of high-heat canoodling. "Extreme petting," that
is, intense no-fuck fucking. I'm gasping over her

dozens of comes and her -- her -- well, just, yes, her.
But especially on this night the rap. "Pillow talk."
She acknowledges she's worked up a major, major case of
the zazzles for me like nothing she's ever known. As
have I for her, of course, and I just wish she could
believe the freakin' e-dys doesn't mean otherwise.

   But do I really believe this myself? How the hell
could I? And yet I do. It's as strange as anything in
my life. Talk about enigmas. The erotically
supercharged state of love-drunk puzzlement I stagger
around in day after day, week after week. Swollen
gonads too, I swear, far heavier than usual and
annoyingly adroop in the heat and sometimes painfully
knocking about or getting squeezed by a jeans inseam.

   Today before she left for the tea party we strolled
the street fair in the Asian quarter. As it happened, a
hula group was performing when we came up to the main
stage. For the first time Z was able to overcome the
Lady U jealousy fits to ask a question about her (and
was mighty proud of herself for doing so). Yes, I
confirmed, Lady U had been a hula performer at one time.
-- A previous "insight" of Z's this week, Lady U and
failed erections must somehow be connected. Lady U must
be sexier, more attractive. (Well, is it true? No way.
No one ever in my life even approaching Z in physical/
sexual magnetic power. -- And just can't prevent myself
from saying this, conceding thereby the relativity of
all superlatives expressed in bygone eras, falling into
invidious comparisons which I'm always saying I'll never
do and most definitely hoping Z won't either.)

   The Asian quarter for me is no longer Lady U turf.
Not even the big Japanese department store -- and we hit
that too, and there as elsewhere kept running into
friends of Z's. A community pillar she is, though she's
never actually lived there. Chiusan Evan W. in his
greengrocer's outfit stops her on the stairs to ask if
she'll review a certain book on biodiversity for the AQ
newspaper he edits (and he's a fine poet and painter as
well). Upstairs in the bookstore, the Japan section --
which is most of it -- now seems much less enticing to

me. -- We stop and pose for pix in a booth outside the
entrance, a new form of instant contact sheet, and of me
with my scalped "straightforward" look they're so
horrible even she says, "We're going to have to work on
making you feel more comfortable in front of the
camera." -- Then ambling along in the crowded street
she suddenly tugs me into a doorway to announce she's
hit on a "piece of the puzzle" which helps explain her
upsurges of Lady U jealousy: when Z was a kid her mother
was constantly comparing her with her blond, blue-eyed
cousins on the Polish side, wishing she was more like
them. Envy. Intimate love of her mother. Yet another
family-of-origin aha. Maybe even FOO of the week.
     Zoelie in her outrageously sexy blue-denim cutoffs
and a sparkly scoopnecked top. Comes on like a tough
big-city driver (even though, as noted before, she
didn't start driving until roughly age 10K, several
years after leaving Mentoka and the heartland for good).
Crows over finding a parking spot her way, scorning my
advice. "City girls eat suburban boys for lunch," she
likes to remind me from time to time, and not always
just for laughs. As we're heading back to the Z-mobile
she announces out of the blue (another familiar gambit
of hers) she'll never fit any mold I might come up with
for her. "Any boat you float I'm gonna scuttle it,
Buster Brown!" (And I admit I'm feeling more pushed out
of shape than before by her continuing displays of
suspicion about my motives in being interested in this
or that about her. And she admits she's in an unusually
rebellious mood these days. "Loverence," she declared,
"is moving into the reality stage." And earlier: "The
thing is, I do know how rare you are and I won't give up
on us no matter what. But when I was twenty I
wouldn't've realized it and at some point I would've
dropped you because I'd've thought it would be easier
with someone else" -- all this in the context of the e-
dys enigma. -- And my reply in essence was that when I
was eighteen or nineteen (as I was when she was twenty)
there wouldn't've been an e-dys enigma. -- But am I
really sure about that? I like to think I am, but let's

face it, maybe I'm wrong.)

    She's constantly turning things over in her mind, including the good things. Sometimes this leads to a release of fearsome bugs and demons, to eeks and flip-flops and backward lurches. Irksome, yet I can't be displeased. Not if I hold fast to a balanced outlook. Yesterday seven Z phone messages with her latest plans, insights, love words, seductions, provocations. Contradictions so flat-out she too laughs at their absurdity. Moves on. Becomes wary. Leaves a poem on my hideaway chair, a double scroll tied with a yellow ribbon -- I make sure to hit the hideaway every day just so I won't miss anything she's dropped off there. Yesterday's scroll poem (tacked now to the loft, though tomorrow I'll be taking it and all the other writings and drawings and some of the posters down in prepping the place for Jim Q.'s stay here): "the palimpsest of my desire / is deeper too / and I bloom in our seasons / and laugh in the metaphors of our field."

    Crazy in love am I. (But also, at this moment, growling in gut. As the radio blues show boogies on, literally, the reigning boogie grandmaster banging it out on an old-timey barrelhouse eighty-eight. Phone turned off because I'm happy to have this break but I do keep checking for messages regardless. -- And will return later to lay down another patch of jyze with hopefully a bit more perspective wrenched into it. Disimmerse myself. Crawl out of the sea of love to charge back onto teeming fields of jyzaphor. -- And thanks for the trope, Zoelie B.!)

*   *

    Now a little past one a.m. Alley window open, vehicles whooshing by on the viaduct, jazz softly playing in here. B-2 lamps warmly aglow and jyze poster gallery too. I plowed through some periodicals (including one I usually skip these days, but this time it's tackling a topic of immediate interest: the latest choosh on "What's Real"). I swung my hand barbell around a bit, I wallballed, I nerfhooped, I nuked a soy griller for dinner and nibbled on red flames for

dessert. And stripped the loft and walls of all Zoelie-
related items so that Jim Q. won't be shocked out of
his jockeys. (Nor has Z tried to call. Sure hope she's
not taking herself too seriously about this "moving into
the reality stage" declaration.)
     But the larger picture. I'm uneasy with myself.
Do I possibly want to revisit a Mentoka-series fictojyze
project or do I not? Maybe try my luck on some other
form of JIFT, possibly even a new one? Despite my
disavowal of all forms of same back in February? I'm
also mulling a pure JIRT blitz -- an expansion of this
year's real-time annal by a full volume. For one month
jyze it up every other day instead of every eighth day.
Wish the idea had struck me before starting up this
volume right here. For once I have a personal story
with legs, meaning one worth exploring in depth. -- But
then how much does jyze want to be going for depth? And
especially if it's being nudged into "the reality stage"
(and never mind just which reality or whose or how
metaphorical or jyzaphorical the field).
     Meanwhile I may soon be up against a new money
crunch. A death in reporter Naomi's husband's family
means Jyzer Ink will have little scoping work next week
and possibly the week after. In romancing Zoelie B.
I've reduced my financial cushion to the bare minimum:
one month's grace. Most of that, it appears, will now
be needed this month. If Jyzer Ink's income again falls
short next month I might not be able to pay my bills.
Might have to hit the deep reserves again, thereby
ensuring that the era of my twenties (of days in K's,
this is), including my retirement years farther down the
road should I happen to make it that far, will be even
more po-boy than anticipated. (But in truth I can do
little about any of this other than hang in there and
hope for the best. -- Or I could look for a second job.
But no, I won't be doing that. Not unless the walls
start to crumble.)
     And health. It appears the herpes alarm for myself
was false (but I expect my current hyper-alert state in
matters genital will trigger more such alarms and likely

before long one will prove warranted). I'm seeing
occasional flashes in my right eye, especially after
overworking it at the computer screen, and I'm reminded
of Popeye's detached retina; similar flashes were among
his early symptoms. Otherwise I seem to be holding
together all right. I worry about prostate cancer and
skin cancer. I wonder if the e-dys might have some
physical cause (though this continues to seem unlikely).
I notice that disruptions created by the new life with
Zoelie B. make maintaining a steady weight a lot tougher
(but then my incentive to do so is much greater).

I've been letting sister Barb's letter of over a
month ago remain unanswered. Haven't written any
friends in months. Everything's on the slide except,
that is, the truly important thing.

(One very sexy night last week, riding out to J&G's
on the last bus at one-fifteen a.m. after a long night's
scoping work, Z awaiting me in bed wearing -- as she'd
revealed on the phone -- the new black satin teddy J&G
gave her as a graduation gift. Wonderful loving moments
as the doggies snored and groaned, two spooning moments
especially: one with me at her back, one with her at
mine, she getting off both times through tiny movements
or none at all: just thinking about doing so.)

My life changing. Lots of small adjustments adding
up, though the basic overall form still seems to be
holding. I'm experimenting with doing my vittles
shopping during prebreakfast walks. Too often I find I
need to make up for lost sleep with naps during the day
(but I'm certainly not about to trade the erotic loving
for more nighttime sleep).

Pocket-watch fob broken -- the watch now rides in a
zip pocket of my pack. The inner/under-sanctum computer
remains unloaded -- no time to figure out why the first
two attempts failed. And Z's in the process of
installing brand-new water purifiers on the B-2 kitchen
faucet and shower nozzle, both of them bought by her
through a utility discount program in hopes I'd later
agree, as I now have, albeit perhaps a bit grimly, to
"go with the healthy flow."

[Jyze in Love]

     Our new "policy," Z's and mine, is never to sleep
apart for more than one night in a row. Tonight she's
borrowing one of my sleeping bags for the sleepover with
the kids. Tomorrow night, back to her place. "I admit
it, I hate not sleeping with you, I can't stand it."
She said that. And my reply: "Me too with you!" And
it's true: sleeping with her is marvelously good. Her
warm body. The way she presses her breasts and lips
against my bare back, lays one arm in a V across my lat
zone with her hand dangling above my heart, her
fingertips barely touching the skin so that each breath
I take elicits a light caress even though her hand
doesn't move at all. (Can feel one of those caresses
right now. Mmm, press in closer, Z-woman, closer....)

26

     So now we're halfway there. I came. She got me
off. "The fountain." Not just one; three of 'em, one
each for three days in a row (but the streak came to an
end this morning with an oiled handjob that had an odd
overstimulating effect, reducing full veins-a-poppin'
hyper-rampancy to strange glowing semiswollen quasi-
lankness).
     The first time was Friday morning at her place and
later in the day we each sent the other a card
commemorating the grand event. Mine to her was the one
I'd been saving for just this occasion: the cover
showing the two kids, boy and girl, holding hands while
gazing in awe at the eruption of Old Faithful, the
preprinted words inside reading "Faithful friends
forever." Her card to me said (in her own words), "Hip
Hip Hoo Ray, It's a Special Day." And then, because

242

she'd mistakenly noted the date as 7/17, she sent a second card correcting herself: "Time stood still for me...it was actually 7/18, 6 a.m.-ish."

Just so. Both of us naked and lying on our sides facing each other. Silvery dawn and she employing a nifty two-hand torquing technique, I'll call it. This following an electric full-body caress as I floated in and out of sleep. The gusher, I was at least as surprised as she was. And in the morning! (As were the following two.) And what glee and chortling and sticky good times afterward.

Meanwhile quite an eighter elsewise too. Only today am I reinstalled in my own room after lending it to Jim Q. for four of the past six nights. He slept on a thick foam pad borrowed from Jess and Gwen. B-2's first overnight visitor other than Zoelie during my incumbency here. And because he was saving a bundle on hotel costs he took care of all our mutual expenses and the week became one of numerous firsts for me, including visits to my favorite jazz club in its excellent new downtown digs (for a performance by the touring "Guitar Greats"), the seafood diner out on the new pier, a fancy breakfast cafe with scrumptious cinnamon rolls a few blocks north of here (B-2), a book-lined bar near the hideaway: all of these being high-class joints normally way out of my price range. Also a major league baseball game with brother Rob and nephew Zach, watching the premier lefty fireballer of the current era whiff sixteen as the hometown boys triumphed.

More important, Zoelie for the first time meets someone from my life. Finally. After I've met scores or even hundreds from hers. First Jim Q. at the train station (where, as she and I waited inside, a huge flock of starlings frosted the Z-mobile with droppings from the tree she insisted we park under to avoid the sun "just in case" even though it was hidden behind a huge cloud), then Rob, Gail, and Zach at the barbecue they fired up for Jim Q. Saturday night on their garage roof. Then Jim Q. again at the jazz club Sunday night (Zoelie glamorously gorgeous -- quote quote, but truly -- in her

big-bucks white pajamalike outfit). And it all goes
swimmingly well. Everyone gets along. Z seems
impressed. My only surprise is her relatively subdued
state afterward and in the interstices when we were
alone. For so long have we been building toward these
meet-ups I'd expected some intense colloquy about them.
For instance, what did it all mean? What was going on
here, here, and here? But no. Maybe because this was
also the ludicrously delayed first-ejac weekend? (And
how curious it is that this arrived almost in exact
synchrony with her exposure to extended portions of my
"history" through these four witnesses of same -- first
independent confirmation for her, could say, that I'm
real and have existed by and large just as I've told her
I have.)

Also some squabbles. Several. But later for
those. No serious damage done or deep flaws revealed,
or "Deep" flaws either, as in domestic partners
(prospective), so far as I know. On the contrary I
would assert.

(This is jyze? "Girl from Ipanema" playing, one
of those same Guitar Greats featured because he's still
here in town. And it's one a.m. It's taken me all day
to refocus myself. Both Sunday and Monday Jim Q. and I
were together upwards of ten hours straight, and
Monday, yesterday, it was just the two of us the whole
time. Enjoyable but after a while a strain as well.
-- And the breeze sifting in tonight is cool. For the
most part it's been a cool summer so far. Oh but those
warm nights lying naked and coverless in Z's bed with
the naked Z herself -- who else? -- snuggled in close.)

Yes, it's still sensational, the romance. She
frets energetically and often inspirationally over just
about every little thing, and usually the results are
positive. Amazing, this. How preternaturally alert and
alive I become thanks to her. How bursting with lust
and strange solicitudes. How I can't keep my hands off
her. (And she me. And says so. "I have lust in my
heart for you." The quality of attention she can bring
to bear! And attention to her pays extraordinarily well

too, that is, mine. Or anyone's, I don't doubt.)
    This be gibberish and why not. Jyzish gibberish
and yet all of it gospel, more or less. -- And really
what other kind of jyze could there be right now?
    "M'bao" she's lately taken to calling me.
Acronymic for "My Beloved & Adored One." One night she
let slip "I adore you!" -- and I adored her doing so --
but she was embarrassed by the insult to principles of
postconfluent love (or postromantic feminist type
anyway) and then recovered by proposing the acronym
sounding almost like "m'boy" and thus putting a loving
satirical spin on that "adore" while still retaining its
effect in abbreviated form. (She's plenty sharp with
such improvs, consistently, and makes me sweat to keep
up, even makes me worry sometimes I can't -- but in
general I think I can and give her as much trouble as
she gives me and so we both relish the exchanges. Good
thing too.)
    It's still at least two shag sessions every day
we're together, which is most days now -- at least five
days per week. Still Z coming like crazy and me wowed
over and over. She frets about "balance" when she's
come a dozen times or more three sessions in a row and
I've come only once during that whole period, and in
this sense it doesn't really matter whether I get off or
not, since actual equivalence or "come symmetry" is
clearly out of the question; but I think I'm doing
better at riding out her spells of worry. And I still
have little solid ground to stand on so long as we
haven't truly boinked (the going yuk-it-up term). Then
again at least I've now demonstrated I'm not wholly ejac-
dysfunct and she's demonstrated (as she sees it) she's
not wholly inept or incompetent as a strokesperson. And
how good it is to find our bellies stuck together with
dried essence d'brut. Now we must have (and do have) a
bedside "sperm towel." (All three eruptions came in her
bed. All three at the same time of day, bodies in the
same positions, Z-woman using the same hold and rhythms
and torques. -- Go with what gets you to the geyser, I
guess.)

[Jyze in Love]

    And I'm wondering: could I make something
fictojyzey out of all this? Something JIFTy? Could
this right here be a new form of JIFT? She's already
given me permission to go for it. Truth is I'm feeling
more and more uneasy drifting along in suspension mode.
And Jim Q.'s questions about my progress on the Mentoka
series rankled. And an essay in a current lit review
piques my longtime interest in exploring scribbly
borderlines. How about something along the lines of
"JIFT for JIRT Days Off"? While moving forward in the
JIRT I could be moving backward during the off days on
the JIFTing of the JIRT. The JIRT itself wouldn't be
part of the JIFT except as a felt (if all went well)
absence, that is, something to be superseded or jacked
right out of itself. Which is to say: imagination could
take over. Probing the fantasies and pains (loving in
the solitary aftermath) (hashing out the return(s) from
the long hard scribble/scrabble in the wilderness).
    Well anyway I'm starting to think about such things
again. But -- now it's bedtime.
                    *   *
    -- And two days later, the hideaway. She's due
here in just under an hour, Z is. It's Thursday and on
Thursdays she almost always stays over at B-2, dinner
included. It's penciled into her daytimer for weeks or
maybe even months to come. And for this reason my
freezer is packed with a dozen special "healthy" TV
dinners bought just this week. The sorry non-frozen
stuff I ordinarily rustle up for us is losing its luster
of the primitive/exotic "nostalgie de la boue" for her.
    Her arrival time today will be different: half past
five. This is part of a new experiment to see if she
can carve out a solid block of at least seven hours'
sleep on the nights we stay together. I proposed this
one, or anyway most elements of it. But since it has
her rising at six-thirty a.m. instead of her accustomed
six or five-thirty or even five, she's decided to go in
to the office half an hour later on these days, or
actually every workday, and also to stay there half an
hour later in the evening. She's high enough a muckety-

muck at the utility to make the call on her own.

The idea this time is for her to hit the loft at ten, tumble back out at half past six. Responsibility for seeing that she does so has devolved upon me. "Sleep coach." In theory we have forty-five minutes for horsing around at each end, an hour and a half in all. Or if she's tired (or for that matter if I am, I suppose, though this hasn't come up yet), less. (But my tiredness doesn't matter as much because I can usually nap during the day if necessary.)

The first night of this new regimen didn't go so well, except technically. She logged her seven hours, with loving at both ends. But despite being widely acknowledged as the queen of schedulers, she's not happy with the scheduled aspect of this experiment. (Nor am I, but what else can we do? If we don't watch ourselves we slide into the sexual "magnetic field" and wind up amourizing away most of the night, and the next day she runs low on juice and feels miserable at work and vows not to let it happen again.) She: "I want to find a way we can have more time for loving." Also I'd told her I didn't want her to be worrying so much about getting me off, especially on weeknights, because then I feared she wouldn't look forward as much to staying with me. On weeknights I wished she would, for now anyway, just let herself be loved and let whatever will happen with the G-man's gen set go ahead and happen.

Yeah. So. Often when we're first together again after a day or two apart she feels awkward. This night was no exception. Yet at the same time, oddly, the "longtime-coupledness" of the evening troubled her. "It's not like a hot date anymore," she pouted. (For spouting which words I mercilessly denounced her, she vowing in revenge never again to let me know her true innermost thoughts however much she does or does not regret them. But this is just our normal back-and-forth; she goes after me the same way; and it's usually all to the good.) She also wanted, she declared, "more drama." Once again she was picking fights just because the laid-back peacefulness seemed "too good to be true."

And she defiantly proclaimed this.

     Not serious fights. Squabbles. Probably this is
how it will generally be. She frets a lot. "Micro
manages." Finds it hard to be content with anything for
long. Is "insecure" and has an "overactive amygdala"
and is hugely proud of both. Grapples at times with
deep abandonment fears. Nurses lots of suspicions about
motives, mine and just about everyone else's, especially
if they're Cawk males of USAn invader/colonial/settler/
suburban provenance. But our dynamic is such that most
of this touchy stuff converts painlessly into wordplay
or even "productive dialogue." Things stay interesting.
Sparks fly.

     She also announced she probably has "more of an
introvert streak than you do." This came after I'd said
I wouldn't mind if, as we went about our "parallel
play," she paused every now and then to bestow upon her
Beloved & Adored One a loving touch or two. Earlier
this week I'd said something similar about the way she
is with me in public. Aida had observed how "openly
affectionate" I am with Z (and seemed to view this
positively). I pointed out that Aida had not mentioned
anything to the same effect about how she, Z, is with
me. I said I'm uneasy with the imbalance, perhaps even
in the same way she is about the orgasm imbalance; after
a while it makes me feel I'm slobbering all over her.
"You may be creating a monster," she warned me, and
thereafter was at least a bit more demonstrative. Now,
though, she was saying maybe she just doesn't "interact
as well" -- meaning she's more private or maybe just
more accustomed to being alone at home (no, undoubtedly
a whole lot more accustomed to that). -- And this is
dangerous territory because it brings up the Lady U
connection. "I hate for you to be the family expert on
long-term love," she gripes, as she's done several times
before. But how can I not come across that way when
she's never had a truly long-term love and often brings
up this fact herself and then asks for my opinion on how
we should handle various relational matters? (Sure, I
know my own long-termer was a fluke, but Z doesn't

necessarily believe this.)

Squabbles. While on the topic, several others of note broke out during this eighter.

Over Aida. Z passed along to her my joking remark that I'd had to "brutally suppress" my normal self at the D-clan's gathering at the spaghetti house last Sunday (which I did have to do, sort of, but I enjoyed myself anyway and also enjoyed every last one of the D-clan -- amounting to a full baker's dozen plus one or two including mates and dates and four of those super-cute little girls pictured on Z's fridge door now come raucously to life -- and really I was just hyperbolizing with Z). But this led to a dispute about how can she continue being "completely open" with her decades-long best friend Aida without at the same time betraying things I say to her, that is, to Z, in presumed confidence. And so far no real solutions. Z talked the matter over with Anita, her paid "counselor"; the solution they arrived at sparked still more sparring between us when Z explained it to me. It was a "woman thing," Z and Anita agreed, to talk openly as Z and Aida had done. I found that unacceptable. Declaring something to be a "woman thing" or a "man thing" shouldn't be the end of the conversation, I pontificated, but the beginning of one. Eventually Z rather grumpily went along with this. (Today she had her first luncheon with Aida since the dispute surfaced. Maybe we'll be going another round on it tonight.)

Second squabble, the Lady U connection (again). Z decided she hadn't felt so good after all when we briefly discussed Lady U during our visit to the street fair with its hula dancers. So she reversed herself once more: said she still wasn't quite ready to dig into all that love-history stuff. (Ironically during Jim Q.'s visit we took him to see -- Z's idea -- the annual Bon Odori festivities in the AQ and found ourselves facing all the same issues again. Lady U, of course, had performed regularly at Bon Odori and helped lead the street dances there. But this time we kept silent on the matter -- as the taiko drums boomed and the dancers

paraded by, including several kimonoed instructors whom
I knew a little through Lady U -- but I said nothing,
and fortunately the instructors did likewise, though one
nodded discreetly -- and thank the kamis, all of them,
for the hyperdeveloped Japanese sense of discretion.)
        Third squabble, a slap in the face regarding
living together. Sunday after seeing "The Pillow Book"
(a dispute over which will be explored as squabble
number four if I have time for it) we stopped by a
real-estate office near the theater to check out
apartment listings for the area (atop the big hill east
of downtown). While doing this Z suddenly let it be
known she'd be wanting to have Friday nights and
Saturday mornings to herself even when we're living
together, and this would mean sleeping separately on
Friday nights. Maybe not a completely outrageous
preference, but the way she announced it -- this is how
things would be, period: ukase: "Thus spake [yet
again!] Z-thustra" -- made me fume. But I managed to
keep most of it to myself at the time.
        -- Over.

*   *

        "Over"? Meaning "Take it from here, reality." For
at that moment Z knocked on the hideaway door. Slipped
in. I said I was ready to go, but she wanted to talk
first and knelt on the rug just inside the door (this
after bestowing a kiss as per "the affection rules," as
she's now dubbed them) and I too slipped down to floor
level and we talked about some of the same things this
jyze had just been wrestling with.
        (No, she and her best bud Aida hadn't delved into
the confidentiality issue at their luncheon, but she had
told Aida she was thinking her relationship with me
would be "long term," and Aida had observed this was the
first time she'd ever heard Z talk like that; and I said
I was surprised only because I'd assumed it would all be
old news to Aida and I kidded Z that the words "long
term" seemed a little weak; I preferred "lifetime."
Then an odd question from her, or at least oddly timed:
she wanted to be sure I wasn't just expecting her, Z, to

250

be like Lady U -- meaning in my quest for more open
expression of affection and so forth. Absolutely not, I
said, and that's the truth, though another truth is that
Lady U was generally quite openly affectionate. In most
respects, however, Lady U and the future Lady Z -- if I
may presume -- are about as different as two people can
be; and in no way am I expecting or wanting Z to fill
some kind of shadow of expectation left behind by her
"honorable predecessor," as Z once called her, with
blatant political incorrectness and a classic glower.)

So then to my place, slowly, on foot, with stops at
various downtown emporia (she bought a bra at one while
I read in a chair in the lingerie section, a life-size
"femikin" dressed in sexy black undies standing watch
on a pedestal immediately behind and above me: would've
made a great photo, Z said). Dinner. Reading. (The
manhunt for the half-Filipino murderer of a famous
fashion designer and several other prominent gay men is
canceled when his body's found: suicide.) Loving up in
the loft (but very cautious because she's again in a
"prodomo" state, sensing a herpes outbreak coming on).
Naked dancing in the kitchen, ballroom type, G gen set
pressed against Z navel and vicinity. She gives me a
poem asking for more written words of love from me as an
addendum to "the affection rules" and also requests a
replacement for that passionate letter I sent her at the
mountain resort over two months ago and then supposedly
"took back" because of the equivocations in her "green
letter." I said no way did I ever take back what I
wrote in that letter; rather what I'd told her at the
time was I wished I could've had the letter itself back,
that is, had never sent it, given the dismaying contents
of her green letter that crossed in the mail with it. I
said this again now, tonight, as strongly as I could --
quiet fierce intensity -- and she said, "When you get so
serious like that it makes me feel really squidgy." And
just what, I asked, did she mean by "squidgy"? Uneasy
and embarrassed was part of it, she said, but by no
means all, and since it was late and I had to be leaving
for work, she'd think about the rest of it and let me

know when I returned -- or maybe it would just have to
remain a mystery.

So now a couple of hours later, work finished, this
jyze. At the scope-office conference table. Same one
where I've been taking breaks for a dozen years or so.

Squabble number four over "The Pillow Book," though
it seemed important at the time (yeah, and still does),
I'm dropping it for now. Almost certainly the issues
involved will be coming up again in one form or another.

So these scattered items to top off the eighter.
Bullet-head nephew Zach playing with his huge collection
of Goth cards in the cluster of chairs on brother Rob's
garage-roof deck as the rest of us chatted and the
charcoal heated up (for pork ribs), and then some
unexpectedly lively conversation at the dinner table
inside. Rob telling Zoelie I've been a mentor and
almost a second father to him all his life -- this
touched me deeply. Jim Q. confiding when we were alone
together how impressed he was by Z, "her wonderful smile
-- and she's certainly not lacking in high spirits, just
like your mother"). Z waiting for me in bed at her
place and flinging aside the sheet to display her naked
self: "Surprise!" (Thinking she was asleep, I was
literally crawling bedward in the semidark, exhausted
from working late -- but then suddenly as the sheet flew
up I wasn't exhausted anymore.) Jim Q. and I both going
watery-eyed as he recounted tales from his lengthy
travels around the country with ol' Mom. His huge
pillbox, five or six cubbyholes for each day of the
week, hundreds of pills (and bronchitis causing him to
suck on an inhaler from time to time) (but he gamely
trekked with me to all three tips of my tripolar turf
and various points widely scattered inside it, bad hip
and all).

Z, meanwhile, moving into her new office at the
utility, just a few doors down from the old one but this
time a whole room of her own -- roughly five times the
space -- after almost eight years of sharing an office
with Leola or Leola's predecessor. Z professing
amusement that people at work are coming up to her all

the time, "Are you still madly in love with that guy?"
(She swears she tells them yes but I'll bet she just
flashes one of her twisted quizzical smiles featuring a
single raised eyebrow and says nothing. Or maybe gives
a knowing look and wiggles her ears.) -- And just
tonight the beauty of her arm pressing against mine on
the pillow as she lay atop me in the loft nibbling at my
back and nape. And I'd like to mention her terrifically
sexy armpit, a light pelt there seeming almost vulvar
when her arm stretches back over her head (the guys
upstairs on this same night getting likely the best
earful yet of her tumultuous lovesounds).

27

    For shame. Just blew an hour or more (all right,
more) stalking fruit flies. I'm sweaty and irked, in
drenched red shorts and green henley, cheeks grizzled
and pits stinking because last night was an off night
from Zoelie, being Monday night, so why bother to clean
myself up? It's half past three and the bigger part of
the afternoon is shot. And I didn't make it to the
public market for the produce/bread run, nor did I make
it to the northern tripolar turf for groceries and mags
or even just for exercise's sake, and I do need that
exercise. And I still have a home workout to do, so
this jyze session will be abbreviated at both ends.
    But here the J-slinger in all inane glory. Fruit-
fly population down from thousands to maybe a few dozen
savvy stragglers with exceptional reflexes. During the
two hot, muggy days I was at Z's place my kitchen trash
bin (whose lid is very loose) incubated a population
explosion. And the alley window was open, the gap at

the top of the screen being like a well-lit tunnel on
the fruit-fly freeway from alley dumpster to B-2 trash
bin. -- Leaping about, pouncing, flailing (J-slinger).
Pathetic when you catch yourself in the act of trying to
outthink a fruit fly. Squinting intensely. Eyes
darting about. Suddenly spinning 180 degrees with a
karate cry because you sense a flight of flies is
sneaking behind you. Swoops of the Valkyries.
"Apocalypse Now" all over again as farce, miniature
black helicopters zipping about everywhere.

     So, workout, yes. I'm into the program now.
Wallball is down to fifteen minutes but only to make
room for thirty minutes of pull-ups, dips, push-ups and
the like. I refuse to be flabby. (Z's alarmed because
the scales at her fitness club say she's up two pounds
in one week. Asks me if I've noticed any evidence of
this. In truth I haven't, but I have noticed she snacks
a lot. She figures she's doing this, oversnacking, not
just because of all the 'gasming but also from lack of
sleep -- though the two are clearly symbiotic.)

     At dinner last night her coworker/friend Tabitha
told her about studies showing that sleep deprivation
kills off brain cells by the millions. Z, horrified,
announced in our phone talk later that from now on
she'll be racking up eight hours' sleep every night,
period, no exceptions. Hossing around will be cut to
one nightly session tops. You got that, sleep coach?

     The call turned bristly. Again she was saying she
really needs only one or two O's a session, although a
few weeks ago she repudiated this very same line as
something she employs only to keep men from freaking
over her sexuality. I was joking about what the guys
out in the alley must be thinking as they overheard my
side of the dialogue, the weirdly prurient sentences I
was spewing. In the end we managed to agree to stay
within the experimental sleep protocol we were already
trying to abide by, except for one new codicil: we'll
limit ourselves to just a single shag session per night
unless she happens to wake up early in the morning and
feels like going for another. It's her call. I'm her

adamantly willing sex slave.

    Ironic, I was thinking, getting back to the workout: if my arms are now my best part (as she seems to think), it's because (A) I whacked away manually at huge yardfuls of weeds and grass for all those years during the Lady U era, and (B) the bursitis in my shoulders forced me to keep up the hand-barbell exercises which as an unintended byproduct kept the arms in shape. -- Funny how you have to have something to feel vain about. You'll settle even for arms. (And cut the sleeves off more henleys, to be sure, so you can be showing off your new best feature all the way up, though they're still the same rags they always were, the henleys, except now even raggedier with the jagged scissor-cuts around the shoulder holes. Not T-shirts but Z-shirts, call 'em.)

    Nor have there been any more ejacs for me. Are we back to square one? Maybe. "You're most definitely a challenge," Z says. And what irony in this too. Yet for the first time she started joking about her own ineptitude as a lover (as opposed to a lovee). She's such a rebel she refuses to do anything if I say it gives me pleasure! And yet: she said the other night, between canoodlings, "I really do want to marry you." I reminded her she'd said this before and I'd believed her then and ever since and so she didn't need to convince me now. "Yes," she said, "but back then I was wanting it as an idea. Now I'm feeling it viscerally."

    And how could anyone not be crazy about a woman who can come up with -- on the spot! -- a line like that?

    Half a dozen of her friends have independently told her they want to plan the wedding. She's still flabbergasted to see how people she scarcely knows are so interested in the status of our relationship; how they seem to feel they're entitled to hear all about it; and most of all by the number who're openly astounded that she'd take up with a guy at all, as if she weren't a sociable type or weren't even capable of attracting a man. -- And then there are the others who regard her affair with me as almost a betrayal, as if she's become

a kind of scab crossing picket lines set up by,
especially, a certain faction of the Sapphic subset of
her women's guild (but Jess and Gwen emphatically not
among them).

And this. Best news of all. She's agreed to join
me in a jyze spree for the month of August. Starting
the 1st and going through the 31st we'll both be jyzing
every other day, sometimes together and sometimes not,
with the goal of filling up a whole volume each,
companion jyze volumes which we'll later type up and
present to each other and maybe even combine into a
single volume. And while at it we'll be flashing back
to key moments in "The Z&G Story" in hopes of gaining
new insights and thereby keeping the pot aboil (and the
plot astir) in the months ahead.

My idea, most of this. Behind it is a new way of
thinking about the rest of the year. I figure with 20K
Day at the end of May and the rollover to Glennarian
Stage III in early December, the period between the two
grand occasions should be considered the real Peak Prime
Time of J-slinger G. Speaking adult lifetime here now.
And at the exact middle of this period would be the
Absolute Pinnacle of Peak Prime Time, and by sheer
coincidence that happens to fall quite close to my
birthday on August 30. One full month remains until
this supreme crossover event. What better occasion to
jyze things up to the utter max?

And I loved the way she immediately agreed to
participate in this project. It's a dream -- it's
itself an instance of the miraculousness of the story.
She's already binding together her own blank book of
"reused" paper from work, a hundred sheets. And of
course she'll be jyzing them up in her own way. Her
pages won't always be fully written on, top to bottom,
like mine, she's let me know. Some will feature poems
or drawings or whatever else may come to mind.
Splendid, sez I.

What delight! What a spectacular turnaround in my
fortunes in the past six months! What fun August will
be! (Today is July 29. Two more days to clear the

decks. -- And for her, obviously, the strain involved
in churning out a dozen pages every other day will be
far greater than for me, simply because her job eats up
forty hours a week and her workouts and political
activities and friendship circles take many more. And
she'll be trying to score that "mandatory" eight hours'
sleep as well. So from time to time the tensions might
torque up a bit beyond the usual, especially as we
explore touchy issues, which of course we're both
intending to do.)

And then we'll have the ongoing prime dramatic
issue: will we ever manage to consummate this consummate
relationship? My birthday in particular -- the
"Absolute Pinnacle," on which day we're planning the
penultimate tandem-jyze session -- would be a supremely
apt occasion for the breakthrough. (She did say one
reason she thinks she's been wanting to get it on so
much is fear she'll lose me -- to death, she means -- as
she did her friends Manny, Ruth, and Julie, and all
three not long after they found their big new loves.
But now she's decided maybe it's not so good to be
acting every night as if, because it could be our last
together, the Big Deed must occur right then and there
or it never will.)

So -- something new for jyze. In its protojyze
form it's spawned a few sprees before, true, but never
one in tandem and certainly never one in Peak Prime Time
with the Absolute Pinnacle looming climactically therein
-- and as a dramatic conclusion for the tandem spree
itself. Anything could happen!

-- But back to the abbreviated J-week just past.
Four days only. Meeting brother Rob at the hideaway
Friday night. Then the weekend with Z, including a
rousing dinner at Wei and Alison's place Saturday night
and a busy Sunday, most of which had to be improvised
owing to a flat tire on the Z-mobile (when the spare
also proved to be flat, her auto-insurance tow-truck
service had to be called in, and they took their time
coming). And Monday, yesterday, nothing at all notable
about it except that the bulk, for me, went to catching

up on lost sleep, lost reading, lost exercise.
     -- And by the way, in late October Z is scheduled
to attend a conference at a "surprise" out-of-state site
(she won't tell me where) and I'll be traveling with
her, for four days in all, one day to be paid for by the
utility and another by Z as a birthday present and the
third by me even though I may have no money at all by
then. And the fourth day we'll be driving back. One
reason she's happy about visiting this site in
particular, she says, is that "you have no history
there."

     I guess this is all I can do right now. -- No, I
don't guess. Time's run out. Next squeeze in some
wallball and then a shower (I'll be sweating like crazy,
drenched, and happily so), no doubt some more hunting of
fruit flies, though only a quick mop-up operation. Then
swing by the hideaway to water the plants and check for
notes and poems from Z, then up to the scope office to
do finals and maybe some actual scoping, then a bus ride
out to Z's. Because she needs to be home tonight for
some reason I forget (or no, a last-minute opening for a
doctor's appointment tomorrow morning, I now recall) and
last night we were apart and never, never, never will we
ever again sleep apart two nights consecutively.
(Really do enjoy whacking that nerfball around with my
bare hands as paddles, by the way, just as I loved
tossing a tennis ball against a wall or a staircase as a
kid. Another way, besides romance, in which I'm
emotionally retrogressing into a kind of fantasy world
these days and getting a big kick out of doing it.)
                    *   *
     -- At the hideaway for some kwikjyze and it's not
an hour or two but almost a day and a half later. And
I'm hurting bad. That bristly phone call with Z turned
into a nasty incident last night. A serious fight.
Some ugly words she laid on me, especially in a note
left on her pillow this morning. As she muttered at one
point: "Looks like we're moving into a different third
phase than I thought."
     Tonight she came over as per usual and we tried to

work it out. It would appear we're now back to exactly
the same experimental sleep program she rejected on
Monday night. In any case we'll keep trying. And the
tandem jyze spree is still on. But it won't be starting
out in anything like the mood we'd been expecting.

Took all the heart out of me, this battle.
Certainly I don't have enough left right now to try to
describe it. Or anything else for that matter.

I put her to bed in B-2 and left just to get out
(but to avoid making matters worse let her assume I was
on my way to work). As she remarked during an otherwise
sad and silent period of attempted mutual consoling up
in the loft: "Maybe I'm going to be even more difficult
than you thought." (And even in this remark a spiteful
edge. "So you thought I'd be difficult but you could
handle me? I'll show you what difficult is.") Yet also
she said this: "It's my intent to love you in a really
wonderful way." (And an example of this: she gave me a
"Zoeku" she wrote going in to work, "Lipstickless on the
bus." A Zoeku is a new form she's invented, a kind of
haiku by Zoelie in which she's not too worried about the
exact syllable count or any other formal rules except
"real short." At my request she's been holding off on
applying lipstick until she gets to the office so we can
canoodle at home and on the bus riding in from her
place; that's what the first Zoeku is about.)

I want to believe the power of love will pull us
through. Determination alone obviously won't be enough.
Badly wanting this love to work obviously won't do it.
-- And now I'm wondering if the question of our survival
as a couple might turn out to be our main mutual topic
during the spree. (Her new bound volume bears the
handwritten title "Jyzin' with G." This by itself ought
to be enough to ensure our survival. -- So then maybe
it is. Or if not in the flesh, at least in the jyze.
And therefore I'll now add "Jyzin' with Z" to the title
I had earlier settled on for my own spree volume.)

BOOK III

[Absolute Tiptop Pinnacle –
Jyzin' with Z]

Just grateful to be doing this at all. Only a day
late with the launch but already way behind and catching
up will be tough. But when the going gets tough --
yeah. "Just jyze it."

At Z's. we're back from a B-2 run to pick up a
crucial item I'd intentionally left behind because I was
sure I wouldn't be needing it. The tandem spree was
dead on arrival! Even before arrival! So who needs a
J-stick! (Can't think. Pressure's on. Her dinette
table, ten p.m., railroad blues clickety-clacking down
the boom-box track. Already I've been reminded her
normal bedtime is exactly what the time now is. She
doesn't know how much longer before she starts fading.
And when that happens, though she doesn't say this --
not in so many words -- I'll be facing a dilemma.
Jyzin' or lovin'? -- And then how much longer can jyze
tough it out?)

On the way back here a stop at Z's usual co-op
market for upscale organic grub (which I could easily
refuse to eat on principle -- principle of dietary
consistency if nothing else -- but being "crazy in
compromise" right now I'd better not).

Earlier, before the trip, a five-hour "conflict
resolution" session. Yes, five hours of nonstop
haggling, Z and I. To my surprise it appears to have
accomplished something. we might even be right back on
that clickety-clack track. In any event, all sorts of
new vows and guidelines are firmly slotted into place,
somewhat like railroad ties, could say (have!).

Earlier yet I hiked over here, over the hill, again

the same path as Meet Day. In my foul mood the symmetry
was morbidly appealing. In all probability, I was
thinking, this would be the day of the breakup. Again
the long arc of the Asian wars rose up, the deep
structure of our story line, Z's and mine and for that
matter a whole generation's (wouldn't want to neglect
the big picture here). All that wondrous and terrible
stuff. And probably jyze will be referring back to
these matters regardless. Because right now -- well,
clear thoughts should never be this hard to come by. To
struggle on under such a handicap!

But -- surprise. Celebration's in the air. Love
celebration! And isn't that what this spree was
supposed to be all about in the first place? Maybe the
one chance jyze would ever have to engage in such a
blowout, at length and in depth and with the celebratory
substance freshly in mind and also to hand.

How sure was I until just hours ago it was over?
Pretty damn sure. Sure enough to be pondering seriously
what city I should decamp to next to try to put it all
behind me (ha). Day of catatonic grimness (and this the
inaugural day of our shamelessly kitschy summer festival,
citywide, splendid blue-beyond-blue skies all day and
then the massively popular torchlight parade downtown
with hundreds of thousands attending; but I never made
it out of B-2).

Before that, three nights of no loving. In a row.
(And in all our previous time together only one stretch
so sexually impoverished, her graduation week.) Battles
of the intense quiet-fury kind. No raised voices.
Withdrawals. Dueling cancellations. Silences. Backs
turned, in bed and elsewhere. Glazed eyes. Red eyes.
Thin bloodless lips. Teeth filed into daggers.

I could take a crack at detailing some of this and
maybe will. Tomorrow? For sure not now. These quick
scribbles just a series of jabs: hoping to startle
"Absolute Tiptop Pinnacle" into flight, however wobbly.
Kwikjyze intro. -- I'd been thinking maybe try for
more, but now, no. Reconciliation time! Saturday
night! When we get some! Combat pay already earned on

both sides!   -- And she's just closed herself in the
bathroom. Toothbrush sounds. I'm gonna jyze on now?
    (Meanwhile her head start's already ballooned to
ten pages. Tandem jyze, did we say? -- And so
disappointed was she at hearing I'd scratched the
project, I had no choice but to restart it. Instantly.
The makeup moment. Or -- too pat. Still, I think so.)
    And say forget all this. Jyze here at the start
will be notable, if at all, only for its embarrassed
absence. Hardscribble beginnings -- but better this
than nothing. (She's out. Now I spring my surprise.
Guess what, I'm crashing too! Four hours early!
-- Even while closing it out here I'm using the other
hand to strip down to bone. Well, or the hope thereof
anyway, knock on wood. Well, or -- simple flesh, that's
what. Exposed vulnerable refractory J-slinger man-flesh.
Knock lightly with J-stick. Or don't knock the thing,
no no; rather tap. Tap, tap, tap. The real megillah,
right there. This tap of the G-wand with the J-wand
just for luck. Because here we go.)

S2

    Twelve hours and a whole lotta good lovin' later.
Back at the same new stand: Z's dinette table. The
splendid peaceful Sunday urban view stretching out
before us, greenery and lake and skyline and all the
rest. Hills. Birds. A human contralto warbling scales
in the house across the street. A jerk of a dad ranting
at his kid downstairs.
    -- Hold on now: someone else downstairs, or maybe
it's the same dad, fires up some extremely loud rock
music and Z mutters from her parallel perch around the

corner, "I'm turning on the radio if that's okay with
you." Swoops by in her undeniably eye-catching powder-
blue diaphanous floor-length nightgown. Sez, "Even if
I've had a zillion O's I don't like listening to other
people's loud music" -- this alluding to the advice her
friend Olwen gave her, back when Z was off men and
romance and becoming more and more irked by other
people's loud music blasting through thin apartment
walls: "You should pleasure yourself more often."
     The jazz station. Same one I'd be listening to if
this were B-2. She never changes the station either,
and didn't before we met. She has another radio, a
smaller one by the bed, for 24-hour public news and
talk, whose station she also never changes.
     Reconciliation loving: delightful. Night session,
two morning sessions, with some deep dozing in between.
Oh how she can come. And oh how I can't. Nor do I
even try to "enter" now, as in fuck. But the loving's
so fine it doesn't matter a whole lot, to me or to her
either, except sporadically and, in the long run, deep
down, bedrock level, at which of course it matters a
great deal. And of course we both know this well. But
we're ignoring it for a while. Doing our best.
     We're agreed: this past weekend's battle will count
as the regularly scheduled meltdown over the no-fuck
issue. The next one's not due, again by mutual consent,
for another six weeks. In the meantime we'll go back to
"letting nature take its course" and try not to be
discouraged by flops and failures. She's being terrific
about this. What can I say. Such a sexual schlemiel
I've become.
     Mostly blue skies. August weather. Balcony door
open. (I should note it's now two weeks and two days
since she got me off for the first time, and then did it
twice more in the following two days, all by hand and
all at dawn or shortly after. And no more since. But I
have high hopes for our spree month here, yes I do.)
     -- Now she's set aside her own J-book and is
pounding away at her computer. She's typing up the list
of new agreements and understandings we reached

yesterday. (And she's turning the boom box way up and
putting in earplugs. I've already assured her I don't
care how loud it gets. More mutterings. A long-running
feud here, Z and her neighbors. "Why do you think they
call me Feisty?" Retaliation threats -- but we talked
this over yesterday. At one point I almost asked her to
return the key to my hideaway office for fear she'd
shred some manuscripts in a fit of vengeful fury. But
not to worry. She thoroughly persuaded me. She even
recognized that my jumpiness stemmed at least in part
from long-lingering bad vibes of the Lady V era.)

   -- This list she's typing up, I can't remember what-
all's on it. No doubt she'll be providing me a copy,
perhaps to be signed in blood. Nothing too upsetting
though. All reasonable stuff. We've both learned some
useful things, I do believe. I mean, we must've;
otherwise we'd still be thrashing it out. Or worse.

   (She creeps by, forgets to bestow a loving touch.
More physical affection outside of bed is basically all
I've asked for -- again -- as her side of the bargain.
I grab her knee through the diaphanous nightgown and
flash what's supposed to be a playful mock pout. Oops,
she says, in effect, and gently squeezes my shoulder.)

   Now, with the list presumably ready for printing,
she's settling into the view armchair a couple feet to
my rear, about to tackle the local Sunday paper. How I
do groove on having a lover who's a heavy-duty reader
and what's more politically alert and active. -- And
trust is deepening. She's singling me out from the
crowd: I'm being officially designated an ally. And
what's more I like her new haircut, acquired yesterday.
Punky modified bob type, sort of, I'd say, probably
inaccurately. Short, close, semi-spiky, isolated
fringes angling down onto her forehead. Hereafter, she
tells me, her trims will come every six weeks instead of
every four, as part of her ongoing thrift drive. Cut
down on expenses, pay off the big education loan, save
money for a rainy day, one most likely to involve her
aging mother's failing health -- although Mama E (for
Elza -- yes, with a, it turns out, Z, Polish style) --

Mama E, I say, seems to be holding up quite well at
present. (And today's the day for the weekly call to
her back in Centropolis -- in Mentoka lingo; I also may
need to note again that this is the city of Z's and my
raising -- a/k/a C-town -- where last Sunday the heat
index soared way beyond anything ever seen here.)
        She sang marvelously in my ear. She worried about
another canker sore in her mouth (and wondered aloud if
I could be the source of these, which she's never had
before, or if they might somehow be related to her own
type of Big H nether canker). (Now while slipping
behind me, again on a fridge run, she plants a big wet
kiss on my neck: all right!) She proclaimed herself to
be "completely, gapingly, unbelievably open to you" and
asked if I grokked this (yes, I do; and what's more, I
like it a lot). She declared she wants "more
surprises." She advanced new psychosexual theories for
my phallic failings, a/k/a "nonperforming endowment"
(her pun, yuk yuk); and her theory about my being unable
to trust her fully at the unconscious level, well, there
just might be something to it, I'm not denying. I'm so
perplexed myself I figure I lack any grounds to be
rejecting out of hand even the seemingly most unlikely
of possible explanations. (Major distractions erupting
now: the same jerk dad is banging on his pickup in the
street four stories below, cussing out his wife who's
inside the building; he's revving his engine, belching
out clouds of noxious black smoke which billow all the
way up here and roil around angrily and quite visibly
just beyond the balcony. To Z's friend Jess -- working
class herself -- this guy is "Mr. White Trash.")
        The skyline. The lake. The trees. The hills.
Take in a view like this and no matter how awed you may
be, you still feel ashamed for not being even more
awed. (I do anyway. Question whether this is a sign
of urban jadedness or what.) -- But how lucky we are!
We take note of this frequently and I do feel strongly,
deeply, fervently it's so. Will confess a twinge or
two of what I believe is authentic guilt about it
occurs from time to time.

[Absolute Tiptop Pinnacle - Jyzin' with Z]

     Then again we've just barely made it to four months
so far. But in her introductory remarks for the
"conflict resolution" session yesterday she declared
her belief that we'll have at least half a century
together and only death will "do us part." (And also
proclaimed herself to be strong enough to handle
anything I might be needing to tell her. And if I were
needing to tell her we were splits, she thought she'd be
able to persuade me otherwise, if not right away, then
eventually; and I don't doubt that at all, that she
could do it if she wanted to, though at the time I did
doubt whether she'd ever actually want to.)
     Well, but what about those earlier pronouncements
of hers, those broken agreements? And what about my
charges of gross hypocrisy and insensitivity? What
about her walkout threats and ominous references to her
"dark side"? -- And, she acidly asked, had I noticed I
was starting to talk like the lawyer's son I am? Were
those forensic matters I've been laboring over in my
night job for all these years messing me up more than
I'd been aware of? Well, if not, could we then please
start exploring where all this skanky stuff was coming
from? (So, did. With many digressions to look into the
ways of exploring, the meta issues. And in time all
issues, meta and otherwise, seemed to be exhausted. Not
resolved, though, of course, fully. I'll try to be more
this way, she more that way. At least now we each grok
more deeply the other's grievances -- if we can just
hold on to some working day-to day awareness of them.
Reduce tensions, say, to tolerable levels.   Okay,
fine, I'll try to do better at saying "ouch" when she
causes me pain. Not too much better, though, because
harmony matters too, as I pointed out and she grudgingly
conceded. -- And gradually we warmed up. And were
laughing. And were gut-rumbling for grub.)
     A fight though. Our worst so far, maybe not quite
in intensity but without doubt in length. As soon as
it's over you start busily suppressing all memories of
how bad it was, how sick at heart it made you feel, how
truly you believed the end was near. Typical fight, I

suppose. Will we make them a regular practice? To be
realistic, I'd say two or three a year would be okay,
terrible though they be, rather than try to stay fight-
free as Lady U and I generally did, and for the most
part were, for our entire time together, and more so
than ever toward the end. "Conflict resolution"
programs invite mockery with all their psychojargon and
simulated legalisms but I do believe conflict needs
airing from time to time. Flawless and unending harmony
can't be a realistic ideal for anyone and especially not
in a mongrel society like ours (for on what principles
acceptable to all could it be based?).

Jyze spree beginnings. Enough for now. Under the
terms of our newly readjusted weekly schedule she'll
soon be booting me from the premises here. And later
tonight I won't be able to do much because for the first
time in a couple of years Jyzer Ink's been asked to take
on a special government "real time" job, three full days
of scoping, and as J. Ink's CEO I've accepted with
alacrity and also relief owing to (in more ways than
one) my personal financial crunch. With luck I'll now
be able to get over the hump this month, and when the
quarterly booster shot from the deep reserves arrives
late next month I should be coasting again for a while.

But before going in for a long scope session
tonight, more jyze. Catchup stuff. And then maybe a
nightcap afterwards. Even a dream sequence, who knows.
Followed by two heavy workdays Monday and Tuesday while
Z and I are apart under the new regime. And by the time
we meet again late Tuesday night this spree thing should
be back on track again. Or by gum that's the plan.

*   *

Home now. And here's one more clue as to why I'm
so crazy about this Z-woman. She left a brief sexy
voicemail at 5:11 p.m., just moments after we parted at
the bus stop. "M'bao," she says in her lovingest voice,
low and husky and musical, "I just want you to know" --
and then declares that in her view we've made a real
breakthrough this weekend and she's sure the sailing
will be much smoother from now on (almost the same way I

270

described my own view earlier!). Says she'll miss me the next two days and indeed already does but won't really be alone, she'll be sleeping with my "animal spirit" as evoked by certain funky clothing items I left behind at her request. "Pheromone saturated."

But the tone's what really made it. More loving than ever before. Left me stunned, jaw literally hanging. Just like in the comix! Lurching about with little curlicues popping outta my noggin!

How can it be this Z-person exists and life is so good after all?

-- Unit B-2. Open the door and BAM, a wall of heat. Strip down to all skin (plus hair in isolated scraggly patches) while still in the hallway. The place looks dusty and the plants are crying for water though it's been only about twenty-five hours since their last hit. Brew some coffee to torque up for the hard night ahead. Toast a couple of slices of weeks-old cinnamon-raisin bread, both of them exceptionally tough heels. Nail a few fruit flies but praise the kitchen god: a smart rap on the lid of the wet-garbage bin raises no new swarms. Allot ninety minutes for jyzing in the green armchair. Push on with just that, as confirmed by these sentences. (But flick on the fan first, aiming it so that one extreme of its hobbled sweep will aerate soggy/droopy J-slinger crotch, legs spread, right here.)

Rode the bus home. Held a book open in my hand the whole way but read not a single word. My mind's buried under a headful of flotsam and jetsam blown in by the weekend Z-hurricane. And so it almost always is. The Z-daze. Lost in a Z-daze in the Z-maze.

She walked me over to the bus stop after we'd taken down the recycling. I'm noticing how fine and foxy she's looking in her short white skirt and pink off-one-shoulder top. Her uniquely sexy shambly amble. Traces back to the sixth-toe removals, a crucial formative childhood event -- FOO to you! -- if ever there was one (and she just ten months old at the time of the first amputation). -- And I'm praising her again for the skillful work she's done in guiding us through this

fractious weekend. Squeezes and tongue rassles follow.
Amorous explorations back in the shadows of the bus
shelter. And off she saunters. I love watching (even
if this time she forgets the new affection rules and
fails to wave before turning the corner).

     -- Getting lost here. So far just floating along.
Is this maybe how it'll be for twenty-eight more days of
spree? If so -- okay. Drift on! And to show for it at
the end, a jyze testimonial about half a mile long, if
my figuring's right (at six inches per line in this
J-book), and all of this likely to reveal little else
beyond the extreme state of my zonkedness over Zoelie B.
"I'm a Zonked-out Zealot for Zoelie" -- to the tune of
"Ding-Dong Daddy."

     As I'm hauling her bins down she warns me to be
careful. Despite determined efforts I can't shake my
rep with her as a klutz. Tripping on stairs,
misbuttoning shirts, pouring wine that misses the glass
entirely. The slapstick moments just won't stop
slapping, like a highlight reel complete with rimshots
from a TV boners show. Another one last night, an elbow
again, suddenly the table on which it was about to brace
itself as a prop for my chin shifted a foot to the left,
so it seemed, and the elbow had no place to go but down,
down, down, taking much of the rest of me with it until
I finally caught myself halfway to the floor.

     Well anyway we cleared the deck. Her deck, that
is, or balcony, where she stores the full bins. It's
the second time we've done this. That's how far we go
back now: two recycling cycles. Earlier today she was
wearing another red utility-issued T-shirt; the front of
this one reads "You want to talk trash? Talk to me."

     (As I changed out of blue shorts back into khaki
workshirt and jeans she said, "Mmmm, I like when you're
standing there with your pants still unbuttoned and your
shirt open like that -- very sexy!" Ooh do I go for her
telling me I'm sexy to her! Could it be my sexual
foozles are leaving me in dire need of strokes? And she
deals them with such flash and panache. This time she
pressed her palm flat against my bare lower stomach and

then slowly slid that same hand down as we went into yet
another clinch like two punch-drunk boxers in the
fifteenth round. -- The shorts and Z-shirt, by the way,
along with a few other items I'm keeping at her place,
go into a green plastic stackable box she's labeled "G's
Box" in her bogglingly cluttered and box-stuffed "extra
bedroom" which in fact is her only bedroom (she sleeps
in the living room). And earlier in the afternoon we'd
dug deep into a corner of that bedroom to unearth three
boxes of old albums and tapes she'd been promising for
weeks to show me. One by one we went through them.
Fabulous stuff. Warped vinyl! Album covers I recalled
from my teen days! Her taste every bit as eclectic as
she'd declared back in our very first phone talk! And
best of all: she has several albums of jazz standards,
instrumental only, intended for singers to rehearse
with, and she promised to rehearse with them for me!)
     -- But does she have a jyzey kind of soul? Well
yeah, amazingly, given how much else she has.
     Earlier yet she'd handed me the printout of her
list of our agreements, now titled "A Little Light
Music." Did I want to make any additions or
corrections? Last chance! I came up with a few minor
edits just to show I'd done the required reading and
then she printed up final copies for both of us, at my
request, because originally she'd put together this list
just for herself as a memory aid. "I'm a very visual
person and I can't really think of things as being real
until I see them written down." -- See, the soul of a
jyzer. (And often when talking she'll pause to think
and roll her eyes upward to gaze at a patch of ceiling
or sky, always slightly to her right -- and she's a
lefty! -- and she says she does this to visualize
whatever it is she's thinking about. If I say something
and she wants to think about it, even then, she insists,
she visualizes it written in a cartoon bubble above my
head. Just joking, though, probably, or at least maybe,
I presume.)
     As for the items on the "Light Music" list, I'll
try to take a closer look at those later. Most

important to me, it seems she's finally grokked what's
been bothering me most -- I suspect, anyway -- in the
sexual realm, and that is the hostility she shows at
times to collective colonialist Cawk malehood without
singling out my own personal colonialist Cawk malehood
as at least a provisional exception. So does this mean
I'm suffering from castration anxieties or something?
Maybe so. Or just say I've been slow to trust her in
this realm, and I think for good reason, just as I think
she's hostile toward colonialist Cawk males as a group
for good reason. But today I sensed I'd finally risen
to the status of beloved exception, even if it's still
resolutely provisional. And it felt real good, yes it
did. (But the proof will be in the pud-pulling.)
      Another item: as we sat in bright light at the
dinette table chomping on watermelon slices I noticed
for the first time a faint baseball-size burn scar on
her inner left thigh. She told me what had caused it --
an accident involving a boiling-hot tea container caught
against her tights at a theater, forcing a trip to the
emergency room -- and then as an afterthought promised
to tell me the whole "unexpurgated" tale someday. In
other words, a lover was somehow involved. And we can't
talk about her lovers, see, because doing so would be
asymmetrical, since she isn't ready yet to talk about
mine. "I'll tell you about it in seventeen years and
eight months," she said. I was slow to catch on; why
that particular number? "Because eighteen years is how
long you were with a certain someone. When we've been
together the same length of time so I feel we're on
equal grounds, then we can talk about love histories."
      She wasn't joking. Or at least not much. She's
still not ready to grapple with these things, period.
-- And does this matter? I'm not sure. I think it
might. But I'm prepared to assume it doesn't and won't,
especially if she continues to insist such intimate
disclosures would be more than she could bear to hear.
      And this: she mentioned casually she'd decided to
stop seeing Anita, her "counselor." I'd already known
about her intention to cut back -- on the grounds she

was no longer attending school, and she'd sought out
Anita's advice mainly to help her deal with the stress
of adjusting to the "WASPy" atmosphere in her classes --
but this was the first time she'd said anything about
going cold turkey. For someone who's been seeing
counselors/therapists/shrinks virtually nonstop since
early college days this must be a major step. It's
probably something of a concession too, in a way, since
I've been taking a fairly explicit antitherapy stance
with her even while trying to remain neutral about her
seeing Anita in particular. But she didn't act as if
she were yielding to my preferences or way of seeing and
I didn't act or feel as if I'd scored any points.
Because: I don't really have a good sense of whether the
results will be positive or negative.
     But -- yeah. I'm pleased about this counseling
shutoff. I see her as feeling stronger and more self-
confident. I see her as believing she can handle a
loving relationship without outside help and do her part
to keep it on an even keel, at most times if not all.
     -- And now to work. Same jeans and workshirt go
back on though they're hot and sweaty. Same socks too.
And I'm not forgetting that during these three days of
real-time scoping I'll be dealing with some reporters
and staff who've been a royal pain to work with in the
past. But what the hell. I need the dough. And who
wants to act vengefully now -- cut off my nose to spite
my face (which is what Z says she used to do to herself
constantly even as a child and her parents often used
the phrase in admonishing her: this was Weezie the
rebel. The spirited one. Has a lot to do, I'd say,
with why she's so vitally alive today, including
sexually).
     -- A joke this afternoon: I tell her I too think
sexual symmetry would be wonderful and I'd like to come
and come and come just as she'd been saying she wanted
me to, but then again I think she'd be wasting a lot of
time if she tried to get me off by, say, stroking my
armpit. -- As I've been able to do with her several
times. Her electric jolts, her arching body, her

deliciously juice-brimming female seam. The touch of
her marvelously soft and smooth skin. Her cries of
pleasure. Her jazzy love talk. Ooh ooh ooh, I can't
get any of this out of my head, I can't stop jyzing
about it any more than I can stop the loving once we're
into it -- or anyway I have such a hard time stopping
but eventually somehow can when I know I must. -- As in
the jyze realm I must right now.

*   *

Kwikjyze next day:

A wake-up message from Zoelie. A reply to a fried-
synapses message I left her at three a.m. last night;
and that in turn was a reply to her terrific "smooth
sailing" message of yesterday afternoon. She recorded
the wake-up message early this morning, right at her new
rising time of six-thirty. I have to say she no longer
sounded quite so thrilled about our reconciliation. But
then why should she? Got to get back to work just like
me. And she directly addressed the matter of
thrilledness: "Now that I know you love me it's not the
same kind of sleepless night focused solely on us."

It's natural, I think, a little post-conflict-
resolution letdown. A return to unheightened normal
reality. But we'll still be visiting the heights plenty
often enough, I do believe.

Thinking back then. Yesterday. A couple of things
I neglected to mention. One, she brought out her
calendar for August and we went over it day by day,
making changes as needed to accommodate the new weekly
schedule which keeps us apart Sunday and Monday nights
and brings us together again for all the others. Lots
and lots of adjustments and yet we were able to agree on
them quite easily. "Hey, I'm an easygoing guy."

Alas, for the next several weeks I won't be seeing
much of Kathryn C., "the Katgrrrl," because Z takes care
of her on Tuesday nights and -- well, it's complicated.
I'll just say I'm already terrifically fond of this kid
and expect her to remain a major presence in my life for
years to come. My new wallball partner. Whose self-
portrait in crayon done especially for the subunk

(that's me!) now graces the side of the loft stairs
(whose steepness, I realized the other day in one of
those "aha!" moments, resembles that of the creaky
wooden pulldown attic stairs of my grade-school years;
and at the top of both sets of steep stairs, an equally
woody, stale-aired, low-ceilinged paradise of sorts).

    -- And at the very end of Z's August calendar, the
weekend of my Absolute Tiptop Pinnacle birthday (and the
final few days -- the climax if climax there be -- of
this jyze spree right here), she's written in "Mystery
Weekend." I guess she's planning something for the
whole weekend, which this year includes Labor Day.

    Oh the conundrums of jyze planning.

    -- Traffic picking up out there. A jet roaring
overhead. And I'm reminded: a year ago this week my
hood here was a madhouse. This year the epicenter of
the festival has shifted elsewhere. Hurrah! With all
the nightlife (and in the past month no fewer than three
new clubs have opened nearby) plenty's always going on
anyway. (But do I want to leave this area? No. I like
it fine and it remains almost ideal given its proximity
to my two workplaces and given my lack of wheels and my
puny income. But for Zoelie I'd do it regardless and I
expect soon will. At one point over the weekend we
talked about the end of the year as a possible target
date for moving in together. That would allow her the
prep time she wants -- for fear of rushing into things
-- and it would enable me to keep this year's jyze at
least technically within the form I intended it to have
at the start, although the more apt title now might be
"Jyze Around Zoelie" rather than the original "Jyze
Around My Room," that is, JAZ instead of JAMR. JAZ
JYZE! -- As if sticking with form matters a whole lot.
By itself it shouldn't, I'd say, so maybe it's standing
in for some other concern. Or just for reluctance to
move out of B-2. I think of all the work I put in on
tearing down and transporting and rebuilding the loft
and what a massive chore re-dismantling it will be. And
I think of my certainty back in the early days that I'd
be living here the rest of my life. The recluse. This

the declared year of same.)

*

(Several times Z has openly wondered if I have any
hidden longings to return to the isolato state. So I
ask myself: do I? And answer: probably. In some part
of me. -- But no, I want life with her. She's yanked
me out of my inward spiral, even rescued me. That's the
truth. No doubt this still accounts for a big part of
the neediness driving my love for her. -- And by
coincidence just this week the landlord here has
presented all tenants with recertification papers. If
we want to stay on in our units another year starting in
January we'll soon have to prove our income still falls
below the limit; and even though in my case I don't
doubt it does, providing the proof would likely be the
same kind of major hassle it was last year. The papers
are due by the end of September. Should I maybe just
try to stall until the end of the year?)

S3

Hideaway. Brown armchair. Door open a crack and
both fans on (and unlike the one back in B-2, these two
work the way they're supposed to -- but even taken
together they're too small to do the job back there).
Approaching in the hall I'm surprised to see the
blinds lit up and for a second think Zoelie might be
here. Then I recall I intentionally left the lights on
yesterday as recompense for the plants -- I have two
now, the second cloned off the first -- after the long
dark weekend. (And recall Z told me her pulse quickened
one day when she too saw the blinds glowing as she came
by to take a lunch break alone here, and that time also

278

the lights were on for the plants and I wasn't around.)
    First thing I do in the office is flip the calendar
page to August. Just a few days late, but this shows
where my focus has been for the past week or so, meaning
not here. Then I replenish my traveling "jyze ammo"
from the stock in the desk. In the office of Jyzer Ink
only one full bottle of jyzer ink remains. Soon it'll
be time to return to the source and lay in a new supply
(the source being the grizzled guy up in the mountains
who's grinding away for lone jyzers across the land).
    Feeling edgy today. Could be because this is the
second day in a row with no Z-skin in the game (not
until after work tonight will there be some). Our vow
never again to sleep apart more than one night in a row
has now been broken. It's for the cause of the new and
improved regime. And as trade-off we get to sleep
together five nights straight. (Most likely I'll be
dead tired for the first four, the worknights, but this
would've been much the same under the old regime.)
    No sign she's been here since yesterday. Was today
a workout day for her? Or is she reluctant to use her
key now after my revelation that at the height of the
battle I'd thought about asking her to return it? She
did drop by here yesterday but didn't come inside, or at
least I don't think so. Just shoved a card under the
door. (One of our agreements -- and this one she left
out of "Light Music," I realize now -- is that neither
of us will read the other's private writings without
approval, which is to say: won't pry or snoop. This
office is stuffed with prime snooping material. -- But
would I actually care if she peeked into any of it on
the sly? At this point I think not. What's to hide?
Flattered is what I should be. -- And she might have a
lot of fun flipping through the photo albums. But
never, never would she rip up anything, she swore
Saturday, no matter how great the rage. -- And so stomp
down on this imagining. Ya gotta trust. Or else.)
    Still sweaty from the fast-paced walk down. Funky.
No shower since Saturday, hot weather, a fierce wallball
session. Grizzled too. (A glance in the mirror in the

men's room down the hall and I wondered if she might go
for this stubbly look. "Jyze Vice Retro."   -- Reminding
me she mentioned on the phone this morning that the
photos have come back from the D-clan's birthday fling
at the spaghetti house and in one of them, she said,
"You actually look kinda cute.")

On the desk a bunch of flowers, just about gone to
seed now, she left here a week ago today. "Tit for 4,"
says the card for those flowers, and it's signed with
"M'bao" inscribed inside a heart. I had to ask her what
the "Tit for 4" means. It's a play on "tit for tat,"
she said, and it refers to the four pronouncements she'd
made on the phone the night before and to my agreeing to
go along with her on all four. And that, as it happens,
is what really triggered the fight. (She told me this
about "Tit for 4" on the phone just prior to my riding
out there on the bus. That night I stayed up and read
instead of hitting the rack with her at ten, four hours
ahead of my current normal bedtime. To her, it turned
out, this was an unforgivable insult, a slap-in-the-face
payback. To me it was taking seriously what she'd said
about scoring eight straight hours of sleep. And maybe
just a tap of payback in there as well. I was not all
that pleased with her unilateral pronouncements.)

-- But no, jyze will not attempt a blow-by-blow
account of the fight. At this late date that would be
folly. Of course it's true she did me wrong, no
question about that, but it's also true by personal-
relations axiom that the blame must fall equally on both
parties if you want the relationship to continue. It's
just that I've failed to come up with any wrongs of my
own in this case that meet that high standard. Must've
been something though. Or I could always make my
psychosexual malfunctioning the fall guy. In any case,
invoke forgiveness. Move on. Assume love and good
faith on her side too. (Because do I want to assume
otherwise and risk losing her? Hell no! Especially not
after all the trouble we've both gone through this past
week trying to thrash out our differences -- while also
respecting, yes, those same differences.)

[Absolute Tiptop Pinnacle - Jyzin' with Z]

    And right here folded into the back of the J-book
is my newly revised copy of "A Little Light Music."
This copy was tucked into the card she shoved under the
door yesterday. On the earlier version she'd neglected
to type in a few of my suggested minor changes, which in
truth I hadn't even noticed were missing on that other
copy and will now acknowledge add absolutely nothing to
the current one. In fact they detract from it -- uglify
it with some superfluous paraphrasing.
    Time slippin' by. I need more time! In another
half hour I'll have to close up shop and head on back to
B-2. More wallball. Dinner, but a light dinner. Stay
at all times a little hungry. Stop physical decay in
its tracks. Image wolflike leanness. Present to the
Z-woman the very best G-man possible without becoming
compulsive or ridiculous about it. Nobody except the
jyze gods need know I'm working up some real sweat over
this. (And still I'm trying to keep the process itself
idiosyncratic, by which I mean sweating it out far from
the beaten fitness treadmill.)
    Throngs of tourists out there. Summery stuff,
including lots of nubile fleshy jiggles. The month of
maximal body display. (Z jauntily referred to last week
as "the Week of Loving Dangerously.") Dripping cones
and flashing eyes. Kites swooping overhead. Doo-wop
singers belting outdoors at the public market right next
to a chamber-music quintet sawing antically away in
uber-serious fashion, the overall effect a strange and
wondrous cosmopolitan cacophony. And at the market
newsstand the new newsie makes a mistake in his own
favor when I'm paying for the usual stack of newsprint
(which then blackened my sweaty hands during the walk
down here and this is why they too are funky now) and I
say, "Hey, no big deal, a month ago I was thinking about
applying for the very job you have now." He laughed,
probably because my remark made no sense at all. But
it's true, I even took home an application to fill out.
    News. Widespread famine in North Korea. Looks
bad, even after factoring in the usual probable media
distortions and also those of the South Korean and U.S.

281

governments. And the Z angle on this news, my Asian
blood connection. My probable kid who's half-Korean
just as she's half-Filipina. Racism and culturism and
Orientalism and Confucianism and Taoism and colonialism/
neocolonialism and all the various ismic backlashes and
overrides. Korea a bridge between Japan and China, a
kind of quirky blending of the two with its own intense
peninsular particularity. Lady U and Lady V, Japan and
China/Vietnam, my other blended Asian love connections.
And how East Asian are Filipino values with their heavy
admixture of Spanish and Roman Catholic and USAn
colonial/neocolonial influences? (And how many people
die of starvation even while jyze ponders these abstruse
matters? But then how many so die during the pondering
or even the actual doing of anything for any reason
whatsoever? -- Not that I'm buying this as an excuse
for disengagement. Always engage! -- But engage
thoughtfully as well as heartfully and artfully, yes.)
     Preach!
     Another news item, the oldest living human is dead.
She croaked yesterday at age 122. Now the oldest living
(and adequately documented agewise) is a mere 114. Z in
her fierce pursuit of "healthy stuff" says she expects
to make it to 105 and I'd better change my unhealthy
ways so I'll make it that far too, or at least to 103.5
(when she'll hit 105) so she'll never have to be lonely.
105 is her stated goal, but I suspect she harbors a
secret intention to attain "oldest living human" status.
I worry about this form of perfectionism because I think
it would take away too much from living now -- at least
in theory. But if you've got the bucks, maybe not.
Except then what about your priorities? How justify
such ever-steepening trade-offs to live the merely
hypothetical extra time?
     This love, another good thing about it is the way
it always seems to be raising one or another of the hot-
button issues of the day. We can square off on them and
maybe educate each other a bit. Jyze can feast on them.
     -- But no time for that. Not now anyway. Will
return later but probably only long enough to catch up.

[Absolute Tiptop Pinnacle - Jyzin' with Z]

with what? The spree plan!
                *   *

     Scope-office kwikjyze, half past midnight. In
forty minutes I'll be heading down seventeen stories to
the corner stop where my bus will be standing dead and
dark at the curb except for parking lights flashing, the
driver, assuming it's the regular one, taking a smoke
break while locked inside -- holding the cigarette out
the side window to be in technical compliance with no-
smoking regulations, pulling it back to the opening for
each drag but blowing the smoke back out into the street
-- reminding me of a guppy nibbling at the surface of
its tank, only lips showing -- before embarking on the
last run of the night (the bus visible almost straight
down from the north windows of the computer room if I
press up against the glass window of my own tank right
here).
     Spoke briefly in person with reporter Verna earlier
tonight, first time in a couple of years. She offered
this morsel: my old staff nemesis dayscoper Amy has been
fired. Why? "Basically for being such a creep."
(Technically for refusing to speak with a coworker to
whom she took extreme umbrage over some petty offense.)
So finally it's become the case, after several prior
false pronouncements: I'm the last of the old scoping
crew still hanging on at the old pop stand. Outlasted
them all. Got the last laugh, yo ho ho. (And boy does
this prove a lot.)
     Going back, a few notes on contacts with Z during
our two days apart. Her message recorded at six-thirty
a.m. today, yawn-filled, saying she's making good use of
"horse-o-meter time" and she's now almost fully adapted
to her new ten p.m. bedtime. Then a couple of hours
later another message, the daily dish, short and
whispered: first, as she'd thought might happen, Leola,
her former officemate (until last week), has canceled
the barbecue scheduled for this Sunday (all kinds of bad
things going down in Leola's life right now). And grad-
school friend Lee M., the one who warned Z against
getting involved too fast with me, tells her in an e-

mail of a separation from his wife Carol (though we saw
no hints of trouble at our commencement luncheon with
them last month). And Z's USAn indigene friend Irene
would like to meet me after all, but "not in a setting
in which there's nothing else to do but talk"; so how
about, Z suggests, we take her along with us to a movie
Saturday night (though Irene mostly goes for Hollywood
laff-riot stuff). Thus it appears a big shake-up of the
weekend plans is in the cards. -- But fine. Hey, jyze
thrives on chaos and confusion!

    -- And from the office receptionist's desk here
tonight I called at the current nightly call-when-apart
time, 8:45, and she was there, just back from doing her
laundry at J&G's; but that was when reporter Verna came
in and so I said I'd have to go but I'd call again in a
few minutes, and did, but still couldn't talk freely
because Verna was camped at a desk nearby and scope-job
pandemonium reigned, so I just said I'd see her later
and reminded her not to deploy the burglar brace in the
usual spot against the inside of her door and to leave
the safety guard off the doorknob.

    -- And should mention I talked briefly with the
Katgrrrl during the earlier call. She's becoming highly
conscious, Z tells me, of the brownness of her skin.
And Irene, who's full-blooded Cherokee, I think it is,
and Kat hit it off right away and as "kindred indigenous
souls ganged up on me," that is, on Z. -- And her card
from yesterday, Z's, said she wants to be "grabbin'
those Glennarious glutes." -- And the two poems she
sent me last week (prefight) are now pinned to the loft;
one starts "I want to live with you until I die" and the
other "Heart still hurting big-time." -- And she
confessed that as a teenager she sang "Now I've Got a
Secret Love" at the top of her lungs while washing the
dishes at home, intentionally trying to drive her
parents mad. This was during the period when she was
forbidden to date, which because her father was very
strict and old-school lasted until she left for college.
    Must stop.

S4

      Tight quarters under here now. First jyze visit
to the inner/under sanctum since installing the desktop
computer (and the damn thing's still not working right
and I can't free up enough time to try to figure out
why, nor is it likely I'll do any better on that chore
until the second week of September at the earliest).
      Time constraints. Of course I'm the one who's
laying the bulk of them on myself so what's to get
worked up about? And I'm not worked up. Feeling good!
Maybe even verifiably so by peptide measurement! And
why? Because the special real-time scope job is a wrap.
And better yet, I'm all caught up with the jyze spree
plan. Back on schedule. Cookin'. And so now the new
history/origins feedback loop is about to kick in -- is
doing so, in fact, just by virtue of my being holed up
where I am.
      I'm catching up with history (by which I mean Z's
and my mutual history, which goes back a full six months
as of next week) at entry #10 in Book I of this annal.
That was the eighter of the first call, our first
nonwritten, "live" contact, and for me it took place
right here. This phone. A big surprise on a Monday
evening when I just happened to be home at seven p.m., a
rarity under my then-current daily regimen, and I'd
pretty much given up hope on hearing from her, and the
phone rang. This one right here. White squarish thing.
Big double zero showing right now on its message display
panel (but it was "04" when I woke up this morning, and
all were Z messages). And I picked up the receiver and
ninety minutes later, give or take ten or twenty or

maybe even thirty, we were still talking and my life had
changed. (So there. Big deal. But -- seriously.)

As now, I believe for the first time ever, the
microwave's nuking away while jyze is blazing out. Both
are set for forty-four minutes. When the five-beep
timer sounds I'll need to start getting ready to meet Z
at the hideaway, where she'll be arriving at half past
five. I'm giving myself an hour to do a drastically
abbreviated wallball workout, shower, dress, and hike
down there, and I've already left her a message warning
I might be a few minutes late.

And then dinner here with her (though likely first
some shopping, as one of her messages proposed), and
then I'll head back downtown to scope a short back
order. But it's J-day! And one must keep one's jyze
commitments! (How marvelous is this spree life in which
every other day can be J-day, which to me is almost like
every other day being -- Xmas! Or Zmas!) -- So
therefore I'll continue with this entry at the scope
office, even while Z will be sleeping here -- I mean
directly above where I sit now, so I should say "up
there" -- but this is okay because it's how we've agreed
it should be. Sleep comes first for her during the
workweek, and jyze comes first for me when she's asleep
and I'm still up (this of course being jyze of, with,
for her -- spree jyze! -- as hers is of, with, for me).

And some good stuff to jyze about this round. A
relapse averted, a lusty morning. -- But later for
those. (Already halfway to the five pings.)

-- Before starting this entry, the grub run. My
khaki workshirt, now hanging on a chair by the fan,
still bears a big backpack sweat patch. Summery summer,
yes. Urban too. Saw a tiny red car sail cinematically
into an intersection from the steep hillside below and
execute a hard-left turn with smoking-rubber squeals.
At the same time rail cars were rolling along down by
the waterfront and a helicopter was zipping wasplike
overhead directly beneath a blimp suspended motionlessly
in blue haze high above the fairgrounds. A crowd of day
workers lined the curb, most of them brown-skinned (and

bringing to mind Z's comment about Kat's burst of brown-skin awareness). Issues popping into my head -- such as, for instance, a clip Z gave me on "affluenza" -- and euphoric moments, extended, all one really; I'm thinking yup, yup, dig it because this is as good as it gets. Issues on a hundred burners. Loving. So many realms of life this Z-phenom's engaging. Fight's over. With luck we might even find our separate euphorias still firing an hour from now, maybe even in sync.

Red-flame grapes. Stack of freebie print stuff from the "north pole" bookstore. Flashing red lights of two aid wagons pulled up face to face at curbside an hour ago just at the start of my hike home, a throng of gapers gathered, a scraggly denim-clad drifter laid out flat on the sidewalk in front of the TV-shaped box rack of the disgracefully bad national news sheet, almost as if he's taken one look at the front page and keeled over. Old Asian-looking guy leaning on a cane in the throng chirps "Good afternoon!" to me with a crinkly smile as if we're pals, though I'm pretty sure I've never seen him before. I'm a pack animal slung wide and high with groceries. Need these brisk daily walks and need 'em bad. At least four miles -- so I'd prefer anyway. Plus wallball. Nerfhoops. Hang together. See what I can offer up to keep things sizzling with the Z-woman, do my part (as she pushes ahead with hers).

-- There they go, the pings. Brief grace period follows. Say what? Say again, right here's the best of the bliss. And now, keep it rolling. Ride with it. Be alert. Be humble and grateful. Be ready to toss aside anything and everything. JYZE ALL OUT & LOVE ALL OUT.

*   *

Indeed I'm back. Scope office again, the conference room freshly vacuumed (dust still visibly resettling) and the usual shiny red telescope angled downward roughly forty-five degrees on its floor tripod, pointed at a rooftop famous for sunbathing, though not at this hour: round about midnight. A new janitor hard at it in the front office at the moment, obviously a vet of the trade to be able to execute such near-perfect

diamond vacuum sweeps as I observed traced on the carpet
out there. He's maybe the thirtieth or fortieth I've
watched go at the task over the years in this office and
its predecessors and for sure he's one of the best.

    Didn't get here until almost ten and then I was
still a little ripped on the old "Sandefjord family
rose'." Must've been an extremely special occasion
because I hauled out my last jug of the stuff and Z
agreed to imbibe, unusual for a weeknight. And then
after she took mock offense at my observation that
alcohol makes her amorous (and this has happened a
couple of times before), it did so again. As we sat
facing each other at the redwood worktable. Z in
unforgivably sexy side-slit black short-shorts and loose
scoopneck black top. A nipple come (black bra too -- I
hadn't seen her in all black before except for the teddy
(when she wore the teddy only) -- and I liked the look a
lot), then for symmetry one for the other nipple (at her
urging). Then she was famished for real food, not just
more grapes and gingersnaps, and we zapped one of her
super-healthy frozen dinners and one of my own hazmat-
fed chicken pot pies. And by the time we finished with
those I was already an hour late for work. As I left
she was seated on the couch, granny glasses on, digging
into the stack of clippings I'd saved for her.

    Earlier -- or no. Or yes, but way earlier. Night
before last, I should say something about that. Tuesday
night this was, and I arrived at her place a little past
one-thirty a.m. after again riding the last bus out.
Another row of pup tents -- this time made from utility
recycling handbills themselves recycled or rather reused
-- greeted me on the hallway rug inside the door, and Z
was awake in bed, having just gotten up to pee, and with
the sheet drawn tightly around her because she was naked
(which is not standard for her when in bed alone but
indicates she's ready for loving, or anyway she's doing
it for me because I always sleep in the buff for her and
she knows I like it when she does the same for me). So
I stripped down, joined her. But she was oddly
unresponsive, or call it oddly sluggishly responsive,

even while denying this was so. Only after coming --
taking much longer than usual to get there -- did she
admit otherwise. "That was very strange," she said.

What it came down to, she was still shaky from the
fight. She said exactly this: her trust in us had been
shaken. Of course couples have to fight sometimes, she
granted, but this one had been especially bad. Had I
really been ready to end it all, as it seemed? What was
this "brinksmanship" (as she called it)? -- For a few
moments getting me down. Oh geez, I'm thinking, not
again. Why's she not ready to let it go? We gonna have
to slug it out a second round? But managed to pull
myself back from this particular brink, and so did she.
We agreed to let it drop for the time being and try to
score some sleep -- she pressing in from behind,
"spooning." And soon, zzzzz, special Z zzzzz, warm and
moist, lips pressed loosely against the usual spot right
between my shoulder blades.

The alarm was set for her new default time, half
past six, but we were awake (or in my case, semi awake)
well before that, nuzzling, murmuring, canoodling, but
nothing much was coming of it and she started to crawl
across me to exit the bed. Stopped for a last kiss
while on all fours, nipples brushing my chest as I lay
on my back, and my right hand was stroking her legs and
rear and the kiss kept going and then she said, "You
could touch my clit just once." So did, from below as
she knelt, and it turned into a very long "just once"
during which she quickly came a first time and soon a
second, and then a movement of mine cued her in that I
was turned on too (she seemingly hadn't noticed this up
until then) and she reached down through her legs to
grab the fully rigid G-member with her right hand,
backhanded I think, or anyway in an unusual manner, and
started pumping away and very quickly (or so it seemed
to me, and so it certainly was by the standard of our
earlier times) I shot off. Ejacked. Six or seven or
maybe even eight respectable spurts and most of them
fully visible, almost like imitations of the geyser on
the card celebrating my first such eruption with her

(and that card is now tacked up on the wall by her bed).
Wotta surprise! And for her wotta triumph! (And sure,
at least as much for me.)

Earlier she'd been grumping about how haggard she'd
soon be looking -- how wanting to avoid looking haggard
is at least part of the reason, "even if politically
incorrect," for her needing to rack up more sleep -- and
now she said I'd given her another way to avoid
haggardness and she slipped down to rub the jizz in her
face. And suck out the last drop. "Going down for a
facial." Very sexy. (And for her I think a third come
happened just as she got me off. My hand was drenched
with her juices and they were literally dripping down my
arm as I worked on her from below. Ooh, I liked it.)

After that things seemed a whole lot better for us.
(But I've mulled what she said about brinksmanship. I
think maybe she's onto something. In a sense it might
be my own way of panicking. In an earlier phase of our
budding romance it may've been justified as a means of
jolting her out of a kind of excessive caution or
reluctance to engage fully. Now, no. It's more habit
on my part, related to the pride I take in tackling
things head-on. Not to mention fear she'll give up on
me because of my foozly phallus. In the context of a
loving longtime liaison with the proud and feisty Z-
woman such gamesmanship is too dangerous and I need to,
and intend to, find new ways to defuse it. -- As I was
telling her this afternoon during our walk home.)

That same night, by the way, "white trash" Jimmy
was in top bad form, ragingly drunk, bellowing and
roaring, working on his pickup at two a.m. on a
weeknight, and I learned something I hadn't understood
before: this is the same landlord's son she's been
feuding with for months, the one she suspects broke into
her room via the rooftop and balcony and stole her
backpack. "I wish you'd go beat him up," she said, and
not entirely jokingly. My response (not entirely joking
either): "Yeah, right, and within an hour you and I'd
both be shot dead." And a moment later I asked: "So
have you tried any of your new 'conflict resolution'

techniques on him?" She: "Believe me, this conflict is way beyond any possibility of resolution."

     Also I want to note Z seemed to go for my "Jyze Vice" stubble until she viewed it outside in the morning sun, on the way to the bus stop with its crowd of dress-for-success clean-shavens, including one she knows from the utility. The message I got, it doesn't do enough for her to outbalance the social static it might cause for her, though this message was not unkindly delivered. Nonetheless I declare the experiment to be over. (Today I'm again a very easygoing and clean-shaven J-slinger.)

     -- And up here in the conference room nothing at all is what's doing. It almost always is during the swing/graveyard hours when I'm around. Sterility. Yet I still like my work life, I surely do. The rounds, the nightscoping. Dress how I want (for jyze, that is, not success), show up and leave when I want and have the full run of the place, take breaks when I want and for as long as I want, listen to whatever music I want and as loud as I want, avoid almost always most of or all the usual workaday office nonsense, including, best of all, the presence of a finger-wagging, order-spouting boss. Sometimes I forget just how good I personally think I have it. (Fine with me if not too many others would think so. -- But does the Z-woman? Maybe not wholly so just yet. But I think she's wising up to it.)

     A noisy thunderstorm yesterday afternoon, rare for these parts. In just minutes it delivered close to an inch of true thunderstormy rain, a big splashy downpour, and then a hailstorm, unit B-2 suddenly sounding as if it were under attack by an army of kids with BB guns (or caught behind a heavy truck on a gravel road, pebbles spraying up in volleys -- and a few of marble size). At that point the outdoor blues concert we were planning to attend in the evening looked like a scratch for sure. But then a few minutes after the deluge, blazing sun. (In the middle of it all, a call from Z: we were listening to the same thunder! And was it not like a contemporary version of distantly separated lovers gazing at the moon in ancient Chinese poetry?)

[Jyze in Love]

    An hour later, meeting Z at work, riding out with
her on her usual express bus, packing the picnic dinner,
dropping by J&G's a block away to meet Jess's brother
and his wife and two kids -- he a prosecutor in the very
DA's office I used to cover as a cub reporter way back
in the long-ago, the gang unit, not exactly known then
or I'm sure now for its social progressiveness, yet the
whole family handling the delicate scene seemingly quite
well as they were meeting Jess's female live-in lover
for the first time -- and the trek ten blocks north to
the zoo, outdoor natural auditorium, everything just
about ideal, the grass almost dry, the crowd not too
big, a terrific up-and-coming acoustic bluesman (new to
me as of this year but strongly reminiscent of my man
Taj), folding legless chairs on which Z and I sat, she
at my left and slightly to my back, her arm around my
shoulders much of the evening and I was feeling very
loved and loving (and enjoying the sight of J&G being
lovey-dovey in front of family and friends and a mostly
hetero crowd -- and telling Z how I like it that with so
many of her friends she and I are in one way or another
a token couple, so to speak, either genderwise or
racial-mix-wise or both -- or seemingly anyway).
    And I've been thinking history and our origins
myth, how it's shifting and growing. Five months ago
this week, in fact day after tomorrow, that first call.
Looking back now I'm struck most by those long silences
of hers (during a talk which nonetheless kept going on
and on) when, as I know now, she had no idea what to
make of me and at times was stunned by what I was saying
(though lately she's been pooh-poohing this explanation
after seeming to affirm it for quite a while) and how I
consequently tied myself up in knots trying to fill dead
air or draw her back into the conversation (fearing I'd
mortally insulted her a number of times). How
mesmerized I nonetheless was, and not only by what a
fine match it appeared we might make but also just by
that incomparable phone voice. The hearty laugh. The
voice so musical, vibrant, sexy. How jolted I was! How
perplexed too, when she couldn't come up with a time

less than two weeks away for us to meet in person, and
nonplussed by the cavalier way she shrugged off my
squawks about this. -- Even in the first call the
courting dynamics of the months ahead were already
firmly set. Mainly my desperation, my frantic efforts
to find ways to break through to her without totally
blowing my cool.

(Last night, talking with Gwen about all this at
the concert, she assured me it was clear from the start
I was "the pick of the litter, ears and snout above the
rest." Not only had I gone beyond the others in the way
I answered the ad -- many sent a mere form letter -- but
I'd obviously put a lot of effort into the next several
steps and produced some funny, interesting stuff. Damn
right! -- But did Z realize this at the time? I'm
still not persuaded. If she did, why such a slow and
cautious response?)

The sheer blindness of it all. The thrashing about
in the dark. (And still how hard it is for me now to
remember, already, what life was like before Zoelie B.)

And what if I hadn't happened to be home the night
she called? I tend to forget how close I came to giving
up on hearing from her. What if one of the others I'd
contacted had responded and been seriously interested?
In that case I might've reacted very differently to Z's
call -- given her a hard time for waiting so long and
playing it so cool -- and I might never have recognized
her extraordinary qualities. Or she might've decided I
was hostile or too abrasive ("smart-ass") and written me
off right at the start. Could easily have happened.

-- Now she awaits me naked up in the loft at B-2.
I'm hooked and I'm convinced she's hooked too. To most
of her friends we're such an obviously splendid match
the entire support network (also known as the "vetting
corps") would go into shock if we didn't make it (and
then after the breakup would face a tough rehab job with
their Zoelie). And -- well, I haven't touched on our
talk about the delicate situation with Aida, the best
bud who appears more afraid than ever she's being booted
off the ever-spinning Zoelie Trope. But must go.

[Jyze in Love]

S5

Jyzin' with Z. She's right here. In blue-denim
cutoffs, purple tank top, gauzy lime shirt. Nibbling on
an avocado sandwich, gearing up to start in on -- jyzin'
with G! (Dons her granny specs and draws her bare feet
up on the bench, leans against the old brick wall to her
right.)

This at the ORB cafe, basement of the only real
bookstore, the hidden corner way in back. Not my usual
favorite table (which stands empty and better lit
directly across the room) and not the one adjacent to it
where I dressed down, so to speak, her ghost on the
night we were originally supposed to meet for the very
first time (until she canceled the meeting), but rather
the one where we did the short bristly lunch of our
second meeting.

And how come this table now? Because here's better
for sneaking a little nookie, that's why. Crass idea
but also inspired. (And not even my idea. Hers, up in
the loft a few hours ago.)

Fine afternoon for a stroll, blue and summery, and
so we took one. Hunting the whole way for a birthday
gift for Z's friend Tobey. (Finally found an African
necklace at a shop just up the street from here, thirty
bucks for thirty beads for Tobey who's at least partly
of African origin herself and turning thirty.)

Ooh, this Z always does blaze away so impressively.
Born to jyze, I'll say it again. Zip zip zip -- as with
the sword of Zorro slashing out that other celebrated Z.
(And I count eight, nine, yes ten neatly pedicured toes
on the bench, each bearing a perfect little candy-apple-

red toenail in the shape of a waning gibbous moon. Feet
of the fabled twelve toes of yore, and only now, as of
yesterday, am I clear exactly where the extra two used
to be: between big toe and standard index toe -- if
"index" is the correct term for a toe that's seldom
needed to point with) (she doesn't know about that for
sure, she says now, but she knows the toe I mean).

At least an hour we've got here, two max, by mutual
collaborative agreement. (And I lean left to do some
"reiki" on her left calf. Reiki, the healing touch: in
which she once took a certified training course. And
what's to heal? Right now not much, calf or elsewise.
Other hours, maybe something. But later for that.)

Big this entry, news of Z's meeting with her lawyer
friend Jenny L. Jenny will do a proper internet search
for evidence that Lady S has actually divorced me (as
opposed to merely threatening/promising to). If she
can't find any, the easiest and wisest next step for me
is to file for divorce just in case. As part of this
process Jenny will arrange to run newspaper ads
attempting to locate Lady S in her latest known city of
residence in the U.S. and her city of birth overseas
(which is probably where she is right now, but I have no
address or phone number for her and no way to track down
either). Such ads almost always fail, but, says Jenny,
"The judges do like to see you jump through that hoop."

The basic cost of such a fail-safe divorce would be
$130 plus the price of the ads. And Jenny's making a
gift of her services in the name of her longtime friend
and Asian women's group cofounder Zoelie B.

But next week for that, when I'll be talking with
Jenny. Meanwhile, since last jyze session, lots and
lots of loving, a couple of comes for me, including the
first ever up in the loft (with Z, that is, and for that
matter with anyone, at least in its present location),
and a couple of dozen for her, and also a couple of near
meltdowns over the sex issue, each headed off by a
timely J-slinger ejac. "It just kills me that you won't
put your penis in me." ("Won't" isn't quite it. But
still haven't for more than a few brief visits, and all

of those ending ignominiously. "Wilts the stilt."
Handjobs only for ejacs. This morning she attempted a
blowjob, came close to popping a third G-come for the
week, but then another inexplicable G-wanger foozle.)
     -- Hi Zoelie! She be jyzin' away. But I do know
she's a bit uneasy about the way our tandem spree's going
so far simply because we're keeping the results private
on both sides until after it's over. The things she used
to tell me, the poems she used to write me, the notes and
lists and cards (and poems!) she used to shove under my
office door, it appears she's now diverting the impulse
and energy that once went for all those into jyze. And
suddenly she seems to be feeling much more self-conscious
about virtually everything she's doing. (Jyze alertness,
I'd call it, and say it's terrific.) But is she happy
anyway? Well I'd sure like to believe so.
     Back then, four and a half months ago when her
ghost sat in for her here (as noted in J-week #12), that
was the eighter of the first brinksmanship, no question
about it. And this weekend right here, the current one,
she's now dubbed our "first post-brinksmanship weekend."
She's appreciating my vow to swear off the nasty habit.
Or anyway says as much as of a few moments ago.
                           *
     -- I've just fessed up to her I'm spewing total
nonsense in here. And though we leaned in close with
nookie hopes, the unforeseen presence of an interloper
who suddenly appeared and stretched out supine on the
same bench we're sitting on, his head a foot from my
right hip, his cheeks stubbled and his red-rimmed eyes
wide open and staring up at the ceiling, is proving to
be a major inhibiting factor. Impressive mop of curly
black hair he has, though, undeniably. -- And Z's
saying she's already all jyzed out for this session.
But the good news I'm also just learning is she's
decided to stay over at B-2 again tonight and thus we're
no longer so pressed for time. (And I did come up with
a name for a certain facial expression of hers as we
walked up here: "pricklenose." It proved to be a kind
of self-fulfilling coinage: hearing the word made her

wrinkle her nose in just that way and unawares, I'd
wager a bundle.)
*   *
Will try to do better; can't do much worse (but
maybe the only way to do better is to try to do worse --
meaning jyze away and forget all else). -- But don't
leave out that glowing crescent, say like a trimming
from one of Z's toenails but with the red polish scraped
off, hanging right now in the upper right quadrant of my
peripheral vision, high in the nearest B-2 alley
windowpane. Or call it a hangmoon. Just as back in J-
week #12 Comet Zoelie was roaring into view out there
with seemingly high symbolic import, except in that case
I never did view the astral body itself.
What's new? Fine weekend. Finest yet maybe. Full
passion again burning, both parties, I'm convinced.
Last night we polished off the rest of the
"Sandefjord family rose'" and she sang for me, though
not until I turned my chair around so she faced my back.
Warbled into my ear and with lots of amorousness too,
loving tongue action, lips exploring nape, "Embraceable
You" five straight times. (The other tunes on the
rehearsal albums she either didn't know well enough or
we lacked the lyrics for them or both.) Then up to the
loft, eleven o'clock already, but she wasn't too tired
for a little horseplay if I didn't take too long getting
up there. I didn't. Again it was a case of my hard-on
foozling but this time she was in "selfish/lazy/spoiled"
mode and the foozle didn't seem to matter much, if at
all (well, surely at least a little, or I hope so); and
then in the morning she set out to right the balance --
and with her tongue yet -- and this time the foozle
mattered more, but still probably not a helluva lot.
She'd like to roll the dice again for a new I-Ching
reading, this one to clarify the existing "innocence
hexagram." Just what can she and can't she talk about
with me? I keep trying to persuade her to let go of her
worries about this vexed foozle factor (recognizing it's
no easy task) and she's again agreed to try. The next
meltdown, she vowed, won't occur for either three or six

weeks, depending on the dictates of the revised hexagram
(and what the criteria are this time I have no idea).
     Original plan for the day: no horseplay, back to Z-
turf by bus in the early a.m., "parallel play" while
she worked on her "biopiracy" review, then at one p.m.
to Paz and Tobey's for the birthday party. After that
a mall stop to pick up an ordered book that had come in,
then back to her place for more "parallel play" while
she finished up the review, and I'd leave at five p.m.
to begin our two days apart as per the new protocol.
     What actually happened: horseplay at the beginning
and end, the bus ride late in the morning rather than
early, no more than a couple of hours of "parallel
play" tops and I left at seven p.m. instead of five.
Otherwise, as scheduled. And in any case, delightful.
     Cloudless day it was, mid eighties, U.S. Navy jets
screaming overhead in performance for the summerfest
multitudes (and just barely overhead in Z's hood; low
enough and loud enough to trigger half a dozen car
alarms near her building). At the birthday party
several attendees set up their folding chairs in a
wading pool the better to cool badminton-scorched heels
(and Z and I both flailed crazily about on opposing
teams, completely missing the birdie more often than
hitting it). The birthday girl seemed to go for the
African necklace (she being of entirely African descent,
it turns out, though raised as an adoptee in a Eurusan
family). For Paz, Tobey's partner and a recent
graduate, Z brought a bottle of champagne (Paz being
Asiusan, mixed Japanese/Filipino descent I think,
female; and perhaps half the attendees hetero couples
and half gay or lesbian, including Jess and Gwen) -- Z a
good friend to a lot of folks and in any case a very
good friend to have, warm and lively and generous and
thoughtful (she handmade a card for Tobey, her utility
coworker who until recently assisted her with the
newsletter).
     This a barbecue, I gobbled down stick after stick
of savory chicken shishkebab. And after badminton Z
announced she'd discovered a previously unknown sports-

related competitive streak in herself and she wants to
take me on one-on-one, but it must involve a sport which
neither of us knows anything about. (She did laugh big,
as did most everyone, when one of my crazed attempts at
a birdie fetch brought down the net while also landing
my foot in a large puddle with a cannonball splash.)

A stop at the usual co-op market on the way back to
her place and then outside as we nibbled on ice-cream
bars (half the chocolate dip slid off mine and plopped
onto my dressiest summer shirt) she said her auricles
and ventricles were aching because we'd soon have to
part. Lots of smooching as we drove along, she at the
wheel and her hand in my crotch (making a sexy sight for
a bus driver, she remarked, as a bus rumbled in place to
my right with the driver peering obliquely down through
our passenger window while we waited at a stoplight).
Talked about boy was she feeling lusty, too bad we had
the five o'clock deadline and it was now four-fifty.
Then at her door she said, "You know, it's been a long
time since we've horsed around in my bed. You wanna?"

Two hours of deadline-busting loving followed.
Sweaty, sticky, red-faced kind (especially me, pale Cawk
night worker now laughably sunburned). Open-eyed
orgasms (hers) and fierce passionate gazes and out
popped a couple more tears (mine) of bliss. Truth! And
a glorious hard-on popped out too -- veins, ridges,
twisted craning head -- bells and whistles -- the works!
-- but, sure, again deflated way too soon. I did show
her some more secrets of how to pleasure me, though, and
this time she was more receptive even while noting that
one of the topics for her next meltdown would surely be
the extreme jealousy she's feeling toward my lovers who
succeeded in ways she's been failing, turn-on-wise, as
she sees it anyway, and understandably (but I swear I'm
plenty pleased with what she does, possibly because,
it's true, she makes me feel as though I must be the
most skillful and sexiest lover ever for what I can draw
out of her almost without trying).

Don't think either of us has any doubt now we're
paired up forever.

    -- Meanwhile she's facing new troubles with her pal
Aida, who's being "pookie" because Z's seeing so much
less of her, and they're best friends of some twenty
years' standing. Aida wants more time with her and she
also wants Z to dish to her about us, Z and me, with the
same unconstrained openness she's shown in dishing about
(or dissing?) past lovers. And Aida unhelpfully (from
my perspective) tells Z that she, Z, is "naive" in
certain expectations she has about our relationship and
also in trusting me too much too quickly.

    My take on all this? Mainly I'm trying to avoid
causing further trouble between these two (liking Aida
a lot except for this one crucial area) while also
trying to protect some "sacred private space" for Z and
me. For a while no doubt all three of us will be
ruminating on this matter. Z will spend more time with
Aida (starting next Saturday afternoon or the one after
that), Z and I will invite Aida to go out with us,
either as a threesome or double-dating if Aida's on-
again, off-again lover Pavi should happen to be on-again
at the time. (Pavi's a playboy type, Z tells me, from a
wealthy clothes-importing family of "India Indians.")
And Jenny the lawyer, who knows both Z and Aida quite
well, on Friday told Z she thinks the onus should
primarily fall on Aida to adapt to the changed situation
with Z, and Z seems to agree at least for now.

    (Regarding my own divorce dealings with Jenny, by
the way, Z has taken herself out of the loop. She's
done her bit to help out and now it must be entirely
my thing. Which I think is exactly the right move on
her part and told her as much and thanked her for it.)

    -- And how boggling it is to realize, as I'm still
capable of doing though just barely, only five months
ago I didn't know any of these people, and now, already,
I feel my life would be painfully diminished if not just
Z but the group as a whole and doubly so certain members
in particular weren't part of it. And not just the ones
I've mentioned in here but at least a dozen others as
well. So no doubt about it, you, Zoelie B., you've
turned my life right around and filled it up in splendid

ways. (And I'm recalling how I wrote in that wild week
after her first call that I hoped my deviant doings
would at least serve to appeal to her social-worker
side. I don't know that they have -- maybe so, though,
I must admit -- but I don't doubt at all the results
have been highly therapeutic for me.)

Also: she says she's now ready to talk about the
other women in my life "up till you-know-who" (meaning
my "eighteen-year locus," that is, Lady U). My own
hunch is that the topic of former lovers will prove too
hot to handle (and I'm including hers in this too) until
she and I have managed to become bona-fide, fully carnal
lovers ourselves. (This bizarre coupling. More and
more I lose sight of just how odd it is. The way we
met. Our hot but weird sex life. Our extreme
differences and extreme similarities. The way we carry
on like moonstruck teens. But drop all the outer-world
context and we just blend into each other's interior
comfort zones. Weird and yet wun-wun-wunnerful.)

What other quick items? She'd like me to write her
a five-page autobiography like the one she did two years
ago for grad school. (Huh-uh, no chance.) She thinks
I'm "cutest" in the morning, when I supposedly look more
than ever like that rumple-faced French actor with the
big nose and my voice sounds like that of what's-his
name, the Hollywood B-movie stalwart from way back,
Waldo something ("hoarse and throaty and foggy").
(Groan and rolling eyeballs.) During our schedule-
busting nookie session earlier tonight she announced we
deserved such a romp as a reward for having successfully
made it through "our first post-brinksmanship weekend."
(But is she even slightly aware how she does a form of
brinksmanship herself with her cool cutoffs?) She likes
to point out women "of a certain age" who "have fun with
their looks" (and of course doesn't fail to mention you
never encounter the phrase "a man of a certain age").

And: she lost a bet with me about the spelling of
"petard" (as in "hoist by one's own --") and so I now
have a Y up for an "unqualified YES," meaning, she says,
when I have all three letters I can ask her to do

anything I want and she'll do it.

     (Aldo, not Waldo, Ray, that should be, the foggy-
voiced actor. How could I forget Aldo Ray's name for
even a single paragraph? And then why break a jyze rule
to mention it? And then mention it again! The shame!)

     (And now at almost midnight it's still hot enough
that I'm sitting here in just shorts and the sweat's
dripping down my chest from where my chin's pressed
against my lower throat because of the odd jyzing
posture I've somehow twisted myself into with the cedar
board balanced against an arm of the chair while tipped
upward by my right knee.)

     As for the "selfish/lazy/spoiled mode," this was
her self-description for the way she is during
lovemaking. And: by and large it's true. Not all of
the time but much of the time, and especially when her
engine goes into overdrive. And I just shrug at this
truth. Doesn't matter! Because: it's the flip side of
her extreme responsiveness and her mondo orgasmic gift.
These she can tamp way down in trying to do right by me
but at doing right in this respect she remains almost a
beginner. As noted before, she simply never had to
learn how it's done: she was that much of a turn-on for
just about all her many bed partners. And is now for me
as well, or should be, except for my "psychosexual
pookieness," which is to say I'm a big frustration to
her, a vexation, a challenge, indeed just as I am to
myself. I make both of us pout and fume and scheme.

     But I do believe I'm getting there, slowly,
gradually, incrementally; and I think she is too. It's
reciprocal! We're moving right along! And meanwhile
having a helluva good time! (The metaphor I used in
describing how I'd change my ways for her featured a
bush or small tree we saw near her house last week, its
branches weighed down by small stones dangling on twine
slings for bonsai-like shaping. "Topiary art." At
first the stones looked like unusual gray fruits. "The
stone tree." Shape me, baby, eight to the limb!
-- Also likened the branches to the melismatically bent
notes of the fabulous jazz and jyze diva Zoelie B.)

S6

Being bad for the good of jyze. Or just for the
good of bad, period. But here I am at our "Meet Cafe"
out in Z's turf, I'm plopped down in the same spot
across the table from the same wooden bench where she
sat that first day (and burned those gorgeous peeps into
mine as we absurdly disputed whose were darker) -- but
the joint will be closing in less than thirty minutes,
I've just learned. Poor planning. Laziness.

(The half moon dangling overhead tonight is an
unusual sight, looking raggedy in the haze like one of
the hemiglobular loaves of homemade bread for sale here
but after being torn down the middle by hand.)

Tuesday night. (This was supposed to be going down
yesterday.) Just rode the bus out. Moments before that
I called to let Z know I'd be arriving after she'd gone
to bed. She pouted (did a "phonemoan") and I'm feeling
almost depraved not to be with her right now.

Got to get my sorry-ass jyze act together. Got to
make this spree work right. Got to render this truly
the Peak Prime Time it proclaimedly already is (and the
Absolute Tiptop Pinnacle of same being just eighteen
days away).

Haven't seen the woman since Sunday. These have
been the two off days. But we've talked on the phone
six or seven times, exchanged numerous voicemails, and
I've sent her -- (and now my J-stick goes dry and I have
to switch to the scratchy backup, No. 6 -- criminy!) --
sent her five postcards and a vamp letter and received a
card from her. All's well with us, I think, or at least
as much so as it can be given my ongoing e-dys. Which

is to say: we seem to have regained our basic precarious
balance. -- Or quasi-choate symbiotic homeostasis,
could say.
     Before coming here I stood in the doorway of the
magazine shop as I did on that first day (and have done
quite a few times since). Reliving. Nothing new to say
about it really. (Best moment of my life? Could be.
Certainly it's a major contender.)
     -- All chairs except mine have executed half-flips
onto tabletops while I wasn't looking. I'm forced to
move on. (Hot muggy night too. Can I find another spot
to keep on jyzin' before starting the long uphill hike?)
                              *
     -- This might work. Nor was the search all that
arduous. It's a table in the sidewalk-cafe section of
the same establishment, maybe twenty feet due north of
the seat I've just abandoned. White metal lawn
furniture out here, a large parasol planted in the
middle of each table, mine blocking all usable light
except the foot-wide arc of street-lamp lumens in which
the J-book basks, the shadow of the refractory J-stick
No. 6 jerking sharply and scratchily along.
     I'm guessing they leave this furniture out here
overnight. As of right now most of the outdoor tables
are still occupied even though the cafe itself is empty
and officially closed (but the lights are still on) (and
yes, I see my former chair riding upside-down on the
table now -- table of our Meet Day! -- and a shaven-
headed cleanup dude's about to push a mop under it to
clear away all J-slinger leavings, if any, along with
those of previous occupants of course, sanitizing it for
the early-morning shift of, I presume, mostly techies).
     Such a sweet summer night. Such sweet memories
lurk around here. And of such recent vintage too! Is
this premature nostalgia or what? (And if so it's no
less sweet. Maybe even sweeter.)
     And will this soon become my new hood? A good
chance it will. Glancing around, I say I like it just
fine. It's gentrifying, yes, but all by myself and
without even trying -- just by showing up -- I might be

able to set the process back a year or two.

Zoelie on the phone today floated an "immodest proposal": she'd like us to live in a hood where we could become active community members. This is something she's always wanted for herself -- to put down roots -- but she's moved too often to have a real shot at it (and been too distracted with other interests). -- And me too; I've harbored the same sort of participatory yearnings. Admittedly I fear having to give up too much time. Wastage. Other ideals may override. Be wholly devoted to jyze (itself a form of social responsibility, I'd like to believe, and usually do, though never without a caveat or two). -- Or maybe not. Maybe a way to be out and about with Z.

-- And now I see these sidewalk chairs and tables will be moved inside after all, and soon. Stacked in the entrance hallway. If I don't skedaddle I'll be next, to emerge tomorrow in zigzag shape, a foldable two-dimensional version of myself ready to joust with the techies. Handy for compact apartment living too.

Pause again right here ---

*   *

-- So now try this. Top of the outdoor staircase at the east end of Z's apartment building, back side. Sprawled crosswise, leaning against a railing, feet resting on the top two stairs, thigh-tops serving as jyzing platform. Able to go at it here because the wall lamp mounted outside unit 400's door a few feet to my left is quite bright -- maybe twice the lumens reach the J-book as did from the cafe street lamp (which to be sure was brighter but considerably farther away).

Next door down, meaning westward, No. 401, opens on the pad of one Zoelie B.

Strolling up the long gradual incline on this splendid flower-scented night I passed several large apartment buildings whose mailbox names I checked out back when I was trying to come up with an address for Z -- my "stalker" days, now grown to near Jack the Ripper proportions as the legend takes on a life of its own -- and that address I was searching for then of course turned out to be this one right here. I gave up the search about two blocks too soon.

Enjoyed tonight's stroll. Tranquil residential streets, just at the hour when a few interior house lights are blinking off here and there but most are still shining. And on a night like this lots of windows are open and you can sometimes hear snippets from soundtracks of real lives in action (though mostly just active enough to be watching TV or playing computer games, it would appear, and mainly just TV or bang-bang game sounds audible along with the occasional toilet flush). Ran into no fewer than four cats squatting on driveways or sidewalks still warm from the August sun. Twice almost blundered into thorny stray shoots emerging at eye level from blackberry patches and rosebushes. Several yards were so overgrown or the flower gardens in such climactic state I had no choice but to make a wide detour into the street.

Passed J&G's house. They were asleep already, apparently, and I was flashing back to the delicious if also somewhat fraught times Z and I house-sat there and slept with the doggies in their, J&G's -- but also the doggies', yes -- bed. Also noticed a pair of apparent lovers going at it in a car across the street from J&G's place and wondered if this might be an instance of the late-night "hooker invasion" Jess has reportedly been fuming over, caused by the opening of an XXX-rated video store on the main drag several blocks to the west (but to me the lovers looked too young for that). And passed Z's car parked in its usual (if no one beats her to it) shady spot right across from that nasty Jimmy's garden apartment. (Sunday afternoon we heard him bellow, "Tonight I'm gonna get me a mouthful of titty!")

Gazing out at the neighborhood. Mostly single-family houses, some quite large. Residents of Z's building, J&G say, are looked down upon as "the apartment people" by the homeowner types, which of course J&G are themselves. (But just a few feet behind where I sit now the Katgrrrl had a great time on the Fourth with Aida's kid, Charles, watching Jimmy set off

bottle rockets in the street below.) (And now I'm
contributing to this joint's scuzzy rep, holding forth
out here looking like a brazen voyeur or maybe a note-
taking nark, because you can see into all sorts of
windows from this vantage and I've actually spotted one
woman glancing curiously and maybe anxiously at me, a
thirtyish spiky-haired pajama-wearer (blue and white
horizontal prisoner-like stripes) straight across on the
top floor of the annex -- where Z has suggested, by the
way, we might find a suitable apartment for ourselves.
-- And would this pajama woman or anyone else call the
cops on me? I doubt it. But it could happen. "Jail
bait." If there's a sudden break in the jyze here,
that'll be the likely cause as I scramble for unit 401.)
     And what's been going down since the last general
update? Let's see. -- First note this: Z's friend Lee
M. appears to be reconciling with wife Carol -- already!
-- and that's a relief (he and Z have been engaging in a
torrid e-mail exchange during the crisis and he's called
her twice to talk about it but I'm okay with this, being
persuaded no rivalry's involved here). Matters with
Aida, though, are still not looking good. She bridled
when Z wanted to see her alone only Saturday afternoon,
not also that same evening for dinner and a play at the
Filipino center (and seemed as well to take offense at a
card Z sent her). So now I've suggested that Z see Aida
alone in the afternoon and then I join them for the
evening portion, and Z will propose this when the two of
them meet for their more or less regularly scheduled
weekly lunch tomorrow. (But their dispute may get
worse, I'm afraid, before it gets better.)
     (Oops, a cigarette's poking out from the balcony
just a few feet below. A glowing ember, a little
curl of smoke. I could almost reach down with my foot
and tap the ash off. A right hand, quite large but
triply or maybe quadruply beringed and with nails
painted incandescent blue. She, I'll say, doesn't seem
to realize I'm up here. Would likely drop dead of
fright if she did. -- Cigarette now waving like a
miniature conductor's baton, rhythmically, as if in

time to music I'm not hearing (maybe she's wearing buds
or earphones?). -- And more lights blinking out in
surrounding houses and apartments. And the kid's
wailing in unit 402, the Lummi couple living on the far
side of Z's place, the ones we worry about keeping awake
with our rutting racket.)

And Z herself snoozing away maybe two dozen feet
from here at most. Waiting for me, in a way. So why am
I not in there? Well, because if I were I'd face a
familiar no-win situation. She needs her sleep but
she's not pleased if I stay up by myself (though this
might be changing, and I hope it is). It's simply far
too early for me to go to bed. If I did I'd be restless,
she wouldn't be able to sleep either, we'd start in on
the loving and once started we'd probably be unable to
stop for hours. That's just how it is. And I'm the
sleep coach. It's my duty to see to it that she gets
her solid eight.

(Cigarette discarded now -- flicked unceremoniously
to the sidewalk two stories below, exploding in a sparky
little burst before bouncing into the weeds. No
brushfire smoke so far. -- And heard a door close down
there, seemingly right below 401. Which may explain why
Z sometimes sniffs smoke coming out of the vent in her
bathroom. -- And I guess I'm the last line of defense
out here, the de facto fire warden. "That's right,
officer, it's my job to make sure the place doesn't burn
down. That's why I'm stationed out here.")

A few notes:
** Last night Z told me about a book she read as a
kid and the profound impression it left on her. It was
a story about two little Afrusan girls exposed to racial
segregation at a water fountain which bore a "whites
only" sign. One of the girls wasn't bothered by this
but the other became angry and stayed angry and couldn't
suppress her rage and as a consequence soon got into
trouble; and this second girl was the one Z identified
with. Her own rage over racial injustice in particular
has both energized and stigmatized her all her life.
How to handle rage and a tendency to lose her temper and

alienate potential allies has been a focus of her
therapy over the decades and also of her grad studies in
the past two years. Currently she's "trying to see
everyone as a potential ally and treat them that way."
Fortunately for me, I'm included. In fact the new
campaign, she says, is an attempt to universalize her
efforts with me. "If you," she jokes (I think jokes),
"why not the world?" She's even trying it with her
boss. No discernible results there so far, she reports.
     ** Also she talked about how her independent
spirit sometimes conflicts jarringly with her attempts
to get more in tune with her Filipina side. As she
says: "Most Filipino men can hardly stand me." Aida,
she noted, has pretty much the same problem and this has
always been one of the bases of their friendship.
They've both had roughly the same number of Asian lovers
-- two or three -- and Aida's one and only husband, now
ex, is a Cawk. "And you remind her of him maybe a
little too much -- especially your ideas about money."
(I compare Z's love/hate problems concerning her
Filipina heritage with my own regarding my maternal
roots in the antebellum U.S. south. Both involve the
opposite-sex parent and the nostalgic appeal of certain
aspects of politically retrograde "traditional" values.)
     ** When Z stays at my place she now does her
morning meditation sitting cross-legged on my blue
plastic gym mat. So yesterday in a phone message I said
we'd been apart so long I'd been reduced to sniffing the
blue gym mat. Her return message: "Better you should
sniff my nightgown or my pillow like I sniff yours here
when I'm lonely for you. You're already getting too
much exposure to plastic." (She takes very seriously
the possibility such exposure could be causing impotence
in human males, and especially this one right here, just
as it appears to do in certain bird and amphibian
populations. And she wants to lay out forty bucks for a
special window screen which will reduce the flow of
exhaust fumes into B-2 from the viaduct and the alley:
she suspects these too could be devirilizing me. And
she thinks I shouldn't be eating meals microwaved in the

plastic containers they're sold in -- which actually I
don't do, but only because the chicken and turkey pot
pies I buy are sold in cheapo cardboard containers.
-- And besides, my reproductive apparatus has worked
just fine whenever I've auto-tested it. I'm all but
certain plastics are not the culprit. Which of course
isn't to say they're not the culprits for a whole lot of
other bad stuff going down worldwide these days.)
     ** To me and the Katgrrrl both she likes to say,
"I love you wildly, madly, passionately," imitating the
bad movie actor -- who was it again? (Not that Jyze can
say anyway.) She thought she detected displeasure on my
face when I overheard her use these words with Kat on
the phone, but not so. Rather I was touched. Just as I
was when she called Kat "my little chickadee," which she
also sometimes calls me but playfully substituting a
sultry "big bad" or "big freakin'" for "little."
     (The Lummi baby's crying again. Maybe I'm tired
enough to go in now? Surely any danger of a fire has
passed.) (But I do love to climb into bed with Z
regardless of my sorry shag performances. That's
what's so strange. I almost don't feel like the e-
dysfunct klutz I've actually become. For hours, even
for days at a time I can and do forget. Or almost.
Somehow bracket it off. Know the hex is there, know
what it is, but pay it minimal heed.)
     -- Well anyway the height-of-summer festival is
over. Now we're into the dog days, I guess, except
hereabouts true specimens of same are few and far
between. This afternoon, though, I was dragging a
little from the heat, probably about as much as I ever
have in this city.
     Yeah, time to stop. Belt buckle biting into belly
from my bending over this J-book too long, glutes
cramping up, eyes burning, and I thought I just saw a
mosquito. And I'm hungry. So the rest of the stuff
I've been saving for tonight I'll keep on hold.
Shouldn't do this but must. Hope the next round will
provide some openings for me to tend to "old business."
(And by the way: no more smoke down there and no fire

either as far as I can tell. And the window where the
woman in the prison stripes appeared has long since gone
dark, so no remaining potential thrills there either.)

S7

(And it's mushy. And it's sappy. And it's goopy.)
     For starters only. As here I lounge pretty much
naked in the green armchair (except for a towel draped
around my neck) just sixty-three minutes before I'm due
to meet Z at the downtown library. And then to walk her
home, that is, to unit B-2, right here, though she
insists such escort service is unnecessary during
daylight hours (but does appreciate being escorted at
all hours regardless, and each time she's tried walking
here alone even in midafternoon she's wound up with a
gritty story or two to tell).
     Not a word from her all day. I was tempted to ring
her up at the office but thought better of it. Today
she lunched with Aida -- a kind of showdown, from the
way she described it in advance. If it turned out
badly, the fallout could harm us. Or maybe not.
Certainly she wouldn't want that, but her ties with Aida
go deep. (This is the same Aida who once said she'd
marry Z in a heartbeat if she, Z, were a man.)
     Meanwhile the story of last night at Z's place.
Want to lay it right out. (Nothing at all earthshaking
about it. Just a frame to hang some jyzey details on.)
And will do so -- but later, for both frame and details.
Or anyway will try. If new stories don't arise to crowd
out the old. As I've noticed they tend to do more than
ever under spree conditions.
     Now dress quickly, dry hair, charge almost exactly

one mile down to the hideaway (and even while still
licking peanut-buttery lips and suddenly realizing I'm
tired, as indeed I should be given that last night's
sleep totaled less than four hours, plus one more after
I staggered back here this morning) (and I'll mention
I'm keeping up so far on the to-do list for the week
which I drew up Monday morning, although I've still
failed, despite several attempts, to reach Jenny L. to
authorize the search on the divorce -- and laundry I've
put off until next week).
*   *

Kwikjyze again, yes, and no doubt under even
shakier auspices. Hideaway. The hole's twenty-five
minutes this time.

Oddly enough a party is rollicking away in the
south-atrium lobby forty or fifty feet down the hall and
even odder it's a campaign kickoff for Merrill F.,
sober-sided city-council candidate (and not one of Z's
favorite politicians despite his advertised greenness,
because on her other pet issues of race and class he's a
late starter, poorly informed, pretty much your typical
liberal Eurusan guy -- same lamentable type to which I'm
now an officially Z-sanctioned exception, though still
being that type, of course, in many respects, Cawkness
not least; and she's been following through admirably on
her campaign to see "the world" this way, incidentally,
but for sure Merrill F. presents an unusually tough
challenge). -- Z herself, meanwhile, is serving on a
panel at the mayoral candidates night for a women's
group, I hope asking lots of tough questions as I can
personally attest she's highly skilled at doing. ---
*   *

Home now, B-2. And what's happening is: true
tandem jyze, she on the couch and me in the green
armchair. And outside in the alley a few feet away a
wailing woman Z says she identifies with is pathetically
begging a guy named Tim to tell her exactly how she
supposedly did him wrong (this coming from the cab of a
maroon pickup with idling engine and open driver's-side
window in which a backward-facing red ball cap is

visible). Yeek, sure does sound like something they wouldn't want a couple of material-hungry jyzers to be listening in on.

Z in her gray "Mestizas Rule" nightshirt. She's asking me when was the second time I "threatened" her with my alleged brinksmanship stuff. "Do you beat your wife?" kind of question, innit? (Her right foot resting on mine. Me in my "punky" torn black running shorts, the gear of last resort; she says she likes them because she can see my "gnarly whatzis" hanging out.) -- Now declares she can jyze only what she remembers and she simply can't recall my inviting her during J-week #13 to come see me after her graduation when, as she'd told me before, she could finally "be spontaneous," say some Saturday night in July or August.

And here we are, a Wednesday night in August. And mama, look at us now! (And VAROOM off roars the truck.)

-- Her granny glasses. Even with them on she still jyzes big. And fast. Flipping page after page, almost like the riffling calendar in an old-school movie transition. The very image of a jyze spree. Or equally apropos, the very image of the Z-woman in search of a daytimer opening for our original meet date.

-- In her sexy white pajama-style outfit she met me at the library tonight. I escorted her home by my usual perilous two a.m. walking route, but at eight p.m. in high summer it's almost a stroll in the park. She told me about the day's hissy fit at work, a utilitywide meeting having to do with hazardous waste, and when one of the speakers pulled out a can of spray glue to use on her visuals, Z objected: toxic chemicals in that spray! Moments later Z briefly left the room and on her return encountered a big new cloud of the same spray. One of those legendary Z tirades followed. Shortly after that the group broke up into discussion subgroups and the guy who came up to sit next to Z asked, "Do you bite?" "Not if I can have a bite of your bagel," she said, sparking loud laughter that dissipated the tension. "After that I said some really good stuff and I was charming all the way to the end. Before grad school I never could've done it -- I would've stomped out."

Once every week or two, sometimes more but rarely less, I hear about incidents like this one. The woman can be a load and then some -- a fiery advocate for sure -- feisty as they come, yeah. Doubly or triply feisty at times, I'll venture to say. (And of course I'm pleased she tells me about these incidents in depth, though sometimes I'm also discombobled -- if not chastised and nonplussed. And glad as an officially designated "beloved ally" I'm now only a secondary or accidental target of such outbursts myself, at least in theory.)

"It's almost ten," she tells me. Meaning: bedtime.

(First a "hnn-hnn-hnn." This is the "pant-grunt" made by chimps to indicate subordination to higher-ranking chimps. We read about it in the science section of last night's paper. "First one to pant-grunt is a devolved primate!")

*

(She's in the bathroom now. Guess I'll make ready to join her in the loft. Will I be tired enough to stay up there for the rest of the night? Maybe. If not I'll try to return to these pages to say a few words about last night. Or tonight. Or both. Otherwise tomorrow an even bigger backlog. The slippery slope. -- But here she is. And says, all bright-faced and foamy-mouthed (toothpaste kind): "Should I invite you to come to bed?" "Hey, not a bad idea." "Well then consider it done." "Well consider me up there RIGHT NOW" -- and UP HE MANIACALLY LEAPS.) ---

*   *

Next afternoon. And an hour ago she called "Just because I was feeling mushy and I couldn't stop myself." We chatted for a few minutes (nonmushily on her side, or so I thought; finally I asked when she'd be getting to the mushy part and she said she'd been "oozing it silently the whole time"). And earlier yet, when I awakened, not long after she'd left for work some two hours late, I found a series of her pup-tent signs starting in the loft and leading down all the way to the

314

hall door, and they said this: "Guess / what / I love / you / here & now / all / of you / with my / whole / heart" -- and then a yellow stickie attached to the last tent saying, "No ifs ands or buts!"

Yet...last night in bed another near meltdown. When my sorry old man-flesh showed few signs of life in response to her ministrations (trying out some new moves I suggested over the weekend) she went almost catatonic for a while. When I asked why (more as a protest really, because of course I knew all too well why) she said, "I can't tell you because it's what I'm forbidden to talk about" -- by our "Light Music" treaty, she meant. A long silence followed. Finally I asked: "Is there anything I can do?" She: "No."

For an hour or two, misery -- restlessness, silence, thrashings. But then somehow we beat it. Again I asked her to bring the matter up for discussion less often. Again she said she feels like a miserable failure in bed and she's never felt that way before. Again I tried to convince her she makes me plenty happy even when I don't show it by erecting or ejacking or introiting or intromitting or whatever (you know, PUSHING ON IN AND SPURTING) -- and that, yes, I still believe all that'll work itself out eventually. And in the end we made up and shifted back into loving mode, for much of which time I was in a surprisingly erect or semierect state which she in turn completely ignored -- and truly it didn't matter. (But how bizarre all this e-dys stuff is, and true, I really can't blame her at all for losing it every now and then as she does; I'm just grateful she can find her way back to a more merciful view. -- But I still wish we could hit on a less volatile way to deal with the matter. As she pointed out, though: "At least I got through it without going totally hysterical.")

A couple of oddities in the lovemaking. For the first time she was almost completely quiet during a series of O's (she'd told me she could be and she disliked the look the guy who lives in the unit directly above B-2 -- "Claire Voyant" when in drag -- gave her in

the lobby last week). And I told her I like her kissing
better when she doesn't open her mouth too wide, since
that overly tightens her marvelous full lips and
effectively removes their inner surfaces from the
action. She grumped a little about my becoming a "kiss
coach now" but immediately tried out the suggestion and
poutily said she "sort of" liked it. (She still opens
wide when she comes, though, jaw clenched, lips tight.)
    -- Earlier, I should note, she reported the lunch
with Aida had gone surprisingly well. Aida didn't even
mention her previously expressed displeasure with Z's
alleged inattention to her and so Z decided to let the
matter drop. (The previous night I'd learned of several
more upsetting things Aida had said. For Z the worst of
these was what appeared to be a hostile rhetorical
question of sorts: "Are you seeing him [me, this very
jyzer] as your last chance for romance? Because he's
really not, you know.")
    -- But time to start packing up. I'll have back at
it at the hideaway.

*   *

    And am ready to do so! And again in tandem with
Zoelie B.! Jyze in the key of Z!
    She who refused to enter this office the first time
she visited it -- claiming "shyness." Stood just
outside the door nervously pursing her lips and rolling
her eyes ceilingward. (Think I'll step over right now
and lay a big long juicy kiss on those fabulous lips.
See if it'll show up in her jyze account. Of course I
may not know for years, if ever, whether it does.
-- She's sitting in the brown armchair in the corner
beneath the floor lamp, feet tucked under her, black
calf-length skirt and gray blouse -- about four feet
away. Mmm, looking so fine. The row of jyze heroes
raptly gazing down at her from their frames on the wall
like first-row box-seat fans at a ballpark beholding a
superstar. -- And by the way, she'd misplaced the
building's after-hours combination and was lucky someone
happened to be leaving and would let her in. -- And she
still hesitates to come into the room, and not just

because the overhead lights are on. A touch of
claustrophobia maybe. Or maybe another irrepressible
shyness relapse.)

*

Did. Long full-lipped and almost full-tongued kiss
and then I pulled back to dub it "the kiss of
reflexivity." She: "Huh? What's that mean?" "You
remember, that book you put all the stickies in." "Oh,
that. ...That was a lot of meltdowns back."
     -- "By the end of this page," she's now saying, "I
won't be able to stand this music anymore." Some rowdy
hip-hoppy stuff from the next office south is rattling
the windows. A crew of Cawk computer geeks has recently
moved in there, and I guess at five o'clock they figure
everyone's gone home and therefore they can turn the
music way up. Shows how little time I've been putting
in here lately; never before have I encountered an
outburst this raucous. -- The place where we eventually
take up living together should be on a top floor, she's
just let me know. -- But the apartment she has now is
top floor and what's that gotten her? A cross-roof
prowler, that's what, along with huge heating bills.
-- And now she's turned my chairside radio back on,
classical music because the jazz station is in news
mode. Up, up, up goes the loudness until classical
succeeds in drowning out hip-hop (but only because hip-
hop must first pass through a brick wall).
     -- Tonight maybe she'll sing in my ear again.
We're set up for it at B-2, including a bottle of "our"
wine (the cinsault of our breakthrough day) and the
fakebook. (For my last letter to her I used a postage
stamp portraying a jazz great with whom her former jazz-
pianist boyfriend -- in whose ear she also sang, she
admits -- once studied. "Stamp with resonance!" I wrote
on the back of the envelope, with an arrow pointing at
the jazz great. -- Trying to suggest I'm in no way
reluctant to discuss romantic histories with her.)
     (And what about night before last after I stopped
jyzing on her balcony? Last chance to touch on that.
Right inside the 401 doorway another loving row of pup-

317

tent signs, a tray bearing fresh blueberries, a note, a
display of the five postcards I'd sent her which had
arrived in one big clump that day, and a stack of clips
(including an article titled "Care-to-Dance Team Rocks"
from the utility's internal newsletter, with a photo in
which she and I appear -- and I can just barely identify
with the guy who's me in that photo, and this is how it
usually is with photos of myself these days, and mirror
or window reflections as well, and even with my hair
almost fully recovered from the punk scalping she gave
it). Shoes off, in I go to give her a quick kiss which
lingers and lingers, four or five comes' worth
eventually -- just par for the course, pretty much,
really -- and at the end I'm still fully dressed above
the socks. Then talk, lots of it, mainly about the
troubles with Aida (I can almost hear the Z-Trope
roaring right above our heads as a kind of soundtrack --
one of the best belts for it shows them chasing each
other on motorcycles). And Z points out it's hard for
us to sleep on our first night back together after two
apart because "we're horny for words too -- to catch
up." Also she offers a new theory that my psychosexual
malfunctioning may be owing to "overstimulation of your
penis" and therefore she should cut back on the strokes
in that area, a notion I emphatically reject. And so to
sleep. And so to awaken three hours later -- she
already up. Meditates, stretches, showers, dresses as I
doze fitfully on. Then I suddenly cry "Swedeheart!,"
throw off the covers and bound naked into the kitchen to
embrace her. Gobble cereal. Dress. Load up, including
lots of her stuff to carry to my place, where we'll be
sleeping the next night (that is, last night). Leave
with her. Ride into town groggy and gasping for air on
the crowded bus she dubs "The Perfumed Nightmare" after
the excellent Filipino movie of that name (still one of
my all-time favorites just as it's one of hers). Then
stagger home as she rides on to the utility.)

     In brief, this is it: story of our days. Get down,
pack up, move on. Here too now. B-2 next.

[Absolute Tiptop Pinnacle - Jyzin' with Z]

S8

    Out for a stroll, it turns out. This not at all a
surprise either, since in advance I'd ruled out a
supermarket run. No need for one. And also, more to
the point, not enough cash (for no subsistence-living
hoarder's ever truly short on need). Instead just the
hollow form of a supermarket run, up to the "north pole"
and back, nothing bought, no stop at a market of any
kind, not even the bookstore. Exercise and that's it.
    The urge was upon me, though, to lay down some jyze
in one of the local watering holes on the way back (and
had been even before I left B-2, so I was prepared).
The semi-retro bar I tried first, but this being happy
hour on a Friday the place was too crowded and noisy
(and a baseball game was showing on all three TV
screens, our local lads who're caught up in a hot
pennant race). Kept on walking to the one other
neighborhood hangout in the top tier of jyze venues,
this one I'm sitting in now: the digi-cafe.
    No happy hour here. Lots of video monitors but all
are hooked to keyboards. No baseball game in sight.
Light crowd, the usual nerdy/arty mix. Really it's far
too fine a day to be inside at all, even for nerds and
artists not to mention jyzers. (A string of splendid
days spooling out, yes. For the past week I've been
looking to walk in the shade whenever possible, and for
most of the year I try to avoid it -- and doubly so, be
it noted, when I'm on my way home at night and there's
so much more of it: planetary-revolution shade of
course: Earth shade.)
    Also thinking how horny I am. The heat makes me

319

notice this more as I'm walking. Flesh swells and
droops, gets sweaty, prickly; abrasive rubbing provokes
lunkerish semiarousal and makes jeans seem tighter (and
they still seem that way now as I sit at a small round
platform table, traffic rolling by outside as refracted
peripherally through the seventy-two-pane "fly's-eye"
industrial windows, the only visible motion inside the
room being fingers stroking keyboards, one of which I
could easily punch the keys on myself through the
railing, a foot below the level of my table; the stubby
ringless and un-nail-polished male fingers down there
are now absentmindedly caressing a mouse).

Why particularly horny? A very sexy night with no
"release" for me (this being a weeknight) (and just the
way events unfolded) (the bizarro music now playing --
and it's been boisterously bouncing around the brick
walls since I came in, monster dueling church organs,
sounds like, with interspersed horror-house shrieks --
this bedlam has just got to be influencing the way these
words are going down).

-- Back at the hideaway last night, Z stepped over
to the desk when I snapped shut the J-book and kissed me
much the way I'd kissed her in the armchair, but she
kept going and started unbuttoning my shirt, slipped in
her hand and rubbed my stomach and chest (nipple
tweaking), then unbuckled my belt. First time she's
ever done this -- with me, I'm saying -- in a nonbedroom
setting. Leaning against me between my spread legs she
felt me stiffen up pretty much to the max, a tubular
ridge arcing diagonally across my left pants pocket.
Said she: "Well lookie there! Are you happy to see me
or...." Said I: "We could nurse that until we get home
or we could close the door and improvise." She
surprised me again: stepped over and closed the door.
And again: sank down to the carpet and pulled me down
with her. And again: pulled my pants down to mid-thigh.

Tight quarters down there, her head pressing
awkwardly against the hassock. Hot loving. What
happened, though, as she heated up she lost track of my
priapic state (though at least kept a hand there, albeit

motionlessly). A nipple come for her, a couple of clit
comes, a vagina come. And then noises out in the hall
-- vacuum cleaner approaching -- the janitor would soon
be barging in (not suspecting anyone was inside since
the lights were off). So, we hastily rearranged our
clothes. Packed up. Moved on.

But very pleased, yes. Up our hottest avenue, the
"low road." Torrid hooker/sailor kisses in doorways:
it's a tradition now. A stop at the big import shop
(buy gummi worm candies for Z's young eco-interns), then
at B-2 strip to shorts and she's ready to warble. I
pour the wine, cue up the rehearsal album, position
myself in the wooden chair with my back turned to her,
as is now de rigueur; she does "After You've Gone" a
couple of times and then (because, disappointingly, the
fakebook yields up lyrics for only one more of the
rehearsal cuts) "Embraceable You" again. As we both sip
cinsault. Her marvelous voice, low and throaty and
vibrant yet sweetly girlish in the higher registers: how
I love it. My eyes closed. Her hands on my bare
shoulders or neck, running through my hair, reaching
around to embrace me and caress my chest. Oh yez, as
good as it gets and beyond -- rapture me up, O Z-bird!
(My only duty, to rush over after each cut and
reposition the tone arm on the persnickety near-antique
stereo whose tone-arm-lifter lever no longer works.)

By now it was fairly late (and by the way, our
hideaway eroto-scene had caused us to miss the annual
public barbecue up in my hood, which we'd seriously been
planning to attend because the new chief of police would
be present and Z wanted to meet him: she had a few grim
tales from down in the AQ and the south end of town she
wanted to be sure he'd heard). -- It was late and we
hadn't eaten and she said she was about to throw a
hypoglycemic fit. So it was tuna sandwiches and red
flames for dinner (her friend Leola was gleefully
horrified to hear how Z's been eating lately, Z the
"healthy stuff" freak who's forever chiding Leola about
her southern-fried tastes). Then some required reading
on the loveseat (Z) and green armchair (me) with toes

interlocked on the footstool between us, about twenty
minutes' worth, and all of a sudden it was nearly ten
and Z's bedtime.

We cut a deal. I would slip into bed quietly when
I arrived home from work at two a.m. and let her sleep
on undisturbed, and then we'd have a full hour on the
horse-o-meter for morning loving. But after sealing the
deal I followed her up into the loft to tuck her in
properly before leaving and -- yeah. But only for
thirty minutes or so. And then when I returned at two
a.m. and slipped into bed, just one light kiss and --
again. And I loved it, yes, but I was being a bad sleep
coach (as she gently reminded me) and now no time was
left on the horse-o-meter for a morning round.

And in all that the usual cascade of Z O's and not
a single G O.

So is jyze about to freak out over the lack of G
O's? Again? Iz not. The stoic approach this time. At
least for now. If Z can limit her meltdowns over the
issue, as she's promised, to intervals of three to six
weeks, G can certainly do the same with jyze freak-outs
over it.

-- Darkening out there. And scoping work awaits me
before I head for Z's place. Probably I'll take the
last bus so I won't have to face the dilemma of how to
deal with my unsleepy night-worker restlessness in the
gap between arrival at 401 and bedtime. Tonight we've
already agreed will be a sexless night -- or rather
we've agreed the morning will be sexless, since she
wants to have all her "jizm," as she said, while banging
out another book review before seeing Aida at noon.

*   *

Scope office. Whose desk this is, if anyone's, I
don't even know. A bit past midnight. (A rubber stamp
here says in big red letters, "ORIGINAL FOR THE COURT.
DO NOT OPEN." I just stamped it a few dozen times on
the inside cover of this J-book. One of the many
valuable perks that the firm, albeit unknowingly,
accords its one and only nightscoper.)
-- I did inadvertently leave out a scene from last

322

night's sexy doings. Before we climbed loftward I
started kissing her good night near the foot of the
stairs. The kiss went on and on, deeper and deeper,
started involving other body parts. "Is it all right
with you if I lean back?" she asked in her seductive
teasing way. I said fine with me. A leaning come
followed. ("Slapping an O on the loft of love.") (And
later in bed without my asking she put her hand on mine
as I was massaging her clit and showed me a way she
likes which I hadn't hit on before. With my hand fully
under her control she essentially towsed herself off. A
big turn-on for both of us.)

   -- But isn't this sex stuff being grossly
overplayed here? Could try to surface and take note of
a few other things. Like, what's happening in the
world? But no. That's not what this jyze spree is
about! (Well, but maybe mention a few things. So start
with the big union strike against the premier USAn
parcel-delivery service. Nationwide. Truly important
issues at stake. And of considerable interest to Z,
because she comes from a proud union family -- her
father, a linotype operator in his later working years,
was also a union steward -- and she herself helped found
a union of government employees during her time as a
social worker in Centropolis and even served a day in
jail for the cause. -- And for me, it's embarrassing
but I'll note the stock market's back on its crazy ride
and as a result last month my legacy deep reserves grew
by over three thousand bucks, or about four percent --
in a single month! And for that same month my total job
earnings were the lowest they've been since I began
freelance scoping as Jyzer Ink: not quite five hundred
bucks. So -- serious ironies piling up here.)

   This morning Z left me just a single pup-tent
message, on the floor by the door: "Yup. Love you."

   (A new study shows I need to boost my calcium
intake, maybe as much as double it. Have my bones been
quietly hollowing out for the past several decades?
-- Long ago I placed my faith in my Nordic dairy-
tolerating genes but it seems I wasn't letting them do

their thing anywhere near enough. -- But I have been
ingesting a daily bowl of cereal all along, with plenty
of whole milk, or otherwise I might've melted away
entirely. So does this mean I should start gobbling ice
cream again? Or do what? Scarf down calcium supps
maybe. But at what cost financially? And do supps
really work? All of them? Any of them? Truth is we're
still in the Dark Ages on most of this stuff. It's
about ninety-five percent crapshoot right now. -- But
not to Z. She rests her faith in a certain kind of
expert -- mostly naturopathic, really, or "alternative"
-- and I just can't do it. And don't. And won't. But
for sure I'll keep trying to hear them out regardless.)

     (And I'll say this: the organic fruit Z brings home
tastes far better than the standard chemical-stuffed
fare I buy. I'm trying not to let myself become too
spoiled. Those organic blueberries, though -- which
I've been sprinkling on my mainstream corporate
cornflakes for most of the past month, the season just
now starting to wind down -- sensational! And the
organic red-flame grapes too. Of course they cost a lot
more, sometimes two or three times what I ordinarily pay
at the corporate supermarket. -- And here they are
again, those painful ironies. Trade-offs. Give up
jyzing -- JIFT or JIRT not to mention JIFT/JIRT -- so I
can make enough money to eat maximally healthy? Ain't
gonna happen.)

     -- Time running short and I still haven't flashed
back. During J-week #14 she and I didn't see each other
at all but it was a crucial one. Tempestuous. Her
seeming indifference was driving me crazy and so were
her outrageous questions and demands. -- But I haven't
even reread the jyze account yet. And the bus pulls out
in twenty minutes.

     Top off this entry later -- but where? Maybe on
the balcony staircase outside her door again? Don't
want to risk missing the bus. (And I was in such a rush
earlier I didn't shave or shower or change clothes.
Tonight I'll be hitting the Z crib drop-dead funky. The
thought was I could clean up when I got there. Hmm.

               [Absolute Tiptop Pinnacle - Jyzin' with Z]

-- But "twenty" this, by which I perhaps should say I
mean end it with two stars. Worry later.)
                         *   *
     -- Oh yeah, an extraordinary eighter it was, #14.
The world changed that week. I even wrote it at the
time and I believe it's proving true: if (paraphrasing)
I do this (mail a letter, return a call) I'll love her
and be with her the rest of my life; if not, I'll be
loveless and unloved and scraping along alone in B-2 the
rest of my life. (And she agreed to give me her address
and to stop seeing other guys, even though we'd been in
each other's presence a grand total of under four hours.
-- And that was also the week of her "blue-shirt
meltdown" and also the tearful late-night herpes
revelation, but never mind those. For now, that is. No
doubt jyze will have more to say about them in upcoming
entries. Ramifications galore! -- Or maybe not, is
another possibility.) -- This kwikjyze jotted at an
intersection three blocks from her apartment and itself
another historical spot for us: where I stood in the
very gutter in which my right foot is now planted as I
commandeer the top of a green storage mailbox for a jyze
platform -- stood and told her with maximum intensity
how tremendously attractive she was to me -- (under a
dazzling gibbous moon now, and I might note it's of the
waxing kind, not a selenotilla of wane to it).

                        S9

     Stumbling off to a late start today but at least
the day is the right day. Which is not to play down at
all the weariness of the mid-spree jyzer. (But blowing
in through the screen is a kind of second wind, cooler

                         325

now after quite a hot afternoon.) (More hot weather
news! Jyze right on top of it!)
     End of the weekend. In about five hours the
Monday-morning rush begins out there on the viaduct.
And a most excellent weekend it's been, except for
another big fight with Z. And even that could turn out
to be a plus in the long run. Maybe. I'm hoping.
Which itself is a plus. And on top of that, a couple of
worthy ejacs. I'm very proud. The rehab seems to be
moving right along. And also a likable movie about a
doofus midlifer guy not totally unlike the jyzer
himself, a lawn party (for the Katgrrrl's "Uncle Nick,"
who's actually her adoptive half brother-in-law),
another book review successfully churned out (by Z) for
the usual AQ weekly, and lots and lots of loving.
     Right now trying to gird up for the week ahead.
Three grand-jury sessions in one week, plus a number of
chores to tend to (many of which I had to let slide last
week but must tackle soon, including a massive load of
laundry and renewal of my driver's license), plus this
jyze to keep up with and a whole lot of calories to burn
off after overindulging all weekend long (most
egregiously on buttered (real butter) oven-warm homemade
coffee cake at Betty's lawn party -- and no one even
knew I was doing it, least of all me, until too late).
     Friday night I finally proved to Z I'm capable of
shooting off before five in the morning. She'd been
wondering about this. (In fact it happened at about
three a.m.) A great relief for both of us and in more
ways than one. Such sweet impassioned loving it was.
     Greeting me on arrival at her place that night, her
most elaborate array yet of message pup tents, including
several made from pages torn out of her spree jyzebook
(so as not to leave any blank pages at the end of volume
one before starting in on volume two, which puts her way
ahead of me, although then again her handwriting is much
bigger). Also another offering of blueberries and red
flames, and an explanation that in her "family of
origin" (back to FOOs again) such tenderings of food
were a standard way of expressing approval, love,

gratitude, and amends, almost like oblations. Also a warning that she'd developed what appeared to be a heat rash near her "bahookie" (anus) but it could possibly be a herpes outbreak, though she was almost certain it wasn't (but was feeling anxious about it nonetheless) (and yet she's never passed along the disease to anyone as far as she knows, and this despite her very active sex life: things she'd told me before).

So I avoided, as instructed, her bahookie. And in bed she told me about overhearing a phone call in which her naturopathic counselor was recommending "The Tao of Love" to a sexually troubled couple and advising each partner to put an equal amount of energy into loving the other partner, and Z took this as a message from the gods intended for her as well: and therefore she would latch onto both prongs of that advice. And best of all when she assumed a more active role in canoodling right from the start that night its effect was immediate and I ejacked much more quickly and easily than any prior time with her. (And out came the black hand towel we'd placed on the bedside table a few weeks ago for use on such occasions, but which since then had stayed sadly pristine.)

I sensed a change in the alignment of the psychosexual heavens. Easier going ahead, I thought. And still think. Greater sensitivity and attentiveness to her touch, which in turn seems more assured (and did again this morning for ejac number two).

-- And the high point of the relevant jyze anniversary some four months back, J-week #15, has Z sitting in the brown loveseat right here, facing me now, during her very first visit to B-2 (and only our third meeting ever). Some big turnarounds that week. Later that same afternoon she showed me her apartment, though the cost was extremely high: loss of most of my hair the following week. But well worth paying. (Only now is the hair growing out to the length it was, although some seems to have disappeared permanently. But I suspect this would've happened anyway. Can't blame it on her. -- What, when I'm so crazy in love?)

[Jyze in Love]

(Also on Friday night, by the way, she asked if I'd
done "anything strange" in her bathroom before leaving
Thursday morning. It turned out she'd found some foul
reddish matter marinating in the toilet bowl, maybe shit
and maybe vomit and maybe both, and it definitely wasn't
her own. Not mine either, I assured her (truthfully!);
so it must've been left there by one of the two friends
who occasionally stay overnight at her place when she's
not around, both of whom have keys: June or Paula. In
the course of talking about this I seemed to shock her
by revealing I sometimes go two or even three days
without taking a dump and in fact I've never taken one
at her place. The term "taking a dump" all by itself
seemed to shock her. Or weird her out anyway.) (All
that clutter I was so relieved to find in Z's place
during that first visit? Turns out it's been Paula's
task all along to make sure Z's clutter stays clean
while also staying right where it is. She's a former
member of Z's radical-therapy group and Z pays her big
bucks -- double the going rate -- for "tidying up," as Z
puts it, unit 401 once a month.)
    -- Best not to push on any further tonight. I'm
beat. But pleased. (And most pleasing of all, maybe
even including the ejacs, was our success in keeping the
fight out of bed last night. In my view an extremely
promising sign.)
                      *   *
The semi-retro bar this sure isn't. Naught but the
same old funky green armchair yet one more time. (And
so it's becoming clear this spree is flouting a prime
jyze principle: variety of venue. -- Or no, not
intentionally flouting. But falling far short of ideal
or even just adequate implementation.)
    Upon return from the Department of Licensing I
wanted to walk up to the "north pole" just to put in the
miles. Instead I found myself low on energy, burned
out, despite having slept a solid seven and a half last
night. And mystified as to why. Too much rich food
yesterday? Too little coffee today? Or the cumulative
effect of five straight nights in the sack with Zoelie

B.? (A drawback to our latest "2-3-2 plan" emerging belatedly?) (Sure, most likely this; I should've realized it before.)

So a nap. One hour intended, two taken. Therefore zap the northward walk. The costume shop would be closed by that time anyway and the semi-retro bar too crowded. Instead thin out the B-2 fruit-fly population a skosh and slap together a mainstream corporate peanut-butter sandwich and gnaw on it at the worktable before the wallful of jyze posters "in reveram assembled." Fewer than ninety minutes until Z-calling time. (And this my last free night until the weekend, most likely.)

Two messages from her this afternoon. And here's a quality I much admire in her. In effect she's reversing herself, admitting she was wrong about something we quarreled about this weekend just past, and then (here's the real Z difference) she's doing something about it. Storming right back into the dragon's lair, this time wielding a portable heavy-duty fire extinguisher to neutralize the monster's scorching breath.

Saturday she freaked a bit when we returned to my old stomping grounds out near the U to see the midlifer movie, with a stop at my favorite lakeside fish house on the way. During our fight that night it seemed we might have to declare large swatches of the city off limits because I'd once visited them while living with Lady U, of whom Z stated flat-out she wanted no further reminders. Now she's reversing herself: she's saying let's go right back out there and tackle this thing head-on. Let's make over that turf, from U&G turf to Z&G turf.

Or anyhow this is my reading of her proposal. And I hope it's accurate. I think she's hit on something that might work. And just when I'd run out of ideas. (This particular plan of attack I'd never even considered, probably because it seemed off the chart entirely, which is to say: too radical. In this I sold her short. Taking the radical step is just what she almost always likes to do. In the absence of a shy attack, that is.)

[Jyze in Love]

    She's saying let's have Wednesday's dinner with
Betty, Kat, and "Uncle Nick" out in that same contested
turf and at the very same fish house where Lady U and I
so often chowed down. And even though this could cause
big scheduling problems for me because of the heavy
workweek, I want to do it. It could be important.
    Five messages awaited me when I awoke this morning,
all from Z. In the first and best she said (in her
supremely sexy drowsed-over wake-up voice) she'd jyzed
nine pages "while pining for you" when she'd arrived
home last night and she'd figured out the reason for her
meltdown Saturday night was that "I've leaned so far
into you, I had to recalibrate my equilibrium." Then "I
love you" with so much feeling I had to believe she'd
truly succeeded in working things out for herself.
    (In the other messages she was alerting me to an
enviro demo unfolding on the high bridge near her place;
teasingly encouraging me to answer an "Open Call" ad in
the newspapers for men to model underwear ("Virile Bulge
brand, I think it was"); asking if I'd really be
available, as I'd told her I would, to kid-sit for Kat
for an hour or two Thursday afternoon; suggesting we
start wearing pajamas in the streets as they're doing in
Shanghai these days; and ranting about a newspaper story
on the shamelessly condescending "voluntary simplicity"
fad. -- Oh, and she said "Uncle Nick" likes me a lot
and thinks she and I are "a real mitzvah" together.)
                        *
    As for the quarrel itself, by an odd coincidence
(or at least semicoincidence) we wound up parking for
the movie Saturday evening directly in front of the spot
where Lady U and I first took up residence in this city
(although the old redwood farmhouse in which we lived at
that time -- in a small first-floor portion of it -- was
demolished shortly after we moved out and replaced by a
much larger apartment building). Then we ate our salmon
takeout dinners in the minipark right across the street
from that same property. Z showed no sign of being
upset about any of this -- from a prior visit she knew
I'd lived in the area, and she knew the movie theater

was just a block away, and she's the one who picked the
movie; and we'd cruised for blocks looking for a parking
space before hitting on the fateful one -- and so I
assumed all was well, we'd dodged the bullet (though to
be sure I was saying nothing about Lady U).

At the movie a possible danger sign flashed: she
left her seat when a violent scene seemed imminent and
didn't return for forty minutes (and during a mildly
violent preview she abruptly grabbed my arm, spilling
soda all over my pants) -- but then she's known to do
such things from time to time and I was only momentarily
surprised or alarmed by either. In fact I thought I was
doing well to stay calm (except for an initial sharp
"Yike!" which caused twenty or thirty faces to spin
around when the icy drink splashed on my lap).

As we left the theater, though, and crossed the
main road, something I said set her off. And ironically
it happened because I was trying to avoid trouble.
Rather than walk straight down the street of lurking
memories (which is to say: provocations) I suggested we
take a slightly longer route one block to the east.
"I'm curious to see how it's changed over there," I
said. And somehow that remark did it. She ripped away
her hand and stormed off -- and just as I was silently
commending myself for sparing her! By the time we
reached the car she was weeping and lashing out at me
with some choice phrases and the foot traffic in the
area was giving us a wide berth. (Can't remember any of
the choice phrases, though. And maybe it's just as
well.)

I managed to soothe her (placate, yeah, or pacify)
and was damn proud I was able to. For a time it seemed
we'd escaped with no serious damage done. But on
arrival at her place we broke out the wine and the
quarrel started up again -- and in her view I was the
one reviving it. (In my view she was still retaliating
in not-so-subtle ways after promising to stop entirely
and I was calling her out on that.)

So then several hours of verbal battle and a search
for solutions. Does my entire history in this city,

every single mention of it, have to be expunged because
I was living with Lady U for all but the first summer
and the last year and a half of it? Will Z be raking me
over the coals every time I mention a memory triggered
by something I see around town, even when Lady U doesn't
figure in it at all in any direct way?

No quick solution emerged. But at one a.m. I said
I hoped we could avoid taking the fight to bed with us.
"You'll never be able to," she said. "Just try me," I
said, and went on: "Give it a chance. I implore you."

And she did and we were able to do it. At first it
was tough and we talked awkwardly about other things,
but meanwhile a physical rapprochement was stoking up in
a kind of parallel reality. "Maybe we wouldn't fight,"
she said, "if we stripped off our clothes every time it
seemed we were about to." -- And loved each other up
(and down and around and all over) for most of the night
and morning, finally arriving at Betty's at two-thirty
p.m., more than two hours late for the welcoming party
for Nick, because we'd tumbled back into bed for "one
last quickie" just as we were about to leave when we
were only a few minutes behind schedule.

(Now it's time to call.)

*   *

Boy did I get that one wrong. And how depressing
it is.

Now almost three hours later. The call dragged on
for more than an hour. Am I ready yet to say anything
about it? Recovered enough?

Wrong in two ways. Her previous suggestion that we
return to the fish house Wednesday night, it now turned
out, wasn't advancing a radical new proposal to resolve
the "usable history" question, as I've dubbed it. On
the contrary, she thought the matter had been put to
rest when she apologized on Sunday for her meltdown the
night before (even though after her apology I'd said as
intently as I know how that I couldn't take any more
personal-history blowups and we needed to find a new way
of handling the issue and so let's both be thinking
about it).

332

[Absolute Tiptop Pinnacle - Jyzin' with Z]

    Amazing to me, it now became clear she was
proposing we swoop right back into the same minefield
just four days after the disaster of our first visit
there -- and with no new safeguards in place! It was as
if she were intentionally kissing off everything I'd
said. Either that or she was colossally insensitive (or
oblivious -- a frequent charge leveled against her on
certain kinds of emotional matters, even an often
justified one, and she's told me this herself).
    The other way I got her wrong: her comment about
"recalibrating equilibrium" had nothing to do with the
incident Saturday night. On the contrary (again), this
dealt with a whole new issue about which until tonight I
knew nothing (or at least not in its new manifestation).
Sunday had gone so well she didn't want me to leave when
the appointed hour came, and this yearning in turn set
off her alarm bells about what she calls "co-
dependency." Those nine pages she jyzed "while pining
for you" after I left were also about her wish not to be
pining so much. As she pointed out -- not for the first
time -- she's used to being independent and it's hard
for her to give up that status or to see herself bound
by ties of "co-dependency" or "interdependence."
    To illustrate her point she offered the analogy of
an "Italian doll." This is the pop-up, self-righting,
bottom-weighted kind; when you tip it in one direction
and let go, in righting itself it'll tip just as far, or
almost, in the opposite direction. (To me it's known as
a "Daruma doll," the Japanese name, because Lady U had
several of those, but for sure I kept quiet about that.)
Z's "recalibration," she said, had to do with trying to
find a way for us to be close that didn't involve her
tipping, or "leaning in," so far that it later caused an
equally drastic, or almost, "leaning out." (Presumably
she'd say the reactive tip in the opposite direction
("leaning out") is what I'm mistakenly calling self-
destructiveness, when she appears to be lashing out at
me for no other reason than superstitious fear of her
own happiness and contentment.)
    Worse yet, the nasty fighting animals we thought

333

we'd safely caged Saturday night broke loose again.
Suddenly she sounded hostile and suspicious about my
motives in wrongly interpreting her phone messages. I
in turn no doubt sounded incredulous and confused when I
learned she was proposing no such "radical solution."
She then decided I must have "other stuff" going on
behind this. (Yeah, like I'm flipping out over her
jerking me around on it!) The dispute started rippling
out to other areas. She thought I sounded disgusted
with her (I was). She adopted an exasperated, weary --
agh, forget all this before it becomes pure rant.
     What do I do now?
     She's still coming over tomorrow night. We just
barely managed to salvage that. But with the heavy work
demands facing both of us this week we'll be able to
spend only an hour or two together aside from sleep
time. And I'll be staying at work three hours later
than usual that night in order to free up early
Wednesday evening for dinner with Nick, Betty, and Kat
(and that dinner will no longer take place at or
anywhere near the lakeside fish house or any other part
of the old D&G turf) (D, that's Dani, Lady U) -- and so
I'll be exhausted when I do get home.
     Dismaying, all this. The manic swings -- can we
keep matters from flying permanently out of whack? The
danger is we'll both start holding back in significant
ways -- whether out of self-protectiveness or
retribution, it scarcely matters (and maybe they're
pretty much one and the same thing anyway). And we'll
each take offense when the other does this and thus
spur a vicious downward spiral.
     Sick at heart. Just hoping I'll feel better after
sleeping on it, or trying to. Unable to do anything
else just now, and that includes grinding out more jyze.

[Absolute Tiptop Pinnacle - Jyzin' with Z]

S10

    Now I've gone and made matters worse. She called
at eleven this morning trying to be loving and
conciliatory; I couldn't reciprocate to the extent she
wanted and said I was still bummed out over yesterday's
call. Almost immediately we were back at it. Soon she
was weeping. She couldn't be talking to me from work,
she said, if I was going to "make" her cry; she mustn't
be walking around the office red-eyed and puffy-faced.
(I wasn't weeping, so I must be the bad guy. And if I
was despondent, it didn't matter because I was at home
alone.)
    Then I really did it: in referring to her tendency
to freak out and go hostile on me when I let slip with
even the slightest, most oblique allusion to my time
with Lady U, I used the phrase "totalitarian
revisionism." Seemed like some version of that, I said,
was what she wanted me to apply to my own life story.
This seemed to shock her and in a way I'm glad it did,
though it really wasn't much different from the things
I'd been saying Saturday night.
    She's trying to erase eighteen years of my past
with these outbursts and to do it in a way that controls
our relationship. Or so it's appearing more and more to
me. They've occurred I don't know how many times now,
and she refuses to be pinned down on what's acceptable
and what isn't in my references to my past. Every trip
outside of our two separate home turfs and our mutual
downtown work turf becomes a venture into, yes, a
minefield. It feels almost like a kind of terrorist
extortion: I must behave in just the way she says or

she'll blow herself (and us) up.

That's my gripe. To her it's unreasonable or unfair because she really does feel what she feels. I make some negligible reference to my time with Lady U and her heart goes through the floor. (Only rarely is this a reference to Lady U herself, as I hope I've made clear by now; usually it's just to something that happened during the time I was with her, for example, "I used to play pickup hoops over there" or "That place on the corner has great apple fritters.")

So this is how she loves -- or an important part of it. And it very clearly follows that I'll have to find some way of riding out her blowups/meltdowns or we won't make it.

Why are they so hard to take? Because she turns cold and nasty and starts attacking me in vulnerable spots. Suddenly all my motives are suspect. I'm expecting her "to live up to these impossible ideals." I'm becoming "this awful judge person." I become self-protective and thus I'm "not warm and affectionate anymore" (I'm supposed to be warm and affectionate when she's attacking me!).

-- But so what. So we've got a conflict here. Am I surprised or something? I knew she'd be tough to live with in some ways ("feisty," "'tudinous," "high maintenance," "Zoelipsistic," "Zoeliethustraical"). And it turns out this is one of the ways. Simple. The "usable history" issue freaks her out. It will continue to do so. This is what I have to be able to accept as part of loving her. Simple.

So should I tell her she has to allow me a meltdown every three to six weeks over this issue? (As I have to do for her on the matter of my futzed-up psychosexuality or whatever it is that's keeping my gen set from functioning as it oughta.)

I don't know. This is horrible. The jyze spree going down in flames. The wondrous new love once again careening into serious jeopardy. All I can do is stumble around obsessing on this one stupid concern. If any picture of Z at all is emerging from these sentences

it's so one-sided and misleading I'd never want anyone
to be exposed to it (least of all her).

    -- So now one last run to the laundry room. Then
folding and hanging. Clean sheets for the bed, clean
pillowcases, clean towels. Clean gray "Mestizas Rule"
nightshirt for the lady herself (it's already hanging on
a chair over by the worktable and the fan is doing its
blowsy thing on it, just as with the dancing pants a
month or two back: the spectral countenance of the lady
herself, I'd swear, glaring at me "red-eyed and puffy-
faced" from just above the rippling garment).

    This laundry business started at half past ten even
before my breakfast and it's now half past three. The
machines were in high demand today. Arrive two minutes
after your dryer stops and your load's been dumped in a
cardboard box and someone else's load is spinning where
yours was. (Making matters worse, the meters on these
machines accept only one coin at a time; there's no
additive effect. You must either hang around in those
muggy, linty confines or be frequently dashing from one
side of the building to the other to feed the meter.)
*   *
Just out of the shower. Thirty minutes, forty
tops, to hit on a stance to take with the Z-woman when
we meet at the hideaway at five-thirty (she schlepping a
big bag of clothes, she's warned me, because our
schedule calls for her to spend the next three nights
here). A "stance." A whole new gestalt would be nice.
Barring that (and it plainly is barred), just a way to
avoid more fighting. Or at least to postpone it. Call
a truce, I guess. Or rather ask her to join me in
calling one (don't want to be unilateral about this --
about a truce least of all).

    "I want us to have this miraculous relationship!"
she cried on the phone (literally, tears all but audible
in their spilling). Also she pointed out that couples
who've been together forever, as reported in an article
she came across somewhere, always say they never take
their fights to bed (and after all, we've done pretty
well on that score so far). But she's been no more

337

successful than I have at stopping the fighting. Less,
I'd say. But then of course I would say that; we're
fighting! I'm blaming everything on her!

Then with fine irony two postcards from her arrive
in the mail, a message in her trademark backward-looping
purple handwriting starting on one card showing a wild-
haired woman -- "Yup. I'm electrified and" --
continuing on the other card, whose picture side shows a
chipmunk-cheeked jazz trumpeter -- "blown away by you/
us/how I feel about you...." Of course she mailed these
before the Saturday-night eruption.

Now a grim effort to lift my spirits so I can then
try to lift hers. A truce until the weekend. I'm not
sure but I think our "Light Music" agreement (struck
less than three weeks ago in the aftermath of the last
serious fight) permits such a move.

Would she just walk out on me? Quit on me? "Do a
Nine-Oh"? (More obscure grad-school psych jargon. Or
maybe I got it wrong earlier when I thought she'd said
she "Nine-One'd" me.) -- But yes, I think she would.
She's done it with others, again and again, putting an
abrupt end to lord only knows how many burgeoning
romances. Yes, I believe she loves me, but I also
believe she might find the pain I'm causing her
unbearable. Or just -- vent her hot temper and maybe
unleash some massively intemperate actions. To see what
I'll do. Could happen at any time and could blow us to
smithereens. (She'd deny this to my face. She's vowed
not to act that way anymore. Grad school taught her
better. But clearly a relapse is possible.)

How bizarre that the impasse should arise over this
particular issue. Yet so much else about us is bizarre
so why not this too.

My history. Doesn't she realize how its
"usability" connects with my writing, my jyze, my work
in general, with everything I stand for? Doesn't she
remember our talks about how the showdowns I had with
Lady S and Lady V over this same issue helped scuttle
both of those relationships? (All right then, how well
do I remember those showdowns myself? Do I want to go

down a similar path with Z? Did I learn anything at all from those earlier disasters? Can I change anything now?)

Memory. Must one erase all memory to be able to live fully in the present? I don't ask or expect her to do this; why does she require it of me? Does this make her love more admirable? Or would it be more admirable if she were more accepting and even approving of who I am and what I've tried to do with my life before meeting her? (At one point she said this herself: she'd learn to love my past because my past made me the person I am. But even then the fiery way she stated it made it sound like another quest for an impossible purity, to be abandoned at the first sign of an ineradicable contaminant. And for sure my messy history will always be kicking up plenty of those. As of course so will hers.)

-- This has to be it for now. I'm still feeling shaky -- shaky and then some -- but it's time to go meet her.

*   *

A full day later and -- time crunch. Too much work ahead to be able to hold to the spree plan. (Last night a brutal scoping job kept me downtown until almost four-thirty a.m. Today my knuckles and wrists are sore and my eyeballs creaky just as in the bad old days of maximal full-time-plus nightscoper keyboard bashing.)

And now? Four in the afternoon, a gray, chilly day after a weather break last night. Gone is the long spell of fine summer days. Immediately ahead at six-thirty is the long-awaited dinner with Z, Betty, Nick, and Kat at the new waterfront seafood diner a few blocks straight down the hill from B-2 (chosen for this occasion partly because the diner has outdoor seating with a superb view of the bay and points west and we were expecting high summer to last a bit longer). Then, for me, another night of heavy scoping.

Meanwhile a precarious truce. Z and I have agreed to wait until Saturday to thrash out the thorny matter of usable histories, and at the same time we'll also

339

tackle once again, at Z's request, the equally prickly
question of "conflict resolution," this time trying to
come up with some sort of structure or protocol for it.
In fact we'll do that first. (What, have we become
agents for brawling megacorporations? No, we're talking
about dealing with our own conflicts. She's concerned
about "the tyranny of structurelessness." Me, I'd like
to keep things a little more informal, but I guess it's
not in the cards. The price you pay. Am I not willing?
I'm willing! Or at least I'm doing the best I can to be
willing, that is, I'm willing myself to be willing. And
does this not count as being willing? I think it does.
Or should anyway. Partial credit if not full.)

    -- Took about three hours to reach this point,
slugging it out all the way (verbally, I'm saying;
always only verbally and never physically, I do hope,
and do expect). Hiking up from her office to B-2, she
"too stressed" to want dinner. Outraged at my
suggesting that her equivocations on personal history
could pose a threat to me as a writer of whatever kind,
jyze or otherwise. I had to convince her that what
worries me most is the damage we might do to ourselves
as a couple if we continue down this path. I'm not
talking about leaving her or giving up on us; on the
contrary, I'm totally committed to staying with her.
Nor do I pretend to know what the "real" underlying
causes might be of our difficulties with this issue
(usable histories), nor when it gets right down to it am
I assessing blame; I'd rather assume we're equally
responsible and the difficulty arises out of quirks in
the way we interact and not out of major personal flaws
and shortcomings or hurtful intentions on either side.
I want our focus to be on finding a workable solution.

    (None of which is to say I don't get angry, I don't
misread her motives or misinterpret her words, I don't
go irrational or hyper-rational, I don't overreact, I
don't turn self-protective, I don't bleed when I'm
wounded. But why should I have to remind her again and
again she's not the only one who might be humanly
flawed or vulnerable in this relationship?)

[Absolute Tiptop Pinnacle - Jyzin' with Z]

    Shaky truce, yeah. The first time it didn't take
and I suppose this was mainly my fault. When it
appeared it was about to, I muttered something meant to
be funny -- swathed in affectionate irony, so I thought
-- about she "sure can be a load sometimes"; she fired
back that this didn't sound peaceable to her and huffed
off. I said I thought it was beyond dispute that she
could be extremely hard to get along with when she's
feeling stressed; she'd told me as much herself in
numerous ways and on numerous occasions, and I cited a
few of both. It didn't fly. (She hates the way I quote
her own words back at her. It's "lawyerlike." Not only
that, she insists I rip them out of context, use them in
ways she'd never intended them to be taken. -- Which to
me is exactly the point, that she sometimes seems
unaware of the wider implications and ramifications of
what she's saying, but never mind. No doubt I can be
tough to take in my arguing, especially when I'm upset.
But then who isn't that true of? Does she think she's
so pretty at such times?)
    My long face. Forcing down a sandwich while
sitting alone at the worktable. (And does she think I
shouldn't care about what she says? I shouldn't listen
to her and remember her words and think about what they
might mean? -- These were the points I was making at
the time and I think she eventually heard them at least
somewhat.)
    Already I'd stuck around B-2 an hour longer than I
should've. Leaving her during a fight is almost as hard
as leaving our bed once the loving's begun (as was true
this morning up in the loft, the loving part, and for
her too, a projected half-hour session which stretched
to almost an hour as she lay atop me saying goodbye over
and over, both of us naked, her crotch pressed wetly
against my raised left thigh: and she came once in that
posture, slowly moving against me, and stayed there
cooling off, and then another goodbye kiss and a new
round began with an almost identical result). -- And we
sat facing each other right here, chair and couch, room
darkening with twilight, no lights on, and broke our own

341

truce to start speaking directly to the issues again,
and this time we found at least a temporary way out.
How, who knows. Or why this time as opposed to the
others. (She figures we're going through a kind of
advanced shakedown period, learning how to fight in
productive, nonhurtful ways, or minimally hurtful.
Could be true, I guess. I'm hoping it is.)

I need to do better at remembering what matters
most: loving her the best I possibly can. I hate it
when I suddenly realize I've again been victimized by my
own stupid preoccupations. (Meaning exactly what here,
I wonder. Maybe it boils down to letting myself feel
threatened or thrown off balance by the emotional
intensity and complexity and the verbal dexterity of
this fabulous woman. "Fabulous woman"? I say that at a
time like this? Oh but she is. Enriching my life in a
thousand ever-changing and deepening ways. Even a fool
could see this. Even this fool. But the last four or
five days seeing this has been a little harder than
usual. Or a lot harder, yeah.)

As we embraced near the door before I left for work
last night the Z-woman whispered in my ear, "Just a
quick nipple-tweak first," and guided my hand under her
shirt. First time she's done this under such conditions
(and standing up) and it was powerfully sexy, and she
had to lean against the wall because her knees went weak
and she murmured sweet words as she came: "Oh God this
is so, so good...." (She recalled hearing brother Rob
say I'm the natural athlete in the family and she said
for her I'm the natural lover, and I can't deny when I'm
with her I feel like that myself, and this despite the
blatancy of my ongoing near-total joystick flop -- which
is to say she's one helluva lover with one helluva
exceptional sexual gift to be able to make me feel this
way under such personally humiliating circumstances.)

Is a big battle in store for this weekend? I don't
know, but I'm thinking maybe not. Seems we might've
turned a corner here -- started turning it several weeks
ago and a number of times through that period undeniably
thought we'd made it all the way around but then the

corner itself turned out to be much longer and yet also
somehow much sharper and more complex than expected.

     (Now rain's starting up and the breeze is blowing
even cooler. Drat the luck!)
                              *

     As for the jyze flashback, we're now on J-week #16,
the first entry in the second book, and it's our fourth
meeting, at her place, where she delivered the dreaded
tonsorial transformation (agreed to the previous
eighter) as I cowered on a chair in her kitchen. We
were talking about this the other day: it was very sexy
for her too, she now reveals. And then on her couch my
failure to bust a major move on her, anything more than
holding her hand or placing mine impassively on her
thigh. Awkwardness. Was I uninterested or what, she
wondered. But to me she was utterly unresponsive. It
was a kind of high-school makeout game in which we were
simultaneously the sweating, nerve-wracked kids and also
our jaded older selves commenting on the proceedings and
milking them for laughs.

     And then the drive back here and, in her car parked
outside, the first kiss. And how pleased and surprised
I was by the sensual things she did with her lips and
tongue (which I unintentionally left embarrassingly
exposed, hanging out, literally waggling and twisting in
the new romantic rapids, so to speak -- ha! -- when I
pulled back before she was expecting me to). And then
for the next week I could think of little else, except,
that is, when I forgot to put my jacket hood up and
happened to catch a reflected glimpse of my butchered
hair and patches of pink scalp. Of course I was hooked
already but the barb sank in deeper and I was scarcely
even noticing the pain.

     -- All this strictly from memory. And now will I
have a chance to check the actual jyze? Maybe not. And
no more time to say anything right now; must hit the
shower. (Sudden ending. Crudeness and rawness. Next
entry probably the same level of incoherence because
this week I lack the time to do justice to anything.
The risk you take! -- And I'd hoped to pull back during

this present entry, adopt a detached view, try to see Z
whole, look at not just her singularities but her
similarities and differences with respect to the other
women I've loved -- a risky proposition at any time to
be sure and perhaps best jettisoned right now. And in
any case, best or not -- jettisoned right now, and maybe
for good. If I'm smart. If I can talk some sense into
myself here.)

S11

   For a quick jyze romp, the semi-retro bar. Pocket
watch poised to warn when half past five's coming up.
And it won't be long. About forty-five minutes.
   From the perspective of the day before, the next
afternoon always looks to offer a big jyzin' hole to
splash around in. By the time the afternoon arrives,
the hole's usually shrunk up to a tight little puddle.
And why's it so this time? Just one thing after
another, that's why. And not even one a real surprise.
   Window booth. Clouds in view. Soft drink to sip
on, cost just a buck. A black ashtray pretty much
identical to the one I liberated here last summer -- and
then chickened out and asked the bartender's okay to
make off with it, which he granted -- so brother Rob
would have something to tap his pipe into when he came
over to celebrate my birthday. (How relieved Rob must
be to know I've found someone else to celebrate with
now, taking most of the pressure off him. -- And I'm
sorry to say he still hasn't written from Mentokaland.
Could even be he's back home by now. I hope he at least
paid my respects to those restless ancestral spirits --
and of course without neglecting the fictive ones.)

[Absolute Tiptop Pinnacle - Jyzin' with Z]

    Only a tiny bit of loving last night. My workload
turned out to be lighter than expected and so I was home
by two, the normal time. (I'd been thinking I'd be
revisiting my pre-Z regimen this whole week, hitting the
rack at four a.m. or later.) Some "lofty" (meaning up
in the loft) small talk, a nipple come, she saying
"You're just so incredibly seductive" -- but I couldn't
seduce anything more out of her. Sleep coach in fact,
and for once, prevailed. (But she'd told me the night
before that she thinks our bodies are finally moving
into sync, which was her way of explaining why on this
occasion she'd held off so long on coming herself while
trying to get me off. Funny thing, the effect was just
the opposite of what she'd intended, because I'd thought
something I'd done had turned her off.)
    Football talk in the background here. Now baseball
talk (sudden segue). Jukebox music itself jukes from
neopunk to corny contempo pop. Fans spin. Soundless
mimelike baseball plays on the usual three screens.
Youngish homewardbound downtown workers stride
purposefully by outside, all headed in one direction at
pretty much the same speed. Across the street stands
the same old dowdy brick apartment building as always,
but now I look at it differently because Z and I have
considered cohabiting there. But rejected the idea,
because even this relatively upscale part of my turf is
not walker-friendly enough at night for women, she
thinks, and she's probably right.
    Things on the upswing. Everyone agrees the diner
dinner was a grand success. Saturday Z and I will
grapple with our issues. In talking with Aida yesterday
Z dubbed what we're going through a "storming period"
(and the puckish Aida in turn suggested maybe Z and I
should see less of each other for a while, and I
couldn't tell for sure whether Z thought this a good
idea, but I know I didn't, and said so). To me the
"storming" already seemed dated. Yup, I'm hoping we've
blown past the worst of the trouble. But maybe I'm just
needing to look on the bright side or something.
    Walking along, it occurred to me I can probably

risk hanging a little looser with Z now. I know my
attachment to her is strong -- even if I sometimes
forget this momentarily (under duress, say) -- and the
chances seem good it'll stay strong. Paradoxically this
frees me to be a little angrier with her if necessary,
and I think this may even be a good thing.

Love stuff. She's taking an interest in the book
on love I've been reading. Wants us to read it together
this weekend, and also to revisit the one on "postmod
intimacy" (with its clusters of colorful Z-affixed post-
its sticking out like exotic squared-off feathers). Nor
has she failed to remind me both books are the work of
white males or to say she'd like to find something on
the subject by a woman of color. (I suggested "The
Pillow Book"; she was not amused.) And then in came her
favorite glossy far-coast weekly mag with a "Special
Double Issue on Love." And a note she left for me today
offered this "beginning definition of love (mine for
you)...feeling attraction, admiration, fascination,
desire, enjoyment, safety, matching, comfortableness,
lust, curiosity, stimulation." (I'm especially pleased
to note that three of those words openly admit to a
physical interest: attraction, desire, lust.)

So time's up. Alas. Rompety-rompety-romp. (I say
that just as a way of sneaking in part of the name of
the place. Should result in a jyze demerit I suppose.)

*   *

And on over to a new stop for jyze, a small market
five or six blocks northeast of B-2. (I smell smoke and
check to make sure the hostile Cawk drifter dude who
briefly sat down at the next table didn't try to set me
on fire. -- But he staggered off and I couldn't see any
smoke or flames and now I notice a vent behind the chair
is blowing hot smoky air out from the market itself and
that must be what I smelled then and still smell now.)

Almost literally in the shadow of our local mono
version of big-city elevated tracks. No doubt part of
the market itself is so shadowed. And probably also the
building half a block farther east where Z at this
moment is attending a women's caucus meeting. I'll be

picking her up over there in about ninety minutes. For once I've got me a decent jyzin' hole.

(Now an obnoxious Cawk punk kid swaggers up and flashes a wad of bills. Wants someone to buy him a pack of smokes. I give him a half-smiling, half-weary turndown. -- And up above a train whooshes by, and when I look back to see if the kid's found a taker, he's gone.)

-- That same drifter dude, earlier he'd lunged at my bottle of root beer as if trying to knock it over. Muttered something about "fucking lasagna" (if I heard right), then sat down at the next table and scavenged in the sidewalk gutter for butts, and when he found one, lit it up. Dude's maybe around my age, dirty gray overalls, several days' growth of salt-and-pepper-and-food-scraps beard. I'm not exactly thinking there-but-for-the-grace but rather how time has pulled some of its usual nasty tricks on me too and I'm not bearing up under them any better than this guy is and maybe worse. In the sprezzatura of proper aging as decreed by the tastemakers of the First World Third Age I'm sadly lacking. -- As I had to concede yet again while glancing at some photos "Uncle Nick" took at Betty's party the other day. I just don't do well at accepting I'm that older guy. "Peak Prime Time" indeed. -- And the damage isn't even all that bad yet. I'm still recognizable to myself as myself if only just barely.

So then. This area may be gentrifying at Potemkin-village speed but I still feel extremely uneasy letting Z walk it unescorted at dusk or later. (And right on cue the drifter dude is back, panhandling table to table, clearly unaware he's hit on me before. As he threateningly pushes up close I fix a glare on him and rise as massively as possible out of my chair and mutter reflexively, as in some bad movie, "Hold it right there, pal," and he veers away and lurches around the corner.) (Jyze exception up there on Potemkin.)

-- Z in the creamy-colored sweater bearing the small block G lifted from my high-school letter sweater. "Dungaree Polapina, Dungaree Polapina...." She sewed

the G on this sweater of hers the other night, partly
before our disputatious phone call of that night and
partly after, "undeterred by it all," as she proudly
informed me the next day. Monday night that call was.

Tonight she was already kicking back in B-2 reading
the paper when I arrived home. I rustled up our supper.
Spirited dinner-table talk followed, including some from
me about the insight regarding my deep-down belief,
always there to fall back on, that we'll be together
"forever and ever and ever" and what effect this might
have on my style of quarreling with her. She caught my
meaning but not the intensity with which I was feeling
it at that moment and I realized of course she shouldn't
be expected to: this was really my own thing. I'm the
one who's sensing I've finally reached a kind of
emotional bedrock; no one else could understand more
than superficially what this means to me. (Of course I
could also lose the feeling, so best not to make too big
a deal of it. But I don't expect this to happen. I've
stumbled upon a new way of seeing things here -- new for
me anyway -- and I think I'll be able to hang on to it
and build on it.) (And I'm afraid I'll jinx myself if I
say one more word about it.)

Other talk: about what's in the news, about a zany
meeting Z attended today. I searched through a stack of
discarded newspapers hunting for certain cartoons to
show her but they turned out to be less funny than I
remembered. She told me about the distinctions she
makes among "attraction," "desire," and "lust," the
words from her "opening definition of love" (in essence,
growing hormonal involvement moving from left to right),
and said she was planning to jyze about this matter in
depth so she could understand it better herself, since
she never really understands anything until, as she
reminds me regularly, she sees it written down.

And lots, lots more. Political stuff at the
personal level, always plenty of that. Her problems
getting along with Eurusan environmentalists whom she
always assumes to be elitists -- can't help herself. "I
keep trying to see them as potential allies but maybe

[Absolute Tiptop Pinnacle - Jyzin' with Z]

I've just had too much experience with them. I can't do
it anymore. I was thinking about this today. Back in
my twenties and thirties it was much easier."
     And she remarked on how at meetings she's often
aware people expect her to react more rationally and
linearly than she does. "It's like they're always
surprised someone can be emotional and still say
something intelligent." (In this instance as well as
many others I'm all too aware she's likely to level the
same type of charge against me -- being overly rational,
judging her by those same male Cawkazoid "suburban
neocolonial" values we've squabbled about before -- and
I try not to let my bristling over this be too obvious.
I don't want to be fighting with her too much about such
stuff. Instead I try to find ways to let her see I'm on
her side and I look for signs that she's aware of it,
that she's not forgetting to accord me that all-
important "exception" status. -- And in fact one of
the clauses in our "Light Music" treaty calls for her to
verbalize this status -- "the exception" -- anytime she
makes some categorical comment about male Cawks.)
     More talk. About whether she should ("Do you
mind?") put on some lipstick before leaving for our walk
over here. The trouble is, sometimes at work she
realizes with a start she's forgotten to do it and has
been bouncing around the office lipstickless for hours.
Yet she doesn't like being thought of as someone
dependent on makeup. Only recently has she begun
wearing lipstick regularly. And the other day she
looked around at a meeting and noticed most of the women
present were lipstickless. I said my personal view --
ooh, being careful -- is she looks better without it but
of course she also looks very fine with it. In general
I think as she comes to accept that I find her plenty
attractive as she is without cosmetic enhancement she'll
be moving back toward a more natural, relaxed way of
being with me, since this seems to fit in better with
her overall views ("healthy stuff" and the like).
     This morning while I slept she left a message on my
machine saying she has a Catholic/Jewish guilt thing

which causes her to worry that if she leaves too many
little messages or signs for me I'll expect her to do it
all the time. (I reassured her on this: I don't want
her feeling that way because then she'll never leave me
any. -- And she observed: "Boy, you've been thinking
about a lot of stuff today, huh.") And she ended the
message: "Here's a big loose-lipped slurpy smack on your
gooeyduck." -- And in the morning as she's sliding
backwards toward the far end of the loft to climb down
she always does bestow a slurpy smack on said gooeyduck
in passing and I always do look forward to it even if
said gooeyduck isn't stretching as far out of its shell
as it sure as heck oughta be, especially at morning-wood
time -- except for me it's actually middle-of-the-night
time, so I do have that excuse. Chalk it right up!
     (Yike. Time to run.)
                    *   *
    Taking a break down at the scope office. Again the
workload is lighter than expected, and this means (A)
I'm still in financial trouble after all, and (B) I'm
faced with the familiar dilemma of whether to go home
and disturb the sleeping Z-woman or hang on down here
and feel bad about not being back there when I could be.
    Resolved: that I should stick it out here for an
hour or so and then try my luck at home -- see if I can
coax Z into donning her sleep mask up in the loft while
I do a little down-home jyzing in the green armchair.
    Janitor's rolling his cart in right now. Another
new guy: probably wonders what the hell I'm doing here,
all alone in the big fancy conference room in my scruffy
nightscoper garb. Well, listening to the buses go by
down below, that's what. (Salt-and-pepper beard on this
dude too but without visible food scraps. Fellow Cawk,
again around my age or maybe a little older. And what
does he think when he sees photos of himself? And what
are the probabilities I'll someday find myself saddled
with a physically demanding job like his? Certainly not
negligible. -- And I find myself worrying about such
matters quite often these days, virtually every time I
see a help-wanted sign, and a lot of them are going up

in this era of economic boom. Most of the jobs on offer
are subsistence level to be sure, but then subsistence
is all I'm interested in. Just something to pay my room
and board without exhausting me while also keeping me
out of the public eye if at all possible, and also
something not too grossly humiliating. -- Or maybe I've
reached a point of personal equilibrium where nothing
could be too grossly humiliating.)

     Z's adrenaline was coursing when we met after the
caucus broke up. She'd winged it on a speech in support
of the candidate with the best record on environmental
justice. The crowd liked it and gave her a big hand.
Her excited eyes. It's tough for her to address large
audiences but once begun she usually gets into it,
especially if she feels it's going over well. Wish I
could've stuck around at B-2 when we returned there to
help her unwind. (As I left she was making herself some
"calming tea" after failing to locate any appropriate
remedies in the herbal stash she hauls around everywhere
in her infamous rattling netted "trick bag" -- and she
used that term for it long before we met.)

     At times I wonder if at some point it'll bother me
to be the one who tags along as she does her political
stuff. It could, I suppose. The old power-hunger of my
own politics/journalism days might reawaken. Or worse,
shame might start percolating up because I have so
little to show for my decades of devotion to writing --
in the way of public recognition, I mean. Could happen,
sure. But I'll do my damndest to stomp it down if I
ever do sense it rising. (And in truth I don't expect
to. I think I can find plenty to be proud of. Just
have to keep my head screwed on right and, even more
crucial, keep on jyzin'.)

     -- At last night's farewell banquet for Nick at the
diner the most interesting moment came when he asked
Zoelie, "So how did you two meet?" She and I offered up
the tale together in what's become a kind of vaudeville
routine, all but completing each other's sentences. Z
told me later she noticed Nick seemed a bit taken aback
by it. This scarcely surprised me but it did her and

I'm wondering why. Seems to me certain types of people
will always attach a stigma to our way of meeting no
matter what kind of spin we might put on the tale. Best
just to ride with it, I think -- laugh at our needy
lonely-heart selves. Yuk it up. "We're damaged goods
and proud of it." (Not that I'm always so good at doing
this myself. But I have no illusions: a whole lot of
folks will be looking down on us. And maybe I'm more
prepared than Z is to shrug off such views. Could be
she sees this as another of those vexed class issues.)

Just a two-block walk down to the diner. Four
visitors to B-2 at one time -- a first. The Katgrrrl
clambering excitedly up into the loft. She rode atop my
shoulders most of the evening when we were on the move.
Two delicious desserts, blackberry cobbler and peach
slump, and I pigged out on both, startling poor Z who'd
never seen me do anything quite so blatantly gauche.
(Peach slump, she told me later, ranked right up there
with warmed-up peach cobbler soused in cream as a simile
for the way post-sex wind-down feels for her genitally.)

I hadn't realized it's been only six months since
Nick's wife Ruth died (totally unexpectedly, of a heart
attack, at home in bed, while he was briefly out of the
room, and she just barely past her 10K day: what a
shocker!). His occasional off-kilter responses and the
spells of woodenness I'd been noticing this past week
suddenly became much more understandable. (Ruth's
father, Manny, who was Betty's husband and Kat's father
through adoption and Z's "blood brother" with whom she
shared a house, along with four or five others, for
several years, also died unexpectedly while undergoing a
liver transplant about a year before Ruth's demise, and
thus the special connections among the group I was
dining with -- lots of sorrow in evidence but also lots
of love and courage.)

"Subunk G." This Kat still strikes me as one
terrific little kid: smart and funny, cute as can be,
spirited, warm, lovable. Z is her official fallback
guardian on all the papers and I'm hoping I too can soon
start to play a similar role for her. Such a delight

(the serendipitous kind too) this aspect of joining my
life with Z's is turning out to be, a wholly unexpected
dimension, a way to close an aching gap in my own life
which I'd long since given up all hope of doing.

Or is this just super-idealistic hokum? Well I
guess we'll see. But I do know what I want here and I
intend to keep going after it as long as doing so seems
acceptable. And right now it definitely does and it
looks as if it will continue this way as far as the eye
(this blurry red-rimmed myopic organ) can see.

-- And finally, before I head on home, the
flashback. Entry #17, "the WOW week." Only our fifth
meeting (though some ten or eleven weeks had gone by
since our first contact) but we tumbled onto her bed and
-- WOW. Her sexual gift. On top of everything else,
all the other gifts, it was stunning beyond belief. I'm
still stunned by it. And later that same week, when she
hinted she was having second thoughts about proceeding
further with me, I wrote her the intense ten-page letter
which she still refers to even now as being the ultimate
expression of what she wants from me: all-out crazed
passion. And it's just as ultimate for me -- not the
letter itself, necessarily, but the way I felt when
writing it, devoting myself wholly to her and offering
everything. This was the week the miracle revealed
itself fully for the first time.

Yeah wow like what preposterous stuff this is. No
doubt. The dude can't help himself. Wotta stroke of
luck and at wotta time. Still pinching himself so hard
his marrow's compacting and still it all looks true.
Feels true. Keeps holding true. Just gets more solid.
(Any doubters left out there? Thinking of last entry's
struggles perhaps? Just remember: "All Jyze Is True.")

-- But in truth (truly true truth now) no one will
ever believe any of this because it simply is not
believable. If I look at it just slightly aslant I
don't believe it myself. The world, to the extent it
ever finds out about it, will, if anything, hate it.
The bastard, why did he deserve such bliss? The world
will try to tear it apart. All the world loves a lover?

[Jyze in Love]

Ha! How about two lovers in an amazing love? (What we
do have going for us, though, is our generous allotment
of flaws and weirdnesses and twistednesses. The
frictions. The reversals. The scars. The buffoonery.
The pathos and the bathos. The whopping ironies. The
soap-opera flipperoos. The foozle factor. And all the
endearing and complicated bit players around us, if only
I could jyze them up the way they deserve. The
belatedness of it all. The boggling good intentions.
The sappiness and the smarm. Ya ya and blah blah. So
it's the only act on offer in the only ring still
standing in the jyzer's personal circus and so he tends
to wax a bit demento over it, and so so so wot?)
                    *   *
     Not at home in the old inner/under sanctum, Z-bird
slumbering overhead (perchance to dream of G "with a
giant gooeyduck erection," as I learned later she was
doing, or claimed to be, though she never did explain to
what use, if any, the G-man was putting this monster).
And not at the semi-retro bar either, the next afternoon,
although I did try for an encore there and found the
door locked and the chairs riding the tables. At four
o'clock on a Friday afternoon! (This as an enormous
blimp slowly circled overhead -- so slowly you could
almost see the propeller turning, like that of a toy
submarine winding down in a bathtub -- and emblazoned on
the blimp, "You'll Love 'The Z&G Story'!" -- or no, "#1
in Tires.")
     So onward I trekked, stopping at the "north pole"
bookstore to hunt for a title I told Nick about (written
by the son of a famous physicist -- Nick himself being
the son of a distinguished college professor of physics)
and finding instead my old journalism buddy Pete H.'s
new book on environmental justice which Z will presumably
want to look into, so I bought it for her. And crossed
the street, bought shaving items and shampoo at the mall
drugstore upstairs (I'm going through razors much more
quickly now in an effort to spare Z whisker burns, and
going through shampoos quickly too in an effort, almost
certainly futile, to find one that will stop my hair

354

from falling out) -- and grabbed a deck table outside.
White plastic. Nice. Comfortable too, oh yeah;
contoured even. From a distance the cluster of white
chairs and matching white tables and white deck
umbrellas up here shimmered almost oasis-like.

By the time I arrived at B-2 last night it was
nearly two a.m., too late to begin another jyze session.
I went straight to bed (after snacking on butterscotch
pudding and gingersnaps, my main squeeze of a dessert
combo for the past year and most likely for the coming
year as well, given my large stashes of both) and Z was
awaiting me up there, awake or semiawake, and we had a
fine hour and a half of loving which later caused her to
be an hour late for work (and so: another slipup by the
sleep coach even if she did insist on overruling his
warnings in medias res).

The loving began with nipple licking/sucking/
nipping as she drowsed, a come for the left and a come
for the right, and then on to the grotto for several
more (she kindly assisting on one) and then a couple of
"one last one"s with muff pressed against thigh, and
interspersed was lots of loving talk, sexy talk,
seductive talk -- both of us totally gone, immersed,
love-crazed, reminiscing about our very first time in
bed at her place (she remembering especially "when you
jumped my bones and said something like, 'I know you
won't like my saying this but I'm flat-out crazy about
you'" -- and I inanely and pedantically amending the
first part of my quote to, as I recall it, "You might
not want to hear this but" --).

I told her more about the feeling of reaching
emotional bedrock and she told me about her own sense
that "the cosmos made you just for me." Such a sweet
and emotionally intense and loving time it was! (And I
fully or nearly fully erect for much of it and she not
tending to me at all and then apologizing: "You have
such a lazy, sleepy, selfish lover": and I truly not
minding a bit except briefly when I wondered if this was
part of a new tactic of hers, "Don't touch him at all
until he goes mad with frustration," but she assured me

it wasn't -- and so I found myself thinking my rehab is
still proceeding nicely, the Taoist sages of loving
would approve of it for sure, and who knows, maybe this
weekend will mark the true immersion, the baptism by
copulation, the consummation: or anyway may be a good
time to launch the first serious attempt in a while,
with the equipment apparently primed and ready (and even
halfway there right here and now, this moment, swollen
and twitching and making me restless, yes indeed, as I
prepare to abandon the white-plastic oasis).)

*   *

Now fuming. For various reasons (mainly it was
time to hit the road) I'm back home and I've discovered
the new blades don't fit my razor (which is less than
five years old!) and so I'll have to buy another one.
Grump grump, six more bucks gone, I'm the victim of a
marketing ploy not even a grade-schooler would fall for
(or so I suppose people would say, this being allegedly
such a media-hip age; yet I see few signs of media-
hipness around and about, mostly just media-jadedness).

Zoelie's morning phone message, she'd seen a news
report about a study showing "aggressive" women are far
more likely than "meek" women to suffer heart attacks.
"Looks like I'm in deep doo-doo here." And then later
she called again, "I can't find anyone to schmooze
with." At lunch her buddy Wei had presented her with a
collection of feminist essays about desire (I recognized
one of the editors as being an egalitarian pro-sex type,
so there's nothing to be uptight about here). (And this
morning she reused the same pup-tent sign she'd left for
me last night: "Yup. Down deep." -- And I'd better be
on the lookout for a way to reciprocate on her pup-tent
pitchings or else I'm afraid they'll soon go extinct.)

A stop at the party shop on the way home. Some
nifty new costumes. If I had the money I'd stock up on
several, with a wacky full-body clown outfit, green and
orange, topping the list. Might spring for some rubber
animals and life-size movie-star cutouts too. But since
I'm extremely short on funds right now I didn't even go
for the kid's flashing-light marquee or the giant "I

356

Love You" card. Later maybe. Or make my own.
     And this time the semi-retro bar was open again and
packed as usual. In fact that's where I finally found
an accessible head. Whiz kind. By then my need was
great -- it had been one source of the "halfway there"
noted before -- and so the whiz was truly a romp even
though chaste.

S12

     Jyze in real time, the bed. (Also the rain
pounding on the roof.) Her bed this is, the full-size
wood-framed futon with flowery gray sheets bearing a
good many funky body traces from two nights and two days
of more or less nonstop free-style loving, to wit, our
own. She to my right at the moment, sitting cross-
legged in a red robe with her back propped against the
wall next to the built-in bookcase and the brightly
colored Zoelie Trope. She's hard at it too. So JIRT
tandem type with throttles wide open.
     Even though I'm kneeling on the floor and my
torso's laid halfway across the bed just beneath her
knees and I'm bare-assed beneath my brown Z-shirt, she
assures me (when I inquire) I'm looking quite dignified.
     Six inches to the right of my jyzin' hand, her
celebrated toes, right foot. One, two, three, four,
five -- just right! Standardly dactyled! And a
handsome network of very fine veins laid across the top
of that same foot above the arch (and throbbing away,
no doubt, maybe even visibly if I stared awhile).
     Scratch of her J-stick. I teased her about toning
it down, likening the sound to a braying Jimmy finger
puppet (he's out there again doing his usual fumey,

raucous weekend thing with his truck and boom box -- and
therefore we've closed the windows and balcony door --
and Z's said she'd like to tell him to his face that he
himself is -- in a phrase we earlier heard him bellowing
at someone unknown to us -- "a certified peckerwood").

(Now she's up and proclaiming her own entry S12 a
done deal -- already! -- with some catchup jyze next
after a short break. Grumbling: "I'm very uncharitable
about Jimmy." And with mock wonder, as she opens the
lemonade: "M'bao! We didn't drink any wine this
weekend!")

Didn't fight either, and engaged in only a little
bit of "conflict resolution," wrapping it up maybe an
hour ago. In essence we've agreed to try harder to
postpone the thrashing-out of conflicts to the weekend
while staying friendly during the weekdays so our work
routines, and especially hers, aren't overly disturbed.

Also she's again asked me to dial back on the
"rationality." I don't think it's so bad but I said
I'll do it anyway -- redouble my ongoing effort -- and
then (just to prove how bad it can be) observed it's
tough to resolve conflicts while abjuring rationality.
"How about I won't be over-rational if you won't be
over-emotional?" I didn't say that but maybe I'll save
it for next time. Or maybe we'll never fight again.

(She's back scratching away. I can look straight
up her legs under her robe. Voyeur! But jyze insists.
Officer, we've got a grown woman here wearing no
underwear! -- As indeed was the case all afternoon long
yesterday as we bopped around town: to a branch library
to pick up a novel ("The Good Negress") held on reserve
for her book group, to the hideaway to fetch notebooks
and to water the plants, to several supermarkets to
coupon-shop for bulky items (chiefly cornflakes and
chunky applesauce for me and toilet paper for her), to
my place to unload, to her usual co-op market to do her
weekly provisioning.) (Flashing memory of glancing up
my mother's skirt as she sat on the upstairs landing at
636 in Gatewood, gabbing on the phone, her white undies,
I'm twelve or maybe even thirteen. Funny how vividly I

remember that. What the devil could it mean?)

   Best news, Z hit on an excellent way to neutralize
the "usable history" issue regarding Lady U. She's
never been jealous before (not anything like now) -- so
she says -- and thus she attributes her present state to
her inability to "get" me (consummate the relationship
sexually) whereas Lady U was doing so on a virtually
daily basis (when migraine- and injury-free) for all
those years. I couldn't argue with this. (I'd thought
of it myself from time to time -- that is, made the same
connection -- but suppressed it, I guess, simply because
I don't like to think about it.) I immediately agreed
to drop the issue until such time as we finally start up
with actual tab-G-spurts-in-slot-Z fucking (yeah!). And
by then, who knows, maybe the issue will be ancient
history, not too usable for anything. Though lord let's
hope it doesn't take that long.

   (Now, ahem, I let out a fart, softly but -- despite
my best suppression efforts -- still audibly. "See," I
say, since this issue of farting is a slightly vexed one
for us, frequently deployed by her to illustrate alleged
class differences, "I too can fart." And then add: "And
mine are at least as fragrant as yours." At which she
brightens: "Aha! So, are we measuring now? You been
measuring mine? The sniff-o-meter?")

   Oh such banter. Laughter bouncing off the 401
walls at all hours. (Can Jimmy hear us and is he
cursing? Nah. But the Lummi couple, quite likely.)

   And much loving. On number of comes for her during
the forty-hour period up to now I offhandedly guess two
score at least, maybe closer to three. She pooh-poohs
but we agree: "lots." (I offer to let her use my naked
ass as a writing stand and now she's offering to let me
use hers. This is for next weekend. The climax, jyzewise, of both the spree and Peak Prime Time: "tandem
jyze in the raw." She says maybe she'll use my biceps
too -- monsters that they are. And my "pud-dick-ament
area." She's planning some in-your-face interrogation
of the refractory appendage, and more power to her.)

   For me two comes, both Friday night and just a few

hours apart. The first was a lollapalooza, fantasy
fulfiller, she pressing in from behind as we lay on our
sides up in the loft, my lower body twisted so it was
facing the ceiling, she reaching around to wank me real
good with her left hand (as I fantasized way back in the
beginning several months ago while lying on my side
alone up there after she'd first mentioned her aching
nipples and love of spooning, her preference for the
behind position) -- and she a lefty, of course.

-- But she's done for the day and gazing blankly at
the wall. Soon I'll have to be shoving off. So best to
stop now and try for a comeback later, at home, though
by that point I'll likely be glassy-eyed and lethargic
just like last Sunday.

*   *

-- And am. Can't even get it together to put away
the groceries (all those boxes of cornflakes to
supplement the dozen already stacked in the internal
hallway) not to mention doing a little wallballing to
burn off some of the calories derived from the sack of
half a dozen large oatmeal-butterscotch cookies I
discovered on sale at Z's co-op market this weekend
(after years of checking out every bakery in sight for
this, my all-time favorite type of cookie, to no avail).

Did manage to plow through another third or so of
the "Special Double Issue on Love" (not appreciating at
all what appears to be an attempt to discredit, and from
what I see as a reactionary antigay standpoint, a
pioneering sex researcher). Now this. The truly
crucial stuff. It must be tended to even if it feels as
though I'm pushing the J-stick through a thin layer of
wet cement.

The futon bed she and I were jyzing atop back
there, that's the one. Site of the life-changing event
as flashed back to during the previous two jyze accounts
(the bed that birthed this last-chance romance).

An interesting moment during our post-jyze roll in
the sheets right before I left today. After a talk-come
she told me I'm the only one who's ever been able to get
her off that way, just by talking, but then a few

seconds later (sort of like a radio bleep delay) she
amended that. "Bradley did it once by reading out loud
from 'The Story of O.' But only once, and you've done
it lots of times. Still, I had to correct myself
because I always want to tell you the truth."
     Very admirable no doubt, and oddly enough I didn't
feel too stung or jealous -- maybe simply because she
appeared so genuinely worried I would. And besides:
unlike Bradley's, my pillow talk is all improvised.
"You just know intuitively what to say to turn me on."
Amazingly enough, it appears I really do. So is this a
kind of karmic compensation for my dysfunctioning jing-
jang? (Today several more fizzled handjob attempts.
But this time we shrugged them off.) ---
                         *
     Phone rings, it's Z. Three quick points she wants
to make (and this an hour past her bedtime). One, her
telling me about Bradley today was a lot different from
her telling me about Kirk M. on Friday (this I haven't
even mentioned in here yet). Second, she realizes she
drops these little tidbits of her own romantic history
on me "out of fear you'll start taking me for granted,
and I'm going to work on not doing it anymore." Third,
and the reason she was up late, she'd started reading
the latest book on love (the one I gave her yesterday)
and she liked the opening section, especially the
description of love as "gentle engulfment," which also
nails how she feels during a certain kind of orgasm.
("A kind you have with me?" "Oh yeah, baby.")
     A fine list, I'd say. Offered lovingly in her
seductive drowsy late-night voice. (Don't think I'll
ever be taking her for granted, I said. At the very
least I hope she'll wait for some tangible sign I'm
doing so before delivering the next jolt, and I can't
believe she's seen any such sign yet, and she agreed she
hasn't.)
     -- Interestingly, the flashback this time is to J-
week #18, the eighter of my impassioned letter crossing
with her "hiccup of doubt" letter while she was off at
the final grad-school session, followed by our big fight

when she returned (starting in the little pocket park
and now forever associated with it), and that leading to
the big reconciliation, the wine-besotted loving at her
place (beginning with the takeout dinner devoured at her
dinette table with the spectacular view, and she
spectacularly amorous for the first time), and to my
scrawling on my calendar "There's no turning back now"
(which I had to explain to her later when she saw it
because to her it suggested I was thinking I'd, as she
put it, "just passed the halfway point on a desperate
mission in hostile territory" -- whereas for me it
signified, on the extreme contrary, a kind of internal
commitment which it would take a great deal to undo).

        For a time the conflict or "storming period" that
began toward the end of last month appeared severe
enough to undo that commitment. But now I think it
never really was that bad. I think I just needed to
believe it might be for a while in order to convince her
my objections on various points were serious. That is,
she's right, it was a kind of bluff or brinksmanship. I
wasn't aware of it myself at the time, but it was. And
as a result of our struggle over this issue I've come to
believe I could convince her of my seriousness without
actually going to the brink -- if only because I now
realize I can't reach the brink simply by persuading
myself I'm ready to give up on her if she doesn't see
the light. The true brink lies way beyond that. I'm
too attached to her now to be able to reach it simply as
part of a bluff. And I'm persuaded I'll never be able
to reach it, period. (Nor can I believe I'll ever want
to.)

        -- Is all this nonsense? Maybe it is. In that
case it's nonsense I'll be living by, and pleased to be
doing so. (I betcha, I betcha.)

        "The Story of O," I learned, has figured in her
life in a fairly important way. Out of concern over its
being such a turn-on for her she sought help from a
women's radical-therapy group some years back, about the
same time the incident with Bradley occurred. Bradley:
her "quintessential lover" from a strictly physical

362

point of view, the college classmate she saw
episodically over the years, the one who made her
realize her sexuality was truly rare and special. She
also saw him as a lover for the last time in that same
period, roughly fifteen years ago (though they met up
for a reunion that turned out to be nonsexual "about
four years ago").

Fifteen years ago is also when the crisis with
Arvin ("the charming sociopath") and the broken
engagement occurred, and roughly when she began seeking
treatment for sex addiction (or maybe the women's group
led to that a bit later). During that same period, or
leading up to it -- she's so often vague on years and
chronologies -- she'd been seeing several men with whom
she was being intimate simultaneously and for a
protracted period (and I suppose this may be why she
reacted strangely the other day when I played her an
exceptionally raunchy version of "My Monday Man") (that
and the fact, as I already knew, that people used to say
her mother was the spitting image of the singer on this
cut -- a certain buxom blond 1930s movie star of "My
Little Chickadee" fame -- and indeed she does look like
her in some of the photos I've seen, and Z likes to toss
around quotes from the singer's movies, for instance,
"When I'm good I'm very, very good, but when I'm bad
I'm better"). -- And at the same time, that same year,
Z was still in a daze of mourning over her father's
death, trying without much success to write her novel,
and soon to morph from Louise to Zoclie -- with a
bullet!

On Friday when she met her old crony Wei for lunch
they discussed the jealousy matter. The first essay in
the feminist collection about desire he gave her (which
I'd read myself, as it happens, when it first came out)
explored the erotics of "The Story of O." Later she and
I talked about some passages she'd marked in this essay
as a prelude to her writing about them in her own J-
book. Thus it's not so surprising that the incident
with Bradley would pop into her mind today (if indeed it
didn't do so Friday night). (Not long after Manny died,

I should mention, she asked Wei if he would step into Manny's role as her best male friend. He said he would. And he has. As was the case with Manny, they've never been lovers -- or so she says; and yes, I believe her.)

     -- Also Friday evening after work she'd attended a rally downtown protesting the draconian new welfare laws (joining Aida there) and that was when Z had caught a glimpse of another former lover, Kirk M., and later that night she let me know about him too, and she did that in a kind of taunting aside which troubled me at the time. (How can she allow herself to be tormenting me even mildly by invoking former lovers when she's refused to let me speak Lady U's name and we've "stormed" so majorly over the issues of jealousy and "usable history"? It's almost as if she's daring me to counterpunch. -- This matter now being cleared up, however, I hope.)

     Kirk M. is a kind of name drop. He's the brother of our longtime local left-liberal congressman who's been in the news so much lately. She and Kirk go back more than twenty years, to shortly after her arrival here in Jyze City, when he was a highly educated political radical toiling full time as a low-skill laborer for a shipbuilding company "to show solidarity with working people," and they broke up over the issue of her "dabbling in spirituality," which he deplored. (Years later she saw him on the street downtown in a suit and tie, now a cut-and-trimmed businessman and a pompous-looking one to boot, "and I laughed out loud and he's never spoken to me since.") (Most interesting to me was the revelation that only when she got out here -- meaning away from Centropolis/Mentoka and the rest of the heartland -- did she develop an interest in what she calls spiritual matters. Before then "I was strictly an atheist.")

     I look forward to learning more about her past. I also dread it. A high risk here of causing wounds (to me or to her as I reciprocate with info about my own raunchy pre-Lady U era) and leaving lasting scars. I'm much more leery of this sort of thing than I was, say,

364

twenty years ago. Is anything we might learn from such
explorations really worth the risk? Yet at this point
-- or at some point not too far in the future -- I
think we'll have to risk them anyway.

*   *

Continuing on this unusually cool summer night
(could almost say autumn's in the air and so this jyze
spree will soon reach its Absolute Tiptop Pinnacle and
shortly after that terminate -- but then the fourteen-
week run-up to the Glennarian Rollover will be getting
underway, and Peak Prime Time will continue right along
with it). Did my supps and vites. Plucked red flames
from the vine while revisiting the flashback jyze from
J-week #18 -- and realized once again, even more
strongly, that #18 was the turning point. That showdown
in the pocket park did it. A big gamble but it paid off.

Or is this reading too crude? Could I have done
anything else? And am I back to valorizing
brinksmanship again? And beyond that I don't want to be
analyzing too much anyway. And even if I did want to, I
couldn't be. Not now. I'm zonked. Wasted and then
some. And all that taking place in J-week #18 was then
and this is -- now. Yes it is.

-- We did take a nap together this afternoon as a
shakuhachi CD I gave her played. Such a splendid loving
nap it was. And all day I went around wearing just that
same sleeveless brown henley ("Z-shirt"), no shorts,
because she'd said she wanted us to go naked all day but
it was just a shade too chilly for that. (She wore her
thigh-length red robe but kept it open.) She deployed a
familiar word in a modified form to describe her present
condition: "rebesotted." With all the sweaty loving we
both became noticeably funky and were enjoying this.
Her attraction to and comfort with funkiness I consider
to be among her finest qualities.

Once in the hall she surprised me with "You really
are pretty" (I still haven't decided whether she truly
means this and, if so, whether she thinks it's good, but
on both scores it would certainly be pretty to think so
-- and take that, Jake B.!). If I start making didactic

(or as she says, "avuncular") pronouncements she teases
me with a mocking German-accented "Ja, ja, I understand,
Herr Doktor," and then goofily paraphrases what I've
said (and then again sometimes this isn't so funny --
but often it is, and in any event such gentle needling
keeps me on my toes and so I encourage it).

The story behind the farts: we bought a huge five-
buck box of blueberries (was it four pints? eight?) and
I was gobbling them all day.

-- Oh man oh man am I bushed. Yet I want to say
one last thing. I think we truly bolted it down this
weekend. Like J-week #18 but now with a bedrock
foundation of shared experience. So many times she told
me how much she loves me, how deeply, how fiercely, how
tenderly, how trustingly, how safe she feels with me,
how I'm her soulmate/zolemate; and I saw -- acccch, to
heck with it. If this jyze spree ever had any suspense
in it it's gone now. This love's a lock. It's a wrap.
It's a done deal. It's...it's...aw shoot. It is!!!
(Chew on that, Anti-Smarm Overlords.)

S13

Starting this one up in the loft with a dream just
so I'll have done it once during the spree. A dream
fragment. Reported on purple sheets. And here's a
particolored mound of pillows, seven in all. And here's
a black sleep mask, a box of white earplugs, and a small
wicker basket full of bottles, all containing oils
(mango-coconut, calendula, Jamaican dogwood), all
belonging to the Z-woman. Also a small spray tube of
"natural breath freshener." (Hmm, this one I hadn't
noticed before. At some point she may've been thinking

I couldn't take morning-breath kisses. But if so, I
fooled her. Or at least the tube's still sealed.)

Also three books of mine she picked out for bedtime
reading: a collection of stories about Catholic girls,
another about lesbian lovers, a novel about life in a
far-coast redevelopment housing project. (I don't think
she's ever gotten around to looking into any of these
books. She usually brings over her own preferred light
reading -- whodunits mostly, usually featuring female
private eyes -- but none of those are in view now. Many
come from the library.) Also here's something she
stashed between futon and wall, presumably for self-
protection when I'm away: a thirty-inch hunk of two-by-
four. It used to be down in the internal hallway.

The dream fragment features a big image but not
much else. Z and I are aboard a two-block-long
oceanliner which is plowing through the streets of
Centropolis, the city of our mutual raising (hers inner
C-town, mine outer, that is, the burbs). Why the
liner's there eight hundred miles from the nearest ocean
I don't know, but no one on board is panicking.
"Eventually we'll find our way out of here, don't
worry." Meanwhile city dwellers seem to be taking no
notice at all of the massive marine presence. The
streets are made of normal materials but for our ship
they act like water, while for the motor vehicles to the
front and rear of us they're solid pavement.

That's it. End of dream report.

-- I'm shifting positions often. Jyzing in a loft
with a low ceiling, it's becoming clear, never does stop
being bad for your back. And by the way, for the first
time since maybe April I didn't go to bed naked. Wore a
heavy green long-sleeved henley. Cold night.

Now half past ten a.m. Gray day. I know this
indirectly from light seeping in the two alley windows
down below and bouncing off the walls in odd ways,
almost visibly, like arrows on a flow diagram. Traffic
and a few birds: no other sounds except the ticking of
the two clocks up here -- and they're still in sync.

Also the mound of pillows contains one more than

before. Z's own. Wish I could say "I bought her a pillow so she could lay her head just right," but she beat me to it and brought one over herself.

*   *

I've been so bad, letting the whole day go by without jyzing a single word (other than those about the dream, which from this distance seem more like part of the dream itself). Now I finally start up again just as the grooveyard jockey announces it's two a.m. at the tone -- meaning bedtime. Return of dreamtime.

Here are the main elements of the day (testing my bleary recall): a wake-up voicemail from Z, a personal provisioning trip on foot with a stop at the hideaway, a voicemail from Nurse Betty, a call from Z, another personal provisioning trip on foot going in the opposite direction, a call to Betty, a call to Z. Also mixed in were the usual at-home meals (breakfast and dinner), a home workout session, a home reading session. Empty mailbox today. -- Ah, and I almost forgot: I oiled my old boxy leather briefcase, stopping about halfway through when the oil ran out.

So now I'm guaranteeing myself a cramped day tomorrow, starting with a late rising hour. Gonna be tired and grumpy -- either that or work in a nap somewhere. Or fool myself.

Z's wake-up message today had two parts. She said she too thought our relationship had turned another corner because last night for the first time she'd had a harder night sleeping without me than with me. And she said she truly loves the way I make her come by words alone and this was the message she wanted to be sure I'd grokked from last night's phone talk. (She does have a special fondness for that word "grok" in all its forms, which just might have something to do with why I'm using it so much myself. Same with "suss" and "choosh" and probably a slew of others I'm not even aware of.)

(In our phone talk tonight she was much less sure we'd turned a corner on sleeping. Didn't want to stand by that anymore. "It's true I didn't sleep well last night but it could've been for any number of reasons."

368

I figure the main cause was probably that same "Italian doll" effect she talked about a couple of weeks back, just a slightly delayed version.)

-- Shopping today, I blew about sixty bucks on books as a birthday present to myself even though it pushes me that much closer to the financial brink. Also bought a new bottle of oil for the briefcase, a new razor (since I've dulled all my blades in the effort to spare Z's peachy complexion and now I find my old razor is obsolete), a dozen cans of tuna at a two-for-one sale (because the larder of a person in my financial condition can never stock too much tuna), a box of whole-wheat fig bars (just on impulse, to which I'm more vulnerable than usual because it's birthday week), and two bottles of permanent black ink (because I've been going through ink even faster than blades).

The call from Betty, that was to ask if I'd be interested in doing some paid editing of her papers for a nursing-upgrade class she's taking. I successfully begged off for lack of time. We had a good talk after that, and she invited me and Z over for post-birthday raspberry pie. "Kathryn loves to help, so if a berry's missing here and there I hope you'll be forgiving." Kat came on the line to say hello and after listening to my spiel for a moment interrupted it like so: "You're goofy, Glen! You'd better start behaving yourself!"

Too late now to go into the afternoon call from Z. Tomorrow for that, if it's not superseded by then (which would be a shame since it was revealing in a number of ways; so I guess I'll make an effort to keep it high on the to-jyze list).

Before turning in for good I'll call Z's answering service and leave a wake-up message for her. I'll be proposing a jyze session in her office sometime this week (meaning before spree's end) and reading her a short poem I came across tonight about the torment that can result from hearing about a lover's love history (recognizing that doing this is risky, if for no other reason than the identity of the author: a woman of Lady U's cultural ancestry). And then I'll be winging it

(and just today I was noticing I've become much more
comfortable now when talking to an answering machine;
for the first few months I was bumbly and tongue-tied
as if addressing a crowd of thousands).

Before stopping, just a couple of thoughts about
today's jyze flashback. It goes to J-week #19, the
eighter following our big breakthrough. Now the AIDS
test came back negative, she said she was willing to
forgo use of condoms, we "fucked" for the first time.
And I was actually erect and inside her -- twice! -- but
both times it was causing her lots of pain, and both
times I pulled back and found myself wilting and that
was when the e-dys troubles truly began.

First thought: I doubt she or I could've done
anything differently that would've led to a better
sexual launch. In a sense the launch (full-raunch
launch) might even have been the best possible one,
because to compensate for the ensuing foozles I had to
work harder at loving her physically, and this gave her
a chance to show off a wider range of her astonishing
sexual gift; and once we'd canoodled our way "over the
hump" into wonderland, the astonishments just kept on
coming (and coming and coming) and that might not have
happened otherwise, or at least not to that degree.

Second thought: has to do with what we were talking
about last week after telling our "meet story" to Nick,
namely the stigma attached to answering personal ads.
Even before meeting Z I may've had to admit to myself at
some deep level that I was no longer the desirable
fellow I'd hoped I still was, and this in turn may've
had (and may still have) a lot to do with my e-dys (from
the "damaged goods" angle).

Just thoughts. Next I'll read the actual jyze
entry and see what kind of reaction it kicks up. But
before that: the call, sleep, maybe another jyze dream
session if I'm lucky, breakfast, possibly another
attempt or two to reach Jenny L. to see if she's found
out whether Lady S and I are, ahem, still hitched.

*   *

-- Now seven in the evening, next day, and I never

did call Jenny L. (but I will, I will) and neither did I
fetch up another dream (but I've dreamt plenty in the
past few weeks, including a wrenching one in which Lady
U featured, though its details are long gone).

Sun's shining now, suddenly, and rain's still
falling, as it has been most of the day. An unusual
throbbing parallelogram of sun has popped up on the wall
opposite the armchair here in B-2, the glow brightening
and fading and brightening again, the effect much like a
distorted TV screen. The angled pinstripe shadows cast
into the parallelogram by the blinds might almost be
horizontal hold lines as in the early days of the tube.
And superimposed on those lines are shadows of vines
from the fence outside, leaves frisking in the wind --
and in the parallelogram they look like the hands of
dancers (line dancers!) raised overhead, as in TV teen
dance shows in that same era way way way back. "Do the
Hokey-Pokey and you turn yourself around...."

So then yesterday afternoon's Zoelie call. For
reasons unknown I was all amped up, to the point she
said she was reminded of our very first phone talk.
(And toward the end of yesterday's call I proposed we do
lunch together sometime soon and she had to consult her
daytimer and as she unzipped it and riffled through the
pages searching for an open slot a strong sense of déjà
vu seized me -- it was indeed our very first phone call
all over again. And just as back then she wound up
proposing a date two weeks in the future -- for a simple
lunch! With her M'bao! And just as back then I
squawked but wound up agreeing to the proposed date.)

I started out excitedly reporting on the books I'd
bought an hour earlier, especially one about "the
philosophy of rapture" which I thought she might like to
look into -- not least because the author is a woman.
As I raved on she suddenly said, tone admonishing, that
she hoped I didn't expect her to agree with the thoughts
expressed in all these books and articles I was laying
on her. I in turn admonished her for entertaining such
a libelous notion. But she kept on with the theme,
saying she likes to figure out by herself what to think

about things (thus repeating, and unawares as far as I could tell, the very case I made to her back in our early days against psych categorizing). Least of all did she want to be told by this woman I was telling her about (who does go on and on about jouissance) how to feel and/or think about her own orgasms.

And while on the subject, she added, she was finding some objectionable views in the chapter on environmental justice in the Pete H. book I'd given her. "I'm going to talk about privileged-white-male colonial perspectives," she announced, "so I want to honor our agreement and say I'm not talking about you -- you truly are an exception. But his view is so typically privileged white male colonial," and she went on to spell out why she thought so. And I didn't disagree. I even beat her to the punch on a couple of points, including Pete's failure to situate himself as Eurusan in the EJ chapter (though I wondered if maybe he'd done so elsewhere earlier in the book, since neither she nor I had read anything but the one chapter).

Unfortunately I pushed further and also said I recognize she might see the way I champion my personal views, including by deluging her with "PM" (printed material), as an intentional challenge to her own hard-won perspective. Even though she'd made this same point to me earlier, she now said I was being "borderline presumptuous," and I had to do a lot of energetic wriggling to free myself from that charge and bring her tone back from near-combative.

But yes, soon enough we were "friends again," as the bathroom protojyzist would say (meaning the one whose book rides my toilet tank). And she told me a story about Jess and Gwen. While doing her laundry at their place she'd answered a question about how her weekend had gone by saying we'd lazed around in bed most of the time. And we were also, she told them, "learning how to fight less disruptively." (J&G say they've tried to do this too, and they're still working on it.) So then Jess was teasing Zoelie about how fast we're moving along and asked if it's likely we'll be tying the knot,

and when Z said yes, Jess said she wanted to be "dyke of
honor" at the wedding. (Trouble is, from Gwen's earlier
objections we know she'll want to be "co-dyke of honor."
And then what will Paz and Tobey think? Z's solution:
Gwen and Jess will be "dominant-culture dykes of honor"
and Paz and Tobey will be "dykes of color of honor.")
(What had started all this, reminding her of the talk
with Jess about fighting, was my remark, semi tongue-in-
cheek, "Looks to me like we're settling into a fine
strong steady and utterly peaceful and harmonious rhythm
-- what you think?")
     -- Yeek, it's late and I'd better be moving on.
But one way or another I'll be back later tonight.
                    *   *
     Jyze in the wee hours at Z's place. On the phone I
asked if she'd prefer I do this here or somewhere else
and she said here. But she also reminded me that a week
or two back I'd agreed to hold off on middle-of-her-
night loving on those nights when she needs to be
"perky" for work the next day, and this, she said,
would be one of those nights.
     When I came in she was asleep in bed wearing a Lone
Ranger face mask (minus the eyeholes) and her signature
white earplugs. One of her floor pup tents warned me
about this. But then when I started tiptoeing over to
kiss her hello, she whipped off the mask and yanked the
plugs well before I got there.
     What I intended to be just a quick kiss turned out
otherwise. Not too much so, though. A few minutes,
that's all. Z naked beneath her coverlet, as she
usually is nowadays, at least when I'm around to check.
     (Those earplugs of hers, I often find them rolling
around in the sheets at B-2. They look like little
white gumdrops with the sugar licked off.)
     Now I'm hunkered down for the duration in her "view
chair" over by the sliding glass balcony door.
Scattered lights of the postmidnight city sparkling out
there. In here, the cool light of a fluorescent study
lamp Z set up solely for my benefit atop the bookcase
behind the chair. On the dinette table another of the

floor pup tents, and an unusually large one (like twenty by thirty inches folded over) which I found just inside the door when I arrived: "Welcome home, Honeybee," featuring a pretty damn good hand-drawn likeness of a swaggery specimen of said insect with a block "G" on its chest and a somewhat G-like countenance.

No sounds at all from Z thus far except in the very early going when my attempts to pluck grapes one-handed from the vine produced a rattling noise, the inner colander scraping or sometimes banging against the outer bowl, metal on metal. "Hey!" she objected, fairly good-naturedly all things considered, and after that I did my plucking two-handed, one hand holding the bowl and colander firmly together while also steadying the grapes for plucking, and everything was fine.

This morning she left me a long voicemail which she herself declared to be sexy. She'd forgotten to turn her phone off last night and so heard the rings for my calls coming in at four a.m., and then from fear they might signal an emergency she checked them. After listening to the poem about a woman being tormented into sleeplessness by a lover's reciting love-life history she was, alas, unable to find her own way back to slumberland. Not even a hit of Jamaican dogwood could do the trick, though it did leave her feeling "dogwoody." Now in the call she was telling me about her attempt to dispel the "dogwoodiness" by playing with her nipples. "I really do have cute breasts, don't you think? Hmm?" Those nipples yearning, she went on, for her G-man. "So...this is a nice sexy message for you, wouldn't you say?"

A second message, from the office several hours later, started out, "Grump grump grump!" She'd lost her reading glasses on the bus when they fell out of her pocket. She also had two things she wanted to talk about, she said, "but maybe I'd better wait until after your birthday." Terrific, I thought: now we've got a threat hanging over the climactic birthday weekend!

(Here she calls out from her dark corner, "Jyzeman G, come to bed!" Her tone, at once affectionate and

vexed and slightly peremptory, reminds me of old Mom's
when she stood at the top of the stairs in her bathrobe
back in Gatewood calling Dad up to bed after he'd
lingered late in his study. "I'm not done yet!" I
protest to Z. "When?" "I'm done when I'm done. It's
not even close to two yet. How come you're not
sleeping? I thought you said you wanted to be perky
tomorrow." "I was sleeping until you started doing that
thing with the grapes." "Well sleep some more, the
night is young. The grapes are history. I've got jyze
to do here!" She muttered and sputtered for a while,
"Schlubbedy-schlubbedy-schlub," but now she's quiet
again.)

In her call this afternoon she revealed, at my
urging, what those two things she wanted to talk about
were. They turned out to be not all that bad, or at
least so I'm thinking now. Aida had told her about some
friends of hers who'll soon be moving out of their
"great" two-bedroom apartment which rents for just $775
a month and is located atop the big hill immediately
southeast of downtown ("south hill," jyze calls it), not
too far from Aida's house. If we wanted the place we'd
have to move fast, and Z in her message was admitting to
hesitancy about doing so. Cold feet. Last-minute
shakiness. And she was concerned about how we'd handle
the financing. She no longer thought it was such a hot
idea, though she'd proposed it herself, that she pay
more simply because she makes more and carries a higher
rent at her current place than I do at mine and also I'd
be giving up my sorry-ass city low-income subsidy worth
a couple hundred bucks a month.

But -- to me her doubts didn't sound all that
serious. Mainly it seems to be a question of whether we
want to be living in that particular hood. And when I
checked on a map and discovered it's a little under two
miles from the hideaway and thus I could continue
walking there and also to the scope office, which is
less than a mile farther north of the hideaway, I was
sold. We both like it that the entire hilltop is
racially diverse and mostly working-class and so

engaging in local politics might actually be worthwhile.
    Is she ready to take the big step? It's almost
September. Her friend June advised her to wait six
months after Meet Day before deciding whether to live
with me (with any man) and Z seems to have seized upon
this advice as gospel. As of September 10th we'll have
known each other six months, starting from the day of
the first call. (June also counseled Z to hold off
for a full year before seriously considering marriage.)
        -- So then after our phone talk this afternoon I
went up to check my mail and found a pre-birthday card
from her. It asked me to set aside Saturday afternoon
and evening for "mystery doings" and offered a "free
yes" for the rest of the weekend and asked what I'd like
to do. -- And later while thinking about this in the
shower I decided what I'd really go for, beyond the
"tandem jyze in the raw" already agreed to, would be a
showdown on our most explosive issues of the moment --
I'd like to see "The Pillow Book" again and then thrash
out our differences on it. But I checked and it's no
longer playing anywhere in the area. Yet I'd still
relish talking about it if for no other reason than the
timing is right jyzewise. I don't want us to keep
ducking these tough issues. (What are the issues?
Exoticism. Orientalism. Incest. Aestheticism. Art/
life conflicts. Cawk males and fetishization of non-
Cawk females. Domination. Addiction. Japan and Lady U
and "The Story of O." My years overseas. Neocolonials
v. postcolonials. The alleged advantage "beautiful
young bodies have in making cocks hard." -- All
toughies for sure.)
    When I proposed this on the phone, she immediately
agreed. (I also said I'd like to discuss in depth the
various "books of love" we've both read in the past few
months and our personal love ideals, so those'll be on
the agenda too. -- "On your birthday you want to do
this? On your 'All-time Absolute Mountaintop Pinnacle'
or whatever it is you're calling it?" "Could any time
be better?" "Well, okay. I mean, it's your birthday
and it's your mountaintop.")

[Absolute Tiptop Pinnacle - Jyzin' with Z]

    And then finally, quickly, I did reread that jyze
flashback section, entry #19. It stunned me -- the week
of our first and only true copulations so far (except
for a few even briefer and more pathetic attempts) -- it
stunned me, I say, with its excitement and confusion and
its zonked-out display of "limerence." That was when we
first began using the term, and soon thereafter we
pretty much stopped using it, mainly owing to the foozle
predicament, I'd say now (though who can really know),
and I'm thinking we ought to revive it. If not for all
time, certainly at least for the birthday weekend.

    -- And though she hasn't said anything more about
my coming to bed and appears to be soundly asleep, I'm
feeling a strong pull anyway. -- So g'night, jyze fans,
wherever you are. Yes, and even those of you who've
dropped out before getting this far and so might never
know you're being addressed here. You matter too -- for
at least having given the stuff a try. Thank you very
much!

                      S14

    Tandem jyze drops in at Z's office. It's thirty
minutes past closing time and her friend Jess just took
off for home after changing into biking gear (including
rainwear, for the sprinkles started up again just as I
began walking down here and therefore my hair and
shoulders are still damp right now, even though I rode
the free bus part of the way and unfurled my umbrella
for the rest) -- and so we're all alone in here now, Z
and I.
    Out in the hallway the three of us were joking
about who'll be what kind of "dyke of honor" at the

wedding. As Jess herself pointed out, "Hey, this must be getting really serious if you're talking about it openly." "You betcha," said I. Z blushed. The ears of coworkers passing in the hallway perked up. Their eyebrows rose. Their jaws dropped. (Literally, all of these. I swear!)

Jess confirmed that Z's presentation to the highest of the utility's high honchos earlier today had gone splendidly. Afterwards the energy-conservation people took Z out for lunch and she saved me her dessert from that, and so it is I'm still tonguing out tiny chunks of fudge from the creases at the corners of my lips. And how sweet they are!

-- Now I once again tell Z she has great jyze style and she takes it the wrong way, as if I were making fun of her. I'm serious! Such concentration, such a fast hand, such a rare ability to go at it any time and any place and with no advance notice at all -- like now, as an instance, sprawled out on her wheeled desk chair, leaning back, feet resting on the open bottom drawer of a filing cabinet. Z in calf-length denim skirt, green Chinese-looking blouse, dynamite high-topped and high-heeled gold-dragon sneakers (for the walk to B-2), reading glasses perched on the tip of her nose.

"I don't like to be complimented too much," she ripostes with a laugh, "because then I feel too much pressure to keep doing what I'm being complimented for."

And as I lean back to ponder this remark I see a trace of J-slinger influence hugging the ceiling: one of the three dragonfly kites we bought at Z's co-op market in honor of a major component of my old (abandoned) fiction series, "Blue Dragonfly," and later the Katgrrrl and I each colored a kite using my markers, and this is the one Kat did. All by itself it's nearly enough to inspire me to take a shot at another rewrite of "B.D." -- But still not enough, no. Not for a good long while anyway.

My inaugural visit to Z's new office. She's going solo for the first time in years. It's roughly six times the size of my hideaway office, but with many fewer bookshelves and many more filing cabinets (twenty-four drawers in all: I just counted), less wood and more metal (though I'm sure she'd prefer wood too if the utility had any to offer). A big light-table for viewing newsletter layouts. Several years' worth of newsletter back issues mounted on the walls. A dozen cartoons taped to the door. Photos of all seven of the kids for whom she's an honorary "auntie" and/or godmother arrayed on her desk and a nearby shelf. A batch of award plaques displayed here and there, including one for "VIP" from a national Filipino association (it stands for "Very Important Pinay" -- and she'd never even told me about it before -- a Pinay being a female Filusan). Also a hanging basket (attached to a ceiling light fixture) containing organic foodstuffs: fruit and power bars. A plant, no, two -- no, three plants, one of which is barely visible and barely surviving in a dark back corner. A jam-packed bulletin board. Lots of the utility's energy-conservation magnets and mobiles and whatnot hanging about (she gave me a mobile and two magnets to pass along to Rob and Gail).

Also taped to the door, I just noticed: a sign saying "Love me, love my junk."

Why haven't I been here before? The way things are shaking out I feel she wants her work world (day world) to be a place of independence and autonomy. Not that she's barring me from it, but I think she's more comfortable if I keep my appearances here to a socially amenable minimum. (We've talked about this a little bit. I don't think it's really an issue with us or likely to become one.)

Her old office is just three doors down the hall. Her relations with former longtime officemate Leola seem solid again after a shaky period probably caused by my arrival on the scene. (We're scheduled to attend a barbecue at Leola's house weekend after next. Her husband of several decades, Gerry, also of mostly African and Afrusan ancestry like Leola herself, is a jazz and blues fan and Z's painted me to Leola as being

deeply into both (of course closely related) genres and
I'm mulling how to handle the situation -- me the pink
dude from the burbs: don't want to be coming on like
some big braying Cawk aficionado.)
     On the ring finger of her left (jyzin') hand is the
octagonal blue Chinese "Love" ring I gave her around the
time of the punky haircut to betoken our "going steady."
She recently clipped it from the black leather thong of
"wear my ring around your neck" intent. (I still wear
the ring she gave me where it was intended to be,
although I did notice the other day my own matching
black thong is starting to funkify a bit from summer
sweats.) A moment ago she flashed the "Love" ring at me
and said, "For Christmas or sometime maybe you could
come up with one that would go with my other jewelry a
little better?" "I think I have a phobia or something,"
I grumped, "about spending big bucks on jewelry."
"Whatever," said she. -- So maybe make her something?
     -- This morning she confirmed my hunch that she's
feeling shaky about our living together quite this soon,
with the question of whether south hill's the right kind
of neighborhood also being part of it. She knew she was
shaky because her stomach started bothering her as soon
as she began seriously mulling the matter (in the same
way it did back in her late teens and twenties when she
faced similar kinds of questions, causing her to seek
psychiatric help -- though most of it cleared up as soon
as she moved away from Centropolis and her parents,
first to Mentoka and then here -- but then it, the
shakiness, returned when she started living with fiance
Arvin ("the charming sociopath") fifteen years ago --
and the Arvin association of course is the real reason
she's disturbed by its reappearance now after such a
long absence).
     But then this afternoon she said the upset might've
been brought on by an overdose of peanut butter, so
maybe she's not so averse to living together as she'd
been thinking.
     "Okay," she announces, clapping her J-book shut,
"I'm twenty minutes over my time limit." -- She's been

here all day (and all week, all year, the past eight or
nine years, basically, during working hours, this same
hallway or another one nearby), she wants to get outta
here (and can stand overhead fluorescents for only so
long, and for my benefit she's tolerantly turned them on
and then left them on this whole jyze session because
the chair I'm using is too far away from her desk lamp
for adequate light with the overheads doused) (and now
she's all packed up and ready to go).
    So onward. I'll get back to last night -- my
shameful confession -- and other developments -- in a
bit. Or tomorrow. We'll be taking a ferry ride then,
by the way, "deep into the region of the perilous past."
                          *
    One last note before leaving (as she's now hitting
the head): her office boasts a big window looking out on
a narrow stretch of recessed roof, and by leaning up
close to that window one can look southwest toward the
hideaway building, which, however, even though it's the
largest building on its block and less than a diagonal
block distant, isn't actually visible -- a slightly
shorter building across the intersection blocks the
view -- but still the sense of our geographical
closeness is very strong here. Odd to think that for
fifteen months or so we were cooped up as much as five
days a week in such proximity yet totally unknown to
each other. Surely we must've come close to making
contact at least a few times on the street or at the
ORB, which in that period she visited almost as often as
I did -- though usually during her lunch hour, well
before I made it down there.
    -- And now she's back and listening to voicemail,
which includes personal appeals for support from two
city-council candidates. "Boy, ain't I the popular one
all of a sudden," she chirps. "And both of 'em white
boys too -- oops, sorry, present company excepted -- and
I'm not just saying that, I mean it!" ---
                    *   *
    Here's jyze with Z's lips pressed against my bare
back. And with one hand reaching through just beneath

my nether cheeks, gently palming "da jewels."

This is live, some thirty hours down the line. "I can hear your J-stick. I thought I wasn't supposed to be able to hear your J-stick."

"Like the brushes in 'The Pillow Book,'" I reply.

Up in the loft. Both of us naked. She's supposed to be jyzin' too but she's too tired, or not in the mood all of a sudden or in the mood for something else (as she licks my right flank). Ooh, slow and seductive. And -- agh, what a time for the ink to run out ---

*

Good thing I brought the bottle up here. Must be my alleged Calvinist streak she was just teasing me about -- "preferring jyze to sex." (Well, preferring, no, but this'll likely be our last chance for loft jyzin' during the spree. Can't let it slip away.) (And used the black hand towel, hitherto reserved for jizz mop-up -- and in a prior life, for keeping the light out of my eyes during daytime sleep hours in a very bright bedroom -- used it, I say, to wipe off the dipped nib and lower barrel of the J-stick. -- Just wish we'd had more occasion to use that black towel for its current designated purpose. But we will, we will: I don't doubt it at all. -- And I'm reminded of her salaciously posed query earlier this evening: "So is the ideology of jyze called jyzism? Are you pumping me up with your doctrine of jyzism? Or...should that be pronounced jizzism?")

Now it appears she's about to yield to the sleep demon. She's lying along my right side as I stretch out prone, my head up by the lamp. Hers is near the bottom of my rib cage, her left arm reaching down between my slightly spread legs just as before, her fingertips gently pressing the same "silky-smooth," as she describes it, inner or ventral (if that's the word) or perineum-side scrotal zone.

Slow warm breath on my right flank. Her left leg bent across the back of my right thigh, then bent back across it at the ankle.

Lovers, us, except still (drat) not truly consummated, but what the heck, a minor matter, or

anyway so we're both hoping (always hoping -- not to
mention vowing). "Absolute Tiptop Pinnacle" birthday
now just one day away, this being a very early hour of
the eve of that day, that is, of the day before. And
she's taking a vacation day tomorrow, or rather later
today, technically, Friday, which means our long
celebratory holiday weekend has already begun. Today
we'll be riding the ferries to my old stomping grounds
"in the far province across the waters." Storage unit
161. Best to get some sleep tonight.
     But not quite yet.
     This the realization of a longtime fantasy. Also a
foretaste of this weekend's planned "tandem jyze in the
raw," a/k/a "tandem birthday jyze in our birthday suits"
-- also a venerable fantasy. (Steady rhythm of her
sleep-breathing, sound and movement and the circle of
warm breath spreading and shrinking like an ultra-slow-
beating heart on my back.) (Earlier I told her the
notion that I was showing a Calvinist streak by
preferring jyze to sex struck me as being analogous to
"a reverse Albighensian heresy" -- whatever that might
mean. Wonder why that term popped up and what it really
conveys. She seemed to think the comment funny, though.
Maybe I tickled her Our Lady of Transfiguration streak.
(Jyze exception right there.) -- OLT being the
neighborhood church she attended prior to her bolt-from-
heaven moment of antireligious enlightenment. One of
the priests at OLT, she let me know, was young and "very
cute" and had a big crush on her. Possibly for that
reason she lasted a bit longer there than she otherwise
would've, although she assures me nothing physical ever
occurred between them. Then that other, older, crankier
priest told her in confession she'd have to give up
"Lady Chatterley" and books like it and this convinced
her it was time to move on: and thus OLT inadvertently
transfigured her life and also she truly transfigured
herself.)
     Lots of loving up here late last night despite all
the sleep vows. Mondo comes for her, none for me, the
usual, but no new meltdowns. New nicknames popped up,

however: Slow-Dick Jeep, Fast-Clit Weezie. Not quite
accurate, though, that first one. Performance-Anxiety-
Dick Jeep might be more like it. Or Low-Jizz Jeep.

     Did I say "no new meltdowns"? I did, but only
because the night's meltdown had come earlier, before I
left for work. And of course it was over another of my
sorry genital failures (to come, to harden up, to stay
hard, to "penetrate," to stay hard while "penetrating,"
etc. -- but this one primarily over coming). And it
happened after another session of gorgeous loving right
here in the loft, she dressed and me fully naked (this
by happenstance; I'd assumed she was already undressed
and I stripped before coming up); and this state of
differential dress turned out to be a turn-on for both
of us. (It began as a total surprise. We'd been
reading the afternoon paper, she in the green armchair
and I on the cluttered loveseat -- reversing the usual
arrangement just for variety's sake -- and it was time
to make dinner. As we headed for the kitchen she said,
"You wanna go up and horse around some first?")

     As for the meltdown itself, it was much like the
others. 'Nuff said. -- And same goes for the foozles.
Why keep beating myself over the head with this stuff?
Or over the genitals, right. Or over the head with the
genitals, figuratively speaking, yes of course. (It
just so happens that the shameful confession I mentioned
earlier had to do with beating myself about the genitals,
which is to say: wanky-panky. Fessed it up to Z. An
attempt to jolt the mechanism into action by a kind of
reverse psychology earlier in the evening, that's what.
And it was no more successful than the dozens of other
ways I've tried to get the thing up and fucking --
unsuccessful except for the onanistic action itself, that
is, but then that's never been a problem.)

     -- Today at work she definitely was not perky.
(That was her afternoon phone message: "I'm not perky,
I'm not perky." And since she'd learned about the
unexpected availability of several vacation days, she
wanted to take one tomorrow, meaning later today. "You
want to play around together?" Took me a few minutes to

[Absolute Tiptop Pinnacle - Jyzin' with Z]

let go of the plans I'd already made to visit the
storage unit by myself, but I did. Of course having her
along would be far better. "Yah'm sure!" But yes.)
     (Just hit on a new position for jyzing up here.
Laying the J-book on the foot-wide strip of platform
wood between the head of the futon and the wall, thus at
a level several inches lower than the futon top --
having swept aside the pillows which were stuffed into
that strip -- takes most of the pressure off my back.
If fatigue weren't closing in I might be able to go all
night.) (By the way: visitors to Tokyo these days can
rent hotel rooms "the size of a broom closet laid out
horizontally." This according to a newspaper clip Z
gave me yesterday. And possibly because this loft-top
area here is roughly equivalent to a couple of those
broom closets laid side by side, but with the internal
wall between them knocked out and the resultant single
ceiling lowered a foot or so, the one in Tokyo pictured
in the clip looked almost like home to both of us.)
     -- Obviously I'm having trouble holding to the plan
on flashbacks. I'll just say the one assigned to this
entry, J-week #20, of course goes to 20K Day and the
jyzo album she gave me on that occasion -- and I said
then and I repeat now, for me that was the finest gift
ever. It sealed us, joined us at the heart. I moved
into the third 10K era of my life -- into Peak Prime
Time too, I'm not forgetting, and also the six-month
transition to Glennarian Stage III -- moved into all
this, I say, feeling almost as close and permanently
attached to her as I do right now with her naked body
pressed against mine (noticing we're both getting a
little moist where we're in contact, especially between
the legs -- and my god is this sweet) (in the warm
yellow loft lamplight as the fan spins just barely
audibly down below, an occasional lick of cool breeze
reaching up here).
     The first ferry trip also took place during J-week
#20, but I'll save that for tomorrow too as we seek to
replay it in real time (just as then) for this JIRT.
     -- So tonight we met at eight up at the old

Japanese theater. It was mayoral candidates night for
her Asian/Pacific Islander women's group (APWA) and
seven of the wannabes were seated at tables on the
stage and in the middle with a mike stood -- Aida.
Wotta surprise! (And she made a superb moderator too,
from the few minutes I saw, and Z said she'd done just
as well earlier.) (And someone I didn't even recognize
said happy birthday to me -- turned out it was Aida and
Z's friend Emiko, who'd organized the refreshments for
the occasion. "I'm sure Aida keeps her fully apprised
of what's going on between us," Z explained. "Well, I
hope not 'fully,'" I said; "I hope Aida doesn't know the
'fully' fully enough to be apprising anyone of it." And
Z again assured me she's keeping her word on this --
meaning she's not talking with anyone about our private,
"intimate" life, and especially the sexual portion of it
-- although it's not so easy to hold to this vow with
Aida in particular, as Z's let me know, because they're
so close and they've always been open with each other
about "everything.") (Emiko and I met at Z's graduation
shindig at Aida's house, but I OD'd on introductions
that day and remembered her only vaguely as a face and
tonight had to ask Z in a whisper for her name. The
same happened with several others we ran into at the
theater. But I swear the incidence of these forgettings
is slowly shrinking.)
     So then a stroll home together through the downtown
canyons. Dinner here at B-2. Reading. Just after
she'd changed into her "Mestizas Rule" nightshirt I
coaxed her down onto my lap in the green armchair and we
spiraled into a long loving session there, four or five
Z-comes. Then up here supposedly to jyze but she was
suddenly strange -- didn't seem to want to -- and when I
said I still did, she hit me with the "Calvinist" remark.
Then in shifting positions so I could be closer to the
light I paused while atop her, we began futzing around
again (because it's unusual for me to be atop her --
since being there would almost oblige me to perform and
I don't trust my goddamn magic twanger right now, and
haven't for all these months), and then -- and then good

good loving, yes, except for the one thing. That, yeah.
Of course. And this morning another round, the same.
Except -- the one thing almost worked. Bizarre. Very
close. Even at the time I was thinking, "This is good
enough, we're another step closer, gradually getting
there, eventually it'll happen, best not to rush it,
don't want another humiliating in-vaj foozle."
     And this note: yesterday morning for the first time
during one of our workday bus rides in from her place
she took out her newspaper and (after asking whether I
minded) started reading it. This is her longtime
practice -- and she does it like a veteran too, folding
the paper into quarters, and takes special pride in
doing so -- but she'd abandoned the practice from the
start while riding in with me. Thus it would seem we've
crossed another significant barrier on our way back into
the land of normalcy, but this time together, and I for
one am glad of it.
     Also she cited, as evidence of "the effect you and
school have had on me," how much more "approachable"
she's become on the bus, where people have actually
engaged her in conversation in recent months, whereas
before they shied away because "I always acted like this
aloof big-city person" -- that is, she who routinely
eats suburban boys for lunch -- and who back in her late
teens and twenties sometimes scared off creeps on city
buses by warning them she was a cop and flashing a fake
badge -- she in a miniskirt -- a method which she grants
would be more like waving a red flag today.
     And she wore a new transparent lip gloss, thus
resolving the problem of how to feel "fully dressed" for
work and yet also be able to smooch with her G-man at
the bus stop and on the bus without leaving flagrant
lipstick stains on both of us.
     -- Now she's disengaged except for one hand on my
thigh. She's rolled over on her back, head turned away
from me and the light, her other hand thrown behind her
head so it's the only part of her I can see, far right
visual periphery. (Such a handsome hand too: lean,
shapely, strong, tapered, expressive. No nail polish at

the moment, I see. I love this woman whose hand this
is, yes I do. Touches my heart in a thousand ways, yes
she does. As I do hers, yes, she says so and I believe
her and I see all kinds of confirmation. Her latest
pup-tent sign, for instance: "Yup. Open. Now.")

    -- And her nipples. Time to put a stop to
tonight's JAZ-jyzin' and get my priorities back into
whack. Lightly graze those nipples with these same JAZ-
jyzin' fingertips and see at what point she awakens.
(And chases me away maybe. She must be very, very
tired. So maybe drop the grazing notion for now. But
then again she's not working tomorrow. And right from
the start she's always said no matter how tired she is,
as long as she's not working the next day....)

S15

    Aboard. Summoning the wiles of the former ferry
regular I bolted ahead of the pack to grab the best
booth of all. And on the bench opposite right here, Z's
going "haa-haa-haa," steaming up her brand-new reading
glasses before wiping them off in preparation for a
cross-drink ferryboat jyzedown.

    We'd hoped to catch the 11:45 but a few things came
up. One was another Z-meltdown. A well-earned meltdown
this time, no question. "I'm a total failure! It's
cosmic retribution." (For what? "For being so mean to
all those men.")

    Three times during the night she went at the
aroused G-joint with everything she had and all three
times it deflated in her hands. "I want to throw myself
from the loft, beat my head against the wall."

    She identified the FOO which she sees as being

behind all this (or reidentified, but for the first time
in at least a month): the feeling she's letting her
father down. She could never be what he wanted her to
be, which was a son who would become an engineer or, as
a lesser hope, a daughter who would be dainty and demure
in the traditional Filipina way (though I suppose
"dainty and demure" isn't quite right; more like
spirited and vivacious but submissive on patriarchal
request or demand).

(We're chugging out now. She's blazing along in
her own jyze -- then pauses to ask, "So, during your
commuting days were you this spectral figure haunting
the ferries?" -- Yes, that was me, that was me! And
often doing it in, or from, this very booth on this very
vessel.)

(And she told me her father on his deathbed
apologized for not having encouraged her to become an
artist. -- And he often ate with his fingers. My
saying "Excuse my fingers" at dinner last night evoked
this tidbit and also the deathbed story -- and buckets
of mournful tears the operatic production of which
anyone who didn't know her at least a little would
think was grossly exaggerated.)

-- Then a remarkable turnaround. And it came when
I'd just about given up hope (and she'd even told me
things seemed hopeless, and for the first time said,
"Maybe it's not such a miracle after all, you and me").

Earlier I'd recalled that night at her place way
back in the first few weeks when she'd repeated "I love
you" about a thousand times while being towsed. Now
without any further prompting she started into another
"I love you" mantra (both of us lying on our backs
naked on the purple sheet up in the loft) and went on
and on with it, and before long it somehow began turning
me on, and I put her hand on my sex and said, "Say it
with your hand too," and she did and it worked: the
jyzerman came. Again. Finally. "Shot off." (Such an
abundance too, and it flew all over the place, including
up to the ceiling -- which of course is only twenty
inches above the futon -- a couple of the gobs dangling

like stalactites.) And still she kept on with the
mantra and then I reciprocated a come for her. Several.
(Come come now, surely you exaggerate, Jyze Guy. But
no. Her climax cascade was only beginning.)
     -- Now she's stretching out on the bench across
from me. "Sleepy." And asks: "Wouldn't it be fun to
lie next to each other here?" Reaches under the table
to squeeze my thigh.
     Bending into the narrow passage. Loving her.
Sneaking glances. This morning she caught me doing the
same from the loft as she wandered around naked down
below and said, "You think I'm cute, don't you." This
led to my learning that the adjectives she's heard most
often from men are "striking" and "sexy." "Not
ravishingly beautiful?" "That too."
     A bit later a standing come for her as we showered
together. Then as she sat in the green armchair I
reacted to something she said by assuming a mock-macho
pose and she responded by grabbing her crotch in mock
heat -- but then I began kissing her and allowed as how
I liked what she was doing with her hand, so she kept
doing it as I talk-kissed her, and WHAMMO, another come
for her. Comes galore! Minutes later, standing next to
me in the middle of the room, she flipped up her T-shirt
to indicate her nipples needed attention. -- Did it
with such panache too. This was the "Brown" T-shirt:
the first time she showed it to me I was bamboozled
enough to ask if it had been a gift from someone who'd
gone to the university of that name (the words "and
Proud," which I hadn't noticed at first, appear well
below "Brown" and in place of "University," all laid out
in large gothic font). Another come. (And another jyze
exception -- maybe -- on "Brown.")
     -- And the birthday weekend's just beginning. Big
mysterious doings scheduled for tomorrow. She's
tantalizing me: "Aren't you just dying of curiosity to
know what's going to happen?"
     -- But the "I love you" mantra, it struck deep for
me. Immediately I proposed we switch paradigms, from
innocence to love. And I was linking what happened as

she mantra'd to what impressed me most in reviewing those early flashback sections, how during such a short period I'd lost in one way or another all the women I'd loved -- Mother, Lady U, sister Barb, even Yo and Lena, the main female characters in "Jyzer" (and the briefly resurrected Lady K, upon whom Lena is based, in JIFT and in real life -- via correspondence -- as well). More forcefully than ever I realized it could be unconscious grief over such concentrated loss that was messing me up sexually, and that taking this grief into greater account could perhaps help repair my damaged psychosexual soul.

    -- Last turn. And here she is, back from the women's head. "I saw myself in the mirror. I look all washed out and dissipated." "You look fabulous." "I look like I've been fucking all night and all morning. -- Hey, are we here already?"

    -- As the ominous gray line of U.S. Navy warships fills the windows. Because that's the main "here" here.

           *   *

    -- So now some nookie deep in unit 161, brushing up against the support studs (where else?) back behind high stacks of boxes and beneath the makeshift storage loft -- one false move and the whole structure could come crashing down on us. (Meaning symbolically we're in such a fragile condition too much knowledge of the G-man's past could crush us? No no no.)

    Up comes the "Brown" shirt, down comes the "Pink" zipper. For her, one come per nipple and a third for the clit, and this last happens almost instantaneously and I say, "Fast Weezie, you're amazing me again," and she does a major pricklenose and says, "I don't think I like that 'Fast Weezie' anymore." So I say, "I don't mean it bad, I mean it good" -- and do I ever -- but I'll drop it anyway. (But the second nipple come is the best, eyes open and locked, hers so meltingly amorous, I feel this love's at a new and even deeper/higher pitch -- and the birthday blowout's scarcely even begun.)

    "Why is it we're so hot for each other all the time?" she asks as we work our way back down the aisle

between high stacks of boxes, and she's not asking
rhetorically, though she knows as well as I do -- or
probably better -- that we have no noncircular or
nontautological answer and what's more don't really want
to have one, or maybe better to have lots of them of the
partial type and all clashing and producing plenty of
sparks making things even hotter.

Fire safe and file drawers open for airing as we
sit outside. She's perched on Nana's shameful antique
"mammy chair" across the asphalt drive in the shade.
My clothes are still arrayed just as when I laid them
out for her inspection during our first visit here (even
though, unbeknownst to me until now, the ministorage
outfit has changed hands since then -- I found a fresh
sticker bearing the new corporate owner's name affixed
to my lock).

"I'm on a JAG jag," she calls out. "JAGin' off!"
(We've discussed it: if JAZ is Jyze Around Zoelie, JAG
is....)

(The two times a car drove by while we were
nookying back there I instinctively pretended to be
inspecting a high-up box, since I was visible above the
waist from out here. Such high-school stuff!) (As we
crossed the street from the mall after hopping off the
bus she said, "My nipples really really need doing
again. Before we pump the jyze if that works for you."
At the corner while we were waiting for the light to
change, our eyes were drawn to the sight of our own
stretched-out, distorted "Giacometti" shadows -- another
jyze exception there, but quoting Z so maybe it's not
necessary -- swaying together at an odd angle atop a
ten-foot-high, forty-five-degree embankment overlooking
the parking lot: "Seeing ourselves oblique.")

So marvelous this is, I'm reduced to dazed
transcription of snippets of dialogue and the simplest
chronology and otherwise it's almost all sex stuff.
Once again we're both totally caught up in the hormonal
cascade. I might even have ejacked again myself back
there under the loft had I not lost my balance a little
and set the loft to ominously swaying and creaking

overhead, causing a panicky moment for both of us.

     -- Riding across the inlet on the foot ferry with a
full load of shipyard workers, many with familiar faces,
every last one male and most dressed much like me, the
real working-class dudes versus the declasse' impostor
(who in weekly wages makes maybe a third or a fourth
what they do). She and I sitting on the prow deck, atop
the engine box, she enjoying the engine vibrations just
as she had back on the big boat. Rubbing her braless
breasts against me "discreetly" (the pilot looking down
on us with voyeuristic glee, no doubt, we shameless
exhibitionists -- but discreet, yeah, as if the whole
boat weren't about to start spinning in tight little
circles of Z-inspired lust out there in mid inlet).

     So...history. Here it is. My former life. My old
bike route, all the old highways and byways, the shops
and eateries and movie theater and whatnot. All kinds
of phantom selves, my own and others', go whizzing by.
Can't focus on them at all (especially not with the Z-
woman's tongue in my ear as it now is, lubriciously
aswirl. -- Her tongue aswirl that way, I mean, but my
head too, as has been the case for pretty much the past
five months nonstop). -- But we're talking some about
this history stuff, yeah. And of course with extreme
caution. But anything "usable" here? And if so, usable
in just what way?

                      *   *

     -- Now back lolling on the big ferry as it chugs
homewardbound. Z's perched across from me, her J-book
laid out on the booth table but not yet cracked open.
"I don't know if anything's built up yet," she explains.

     -- Hello. She's joining me on this side of the
table. Is stretching out in comely fashion on the
bench (which is about six feet long), her head tilting
against my back as I lean into the table, her hand
reaching around to rest on my inner thigh. -- And now
she's sitting up, her arm around my neck.

     Am I loving all this? Oh am I! -- And it appears
we may be caught up in a bit of a canoodling contest
with another couple roughly our vintage, give or take a

decade or so, facing us two booths up with the one between us unoccupied. Z noticed this couple too. The "when I'm bad I'm better" voice: "Wanna do some clandestine nipple stuff, big boy?"

Rounding one of the points -- now I have a good excuse for not remembering its name. How my life is different: this trip I was making five or six times a week for close to seven years, and weekly or fortnightly for most of last year, I'm currently making once every three months. (Sun's all but blinding as we groan around the first sharp bend -- in what I've long called the Z-narrows, starting well before I'd met the Z-woman -- should've mentioned this earlier when we were going the other way -- and now plowing almost due south down the twisty narrow inner passage. And the other raunchy couple has handed a fancy camera to a passing deckhand to memorialize the dazzling moment -- same thing this jyze right here is trying to do but in ink.)

Now churning out eastbound into open water and leaving behind my old stomping grounds. And maybe for a long while; maybe even in a symbolic sense -- or just about certainly -- forever. Nor am I feeling any pain over this. Well, not true, some twinges, but at most they're few and far between. This Z upheaval is casting the landforms behind us and "the past" into a grand metaphorical darkness (as indeed the mountains are doing also as the sun slips down behind them some fifteen miles to our rear, melodramatically dipping the vessel itself and all its riders -- not just us! -- into a sudden and very lengthy stretch of alpine shadow).

In my ear she's singing "What a day this has been / What a fine mood I'm in...."

But the other raunchy couple is making us look bad. Time to focus. "The mush mudra," Z says. Let's get it on, boys and girls, I say. Be over-the-top obnoxious here. Yes! Just do it! Express yourself!

[Absolute Tiptop Pinnacle - Jyzin' with Z]

----

s16

     The big day finds me once again back where we
began. I'm holding forth now where Z sat then: a worn
wooden bench resting at the base of a high white plaster
wall hung with roughly a dozen oil and acrylic paintings
on unframed canvases of various shapes and sizes
including oval and triangular. Maple tabletop. The
wooden chair to my right is where I sat on that day,
and just as it was then it's facing the next table over,
the window table. It was Z's idea on that day to turn
the chair around so we could sit closer together rather
than face each other across the wide expanse of table.
     (Almost unbearably warm in here right now. Most
everybody's sitting outside. You gotta have a damn good
reason to subject yourself to such an indoor heat bath.
And I, as it happens, have a damn good reason.)
     So now I'm officially a year older. I'm also at
the self-declared "Absolute Tiptop Pinnacle" of my adult
life (self-declared but using perfectly legit actuarial
and calendrical principles). -- Which is also to say
I'm halfway across the Peak Prime Time transition phase
between 20K Day and Glennarian Rollover into Stage III
-- and I've never even gotten around to explaining what
the Glennarian calendar is all about, or at least not in
this year's jyze. -- But later for that. Or not.
Certainly doesn't seem to matter a great deal just now.
What does matter is my strong hunch that I'm moving into
a new personal era which will probably last in much the
same form -- or at least I'm sure hoping so -- the rest
of my life. Or better to say: our lives.
     Zoelie. Zoelie B. What a blessing she is. Again

395

I'm dazed by the sheer magnitude of it. Not to mention
its extreme, I mean space-warp transport to Galaxy
Jyzomeda EXTREME improbability.

I'm down here right now because she ran me out of
her apartment. She's readying the place for tonight's
festivities, the exact nature of which remains unknown
to me. I'm not even guessing what it might be.
"Surprise birthday party" is all I know.

Last night after our return to her place from the
ferry terminal we drank wine and loveplayed until
midnight (me in the blue shorts and then out of them; Z
seated between my legs on the floor to suck me off as I
sat in one of the rattan chairs -- though "off" didn't
quite happen, then or in bed later or this morning, for
me anyway; but for her it did, over and over, as per
usual). At midnight I opened one of her three gifts,
which turned out to be a book of charts of the music
kind, lyrics included, for a hundred jazz standards.
Then she sang two of the tunes in that book -- "My Funny
Valentine" and "You Do Something To Me" -- and it's hard
to imagine any "off" better than what those did to me.
Especially the way she nuzzled my scalp as she delivered
the key line of them all: "'...don't change a hair for
me' -- because I'm gonna shear them all off anyway!"

(An hour earlier she'd secluded herself in the
bedroom to wrap the gifts in newspaper and blue straw
ribbon. I'd've preferred to wait until tonight to open
them, but so eager was she to go ahead right away that I
couldn't say no. "Christmas and birthdays," she
acknowledged, "are big big deals for me." And added: "I
really like to be fussed over on those days, and my
suspicion is that you do too.")

Everything seems shot through with meaning right
now. What I'm especially noticing is that the move into
the love paradigm has her wondering if I'm totally,
absolutely sure she loves me. Her doubt about this has
me focusing on ways we might push the love still further
and deeper. It was just five months ago yesterday we
met in the flesh and she was sitting on this bench where
I sit now, but in these months I feel I've already gone

well beyond the ways I've loved in the past. The
question is how to forge on into even more radically
unknown territory. I'm determined it'll happen. Looks
to me like it'll be fabulous.

The other big question is how to forge on in those
same ways but in the sexual realm. How jelly that jelly
roll? It's ridiculous, maybe, but I still believe this
will answer itself. In its own time to be sure. Which
I guess is okay, just so long as its own time isn't too
big a portion of our cumulative time together in total.

(Another meaningful moment: in bed she whispered
she feels completely safe in letting herself be
"submissive" with me. And I said I feel likewise in
letting her know I need her big-time.)

*

(I told her I'd be back around four-thirty, five at
the latest. It's almost four now -- later than I
realized. The walk to her place takes roughly twenty
minutes, so I'll have to be wrapping this up in forty
minutes or less. I wasted too much time browsing at the
magazine shop -- same one where, at its entrance, we
first laid eyes on each other before coming over here,
to this cafe, although by an extremely roundabout route,
to "get acquainted.")

-- Last night she brought out her high-school
annuals for the first time. The Vikings, of all
possible mascots. Such a heartbreaking beauty, the
teenage Zoelie (Louise then of course) looking so bright
and energetic at her editor's desk for the school
newspaper. Maybe not quite yet at climax glamour state,
but you can definitely see it coming. (In flipping
through the pages for the first time in years she was
surprised to discover that two of her classmates were
Asiusan -- in her own mind she'd reduced the situation
to one even more stark than it really was (that is, to
one all Cawk except for her).) (And today in talking
about Kat's beauty and how to speak about it with her I
was astounded to learn Z's parents didn't see her as
being exceptionally beautiful while she was growing up.
She had to wait to hear it from lovers.)

                    [Jyze in Love]

     She's convinced our paths crossed at least one
previously undiscovered time when we were in our mid-
twenties. It was at a certain party during a period
when I was often in the city (Centropolis) and
occasionally partying in an area where she did also, and
our eyes caught and flashed; she's almost sure of it.
But in those days, we now agree, neither of us would've
been anywhere near ready to cope with the other. The
volatility would've done us in for sure. And for the
next fifteen or twenty years the story might well have
been the same. In a sense we met at the best possible
time for both of us. (In the past twenty years while
working and usually living here in Jyze City we must've
crossed paths scores or even hundreds of times. I
learned about a new one when I picked her up at the
Japanese theater the other night: she and I were both
present -- in a crowd of hundreds -- for the dedication
of the new curtain there maybe ten years ago.)
     This morning loveplay in bed until eleven. Best
moment for me: when she agreed to do her daily
meditation stint right there, lying in my arms, one hand
cupping my "G'nads" -- another snappy (ballsy) Z-coinage
-- "as the manly equivalent of love beads." Then over
breakfast I opened the other two gifts. One is a
marvelous hand-painted (by her) dinner plate bearing the
words "M'BAO MUSH" and showing two lovestruck camels
rubbing noses. The other's a handmade pop-up card
reminding me she'll be footing the hotel bill for two-
thirds of our first out-of-state (just barely) trip, now
firmed up for the first weekend in November -- which
means this already extended birthday weekend will be
stretched out much further: another seventy or so days
before the final curtain falls at the end of that trip.
     And more good things. Kat and Betty called and
sang "Happy Birthday," a duet, and a little later they
dropped by bearing the promised home-baked raspberry pie
(berries from their garden). Kat gave me a pop-up card
she made with Z's assistance. "I like you, Glen!" it
says. We gobbled down half the pie (which was decorated
with flowers and the same small Norwegian flag I

                          398

originally bought for Kat at the Independence Day
parade) and as usual Kat charmed me through and through.
How moved I was! (And afterwards I assured a suddenly
weeping Z that Manny would've been deeply grateful for
the way she's helping Betty raise Kat.) -- And Z
sobbed, "You're family to them now." Well, maybe not
all the way just yet. But I truly do feel it's moving
in that direction, and I love the feeling.

     Oooeee, the mush. And more ahead. Seems unlikely
now the talk about "The Pillow Book" and the various
hot-button issues will lead to anything too disruptive.
We're even planning to do some body-writing on each
other as part of "tandem jyze in the raw." And maybe,
presumably after getting dressed again, we'll try to
squeeze in dinner at an authentic restaurant and then
catch a movie somewhere.

     But what's tonight's surprise? Time to climb the
hill to find out. -- I'm not sure but I think, even
though it's not fully a surprise, this is still my very
first surprise birthday party ever. (Awww....)
                    *   *

     Suddenly it's very quiet as I turn the radio off.
Absolute Tiptop Pinnacle Birthday -- the day itself --
already almost over, just ten minutes of it remaining.
Only this one light on in Z's apartment (the
fluorescent desk lamp atop the bookcase).

     We started reading together (parallel) in bed but
she faded quickly. A few plaintive little murmurs at my
side and off she dozed. After her breathing evened out
I slipped over here, to the dinette table, which is
still in its state of maximum party-time expansion, with
two extra leaves inserted in the middle.

     Glittery dark scarves, night city. They bring to
mind the biggest question Z and I face right now: will
we one day be living together on the far side of those
big downtown towers -- or on this side?

     A wonderful birthday party. She worked hard to
pull it off and should be feeling mighty proud. (Her
comment when I told her this maybe half an hour ago:
"Yeah, and now I'm gonna coast awhile." And then with

a hearty laugh: "D'you think I'm a pookhead for letting
you do the dishes on your birthday?" Heck no, I said,
as long as she doesn't think I'm a pookhead for putting
off the actual washing until tomorrow.)

    Nibbling at a bowl of fresh birthday blueberries.
Here's the bottle of cabernet merlot, now empty, brother
Rob brought over (yes, he and Gail were two of the
surprise dinner guests, as I'd been secretly expecting,
and hoping too, because otherwise I might've been miffed
not to have heard from Rob for my birthday, and
especially after he failed to write during his Mentoka
trip, which he returned from last Sunday).

    On the counter are several large bowls which once
contained the chicken stew Aida brought over (yes, she
was the third guest, which truly was a surprise, and I
was delighted by it; and from the way the talk went I
felt all was okay between us again, though maybe not yet
as good as it could be) (she's now thinking about moving
up to this end of town to be near her family, by the
way, so we probably won't be neighbors on south hill
after all -- and maybe that's just as well).

    Five partiers in total, myself included. With two
of the other four being certified "facilitators" (Z and
Aida) there was never any danger of conversational drag
or lag, not even when Rob stepped out on the balcony to
smoke his pipe. (From time to time he pitched in a
comment through the screen door -- which, incidentally,
jumped its track at some point tonight and thus
tomorrow will become the object of my first-ever
"manly-man repair-mission thing" for Z here in 401).

    Highlight of the evening was Z's homemade cobbler.
It started out as peach cobbler in honor of her favorite
analogy for postcoital vaginal good feeling (though only
I'm in the know on this, she assured me). Then she
added a box of fresh blueberries because she knows I
love them. Then after hearing me talk about our family
tradition of strawberry shortcake on birthdays she
tossed in a box of sliced fresh strawberries too. The
result was scrumptious, every bit as good as that out-
of-this-world peach slump we had at the diner last week.

[Absolute Tiptop Pinnacle - Jyzin' with Z]

     "So now do you believe I can cook?" I believe!
(I also believe, given her priorities, she's making the
right choice in limiting it to special occasions.
-- And yes, I believe in her priorities too.)
     (A couple of birthday stories she told spring to
mind. One: friends threw a big party for her on her
thirtieth and she missed the whole thing, passed out
dead drunk in the bedroom (this was back in Lahontan).
Two: for her fortieth she did a scantily clad belly
dance atop the bar at the same infamous dive atop east
hill where jyze once held forth roughly a year ago. She
does like to party and though she may have a shy streak,
she can overcome it; and once she does, look out:
inhibited she ain't. Three times in the past four days
she's wanked off in front of me. It turns out -- no
surprise really -- I'm the inhibited one, at least in
some respects, including that one.)
     The party didn't go late. Rob would have to be up
at five-thirty a.m. for work. And Aida was exhausted
(like Z, her self-declared role model, she's forever
juggling projects; just yesterday she was appointed
diversity manager for local state offices -- I listened
to Z sing, literally, her congratulations to Aida's
answering machine). -- So after dinner thirty or forty
minutes of lying around like life-size stuffed animals
on the futon and couch and Tibetan (Nepalese?) dragon
carpet in the other part of the room discussing city
politics (mostly) as the figures in Manny's terrific
Zoelie Trope went round and round, much to Rob and
Gail's fascination (Aida providing some riveting engine
and exhaust sound effects for the hilarious loop with
her and Z on prop motorcycles chasing each other over
hill and dale in a studio at the state fair).
     Any conflicts left between Z and me? Of course!
Maybe we'll try to discuss some of them tomorrow. Yet
I'd like to think (this occurred to me as I was hoofing
it up the hill from the cafe this afternoon) this spree
has been showing something else: namely, that the love
bonds between the two tandem jyzers have strengthened to
the point where most of the "hot-button issues" I listed

earlier will gradually disarm themselves simply through
growing trust.

     I'm not saying I'm sure that's happening. But I'm
hoping it is. Or if it's not just yet, that it soon
will.

     -- Z's now softly snoring. -- Suddenly, though, a
snort and a thrash and then she's almost silent again:
just a little sporadic plopping sound, barely audible,
something like a bubble breaking the surface. Ploop!
Ploop! (Or maybe like the jyzer plucking grapes one-
handed sounded to her a cycle or two back.)

     The night's no longer young. But neither is it
old. Say it's, like our adult lives, Z's and mine, at
Prime Time Peak. (Okay, okay, it's shortly before one,
and so just about halfway between sunset and sunrise.)
-- "Truly middle-aged" is how Z thinks of us "in my
rare realistic moments" (as opposed to the frequent
romantic ones, in which we might be any age at all, with
high school and college predominating these days, it
often seems, or that "ageless" category of hard-to-
pinpoint barely-post-youth). -- True, a different sort
of realism would classify us, by some measures anyway,
as proto or premature geezers. As of today I'm eligible
for an early senior discount or two, I do believe. And
of course that's been true of her for a good while:
about 525 days, if my calculations are correct.

     But so what. I'm not pursuing the matter. Don't
want to be denying it but still less want to be calling
attention to it. What is, is; what's going is going;
what's gone is gone -- and meanwhile, boys and girls,
let's get it on while we still can. If, that is, we
still can. And I say -- we can! Or at the very least:
she sure can!

*

     -- And what a note to end a birthday entry on.
"Absolute Tiptop Pinnacle" indeed. But Z's up again
and needing a snack and I'm calling it quits in here
(and reminding myself this entry still has tomorrow's
stuff to tack on since we'll be doing it real time --
the truly raw birthday-suit body writing and whatnot --

unless that winds up being postponed until Monday).
*   *

Coda opens on the red couch. (It's early evening of the next day, third day of the celebratory four-day weekend, and radio blues are playing and we're both revved up and ready.) -- She wanted to move over to the bed before starting into "tandem jyze in the raw," the acronym for which is TJITR, but is now retracting that.

"I think the moment's come for you to take off your shorts, M'bao," she says, "and bring out N'dow" (another clever Z-acro intro'd just today). She in her wicked black knit dress, no underwear -- and lifts her legs, both sides of me, one now resting on my thigh. ("Beaver flash," high-school thrill.) "Just one moment," I say. (Ooh I do like how she looks down there.) (Shorts off.) (We heated up first. She's juicy. Finger-dip check. -- I'm maybe a slight bit tumefied but that's about it. A couple of veins protruding somewhat I'm happy to see.)
*

And a swig of wine in a dark blue cup (hers already empty but she wants no more just yet). My legs now straddling her too. Our legs-locked position way too complex for quick description. Oh this woman I love, why did she take so long to show up in my life? Glasses, wire rimmed, pushed down to nose-tip (these are her new reading glasses and just in the past couple of days she's lost another pair and hissy-fitted over it and blames it all on our return to "hyper-limerence," though birthday stress no doubt also figures into it). (She's now laying "N'dow," nee "gnarly whatzis," across the top of her foot by the toes and pinning it there with her right hand while jyzing away with her left. "MIA dick, meet MIA toe." (That's me imagining an intro, with MIA in its military meaning.) -- Or "willy and the Hot Jyze," could call it, referring to the whole scene.)

The red couch. This highly uncomfortable slab of designer ugliness. Here we conducted our first major courting exercise, getting nowhere. All my energy went to pulling myself back up again and again Sisyphuslike

403

as the spongy cushions and lack of a frame kept sliding
me toward the floor just as the Z-woman and I were about
to get into it -- or more like a vaudeville gag really.
*
(Now we've moved over to the bed. Danced a little
slow dance to one of her favorite soul tunes on the
radio. Closed the curtain to make sure we wouldn't be
visible from the street, though it's hard to see how
that would be possible except maybe if a TV van with an
extendo transmission tower happened by and decided to
erect.) (Black dress up over her head.)
It's her call on positions here. I'm lying on my
right side in front of her, facing her, her right knee
above -- no, make that below my left leg, her J-book
resting on my left hip, my genital "package" drooping in
insouciant triune fashion right below the book, with the
package centerpiece maybe slightly more swole up now.
Oooeee, yup yup, this is fun! And I'd say she's
not just being a good sport; she's into this. (With the
back of my fingers, left hand, I'm stroking her fine
soft black muff and she stops to gaze at me, even sort
of mock glare. "Jyze on, grrrrl." 'N she does.)
-- And here's what I've been trying to get to since
the first word of this entry (and I swear this is not a
setup):
On the little finger of my left hand rides a new
ring, silver, three stars and two half moons cut through
it or say punched out of it. On her ring finger left
hand rides another new ring, also silver.
(Pause now to admire some curves as she pulls her
body away and draws her head up to within a few inches
of my still pretty much limp and lank sideways-dangling
"N'dow" whose lipless little slit of a mouth I trust is
grinning sassily back at her as she alternates peering
up close and jyzing -- say like a dutiful student in
biology class inspecting a strung-up bullfrog -- and at
the same time at a deeper level she's probably
addressing it with a few choice words. Now tapping the
puffy cheeks, as it were, of the glans on either side
of the slit with her own J-stick. Little visible

effect but she's smiling -- into it, yup. Tap tap tap
again. "You like that, eh?")

   Both rings bought at the local flea market this
afternoon. Impulse purchases but the impulse going all
the way down. Total cost nine bucks. Symbolizing --
whatever. "Engagement." Or just say big-time last-
chance romance. Or say: this is it. We're there.
We're never going back.

   Best birthday present ever. None better possible.
   -- Getting funkier now. Switch to a 69 position,
but twisted a little so I can prop the J-book against
her ass. Aieeee, so sweet! So smooth! So shapely!
-- This touches on "The Pillow Book" body-writing
controversy too, because I inscribe with my J-stick a
heart in the small of her back and inside it the
phrase "G loves Z." And she twists her hips around
and presents her pretty little puss, calls for me to
make my mark there too, and I do: "For Loving M'bao/
N'dow," with an arrow pointing to the grotto. (These
notes now going down with the J-book spread on her
tender upper inner left thigh -- and here a few quick
licks -- but literally! -- on her truly jyzogenic
snatch. Recalls one of the jyze posters hanging above
the worktable in B-2: "Jyzin' the Groove Thang.")
   -- Mmm, yeah, fine funky strong sniff. Lovely
skin, a tiny vein. Up near the Z-bird navel now, a
fibroidectomy scar here and a mole there and some more
very pretty curves. (Just dipped the tip of the J-stick
gently into juicy vulva -- with her consent, to be sure,
and even urging -- and could be that's what's making
this scrawl so thick and pale. And noting the small
black vulvar violet (flower type), the mark of the
jyzer: and it's permanent ink! -- Now scrubbing it away
with my finger. Or the visible part, let's say. -- And
recalling "Wicked Jyze Licks": another poster.) (Now
she swings a leg over my head so I have the callipygian
view from behind and below. The justly celebrated
little pool-table-smooth buns, ooh ooh ooh ooh ooh ooh
ooh.)
   -- And what's she really thinking now? Still

feeling safe to "submit," to open herself? As, say, I
am? -- Or is she at some level worrying the J-man is
scrawling awful suburban male Cawkazoidal neocolonial
invader nastinesses in her most intimate places,
crowing, conquesting, machoing, patriarchalizing? No,
she'd not be, I refuse to think it. -- But I believe
she may be discovering new things from these new
perspectives. "You're a man," she keeps murmuring, as
if noticing for the first time. "I'm writing the male
body."

     Think she's done now. She's had her fill. Says,
"So?" I hear her capping her pen. -- We'll take a
break, that's what: she suggests and I agree.
                    *   *

     Back maybe half an hour later for round two. Still
naked, this time lying on the gorgeous dragon rug in
front of the abominable red couch. "Sort of like a
Playgirl centerfold," she observes, leaning back, head
tilted, finger scratching chin, an eye cocked perhaps a
bit more critically than one might wish even if she
thinks she just be playin'. -- It's Nepalese, the rug,
she tells me, not Tibetan. She loved it so much she
carried it all the way back from Nepal (where, in a
shocking lapse of cultural sensitivity she now rues, she
wore mainly miniskirts, as also in Afghanistan and
India) -- carried it rather than risk shipping it. (I'm
lying, she's sitting at the moment -- still naked too --
with breasts so perkily protuberant because of how her
back's propped against the lower part of the couch.)

     Not a meltdown then, but suddenly she was looking
at me as if I were a stranger. "Jamais vu." It still
happens every now and then. Detached, frowning,
quizzical. Why? Because a stranger is just what she
was seeing. "Tell me who you are." (Later an even
tougher command: "Tell me who I am.")

     Her spiritedness. Her mutability. Her lability.
"Why is it you're so steady," she asked, "and I'm so
flibberty-jibberty?"

     So I'm the rock here? Well, if she wants to think
so, fine. But might her thinking this way pose a few

challenges, I'll call them, at some point? -- But then
what else is love about? Moving into uncharted waters
now, methinks, she and I. Depths. Currents. Monsters
maybe. Marvels for sure.
     Are we ready?
     I say we're not just ready, we're there. Still!
Again!
     Sez she: "I love you and I careen." Lurches about,
yeah; loses it sometimes and more than I do, or anyway
more than I'm willing to admit I do. It has its dark
and negative side too, my being the guy who knows what
he wants. (Is it just a role I'm accustomed to playing?
I think not. Somehow it's just always been this way.
Class issue, she'd likely say. Privilege. Neocolonial
arrogance. Settler obliviousness. Could be right too,
at least to an extent, but I say I still had to work
like hell and suffer plenty to get here, meaning the
point of knowing what I want now as opposed to what I
used to want in earlier stages, even though the main
things have pretty much held steady.)
     Naked like this. Jyzing each other. "TJITR."
Loving, desiring, wondering over and at each other.
(Over and out? Over and in!) -- As good as it gets.
Prefer jyze to sex, okay, sometimes maybe so and what of
it? Didn't the troubadours prefer poetry? If not for
their bizarre preferences, where would romance be now?
(And yes, yes, it's true, no denying, I'm scarcely the
first to ponder such matters, rhetorically or
otherwise.)
     -- Her portrait in acrylics meanwhile gazing down
at us this whole time. Z in her divine aspect, just as
I'd like to portray her -- if not in these pages, then
somewhere -- and not just this one aspect but all, and
all their morphs and combines as well. (Big, big task
though, and of course never to be completed: I'm not
kidding myself. But then also of course I'd never want
it to be completed, so I wonder what I'm really saying
here.)
     -- She just wrote something on my back. Tells me
what it is too: "My Pillow Book," with "My" underlined.

    Okay, I say, so it is. Inscribe all needs hereon.
On entire being to degree possible.

    The reverse too, me on her. Artful and loving
reciprocity. Or say equilibrating. Or say do what it
takes to make this engagement (in all senses) work
forevermore just as it's working today.

    (There's that cry again -- "Edgar. Edgar." A
woman's voice, high-pitched, down on the street. All
month we've been hearing it. Calling a dog, maybe, or
more likely a cat since we've never heard an answering
bark. Or a boa constrictor maybe? Whatever it is, the
calling sometimes goes on for twenty minutes or more.)

    (Sez now she likes looking at my hand with the new
ring on it. Is twisting the ring. Up by her "tender
buttons," the punched-through crescent moon and stars
lending some kitschy-kinky karessing edge. "That
doesn't hurt?" "They're just about indestructible.")

    -- I was recalling the night we got drunk at her
table, night of the big fight at the pocket park, how
amorous she was then in the aftermath, how I felt she
was welcoming me into her life. Only now am I realizing
exactly why that night moved me so much. (Or at some
level did I know it even then? Quite possibly.)

    -- In response to her expression of doubt during
the break I launched into a corny little speech about
trust. She has mine, I said, and did right from the
start, though admittedly I might've momentarily
forgotten this crucial fact a few times under duress,
especially of the Z-meltdown kind. For her I know it's
harder trusting, it takes longer. But: it's still what
matters most. -- And what did she have to say, I asked,
to all that?

    She, silent. At first. But finally when pressed:
"To quote someone, I'm saying it already if you'll just
hear it."

    "Please, will you just say yes or no? So I can be
sure I'm hearing what I think I'm hearing?"

    Loved what she did: pressed a hand against my heart
and said with absolute eyes-burning-in sincerity: "Yes."

[Absolute Tiptop Pinnacle - Jyzin' with Z]

S17

     Here's the spree encore and the summing up. Same
dragon rug. And we're warmed up for round three. Again
the naked truth. Naked as -- J-birds!
     "Oh my god, they're at it again."
     As it happens my jyzing hand is nestling into her
pubic thatch. Especially when the hand hits the right
margin, as just then with the word "right." And again
now at "again." Heat and her strong female fragrance
(again) wafting abundantly after our warmup canoodling
(again) and two small brown moles faintly visible
(again) through thatch and -- time to shift positions
(again) -- this is too awkward. Not to say pointless.
But...fun, yes, no denying. She says so too (again!).
                              *
     Stretched out on the carpet with the J-book resting
by her left hip. She's flipping through her own J-book
in search of loose threads. I'm thinking, well, it's
true that in one respect this spree isn't coming out the
way I hoped -- we're still unconsummated, even after
spending most of this long weekend in bed -- but
otherwise it's been, yes, fabulous. We're now united in
all the other ways that matter -- even in jyze! -- and
nothing will ever tear us apart. That's just how it is.
This is what I'm thinking. And even willing to write,
the naked words. (Again!)
     So never mind the meltdowns. This morning's was
minor. Weeping and moaning, she, "Please, someday...
please, someday," meaning put the damn bacon in. Then
on into the dreaded topic, "What if it turns out we
really are sexually incompatible? How can we possibly
stay together and be happy?" Like that.
     But I believe we can. Stay that goddamn course!

what, give up all this because of mere copulatory
glitches? -- And just think, what if the refractory
appendage had been blown off in a war or, say, a boiler
accident? Then I still might be wanting to get off
("phantom dick ejac demand") but not only would the
project be truly hopeless, there wouldn't even be
anything for her to hang on to while I thrashed around.

But...we bobbed back to the surface on the other
side of the white water with no damage done so far as I
could tell. Quick breakfast. Then a "nap" which turned
into another nookie session. She was delighted when a
lawn mower started up nearby because it freed her to
scream as loud as she wanted. And she did. Truly got
into it. Once again I say so. (As now an ice-cream van
jingles down below.)

Eating each other's faces and various other
surfaces and parts. First time she's asked me to lick
certain specified vulvar features as opposed to just
"submitting" to eat-outer's choice (encouraged, she
says, by my urging her last night to be more verbal and
more specific about it). "I love tasting my funky
smells on your lips."

More love-yammer about all the ways we know we're
right for each other. More fantasizing about what it'll
be like living together. (A real nap -- conjoined --
was mixed in there too, more than an hour's worth.
We've been doing much better on sleep lately.) (And the
meltdown she once again blamed at least in part on
hypoglycemia.)

-- And here I am lying naked on my belly at her
side, the bottom-up view. Must look very strange to
her. Always new angles on the J-slinger, hey wot? (So
then is a Rashomonic truth soon to emerge? Two of
them, one being hers? Anything could happen!)
("Rashomon" is fiction so no jyze exception is called
for. Don't know why but I absolutely must state this at
least once about what the rules are and now's the time.)

-- Now she runs her hand through my head hair and
I'm reminded it's pretty much fully grown back out again
after the chop job she gave it in April. I'm whole

again, Jake B.! Except, alas, not in the front (of the
skull, I mean). (To me this appears to confirm I'm an
ancient right now and will never again be anything else
-- if I look. But I don't have to look. As advised
to self numerous times before, simply avoid all mirrors
and photos.)

Today's Labor Day, by the way. It's also the first
day of September, yet the third day of the official
three-day holiday weekend which also happens to be the
latter three-quarters of my four-day birthday weekend
(disregarding for the moment the seventy-day super-
extension). This is why it seems right to include today
in the August jyze spree as a kind of coda on the coda.

Mild temp, blue sky, but we still haven't made it
out of her apartment other than the one crucial trip to
the flea market, the "ringing" one. Dinner out followed
by a movie last night never happened. And in an hour
I'll be taking off for home as the new weekly cycle
starts up. She has lots of prepping to do for
tomorrow's return to work.

"I like what I said," she announces, emphatically
clapping her J-book shut. "I'm done." Lies down on her
back at my side, left calf resting atop my bare ass.

*

(Right there I could tell I was about to run out of
ink and so stopped to show her, as previously promised,
my quirky method of reloading J-stick No. 5 -- and all
the other ones too for that matter, all J-sticks being
the same highly ink-thirsty double-broad brand X. This
sparked something for her, I guess, because now she's
sitting up and is back to jyzing again, with an impish
little smile. Encore! By popular demand!)

Last night she came up with a new theory which I
sort of like. "What if it's my own psychosexual center
that's doing it," she said. "What if my center has
decided I shouldn't let you be fucking me yet because if
I did I'd just be totally blown away by you?"

She seemed serious. Could be she's onto something
too. Better we should at least be putting up a united
front on "co-owning" -- as she in particular might say

-- this dysfunction even if it's still basically mine
and we both know this and know it "to the bone" (even if
the bone be all soft-rubbery marrow).

Or it could be, as noted before, our unconsciouses
are just "saving it for marriage." Somehow the way we
relate has reactivated our long-suppressed high-school
moralities, which it should be recalled can't differ all
that much. Can they? Being largely constructions of
that famously uptight era as it played out for the
eighteen years when we were young'uns unknown to each
other living just eight miles apart? -- Any number of
possibilities here.

She starts singing. "You are the tuna of my life.
That's why I'm always biting at you."

Time to do something else. Only half an hour
before departure deadline. -- But later a coda for the
coda on the coda. That's the plan anyway.

*   *

Just poured myself a stiff one. Back in B-2,
along about midnight, and it's time to really do it:
bring this spree to a close.

Background jazz playing. Fan spinning. Viaduct
traffic flashing, whirring, whooshing, thunking.

-- More little miraculous moments with Z before I
left. It's almost embarrassing to recount them. So
this time I won't even try. Except for this one: as we
lay next to each other on the dragon rug, just nuzzling,
girding up for the time we'd be apart (which this week
will be only twenty-four hours owing to the holiday),
she said, "This is always one of my favorite parts of
the weekend." "You mean when you get to kick me out?"
"Ha, very funny." -- And then a literal kick in the
(still bare) ass: "So hit the road already!"

Packing up. What's new is the sack of tomatoes in
my backpack. We bought them at the flea market just
after picking out our rings. Brother Rob's glowing
speech supporting my statement about the health value of
tomatoes finally convinced her to override the advice of
her herbalist and the blood-type diet book she read
recently. She's fixing to give them a try.

We never did get around to serious focus on the books of love or mags of love or "The Pillow Book" or any of those thorny issues. Neither did we work out our criteria for apartment-hunting (this is something she's been hammering away at all week, making herself a very large target for my "gentle teasing" -- which in style and quantity is a lot like hers, we agree, and the synergy between the two styles seems to work like the one between our peptides: leads off into lots of sparky new realms).

Nor have I done well at keeping up with the jyze flashback plan. For some reason this aspect of the spree turned out to be more or less a dud. Already too much dutiful earnestness in these pages, I'd say. And for sure not enough attempted lyricism or free-floating jyze. I stand self-convicted. Somehow I want to change my ways for future sprees. But just how to do it, I dunno. So I'll be thinking on it.

I do assume more such sprees will be coming along, yes I do, and that Z will be part of at least some of them. I also say my current state of rebesottedness with her is a prime contributor to the crimes against jyze I'm convicting myself of. (I'm so rebesotted I'm even stealing her term here, and pleased to do so. "Rebesot me anew daily." -- And she does!)

What's left out from these spree pages? A helluva lot. Some of it intentional: right now it doesn't seem to matter much what city this is or what's going on in the world beyond it (the storybook Cawk princess of our era dies in an auto accident and my only interest in this is learning that Z is a bit more of a royalty groupie than I'd've expected and her mother much more of one; not only does she read the tabloids, Mama E, but she regularly sends Z big sheaves of clips from them, and Z showed me a boxful of such sheaves she's loyally consigned to her storage bedroom). Some of it I just haven't been up to: working in more dialogue, more info about "minor" characters, more probing into the meaning of various twists and turns in "the plot" as it unfolds and of course usually but not always with a mind

entirely its own. Most of all I've failed to paint
a portrait in words that even begins to do justice
to this remarkable woman who's singlehandedly
turned my life inside out and upside down.

   Unit B-2. "Jyze Around My Room." I had renounced
the world and was intending to hole up here forever. No
longer. This joint is history. I'm outta here.
"Reader, I'm engaged to her." Only the details remain
to be worked out. And: three more months of Peak Prime
Time in which to do just that (assuming, of course, the
world doesn't end in October as per the prognostications
of certain religious doomsayers -- which in fact are the
same ones who were predicting the same doom for October
of last year, except some spoilsport historian pointed
out they'd added up the years incorrectly -- I just
heard a radio report on this tonight).

   -- True, I'm now on the downward slope into
ancienthood. Equally true, though, I would've become an
ancient anyway, Absolute Pinnacle or no Absolute
Pinnacle, and likely on exactly the same corporeal
timetable (and barring some premature absolute
crumpling). Now, however, I'm more conscious of not
just the truth but the personal import of the old saw
about "the mind is willing but the flesh is weak." Can
it be I'm already there? Love will have to adjust?
(Ego too?) Yike -- but maybe so.

   (I did tell her today I'd like to try a different
approach next time. Introduction of tab G into slot Z
no matter what the stiffness state of tab G and the
consequent chagrin of tab-bearer G, especially if
deflation should immediately or at best way too quickly
ensue and of course "without issue," as has been the
case every single time so far. She said she's game.
We'll see what happens. In any event, I'm not about to
give up.)

   But this spree, yeah, time to pack it in. I've
loved it but now off with it to the J. Ink typing pool.
Though it'll be a while before the pool can take it up.
Sez I, the pool itself -- sixty percent water, innit,
the male kind?

BOOK IV

[Glennarian Rollover Jyze]

32

     For openers it's back to lofty sentiments. Or
lofty jyzing anyway. But up in the loft late in the
afternoon following several hours of dream-teeming
sleep-catchup nap. I was racing around at some strange
airport trying to see off two lovers at once. One was
Lady S, the other was -- I'm not sure who. Lady U?
Lady K? Someone. But I kept bumping into people I knew
and felt obliged to speak with. These included two of
the W. brothers from high-school days (they were in
baseball uniforms, as was I; and the dry-goods store
where they both worked part-time in real life turned out
to have a branch in the concourse where I ran into
them). The only other detail I recall now is trying to
explain to the W. brothers about the new woman in my
life, Zoelie B., who grew up right down the road from
us; but they kept turning the subject back to baseball.
     Fine afternoon. Like me, Z was worn out from our
strenuous socializing weekend just past -- a full
eighter has gone by since the last jyze of my birthday
weekend, I should note, or almost full; in any case
we're back to the normal octurnal schedule -- and she
went straight home after dropping me off here last night
and slept eleven hours and didn't go in to work until
noon today. I awakened at the usual time and descended
from the loft but stayed down there just long enough to
read the papers (while nibbling on a big hunk of peach
cobbler Leola gave us to take home). Now the day is
pretty much shot and most everything I'd planned to do
out in the world must be put off until tomorrow. But to
heck with feeling bad about it. I'm feelin' good!

    No special reason. Lying here naked (again!). Sun
shining in down below. Sheets still purple up here.
The Z kiri ribbon tied to the ceiling sprinkler nozzle
gently undulating. As is the "Solid Sleep Award" ribbon
I gave her; it's dangling now from the arm of the
bedside lamp. (I also awarded myself a "#1 Sleep Coach"
ribbon which is pinned to the bookcase down below,
right next to a new poem Z wrote one night after
catching a glimpse of me walking along a few blocks from
here as she rode by on the bus -- and in it I'm
described as "full-bodied," I have a "slight limp," my
face resembles a "prow." -- Then later she changed
"full-bodied" to "barrel-chested," which may be more
flattering but regrettably is far from accurate. In the
poem she asks herself if she'd notice this guy were he
not already her love but decides she can't imagine him
not being her love. -- Damn right I was pleased by it
and posted it immediately.)

    This week we made progress not only in sleep. Also
in something else that tends to happen in the sack.
It's a little humiliating to write about, no question,
but so be it -- at this late date why worry about
something like that? Embrace it! Anyway: during our
night off Z evidently decided to take the horn by the
horn, so to speak -- to hop aboard and shove it in if it
became hornlike enough (as indeed we'd talked about
during my birthday weekend -- and in fact I'd long ago
given her carte blanche to do). She tried it three or
four times, and one of the times (yesterday morning at
her place) it worked for a while. It's the longest I've
been inside her yet, and what's more this is true both
sizewise and timewise: let's say seven-eighths rampant
and two or three minutes of action. This is
encouraging, I do believe. It might even constitute
sexual healing of a sort. (Another time, the first,
might've worked out just as well or better, but she
couldn't find her vaginal opening as she tried to guide
me in and my hands were pinned down. Eventually we
dissolved in laughter.) The unalloyed good news is she
felt no pain, unlike those first few times months ago.

Also she wanked me off by hand -- twice. So we just might be on the brink. Just might almost be smokin'. (Both times she didn't want to wipe away the jizz. "Let's be funky and get all stuck together." And we were and we did, most notably the first round when several pearly lines ribboned out across my stomach like spurts of a certain infamous brand of white glue whose packaging features an inanely grinning cartoon bull who to this day reminds me of my father -- "the Old Bull," as we often called him.)

The other news, maybe not so good but then maybe not so bad either, is we've put off the time we'll start cohabiting until after the first of the year. One morning she woke up knowing she didn't want us to take the apartment Aida had tipped us to on south hill. "I think it's because it would be too much newness for me: both a new neighborhood and a new kind of living arrangement." I wasn't all that pleased with the way she was suddenly talking so uneagerly about the prospect of our living together. She suspected anxiety over the possible move was again causing the upset stomach which had been troubling her all week. Eventually we agreed not even to begin looking for another place until after January 1. (But we've asked to be informed if a two-bedroom apartment opens up in the annex of her current building. In that case we'd probably take it, and at any time, including even right now. But it's unlikely such an opening will occur. The annex has only nine or ten units, and some are one-bedroom and thus, by our agreement, not acceptable for us.)

I try not to read anything too negative into this delay. She was burned badly the only other time she took up living with a man. She values her independence. She's accustomed to living alone. Everyone advises her to go slowly (except me). I believe she loves me and wants to live with me. So I'm trying not to be put off by this sudden backward step. Give her a chance to come to grips with her fears. (And most likely her ambivalence would ease at least a bit if we could finally become lovers who do what lovers ordinarily do, even lovers of post-Absolute Tiptop Pinnacle vintage, or some of them anyway, or rather some of us: that is, authentically schtup.)

But that "post" phrase is one I didn't want to be using yet. Just a momentary lapse there. Peak Prime Time is where I still am (until early December) and I figure I'll be proving this any day now, even in the sexual realm. Which I've been saying for quite a while now, true. (So just do it then! Prove it! Simple!)

-- Almost six p.m. A late hour to be climbing down from the loft and dressing to go out. But why not.

*   *

Green armchair. And where have the past seven hours gone (it's now one a.m.)? Mostly to the same sort of thing the hours have been going to for the past week. To writing thank-you notes, making birthday presents, finding goofy thrift-shop gifts and such like. The best of these gifts, in my view, completed Sunday morning, is a kitschy-campy Land of Oz dinner plate, minorly cracked, for Z's friend Leola and her husband, Gerry, with two little Monopoly-like houses glued to it representing the homes where they grew up in neighboring small towns not far from Dorothy and Toto's farm. Tonight's main project was hand-painting odd cartoony bits on a bargain-bin "Old-'Tie'-mer" necktie for brother Jeff's big decadal birthday coming up next week. I discovered this type of painting is nowhere near as easy as it appears it might be (the low quality of the tie's "silk" likely accounting for much of the difficulty).

And then a series of telephone talks with Z. She'd signed on to make campaign calls for a council candidate and spaced out the fact that I'd be ringing her up at nine. As I told her, this pretty much proves we're about ready to start living together. (Just a joke, though.) And lest I get the notion we really should be pressing ahead on finding an apartment, she said she'd thrown an I Ching on the question and it had counseled her to seek tranquility and be extra-cautious about making any changes. "You'll probably just scoff," she

grumped. But I'm not scoffing at all. I may not take
such stuff too seriously, but I know she does. If she
wants to move slowly, it's fine with me. True, I'd like
her to keep in mind that I'd prefer to move quickly --
but only if she also wants to do that. No sense in
being at cross-purposes here. Right, Z-dawg?

    She's asked for a few other small adjustments in
the way we do things together. When we're sleeping at
her place during the week, for one, she wants to rise
half an hour earlier than she's been doing, at six
rather than six-thirty. By "horse-o-meter" guidelines
she should accordingly go to bed at nine-thirty, but I
doubt she'll be able to do that. In practice I suspect
this change will mean we'll be sexing it up less often
on weeknights. One night when I crawled into the loft
at two a.m. I awakened her for loving (starting with
long slow back caresses) and though she said she liked
this a lot (and awakened me the same way in the morning,
whispering "Imitation is the sincerest form of
flattery"), at work later that day she was back to
"Zombie Zoelie" and we therefore decided to try to do
entirely without middle-of-her-night loving during the
workweek. Since I'm often not around when she goes to
bed, and mornings often aren't good for her because she
wants to have her "jizm" for work (and for me her
mornings are middle-of-my-night anyway), it would appear
our sex life may soon be suffering even more than it
already is.

    And yet...I doubt it. "Where there's lust, there's
a way." And almost always one of us has lust for the
other, and nearly as often we both do. Last week we
were crazily going at it all over the place, including a
couple of times in this chair right here and once in
the one at the hideaway (toward the end of our long-
awaited "luncheon date"). Friday we both kept wanting
more and more, starting at two a.m., continuing at six
a.m., again at lunch, again at midnight here in B-2 and
then again here at three a.m., at dawn, and at nine when
we were finally about to get up to rejoin the world.
"Why am I so horny today?" she kept asking. "I think I

need saltpeter or something."

Needless to say I'm not complaining about the lust glut. So far I've never been the one to say no and I'm expecting that's how it'll be pretty much forever. Granted, things may become more difficult when, and if, I'm no longer feeling I owe her something for my being unable to get it up and in for her (that is, when I'm finally able to get it up and in, if ever) (knock on wood so to speak don't I wish yet once more) and/or when I'm no longer erotically powered by "Taoist semen retention" (that is, when I'm expending the stuff mostly inside her). But enough of a strain so I won't be wanting to keep her happy? I seriously doubt it. Simple fact is I love loving her, with or without full, or even any, penile participation.

Saturday morning, I should mention, she started into a meltdown -- wept (this at six a.m.) -- and it led to an interesting reversal (as we both agreed later) in which suddenly I was the one who was downcast and inconsolable and she became the cheerer-upper and indefatigable, irrepressible consoler. This led to the edge of some strange kinky behavior which I didn't go for too much (being reminded of some bad times with Lady V) but I think maybe she did. At one point she was suggesting that neither of us should come, as in orgasm, at all for the remaining three and a half weeks of September (she who'd come literally dozens or more like scores of times in the previous twenty-eight hours, her prime "Why am I so horny?" period). I reversed this proposal, suggesting we keep upping the ante rather than walk away from the game. In the end we simply dropped the matter (preferring to squeeze in a last few quickies before rushing off to catch a bus). In the long run, though, I expect we'll be exploring this realm more fully. (Over the weekend I reread the essay on "Story of O" which had impressed her so much. Power issues and all that. The role of incest in her own childhood, but coming from her mother, not her father. -- And how serious was that incest, really, if it should even be called incest? All things to be grappled with someday

-- and preferably, for me anyway, a distant day, when we're well established and our present sexual impasse has long since -- passed.)

    -- Almost two a.m. now. I'm trying not to let myself drift back into the old sleep schedule. Therefore (on this muggy night, during which sleeping will likely be tough anyway because of the long nap I lapsed into this afternoon, and during which I'll also be tempted by lots of backed-up periodical reading) I'll stop jyzing now and take up some of those other matters.

*   *

    Twenty hours later, the big oval conference table, the night's scoping work completed and a new cycle of Z-days about to begin as soon as I've finished up here with the jyze and caught the last bus out to her place.

    There's news. She's reversed herself again: now wants to live on south hill after all. A kind of negative epiphany powered this new switcheroo, she tells me: listening to some pompous "outreach specialist from the group regarding which you're a beloved exception" (meaning burb-bred Cawkazoids). For Z to be able to live with herself (and never mind with me; I don't think I enter into this computation very much, really, except maybe as a negative prod) she thinks she'd better be "walking the talk," that is, living in a hood which is downscale and racially diverse. And on both of these scores south hill fills the bill quite well.

    Also she's again hot and bothered about applying for a new job -- this time as some sort of diversity honcho for the new regional transit authority. It would mean being less bored and also making more money. But she's let me know she won't be keeping her opinions under wraps while she's interviewing. They have to take her as she is or not at all.

    Admittedly I feel I'm being jerked around a bit here with these frequent flip-flops concerning the move. Nor do I like it too much that she's already making a point of how she'll be needing her sleep and her "perkiness" in the period ahead -- which translates into no hanky-panky during the week unless it's in the evening before she goes to bed (and often during those hours I of course have to be at work, as was the case tonight). However. I'm not so irked I'm ready to start openly griping about any of this just yet. Many more changes could lie ahead before we start wrestling with the truly challenging business of living together in the same eight hundred square feet (size of a typical two-bedroom apartment these days). I'd like to sort of float along above those changes if I can.

This feels like the first real week of fall (starting yesterday, Monday). Because the weekend before the one just past was Labor Day weekend, the working part of the following week, meaning last week, was short, and because my birthday fell on that previous holiday weekend, the workweek simply by virtue of its shortness still seemed to bear happy traces of the celebration, like after-tremors, especially since for much of that time I was churning out those gifts and thank-you notes (while the world was preoccupied with an oddly matched pair of Cawk icon deaths, the "fairytale princess" and the "mother of the poor"). Now, however, comes the grind. My first full week of resumed normality, even if it's also still my Peak Prime Time. And right at the start a serious money crunch. Yet how serious can it really be if all I need do to remedy it is swallow my pride and ring up the keeper of the "deep reserves" and ask her to send a check?

Why a grind? Partly because I was stung by something Aida told Z this week (and Z chortlingly passed along to me) about how "he [I] could still be a good-looking guy like his brother [Rob] if he'd slim down some." And this the same Aida who, as we walked along during our initial "vetting" encounter some three months ago now, dropped behind Z and me for a moment and then announced impishly, "Ooh, yeah, Zo, he's kinda V-shaped!" -- I swear I'm not that much over my normal weight (and I'm talking about my norm all the way back to my early twenties), but on the other hand I also swear I'll soon be shedding every single excess pound. I've vowed 120 days of hunger (and not exactly by coincidence, the 120th day will fall on January 1 of next year -- jyze year five). Z's joining me in this, though she's speaking of a diet and I'm not. I'll eat less, true -- and I do mean true -- but the main effort will go to being more physically active. (Big fucking deal. Stupid stupid stupid. But I'm gonna do it regardless.)

The socializing weekend which I still haven't touched on consisted of two main events. The first was Jess's birthday party Saturday night (at which I was the only male out of fourteen attendees) (and Jess in her woozy intoxicated state kept reminding me of Lady V for some reason I don't even want to think about trying to parse). The second was Gerry and Leola's barbecue on Sunday at their place out in the first ring of burbs across the lake to the east. At group socializing I'm about as rusty as anyone can be but even so I enjoyed both events (what the heck, I'm in love; if Z were with me I'd probably enjoy being locked up in a room full of raving Bible-thumpers...and these were all people I like and not a raving Bible-thumper among them).

Details, let's see. Gerry turns out to be about six-five, a former big-time college jock and current federal administrator within three months of me in age; in fact he should be about three weeks into his own Peak Prime Time right now (but I didn't try to fill him in on this because it would've involved explaining about 20K Day and the Glennarian calendar, and few are the eyeballs such an effort doesn't cause to glaze over). A stream wanders through Gerry and Leola's backyard; a croquet course was set up and I was the only player who managed to mallet a ball into the creek -- my own ball! Gerry doesn't talk much but he's mellow and a pleasure to be around (and he and Leola haven't slept together or had sex in years, Z tells me -- ten years, is it?).

Jess's birthday is the same day as sister Barb's and as it happens I do have a bit of brotherly feeling toward Jess. (Barb I didn't hear from for my birthday, nor did she hear from me for hers five days later. Unless she makes a sincere effort to patch things up

with me -- and I've seen no sign of any such move yet --
she's simply out of my loop. Gone.) -- Jess being the
butch force of J&G, it's no surprise she and I relate
pretty much "man to man." Gwen, femme with a high
chirpy voice, was pretty much straight until she met
Jess (and reminds me a lot of brother Jeff's big teen-
years love Jamie). Z tells me Jess once attended a
party where it suddenly dawned on her that she'd gotten
it on with every single person present: seventeen of
them, and all women. (Dish! Dish!) (In fact she's
never had sex with a man -- not even a kiss.)

Z jokes a lot about my "bonding" with her friends
(the term is another favorite of hers, right up there
with "grok," "suss," etc.). But oddly enough it really
does seem to be happening. The ones I've met so far are
for the most part very likable, smart, aware, easy to
get along with, and to top it off they're, as noted
before, a highly diverse lot: in age, class, race,
gender, education, sexual preference, on and on and on.
It's the kind of "circle" I've always enjoyed being part
of (but rarely been able to stay a part of, usually
because I wind up focusing too much on my own work).

Other juicy bits? Okay. Thinking.

** I accompanied Z to her hairdresser's on
Saturday (and during the week she visited her eyebrow
archer -- and I learned that only the vigilant efforts
of such archers over the years have kept her eyebrows
from growing together).

** I stumbled across a "Mighty Movers" yard sign
in a gutter and hauled it to B-2, setting it up in the
interior hallway as a kind of message board (it's the
size and configuration of a typical political yard sign
with a pointed wooden stake, handy for dealing with any
invading vampires from the housing agency office).
(Jyze exception on the company name.)

** This past month Z has lost more than $400 worth
of reading glasses (three pairs, I think, or maybe four),
and she assigns the blame on this to her love-addled
state and thus to me. (Betty consoled her with tales of
the four times she locked herself out of her car in the

months between meeting Manny -- they were nurses at the
same hospital -- and their moving in together.)
    ** Z opined that one main reason for all the
middle-of-her-night loving that erupts despite our vows
is its "forbidden fruit" aspect. (Did I say? Friday,
her supremely horny day, I tried to drain her of comes.
Couldn't do it.)
    ** On Jess's birthday I left her several goofy
phone messages and she, Jess, said later, "I had no idea
you were such an extrovert" (ambivert is more like it).
    ** Z says she's been startled over the past few
months by the way men have been coming on to her at work
and elsewhere, more so than's been the case in "lotsa
years," and she figures it's because she must be exuding
clouds of pheromones.
    ** And last but not (least, yeah): a whole row of
tabloids in the supermarket racks confirms that the
latest iteration of the apocalypse is slated for six
weeks from tomorrow. This is the big one predicted
centuries ago and dreaded by true believers ever since.
If the world began in 4004 B.C.E. and each of the
creation's six days equals a thousand years as the holy
book says, and it's recalled that there was no year zero
(as the doomsayers failed to take into account until
last summer), October 23 is it: Judgment Day. -- But
yeah, in the aftermath of Absolute Tiptop Pinnacle Day
it seems, I gotta say, almost anticlimactic.

33

So wot's new, Jyze Guy?
    Try this: today Jeff's age hits a number ten times
the size in years of the gap between us. And I remember

when his age was one-tenth the size of that gap -- or
for that matter, one-thousandth. That's brother Jeff
back in Lahontan. Hope my baroque bargain-bin hand-
painted necktie has reached him all right. (Didn't
mention before that brother Rob said Jeff and his wife
Angie are just barely scraping by financially, with Jeff
unable to make a go of it thus far as a newly
credentialed real-estate agent. Combine the incomes of
all four of us siblings, I observed to Rob, and the sum
would likely fall short of the median U.S. income for a
single individual. And all four of us in our peak
earning years! Imagine if Dad were still around to
witness this -- the apoplexy. And the sarcasm. -- Or
would he maybe have gotten over all that? But no, I
think not. Not hardly. And Rob agrees.)

If not for the miraculous arrival of one Zoelie B.
in my life I might well be thinking of moving back to
the Mentoka zone myself along about now -- though I
doubt I'd actually be ready to pull up stakes here. A
few more years of desperation might've been required to
coax me into dismantling this confounded loft (beneath
which, or almost beneath, I'm sitting at present).

But then I'll soon be dismantling it regardless. A
different kind of desperation, but related, and more
powerful, is at work. Wanna live with this Zoelie B.
Got to. Will. Because the decision's been made and
confirmed and reconfirmed several times over. It'll be
south hill. We've agreed to move up there as soon as
the apartment becomes available.

To recap, at first Z felt the choice was too hard
and so she'd "let the cosmos decide" between the south-
hill place and the annex of her present apartment
building. Whichever offered a true opening first, that
would be the one, and if neither did by the end of the
year we'd start looking elsewhere. Fine, nodded I; a
terrific solution.

Two days later the cosmos announced its decision,
though obliquely. Z had the run-in, noted in last
week's entry, with the horrible gentrified kind of hip
Eurusan "outreach specialist" (luckily for me a female

this time) and in a flash realized she couldn't bear to
be living in a gentrifying hip Eurusan kind of hood
anymore. "I wanna walk the talk." South hill, although
it too shows signs of imminent gentrification, remains
largely lower-middle and working class and boasts a
majority person-of-color presence, including many
Filusans. It's in the funky end of the city. It's a
bit more dangerous down there but a lot cheaper. Cachet
it doesn't have -- yet. (The irony being that our
moving there -- along with others like us, of course, as
more and more are said to be doing, folks with college
degrees and pink-skin privilege and maybe even a little
neocolonial-settler clout -- boosts its cachet and the
rents will probably soon be rising sharply.)

I too like the political statement this move will
make. And I like it that I'll be paying less there to
share a two-bedroom, one-and-a-half-bath apartment in an
attractive modern four-story building (on the top floor,
with a sweeping eastern view and a balcony overlooking
the street) than I am to live here in the ground-floor
studio which is B-2 with its severely truncated bay
view. And I like the location there: the hideaway is
just 1.81 miles away (we measured with the Z-mobile's
trip odometer), easily walkable (especially downhill,
northwestward, going in), and the scope office is .74
miles beyond the hideaway. But despite all this I'd
prefer to stay right where I am, except for a single
factor: there I'll be living with one Zoelie B. (more
than one Zoelie B. might be way too much, true).

We've already explored the new hood twice, once by
ourselves and once with Kat and Betty. We've eaten at a
Filipino restaurant and checked out a small outlook park
named for a Philippine national hero. We've walked
around the hilltop and admired its spectacular views
opening up in all directions. This weekend we'll be
seeing the apartment itself. Evidently we're the only
ones who've expressed interest in it. The present
occupants, Doug and Thuy (old friends of Aida's and well
known to Z), need something bigger because a second
kid's on the way, due in December, and they want to be

in the new digs before then. Now it's simply a
matter of how long it takes them to find a place that
meets their needs. Unless their search fails or they
change their minds for other reasons (decide to wait
a year before moving, say), we're in.

     And so I've gone ahead and tapped the deep reserves
for two thousand bucks. Moving will be expensive. And
I need cash anyway. No point in waiting to make the tap
and meanwhile living on the edge. As it is I've delayed
sending in my quarterly tax payment, due today, until
the next Jyzer Ink check arrives later this week; and
even then I'll have -- absent the new infusion -- only
about a hundred bucks to get through the rest of the
month. (At month's end the quarterly deep-reserves
interest check will be coming in, but my three rents
will immediately eat up most of that.)

     So, a couple of euphorias here. I'm flush again
(or soon will be, since the 2K check hasn't arrived yet)
and I'm about to take up housekeeping with my honey.
Also I'm excited about a jyze project I'm working on
(typing up the spree just ended). Also I'm a little
wild-eyed from hunger here in the early days of the 120-
day shaping-up ordeal but I'm starting to adjust to it
now and I'm feeling healthy and good (though with one
new caveat which I'll try to explain later). Eager.
Excited. Erect, even, almost, at times.

     Almost. The phallic front, the news is not so
good. Another major Z meltdown, and once again I really
can't blame her even though I sure do wish she'd get the
damn things out of her system. For a while she was
proposing we drop sex entirely and then she was
insisting we observe a moratorium until next March on
sexual "advice" (mine to her about how to proceed in a
way that might work, for example, though in truth I've
offered little such advice lately, for the simple reason
that I have no new ideas about it) (to her way of
thinking this moratorium would've been quid pro quo for
the one she's granted me regarding medical advice). A
single sentence of mine turned her around on this: "You
mean you want me to go completely passive?"

[Glennarian Rollover Jyze]

So now we're back to the "innocence hexagram."
Sunday morning (meltdown time) she even read it aloud to
me. And the "love paradigm" is still around too: Friday
night she launched into an "I love you" mantra that went
on for at least twenty minutes and included several O's
for her along the way, and each one a jaw-wrenching
gasper. And just today on the phone she promised to
abstain from all personal meltdowns until well after the
gigantic planetwide apocalyptic one scheduled for five
weeks from Thursday, "since it'll be pretty hard to
compete with that." And in this same call she reported
a new insight which she thinks might limit future
meltdowns of her own, should we survive the planetary
big one. "I realized the ability I had to give men
erections and ejaculations was a real source of power
for me back when I was more insecure about myself. Now
I think I don't need that so much anymore."

Otherwise a number of terrific sexual moments and/
or episodes. I'm more agog than ever over this Z-woman.
Especially I liked getting her off solely by caressing
the scars left by removal of her two extra toes (one on
each foot, between the standard first and second, or
biggest and second-biggest, toes). And how I loved
awakening one morning in the loft to find her spooning
in from behind, her hand reaching around and stroking
"N'dow" with a feathery touch as she meanwhile slowly
got herself off by lightly "frotting" her vulva against
my thigh (and that come of hers triggered my own ejac,
and I turned on my back and arched as it hit -- "All day
I was thinking how you arched," she said later; "that
was my favorite time so far").

And Saturday night she was unbelievably hot (said
so herself) after an hour of reading a lesbian novel as
we fondled each other on the dragon carpet by her
dreaded red couch: and a couple of hours of nonstop
Zoelie O's ensued (the neighbors getting an earful for
sure). (And a funny moment one night when she arrived
at B-2 from work and during a long welcoming kiss placed
my hand in her crotch and then said, in her "when I'm
bad I'm better" voice, meanwhile sniffing my fingertips,

"Hmm, have you been eating tuna or am I happy to see you?")

     -- And another time when, while "purging" in her extra bedroom, she stumbled upon a collection of fancy vibrators with which, as she explained later, she'd powered herself through the "slack periods" with men back at the height of the "Love Yourself First" era (and then more such powering in the post-Jerry II "Off Men Forever" years, no doubt).   -- And she announced she'd be keeping only one of those pleasure machines around, and that one "just on principle."   -- The others went into the "Free Box" for Paula, June, Gwen and Jess and anyone else who happens by.   -- This being part of her "purge" preparation for moving, so of course I'm pleased no matter what becomes of her sex devices. (She did mention a certain notorious book on female masturbation which she studied closely back in the day. And she confessed she often used to masturbate -- sometimes with a cucumber -- before going out on dates, so as not to be "overexcited" and thus "too easily manipulated" -- and even owned up to doing this several times when the date was none other than the Jyze Guy himself, "back in the early days -- mostly -- although never with a cucumber -- at least not yet.")

     One other note about doings on the phallic front. For the first time I used the word "intimidating" in describing her sexuality. Lots of qualifiers appeared in front of it, and more after it, but she still didn't like it one bit. "I don't want you to be saying that," she grumped. Her tone made it obvious she'd heard the word a time or two before (and I'm sure not just in sexual contexts). It hurt her and so I'm dropping it posthaste. Nonetheless it still applies, though for the most part in a way I don't, on balance, consider negative: that is, her sexuality can be overwhelming. My own sometimes, or even often -- admit it! -- appears feeble by comparison. And for it to be perceived this way when for me it's always been a source of pride and power as well as pleasure (just as hers has been for her), well, the effect of this is even more enfeebling.

[Glennarian Rollover Jyze]

     Frustrating too, yeah. But I refuse to believe
things'll go on like this forever. (And if they do, I
think we'll make it anyway, but perhaps not without
causing each other a whole lotta gratuitous grief.
-- Grief? Aw, I dunno. Anyway, grief or whatever it
is, we'd both rather do without it if possible.)
     -- It's chilly and rainy tonight. The most
dramatic autumn weather break I can recall in my
nineteen autumns in or near this burg. Last night the
wind loosened some huge tarps atop a couple of buildings
going up a block or two down the hill and the flapping
sound was wild indeed (and when it let up in the early
evening I could hear even wilder drumming and chanting
from a powwow/festival being held at a waterfront pier,
the afternoon session of which we'd attended with Kat
earlier in the day, Z throwing a monumental fit when it
turned out the utility's booth she was supposed to work
in had been closed down at noon and no one had called
her about it. The woman truly has formidable power and
unfortunately does not always, I must say, use it to
best effect. -- But I also believe this means I'm good
for her to have around, because in such instances I can
sometimes jujitsu her out of a blowup before she does
too much damage, most of all to herself.) (She'd
probably throw another monumental fit to hear me say all
this, but maybe I could leverage her out of that one too
-- get her to laughing as I usually can do. (We're
right for each other. Period. I insist.)
     So, bed.
     (But before I forget, next week we'll again be
trying out a newly fine-tuned routine. She'll stay
here Sunday night, then take Monday and Tuesday nights
"off." This way I won't have to be busing in with her
Tuesday mornings on just a few hours' sleep. The other
nights will be as before: Wednesday and Thursday she'll
be here, Friday and Saturday I'll be there.)
     -- And so now it's more or less official: I won't
have unit B-2 to jyze around in much longer. Therefore
in the time remaining I'd like to be jyzing around in it
a little more often (though I doubt I'll be able to

squeeze in any more this round). -- I haven't even
mentioned the impressive calluses which wallballing and
nerfhooping on this rugged carpet have built up on my
feet. (But must stop now.)

*   *

Falling into an unjyzelike rut here. "Unjyzelike"
-- speaking ideally. For this week's continuation I'm
holed up in the conference room at the scope office just
as I was for last week's, except this time it's twenty-
two hours down the road from the previous part of the
entry, not a mere twenty.

The weather's worsening. On the phone earlier Z
was saying she'd overheard something about big winds and
heavy rains, possibly even a tornado tonight. (She also
said she'd imbibe some more of that lesbian novel before
hitting the sack "since I know you'll be coming over."
-- And does this mean she'll be willing to indulge in a
quickie tension-releaser/restlessness-calmer when I slip
in at two a.m.? I failed to pin her down on this but
I'm guessing it does. In any case I'll try for one.
Why not? Surely she wouldn't melt down again if she
were opposed to the idea. Now would she?)

All that's four hours away. The janitor here's
just unplugging the vacuum after an energetic full-
office sweep (usually they skip the conference rooms if
they haven't been in use). I'm about halfway through my
own energetic scan-scope of today's grand-jury session,
with 125 pages still to go. My watch is out and open
(it has a hinged face-cover) and what's more it's
ticking up a storm of its own to rival the one that's
rattling the windowpanes. (Ever since the fob broke off
I've given up trying to keep the watch wound up, except
for special occasions like this.)

Again I'll be catching the last bus out. This
might be the final time, though, if we actually go
through with our scheduled "fine tuning." (But tonight
on the phone she was balking on this. We'd talked
before about the fact that under the adjusted schedule
we'd be staying at my place three nights and at hers
only two, but evidently it didn't really register. Now

434

she's bridling at the apparent asymmetry, even though
we'll be spending two daytimes as well as the preceding
nights at her place -- Saturday and Sunday -- and no
daytimes at mine, and by my reckoning this puts her back
on top, four half days to three. But is any of this
really worth making a ruckus over? Not as far as I'm
concerned. She's a lot more likely than I am to be a
stickler about "equity" in the short run, even at the
cost of convenience and keeping things simple.
Therefore I tend toward temporary yielding -- not
insisting on a fifty/fifty split or anything close to it
on most matters -- in the hope she'll soon see the
bigger picture, and she usually does.)

*

(Pause to say hello to the guard. A new one, a
young guy with a buzz cut who called me "sir" four times
in three sentences. Just mustered out of the Marines is
my guess. Could be he's checking out my bona-fides by
cellphone right now, itching to call in an airstrike.)
     -- I wanted to do a quick friends report.
     First, with Aida, as if matters weren't already
fraught enough, they've now taken another turn for the
worse. In Z's familiar phrase "she's being a pookhead."
Suddenly she all but demanded that Z see her Saturday
night ("She gets this Filipino you-will-do-this tone")
even though Z and I had already made other plans. And
she didn't want to see Z with me; she seemed bent on
making it pointedly clear she's Z's friend and not mine.
When Z hesitated to agree to see her alone (even though
I said I'd be willing to take a powder that night for as
long as she wanted in hopes of keeping the peace) Aida
wound up canceling entirely in a huff. She also showed
no excitement at all about Z's decision to live on south
hill, and never mind the fact that Aida had been the
first to suggest it and tipped us to the apartment
vacancy and herself lives, at least for the time being,
on the stretched-out southern slope of the hill;
"Whatever," Aida said airily. Nor did she so much as
mention the hand-painted card I'd sent to thank her for
the birthday chicken stew and the good company.

Was it possible I'd said or done something to offend her? Z didn't think so, although she did have the impression Aida might think I like her (Aida) a little too much rather than a little too little, as if I were angling to lure her into a menage or who knows what. This was so absurd to me (especially considering Aida's expressed hope that I'd be "like an older brother" to her) I decided on the spot to stop worrying about the whole thing; instead I'll try to pull back -- unobtrusively -- from any relationship with Aida until she clearly shows she wants us to have one (and Z approves of this way of handling the situation).

Then Betty and Kat. A couple of interesting notes on them. Z's convinced Betty has the hots for me, and it's not really a problem because Betty's no threat to Z and isn't about to act on any alleged hots and of course neither am I. But she's frequently talking to Z about me in physical terms. The other day she saw me walking downtown (this is the second time it's happened) and she called Z right away, described me to her as "your studmuffin," said "he has such a forceful walk," remarked how she likes my wearing tight jeans "because you can see what a cute little butt he has" (and hey, I love it, and how come Z herself doesn't say more stuff like this?). So for the rest of the week I was no longer "M'bao," I was "Studmuffin." (And together Z and I worked up a theory for why Betty's talking like this to Z: in essence she's drawn to me as a fellow reforming heartlander of Scandi roots and she'd like to see me become a surrogate father or uncle for Kat, standing in for Manny, as indeed I'll almost certainly be doing assuming I wind up with Z (which of course I do assume); and therefore she's saying all these things in a more or less unconscious effort to make me look more exciting and attractive to Z.)

Then Kat. Such a terrific kid. And so cute, so seductive -- and doubly so with me, as everyone agrees -- that Z finally couldn't constrain herself; she apologized in advance but demanded to know: "You'd never, ever do anything to Kat, would you?" As I told Z

immediately, had I not known she'd been sexually abused
herself as a kid (by her mother!) and therefore could
never completely trust anyone on such a matter, not even
someone she was madly in love with, I'd've hit the roof
over her question. (In truth I was surprised she hadn't
asked it long before now, especially given her reaction
to the -- alleged, by her -- child abuse in "The Pillow
Book.") Of course I told her such a thing could never
happen, period. (And it couldn't. But this isn't to
say there's no sexual attraction between Kat and me, or
for that matter between Kat and just about everyone, Z
most certainly included. But now's not the time to be
looking into the complexities and potential dark sides
here. The point is that for me, protecting Kat's
innocence would be more important than anything.)
-- And I asked Z to tell Betty I'd said this, because I
knew Betty herself (as Z had told me earlier) had been
sexually abused as a kid. (Next day Z said she was very
grateful for the understanding I'd shown in replying to
her question; it bowled her over, she said, much as did
my response last spring to her revelation of having
herpes.)
    -- Going on too long! Just want to mention this,
though. Wednesday I joined Z at "the WOC" as a guest.
("WOC" is acronymic for "work out - club" and she has it
written in on M/W/Fs in her daytimer for weeks and even
months in advance.) In trying out the treadmill there I
discovered my heartbeat when exercising hard is a bit
higher than it's supposed to be for a man my age and
weight -- 120 a minute instead of 107. So now I'm
wondering if my arteries are clogging up -- or what. My
heartbeat's always been a little above the norm but
never quite this much. And so I'm starting to feel more
vulnerable healthwise and in a whole new way. And I'm
wondering: could this even be connected with my
ridiculous phallic "stammering"? Arteries clogging up
there too? What's happening here anyway? And me still
a Peak Prime Timer! Yike! -- But am I going to worry
about this? Well...yes, I think I probably am. But
will I let the worrying get to me? Well...I hope not.

34

Hideaway. Almost midnight. Today during her lunch
hour Zoelie returned here for the first time in weeks
and left me a note and various items (articles on
recycling, bus schedules for south hill, a drugstore
coupon book). She told me about these on the phone or I
might not've made it down here at all tonight. I'm
still not back to my pre-spree routine of hitting this
office for at least two or three hours every day. Maybe
I never will be. (Though I'll soon quit shilly-
shallying around and start seriously trying.)
    It's equinox day. If the period between Labor Day
and the equinox is a kind of false autumn, this year I'd
say it's been considerably less false than usual. For
most of the past eighter we've been close to shivering,
even in bed (and a whole month's worth of rain has
fallen in that time -- an early gift from a massive El
Nino phenomenon taking shape in the usual place, the
eastern Pacific, but supposedly the most powerful in a
century and a half). For the first time Z and I are
doing things in the dark we've always done in the light
-- for example, getting up on workday mornings (or in
my case, except for one morning last week -- my last for
staying at her place on a weeknight -- sleeping on in
the dark after an a.m. horseplay session).
    Or to put it another way: the tilt of that very
large "Italian doll" called the planet Earth is back to
what it was the week Z and I met: straight up. So now
we'll see how we do when it's tilting in the opposite
direction. "Leaning out."
    More important yet, speaking of the heavens, five

planets are "in retrograde" this month. Just what this
means astronomically -- if anything -- I couldn't say,
but astrologically it's supposed to portend a terrible
month for starting anything new or making big decisions.
For this reason Z has decided we should rescind our
decision to move to south hill, and of course I'm going
along with her on this. Why not, since the rescission
is only a technicality? We're still intending to move
there, and just yesterday I overheard Z breaking this
news to her mother on the phone. (Mrs. B., as I suppose
I should call her, took it without batting an eyelash,
much to her daughter's surprise. Similar announcements
in the past have provoked massive maternal tantrums
because in her heart of hearts Mrs. B. would like Z to
move back to Centropolis and care for her in her
declining years rather than take up with a man out here.
Or at least Z herself is convinced this is the case.)
     (-- And in Z's note I found here on the hassock
tonight she says she's still feeling anxious about
living with a man -- as indeed she's already mentioned
several times just in this past eighter -- and therefore
she's "daydreaming" about it "the way they coach people
in speech class to 'visualize' their performance."
-- In fact she informed me of this earlier on the phone
and tacked on a bit of advice to the effect that I too
might find performance visualization helpful, and in my
case the relevant type of visualization would be, as it
happens, the XXX-rated variety. I assured her I already
was into that in a major way, nonstop almost, even when
trying not to be.)
     What kind of eighter's it been lovewise? Normal
tumultuous kind of the present era. By and large
terrific. (So often do I walk the streets in a euphoric
state these days I scarcely even notice the euphoria
anymore unless it's either a special enhanced sort or
the standard one made conspicuous by contrast with a
recent dysphoria -- both types of which do appear, again
including a couple of times this eighter.) For me, four
ejacs in a single J-week (the mop-up towels are getting
crusty, I'm happy to say, the one at her place as well

as the one at mine). Some gorgeous loving scenes. But
also a couple of brief blowups. And at times Z's been
strangely and touchingly near-manic, mostly owing to the
sudden death by leukemia of one of her recent grad-
school classmates (less than a year older, and until her
diagnosis the manager of a nearby satellite city). One
moment Z was weeping and disconsolate, the next burning
to celebrate life while we're still here to do it.

    Both Tuesday and Wednesday nights she overrode her
own abstinence vows to initiate middle-of-her-night and
a.m. loving sessions (and both times after we'd already
gone a round earlier in the evening, one of those taking
place on the floor right here), and both mornings she
wound up wanking me off (the first time as we lay face
to face on our sides, mostly moving very slowly while
pressed tightly together with the G-member stiff and
squeezed between her thighs; the second as I lay on my
back and she caressed my chest and stomach -- truly I
can't recall ever feeling more physically loved -- while
"frotting" her sex against my thigh). Thursday night,
after "nearly dying" from exhaustion during the day at
the office, she took her vow much more seriously -- even
wearing a sleep mask and earplugs -- but then professed
to be miffed in the morning when I slept through her
awakening. "I suppose turnabout's fair play, but...
sputter sputter sputter...I think you enjoy withholding
it!" (And maybe I do sometimes -- but nowhere near as
much as bestowing it.)

    -- Then again one night I had her laughing so hard
she pissed in her pants for the first time since infancy
(or so she said) -- and later she wrote a funny little
poem about the "amber jouissance" of this incident.
-- Then yesterday I made the mistake of admitting, when
she asked, that a "life-companion ceremony" would be
just as acceptable to me as a "real" marriage, and she
nearly went to pieces. More or less constantly for the
next several hours I had to be reassuring her I wasn't
getting cold feet, wasn't hanging a U-ie, wasn't trying
to back out (during these discussions we agreed we'll
eventually look for wedding rings at the same place

where we found the "going steady" and "engagement" rings
we're wearing now -- that is, her neighborhood flea
market -- and we'll spend no more than fifty bucks on
them) (I suggested twenty, she suggested sixty; we
"compromised" on fifty).

      -- Yet at other times she was saying things like
"It's going so well, it's like a fairy tale," "You
really are the man of my dreams," "You're incredibly
sexy," "I always believed someone like you must exist
somewhere but I thought the chances of my meeting this
person had gone from slim to none." -- Yet Saturday
morning she was ready to hit the roof because I'd said I
wanted to sleep in for another hour when she was in one
of her frisky morning-person horseplay moods. (Truth to
tell, I was extremely tired but I was also trying to
make a point: she's not the only one with sleep
concerns. Yeah, the nature of my work often permits me
to be more flexible, but I do have limits, and I've had
to give up lots of other things over the years to gain
this flexibility and I'd like her to show some
appreciation for this rather than take it for granted
all the time, not to say take advantage of it. -- Which
is an old point, and we're into at least our dozenth
round on this thorny sleep issue, and in general we seem
to be doing better with it, except for the occasional
cruel setback, such as the one on Friday morning that
was still reverbing a day later.)

      Two more fabulous sex sessions over the weekend
along with several other "ordinary" very good ones.
(Unbelievably we're shagging away more than ever, almost
always at least three sessions a day during each of
which it would appear she comes at least four or five
times and sometimes a lot or even a whole lot more --
because once she gets rolling she just doesn't want to
stop.) One of these was something new for us: she
implored me to keep my fingers (two at first, then
three) inside her instead of pulling them out after a
vaginal come and then proceeded to come again and again
with them inside, begging me to "stay...stay...I won't
let you leave," climaxing at intervals of every few

minutes for what must've been close to an hour (and
during one of these she yanked me off too, and that
didn't stop her either).

Sex fiends. Both of us. Loving it. Astounded,
even embarrassed, by the extent of it. She worrying at
times that I'll think badly of her or that things are
tipping too far out of balance orgasm-wise (though
clearly this will always be the case for us and would
always have been so no matter what our ages, including
even when I was at my physiological sexual peak at,
say, seventeen) and most of all because she wants my
penis inside her vagina and I'm not putting it there
even if it's fully phallified -- so how come? And I
explain as best I can. In twenty-five words or less:
just don't want to shame myself again with yet another
episode of foozle-inside-her. (Just fifteen words!)
(-- Yet it's also something more. Mysterious stuff.
Adjustments. "Intimidation." Awe. Fear. The sense
that this sex we're caught up in now is so fine I
mustn't "rush" on to the next stage. Once we're into
real yes-fuck fucking, the demands and rhythms may force
us to neglect, even jettison, our current kind of sex.
She might prefer that, but I might not. Anyway: I'd
like to think I'm taking my own sweet time just because
"at some level" not necessarily conscious I want to stay
in the present stage a while longer.)

As I told her, it seems best to let old "N'dow"
sort of hang around old "Peaches" (as we're calling her
vulva now owing to the "peach-cobbler effect") and if
"N'dow" decides on its own to stretch out and pop in,
terrific; if it doesn't, fine, at least I don't have to
go through the humiliation of mounting another big
let's-do-it-now scene and then failing. Tried to tell
her this humorously. And she did find the notion
amusing, without doubt, not to say hilarious. (Also, by
the way, I agreed to her proposal that she be the one to
break off kisses in the a.m. once she's awake on
workdays; and she agreed to try to remember to touch me
genitally a little more often, especially at or near her
own orgasmic crunch time. -- She becomes so engrossed

in her own pleasure and so hesitant to "multitask" that
(in conjunction with my damnable tendency to wilt after
she's come) her pleasuring me tends not to happen.
Oddly I don't usually mind too much; loving her is such
an intensely sexual experience it can literally give me
a kind of super-extended non-ejaculatory orgasm that's
both more satisfying and more exhausting than the "real"
thing. (Or is this just how it is when you're about to
go Glennarian III? -- But I don't think so, no. I
wasn't that much younger a few years ago with Lady U and
that was a whole different world. -- And in the end a
whole different world of hurt as well, though not so
much sexually. But never mind, no comparisons. Better
to declare what's over is over and let it go at that.
-- Most of the time anyway. If I'm not a fool.))

     More to say about the sex thing. Can't say it now,
though. -- All this time total quiet in the building
(bands blasting all around the triangle because tonight
the baseballers are going at it a few blocks away on
national TV; but only occasionally can I hear any of the
live music from here with my fans turned on, as they are
now). And it's half past one and my bedtime these days
is supposed to be two. I'd hoped to finish up this jyze
entry tonight so I could work on the giant-size card
thanking Z for her all-out birthday effort. So more
delay on that. Friday's the next possible day for
taking the card over to her place and propping it inside
the door to flabbergast her when she arrives home from
work. So the rest of the week will likely go to that
project. And next week, in roars October. As good a
time as any to try to shoehorn myself back into a steady
routine, I guess. -- Or until the 23rd anyway, when the
planetary meltdown is still scheduled to occur. (On a
jaunt to the "north pole" this eighter I came across
something at least seemingly non-tabloidal confirming
this: the readerboard of an evangelical church (and also
saw a tongue-in-cheek mainstream news-service story
about it).) Otherwise the world appears to be careening
along toward putative apocalypse in pretty much the
usual oblivious way. -- And more than one apocalypse,

of course. Many. And at least one of those others just
a bit further down the road quite likely real.

*   *

How many hours later? Twenty-four almost to the
minute. During which what happened? Ogled a slice'a
moon as I walked home from the hideaway last night
(through the heart of Saturday night's riot territory,
where hundreds of concertgoers angry at being turned
away from a sold-out show tore up dozens of shopfronts
and did some serious looting, including at one of my old
hangouts, the broiler; and if Z hadn't come along in my
life I'd probably have been working late at the hideaway
on that night and on the way home might've walked right
into the riot and might've been looted, as it were, or
worse than looted, myself).

Here, last night, stayed up unusually late for this
era, sorry to say, reading, until almost four. Slept
until eleven. Made breakfast, read the papers while
drinking coffee until one, took notes from several books
until four, worked out for an hour (I've yet to detect
any results from all these workouts), rambled up to the
old "north pole" and back by seven (bought calcium supps
and grapes, browsed at the bookstore), prepared a quick
lunch (grapes and raisin-bread toast) and grazed in
magazines and reviews until eight, marched to the scope
office by way of the hideaway in time to call Z at the
current agreed hour (nine o'clock), eventually got
through to her forty minutes later, punched up scope
finals until midnight, hiked home, did some dishes and
cleaned up a little, relished every word of a fine new
local radical fortnightly newspaper (but it's only six
pages of standard typing paper size) -- and now this.

Also in there, two messages from Z when I arrived
home last night and a bunch this morning, then a live
call from her at two p.m. Last night's messages, to hit
the high points, said she hated to admit it but I was
right, she's again falling prey to "anxiety flashbacks"
about the first time she tried living with a man: the
debacle with Arvin. Her anxieties back then were so
great she even sought a hypnotist's help (it failed).

444

She also said she's having physical problems she didn't
want to talk about since she'd brought them upon herself
(I guessed these must have to do with her vagina, which
I unintentionally scraped with a fingernail this weekend
during the lengthy three-digit fingerfucking session,
and she confirmed that's what it was).

The morning messages said again (like one last week
after a night when she stayed home alone) she now does
better sleeping with me than without me; mentioned that
certain things about me really touch her but she doesn't
want to say what they are; assured me that her lack of
perkiness at work or elsewhere often has nothing to do
with our time together; and said she'd like to attend a
buffet featuring a reading by a current best-selling
author of seemingly serious intent (for which I received
an invitation in the mail, presumably because I was
until recently a subscriber to the magazine sponsoring
it) "just so I could see you in your element" (but I
vetoed this; I can imagine few outings I'd enjoy less).
-- Oh, and she was worried she'd lost yet another pair
of reading glasses. (She was fairly sure she'd left
them at Aida's on Sunday. The only other possibility
was the Z-mobile, and she'd already looked there. But
later she found them in, yes, the Z-mobile, on the floor
beneath the passenger seat -- where she also found a
wadded-up twenty-dollar bill, so kismet doubled.)

The afternoon call, highlights. I'm definitely a
hit with June, she says; after a long chat with me on
totally unrelated topics on Sunday at Aida's, June, as
Z's primary moral and financial "advisor," has now
okayed our living-together plan. And Aida's sister
Sera's e-mail from Indonesia clearly approves of the
same plan (and also notes that Dak, her husband, three
times packed up and was ready to move in with her before
she finally let the fourth time be the charm). On the
other hand, another of Z's work friends, a devout
Baptist, spoke against Z's living with anyone without
benefit of marriage. (Z: "I should've told her my
mother approved of it.") -- It seems every day she's
the recipient, directly or indirectly, of a comment or

two or three regarding our relationship, mostly pro, a
few con, but virtually all surprising to her because
before now most of these same folks have rarely shown
any interest at all in her personal life. "Lots of them
seem almost openly shocked to discover I'm capable of
even having a personal life, to say nothing of one
involving a man. I think most of them assumed I was
into women but I was sexually inactive or something.
Which was sort of true, but more like across the board
sexually inactive -- except for cucumbers, of course."
     Tonight it was Aida, Z told me, who kept her line
tied up from well before nine until nine-forty. "She
said she really needed to talk. After everything that's
happened I thought I'd better not rush her." In Z's
judgment, again, all of our, and especially my, problems
with Aida stem from troubles in Aida's own life and not
from anything either of us, Z or me, has done.
Personally I doubt this but I'm pleased to go along with
it in hopes Aida will eventually start to see things
differently. "Kavi," Z told me, "is driving her crazy
again." (Last week she tried to break off with him for
good after he'd failed to call for five or six weeks.
Apparently this new tack of hers stirred him into
action.) Also: "Aida and I take turns acting as each
other's therapist." (With her master's in social work Z
still thinks of herself as a kind of licensed therapist/
counselor, although she no longer engages in such
matters vocationally. In her days as a diversity
counselor at the north-end branch of the Jyze City
community college she was frequently called upon to
serve as a surrogate shrink of sorts. "I'm very good at
it. People are always telling me I should take it up
again. But I'm just not that interested.") (Aida
teased her at the beginning of the call: "You were
sitting on Glen's lap at the party! What do you think
my mother thought of that?" -- This was Aida's son
Charles's tenth-birthday party on Sunday, on which more
anon.)

*

Now I've jyzed just about all there is to jyze from

446

the past twenty-four hours and so I can go back and try to fill in some of the gaps for the preceding week.

First, more on our sexual follies. It's beginning to look as though I really do need to eat more red meat. Last week I experimented: cashing in a set of fast-food coupons, I twice gobbled down two cheeseburgers for dinner, on Tuesday and Friday nights. Sure enough I was soon "all spunked up" on both occasions: came easily and quickly later that night or the next a.m. and then came again but quite a bit less easily and less quickly the following night. Therefore I'll repeat the experiment this week and see what happens. If it works again I'll try going red-meatless next week (most weeks turkey-ham is the red-meatiest I get) and see if I seem to have a harder time getting off. (Obviously this is not a rigorous scientific experiment. Conclusions can be only slightly better than impressionistic at best. But I'm more or less (or more) desperate. And I do like cheeseburgers. Always have. It's just I know they're not exactly "healthy stuff" -- the ones from this particular fast-food chain being so clogged with noxious fat they supposedly make your turds float within an hour. Or so I read somewhere.)

And the move? On that we've chalked up no progress at all. Doug and Thuy at the south-hill place for some reason aren't returning Z's calls. But then neither has there been any further backsliding, and Z's having informed her mother of what would be happening, and then obtained friend June's approval on it, seems to have eased her own anxieties at least somewhat. And I think her discussing it with Jess had a similar effect. Now we're talking about checking out want ads in the south-hill district paper should Doug and Thuy's place fall through. Z seems firmly set on moving to that hood and no other. She's even rechristened her ongoing weekly "purge" attempts as "packing" efforts -- though she's accomplishing about as much as before, apparently, which is to say (except for vibrators and a few other choice items): zilch. Or Z-ilch.

Interesting note: when I asked exactly how she'd

justified the move to Jess, she told me and then
wondered why I wanted to know. Well, I said, paranoia
was starting to set in about her friends as a result of
the Aida episodes; I didn't want J&G to blame me for
luring her out of her, and their, current home turf.
She just laughed over this: sympathized even. But what
was interesting, along the way she said, "I just told
Jess the truth. You can always assume that. I'm very
truthful." I offered my view that it's sometimes better
to be a little discreet -- as per the damaging remark
she herself made to Aida about my feeling "stifled" at
the D-clan's spaghetti party a month or two back -- but
in general I was pleased with this statement of first
principles. Because: what a contrast with the Lady U
era. And yet also what a contrast with sister Barb's
rage for truthtelling no matter how hurtful it might be
(and the more hurtful it appears in advance, the more
virtuous you prove yourself to be by engaging in it).

     -- And I can jyze no more tonight. Meaning I'll be
going over into a third day. A long entry, this. By
the time it's done I might be close to a full standard
entry ahead in terms of total pages accumulated. At
this rate I'll need to append a big sheaf of pages in
December so as not to run over into yet another J-book.
Four for one year ought to be the limit. (Sez who? Sez
the world's first and only fully accredited jyzemeister,
that's who.)

*   *

     Next afternoon. Got a ninety-minute hole here.
Then a workout, then a hike down to Z's fitness club
("the WOC") for a charity event at which a seven-buck
donation buys you dinner and a free week's pass to use
the facilities. I want to check the place out carefully
before deciding whether to become a member, as Z'd like
me to be. The real underlying question is this: do I
want to sculpt my body so I can become even more of a
boy toy for her? And the yet realer question underlying
that one: is such sculpting even possible given that my
body's already been around for 20K-plus days and will
soon be going Glennarian III? And if it is, what kind

448

of fanatical effort would be required? How much time?
I mean I want to, sure. But. But.

On the phone an hour ago she said it's actually not
her vagina that's hurting, it's her labia. "Abraded."
I pretended to mis-hear and wondered if this was a new
fad: braided labia. She also joked that she's not like
a coworker friend she told me about yesterday who "likes
to let the tension build for a week" between sexual
episodes: after two days apart she, Z, is ready to grab
me by the hair and drag me up into the loft. -- And by
the way, neither is Jess P. like that coworker friend.
"Let it build for how long?" she roared. "Two minutes?"
But then again when Z staggered in to work the other day
looking "love-drugged" to Jess, Z asked how long it
would go on like this. Jess's reply: "Until you move
in together." (And I learned Gwen once left Jess for
another woman, about three years ago, and Jess took it
so badly she shaved her head and was in a near-suicidal
tailspin for months until Gwen came back.)

So then a few other quick updates.

Saturday afternoon we attended an exhibition of
century-old Chinese photography with Wei and Alison. A
lovely laid-back afternoon. Wei and I have much in
common, especially regarding politics and money, that
is, "frugality"; and Alison, who's an inmate counselor
for the state prison system, likes to talk art (wabi-
sabi kind especially); and both seem to enjoy our get-
togethers. Also Wei knows Z quite well -- has been a
friend (never a lover) for fifteen years, including a
spell as coworkers doing home energy checks -- and so I
learn a lot about her just from the way they interact.
(A touching little intimate scene at a bluffside park
thirty miles to the south, sitting on logs, Alison
handing Wei a tiny pair of fingernail scissors from her
purse so he could snip off a diminutive hangnail as she
stretched the skin of her fingertip. And rising in the
distance behind the two of them at that moment,
coincidentally, a topography utterly familiar to me: the
hills surrounding the town where Lady U and I used to
reside. As I gazed at the scene a bit later from a

point higher on the bluff, the whole era it represented
seemed to be spread out before me -- "almost like a
foreign country now," as I thought to myself. It seemed
impossibly distant even though it was no more than ten
or twelve minutes away across the water.)

   Sunday, Aida's birthday party for Charles, a more
relaxed replay of Z's commencement tea, a similar
fabulous spread, the same setting, many of the same
people, the D-clan prominent among them. Charles was in
bad form, sad to say, furiously indignant over losing
at backyard soccer and eventually banished to his room.
And with me at least, Aida's form wasn't much better:
almost openly hostile, or "confrontational" as Z called
it, apparently as mystified about this as I was. I did
notice my card thanking Aida for her birthday efforts
half-buried in a pile of junk mail atop the piano and
showed it to Z just to prove I'd sent one and it was in
no way offensive, as she agreed after checking it out
(at least it had been opened). Though I made the card
myself and put in a lot of time on it, Aida's never even
mentioned receiving it, to Z or to me. Bizarre. Z says
so too. "Why do Wei, Betty, June, Leola all think
you're fine but Aida doesn't? Why's she the only one?"
I even wondered if Aida might be behind Thuy's failure
to call back about the apartment. Makes no sense as far
as I can see, but then neither does any of the rest of
it. So then maybe it's just a matter of Aida being, as
her D-clan nickname has it, "Laloo," which means,
according to Z: too much.

   Friday night, a brief spat with Z over a card her
friend Irene sent her. It accused me of "disrespecting"
Z in wanting to live with her without benefit of
marriage, and did so in a pious moralizing tone. Worse
yet, Z took Irene's side in discussing this. Irene,
see, is another victim of sexual abuse as a child and
consequently has had a rough time with men. Fine, said
I, I can feel for her; but does her childhood misfortune
mean it's okay for her to be making derogatory remarks
like those in her card when she's never even met me? I
should be pleased to be the target of bias caused by

others' mistreatment of Irene? -- Yes, I'll be cautious
and compassionate with her, but I refuse to pretend I
like being referred to that way. Hadn't Z herself
spoken proudly about being a truthteller? If she and
Irene could be truthtellers with each other, couldn't I
be one with Z? -- And I then had to explain why this
episode would push my hot buttons: the Lady S/Elgie
story, all the years of parrying with similar moralizing
meddlers who had little or no idea what it was all about
with us, and minds closed to finding out, those of my
own sister and mother at times prominent among them.

Saturday afternoon Kat left Z a cute phone message
which Z played back for me. It had to do with her first
viewing of "Josefina," the new brown-skinned Barbie
doll, at a mall. She looks just like me," Kat exulted,
"except her hair doesn't have red highlights like mine."
The search for a non-Cawk-looking doll for Kat has been
going on for quite some time, for all of which Z has
stood ready to lay out a small fortune on a custom-made
doll whose facial features would be based on a photo of
Kat. Now it appears Kat prefers Josefina. Of course
hundreds of dollars' worth of Latina-themed Josefina
accoutrements are also available, and the prices on some
are even slightly discounted. Yes! (Jyze exceptions up
there on "Barbie" and "Josefina.")

Two notable encounters Sunday afternoon as we drove
to Aida's house. The first, while stopping at a nearby
market to pick up goodies for the party, we ran into
Aida's ex, Tom, Charles's father. To my surprise (given
all the grim stories I've heard about him) he turned out
to be friendly and easygoing, even likable. True, he's
about my height and has a longish face somewhat like
mine and his hair color's about the same as mine, but
otherwise he doesn't seem monstrous at all. (He's still
a social worker in the Asian quarter, as he was when he
and Aida first met. It seems his main sin with her is
that his "life goals" are not "ambitious" enough,
meaning he likes what he's doing even though the pay is
low -- and I suspect he's into "frugality" too.)

The other encounter, Z spotted June wandering

around at a yard sale just a block from Aida's place
when we were all on our way there. June's notorious for
being unable to resist bargains. We stopped and joined
her and I'm glad we did because I scored a couple of
lidded microwave dishes for a buck thanks to June's
dickering. June herself (though Z tells me she has a
huge house out in the burbs) couldn't resist buying a
white plastic shower chair for the elderly, god only
knows why. But more than ever I'm viewing her as my pal
now, especially after hearing from Z that June can
always be counted on to stand up for me when Z and her
friends discuss us, including even on matters where
Aida's on the other side. (Of course I'm always tickled
pink -- Cawk color, so doubly pink I guess -- to hear
the old "vetting squad" is still war-gaming us.)
      -- And now some even more miscellaneous tidbits.
Z's nemesis Jimmy ("Mr. White Trash") and his father the
apartment manager have both been evicted by the new
owners of her building. The hundred-dollar rent
increase still stands but, sez Z, "it's worth it to have
them ouddaheah." Also, the press these days is full of
stories about the colossally expensive and glitch-ridden
B-2 bomber and I gleefully clip the headlines, including
this one from an op-ed piece calling for the aircraft to
be junked (lotsa luck): "Flight of the Living Brain-
Dead: Put Stake through B-2's Heart." I'll be taping it
up next to the "B-2" painted in black on my apartment
door.
      And this surprise: during one of the purge sessions
in her storage bedroom, Z sashayed out to show me a
large bagful of political buttons. For years she'd
collected them and I never had an inkling of this when I
was making those buttons for her last spring. Many of
the ones in the bag were the same as some I have in my
box atop the bureau here -- "Eat the Rich" being one.
      One day walking back home along the waterfront I
witnessed a spectacular sunset featuring complexly
layered clouds of various types and shades moving in
different directions at different levels, a stormy,
choppy bay, and stringy columns of luminescent mist

rising like campfire smoke from forested areas miles
across the water -- and all this set off against jagged
mountain silhouettes. For sure it makes my all-time Top
Ten list of fabulous sunsets (though what the other
nine might be, or the one now bumped from the list, I'd
have a hard time saying).

     As a kid Z was spoiled even more than usual when
she was sick. She jokes -- but it's not entirely a joke
-- that she expects nothing less now. One evening last
week she was not feeling good. Since her favorite
"comfort food" as a kid was graham crackers -- or "gam
cackers," as she still calls them at times -- I bought
her a box of them as a surprise while out on an errand.
Alas, it turns out she dislikes them now -- too much
refined sugar. Or rather: refined sugar, period. Any
is bad. But the unopened box still rides a pedestal on
my worktable as a monument to my good intentions.

     Scaffolding has gone up on the facade of the old
building a few feet north of where Z and I exchanged our
first kiss -- an historic structure in the hood, six
stories, same Great Fire vintage as the hideaway
building. It's being gutted to put in condos and
ground-floor retail, but the facade will remain in
place. Interesting changes around here. A new cinema
opening a block up the street, independent, and it will
be showing mostly old art films -- same building as the
ancient honky-tonk sailors' bar, now defunct.

     I'm doing pretty well at staying hungry. Another
few weeks and I figure I'll be trimming down into
territory I haven't visited anytime recently -- say not
for a couple of decades. Emaciation almost.

     And: I think I've come up with a way to dismantle
the loft that won't be too arduous for me or too
disturbing for the neighbors. The idea is to saw it
into sections, then move most of the sections to the new
apartment to serve as bookcases. This would take
several days of sawing, no doubt, but it would sure beat
the several weeks of hammering and crowbarring required
for the previous dismantlings.

[Jyze in Love]

35

      Tomorrow's the 1st of October. Yesterday Zoelie
and I celebrated our six-month anniversary (of the day
we physically met). And day before yesterday, Sunday,
we viewed the apartment on south hill and found it good
and agreed to take on Doug and Thuy's lease whenever
they're ready to move out. It's a done deal. Barring
some freaky accident, Z and I will be living together
there. Units B-2 and 401 are history. Unit 303 is
where it's at or soon will be. And all is well.
      No, all is better than that. All is terrific. And
I mean across the board. Just one major flaw remains:
my recalcitrant male (or neuter now?) member. And even
that might've come across with the goods during this
past eighter had Z not been worried the sore spot on
her labia was herpes-related.
      Something splendid happened on Saturday, we both
agree. In short, we moved up to loverence level No. 2.
Or in Z's words: "I realized you're mine. You're really
mine." She's decided to hell with it, she'll drop her
putatively politically correct stance and let herself be
possessive and possessed and, what's more, proud of
both. No more big anxiety attacks, she promised.
      We also started talking about our pasts again. She
even asked some questions about Lady U (now alias "Nora"
after the previous main squeeze of the lead male
character in the comic strip "Second Chances" whose
storyline over the past few months has amusingly
paralleled our own in a number of ways). More startling
yet, she openly complimented me about something physical
("I really like your body -- I didn't realize it before

454

[Glennarian Rollover Jyze]

[that is, during the jyzerman's high klutzy period with
her] but you have a natural grace") and she also asked
me to do something mildly kinky in bed (to tantalize her
in caressing her breasts, withholding any nipple-
twisting until she begged for it).

     No eighter would be complete without a meltdown, to
be sure, and this eighter did not fail to be complete.
But as Z said herself, the meltdown was closer to a
"mere tantrum." The positive stuff massively
outweighed it. And this even though the five planets
are still in retrograde. And will remain so until
Wednesday.

     Squally day today, gusty, a few sun breaks and a
lot of rain breaks. I hustled down to the hideaway
shortly before noon to pick up a few things prior to
meeting Z at "the WOC." (I now have my "free" week's
pass in return for the seven-buck charity donation.)
Beneath the hideaway door I found a poem she'd left as
further thanks for the giant teddy-bear card and bouquet
I surprised her with yesterday, hauling them down to her
office at eight a.m. (middle of my night) so they'd be
awaiting her when she came in. In return she left me
flowers and two cards at the hideaway, and then the
poem. How this surprise blew her away. How she likes
people at work to know she's loved. How she enjoys
being fussed over. How incredibly lucky we both are to
have met, and doubly so considering the way it happened.

     The word of the week is "forelsket." In Norwegian
it means, she tells me, the same as "salamat po" in
Tagalog, that is, "I love you" or "I'm in love with you"
(my own pocket Norski dictionary says just "in love").
Leola's the one who suggested she use it. Supposedly
the whole office was abuzz all day about the weird sight
of Zoelie's "fiance" lurching down the hallway tousled
and groggy at eight a.m. bearing an armload of flowers
and a card in an envelope measuring two feet by three
feet (and plastered with scores of authentic postage
stamps -- one-centers -- hand-canceled with one of my
old rubber stamps to make it all look official).

     A few more minutes and I'll be leaving to meet her

at half past five. Today's project is a trial bus ride
up to the new hood in hopes of allaying her concerns
about the transportation aspects of living there. An
hour ago I called her to warn this might not be the best
day for the trial owing to the start of the baseball
playoff series at the stadium just a few blocks from the
bus line -- and south hill is served from downtown by
only this one line -- but it turns out I misread the
sports-section headline: the first game is tomorrow, not
today. On the other hand maybe tomorrow would be better
for the trial so we can see how bad traffic will be at
its worst. Once we're living up there (knock, knock,
knock on woo-woo-wood) we'll no doubt want to keep close
track of what's going on at the sports complex. (Soon
that complex will feature two stadiums, one for baseball
and one for football, replacing -- at outrageous public
expense -- the present single dual-use domed facility,
which itself was built at outrageous public expense
fewer than 8K days ago.

Meanwhile I'm plenty stiff and sore. Yesterday
and today also I tried out various weight and aerobic
machines at "the WOC." In the full-length vanity
mirrors lining the walls I was pleased to see I do look
perhaps slightly less flabby than two months ago. On
the other hand the tale of the scale was one I'd rather
forget, because so far my painful campaign to carve off
the pounds hasn't yielded a single one. I couldn't
believe it. So now I'm resolved to redouble my efforts.
And I'm planning to sign up as a WOC member (and at a
reduced rate as Z's domestic partner), although certain
pesky city "regs," she tells me, will likely prevent my
doing so until we actually move in together.

Wore all black today. Enjoyed strolling about the
WOC with Z. Grunting and groaning and sweating.
Discovering some unexpectedly strong muscles and some
unexpectedly weak ones and some whose existence I'd
totally forgotten about (and they're making me pay for
that now). Doing the gym thing again -- kicking up
musty memory clouds from the long chain of gyms that
runs through my history, starting when I was age six or

so, like a series of gritty reform schools (though I
loved them all regardless). Athletics and competition.
Resolution and ostentation. Flashing eyes and glowing
bodies (lots of gay dudes at this gym, no question) (and
Jess and Leola and a number of other officemates of Z's
are members, and Aida is too; and in racial terms the
membership as a whole is highly diverse by Jyze City
standards because it's made up largely of government,
not private-sector, employees).

*   *

    The above entry eked into being right here in the
green armchair whose days appear to be numbered -- Z
doesn't like it; its funkiness exceeds even her limits,
which I'd concede are extremely tolerant -- and now I
return to the same spot twenty-four hours later. Stormy
Wednesday afternoon. Cold too, and with Z's new all-
purpose screen rendering the chairside window
unshuttable I can't do a damn thing but shiver. Or I
could clap an old denim skirt of hers over the opening
-- she salvaged it from her own free bin to serve just
that purpose -- but the suffering isn't quite severe
enough to justify the hassle. How bad is it then? Bad
enough that it bestirred me to put on a heavy long-
sleeve henley. Not bad enough, though, that it could
bestir me into rummaging around in my bureau for a pair
of sweatpants, unused since last winter and no doubt
fragrant from being shut up in there so long. Instead
it's red shorts above goose-fleshy bare and still-sore
legs (groin and back of thighs especially).
    Unexpected scoping work last night, a two-hundred-
pager. My plan to do some jyzing at the hideaway had
to be scuttled.
    Some delicious loving earlier last night. Over and
over again these days it's turning out this way. How
sweet it is! -- Z had announced she'd need to be "semi-
perky" today and so we should confine our sexplay to the
evening. As I was rustling up dinner (pea soup with
chunks of turkey-ham, not a favorite dish of hers, but
her stash of healthful TV dinners had run out) we agreed
to hit the loft at nine before I left for work at ten.

457

But while still seated for dinner we began nuzzling and
she moved over and knelt by my chair, our hands got
busy, and she whispered: "Or we could go up there right
now." Ooh, that was so fine, the way she said that!
And we did go up there right then, for over an hour.
     Always she's noticeably lustier after we've been
apart a day or two. The electric jolts. The spicy love
talk. The seductive pleas. The impassioned cries as
she heats up. (Last night for the first time a
Christian deity combo came into it. "Oh God, oh Jesus,
oh God, oh Jesus." It's all the apocalypse talk that's
doing it, I think. The Rapture, the Rapture!) Also the
retrograde endearment "baby" is cropping up much more as
our mutual perceived need to show political correctness
dwindles. -- And she asked me to say her name more, and
I whispered it in her ear over and over along with a
number of interpolated love and lust words until she
'gasmed on the sound alone. Truly. Amazing. She
pointed it out herself with a kind of bemused pride: "I
can come just from the sound of your voice. Why is it
you're so incredibly sexy to me?" I have no more idea
why than she does -- less, I suspect -- but I can see
it's definitely the case and I sure am pleased it is.
This after-dinner loving, as an instance, she'd already
come four or five times before I'd even reached skin
beneath her clothing. -- She was still fully dressed
but I was down to just my jeans and reveling in the
muscle soreness and pumped-upness from the WOC workout.
     That should've been it for the night. But when I
slipped into bed at two a.m., our attempts to hold back
eventually failed. Then at six when the alarm went off
she was the initiator, and after one round she tried to
leave, started to, began kissing my body parts goodbye
in the usual ritual way as she crawled backwards toward
the top of the loft staircase, then reversed direction
and crawled back up, saying, "Forbidden fruit, I can't
resist." We went at it until past seven.
     For a lot of that time I was turned on to the max,
stiff to bursting, maybe in part because her crotch was
itself forbidden: she was afraid a new rash around her

"bahookie" was herpes-related. "We could dry-hump,"
she brightly suggested, and so we did, with my appendage
squeezed between her legs and the humpy part just below
the head noogling around in the very region we were
trying to avoid. For a time it seemed I might come from
that all by itself. But it didn't happen. Nor did any
of her other efforts do the trick. (I didn't gorge on
cheeseburgers last night; maybe that's why.) Nor did it
really matter. Wondrous fabulous loving. Just can't
stop marveling at it. What incredible good fortune (and
to have it happen when I may soon be needing my very own
white plastic shower chair!).

While on the topic: a flash of memory, we're
standing naked by the loft stairs, facing each other,
and the semitumesced "N'dow" is laid out across her palm
at a diagonal, her fingers lightly grasping the shaft,
the head bending down by her wrist (as if bowing to her,
sort of), and she says: "It's such a beautiful picture,
don't you think?" And she points out my penile skin is
somewhat darker than the rest of my body and also
slightly darker than most of hers, which otherwise is
several shades darker than mine. Anyway: yes, it truly
was a beautiful sight. I love her hands to begin with
and I love even more the sight of them touching me or
holding me in intimate ways. (As also, for instance,
when one of them rests on my chest as she spoons in from
behind, or when one of hers and one of mine rest
together with fingers loosely interlaced above the
pillow, recalling a scene from a certain Swedish movie I
first saw some 10K days back and which has stuck with me
ever since -- and of course it was already a visual
cliche eons before that movie made it even more so.)

Obsession. Obsession. It can warp you in many
ways.

Ain't denying. But to mention some other things.
Saturday's long loving at her place could happen because
her buddy from the leadership institute, Lee M., failed
to call to set a time and place for our planned get-
together that afternoon, and as of this morning she
still hadn't heard from him. We both suspect his

reconciliation with wife Carol is failing to take.
-- And that night, Saturday, with Jessica D. (another
grad-school friend of Z's), we attended a one-person
play at one of Lady U's former prime performance venues.
The production was intriguing and yet also troubling for
the way it seemed to caricature, maybe unintentionally,
some of our generation's more important political
contributions -- on this Z and I see eye to eye -- but
the evening as a whole was a great triumph because we
made it through without letting it provoke another
meltdown over Lady U. This is part of what the
breakthrough on Saturday was all about. I'm hers now
(Z's, that is, of course), she's mine, so we can discuss
personal history again. And we even did some more of
this, disclosing early love/sex experiences and also
again discussing why and how Lady U and I broke up.

About Z's early love life I learned a few new
things. For one, her first big crush as a teenager,
Ronald, was the fellow who just barely edged her in the
race for junior-high class president. And her big high-
school crush, Paul, was a basketball player who somewhat
resembled me physically (as Z resembles one of my high-
school crushes, Pat B., at least a little). This Paul
was two years older and she used to call him at home and
hang up without saying anything when he answered. The
other guy from high school I remind her of -- Floyd? --
was a photographer on the paper "who was as gaga about
me as I was about Paul" but never tried to act on it.

She wasn't allowed to date in high school. When
someone hit on her -- as happened "a fair amount, but
hardly at all compared to later" (more diva dish!) --
her favorite gambit was to say she had a boyfriend who
was off at college. The one exception to the no-date
rule was the senior prom, which she attended with an
older Greek guy (her mother thought he was a dud).

Her freshman year of college included plenty of
dating and necking and petting -- most of the latter
two in the nooks and crannies of dorm lobbies -- but
her first sexual affair didn't begin until fall of
sophomore year -- with Marty, the law student -- and he

had to work on her for six months (much as I did with
Lady K) before she finally gave in. The way it happened
that first time, she made the decision on her own "for
political reasons" (good old Emma G. -- jyze exception!
-- providing the main rationale) and marched over to his
room and said she was ready, she wanted to get it over
with right then and there, but kissing wouldn't be
allowed; it was "too romantic." And that's how it went
down. Her reaction afterwards: "Is that all there is to
it?" (Much like Lady K's back in my own college days --
and she also a virgin.) Not until a few months later
did she start taking real pleasure from vaginal sex.
After that, of course, it was "Weezie bar the door!"
     -- And now back to the present.
     On Sunday we did the AIDS walk, the marchers
assembling some ten thousand strong at the fairgrounds
and hiking several miles down to the waterfront and back
(though we ducked out during the last leg). I joined
the city employees team of which Z was the co-captain
(she's been doing this march regularly since the first
one maybe ten years ago). I met her division boss,
Dale, a short but jockish redhead with whom she has a
long history of mutual antagonism (and yet she's now
considering, among numerous other job options, applying
to become his executive assistant with the goal of
eventually succeeding him). Memories of my own protest-
marching days bubbled up quite frequently. I liked the
feeling of being back into it.
     Later that afternoon we visited the apartment on
south hill. Doug and Thuy had been out of town for a
week; that was why Z's messages had gone unanswered. A
quick tour and we liked what we saw: it's spacious (820
square feet), attractive, asymmetrically configured
instead of boxy, and has a small balcony featuring a
virtually unobstructed panoramic mountain-and-lake view
to the east. It's a fourth-floor walkup, with an
assigned parking space in the gated garage -- which
occupies the whole first floor at street level -- and a
washer/dryer in the apartment itself (imperative to Z
after the years of schlepping her laundry to J&G's).

     "You impressed me," Z commented shortly after we
left, referring to the questions I was asking Doug while
checking out various exotic features such as the garbage
disposal and the fuse box. "That's the kind of thing
real grown-ups do!" (She used that same line the first
time I ordered a bourbon and water at a restaurant.)
     It's still giving her the jitters, though, this
notion of living with someone, and what's more a male of
the species. She commented on this in another way in
bed last night, observing how ironic it is that in part
("a very important part!") she goes for me precisely
because of my most stereotypically masculine qualities.
Given her history as a radical feminist this isn't
something that lots of people would've predicted. My
view is she's always been attracted to such qualities
but she's played this down for legitimate and I think
admirable political reasons. Now she's reached a stage
where she can accept the "atavistic" parts of herself --
and myself -- without fearing she's compromising her
overall values too seriously in doing so. (And I hope
I'm able to do the same with my own and her such parts
-- absolutely.)
     Last night we finally made our trial run up to the
new hood on the bus. It's a quick trip and the
ridership is much different from what she's accustomed
to on her current route: it's highly diverse both
racially (Asians and Latinos predominating) and with
respect to age and class. During the day the route is
safe to walk (essentially there's only one way to access
the hill if you're coming from downtown: first east
through the Asian quarter and then south across a high
bridge and up a long steep incline that causes the bus
engine to groan mightily) but it's probably not so safe
at night and Z asked me to promise to take the bus home,
not walk, after ten p.m. No doubt I'll be doing just
that, at least at the start.
     Doug (Chiusan: USAn of Chinese ancestry) told us
the immediate hilltop neighborhood is "reasonably safe,"
but he also noted the frequent presence of drug dealers
at the nearest bus stop, some van-based prostitution,

several rowdy work-release houses in the area, and
frequent busts at the motel-like two-story apartment
house directly across the street. Our future building
is just eight years old and seems fairly well kept up,
but lots of litter is visible outside; and so Z asked
me to join her in "adopting" the street through a city
program. How could I resist when she assured me we'd
be issued our very own city brooms and "litter spears"
and maybe even official "Adopt-a-Street" T-shirts?

I'm delighted with the apartment, the hood, the
proximity to downtown, the breathtaking views -- our
building stands within a few feet of the hill's crest
(or should I say "absolute tiptop pinnacle"?) -- and
of course most of all with the prospect of living
there with the fabulous Zoelie B.

Maybe we'll be moving in before the first of the
year, maybe not. But in either case I'll try to
withhold further description of the new digs/hood until
we actually make the move. My focus until then will be
on closing things out here at unit B-2.

What else? Z has an invitation to tour Indonesia
for free on a utility junket next month (and to visit
Aida's sister Serafina and her family for a few days
while there), but it's unlikely she'll accept it.
"There's just too much going on here. How could I?"

Kar and Kerani were in town this past weekend,
staying with brother Rob, but I knew nothing about this
until they'd already left. By the time Kar called and
left a message suggesting we meet for dinner Saturday
night I'd already decamped for Z's place for the
weekend. (I'm a little miffed that Rob didn't let me
know sooner. Again I'm wondering if he doesn't want us
to become as close as we used to be. I still fear that
certain incidents stemming from my reclusiveness toward
the end of the Lady U years might've alienated him
somewhat in ways he's never acknowledged to me.)

Yesterday Z felt I was acting "differently" at the
WOC. She wondered if my old jock side was coming back
out. Probably it was, but this isn't too troubling to
me because, as noted before, I think the "jock side" is

part of that "stereotypically masculine" side she admits
she's drawn to. It's like high-school days all over
again: I'm that hoopster she had the crush on but was
forbidden to go out with. She's said as much several
times but only now am I realizing there's a lot of truth
to it: "It's the torrid makeout year I never got to have
in high school."

     Z crying out in the loft (last week and again last
night): "I want to stretch it out as long as I can." "I
want to schtup all morning." "I think we should try to
see how long we can stay in bed making love. How about
Thanksgiving weekend, Friday through Sunday?" "Isn't it
amazing how juicy I get for you?" "It's like we could
just fuck forever." "Promise me you'll never ever tire
of this." "I don't even care if you get a big head
anymore." "I'm your sweet raunchy cunt." ...Ooh I do,
I do, I do love the way she love-talks. And her two
latest pup-tent messages: (1) "...That simply
electrifies me...." (2) "Z [heart] M'bao/N'dow." (And
recalling the time we lay down to take a nap last week,
she after a moment saying brightly: "Wanna do some
nookie first so we can relax better?")

     -- Looking at my hardy fuchsias, seatside, soon to
be retired for good (that is, trashed), realizing I
haven't picked a single mite from them all year. The
contrast with last year when "grooming" them was my
main, even sole, social activity -- well, 'nuff jyzed.

36

     Jyze comes roaring back (after taking a full cycle
off) with a classic good-news/bad-news lede.
     The good news is very good indeed. Once again,

just like last year, the apocalypse has been canceled.
That's right! Or almost right, because it's actually
been backdated by a month, from 10/23, a week from
today, to 9/22, or about three weeks ago. And therefore
it's already failed to occur at the true appointed time
and the world crisis everyone was waiting for -- even
including in some sense the vast majority who most
likely found the whole notion preposterous from the get-
go -- is over before it could begin and everything seems
pretty much the same as it was. Is anyone even
relieved? Or upset? Not that I can tell.

The bad news, however, is a kind of domestic-
partnership judgment day of our own. Astoundingly, Aida
D., the very person who tipped us to the hilltop
apartment and vouched for us to the present occupants,
decided she wanted it for herself after all. We're
still in shock over this. The two best buds aren't
speaking and I'm fuming. Z is so riled she doesn't even
want to live on south hill anymore -- doesn't want to be
reminded of what happened. "Unit 303 it will not be."
We're back to restricting our search to Z's current hood
(at least Gwen and Jess are pleased). And we're also
back to not even starting the resumed hunt until after
the first of the year. It'll take a while to recharge
our batteries. But what the hell: the status quo is
pretty damn good anyway.

And this despite another storm between Z and me.
Meltdown time again. Same primary cause as before. But
we managed to push through this one surprisingly easily.
(It was at its peak just two nights ago.)

-- Jyze going down at top speed in the hideaway and
it might break off abruptly at any moment. The Z-
woman's working on a speech for tomorrow's annual
conference of city employees of Filipino ancestry and
she'll be joining me here when she's finished with it or
at six o'clock, whichever comes first. It's ten after
five now.

In the meantime I can glance up at a fine new photo
of her I found here this afternoon in an envelope she'd
slipped under the door. Zoelie B. looking serious,

thoughtful, heartbreakingly beautiful standing in her
red raincoat in front of a waterfall, probably taken
during a work-related tour of a city reservoir a few
weeks ago (and back in B-2 I have another new photo,
this one showing both of us marching in the AIDS walk --
and I'm taking my turn holding aloft one end of the
banner for the contingent of city employees and at least
I don't look totally alien to myself -- though not all
that familiar either -- and certainly not all that
pleasing to the eye, mine or anyone's -- but then who
the hell else is looking and what difference would it
make if anyone were? -- Other than I'd like Z to be
doing so and savoring what she sees in the same way I
savor what I see in both of these photos of her.)

On the back of the waterfall photo she's written:
"No cookbook / No self-help treatise / I breathe / And
let you play my chords." (And as she's done several
times in the past week, she's dated this wrongly, 9/15
instead of 10/15, perhaps in imitation of those
befuddled end-time experts but more likely because of
stress. Lots of it for her lately.)

-- Or perhaps it actually did happen, the
apocalypse, and we've all been raptured up to heaven and
it's just that heaven looks and feels a whole lot like
planet Earth, including all the things we once thought
were not so good -- war, pain, poverty, disease, looming
extinctions, etc. -- Or maybe it's only the truly true
believers who've all been raptured up but they're far
fewer than advertised and so their absence is scarcely
noticeable, and both they and we will be better off with
us dwelling down here and them up there; that is, it's
a win-win. This at least is my favored interpretation.

(The usual grooveyard DJ talked at length last night
about the end-time snafu. This time around the experts
somehow failed to consider that over the course of six
thousand years the date of the equinox has shifted, just
as last year they counted two years between 1 B.C.E. and
1 C.E. (from -1 to zero, from zero to +1) rather than
just one -- because there was no year zero -- and thus
shorted the apocalypse date by a full year.)

[Glennarian Rollover Jyze]

Meantime anything else going on? Not much really.
Autumn, it's advancing. Zoelie's anti-fume screen for
the B-2 chairside alley window has had to come down so I
can close the window against the nighttime cold. I'm
wearing henleys again, short-sleeved, beneath my regular
shirts, though actually today for the first time in a
week I'm not. Mother's white electric blanket is back
on the loft bed, to one side, not plugged in, this year
sharing honors with Z's small white comforter. The
fruit flies have fled -- "gone south." Z's starting to
grouse about the morning chill. No heater use yet but --
soon.

And brother Rob's birthday has come and gone. I
called him at work on the day itself (yesterday) and
we'll be meeting for the traditional one-on-one
celebration next Friday. The kid brother, right on
schedule, turns the same age I was ten years ago. No
surprise there! But I think of myself as having been
almost antediluvianly young at that age, whereas it's a
shock he's that old now. (All right, all right, no
surprise in either of these cases either.)

My main personal grump, I still haven't been able
to restart my own protojyze editing work. Skipping a
jyze cycle was supposed to help but so far it hasn't.
I'm pumped, though. I'll make it. Surely this week.

Spectacular sex continues, meanwhile, but still
without the big breakthrough. I'm visualizing like
crazy: the deep deep "penetration," the grinding churn,
the ejac that semenically laves her womb and heart.
During this week's meltdown she demanded to know when
I'll finally fuck her good and proper and again accused
me of being "imprinted" on "Nora" (or at least suggested
I might be, although offering no evidence; but she did
profess shock to hear about "Nora"'s three abortions,
thus confirming once and for all I really am capable of
consummating a sex act, or anyhow was until fairly
recently) (and then she objected to the "boastfully
studlike" tone I supposedly adopted while owning up to
all this, even though I explained that the abortions
were strictly under doctor's orders and Lady U would've

risked serious injury or death without them). Mainly I
was just steamed that she, Z, would use my intimate
revelations against me and jump to such a judgmental
conclusion (as she did do) while having so little
knowledge of the circumstances -- just as, say, her
friend Irene did in that letter a few weeks ago
regarding a different matter. In the end, though, she
apologized, Z did, to me, and soon all was fine again.

 -- And interesting weekends. "Doing things." Two
weeks ago a Saturday trip with Z and the Katgrrrl to an
isolated littoral park that's a longtime favorite of
Z's, walking slippery beached logs along the famously
storm-tossed shoreline, picking up scads of seashells
and sand dollars; then on the following Sunday checking
out an art exhibition at the university gallery with Wei
and Alison, seeing dozens of marvelous "Blue Writer"
canvases (all new to me) and a vitrineful of the artists'
letters and cards, many decorated with watercolors (which
sparked ideas for new cards for Z). Then this past
weekend I strolled around Z's hood while she toured an
herb farm with Leola on Saturday; and on Sunday we
visited Z's housebound friend Adele out in the eastern
burbs. (These herbs -- though not the burbs -- stoked Z
up unbelievably, as in aphrodisiacally. The insatiable
one's insatiability cubed. Not that she can't stoke her
own self or let me do it and float us off erotoblissward
without outside aids; it happens all the time. But this
was the limit case. Had to be. Spec-spec-spectacular!)

 Yo, 5:57, best to close the J-book here since she
should be popping up any minute now. Then a slow walk
home hand in hand up our favorite avenue (the "low
road") with frequent stops in doorways for our standard
"sailor/hooker" smooching. Makeshift B-2 dinner.
Newspaper reading, and then (if not before, or if I'm
lucky in addition to before) some early loft loving
since I don't doubt she'll be needing her jizm tomorrow.

*   *

 This second part might be quick too. No, will be.
And should be. How jyze spoze to be. (After all.)
 Sixteen days, a lot can happen in a life. Mine for

468

instance. The new life. The real life, for which the
first two full (almost) Glennarian cycles and,
alternatively, the first 20K days are now looking to be
almost entirely mere prelude. (Am feeling this
strongly.) (And by the way, if things start seeming
anticlimactic now with the apocalypse canceled -- or so
minor as not to be noticed if it did actually happen --
I remind myself I'm still perking along in Peak Prime
Time and what's more our first big road trip, Z's and
mine, is coming up in two weeks -- the last hurrah of
the super-extended birthday weekend -- and a mere month
after that we'll be hitting the pivotal Glennarian
Rollover.)

It's a day later. Six p.m., a Friday, workweek
done, and I'm just back from a hike to the "north pole."
Bought a couple of containers of spun honey and a couple
of used copies (two-bit paperbacks) of works by my two
favorite USAn fictoprotojyzers. These for Z, who's
already zipped through several other works of theirs in
the past few weeks. She's opening herself more to my
interests: trying to see what makes me tick. I'm also
giving her used copies of "Genji" and "The Pillow Book."

No more meltdowns for the rest of the year, she's
vowed (again). Did this just last night. And loved me
up real good, the kind of eros-packed night I've been
agog over for almost five months now. Three separate
sessions this time. The middle one when I crept in at
two a.m. took on a "forbidden fruit" frisson as she was
trying to save some spunk for her speech to the Filusan
city employees tonight. The tension makes her horny
(and so does needing to pee -- "Lots of things do," she
chortled). I improvised a sleep coach's sex-'em-up pep
talk which she found hilarious (said her old buddy Manny
would've loved it). Two hours of this in the middle of
the night, keeping the new guy upstairs (successor to
Claire Voyant as of last month) in whatever state he
enters when we're thrashing about within inches of the
ceiling just beneath him, and Z so bawdily noisy. And
then another round at six a.m., and this time for the
second straight ejac she felt the jizz shoot through the

urethral ridge, which she swore she'd never done before
in her life (and then the mop-up with a cigarette-
company-branded hand towel which some months ago I
grabbed from the laundry-room "free" table). Such
scrumptious sex. "Da fox is fine." I'm totally,
amazingly, miraculously besozzled on her.

And she just as much on me. Now she's saying lots
of flattering things and meaning them, I'm convinced.
She loves this or that body part. At certain hours
and in certain kinds of dim light I'm "kinda pretty."
My heart is a more or less pure heart and yet I can
still see through at least some of the crap. She shows
me notebook pages on which she's doodled my initials
and name during long boring meetings. She moves me up
to number one on her emergency call list (bumping Aida
to number two). She loves my jeans with the button fly
because she can discreetly work a finger in "to play
with N'dow and the rollers" as we sit side by side in a
cafe booth (and weekends, by the way, she's no longer
wearing any kind of underwear). She's greatly pleased
she can let me inspect her "bahookie" because she knows
I dig all her funkinesses. She says flat out, "My
relationship with you has become the most important
thing in my life." And this morning she bestowed upon
me what she herself called "the ultimate accolade": she
said even if Aida were a man she'd love me more. (This
also reflecting, true, her simmering anger at Aida as
they move toward a showdown over the apartment issue.)

In a big confessional moment she revealed details
of her suicide attempt when Marty, her first lover,
broke up with her. First she sliced up her inner thigh
with a razor in front of him. This failing to impress
him enough, she slashed both wrists. He had to rush her
to an emergency room (where he announced to the staff
that she was a "pseudomasochist" -- and a sarcastic
nurse replied, "Oh, you don't speak English?"). -- And
some years later she "semiaccidentally" poured boiling-
hot tea on the same scarred thigh after another love
failed (her first fiance, Gabe, it must've been).

All this trauma was long ago. Now she's stronger

and she's much more together. And yet: the passion's
still there. The wildness. The feistiness. And she's
well aware it's a big part of what draws me to her.
Scarcely an hour goes by when she's not trying to
exploit this fact. And usually succeeding.

For a few days she was close to reversing herself
on joining the utility junket to Indonesia in November.
I encouraged her to go but also grumbled about her flip-
flops on the matter and she said this reminded her of
her father's and also fiance Gabe's objections to her
career choices when she was five or six years out of
college. I was not happy about this. But we worked it
out. And then the Aida apartment shocker settled the
matter for good. (Aida had suddenly decided to go to
Djakarta herself and stay with her sister Sera so that
the three of them could travel the islands together for
a week; she just assumed Z would want to do it. And
then she and Z would fly on to the Philippines, Aida
thought, for another week of escapades.)

So I'm diving right back into denial on the mulish
ill behavior of this hank of flesh dangling impudently
(but still pudendally) between my thighs and declaring
myself wildly happy. Again. Only even more so.

Just about a year ago this week I was agonizing
over whether to contact Lady V and in the end decided to
put it off for a full year. I'll say now I'm not even
slightly sorry I did that. And I hereby declare Lady V
fully dead to me. Z supersedes her. (Supersedes Lady U
too, to be sure, and Ladies S, C, and K as well. But
it's still Lady V she most reminds me of and whose
effect on me hers most resembles.)

Genital herpes has hit the news twice in this
double-eighter period: first a new medical study showing
it tends to fade away as its victims hit the post-peak-
prime years (or say Glennarian Stage III), and then a
new health survey confirming it's still spreading in the
U.S. (as many as two in nine adults have it), and most
of all it's spreading among those in -- yes, the post-
peak-prime years. Where, of course, I'll soon be. And
Z already is.

She bought a new purple beret. I discovered a good
new poet who's also a philosopher of sorts working back
in the Mentoka zone (bought two of his books and read
them quickly and carefully -- with white gloves as it·
were -- so I could give them to Rob for his birthday).
Also bought four "My Journal" kits which I'm planning to
alter into "My Jyzebook" kits before laying them as
Christmas presents on Kat, Betty, Z, and -- of course --
myself. (Or better maybe that one should go to Rob?)
    And what else? I lost my tweezers down the drain
in the bathroom sink (while going after another white
cat's whisker, I'll admit, this one poking out from the
exact same spot on the opposite eyebrow). Also I tired
of fiddling with the "engagement ring" on my pinkie,
where it was way too loose, and jammed it onto the ring
finger using Z's massage oil; now it's doubtful I'll
ever be able to get it off short of taking a hacksaw to
it (and I'm delighted with the corny symbolism of this).
And I noted what appears to be a developing tendonitis
in my left elbow, possibly undermining my shape-up
campaign (which otherwise seems to be going well). And
June and Leola visited B-2 "just to get a gander at it,"
as Z said, prior to all three doing dinner at a nearby
restaurant, and my reportedly high standing with June
and Leola seems not to have suffered too much.

37

    Perched on the carpet outside the B-2 door, a mini
pumpkin. Cute little thing about the size of an apple,
carved by Z to look "just like you at your most dour."
And outside her apartment door squats its mini mate,
carved by me, my take on the Z-woman at her bewitchiest.

472

But it's that week. And earlier yesterday the time
fell back an hour, granting us some badly needed extra
sleep, and -- and. And this Saturday we'll be hitting
the road for our first "long-distance trip" together --
the extended-birthday special -- and that's why this
jyze entry is arriving a couple of days late (that is,
so I can fit in a session during the trip without too
greatly distorting the prescribed gap between entries,
especially with an instance of my doing just that --
when I took a full cycle off -- so freshly in evidence).
    Love love love. And progress too, sexwise (the
Wise Sex Movement). "Fucking like bonobos." We did at
least come up with a copy of the book, finally.
Splendid X-rated stuff, female bonobo genitals inflating
like giant pink bagels and a number of Z's work friends
aghast (reportedly), especially at the sight of the
amusingly carrotlike erect bonobo wanger. Not that I've
gotten around to proving myself truly or even faintly
bonobolike in coital action, no. But I did come twice
within maybe two hours at most, thereby causing Z to
preen and boast and also officially abandon her theory
that I've been rendered impotent forever by hormones
released from plastic.
    "Let's bonobo" is the hot new motto, successor to
"Let's horse around" (though "Let's fuck" is always
available on standby and appears frequently because Z
relishes the term and voices it so raunchily and yet
also so stylishly). On Saturday a week ago we remained
loftbound all day, bonoboing until almost five p.m.
(And that same day I learned that Bradley, the guy who
purportedly taught her the ropes about high-end fucking,
was exactly her height and loved to brag about his
massive member and loved even more to push her to the
limits sexually. This didn't necessarily mean she liked
everything about him, though, she let me know. "I used
to tell people it was like being in bed with the devil."
-- And she swears she never loved him, which also makes
it more bearable for me to hear her talking so glibly
about all this. ("Boastfully studlike" she'd no doubt
call it if I were doing it. Or maybe she'd just say she

was imitating me -- "Let's see how you like it.")

A double-eruption morning. Her bed. It remains true I'm usually easier to get off in the morning nowadays, which reverses the case for all earlier eras. And much of the time it happens the way Z pioneered with me, reaching around from behind as we spoon lying naked on our sides. My theory is the position works because it puts her fingertips into play in the most sensitive frenile zone (or I could say: it's most like the positioning of my own fingers and hand while engaged in a standard wank).

In response to a phone-message plea to let her pursue me "for a change" I came up with a chant for my return message: "Pursue me, pursue me, make me relinquish the spunk." Turned out she didn't catch the allusion to the old high-school sports cheer ("Repel them, repel them...") nor did she, despite her wide reading and even wider experience, recognize that "spunk" has a spermic meaning. But we did have fun with role reversal. This time she didn't need to drive me away first in order to motivate herself to become the pursuer for a while.

Not a single meltdown this eighter (or elevener actually). She's saving them all, or so she's still promising, until after the first of the year. My hope is by then she'll realize life's a whole lot better without them and decide to keep stockpiling them indefinitely, letting them rot away in some forgotten and deeply buried and lead-lined psychic storeroom.

Meanwhile I did it. Both things. (1) Began working on my protojyze stuff again. (2) Began punching in corrections and printing fair copies. Both felt damn good. I'm trying to average three hours or more of editing/writing per day, ten pages (single-spaced and printed on both sides) of fair copies.

Today, for example. It's a Monday, no scoping work in sight, so I should put in six hours on my own stuff and correct twenty pages, to compensate for the heavy scoping days looming later in the week. But I'm also trying to work out daily and walk at least four miles

daily and keep the unread reading matter from stacking
up too high. Busy busy. Socially engaged too.
Concocting a philosophy/politics letter to Z's coworker
Howard at the utility. Serving as a clipping service
for Z (and enjoying it), especially on hot-button issues
such as institutional racism, hazardous waste, global
broiling -- and then the truly sizzling stuff like the
latest updates on bonobo mating behavior.

Brother Rob came by for dinner Friday. First time
in months he's been here in B-2. For this visit I had a
salt shaker and an ashtray ready to go -- pepper shaker
too -- and what's more remembered I had them and where
they were. Tales of his trip to the heartland -- Turtle
Rapids, Gatewood, Lahontan and various other Mentoka hot
spots. Somewhere along the way he saw "The Pillow
Book." Brother Jeff, he reported, was deeply moved by
the Turtle Rapids jaunt, which they made together.
Rob's now determined to pay for restoration of the Buena
Vista monument erected by Great-Gramps Bendyk to honor
the "Learned Pioneer Hermit" (the inscription is
crumbling away) and he's in contact with the current
owner of the general store (or actually the foodstore
which succeeded it in the same building) in hopes the
town council will vote to contribute to the effort. The
store owner has retained a closetful of records from the
early days and offered to let Rob look through them.
Would they perhaps, we wondered, shed some light on the
Roar S. story? Did Roar ever work at the store? Did
his stern older brother (Bendyk) boot him out over some
typical Roar escapade (probably involving women and
alcohol and/or pilferage from the store) and thus hasten
him on his downward spiral? -- This being our current
best-guess theory. (The shocking Roar double-murder/
suicide occurring exactly a century ago as of early
next October, I think it is, or maybe late September.)

Jeff seemed in good spirits, Rob said, but
everywhere they went he was "sucking on a beer," even
while driving. His financial situation was poor, close
to desperate. But then just last week he finally did
make a sale in his new job as a real-estate agent.

[Jyze in Love]

(Sister Barb, Rob said, put Jeff down to his face for
taking such a job. And in reply to a long letter Rob
wrote her about his trip, she could manage only a single
sentence scribbled on a birthday card, something along
the lines of "I'm glad you enjoyed your visit to Turtle
Rapids." Hidden behind the banality of this remark was
another instance of Barb's judgmental savaging of Rob:
for taking an interest in the (undeniably morally
compromised) male line in the family, for following in
his (undeniably morally compromised) big brother's
footsteps in exploring those roots. Appalling, this
purity-obsessed sister. I admire Rob for being able to
keep communications open with her. Me, I just can't do
it anymore. Not now, probably not ever again. I've
given it my best shot more times than I can count and
each time failed miserably.)

     A delayed birthday dinner served up on Mother's
good dishes, the first time I've ever used them on my
own. For cake a big cherry muffin with a single candle
(and lighting it did not set off the smoke alarm -- but
then we had two windows open and the fan turned on high
to vent Rob's pipe smoke). And even though the meal
itself wasn't much, he still commented (while choking
down a chunk of gristly turkey-ham from the pea soup),
"Glen, after what I saw at your birthday party, I'd say
you've definitely come a long way from your 'one-man odd
couple' period." (And as he'd told me several times
before, he thinks Z is terrific. "You really lucked
out, you sonuvagun," he said. "The more I see you with
her, the more I think she's perfect for you.")

     And lots of other out-in-the-world doings this J-
week, the kind of things I rarely did back in the pre-Z
period of the B-2 era. (The days of which overall era
are definitely numbered now, as indeed they have been
for some time, but I still have no firm idea of what
that number ultimately might be. Feelers for apartment
vacancies are out to the farthest nodes of Z's support
network. More and more she's saying this "shuttle life"
between our two squats is getting old for her. Her
anxieties concerning our living together appear to be

fading fast. We fantasize about "the new place" a lot
without having any real idea of where it'll be or what
it'll be like. Joke about the massive adjustments we'll
both need to make. -- One thing I know, I'll be in
charge of lighting. She's even agreed to this.
Otherwise we'd both go blind. How she's avoided this
herself up to now is a mystery.)

    Among the doings, two excellent movies, both with
lots of personal meaning. Sunday before last a
documentary about a northern Cawk guy's exploration of
his family roots in the old south. Plantation houses,
slaves -- what's the moral responsibility of the remote
descendants of slaveholders? Or on the macro level,
what's the responsibility of a nation whose current
prosperity is built on, and significantly attributable
to, a history of slavery, conquest, and genocide? (I'm
proud of how I've dealt with these issues in my own life
and yet this movie still caused me anguish. -- And how
fine it is to be with Z who's so impressively aware of
the way these same issues shake out in daily life for
those affected the most -- and for the descendants of
the oppressors as well as the oppressed.)

    Then this past Saturday night a classic Italian
flick at our new neighborhood art cinema, located just a
block north of here. It so happened Z had seen this
movie with Marty back when it first came out, shortly
after he'd become her "cherry man." And she'd intensely
disliked it then for the admittedly nondisinterested
reason that Marty had thought its blond star "the most
beautiful woman who ever lived" (he was Jewish and
according to Z had a Portnoylike thing for blond
shiksas). As it turned out some 13K days later Z still
couldn't view the movie with any kind of critical
detachment. Only the next day, some 13K plus one, was
she able to admit maybe it wasn't all that bad. Still,
though, she didn't stomp out or blow up later as she did
over "The Pillow Book." Things are looking up.

    -- Getting dark out there. So early. It's addling
in a certain way even though not exactly a surprise. At
rush hour the traffic flashes headlights in here instead

of the glinty sun reflections of high summer. But the
vines growing on the fence outside are still thickly
leaved and so those headlights are just barely visible
from where I sit (green armchair -- all this time).

     To walk. Best to do it now, some of it, so I'm not
forced to do it all at once. So do half. A mile north
to the drugstore where my favorite brand of vegetable
juice is on sale, then a mile back. Funny thing, it
turns out canned V-juice is better for you than fresh
tomatoes -- heating releases the lycopene, the
superantioxidant that will keep you alive forever. A
news story revealed this (with all due skepticism) just
last week. Brother Rob was appalled to hear about it;
he's been focusing on raw tomatoes as a healthy eat for
years. Z wasn't too upset since her vow to override the
advice of her blood-type diet book had gone no further
than the purchase of that single bag of organic
tomatoes, all but one of which I wound up eating myself
when they were about to go bad. (Doc Karen, by the way,
wondered if Z'd like to have her moles burned off to
make her body "nicer" for her new sweetie. Proposed it
exactly that way! -- But I'm fond of those moles and
told Z so. Not only do they look good but they're like
landmarks or raised braille dots -- keep me cued in on
just where my hand is, or tongue is, while bonoboing, in
case I get lost in a sensual trance.) (Doc Karen, Z
says, remembers me from our STD appointment as being "a
really nice guy...but he seemed a bit nervous." -- And
well I should have, it turns out, since I've now learned
Karen used to work at a clinic where Lady U was a
patient and almost certainly was her doctor for a while.
But this bizarre coincidence -- someone else besides
this jyzer right here may have intimate knowledge of
both of their bodies! -- isn't something I'll
necessarily be mentioning to Z anytime soon.)

     -- Reminding me, the latest twist with Aida is she
was supposedly "shocked" to hear Z was upset about her,
Aida's, reclaiming of Doug and Thuy's apartment. She
therefore proposed they pay a joint visit, she and Z, to
one of Z's former "counselors" whom Aida knows too and

try to work it out with professional help. In the
meantime they'll still do lunch together once a week as
they have for years, but they've declared all talk
about the apartment imbroglio off-limits.

     Z, surprisingly to me, is going along with this.
She's also saying we should attend the D-clan's
Thanksgiving celebration. "After all, I'm not mad at
the whole family." So then should I just swallow my own
pique at being treated so shabbily by Aida? I guess I
should. How important is it in the larger scheme of
things? I don't want Z to feel she must give up her
best friend just because of me, or even to feel any more
tension in their relationship than she otherwise would
(or better yet, I'd like her to feel less). So I ought
to drop it, yeah, I think so. But can I do this without
coming off as a wimp? A willing manipulee?

                    *   *

     -- She vintage but she funky. And me too. Thus
Z&G as viewed by Darren the street cartoonist, who now
frames his latest works in cheapo black plastic. These
framed drawings lying on the sidewalk at his new
preferred spot under the pergola in the triangle. And a
blond woman I've never seen before clinging to his non-
drawing arm, adoring toward him but wary toward
strangers such as myself. "This is the guy I told you
about who gave me a pen when I had nothing" -- yeah,
and now that pen's multiplied many times over like the
sorcerer's apprentice, and even so times still look
tough for Darren -- which doesn't mean, though, he's
forgotten how to put up a brave and winning front. And
he did say he sold his nine hundredth work a few days
back and how many artists can top that?

     Meanwhile, since this afternoon I've lost five K.
Or I have if my holdings in deep reserve fell
commensurately with the stock index. A collapse today
of five-hundred-plus points or about seven percent.
Missed the canceled apocalypse date by just four days.
-- But I'd say the good times (in this country, that
is, and mainly for the people who already have it good
anyway, and of course they (we) have it good in large

part because this country makes life miserable in so
many other countries in so many ways and almost always
has) -- the good times here, I say, will likely keep on
rolling (for a while). Analysts will say the market
burped, that's all, as it did on Black Monday ten years
ago, and nowhere near as noisily now as then.

Hideaway for this entry. I'm just back from
phoning Z. Usual phoning place, at times anyway, the
booth in the basement hallway of the ORB cafe. It's one
of a pair, the old wooden kind with windows and a hinged
door and a built-in hardwood seat.

What did I learn? She's afraid my newly emergent
sore throat will ruin our upcoming delayed-birthday-gift
road trip (after the season-opening six-month homestand).
Worries about kissing me and catching it herself. Says
she's a good nurse. More or less orders me to do this
and that: take hot baths, get lots of rest, consume a
staggering array of herbal remedies which she keeps for
her own use in a kitchen drawer at B-2. "You sure it's
safe for me," I ask, "to stick a hand in that drawer?"
(Actually I've already pilfered several thousand-unit tabs
of vitamin C from that drawer with no identifiable ill
effects.)

And: she's worrisomely fallen under the spell of an
essay on the purported death of romance. The longest
she and I can last, it suggests, is a couple of years.
So now I'd like to find a way to calm her about this.
When she feels shaky about us she generally seems to go
one of two ways, neither of which is easy to deal with:
either brusque and brassy or ballistic. Worsening
matters, I'm the one who gave her the essay to read.
My intention, however, was the opposite of what she's
thinking: I mainly just wanted her to know I was aware
of this kind of take on romance and I reject it (though
I do admire the writer of the essay). I thought I'd
explained all these things in my cover note but maybe I
should've talked with her about them too.

In any event I'm pretty sure we've safely gotten
past this little blunder of mine, at least for now.

Last week then. Top of the list, three Katgrrrl

encounters: Sunday when we went out to Betty's for a
meatloaf dinner, Wednesday night when I treated Betty,
Z, and Kat to dinner at the railroad cafe where the food
arrives on model trains (as it happened this was Manny's
birthday as well, and Betty and Z paid to have a quarter
hour of music dedicated to his memory on his favorite
radio station later that night), and then Saturday when
Z and I took Kat to the book fair in a big warehouse on
the downtown waterfront, this followed by game-playing
at B-2 while Z napped in the loft: "nerfpong," marbles,
yoyos. Some lovable mischievous sweet cute smart funny
and truly beautiful little kid she is.

From Z I learn Betty would like to meet one of the
other men who responded to Z's ad -- the one who had a
strong interest in Guatemala. Thus only now does the
story come out that when Z told me she would stop seeing
the other camels and focus on me she didn't immediately
throw out that big stack of replies to the ad. "What if
it hadn't worked out with you? June would've scolded me
for months if I'd had to pay for another ad." What she
did is she put all the best letters in a bag and stored
the bag on the shelf beneath the boom box for "a month
or two" before finally tossing it. "You sure just a
month or two?" I asked. "Well," she replied, "they're
gone now. That's what matters, right?"

Also this past week: Z's book group met on Thursday
(failed apocalypse day) at an impressive fourth-floor
artist's loft in an old brick industrial building across
the street from the domed stadium (reminding me I'd
prefer us to live in a loft -- the problem being that in
areas safe enough for Z to walk at night they can be
found only at outrageous prices, and walkability for Z
is one of our key criteria). And yesterday the whole
day went to "parallel play" as Z worked on her
application for a high-level job in conservation
management that's about to open up at the utility (but
with loving for openers and again for closers before I
took off at five p.m., our usual Sunday parting hour).

And: a gallingly funny scene when Z "casually" took
me into an herbal shop during a north-end shopping

expedition and I found myself face-to-face with a large display touting a concoction designed to cure "erectile dysfunction or virility problems." (I said no way; if she wanted me to take that kind of stuff she'd have to slip it secretly into my food or my vite/supp bottles; and she said she just might do that.)

   And I've been working hard to resist dipping into the overflowing bowls of Halloween goodies at various sites around town, including the usual alluring array at the scope office. And Z had what she called a "venting week" featuring intrigues with several friends still upset because she's seeing so much less of them than in previous years. (And she suddenly realized it was true, she'd gradually stopped calling Aida with the latest hot news when she started calling me with it, because to call two people with the same hot news soon becomes a chore and time is limited. But for six years she and Aida had frequently contacted each other that way, sometimes half a dozen times a day. -- And could this degree of closeness be part of the reason Aida's ex, Tom, feels Z helped break up their marriage, "alienating Aida's affections," "egging her on," as Z told me herself last week? I suspect it could.)

   And finally there was the night when I was an hour late returning to B-2 -- arriving at three a.m. -- and found Z lying on the floor in a frantic state with the phone in her hand, and she was plenty upset because she had no way to reach me at work (and that's still the case, though I've said I'll try to come up with something -- a cellphone or beeper maybe, though I dread the thought of either). Meanwhile she's drawn up a card with her phone number and emergency instructions on it and I'm carrying it in my shirt pocket at all times.

   No, one more thing. She admits when she originally arranged our upcoming trip back during the August jyze spree (which to her was also a fight spree), it was in part because Jess P. advised her you can't really be sure about a lover until you've seen how you get along while traveling together. The crucial "road-trip love test," Jess calls it. And even though Z feels much more

"sure" about us now than she did then, or at least so
she says, she's still not as "sure" as I say I am (and
truly am). "How did you know so soon?" she keeps asking.
"How? How?" -- But to me it's hard to believe she
didn't know right away herself. Especially after that
first hot makeout session on her bed. "Jolt Day."
-- But then she did say yesterday the first time she
really thought she might go for me in a big way -- "When
I started loving you" -- was when she called to reveal
she had herpes and I reacted "so magnificently." And
come to think of it, that may have been later that same
"Jolt Day" night. Makes sense anyway.

      And tonight I'm wearing a heavy long-sleeve henley
for the first time since roughly that same day. About
to walk home. Mama it's cold outside.

38

      From a hallway couch deep in the sanitized and
perfumed entrails of a big fancy motel. By leaning to
the right and peering through an upscale lounge I can
see (out the lounge's back windows) the shadowplay of
auto traffic crossing a high green bridge over a very
wide river. Empty bar, midafternoon, a couple of TVs
droning away. Up the river, visible from the deck
outside but not from here, a sunlit snowcapped volcano
that's not the one I'm used to seeing on clear days when
I look to the southeast back in Jyze City.

      Two hours to blow. Then Z finishes her all-day
toxicology workshop being held in a deckside conference
room downstairs and we head back home.

      A good trip? Proving we can get along just fine
forever and ever? Damn right! Even if it's a little

hard to overlook my own self-disappointment at being
such an eccentric and unsatisfying sexual partner. Not
to be too repetitious or anything, but this I just don't
like at all. I wanna be a damn good lover. Especially
for her I wanna be because she's so extraordinary. (And
she damn well knows it. And I'm glad she does. But
this doesn't mean her wide range of experience is never
disorienting for me, even though mine's probably every
bit as wide, maybe even wider -- but then this might
just make the disorientation that much more disturbing.)

Two nights at a grand old hotel in the city across
the river, then last night here. Lots and lots of
snuffly loving (my cold persists, though weakly) on fine
firm double beds. I've been eating red meat by the
carcassload, I've been focusing, I've been madly
visualizing, I've been trying weird self-stroke (stoke)
stuff in the bathroom and even while lying next to her
as she sleeps, but by conventional standards we still
remain carnally all but unacquainted. Yet I've been
wildly happy. Bizarre. Especially considering this is
bona-fide, flags-flying, bells-ringing, whistles-
blowing, all-out big-time Love with a capital L and all
the rest capitals too -- so LOVE. And not just for me.
For her too. I'm as sure as any sworn anti-absolutist
ultra-romantic radic-prog neoprag can ever be.

Wandering around the handsome downtown of a city
almost new to me, hitting a celebrated bookstore and an
outdoor market, riding the ballyhooed new light rail and
checking out the impressively bricky open-air civic
center and certain alleged architectural masterpieces
(including one which, local legend has it, launched the
postmod movement) -- I liked all of this even to the
point of adding the city to my list of acceptable places
to live, though I'd like it still better if it had a bit
more urban grit and a lot more racial and cultural
diversity of the well-tossed salad kind -- but in truth
I'm scarcely noticing a thing I'm so focused on Z.

The grand old hotel we stayed in stands a few
blocks uphill from the urban core. It boasts a picture-
perfect doorman, himself grand and old, an escapee from

the label on a bottle of stout. Owing to a mistaken
assignment to a smoking room we wound up in a large and
sumptuous nonsmoking double (for the same price) and
then a little construction noise in the hallway enabled
Z to talk the rate down by thirty bucks (oh she can be a
formidable jawboner). We brought our own food, a
heaping tableful, grapes and bananas and tuna and such,
then ate out several times anyway (why not since we were
saving so much money on the hotel?) and ordered a big
room-service breakfast Monday. Z laughing like crazy at
all the TV inanities as she surfed scores of cable
channels using the remote. Z lounging about in her sexy
black teddy, graduation gift last June from Jess and
Gwen. Z waking me in the middle of the night with her
lips "imprinted on" my party-pooper of a joystick. Z
allowing as how she's nipple-come maybe forty times over
the three days but who's counting. Z rapping hard on
the wooden bedpost after proudly observing that she
still hadn't caught my ridiculous cold/sore throat.

     (Last week she strutted her stuff as a caregiver.
No kissing permitted and she did notice sex wasn't at
all the same without it. I did bridle a bit at certain
Nurse Ratchit-isms and she did promise modifications
next time around. One near meltdown occurred over a
probable misunderstanding and we both settled for that
interpretation because the next morning we'd be leaving
for the long-awaited "road-trip love test," as we both
were calling it by then. The issue was power --
starting with her saying she knows it's not politically
correct but sometimes she likes to be overpowered -- and
it's sure to come up again. I also closely examined the
complex scar left on her right inner thigh by the hot-
tea scalding on top of the razor slashing, both of them
self-administered. "Double mortification," she calls
it. Our resumed discussion of these incidents raising
still more Lady V flashback shudders in me (the ones
involving razor blades and self-slashed breasts/chests
just for starters). Interesting times ahead, eep eep.
-- If only my mysterioso clunker of a G-stick were fully
functioning, how much better able to face them I'd be.)

[Jyze in Love]

(And I should mention I got it wrong earlier. It was
the breakup with Jerry II -- not the one with first
fiance Gabe -- that led to the thigh-scalding incident.
We're talking about just six or seven years ago, her
last previous truly serious involvement, the very same
one that turned her off men "forever.")
        -- Still not much happening here at the motel.
Quiet afternoon. Three-forty says my pocket watch.
This setting reminds me a lot of the year my day job was
in sales promotion, the months of the traveling sales-
award show, protojyzing in fancy hotel and motel lobbies
up and down the coast. (How'd we happen to miss this
city? I no longer remember.) -- And while at it I'll
mention that I should've noted an anniversary in the
previous entry. Twenty years on for meeting Lady U.
"Nora." (I sometimes think of her by that name myself
now.) And...I'll admit to a few aching moments over the
past couple of weeks. Ambushes. At one time (and that
time went on a long time) I loved this "Nora" a helluva
lot. Now even the memories are all but obliterated by
the power of loving and being loved by Z. I'm actually
grateful for a few moments of ache over a lost past.
It's a kind of delayed ratification, could say. I don't
want my past to seem worthless nor do I want it to seem
merely a warmup, a prelude. (But for now I'm resigned
to its mostly seeming so, and probably not just for now
but for always.)
        Zoelie. Zoelie B. At noon I spotted her lunching
alone during the workshop break: a little wrench of the
heart. Window seat. Big river out there not really
rolling on, as the song says it does, or not visibly
anyway. An orange lifeboat tied up at the dock. If I'd
come in and seen her and hadn't known her, she asked,
would I have tried for a pickup? Ha! Said I might've
crashed right through the cluster of fully occupied
tables that blocked the shortest direct path to her
booth. (But nah, I'd've played it cool. Only in my own
mind would I have been blasting through all obstacles.)
        An amusing newspaper story about seahorse sex gave
us a new term to complement "bonoboing" as a way of

describing so-called postconfluent lust: how the female
seahorse injects eggs into the male who is the one that
becomes pregnant. "Seahorsing around." Z fucking me:
she says she sometimes likes to fantasize doing so.
Fine with me as long as it gets her hot. True, she
can't inject eggs but then so far neither can I inject
sperm, so we're about as "symmetrically reciprocal" as
can be. She also likes to fantasize we're both gay
males or lesbians -- especially the latter. On butch
mannerisms I have even Jess beat, she says. On butch
prettiness, though, well, never mind. (One day I
clipped a lengthy article on the new "erectile-
dysfunction drugs" soon to hit the market, but I still
haven't given it to Z and maybe never will. Don't want
pressure to try them. Don't want my own e-dys
validated that way. And once you start using them how
do you stop, if you can at all? Nor do I want to be
imbibing powerful little-understood chemicals -- and if
anyone should be able to comprehend this, she with her
brand-new toxicology certificate certainly should.)
     Meanwhile the stock market's been crazily volatile.
The very next day after my deep-reserves stash lost five
grand -- that is, if it performed at roughly the market
average -- it regained three of that.
     Z did observe I've become "skinnier." This means
the 120-day shape-up might actually be working. It also
makes me wonder if she really wants me to be lean and
mean. Did she already think of me as "skinny" to be
able to see me now as "skinnier"? I know she worries
about whether I might think she's "a little plump" (I
don't and she isn't) (she who thinks a two-pound weight
gain after a festive weekend cause for major alarm).
She also worries I'm attracted to body types different
from hers (I've scarcely even noticed another body since
hers came along). (And by the way, last night, for the
first time since we met, she indicated she thought a
woman in our presence was attractive -- pointing out
that a server working a nearby table had a "cute ass" --
but maybe she did it just to see how I'd react.) I
truly hate it that my "temperamental penis" (a term she

used this weekend) seems to stir up her absurd body insecurities simply by its failure to offer timely and snappy, or for that matter untimely and sluggish, salutes. I'm already so imprinted on her it's hard to remember she might be thinking I'm not attracted to her or I am attracted to someone else. This is one of the insidious ways the nonfunctioning of one's genital apparatus can drive one to despair. One thinks one can take it in stride because one forgets it will cause pain to the person one loves, not just to oneself.

(Mention this. The Days of the Dead coincided with the weekend. Since we wouldn't be in town to greet the visiting chthonian spirits, Z hit her favorite "alternative bakery" for a loaf of seasonal "Dead Folks' Bread" adorned with little skulls and laid it out neatly sliced on her dinette table, sort of like a snack for Santa. She also suggested I leave a note in B-2 directing any spirits of my own acquaintance to her place so they could chow down with the ones she was expecting. And with her help I did do that, but without specifically naming any. -- And would Nana and Gram S., two of my prime chow-down candidates, break bread from the same loaf, even now? I seriously doubt it.)

-- In her period of trying to outdo any male in sexual aggressiveness, Z was frequently called not just a tramp and a nympho but, the supreme insult, a slut. She usually told any man who flung such a term at her that she considered it an honor. So many men are intimidated by a woman who really enjoys sex and especially one who goes after it. Naturally she's afraid I'm one of these men. I swear I'm not. I love her love of sex and I love our mutual aggressivity. (Admittedly I don't like thinking of all those men fucking her. Z fucking someone else -- nope, sorry, can't feature it at all.) (She thinks I can, I'm so cool when she talks about it, but I'm that way only because I don't want her to think she can rile me with such provocations, and she does enjoy trying to do that.) -- But lines of men. Some of her housemates back in the day appalled at the numbers, the men

traipsing in and out. "Fuck men before they fuck you"
-- what she scrawled on the motel-room wall with
lipstick during the wild ending with Rodney right here
in this very city (a small one, satellite type). Rodney
the one Asiusan love and the Svengali who enticed her to
move out here from Mentoka; without his savvy tactics
she and I never would've met. -- But the fact is, I
admire the woman for having lived the life she believed
in. What's more: it was also the kind of life I
believed in for myself (though only rarely did I try to
disconnect my emotions from my sexuality, as she
regularly did; but then I admire her for having made
those attempts too because back then women supposedly
couldn't do that, only men could, which of course was
one of the reasons I tried not to do it myself. She and
I were both rebelling against antiquated gender
stereotypes but going in opposite directions. And
probably still are. -- And scratch that "probably."
It's a living fact! Part of "the dance eternal"!)

Ten more minutes. Some possible toxicological
types are wandering around already. Or maybe they're
from one of the other conferences. Up and down the
coast and across the nation, nonstop, the secret life of
conferences. Making the nation safe for its massively
toxic "business as usual" -- could say. (Am saying.)

-- Best hours of the trip so far: the ones we
danced away Saturday night at a nasty little club near a
college campus. Close quarters, good live soul/funk
music, mixed-race crowd, Z the quintessential fox in a
tight low-cut black top and tight short black skirt (and
of course drawing lots of hungry gazes). So sexy she
looks in black, not to mention tight and low-cut and
short. We were not kids out there on the dancefloor but
the crowd was mixed-age too, with several couples well
past us into post-peak-primehood. Just right. And we
did step out, did get down, did work it, did glaze
ourselves up with that good hot "Sex Machine" cold
sweat. Now to find a similar dance spot or two back
home (but they might not exist).

Okay. (Me in black pants and my current favorite

brown-and-black street soccer shoes, green canvas shirt.
Me this late-peak-prime-timer, sheee, I can still hardly
believe it myself. Right now sprawled here jyzing away.
Am pleased still and regardless to be the baddest in-
your-face J-slinger around. -- And so, certified secret
toxicology conspirators, detoxify THIS!)

39

    So much to report. And just six days gone by
since last jyze (because now I'm trying to work my way
back to the original octurnal schedule). So much, and
lots of it truly interesting and revealing, or my name
ain't -- yeah, J-slinger G. Still.
    Yet nothing earthshaking or even close to it.
Except this, maybe, in a sense: we're into double-figure
November days and it's a warm, sunny, summerlike
afternoon out there. Second in a row like this.
Sunbathing, beachgoing weather. Good even for outdoor
jyzing if such unseasonable serendipity as this day
giveth didn't also render me way too lazy to put forth
the effort to get out there.
    From in here. Green armchair. My hunch is Z's
Christmas present for me (which she's said is already
"in the bag") will be a replacement for this chair.
Even for the funk-tolerant and usually funk-loving
Zoelie B. this chair is just too damn funky. And ugly.
The new one'll be like Gerry J.'s chair, I reckon, the
high-backed recliner in which I took a lengthy tilted-
back spin in his family room and raved about in front of
Z maybe a little too much. Expensive too. (It reminded
me of the one Popeye had in which I reclined and spun
for many an hour when I was a kid.) (The other main

possibility for a Christmas gift would be a more or less
formal "dress" suit -- one I could maybe even
respectably get hitched in.) -- I am fond of this old
green armchair, though. Was it five bucks I originally
paid for it? Only a few days after arriving in town, in
the bargain corner of the used-furniture place a block
from Lady U's and my new apartment out in the Yuke.

Marriage has been a hot topic lately. Z even
pointed out I never did ask her officially -- or so she
insisted, though I recall it differently -- and so I did
ask officially just to be doubly sure and then asked if
she'd mind asking officially too, and she also said
she'd already done so, but then she too did it again.
And in response we both said "Hell yes!" But nothing's
imminent. I still haven't been able to reach Jenny L.
to follow up on the question of my current marital
status, and no one else has been able to reach her
either. The suspicion is she's going through a "pookie
period," as she's been known to do from time to time.
On Saturday, Z informed me, she, Z, did "mention" to the
assembled friends of herself and Aida D. that she and I
would be tying the knot one of these days and they all
expressed surprise and delight and clamored for the
right to take charge of this or that facet of the
ceremony or reception or various other offshoot events.
Again I could swear we went through all this before,
back in July and August.

Most surprising of all was Aida's surprise. Z told
me she'd informed Aida about the "engagement" months
ago, but now Aida was saying something like, "Well, if
you're really thinking about getting married, you should
do it before you hit the three-year barrier so you're
committed." And then when Z tsk-tsked that of course we
were "really" thinking about it, Aida pulled another of
the jaw-dropping one-eighties for which she's notorious
and said, "Well, if you're really, really serious, you
can have Doug and Thuy's apartment after all."

Amazement. Z can't figure it out any more than I
can and she's decided to stop trying. What's with Aida?
Maybe a previously deactivated moralizing side revived

by her recent return to the church? (Supposedly Mrs.
D., Aida's mother, to this day remains upset over the
sight of Z sitting on my lap at Charles's birthday party
last month, and I take this to mean a strong streak of
old-country moralizing of the no-nonsense Catholic type
runs in the family. Yet Z says Aida's "rad side usually
trumps her trad side" and that's why she's frequently
upsetting her family -- with her divorce, for example.
"Laloo -- too much"! And since August Aida's reversed
herself again on her plan to move to the north end of
town to be near them. "Now she's back to thinking it
would be unbearable to have them interfering in her life
whenever she turned around. She's seesawed on this many
times before.")

     -- Doug and Thuy's place is still "apato non
grata" to Z; after what's happened, she'd never live
there. But they're schmoozing again, the two friends, Z
and Aida, patching things up. The counseling session's
been canceled. We'll be dropping by the D-clan's
Thanksgiving feast for a post-meal drink (but doing the
meal itself at Wei and Alison's, and Christmas Eve at
Betty and Kat's, and Christmas Day at Rob and Gail's --
this, after much mulling, being Z's preferred way,
unobjectionable to me, of slicing and dicing the most
pressing holiday obligations involving both of us).

     As for Aida's patent antipathy toward me, Z remains
convinced it's mainly because I remind her too much of
Tom, her ex. "She still loves him," Z says. "She just
can't live with him. Five years after the divorce she's
still sleeping with her bed full of pillows. I mean,
why else would she blow up at him so much? And your
values are so much like his and you stand up for them so
strongly. I think she's afraid you'll cause me the same
kind of grief Tom's been causing her all along."

     But I still can't believe this is it. Why was Aida
so warm and friendly the first few months and then
suddenly I'm the bad guy? Yet Z confirms that whenever
she tries to slip a mention of me into their talks, Aida
"just lets it fall flat." Aida's never offered either
of us an explanation much less an apology for her first

flip-flop on the apartment or any of the numerous other
instances of spiteful behavior she's engaged in. So for
the time being I'll continue trying to blend into the
woodwork and let Z take the lead whenever circumstances
place us together in Aida's vicinity. (And by the way,
back in our early days Z told me she herself had been
sleeping with a bedful of pillows "for years." So were
those Jerry II pillows? And did she see my own loftful
of pillows as Lady U pillows? Does she still?)

   As part of her birthday present to Charles, Aida's
boy, Z offered to take him to a movie and this coming
Saturday is when it's supposed to happen. Z asked if I
wanted to join them. I took a pass. I'm hoping this
won't spark new problems, maybe even between me and Z.
(Saturday was Aida's birthday and that was the occasion
for the meeting of the friends: Emiko, Adele, June,
Aida, Z. I didn't send along a present or even a card.
Clearly Aida's let me know she no longer wants me to be
her "big brother," as she more than once said she did
want back in the early days, or her "pal forever," as my
thank-you card for her birthday efforts on my behalf so
grandly proclaimed I'd be.) (And I should mention that
when Aida and Tom were divorcing, Z rather vehemently --
as is her well-known wont -- sided with Aida in several
heated battles between the two and this apparently led
Charles to believe Z was "against" his father; and she,
Z, suspects he's never stopped believing it. This is
why she's now making a special effort to win back his
trust. And I in turn suspected, as I explained to her,
that my presence at the movie might work against that.
Nor did I want to risk coming off to Aida as an evil
Tom surrogate trying to alienate Charles from his
mother, and Z thought I might have a point there too.)

   With everyone else in Z's friends network I seem to
be getting along just fine. The only possible exception
is Irene, her Cherokee classmate at the leadership
institute who was sexually abused as a child and
dislikes men in general and especially pinkskin
colonial-settler men. Z's become something of a mother
figure for her, but the ongoing attempts to arrange a

meeting between me and Irene keep coming a cropper, and
almost always from Irene's side. Friday night the three
of us were supposed to see a movie chosen by Irene, but
at the last moment she pleaded illness (Z and I wound up
catching the movie anyway). I'd even rubber-stamped a
swarm of multicolored dragonflies on my left forearm in
honor of Irene, who'd mentioned to Z that she'd acquired
a new dragonfly rubber stamp of her own. It was
intended to be a surprise: I would turn away from her,
hike up my sleeve, turn back and declare, with a big arm
wave: "Dragonflies rule!"

Another big mystery among Z's friends concerns Lee
M. He's all but dropped out of sight after failing to
show up for our planned late lunch back in September. A
week after the fact he e-mailed Z promising a detailed
explanation when the dust had settled a bit more; since
then, no word from him. We're guessing his fight with
Carol (his wife of roughly a decade) may've had more to
do with his admitted affection for Z than he'd been
letting on (to Z, that is). It's also quite possible
this affection contained a hidden romantic component.
(She's told me there's never been anything romantic
between them on either side as far as she knows, and I
believe she really believes this. But she might be
wrong about his feelings for her.)

Meanwhile -- romance. Ours. As usual we're
"fucking" like crazy. Once for a few minutes on Sunday
we even did it for real, before I foozled again. It was
by far our longest authentic invaginated copulatory
event yet and it did seem to presage good things. Z
atop, this time again mostly without pain, though maybe
in part because her bizarre sidesaddle posture prevented
full "penetration." From now on when I'm erect we'll be
cutting straight to the real fucking or at least the
real attempts. She'll "assist."

Three or four times during the week she jerked me
off by hand, usually in the morning while I was still
half asleep. One of those times was truly a "magic
fingers" spectacular (up in the loft, big gouts of jizz
looping up to my left shoulder and chest). We're both

agog and she's sometimes aghast (if only playfully, I presume) at the amount of canoodling we're indulging in. Truly bountiful physical loving.

One night she left a sign for me on the loft staircase, "LOML Club, Members Only" (that's "Love Of My Life," her newest entry in our ETA contest -- following M'BAO, for "My Beloved and Adored One," and N'DOW, for "Notoriously Defiant Old Wanger" -- oh, and ETA: that's "Endearment Through Acronyms"). -- The next morning, I was about to say, after no fewer than four nookie sessions during the night, each lasting from half an hour up to two hours and all punctuated with half a dozen to a score or more of her climaxes (she appears not to be losing any of her gift even as familiarity deepens, not so far anyway) -- the next morning, yes, she tacked a cryptic line on the sign about "racking up FF points." Only later on the phone did I learn what "FF" meant: "Frequent Fucker." Since then we've been scoring those FF points at an even crazier clip.

Why is this happening? Lots of reasons, no doubt, and clearly a key one, again, and still, is my shameful inability to maintain a hard-on when it's most needed. We're both overcompensating, and we've been doing this so long now it appears we're becoming "addicted" to it. It's led to lots of discoveries which otherwise might never have occurred. It's resulted in the most intensively sexual period of my entire life and I suspect hers too (though maybe not, and right now I'm not all that eager to press for a definitive accounting). Even if a "consummatory breakthrough" lies directly ahead, as I expect (though lord only knows I could be wrong), I don't want to be giving up the kind of fuckless fucking we've become accustomed to. I love our "bonoboing," our "seahorsing around." It's wild, it's electric, it's ravishingly Zoelicious.

One night a brief Z-woman "mini pre-meltdown," in her phrase, caused me to rethink yet again the e-dys question. My conclusion was little changed: I'd defer to the concerns of my body (my wanger, my unconscious) even though well aware those concerns aren't necessarily

right or just or wise, and especially not in the long
run. I'd defer to them respectfully and meanwhile
continue trying to educate those same parts of myself
with the differing views of other parts (call them
"mind," "heart," "lips," "tongue," "fingertips,"
"gastrocnemius," etc.): and in this way the culpable
refractory parts would learn why all my parts, not just
most of them, should trust the astounding Zoelie B. Why
none should hold back. Why none should fear her herpes,
her directness, her feisty attitude, her distrust of
men/Cawks/burbans/colonials, her latest meltdown or
seemingly hostile act. I continue to hope and believe
all my parts will eventually agree to quit squabbling
over these matters. I'm in love with this woman, she's
in love with me, and I expect love to win out in the
end. (What, me romantic? But of course!)

Lots more, lots more. Where are the details?
We've heard all these bland abstractions and mushy
sentiments a thousand times already! -- And starting
with some further details about the "road-trip love
test." The splendid drive back. Two or three -- or
maybe more like twenty or thirty if the jyze rules
permit -- new things I've learned about her.

*   *

That circle of friends at Aida's birthday party, Z
did assure them (or at least assured me she'd assured
them) "this man meets all my requirements." Hey, not
bad! Like I say, these days we're thriving! -- Except
I wish she'd said "exceeds," not merely "meets." And
not merely because the Big Lie would probably work
better (regarding the "consummation piece") but because
with respect to at least some of the requirements this
would be the Big (and yet Startling) Truth.

Now at the hideaway, ten p.m., the desk, slurping
at something Z left for me here several weeks ago: an
all-day sucker, cherry flavor. Out on the streets it's
another balmy El Nino night, this one featuring a three-
quarters moon so bright I was able to read some of my
own tiny scribbly notes in its unassisted light. No
scoping work for me tonight, so I hung around B-2 longer

496

than usual, then hiked up to the north tripolar turf
just to put in the miles (and while there checked out
some sexy pictures at the north bookstore, figuring I'm
in possession of just about the most legit rationale
going: the need to jolt my 'mones alive so I'll finally
be able to sock it to my honey-dripper and thus increase
the odds that we'll soon be segueing into the world of
postconfluent family values). Then hiked back to B-2,
turf central, to call Z at the newly reinstated time for
non-meeting days, quarter to nine (this being the fourth
time I've talked with her today, voicemails not
included). Learned she may be coming down with a cold
(she did fire off a volley of sneezes during one of her
voicemails) but fortunately it's starting out at the
back of her nose, not where mine did, in my throat, and
thus I have a marginally plausible defense if she
accuses me of infecting her. It would even allow her to
continue crowing about successfully evading "my" germs.

Other news, she's now proposing we share the cost
of a new pair of dress pants for me -- used, from the
same consignment shop where we bought the shirts -- so
she can wear her dynamite black velvet dress to the
Filusan association Christmas party and dance on
December 6th (a/k/a Glennarian Rollover Eve -- less than
a month away now). I'm game because I do want to see
her in that dress and even more want her to feel that at
least on occasion I too can qualify sartorially to be
shown off. Wish I could afford to buy the pants myself;
but to be able to do that, or things like that, and do
them consistently over a long period, I'd be forced to
make major changes of a highly disruptive nature to my
life. And so: instead I must suck it up and accept her
generosity. -- And I do believe she understands and
respects me for living as I do, even though (as she
readily admits) a renegade atavistic voice in her calls
for her man to dress like a prince and spend tons of
money on her and what's more be wildly successful and
impressive in all the usual status-grubbing ways. But
she keeps that voice under control most of the time --
stomps it down just as the "money addiction" twelve-step

group taught -- so I'm plenty happy, period, except
maybe on rare occasions such as tonight.

   Then hauled ass down here, the south pole, beneath
that moon. Gorgeous evening. (The 'mones look to be
charged up too. -- And back during the road trip I
showed her how this particular male of the species deals
with awkward protuberances in the groin area when they
become, as they still do once in a while despite all the
evidence she's seen to the contrary, conspicuously
emergent under normal fully dressed circumstances:
inserted her hand in my front left pocket and talked her
through "pud-rolling shift" and "G'nad lift" moves; and
she said she liked that a lot.)

   Trying to think of what non-Z news there might be.
It's sparse, though. I did receive a call from the
housing-agency attorney charged with the dismal task of
checking out recertification applications from some four
hundred income-challenged tenants, myself included. To
my surprise he bought my cover story justifying the
existence of the deep reserves: it's a "retirement
fund." He did so, what's more, even though I let him
know it pays me a small income. He just needed an
excuse, I guess, something to rationalize sending my app
along to the next level, the board. By the time they
look at it -- probably December or January, he thought
-- I figure I'll have moved out anyway or be about to.

   Brother Rob sent over some movie-theater passes
cousin Georgie gave him -- a fine thing for him to do
(and her too), and especially since with Z in my life
I've become a born-again moviegoer. They're good
through the holidays, so I might be able to spend a
little more money on Christmas gifts than I thought.

   Election Day has come and gone. Z and I didn't
disagree on much, but where we did differ, my candidates
surprisingly did better than hers (she supported a green
techie, for example, over an almost equally green full-
spectrum radic-lib, whom she knows personally and
dislikes for allegedly feminist-related reasons, despite
the backing he's gained this year from several left-
leaning feminist groups, including two in which she's a

paid-up member). Most disappointing, though, statewide
initiatives aimed at controlling handgun sales and
securing gay and lesbian rights lost big. And I'm now
in Jess and Gwen's doghouse because Z let it slip to
them that I'm not registered to vote (even though as a
night worker I still have the same practical excuse as
always and also an elaborate political rationale to back
it up; but unfortunately laying that out would take a
lot longer than J&G, or for that matter anyone else I
know, would want to listen). (Z's the exception: she
understands because Manny, who worked mostly nights at
the hospital, used to take the same position for almost
identical practical and political reasons.)

    -- Thinking back to our "road trip," at least a few
more things to mention. Downtown, a smartly dressed
young woman is walking toward us, something falls out of
her handbag and comes bouncing ahead and I stick out a
foot to stop it: turns out it's a pair of rolled-up and
rubber-banded purple panties. Z's comment: "I mean,
was she busting a move or what? Is that how they're
doing it these days?" Another time the door of a parked
car opens a few feet in front of us and a guy leans out
and barfs spectacularly into the gutter, making me dance
as he just barely misses my right shoe. Another time
we're both struck by the beauty of huge golden bigleaf
maple leaves carpeting a plaza -- "like paper stars," I
offer, "stripped from the ceiling after a high-school
dance" -- and she starts crooning, "Say it's only a
bigleaf star...." (Cornball fever the whole trip, both
of us.) -- And how I loved the way she fell asleep in
my arms in the dimly lit motel room as soulful jazz
played on the radio and foghorns sounded from the river
along with the rhythmic slosh and splash of windblown
waves. Also loved the way she let me know that although
her nipples and vulva were sore from the many long
workouts, this didn't mean the workouts should stop:
because she loved the soreness, especially when mixed in
with the "warm peach cobbler" vaginal afterglow.

    Driving back, a stop at a rustic roadside diner for
caramel-apple sundaes. Lots of intimate talk. Most

intriguing of the newly revealed likes and dislikes: the
scar on her lower belly from her fibroid operation is
highly erogenous (since then we've zeroed in on it
several times). And I learned more about her love life.
The one among the "majors" she thinks I most resemble
(though not all that much) is "the first Jerry," from
her mid-twenties; he now writes cultural criticism --
and previously was editor of the Sunday book review --
for the same Centropolis newspaper I home-delivered
(briefly) as a kid. And: Bradley of the devilish bed
presence used to tell her he could come an unlimited
number of times without ejaculating; with him, she says
now, it wasn't so much that she was doing or being done
to differently but rather he was inspiring her to see
her sexuality differently. (Also, I forgot to mention,
in bed at the grand old hotel I discovered she could
'gasm not only from manual massage of the gap between
her big and second toes -- which I'd observed up close
before; "sexidigitation," we dubbed it -- but also by
"frotting" that gap with my own same gap. Freaky!)
     About her fiance No. 2, Arvin, I learned the
marriage was postponed indefinitely only a week before
its scheduled date; her mother and her, Z's, two best
Mentoka/Centropolis friends had already arrived in town
for the occasion or were on the way. For years
afterward Z was running into other women from whom Arvin
had "borrowed" large sums of money which he never repaid
(with Z the amount was relatively small: only three K,
not eight as I'd been thinking for some reason; and the
only positive result of her lawsuit against him for the
return of the money was a "bad debt" document the court
ordered him to sign, thus allowing her to write the
three K off on her taxes -- and the savings from doing
that didn't even pay her lawyer's fees).
     On top of the failed relationships of previous
years this flop with Arvin threw Z into such a tailspin
that she quit her job as minority counselor for the
community college, went into deep isolation for more
than a year, "tore the old Louise down to the ground and
reinvented myself as Zoelie" (and legally changed her

first name); and when the money, which came from cashing
in her state pension fund, ran out, she started a whole
new career at the utility in which she tried to combine
her two major interests, social justice (race, class,
gender) and the environment (helping to define the field
that's come to be called environmental justice). The
Arvin flop also caused her to question her own judgment
in matters of the heart to such an extent that she
avoided serious involvements for the next four or five
years, until Jerry II, the millionaire ex-fireman with
the yacht and the big muscles, came along. Or if she
did get caught up in a few, she swears she can't
remember them, which in emotional terms, I'd say, would
amount to pretty much the same thing. (And I shouldn't
neglect to mention that her father died not long before
that same tailspin period. And that's also the period
when she drove herself even madder trying to write the
novel about what she'd just gone through and was still
going through at that time and the main character's name
was Zoelie -- borrowed from a whodunit -- and she, still
Louise then, eventually decided she liked it so much she
wanted it for herself. Oh, and that's also when she was
socked by a big decadal birthday -- just as I was during
my own year of the big crisis with Marco and Lady U.
Which means that for Z and me the two annus maximus
horribili, hers and mine, were only a year apart --
though I had a second such annus just year before last.)
    And learned this: another of her "majors," Brian
S., who preceded Arvin by a few years, broke up with her
because he decided he didn't like her sleeping with
other guys, though he'd agreed she could do it as part
of an "equality experiment" proposed by her (and then he
didn't see anyone else; only she did). Z says she
didn't realize how much she cared for him until they
broke up and that over the years this was a typical
pattern for her with the "really nice guys" (and she
includes me among them, she said, so I guess I'd better
watch out -- as if I weren't doing that already).
    I also learned more about her longtime practice of
wanking off with vibrators and cucumbers and various

"truly exotic-erotic" Asian vegetables. To pry this
out of her (the info, that is) I had to reveal my own
raunchy Portnoyesque experiments going back to early
teen days. Two of these she refused to believe were
anatomically possible, and in trying to show her they
were (this was back at the grand hotel) I discovered one
no longer is (and for a couple of days thought I'd
thrown out my back permanently).

And then this: the day after the latest mini
meltdown she had an on-the-throne "aha!" which she
called to tell me about moments later. It involved a
kind of romantic corollary to the famous comedian's line
("Grouchy Marxist," she punned): "I wouldn't want to
join any club uncool enough to let me in." The
corollary: "If he loves you, something must be wrong
with him." At certain panicky moments, she said, this
was exactly what she felt about me. This lack of
confidence she traces back to two "FOO"s, both involving
her mother. In the first, Mrs. B.'s saying to little
Weezie (over and over), "No man will ever love you"
(sometimes because she was a mixed-race kid in a white/
pink world, sometimes because she was born with those
extra toes -- as others in Mrs. B.'s family also had
been). In the second -- and this was a real stinger for
me, and she held back a long time before revealing it --
Mrs. B.'s grabbing Mr. B. in the crotch and saying,
"What a lemon you are. I should've married Yago, not
you." Z's rueful comment: "Only recently did I realize
what this must've been about, or at least one piece of
it." (Her father was twenty years older than her
mother. Yago was another Filusan man who pursued her
mother at the same time her father did. And only well
after her father died did her mother reveal Yago was
really "just a womanizer" -- Z's term, not her mother's
-- and she'd never been seriously interested in him.)

-- As for the "lemon" remark, I wasn't about to
tell her how much it hurt. Instead I sucked it up
(bitterly! stingingly!) and helpfully pointed out that
the two FOOs appeared to be closely related and just
might also have something to do with her own sexuality

meltdowns and "who are you?" panics and "let me pursue
you now" flip-flops. "So don't you have any
insecurities?" she demanded to know in return. Ha!
"Let me count the self-doubts" -- but then I didn't
count them. I just said, "Isn't it kind of obvious? I
mean, what have we just been talking about here?" And
she let the talk move elsewhere. -- But about loving
her I have no doubt, I swear it, despite all the seeming
penile evidence to the contrary. I truly believe I'm
the right guy for her -- as right as a guy could ever be
on this or any other planet -- and she likewise for me.
-- So why doesn't my male appendage act like it
believes this? Why does it insist on playing the lemon
instead? That's the question to which an answer simply
refuses to appear -- or rather lots of answers appear,
but no real solution. It's crazy, that's about all I
can say. And we both have to respect that craziness,
like it or not, or at the very least defer to it. No
other tolerable choice exists. Craziness rules!

40

    And this was the eighter. Sort of. Up and in,
yes, and she comes, yes too, for the first time with me
intussuscepted (fancy-pants word I'm probably misusing).
I, alas, still don't. Then after three rounds of this
over the course of little more than a day, no more. One
fribbly attempt. A Z meltdown ensued over failure of
our progress to be permanent and guaranteed. Now it
seems we're back pretty much to square one on the sex
board, meaning the one where the middle-leg bandit ka-
chings mostly lemons.
    But at the time what a triumph. Day after Vets

[Jyze in Love]

Day, up in the loft following our walk home from the
hideaway, a coupla cups of Z's favorite blush wine on
hand and quickly down the hatches. And all day I'd been
looking forward even more than usual to rejoining the
fray because in the morning she'd had to stop while I
was still aroused and she said, "Bookmark it, LOML."
Guess I did. (It's a common computer term now, which I
didn't even know.)
     "The look on your face!" -- she to me as we
authentically fucked away. But hers was something too.
     First time, and two of the first three, she atop.
Why I'm so hard and sustaining it -- was it all that
fast-food red meat? (Or maybe the chocolate shakes, two
of them after none for at least several years, possibly
a decade or more?) Meanwhile she 'gasms again and again
with me in there -- four or five times at least.
     Afterward she thinks we should memorialize the
occasion on my loftside calendar (same one where I kept
close tabs on all the confusing events of last spring
but lately haven't felt the need to note much, but only
because "WT(A)AAIW," meaning "We're Together (Anyway)
And All Is Well" -- yet another Z-cronym -- as in
"YENOM," which is also hers and recent: "Yer Not Me!").
     -- This jyze now issuing yet again from the green
armchair. Circumstances hoary too. Green terrycloth
robe, hair wet, jyzeboard riding lap. Obvious why all
this is so, but I still see it as a rut I'd like to bust
out of. Probably won't be able to, though, or at least
not as much as I'd like, until next year.
     Yes, we're again apartment-hunting. We took a long
walk around two residential neighborhoods not far from
her current place and Z wrote down the addresses of
likely-looking buildings and vowed to draw up a form
letter for mass mailing. The rental market's extremely
tight right now, and of course rents are therefore
soaring. The two actual vacancies we've come across,
both within eight or ten blocks of her present building,
are asking in one case a thousand and in the other a
shocking fourteen hundred (though this second one was
three bedrooms and we want only two), and both vacancies

have probably vanished by now anyway.

She has all her friends out looking as well. In bed these days she's moaning, right in there with the sex talk, "I want us to be living together soon." Now that she's at least semireconciled with Aida she's even willing to consider Doug and Thuy's place again. (The enigmatic Aida is still holding to her offer to defer to us on it as long as (A) we're "seriously" talking marriage and (B) Z's promising never again to sit on my lap in front of Aida's mother.) D&T's rent, under eight hundred, is looking better and better. "But first Aida would have to beg me on bended knee." (That's Z talking.) And the chances of Aida's doing that are poor. The odds she would also beg me on bended knee are of course far poorer, but that's a satisfaction I might be willing to forgo. Hey, I'm flexible! I don't nurse grudges! (Like hell I don't. But in this case I like the trade-offs enough to stomp down the grudge. And the truth is I was quite taken with Aida when we first met and I probably could be again, given some time and a reversion to friendliness on her part and maybe a few somber auto-counseling sessions on mine.)

"First Fuck Week" it was, or almost, and otherwise fine too. On Vets Day we checked out a gallery showing works by an artist hailing originally from Poneeda County (Mentoka styling) and saw an amiable drama called "Miss Nobody" in a cold and drafty theater at the annual Polish film festival and then took a comical stroll through a nearby supermarket, up and down the aisles, while discussing the movie and trying to warm up. The Polish side of Z's roots, class issues, who among her mama's friends and relatives resembled whom in the film, did she understand any of the dialogue? ("Maybe about five words.") Every year she tries to catch at least one film in this festival even though for most of the year and in her general consciousness she clearly makes a much bigger deal of her Filipino side. A major reason for this is the ostracism her mother faced from her own family -- except one older sister -- for marrying a Filipino. "So in my own mind I just

ostrasized them right back and along with them the whole
of Polish society and culture, pretty much. I wasn't
going to let them mess with my mind like that." (And a
few days after seeing "Miss Nobody" she had a nightmare,
presumably sparked by the film, about the Polish parties
her mother used to drag her to, the shame she felt, or
rather was made to feel, as the brown-skinned daughter
among all the snooty blue-eyed blond girls around her
age in their fancy dresses and shiny unclompy shoes.
-- And ooh ooh ooh, if they could only see her now!)
     Weekend, on Saturday afternoon it was early
Christmas shopping with the Katgrrrl in downtown toy
shops. Big fun, I too a kid in toyland buying Z and
myself a pair of wriggly finger-puppets, one with a
brown head and one with a pink head, cost four bits
apiece. That night I hunkered down alone at Z's place
until after ten while she took Charles, Aida's boy, to
see "Mr. Bean" -- I read and napped after racking up way
too little sleep the night before because of way too
much loving plus the Z meltdown over my inability to
replicate the relatively successful near-consummatory
copulations of earlier in the week (and also she was in
a "Denial of 'The Denial of Death'" mode, thinking lots
about mortality, about the final scene with Manny when
she was in the hospital room alone with his dead body on
Christmas Eve and she felt sure he was about to speak to
her, he looked so alive -- except he wasn't breathing).
-- Drank some ghastly rhubarb wine that night (Saturday)
and read in bed with Z until late. Smooched. Pillow-
talked. "Fucked," but fucklessly, our traditional way.
     About her sex history she gave up this new bit:
only with Bradley was her experience similar to the kind
of sex we have (plus she's said he was a superstud at
real fucking and I definitely haven't been that -- yet!
-- but we didn't go into this vexed aspect of the matter
again). With all others the goal (and quite often the
result) was one big glorious simultaneous cock-in-cunt
orgasm; and though she came plenty of times in addition
to the Big One, she usually did so relatively quietly
and almost always without indicating what was happening

and thus in many cases the man didn't even know. (She'd
climax while her breasts were being caressed, while she
was giving head, and many other ways; and no, goddamnit,
I'm not jealous about any of this, or at least not if I
don't think about it -- I mean what's the use? I can
successfully suppress it most of the time, thank god,
and try to do just that.) -- But what would it be like
if I could ejac as frequently as she 'gasms? Just by
thinking about something sexy! Just by associating sexy
thoughts with touches anywhere on my body! Dozens or
scores of times in a single night! One thing for sure,
though: I'd be plenty tuckered out.

(Her vagina was much better this time. All the
fingerwork by me and the kegeling and yam-extract
applications by her have succeeded in opening it up. No
pain at all, she said, though the next day she left a
"sore bagel" message and said she'd run out of
calendula oil. The G-joint had felt softer than
expected inside, that is, its skin did, she said,
especially when compared with my fingers, but in my view
this was because, alas, it wasn't fully engorged, not to
mention grotesquely rockhard veinzapoppin' rampant or
anything approaching that.)

And I learned she's always made lots of sex noise.
Her first lover, Marty, took endless grief for this back
in his law-school dorm. And in later years her
housemates teased her about it too, especially when she
came down to breakfast the morning after. "Which
housemates?" I asked. "Lots of them," she chortled.
"But Manny especially. We had a kind of rivalry going.
He lived right across the hall. Sometimes he was even
noisier than I was. And then we'd compare notes at
breakfast.")

She doesn't like me to forget for a second she's
been around plenty -- "Just as much as you have, Sir
Jizz-a-lot." Or more. Probably lots more. Not that it
should matter. -- But does it anyway? Not that I know
of. -- But does it other than that I know of? Well,
maybe once in a while. But in general, no, I don't
think so. (The other day I was flipping through a new

"post-alt" mag and chanced on a quote from a male porn
star who acts in both straight and gay films. "It
doesn't matter who I'm fucking," he said, "because I
have confidence in my sexuality." Now why don't I have
that? Once it gets going with someone I do, but before
then I may have troubles. Not usually but with certain
types and during certain periods it's been so, as now
with Z. But the troubles are worse by far with her
than they've ever been with anyone else -- way, way,
way worse, probably exacerbated by age or unknown
physical ailments -- and yeah, well, the hell with it.
And a current newsweekly features on its cover the new
"impotence pill." Yipe! I don't like this at all!
-- Will just keep plugging away, though, or keep trying
to. Love the woman and so must. And love my own way of
life too much to go for any remedy by pills, at least
if I can help it. That's for desperation only. If and
only if they're what would keep me from jumping off a
high bridge.) (Boy is this embarrassing. Jyze in
shame. But also jyze shrugging helplessly. As is the
jyzer. What, me worry? When I'm in love?)

     She gave me an amusingly hand-painted "Zole Mate"
button. She sent me an official-looking certificate
(now posted on the loft) confirming that I'm "EAE," that
is, I "EXCEED ALL EXPECTATIONS." She went halfsies with
me on buying a ceramic coffeemaker so I'll no longer be
glugging down hormones leached from the heated plastic
of a filter cone such as the one I've used for exactly
half a Glennarian life stage or, that is, fourteen
years, or roughly 5K days. She said a lot of sweet and
loving things -- and some of these I can detail more
than usual because she said them in a voicemail just
last night and I took notes (it went on and on and on:
she'd decided on a whim to test the capacity of my
message tape).

     She was feeling bad, she said in that voicemail,
because she thought maybe our earlier phone talk about
"my [Z's] pookie-pookie unconscious FOO stuff" (which
was the occasion of the "lemon" remark) "might've given
you some wrong ideas." So she told me she loves me very

much and came up with a long string of adverbs
("utterly, crazily, miraculously, eclectically") and
then launched into an attempt to explain just exactly
why she loves me, breaking the reasons down into two
categories: my qualities and the way she feels in my
presence. The list of qualities was interesting for the
way it's changed over the months and what it now leaves
off. But she cited sense of humor (twice!), willingness
to talk about "anything, and I do mean anything,"
politics, principles I live by, "furry hunky body,"
"hands," "tongue." (This time no biceps, no brain, no
buns, and sadly no N'dow either, post-lemony or
otherwise.) As for what she likes about her own
feelings, it's "being truly seen," "being listened to,"
"feeling safe and warm and loved and all that mushy
stuff."

   The main seed for this outpouring was a comment
she'd made earlier about wanting me to be more
"distanced" with her. (This in turn arose when I asked
to hear more about what she'd meant by asking me to
"overpower" her.) She explained it this way: her father
maintained a distance from her mother. If her mother
nagged him too much as he sat reading the paper after a
hard day at work he might explode and stomp out,
disappearing for up to several days. And Z and her
mother would wail for fear he'd never return. -- Thus
she doesn't like to be "crowded" too much. It can cause
her to become extra-feisty: she turns irascible, wants
to pick a fight just to drive me away -- so then she'll
feel that atavistic emotional urgency -- the withdrawing
father, the withdrawing G of last spring who said "See
ya in August" -- and consequently she'll want to pursue
me, feel panicky about losing me, a powerful jolt to the
heart.

   Said I: this stuff worries me. Dangerous games,
they can fly out of control or become too much or just
too wearing. Best to avoid, I said, if we can. She
said every last one of her counselors/therapists/
shrinks over the years has told her the same thing.

   Talk about out-of-phase dynamics. Perhaps because

509

my mama was highly (not to say overly) demonstrative I
want to be hearing I'm extravagantly loved and not be
sensing massive resentment or hostility which I then
have to analyze to determine whether it's genuine or
intentionally provocative or some combination thereof or
just what.

        (And she did finally ask for more pointers on how
to "pleasure" me, or rather did so again but this time
in a way such that I didn't think she'd flip-flop later
as she's done several times before in recent months. So
I came up with a few. Told her not to expect instant
success. If anything, expect increased anxieties, at
least for a while, both mine and hers. -- So I should
just remember: let go. Whatever'll be'll be
('llbe'llbe'llbe). And she too. We're hooked up for
life anyway, right? So don't sweat the small stuff or
even the big stuff and at the same time care lovingly
and tenderly about all the stuff...or simply do whatever
it takes, okay.)

                            *

        (Hair's dry now, blown by the powerful new blower
she bought because mine's too old and weak and she hates
having to haul hers back and forth. And why the hell,
by the way, don't her blowjobs of the fellatic variety
work equally well on me? She'd like to know and so
would I. For her such failure is almost unprecedented.
Granted she's not too adept at the art despite her
marvelous sensuality and great hands and lips and
tongue. Never had to learn, that's why. She'd hot up
so much herself the blowee'd be ready to erupt before
she could even get in a lick. A couple of licks at
most, and then: gusher. And she does go for that jizzy
stuff, likes it spurting all over her, likes it in her
mouth, on her lips, her breasts, her pubes, her feet --
even begs me in her love talk for all these, and only
occasionally can I oblige, and then not at all in the
spot she likes it best of all. What a nightmare! Can't
wank myself off for her either, though from the start
she's had no inhibitions about doing herself for me and
she still does so quite often, humbling me no end --

though I wouldn't have her stop just because I'm
humbled, no way, and so I try to keep that part of my
reaction mostly to myself.)

    Zoelie B. Love of my fucking life. Can't be at
this late, nearly Glennarian Third Stage; just is. "Am
I pretty enough for you?" She asked this after we saw a
shapely naked actress in "The Master and Margarita"
Sunday afternoon -- a local troupe's live production of
a play it turns out I heartily dislike. Her
insecurities. Amazing she has any at all given her
colossal gifts, not to mention what she's done with
them. Is it possible she really does worry I'm
conventionally better looking or better bodied? It
seems she sometimes does, although often she'll go to
extreme lengths to hide the feeling. She's both
unconventional and exceptional in just about everything
and not always at ease with being either, not even after
decades of intense self-wrestling and therapizing. (But
am I ever glad she does go for such physical assets as I
still may have. She says her insecurities make her
leave them off the list of liked things -- "Don't want
to give you a big head" -- but I know she does go for
them. I also know her physical assets all across the
spectrum are much rarer. She's more "difficult" too,
definitely. More prickly. More suspicious. Quick to
take offense. Anxious. 'Tudinous. Hostile. Sardonic.
"High maintenance." Wild. "Neurotic." Bristly.
Feisty -- for sure! -- But superfine and larger than
life and one of a kind and able to inspire and arouse
unbelievable supercharged love in me. Miraculous this.
Molly me up, Z-woman: YES YES YES YES YES.)

    "Love gush" -- what she says impels her to call,
middle of the afternoon. What hits me again and again
any time of day or night. On the typed page it'll no
doubt look utterly ridiculous to say so but -- doesn't
matter. It is what it is! YES to the fifth power again
but this time with an exclamation mark for each one!!!!!

    Meanwhile, what. Dad's birthday, the twenty-second
since his death and eightieth overall, here and gone
(with just a brief one-day flare-up of my never-ending

sporadic low-intensity dialogue/argument with him; and
no word at all from him during that same flare-up about
whether he liked the "Dead Folks' Bread" of a few weeks
ago) (but then too I also forgot to ask) (Dad who, it
occurred to me this week, was just two months away from
his own Glennarian III rollover when I saw him for what
turned out to be the last time). -- And lots of talk
with Z about bagels and carrots as per the bonobo
phenomenon, resulting in a decision to decorate the new
white porcelain coffee maker with innocent-looking
sketches of same (Z having bought colored ceramic pens
for just this purpose from my buddy at the stationery
shop, to whom she announced, "The editing-pen guy,
that's my sweetie" -- the term "sweetie" being the one
standard one she's at ease with, she's said, those other
old standbys such as "hubby" and "fiance" and "lover"
and so forth happily leaving her cold). -- And my home
hood has suddenly become even more gentriproliferatory,
a disturbing new realtor-sponsored project just getting
underway to rid the area of the day laborers who
congregate along the "low road" beneath the viaduct, the
ancient founder's building now completely demolished
except for its facade, a construction trailer installed
in the vacant triangular lot starting ten feet north of
B-2 where the new condo midrise will go up. (And Z did
declare she likes my old green yuppieish raincoat and
wonders why I wear that ugly beat-up green hooded work
jacket so much. She whose ad sought a working-class
guy! -- And I tell her if she really wants to
understand my wardrobe she must improve her grasp of the
laws of survival in the nightscoper universe.)
　　So now what? She's due here in twenty minutes,
another round starts up. And I didn't note yet, so many
hours of lovemaking are again causing her to request
"collaborative dialogue" regarding her daily schedule,
and here's what she wants: at least one hour of do-her
own-thing time every day we're together, at least seven
hours' sleep every night we're together, and the same
five o'clock splitsville deadline on Sundays at her
place so she'll have enough time to gather herself for

the coming workweek. -- All of which sound reasonable
enough to me. Doable too. The trouble is we slide into
the eroto-zone and all the virtuous intentions go up in
smoke and if I do manage to remember them in the heat
of the grappling she dislikes my reminding her about
them. And I don't like doing it either. -- But nothing
here we can't handle. The ongoing never-ending fine-
tuning or rough-tuning or sometimes even super-rough-
tuning process. (But Lord, Lord please, do let the
yes-fuck fucking continue and keep edging it closer and
closer to the truly consummatory kind, and then let it
reach that same kind, deep and long-lasting and
explosively spurting and most of all regularly
replicable, not to mention as lemon-free as possible.)

41

    Again the same for setting, right down to robe,
moccasins, wet hair. But what an eighter. The
spectrum. New breakthroughs, new meltdowns, new --
well, new stuff scattered all across the spectrum (new
"Anti Horny Patch" poster, a gift from Z, winking down
at me from the wall above the couch right here). A
coupla parties. A movie. A whole lotta lovin'. A sad
anniversary. Not much paid work, sorry to say, but in
its place a new burst of my own protojyzey exertions.
    Two days ago, and then again day after tomorrow
(the Gregorian date and "the day after Thanksgiving"),
the sad anniversary. "Black Friday." Two years now.
-- And if ol' Mom were still among us what would she
make of Z? And Z of her? (Yes, I do keep asking myself
such things from time to time.) -- Doesn't make any
difference really, just an old reflex, I suppose, but

also a way to keep the conversation going with her, just
as with ol' Dad. Or for that matter with my ol' former
selves. To the extent, that is, I can locate any of
those selves still on speaking terms with my current
self. And if I really worked at it I suspect I could
tease out at least a few.

What the future holds, near kind, is Thanksgiving
dinner tomorrow afternoon at Wei and Alison's (hard upon
a double-barreled weekend with them, card-making at
their place this past Saturday night and the delightful
Japanese romantic comedy "Shall We Dance?" at the cut-
rate movie theater Sunday), then a cameo at the D-clan's
annual gathering, this time at Aida's house (and Z
admits she's told her friend Adele I've been "acting a
little squidgy" about this gathering, and I'm worrying
Adele's passed the word along to Aida, as Z acknowledges
is likely, and more trouble's in store), and then a long
weekend of house-sitting at Kat and Betty's (putting
Betty and Manny's fabled five-K imported Scandi bed to
the test). -- But before any of this, dropping Kat and
Betty off at the airport at an ungodly hour tomorrow
morning so they can do some feasting of their own with
"Uncle Nick" at his far-off desert-city abode.

Yuh, I got game. Got family too, new nonblood
extended kind, filling in better than I ever dreamt
possible for that which has faded out in my own life
(pre-Zoelie) or flashed out or never really got going in
the first place. ("Memories of My Ghost Brother"
causing me to bump up against some of my own ghost
relations again this week, not just Mom and Dad but
sister Barb and son Elgie as well. Will either of the
latter two ever be turning up in the flesh in my
Glennarian Stage III era? I suspect not. And continue
to believe -- though with spasms of sorrow -- it's
better for all concerned that this be so. -- And have I
mentioned it? Not too surprisingly, Aida's Charles, in
his East/West "hapaness" (to go with the old Lady U
term), reminds me quite a bit of Elgie at roughly the
same age. Elgie was maybe one year older the only time
I saw him for an extended period after he started school

-- "extended" in this case meaning all of a week or so.)

Regarding Kat, Elgie's ghost cousin of sorts, word comes this week that Z and I figure in the "Family Book" project she's been working on at school, as in stick figures labeled "Aunt Z" and "Subunk G." We're right in there with "Mom Betty" and some of the major ghosts of their merged lives, including "Dad Manny" and Kat's original Guatemalan parents. Am mighty pleased to hear about this. Intend to stay the course for Kat all the way to the end, just as with Z (it's a package deal, matter of fact, which isn't to say I don't like the kid for her own self, because I do, a ton).

Dark outside. Four-day holiday just beginning, though not yet for me. My unorthodox work life -- Z's still having trouble adjusting to it. And for the first time in years it's grumping me out a bit too. But by the luck of the draw I must put in four or five hours tonight and two or three more Friday night. At this moment Z's at home baking dessert for tomorrow -- her famous peach cobbler, which she loves to boast is the one and only fancy dessert she can do -- and I'll bus out after work and stay the night with her there. (It's turning into a big cooking week for Z. Last night she rustled up a whole meal for us for the very first time -- I'm way ahead of her on this score -- and what's more she pulled it off here in B-2 and on my cantankerous stove. Brown rice, brussels sprouts. Doing this shook her up so much -- visions of a gruesome domestic future boiling up from the pots like monstrous steam genies -- I figure it must've been a major cause of her scarifying meltdown later last night.)

Also this eighter a couple more rounds of elementary carrot/bagel fucking. These, alas, were again of the maximally maddening non-ejac type, but even so it appears more than ever that the time of our time is almost upon us. Any remaining inhibitory wariness on either side seems to be fading fast.

"Relationship chess" (another fave Z term), yeah, a few new moves. Setbacks. Her stomach tightens up, her lips turn to wood. She's suddenly vexed because the

magic formula which worked to get the shape-shifter up
and gushing two days in a row won't coax forth so much
as a twitch on day three. I say we'd be better off
kicking back a bit, she says I should cut her more
slack. Through a series of tense negotiations the two
notions merge into the "SLAX" concept (blend of "cut
slack" and "relax"). "Just think SLAX!" So far, for
the roughly twelve hours it's been in effect, this seems
to be working well. (Or: "Got our Jyze SLAX On!")

She's also saying she does better if she regards my
erratic appendage as a kind of juvenile delinquent of
the crotch. All it really wants, in this view, is to be
loved and accepted as one of the gang, so to speak; but
like any teenager (sic!) it entangles itself in moody
suspicions and awkward adolescent self-consciousness.
And quite possibly this happens, she suggests, because
it's received inadequate TLC from its previous tenders
(but I happen to know that's just not the case).

And she's saying something else on the same topic,
something even more shrinkish: that the appendage may be
holding back because of my mother's death. Under this
theory it, the appendage, may be thinking Z is taking
not just Lady U's place but also my mother's (and for
that matter my sister's, I suppose, though Z hasn't
mentioned this), and therefore it, the appendage, being
at its hyper-guarded core extremely moral -- like all
delinquents! -- regards having carnal relations with
her, Z, as taboo and refuses to perform. -- But if this
were truly the case, I ask, why would it be so happy to
gush for her, which it had just done the two previous
nights? Wouldn't that be taboo as well? -- But of
course under the current mortifying circumstances I'm
willing to consider any theory, including even those
whose real-life effects can't be verified or even, truth
be told, identified. And so it is that I'm "thinking
about" this one too.

(The "Dr. Horn-Away" condom poster on the wall
here, she bartered for it, a woman possessed. When
she's gotta have it she's gonna get it. -- Any reason
why that shouldn't eventually hold just as true for

consummatory carrot/bagel matters? None I can see, no.)
    -- Meanwhile it's almost upon us, the grand event
which occurs only about as often as the trough-to-peak
phase of a Kondratieff wave: a Glennarian Rollover.
Yes! A week from Sunday! Stage III here I come! Which
means, of course, I'll be joining Z, since she's already
been rolling along in her own Stage III for almost
eighteen months. And might the fact that we're about to
wheel into Glennarian sync for the first time bode well
for those same carrot/bagel matters? (Big four-syllable
jyze exception on the name of the wave up there.)
    -- And then that other holiday of the annual kind.
It's been creeping up on us for weeks now, setting off
alarms of its own: colored lights glaring from shop
windows, downtown street decorations strangling hapless
urban trees, Yule displays clogging supermarket aisles,
catalogs and advertising supplements stuffing mailboxes
and causing massive rips and wrinkles in magazines and
reviews. At Wei and Alison's we sat around the dinner
table cranking out Christmas cards a week before
Thanksgiving! (Table overloaded with art supplies,
mostly mine from seasons long past, deteriorating rubber
stamps predominating.) -- But yeah, suddenly I'm a
family man again, a man with a "support network," and so
I have this long list of folks I ought to be carding or
gifting. No. Want to be! Cuz I'm just a kid at Xmas!
(Too true. Always will be, even if it just about kills
me. And this year it could. -- Which is probably why
the normal seasonal manifestations are triggering alarms
as noted above.)
    And a quick "La Loo" update. "Li'l Ms. Too Much."
Yesterday we ran into her at five p.m. at the bus stop
outside Z's utility building. A few words exchanged, a
perfunctory hug. "But she did hug you!" noted Z, as
surprised as I was. The nontouching, face-averted type,
however, I pointed out, as if Aida were worrying I might
be, say, a carrier of the new mutant TB. -- So how come
this weirdness with her? I'm still mystified. Z is as
well, she says, though it no longer seems to bother her
all that much -- and so I suppose she and Aida have

discussed the matter in depth and I'm being "protected"
from knowing what it's really all about. Aida still
uses Z as a sounding board, I know that. They schmooze
frequently by phone, meet at least weekly for lunch,
work out together at the WOC at noon a couple of times a
week (though Aida often fails to show). For some reason
Aida's apparently decided to make me into a kind of
unofficial and undeclared nonentity, as it were, off
limits, persona non grata, at best the spook or the
troll in their relationship. It's as if the spirits of
our previous spouses (whom it's now widely known we
resemble more than a little for each other) -- these
spirits take over when we meet, Tom occupying me and
Lady U Aida -- I guess. I don't know. And for good
reason: it's all massively unknowable!
    But that's minor. Or if it's not minor, it's
basically something between Z and Aida; for me it seems
to be mostly better ignored. And barring some major
change, that's how I'll keep trying to deal with it.
    Meanwhile I'm marveling over all these changes --
major for sure -- in my own life. All this new life
here! -- Epitomized, I'd say, by last Friday night,
Jess P.'s birthday blowout for Gwen. First we attended
a women's pro-hoops game and then a late dinner with
drinks and a fancy cake and spirited gift-opening at a
restaurant atop north hill (right on the route of my
early hikes out to Z's turf). Nineteen of us in all,
two guys, the rest lesbians and mostly couples. Lotsa
fun. For Gwen's card I did some unexpectedly elaborate
drawings -- surprising myself -- of a heron and a duck.
The lesbian gang seems pretty much to accept me now as a
kind of auxiliary member, nonvoting, non-flirt-worthy
(of course), but at least preferable to the standard-
issue hetero-patriarchal Neanderthal. (During dinner Z
pointed out two women who she thought would be, if
morphed together, a pretty good stand-in for herself at
age twenty. One, a dark-haired version of the female
lead in "Miss Nobody," was sitting across the room and
to me didn't look that much like Z until she flashed a
wide toothy smile only maybe a hundred watts short of

Z's fabulous thousand-watter. The other was a very
pretty Filusan in our group, Aurelia, and she did indeed
remind me of certain photos of Z from her college days.
The super-glamorous "sex goddess" Z. Whew! And I'd
better not forget for a moment that the Z of now is also
the Z of then, among other Z's, meaning all the others
before and since, and certainly including intimations of
many more yet to appear. So I'll just nudge myself once
again: watch out!)

As my hair where it still exists grows ever longer.
Z says I'm now verging on the Eurotrash look. Talks
ominously of doing me up in a "power ponytail." Talks
witheringly of the "Nero look" I take on when in urgent
need of a scalp hosedown; it reminds her of certain
monkish priests she always tried to avoid as a teenager.
Yeek! But her Delilah-like shearing of my locks last
spring has made me a rock on hair. I'll do it my way,
goddamnit. (But what's my way? Well, that's simple.
What will she really go for? Meaning as opposed to what
she merely says or thinks she'll go for. Because on
such matters she can be very tricky and capricious and
contrarian, even to herself.)

-- Now comes a weeklong feature series on my home
hood in one of the Jyze City dailies. It's turning into
the hot new techno-hip quarter, the articles say, with
its mushrooming clusters of ten-buck-a-bite eateries
and hyper-charming postpunk boutiques and super-slick
Asian fusion discos and all. It's true to my eye as
well: the old G-turf is gentri-glitzing fast.
Residential population is up to fifteen thousand "with a
bullet." All but the most successful artists have
already decamped or are preparing to. One interviewee
in today's installment, close to me in age and lifestyle
and also living in a city-subsidized building similar to
mine, rants depressingly about his room, the rent, the
setting, the dismal future in the area for people like
him (and me). The downtown laboring class must be
subsidized, he avers, or otherwise there won't be one,
and then who'll open the limo doors? Who'll whip up the
quadruple-talls? And who'll scope, I'd like to add, all

those hopelessly tangled grand-jury transcripts as the
city snores?

     So it looks as though I'll be making my escape from
the hood just in time. If only Z and I can find a place
in a part of town that works for both of us. But on
that score, no progress at all to report. Nor will
there be any, it appears, until after the first of the
year. We're now locked into the can't-think-about-
anything-else-but-the-season season. The lady herself
has announced it's so.

     -- I'm still reading books these days, gotta say,
though not nearly as many as in the pre-Z era or
anywhere near as thoroughly, not to mention the quantity
of notes taken from them. Yet even the little I'm able
to do still feels like too much, because I need to be
spending more time on my own work of the protojyze
variety. And will, by gum -- say after the first of the
year.

     Well, yeah, guess I'd be wise to stop this entry
pretty soon here. Anything big I've left out? A couple
of scuzzy incidents in which I didn't like how Z scolded
me in public. No big deal really. It's a "class
thing," she thinks; in the inner-city ethnic turf of her
upbringing, female chew-outs and ordering-arounds of the
husband/boyfriend at the supermarket were strictly
kosher. (Supposedly. But how often did boyfriends or
husbands help out with grocery-shopping chores in those
days and those precincts? About as often in the city as
in the burbs, I'd guess. Which is to say: hardly ever.)

     She also said once, after observing me from the car
as I walked back toward it after a failed hunt for a
newspaper, "If I just saw you on the street I might not
go for you. You look too serious." Said this with an
overlay of snooty dismissiveness. Thanks a lot! But
regardless I'm now scheming up ways to resuscitate my
old "dapper fun-loving foreign journalist" persona.

     And this. I did a "space-alien imitation" to
protest another instance of her suddenly seeing me as a
"total stranger." A pretty amusing imitation, I
thought, and apparently she did too, because it had her

laughing so hard she warned she was about to pee in her
pants (again), and this even though she was naked, up in
the loft. Last night. (It was a busy night.) (But she
caught it all with a tissue or two and we didn't have to
change the sheets.) -- And she said to her mind my
taking offense at these "Who are you?" panics of hers is
equivalent to her meltdowns over my malfeasant member.
And if this be so, why should she alone have to bear
such an onus? Why not me too? -- And on this I'm
grudgingly conceding the point.

    So enough already! I knew I should've stopped
there a page or two back. Shut this thing down.

42

    Big news and I have fifty minutes tops to lay it
out here, as in a classroom essay. Then a quick blow-
dry (in hopes of warding off the dreaded "Nero effect"),
dress, and I'm off to meet my about-to-be official
"Deep," Zoelie B., at her office.

    That's right, we're tying the knot! Meaning also:
we've found a place!

    "Deep": domestic partner: DP. Like "Jeep":
general purpose: GP. That is, like me. Or did I
already explain this? -- But why not a refresher just
to be sure.

    So it's bye-bye unit B-2. All this right here,
I'll start dismantling it before next J-day, including,
for a final time, with a chain saw, the loft. At most
only four or possibly five more jyze journeys around
this room and that'll be it. End of what I expect will
soon be looking like a mere transitional phase between
big loves (no surprise now maybe -- but for sure I

wasn't seeing the B-2 era this way before Zoelie B. came along).

    Wotta twist! And the timing's perfect too, at least for purposes of shaping up this jyze annal: the year ends, annal four ends, my stay in B-2 ends, my "unattached" marital status ends, my Peak Prime Time ends, my Glennarian Stage II ends -- and the first full year of raptured-up post-peak-prime Stage III begins. And (what's more!) the rollover from II to III occurs this very weekend: day after tomorrow. -- And in fact it's way too neat and pat, all this, even to be having any jyzey fun with it. Things should be far messier. But: guess you have to take the tidy with the funky. In any case that's just what I'm aiming to do.

    This on the ninth day of Thanksgiving, so to speak, the Friday after the Friday after. Already! And the Christmas countdown's about to enter a more seriously agitated phase for me, because despite the upcoming move I still want to make a big Christmas fuss over Z (as she'll also be doing for me, unless the rumors prove false; and that seems highly unlikely). Being starved for funds as usual, I'll have to create most of the gifts for her myself. Not that I wouldn't want to do that anyway. But to pull it off I'll need time. And the amount of time I'll have for it has just taken a quantum tumble.

    The impasse on housing broke very suddenly. It happened, as such things will, just a day or two after Z renounced all further searching until early next year. Was it because this turned out to be another of those once-in-a-lifetime astrological weeks, front-page news in all the papers, eight planets "lined up" and supposedly visible right outside my window here (except that the alley crime lights decreed otherwise)? Or because for Virgo it's a "great week for nesting"? Well sure, yeah, why not -- believe!

    The sudden break comes with a delicious ironic twist: the place we're moving into is on the north end of south hill, within a few feet of the crest, just like the place Aida tipped us off to and then stiffed us out

of a couple of months ago. More ironic yet, it's on
the same street. Even in the same block. Even in the
same building! In fact, it's directly beneath that
other apartment, one floor down, and identical to it
in nearly every respect except the rent's thirty
dollars less because it's middle floor instead of top
floor and the view's not quite so sweeping.

No stupendous coincidence here. Aida herself was
the one who told Z about this place too, a couple of
weeks ago, as part of their complex and thorny
rapprochement (and it continues complex and thorny now).
What spurred Z into action on it, though, was the
arrival last Friday of her student-loan bill. Fifty-
eight K and change, interest included. Even though she
knew it was coming and roughly how much it would be,
seeing the numbers printed on official debt paper was a
shocker. A logjam breaker. As ex machina a deus as
could be deduced. Within the next couple of days our
need to find a relatively inexpensive apartment had
jarred loose all previous sticking points regarding
location, aesthetics, safety, pride, so forth and so on.
The chances of hitting on something in or near Z's
current hood in her newly preferred price range would
be, as she said, "slim to hilarious thought." Sunday
night she left me a message announcing that in the
morning she'd be checking city property records and
calling the landlord of the only building we'd seen
where the price was right: the one that Aida had told us
about.

The next piece of news came in at noon Monday: it
turned out the landlord was a guy Z knew slightly from
work, a former electrical power analyst, Min. She
thought he sort of liked her. And now, having sweet-
talked Min, she'd feel better about taking an apartment
in that building because it wouldn't all be Aida's
doing.

We arranged to inspect the vacant unit later that
same afternoon. And did. It looked fine, its condition
every bit as good as that of Doug and Thuy's place one
floor up except for a couple of warped kitchen-cabinet

shelves and some peeling wallpaper and paint above the stove (all likely caused by rumbustious rice-cooking). Min took our application and said he would call Z in a day or two after running the credit check. By yesterday we'd still heard nothing, so Z called him, finding him genuinely sick with the flu (a "brutal hacking cough," she assured me): and he said we'd checked out okay and we were in.

   -- That's all I can report on the matter for now. At just half past four in the afternoon the windows are almost fully dark. Rattling B-2 bathroom fan, storm-trooper stompings overhead, a screechy dumpster-diver rumble in the alley. Hey, I'll miss this place!

   Bring her a couple of anti-horny patches, extra-strength, Z pleaded on the phone. I could use a couple myself for sure, though she might not readily believe it. A wild weekend behind us but no new progress in the bonoboing realm (those hypersexed apes just refuse to relax their death-grip on our bedroom lingo, as in "Bonobo Call, Doodley-ahba"). Nor do I expect any progress this weekend despite the extended no-nookie spell, longest yet for us, lasting basically since last Sunday morning right up to present, except for a quick nipple-tweak trifecta (left, right, both at once) at four a.m. the other night.

   After signing the "Deep" papers we'll bus out for the seven o'clock showing of a reportedly hot Yugoslavian film that's playing for just three days, this being the only time we can squeeze it in. Lots of prior commitments. I have this whole new life of prior commitments now. Way, way, way too many of them (this fact already causing a bit of a brouhaha between us imminent Deeps in recent days -- but never mind about that, at least for now).

   Maximum incoherence here. Yeah! How it oughta be!

*   *

One in the morning finds me unexpectedly back at B-2, a little time to burn before returning to Z's place. If I show up too early out there (before my regular bedtime) I'll face the usual dilemma: either go

524

[Glennarian Rollover Jyze]

to bed long before I'd be able to sleep, or stay up and
offend her (implying I'd rather read than curl up in the
sack with her). Of course it's true she might be
interested in bonoboing too. On a Friday night, in
fact, she likely will be, since she can sleep in
tomorrow morning. But this would be equally true
whether I arrived at one, two, or three a.m. With all
sorts of big time crunches looming it's better to take
the opportunity to do a few other things first.

    Tonight I'm driving the Z-mobile. This means when
I leave I'll be carrying a heavy load: coffeepot,
bread, Z's travel bag, a few games and toys to keep the
Katgrrrl occupied tomorrow. These items and a number of
others almost as crucial are all mounded at the center
of the carpet so I won't forget any of them.

    The movie was truly bad. Massive symbolism
overdose. Great fun though. (Again we walked right by
the site of the first apartment I shared with Lady U in
this city, the same one whose sudden looming proximity
sparked the big battle a few months ago. This time
neither of us said a word about it. The possibility of
a meltdown similar to that earlier one was trembling in
the air, I thought, but Z's state at the moment turned
out to be oblivious. A few other things on her mind,
most likely. I'm not even sure she recognized the
neighborhood.)

    Earlier, on my way down to her office, an impulse
stop at a flower stand to buy her a corsage. Not just
to celebrate the Deep signing and the apartment
clinching, but also to make up for my "laconic Norski"
fade-out last night. Five bucks the bloom cost me but
her obvious delight when I presented it made the price
seem a bargain. A single red rose. I was even given my
choice of holiday greenery to nestle it in at no extra
charge. -- And then signed the Deep papers at her desk
with a grand flourish using this J-stick right here, the
finicky No. 6, the one ol' Mom gave me -- I inadvertently
left No. 5 at the hideaway right before the signing --
and this coincidence has me thinking how pleased ol' Mom
would be to know I'm not only hitching up again but even

planning to make it fully legal this time (though I
should come clean and note it won't be the first or
even the second time for fully legal but the third
lifetime, yes) (as Z well knows).

I've checked my rental agreement for B-2. As long
as I give notice before five p.m. Monday, three days
from now, I'll be able to move out on the 31st -- that
is, the last day of the year -- without paying an extra
month's rent.

My jyze posters (can't stop gazing at them now)
will be coming down and probably staying down. Because
in that realm too it's time to move on. Not to a place
beyond jyze -- no way! -- but to new forms of
"accessorizing" it. Maybe I'll bind all the existing
posters in a large-format book. Thirty-four of 'em if I
recall right. (Yup, thirty-four; just counted.)

This, as noted a few times before, will be only the
second time Z's lived with a man. The first was fifteen
years ago -- fiance No. 2, the odious Arvin -- and
lasted less than six months. To hear her tell it now,
every single minute of that cohabitation (with a few
exceptions, nudge nudge) was, for her, unimaginable
trauma. "This is the real first time ever," she assured
me. "Before now I've never felt I knew enough to make
living with a man work."

The only thing she can remember about the actual
move-in time with Arvin is that she was in "a daze and a
fever." I kidded her about this -- in fact she said it
after the movie just as we were approaching my old abode.
But I'm not kidding her too much these days, about this
or about anything. Truth is she's in a bit of a daze
and fever now too, maybe even a bigger one. I expect
some trying times before we're fully settled in, say two
or three months down the road -- and especially, of
course, during the next three weeks before the move.
Now I'm thinking it's a good thing we've got all the
holiday hoopla to keep us at least a little distracted.

We've agreed to start renting the new place as of
the 15th. That's ten days from today. From the 15th to
the 31st we'll be playing it by ear, sometimes staying

there, sometimes here in B-2 or at her place. But any
stays in the new apartment before the end of the month
will be "unofficial" -- more like campouts. She won't
be bringing on her hired mover (she does have one and
she's been using his services on average every three
years over a period of decades) until the 30th or so.

She's excited though. Me too. But she more so, I
have to say. Frightened too. She mimes panic. Goes
"EEEEE!" very loud and widens her eyes to the max,
waves her hands, grinds her teeth. Makes my hair stand
on end when she does this. But who wants boring?

For rent we've agreed I'll pay $325 a month, she
$420 (for the extra $47.50 she snags the second bedroom
as her own home office and private retreat: a kind of
in-house hideaway to balance my own out-of-house
hideaway). This means I'll be saving $60 compared with
my current B-2 rent, she $230 compared with hers for
401. Not a bad deal at all -- and especially for her!

Since she'll be stashing a bunch of stuff in my
storage unit, I asked if she'd mind helping out with the
rent there -- maybe a third of it, or $30 a month -- but
this request agitated her so much I decided to drop it
forever. She did have those big donnybrooks with Arvin
over the money she lent him. And she's already agreed
to lend me $500 or maybe $600 to help cover my share of
the deposit and moving expenses. -- But yes, I'm
worried about my finances. Living with her will be more
expensive than living alone. It's not any one thing;
it's a lot of little and medium-size things. And in my
experience it's much tougher being frugal when you're
part of a couple. (With us it already is. And it'll be
even more so as of January 1st. -- But I remain hopeful
I can pull it off without any major financial
upheavals.)

-- Now it's past two. Night-owl jazz. Voices in
the alley, doper blather this time. "Hey man, you
lookin'?" The Z-mobile's parked down just off the
waterfront -- not in an area where I'd want to be
walking at this hour with a big ungainly armful of
stuff. What to do? Run down and fetch it and park it

near our building's front entrance for loading? Might
work okay. By now at least an illegal spot or two
should be available up there.

*   *

     -- Talk about anticlimactic. Fifty hours on and
Glennarian Rollover Day's already rolled on through,
except by NUT time. A few scratches here just so I can
say I didn't miss the grand occasion entirely.
     I do mean a few. Thought I'd have several hours
starting at eleven p.m. but the scoping job went seven
hours instead of the predicted three and drove me maybe
seven-thirds mad. Now it's 3:29 a.m. I can barely see
crooked, never mind straight. And before racking out I
still need to scrawl a letter officially giving notice
on B-2 and shove it under the manager's door upstairs.
Sometimes the office closes at noon or one and I don't
want to risk losing a month's rent on a technicality,
say if I should happen to oversleep tomorrow.
     Most of the twenty or so hours I didn't spend
scoping on official Rollover Day I spent with Z. But
since she already had plenty to be stressing about --
and was doing just that, as she pointed out herself
(over and over!) -- I didn't make too big a deal of the
rollover with her. In fact, I mentioned it only once,
and that a passing remark which she scarcely seemed to
notice about my joining her on this very day in vintage
Stage III status. (And after all, how many times should
someone be asked to celebrate a lover's adult-lifetime
peak in a single year? Two should probably be enough.
This is the third this year for poor Zoelie B.)
     But she surprised me. Shouldn't've been surprised
but I was. When she dropped me off here at six she
presented me with a brown paper bag cinched at the top
with red straw ribbon. The attached card, handmade by
her, says on the front, "Roll over, Jyze-hoven"; inside,
"Tell Z-Kedrowski the news!" (Kedrowski is her mother's
maiden name -- but still can be mentioned here only as a
jyze exception.) An arrow points down to "the news":
two figures, a boy labeled "G" and a girl labeled "Z,"
happily tumbling down a long hill together -- the

528

hill labeled "Glennarian/Zoelian Stage III"!

And then this note along the bottom of the card:
"Never forget your Peaches loves you sooooo much and
gets all juicy just thinking about our long life loving
together." And the bag itself containing two smaller
bags, each labeled "Nickel" -- in a nod to the Gregorian
slant on things: my current double-nickel age status
(succeeding double joker) -- and each packed with five
splendid "immortality peaches." (where in the world did
she find them so late in the season? But nine of those
peaches are now mounded in my mother's Chinese bowl atop
the worktable. Juice from the tenth is still sticky on
my lips. Sweet!)

Says it all, this terrific gift. Or says a very,
very large portion of it. Or so I'm assuming and
believing right now. And don't ever expect to stop
doing so. Simple!

When I called to thank her, she'd already turned on
the answering service. But yeah, I'll be thanking her
for the next twenty-eight years, I'll say, give or take.
Or say for as many years as the peach immortals grant.

-- Twenty-eight years. Oh man. That's also how
long I've been waiting for this day and I almost let it
slip by as far as jyzing goes. Imbecile! (And I should
at least mention this: for the entire seven-year
Glennarian quarter just past I've used the numerical
form of today's Gregorian date as my PIN number and
computer password.)

As for the freshly expired and exited Stage II as a
whole -- what to say about such a long period in such a
short time? So I'll just ask myself this: in Stage II
did I cover myself, as intended, with at least a thin
layer of glory? -- And look down and see nothing but
ragged sweat pants and sweat shirt. -- And look around
and see nothing but austere and subsidized B-2. -- So
admit no, didn't. -- And yet also insist yes, did. I'm
here! I scrapped! I scraped! I skimped! I scoped! I
jyzed! I found Z!

(Morning news programming crashes in right now over
jazz and jyze. Snap that thing off.)

[Jyze in Love]

*

So. Back more soberly to the glory question.
     True, by this landmark day "Jyzer" was supposed to
be completed. And it's not completed and neither's any
other worthy piece of serious fiction "of a certain
length" and neither's any ever likely to be. But: in
its (or their) place stand four other works, each with
"Jyze" in the title, including this one right here. And
I like all four better than any fiction I've ever
written. So in a word I'll say (confirm) fiction's
finished for me and jyze is it.
     -- Or maybe I should just declare jyze is fiction
and this right here is jyze fiction (after changing a
few names and other identifying info) and in that way
dissolve the problem. "Jyze roman a clef."
     Consider it done.
     And if that's the first big breakthrough setting
the stage for Stage III, no question at all what's the
second. "The Deeping of Z & G": that's it! -- And
since Peak Prime Time, lasting from 20K Day on June 1 of
the year Jyze 4 (I'm gonna start capping it and using a
numeral) until today, produced this second breakthrough
as well as the first one, I'd say the period
emphatically lived up to its name. Or just call it the
best six months of my life.
     -- And if it's still Rollover Day by NUT time, it's
also still Jyzer G Conception Day. Must be, since
that's the first day of the Glennarian calendar. ("How
could your mother be so sure?" Z asked. I explained. Z
still found the story hard to believe. But with ol'
Mom's diary from that era in my possession, I now have
written "proof." And Z wants to see it -- wants to read
the whole diary, in fact.) (She already knew it was the
grandfathers who long ago inspired the whole Glennarian
business, probably a few years before I turned teenager.
It was Gramps S. who explained that in many countries
one's age is counted from the year of one's conception,
Gramps H. who pointed out that the perpetual Gregorian
calendar recycles every twenty-eight years -- with, as I
learned later, one exception per century, except for

530

every fourth century -- and that there are many
calendrical systems in the world besides the Gregorian.
"If you wanted to you could even make up your own.")

So -- no second acts in USAn lives? What about
third Glennarian stages? In the conjoined lives of a Z
and a G, say.

We're primed to find out. Could not be more
primed.

-- And right here's the daily end-time. Morning
traffic picking up in the dark out there. Need to do
that move-out letter real quick. Tomorrow, if jyze can
squeeze it in, a rundown on any and all major real-life
news left out so far.

*   *

Another night and two more peaches devoured;
otherwise the same setting. Ten to two. I'm still
breathing hard after grinding out four full sets of dips
and push-ups. Yes, I'm serious about this shaping up.
Of course it's loony since it's not an "immortality
project" and here I am already a full day into what's
very likely final-stage mortality -- but then
immortality projects are loony too. So why not do the
best I can to pump myself up for the Z-woman. Or for
myself, or why not say just for the helluvit.

First true post-peak-prime jyzing, this. "True,"
that is, again, with respect to NUT time. And this
therefore also the upside-down extension of the date
when the jyzer's conception day was officially dubbed "a
date that will live in infamy." Whence "the infamous
Jyzer G." Now jyzing right here!

Z, she's weirding out again. Today she stayed home
to pack and started to think she was losing it -- she
was feeling sick, maybe just like, as she's been
thinking -- obsessively -- when she moved in with fiance
No. 2, Arvin. This time she called upon two friends for
moral support. Nurse Betty told her not to worry, "the
big guy is solid," and also said when she and Manny
moved in together he wouldn't let her touch anything,
just as I'm supposedly doing with Z (it's not so!). And
Sufi guru/poet Olwen likewise stood up for me, telling Z

531

my vibes seemed good, nothing at all like fiance No. 2's
(she knew him) -- but then Olwen met me for only a
minute or two at the co-op, as Z is well aware.
     She and I were hoo-hahing over all this during
tonight's call from the phone booth at the ORB cafe. I
said I'm steeled to withstand whatever new glitches
might lie ahead, hers or mine or whoever's or
whatever's, during the "extended transition period" (the
next few months, let's say), and she said she is too.
But I'm also realizing, again, this might not be a
cakewalk, and especially the next three weeks, as I
noted before and may well be noting, yes, again.
     She reminded me she'd just about totally flipped
out during the bad old days with Arvin -- her teeth
started falling out, she went numb, her memory failed --
all kinds of horrific stuff. Worse, she couldn't say
what he'd done to bring this on or even whether he'd
done anything bad at all. Was some portion of his
unacceptable behavior perhaps in response to one or more
of her flip-outs? Maybe even most of it? Could be.
(Not that this would excuse it -- but really now, what
was she doing to drive the poor guy bonkers? Or if he
was wacko to start with, why didn't she recognize this
earlier? -- But then I could query myself the same way
about any number of grotesque episodes in my own life.)
     I still think we'll be all right. From everything
I've heard, Arvin and I have little in common. Still,
I'm starting to worry a bit more. (Not that I'm
planning to let her know I'm worrying. I'm gonna be
cool about this even if it kills me. And I'm hoping the
love daze will be torquing up yet another turn or two
higher, enabling us to whirl merrily above the fray.)
     So her latest thing is this: she needs to take
certain measures to steady herself. Therefore she won't
be attending the utility "dereg" meeting tomorrow night,
and neither does she want to see the reputedly superb
movie we'd been planning to catch at that same hour
before she was informed of the meeting. What she wants
to do is to check out a new batch of whodunits from the
library and immerse herself in them at my place (since

[Glennarian Rollover Jyze]

June by prearrangement will be staying at hers) while
she sends me off to attend the movie by myself.

     But it wasn't a simple matter to establish this is
what she really wants. Back and forth we went on
whether she'd see the movie with me. She didn't want me
to be unhappy with her. I didn't want her to feel
pressured. Well, she did want it to be okay for one of
us to stay home while the other went out for whatever
reason. Well, I did want her to know that I wanted it
to be okay for -- agh, to hell with it.

     At all times I'll try to appreciate this sort of
stuff for, if nothing else, its comedic value. As
domestic farce, but loving domestic farce. I love her,
I want to live with her, the papers are all signed, so
-- chill, Jyzeman. "Slax" it! Have fun with this!
Take notes, who knows, maybe some distant day it'll
provide script material for a low-end sitcom.

     We did a similar kind of Alphonse-Gaston act on
driving a load over to the storage unit next Sunday.
Turns out she wants me to go by myself; she'd rather
stay home and pack. Understandably, I guess: her
daytimer for the period between now and the end of the
year, she told me, is even more crammed than it was
during those early weeks last spring -- when she was
twisting herself into knots trying to find a way we
could meet for an hour or two several weeks in the
future. (Jyze exception on the A-G act up there? I
guess. A&G may be mythical but they're not fictional.)

     -- But I think we really are enjoying it. Not just
me; both of us. We're laughing a lot. Sooner or later
we usually do manage to see the humorous side of our own
absurd melodramas. Once in a while we can even do this
as they're unfolding. (And to think they're all
happening just when for the first time we're rolling
along together on the downhill slope in the "mature"
life stage! -- Z being somewhat like the "old maid"
aunt who's about to be married off and is suddenly and
spectacularly going to pieces. And me, the wizened
buffoon with the dubious matrimonial history, now
cackling lecherously as shack-up time nears.)

[Jyze in Love]

    All day my new Christmas button has been puzzling
folks. "Define Good," it says. And the night paper's
special magazine issue on religion has me gagging: how
is it such medieval schlock can find its way into print
in this day and age, much less in our "flagship liberal
paper"? Z and I talked maybe a dozen times or more on
the phone. ("Second Chances," the comic strip which
seemed to be telling our story, the one that gave us the
name "Nora" for Lady U, has suddenly been canceled. Ill
omen! But it's gone. Z wanted me to call the newspaper
to protest. I told her I was sure in my bones there
would be no second chance for "Second Chances." Why?
Because it's already done yeoman cultural work and she
and I are a shining example of it.) And: she was
worrying I wouldn't understand her "introvert thing."
"When I wanna be alone, I wanna be alone. Do you
really, really grok that?" I kept thinking of passages
from that wretched "don't sweat the small stuff" self-
help book we flipped through together while yukking it
up at Nurse Betty's and wishing I could come up with a
way to recommend some of them to her without sounding
like a complete idiot.

                          *

    Catchup time.
    First the weekend just gone by. All in all a fine
one. As predicted, no hardcore sex, though I did manage
one mediocre "money shot." After dinner at the old
favorite Chinese place of mine and "Nora's" (and,
separately, of Z's as well during the same period and
right up to the present) -- after dinner there, I say,
with Aida and June, a "quiet Saturday evening together
at home," most of it in bed. Bottle of wine, blues show
and then jazz on the radio, alternating bouts of loving,
sleeping, reading, clowning: this continuing all the way
to noon Sunday. Probably it'll turn out to have been
our last "ordinary" evening at home at unit 401 (because
by this coming weekend the joint will likely be close to
unrecognizable). Good good loving too, making up for
the lost week. It was one of those evenings (and nights,
and mornings) when we couldn't stop raving about "the

                          534

miracle." Did a lot of speculating -- planning, daydreaming, joking, even a bit of moderate sparring just to keep things real -- about how life will be in the new place.

At the Chinese restaurant Aida again stunned me. She suggested we should call Doug and Thuy and thank them for letting us know about the vacancy (through Aida!). She even had the gall to propose that as my way of thanking Aida herself I should coach her kid in basketball. And the two of them still might be moving into D&T's place! Charles could be practicing his crossover dribble on the floor above our heads all day long! And Aida could be popping downstairs to whisper thunderbolts into Z's ear about the sorriness of Z's Deep! -- D&T may not be departing for a while, though; their second kid's due any day now and they're still looking for a house and so may postpone moving until the new baby's ready for it, which could mean a delay of six months or more; and meanwhile the housing market is shooting up so fast they may never be able to find an affordable close-in place to their liking.)

-- Fortunately for my own peace of mind, I should note, both Z and June, as I learned later, saw Aida's antics at the restaurant the same way I did: as being surpassingly strange. (I did pull out my old passport photo for the three of them to check out, and they all seemed to find both the act and the photo itself equally bizarre or even more so, not to say mirth-inducing.)

Earlier in the day Betty dropped Kat off and she and I goofed around with the nerfhoop and ball I bought for her at a local thrift shop. Then Z and I took her to play at the lakeside park near Z's place. My nose is still sore from a bonk Z accidentally gave it with her elbow as I pushed her and Kat on a heavy rope swing on the playground there. A remarkable coincidence we couldn't stop marveling about: Kat's running suit was the exact same shade of powder blue as the new nerfball. A perfect match! As if it were meant to be!

*

And on the twelfth and last day of Thanksgiving

(today), back to those fine first four days of same --
don't want to leave them totally unjyzed. Some high,
low, odd lights:
     ** Grace in a hand-holding circle at Wei and
Alison's turkey dinner. Afterwards I ate way too much
(having vowed to extend my "120 Days of Hunger" an extra
day into January to compensate) and enjoyed their friends
Mick and Amy (he a musician and owner of an east-hill
tavern, she a modern dancer and thespian who attended the
same U. of Mentoka in Lahontan as did Z and my parents
and both of my brothers and many of my aunts and uncles
and cousins on both sides -- and she probably knew Lady
U from the Jyze City theater/dance circuit of fifteen
years ago but, I'm pleased to say, I never even brought
the matter up).
     ** Scrabble at Aida's on Thanksgiving evening.
 The J-slinger came in dead last, with Aida's fireman
brother Ray the big winner. Aida again was at least
tolerating me, though in such a phony-baloney saccharine
way my few remaining teeth seemed about to fall out
(just as Z's supposedly did in the Arvin "fugue
period"). What's more, Aida had the gall -- more gall!
-- to mention to Z that I'd never followed up on my
birthday thank-you card to her which spoke of a bigger
thank-you to come (this was the same card that said I'd
be her pal forever -- the one that until last week she'd
never mentioned receiving to Z or me).
     ** Brunch in another Asian-quarter restaurant
Friday afternoon with Lee M. and his amusingly chip-off-
the-old-block son, Todd. Todd's a tall and gawky
college freshman who's intending to do the same double
major I did in college, as it happens, yet is of course
only just beginning, thus allowing me to come on like
someone deeply learned in both fields. Awkward moments
as Lee talked about his impending divorce and Todd
explained his feelings about it; Z and I both had the
impression Lee was hearing all this for the first time.
(Todd's prominent Adam's apple bobbed conspicuously as
he talked, just like his old man's; watching them
converse was like following double bouncing balls on a

TV singalong.) But I do like Lee and I'm glad he'll be
coming to town from time to time and maybe even staying
with us in our new digs. (Should I be worried because
at one time he might've been infatuated with Z and this
may've been -- probably was -- the final straw for his
marriage? I still say no.)
       ** Then the house-sitting at Betty's. A shy
black cocker named Arnold, four frisky cats, thirteen
hamsters (yes!) who kept their treadmills thundering
night and day. We watched the video of Z's favorite
musical ("Grease") twice. Class differences, she said,
account for her liking it more than I do. She'd been
trying to think of the lyrics to "Helplessly Devoted"
for months; now it turned out they didn't fit our
situation so well after all. But Betty's fabled five-K
Scandi bed, originally one of Manny's extravagances,
turned out to be every bit as erotogenically friendly as
advertised. That's where the main wildness of the
weekend broke loose, Z going over the top and off the
charts with "frott comes" as I read aloud from various
books and articles at her request. True hilarity and
also some of the sexiest moments of my entire life.
(She's a sexual marvel! A living treasure!)
       ** Then an appalling gaffe, also hilarious, when,
as we unloaded the car after picking up Betty and Kat at
the airport, Z referred to -- how did it go now? Can't
quite remember. The crucial part was that she came out
with a very loud "fuck" while describing what we'd been
doing. "Mainly fucking a lot," something like that.
But Kat hadn't gone ahead into the house, as Z thought;
she'd only ducked behind the car. To me Kat gave a
wide-eyed and drop-jawed look but then to Z and Betty
she coolly pretended not to have heard. Meanwhile I
turned "magenta," by Z's later account, trying to choke
down howls of glee over her look of extreme chagrin.
Had to bury my face in my arms on the top of the car --
"and then the whole car started shaking!"
                            *
       -- Well, how about it? With Peak Prime Time at an
end am I more worried that my primary sex part continues

to be pretty much missing in action? Or am I less
worried, because we're out of the calendrical spotlight
and so some of the pressure is off?

The real hope, I like to think, is that living
together (Z and me, Z and the MIA appendage) will
somehow make a difference. And even if it doesn't, I
think she'll accept me, and it. I just mainly want all
the agonizing over the "pud-dick-ament" (Z's old pun) to
go away. I'll grant that sometimes it seems it would
almost be better for the MIA appendage itself to go away
and I mean permanently, as in eunuchization. At least
then Z wouldn't feel she's the cause of its failure to
rise up to swyve her righteously and gloriously as she
so richly deserves.

No no no, nothing like eunuchization will be
happening. No chance at all, not even metaphorically.
I'll continue to refuse not to have faith. Short of
giving up on loving Z I see no other way, and I won't be
giving up on loving Z. Even if she said she wanted me
to give up, I wouldn't do it; I'd refuse to believe she
really wanted it. Even with the MIA appendage on
permanent R&R I believe I'd be able to love her right
and make her happy to an extent no one else ever could,
just as I have no doubt at all she'd do for me.

So I'm crazy to think such things. So it goes.
Craziness rules. We're into Glennarian Stage III now.

-- First holiday decorations are up here in B-2.
Five little silver mylar balloons, "Season's Greetings"
and the like. While visiting the storage unit this
weekend I'll pick up a string or two of Christmas lights
with which to tart up the joint for its death throes.
(Z, by the way, brought her camera over so we could take
photos up in the loft. I do believe she's developed a
real attachment to it. -- And I remember when I worried
she might be too shy to go up there. Ha!) Also the
usual seasonal electronic tree is blazing away atop the
city's flying-saucer icon high above the fairgrounds,
shedding its grace on all but the darkest dope-infested
corners of my local turf. The jazz station is playing
some fine cuts from staticky old Christmas albums. And

I want to note that at least one of the many ongoing
mysteries has been solved. The "immortality peaches"
arrived by parcel post, a whole box of them delivered to
J&G's place. Apparently there's a Shangri-La up in a
high mountain valley somewhere that produces them pretty
much year round. And Z learned about this, as she does
about so many other things, from a catalog. She's known
far and wide as a "catalog queen." (Amazing I didn't
get around to mentioning this until now when I've known
it myself since my very first visit to her apartment
when I nearly kicked over a hip-high stack of them by
her view chair.)

        Also I should report (now at twenty past four, a
lot later than I wanted to stay up) Z's decision that
she will after all invite Aida to join her in some
"facilitating therapy" in hopes of easing their
tensions over the apartment issue and various other
matters of dispute. But she'll ask her to hold off on
this until next year, when the city will pick up the tab
(Z long ago used up her limit of six such sessions for
this year). -- And should note I still haven't spoken
with Z's mama but probably will do so during Z's
Christmas Day call home. Z's warned me I'm in for a
shock: Mama E (as I'm calling her now) is supposedly
more working class than a delicate burbazoid like me can
abide. I've told Z I betcha she's wrong about that.

43

    As of today it's me and Zoelie B. living under one
roof, officially, although also still only imminently.
Which is to say it's costing even if we don't have the
keys yet and haven't spent a moment alone in the new

crib. And even though the actual move-in date (the one
with the professional mover assisting) is still two
weeks off. Or rather: thirteen days. And counting.

Old B-2 here still looks pretty much the same. Two
dozen empty boxes stand in lopsidedly telescoped stacks
in the middle of the carpet (I've already hauled a dozen
full ones to the storage unit). And the bookcase side
of the loft is decked out with a string of large old-
fashioned Christmas lights and a couple of bristly
glitter-ropes, I'll call 'em, one red and one green,
hung in the shape (hypercorny to be sure; in fact that's
the whole point) of an interlocking G and Z. Otherwise
it's B-2 as it's been for about twenty months now, with
here and there a few happy additions: the jyze posters,
the anti-horny poster, the foot-high stack of cards and
letters from Z teetering on the loveseat (where else?).

Anticipatory nostalgia. I'm deep into it already,
sappily aglow with it just like the antique bulbs. And
who's got time for this? For sure not me. Two
countdowns are ticking at once, and the move-out isn't
even the more urgent one. (Also I've hung three red-
and-green kiri ribbons from the nerfhoop rim; they keep
catching my eye with their sparkly undulations caused by
heat updraft from the antique bulbs: enough all by
itself to increase global warming by a degree or two.)

Dark rainy day. I've been out of the room only to
pick up my mail, about fifty paces up to the lobby and
as many paces back. And now at a few minutes past four
it's almost full night out there. Rush-hour traffic's
inching along the viaduct like porkers packed in a
gaffing chute (as at Lady C's family farm say about 11K
days back).

My new Christmas cards are laid out on the
worktable to dry. Two dozen versions of "Early Sketch
for Sandefjord's Yule Jyze Suite, Act IV, 'Dance of the
Flame-Red Dreamsicles,'" the 'sicles slashed in at top
speed with a small red calligraphy brush for the dreamy
parts and a black one for the sticks. The time crunch
forced me to abandon the more elaborate design sketched
out at Wei and Alison's. (They threw another party

[Glennarian Rollover Jyze]

Saturday, W&A did, this one for tree trimming, but Z
decided she needed every minute for packing and so we
begged off. But we did call twice to express our
regrets, the second time just as the revelry was revving
up. These are our new good pals.)

        Z cracks wise about these cards of mine. "Who ya
gonna send 'em to? You don't have any friends!" (It's
the latest twist on the "sociopath" gibe of our second
date, back in play now since she's about to move in with
me just as she did with that other sociopath.) But I do
have lots of new friends these days, I remind her -- the
"support network," formerly hers alone (admittedly not
all the supporters may be aware as yet that their burden
has doubled) -- and in fact most of the dreamsicle cards
will be going to them.

        (Let's be clear about this, sez I. It's not that
I'm incapable of making friends by myself. I swear it's
not. Two years back I chose to be as unattached as
possible so I could focus to the max on writing fiction.
Since that didn't work out too well I'm now conceding I
might do better with friends than without. As a result
I have less free time for writing of the nonfictive or
for that matter the jyze-fictive variety, but so far
this fact hasn't been too upsetting. Next year it might
become more so, I suspect, since at this point now all
my normal work rules are suspended for courtship
purposes, as they have been for most of this past year.
If so, next year's when I'll worry about it. But I have
a hunch I won't have to. I might even keep the work
rules suspended indefinitely. It's possible I'll
eventually be able to write better this way -- being
more balanced emotionally and thus less inclined to
drive myself too hard.)

        -- For Christmas, though, I'm driving myself plenty
hard and -- and -- and having a helluva good time with
it! A list of thirteen gifts for Z rides in my shirt
pocket. Most of them involve some handiwork of my own,
and on this I've scarcely begun. But the raw material
is present, mostly, including pillowcases, a lamp shade,
a nightcap, beige cotton panties, blocks of bakeable

plastic, and miniature-book earrings (two sets, each
book with twelve blank pages the size of small postage
stamps). At this stage I'm still mulling themes.
Between now and next J-day (which will move up to the
24th, I'm thinking, because the traditional Christmas
Day entry, even though listed on the schedule, probably
will have to be scratched this year) -- nothing but work
on these gifts.

     And a painful moment on Sunday, two days ago.
While transporting the dozen boxes to storage in the far
province I stopped briefly to check out the old digs.
"U Acres." Though by myself in the Z-mobile (Z held to
her plan to use the time for packing) I was still uneasy
about being recognized and so didn't hang around long --
just crept a few yards up the lengthy driveway. (This
was an hour after sunset but the bright driveway pole
lamps were on.) Ben and Beryl's place next door was
aglow with holiday decorations (same ones as before) but
only a single string of lights was visible at 14421, and
that hung across the front window of my old study on the
second floor, the room Lady U took over when I moved
out. Otherwise the house itself, or at least the part I
could see, was dark, with several unfamiliar vehicles
parked in back and also in a new gravel lot in front
(the yard there having been shamelessly bulldozed and
flattened -- yes, ruining the view from the room where
Jyze first burst into being). And I didn't want to risk
arousing anyone's suspicions by driving farther up.

     Is Lady U still living there? I couldn't really
tell. Our old car wasn't around, but of course the lady
might've been out somewhere. Our old mailbox still had
no name on it, but it did sport a new newspaper box --
and not for a newspaper I'd expect her to be interested
in reading. But has she perhaps taken in some boarders?
Coworkers from the former camera factory maybe? Parked
among the vehicles was a trailer bearing a fairly large
power boat. Would any of those coworkers have that kind
of money? My hunch is her family's sold the place and
she's moved on, either to an apartment in a nearby town
or possibly to one of the half-dozen cities in other

states she used to talk about moving to or, likeliest of
all, back home. But the look of my old study -- the way
that single string of Christmas lights was hung, just as
a very similar string was hanging right there for most
of my years living in that house -- makes me wonder.

     Maybe I'll take another look around during the next
trip over, perhaps as early as this weekend. I'd also
like to see if my writing shed (prior location of the
B-2 loft) is still standing. And if it is, what kind of
shape is it in? I put hundreds of hours into building
that thing and fitting it out! This time I didn't
advance far enough up the driveway to view its site in
the backyard.

     Not much else looked different over there. Other
than in our own yard I noticed not a single change in
the entire town. On the way back I stopped for an ice-
cream cone at the usual drive-in near the bridge; for
what it's worth, the cone cost the same and tasted the
same. On the other hand the distances seemed much
greater: it was hard to believe I could've regularly
bicycled all those miles over all those nasty hills to
and from the ferry dock. I also had a sudden vision of
myself as being touchingly young and innocent back then
-- though of course that's nonsense. It was a stormy
full-moon early evening, big black clouds racing along,
the moon winking from behind shifting veils. The drive
itself brought back the period of lengthy round trips
which started up just two years ago last month, first
the ones to the storage unit ten miles to the north,
later the ones fifty miles down and around to the city.

     (And though I shouldn't be venturing comparisons,
and over these two years I've felt plenty of belated
pangs from the breakup with Lady U and the loss of the
life we had together for so long, I can't help but think
-- and did so over and over during this trip -- how much
better off I am now, happier, feeling incredibly lucky
and fortunate, delighted with almost every aspect of my
new life as it comes into what I take to be long-term
focus. The twists and turns, the surprises of the past
several years -- it's all just boggling. That was

the main mood of the trip: bogglement. -- And for all
these reasons I'm doubly glad I took the extra time to
check out the old stomping grounds. Doing this turned
out to have the feel of a "passages" ritual consecrating
my move into a new era.)

   Oh these warm Christmas bulbs. Ah such fine
ironies. Ooh such bittersweet sorrows. Ooh-ooh such
dazzling new delights.

   Got me a new lover who can dig me in a way no one
else can or could, now or before or ever. One who
fascinates me endlessly and I believe will keep on doing
so always. One who can love me up in ways I never
dreamed of (and also, just as good or better, in ways I
have dreamed of). So bogglement, yeah. Craziness.
Lovestruckness! I'm feelin' it as never before. Slap
me, I gotta be hallucinating.

   Well okay, true, I'm still a sexual flop with this
new lover. Pretty much. Doggedly I must once again
note this sorry fact. But also note she's still hanging
in there too, albeit also doggedly at times. And I do
believe we'll keep getting after it until we finally get
it (on) right. Or if not, as close as can be.
Meanwhile, wild loving anyway. More and more. Go
figure.

   -- Sound of the rain. Popcornlike, almost, as so
often before, on the windows, plus a steady loud cascade
of runoff splashing on concrete just outside. (Haven't
gotten around to opening the blinds on my courtyard
windows in weeks.) (This straggly old Santa Claus
fuchsia here, it'll soon be trying to make a go of it
outdoors on the balcony at our new place on south hill.
Perhaps in gala anticipation, this eighter alone it's
produced three new blooms and they're dangling just
above the J-book like miniature skydiving kewpies whose
parachutes have snagged on tree branches.)

   Zoelie, meanwhile, is still sporadically panicky
about the move into Deephood and perhaps even more so
about the Deep himself. "For my whole life up to now,"
she reminded me yesterday, "I was like a cat on a hot
tin roof." Now all of a sudden, this mate. This one

single focus. "Zole Mate." "This guy I really didn't
think could exist -- so you shouldn't be surprised if
sometimes I seem to doubt that you do." (So of course I
warned her she'd better watch out or I might start
wondering if she's some sort of fictive character
herself -- even if one of her own creation.) (In her
love talk she's still saying things like "You really do
love me, you love to put your hands on me, you love to
fuck me, you love to hear me whisper and sing in your
ear, you ache to have my nipples pressing against your
back....") (Also a weepy night. An upwelling of fear
that "the goddess" would punish her for being too happy.
I'd surely be smote down as were Manny, Ruth, Julie K.)
     My role here for the move: the rock. We'll be
fine, honey! Fer chrissake, we're not a coupla kids,
we've been around the block a few thousand times!
-- Yet in a way she hasn't been around it at all. Not
this block. Sexually, even, she hasn't, or not exactly.
As she frequently points out, for her sex has almost
always been "pretty much a weekend deal." The six-month
shack-up with Arvin was the main exception, but she
insists she's repressed all memory of that period except
for a few sudden flashbacks to keep her (and me) honest.
So now she finds it hard to get used to the notion of
constant availability. "There's always tomorrow if it
doesn't happen tonight!" -- But she does "get it" that
I'm not freaked out by her stupendous lustiness. And
I'm not. She always wants to get it on! And I love it!
And even knowing this she's still astounded that I do!
     -- So a look around. Yes yes yes, I'll miss this
place and I'll miss my solitudinous B-2 life. The
"night paper" from the far coast arriving at two a.m.
The endless sad dramas unfolding in the alley right
outside my windows. The freighters and ferries and tour
boats and many other kinds of vessels chugging across
the narrow slice of saltwater harbor visible to the west
between buildings. The many, many hours of wallballing
and nerfhooping, unthinkable anywhere else in a
building like this except on the bottom floor with only
crawl space and concrete beneath. The books and

journals and newspapers stacked perilously high for so
long on the couch opposite this chair yet endangering
no one except me. The chair itself, ratty old green
armchair with cheapo rugs safety-pinned in place to
cover most, but definitely not all, of the worn spots.

    -- All right, that's it, hunger pangs have grown to
lion-house roars. Time to feed my face. Then must
trudge off to work. Maybe come back for a second jyze
round later, or maybe not. See how it goes. (See what
I've left out here -- probably a lot.)
                    *   *
    -- Checking to make sure these kiri ribbons are
hanging just right. Now they are. And here's a
Christmas cup of blush wine, the kind I keep on hand
these days because Z likes the stuff and to me the
distinctions between wines are scarcely worth a thought
(and for sure they're not anything I'd want to be known
for quibbling about). At a few minutes before two a.m.

    I have two standard ways of walking home at night
and in two weeks both will be history. The walk from
the hideaway straight up the "edge road" is one, the
zigzag walk from the scope office down the "very high
road," then the "high road," then the "middle road" is
the other (and was tonight's). Both routes are a little
risky after the last stores close at ten p.m. and quite
a lot risky after the bars close at two a.m. To an
extent I like facing the risk and I'll surely miss the
walks, especially now having safely survived them almost
all the way to the end (knock on wood -- and I'll note
the loft in its current partially unballasted state
would probably sway a bit if I actually did knock on
it). The walk to the new place on south hill would also
be risky -- even more so, I'd say -- but I won't be
making it, or at least not late at night. The era of
fast-moving, hyper-alert nocturnal treks looks to be
just about over. Now my survival matters to someone
else and so I'll be busing home during the high-risk
hours. (And at other hours I'll be doing lots of other
things I wouldn't otherwise be doing except to please Z,
such as offering myself up for medical mauling as part

of the city's health plan -- which, however, I'll be
joining at little financial cost to myself, which is to
say: as Z's Deep.)

The matter of what will, might, should be happening
next year, better to hold off on jyzing about it. What
the new digs are like, postpone that too. This is the
year of Peak Prime Time, year of jyze courtship and of
jyzing around B-2, year of JAMR and JIRT and JIFT and
TJITR and JAZ and JIL ("JAZ'n'JIL roll down that Stage
III hill"), and these themes ought to prevail, if
possible, until the end.

-- Tonight's call to Z found her in a juiced-up
state. For one thing she's about to interview for a
promotion (as Jess P. and Leola J. are also doing this
week, but for different jobs; so it's a high-tension
week across the whole support network). For another
she's about to move in with a man. And what's more,
with a male Cawkamamie of near-impeccable USAn burbazoid
invader/settler colonial/neocolonial extraction. Talk
about things being out of control! -- But tonight her
take on the Deep move-in was different: "This may sound
Pollyannaish, but it occurred to me why be stressed?
why not be excited?"

Time now for one last news capsule on a Z friend
who's also my friend. Well, but can I still count Aida
as a friend? Maybe this too should be a question for
next year. In any event, she's gone now, on the long-
delayed trip to Indonesia to visit her older sister and
then onward to the Philippines to visit the younger one
(and the families of both to be sure), but before
leaving she and Z tangled several more times. Sessions
with a "facilitator" are again looming. At lunch one
day, Z told me, Aida "was like a time bomb, I was afraid
she'd go off at any second." Especially irksome was the
way Aida kept prefacing everything with "I want to be
sure I'm being totally clear about this," implying all
the misunderstanding was on Z's side.

Z has always sought opinions from mutual friends
about her conflicts with Aida and lately she's been
hearing the same thing from most of them: this time it's

Aida for sure. It's no longer disputable that Aida's jealous because a man (namely me!) has come between her and her best friend. She says herself she feels -- despite Z's many efforts to show her otherwise -- she feels, yes, "abandoned" by her. Healing will take time. Meanwhile Z and I are girding for new incidents when Aida returns.

Z has also concluded that Aida's now feeling she "messed up" in divorcing Tom but is not willing to face up to it. In Z's view the training she and Aida both received at the leadership institute, with its strong emphasis on individuality and self-assertion and confrontation, had much to do with Aida's decision to divorce. (She also thinks that same training provoked Lee M. into separating from Carol. That saga, by the way, has taken a turn for the worse: Carol "has gone into rage" and is refusing to let Lee see Sylvie, their ten-year-old daughter.)

Yeah, I'm glad I went head-to-head with Z on the institute's psych stuff right from the start. Now she's come around to sharing some of my views on it. Not all by any means but enough that we can maintain a kind of precariously balanced mutual understanding on relevant matters. (Or am I blathering here? Maybe it's just that we're both less defensive now.)

-- And it's still the peak of our own high-stress season. The double countdown, Christmas and move-in, goes right on ticking. Z and I are passing up most of the holiday invites, the main exception being an evening with Kat and Betty this coming weekend before they leave for Gramma's farm back in so-called flyover country. Z's newest anxiety, brought on by an accident her office friend Craig A. suffered while working alone with power tools in his basement, is that I'll maim myself while taking down the loft. She'd like me to seek Wei or Jess's help with the heavy work. Yeek! Love, how it can cost! How it can pinch! But I'm not saying I can't take a few costs and pinches for the cause. Cost away! Pinch away!

44

Christmas Day. Z's dinette table with the great
view of the lake and the hills and the downtown skyline,
all of that now shortly after dusk just a huge amorphous
mass of twinkling lights -- but still quite a sight. At
the moment Z's on the phone long-distance with her half-
sister, Camilla. "Why am I moving? I told you, we're
moving in together!" (Yes, real-time dialogue! This is
JIRT! And it has been from word one, page one!)
An apartment chock-a-block with cardboard boxes.
It's always been an obstacle course around here (and I
suspect the story will be the same at our new place) so
it doesn't seem all that different. But it is.
Everything's different. This is for real. Another new
life coming up, and especially for Z. I've been living
alone less than two years; for her it's been more like
fifteen. Or more than double that if you set aside the
one brief exception (Arvin) and the numerous nonintimate
housemates of the pre- and immediately post-Arvin era.
The table piled high with gifts. Z's new lamp with
its brightly colored patchwork "Shade of Hidden Mush"
(made by me!) lighting up the jyze clearing from a shaky
boxtop perch. A cloth Christmas tree (hers) thrusting
up behind it. A couple of newspapers (today's), a box
of fig bars, a cup of java, all of which I just chased
halfway around the north end in the Z-mobile to find.
The stainless-steel locket Z gave me containing
tiny photos of herself from girlhood and "superbabe"
days -- right here, around my neck. Hanging from the
small bookcase, the paper Christmas stockings she made
for us at the last minute upon learning that stockings

always featured in my own family's rites (they didn't in
hers). On the Zoelie Trope next to the bed around the
corner, an amusing new loop put together by her
featuring the two of us alternately leaning down to lick
the same vanilla cone over and over and over (worked up
from photos taken at the party for Nick last summer).
And in my bag, right here for safekeeping, a "ticket"
for her big gift to me: a jazz-singing concert she'll be
performing for just one person -- the J-slinger himself!
It's scheduled for January 10th at eight p.m., and she's
lined up a piano accompanist for the occasion and
they've been rehearsing for weeks -- on top of all the
other things she's been doing in this season of maxed-
out frenzy!

*

A brief pause there while we tried to tweak the CD
player back into action. And succeeded! -- Now she's
taking a break from heating up tonight's dinner which
we'll be carrying over on foot to Jess and Gwen's in an
hour or so ("like a step dinner with only one step").
Flipping through today's newspapers at her usual
breakneck speed. The same Taj-like singer we heard at
the zoo last summer is moaning from the stereo speakers
about the woman who's his "perpetual blues machine."
-- For whom Z's the antithesis, I whisper in her ear,
"perpetual joy machine." -- But it does sound a bit
over the top and also a touch mechanistic, okay, yeah.
But still: how it is.

How it is! What fantastic good fortune! For sure
we oughta be honing that "gratitude attitude" (as she
said too, maybe even more amazed than I am -- that the
"Z&G Story" continues to insist on being for real -- and
we're only just getting started!).

Think of our separate Christmases a year ago. Over
her decades as a single woman living alone she'd come to
dread this holiday most of all (though Thanksgiving and
New Year's came close) for the "pressure" it focused so
sharply on her. Now, suddenly, this. Blink blink.

Family Christmases of long ago. Now it's easier
reminiscing for both of us. Hers, at four a.m. she'd

550

awaken her parents and they'd tell her to go ahead and
start opening presents and would finally straggle in
when she'd torn halfway through the pile. And her
father would always cook the big holiday meal.

My pile for her this year, I worked maniacally to
put it together. Nine items, with the last -- the set
of "jyze earrings" -- finished up at warp speed after
she called at nine p.m. last night, Christmas Eve, to
say she couldn't wait, she was on the way over an hour
early. Everything's either handmade or hand-decorated
except for the controversial big gift, the name-brand
leather shoulder bag. (She suspects it's either "hot,"
as in sold on the street, or somehow associated with
Lady U. I insist it's neither of those and promise to
tell her the true story someday. "Take it on trust, yea
or nay." She gave a queasy yea.)

-- Last jyze in this apartment. One of our two
"early love nests" as I fully expect we'll be seeing
them one day, B-2 and 401. Ah the memories! The
notorious haircut: I was squirming away on this very
chair as she madly hacked off my locks. And she was
squirming on this very chair herself the evening after
our big pocket-park fight (where I was the one who was
the mad hacker, at least as she saw it) when we got high
on cinsault and suddenly were all over each other,
mutually agog.

The slumpy red couch over there. The bed with its
creaky futon frame and skimpy futon mattress. The Z-
trope ever ready to spin out wacky new intrigues. The
knee-high-to-hip-high stacks of books, papers, catalogs,
art goods, clothes, lord only knows what-all. The "G"
kiri ribbon I sent her still dangling up there with its
gold balls on brilliant purple and blue square panels,
even now gently shimmying in the draft from the balcony
door (it's cracked open to vent the heat from the oven
-- the kitchen fan's broken). My green plastic stack-
box of clothes in her storage/dressing bedroom. My one
drawer in her small plastic bathroom chest. Toothbrush
in her glass. Jar of peanut butter in one of her open
and mostly empty kitchen cupboards (probably the only

nonorganic food item in the whole apartment, excepting
the fig bars, and they're almost gone now).

"Mush, mush, and more mush." -- That's me talking
out loud, replying to her question about what I'm laying
down in here. -- And it's pretty much the same thing
I'd be laying down by voice if I were stetched out next
to her over there, whispering in her ear.

(Footnote of note: this sexiest, most voluptuous of
loves I've ever known or heard about or read about or
even imagined, is it consummated yet? No it's not. All
but certainly now the consummation story will carry over
into the new year. Though of course the effectuation of
the consummation, if I may say it thus, would still be
the perfect way to cap off the year. But -- am I up to
such an effectuation? Chances are slim but -- maybe.)

Made her a "Pillow Talk" pillowcase bearing a few
dozen raunchy quotes from our time together. Made her a
"portable meditation kit" featuring a tiny blue ceramic
hippo emblazoned with pithy bits of jyze wisdom.

We've been over to the new apartment only twice
more. The first time was to write up the required
inventory of its flaws, of which we found a surprising
number, but mostly minor (the worst being a fist-size
hole bashed through a bedroom door; during our first
visit it had been covered up with posters). The second
was to perform a ritual solstice housewarming. With Kat
and Betty in the lead, the four of us paraded through
the empty rooms brandishing sage "torches." Beforehand
Z had sprinkled baking powder on all the rugs (to let
any hidden mold know she meant business); for this
reason the procession seemed appropriately seasonal, as
if through snowy fields.

Friday night Z and I and her leadership-institute
friend Irene joined Kat and Betty for a holiday dinner
at a restaurant across the harbor. Kat opened a stack
of presents from all of us, including a yo-yo and face-
painting and fingernail-painting kits from me. Her
favorite was a little game-playing computer from Irene,
who works with kids vocationally and knows what's hot
with them and also plays a mean computer game herself,

as she demonstrated for Kat with the rest of us looking on and marveling (true!).

The next morning Z and I again drove Kat and Betty to the airport. When they return early next week we'll be throwing another party (Betty's birthday is December 29th) and I'll be giving them both make-your-own-jyzebook kits. (I still have the same set of four kits, including one each for Z and brother Rob, and I didn't want Irene to feel left out, so I withheld them from the dinner party.)

Sent out more than thirty Christmas cards this year, quite possibly my all-time record. Most went to selected members of Z's "network." (No doubt on some days I'll regret being part of this network myself. But I think on most not.) All the cards featured "Dance of the Flame-Red Dreamsicles." So far no one's asked what the heck this is all about (as if I could tell them).

Seven or eight cards came in for me alone (as opposed to me and Z), mostly in the past few days. I've been so frazzled I haven't even opened some of them yet. Jim Q., Tom T., cousin Kar, aunts Shar and Shel, brothers Rob and Jeff came through. Sister Barb didn't. (It was just a year ago yesterday I last talked with Barb. It appears more and more likely we'll not be attempting a rapprochement anytime soon. This is the year I lost a sister but gained a lover who in some ways -- but not the explosively divisive ones -- is quite a lot like her.)

*

-- Word's just in by phone: Jess and Gwen are back from snowboarding. We're about to step on down the road.

(But what a fine Christmas. Merriest for me in a long time and maybe ever. -- And I haven't even mentioned yet the Last Chance Romance gag I pulled on Z at her office. One of my all-time best!)

*   *

Next day now, and it's certainly apt that this is Boxing Day. So far this afternoon I've filled up nine double-strength book cartons and I'm only beginning.
-- Except I have to stop at five o'clock because Z's

553

picking me up at quarter after. We'll drop off a load
of these boxes at the new apartment on the way over to
Rob and Gail's for dinner.

Z called a few minutes ago. "You still love me? I
still think you're one of a kind. You still love me?
Was I too easy? Can we be flexible about this moving
stuff? You still love me?" All for laughs but with
some authentic panic mixed in, and not just on her side.
How the hell am I gonna do all this packing and
dismantling and cleaning in just five days?

This loft, for one thing. Right now I'm lying atop
it for probably the last time. Tonight I'll be sleeping
at Z's, tomorrow it'll be coming down (as much as can be
dismantled in one day with a chain saw). It's even
shakier now with almost all the book-ballast gone from
the shelves below; a vigorous stroke of the J-stick is
enough to make the shadows quiver and the boards creak.
(Looking down I see lots and lots of partially full
brown cardboard boxes, something like glancing into the
sub-basement of a department store.) And here's the Z
kiri ribbon, still undulating beneath its ceiling
sprinkler nozzle attachment after all these months. As
is also apt: it represents the force which is pulling me
right out of this apartment, right out of this life.
For Z I'm giving it all up. And I thought I'd be holed
up here the rest of my days!

So why do I love this funky old loft so much?
Well, for one thing, because I designed and built it
myself. And because it's made entirely of solid
unfinished wood, mainly two-by's and four-by's. And
because it's been so adaptable for so long -- this being
its third majorly altered incarnation in the past dozen
years. But most of all because it seems to symbolize
some of my most absurd romantic notions: love and sleep
up here (with a lamp for reading, a radio for music),
writing and editing and art stuff down below (with walls
of books and old protojyze and other writings of my own
enclosing the built-in desk) -- and all integrated into
a single unique, not to say astounding, structure.

-- Phone rings down below, right now. I listen to

[Glennarian Rollover Jyze]

my own taped voice for what may be the last time ever
("Message for the J-slinger? ...at the tone.") and then
Z's live: "Hi you. Will you help me move my computer
boxes on Sunday, pretty please, pretty please? ...Talk
to you later." It has me remembering those calls of
hers back in March and April when I was leaving the
answering-machine volume on high while sleeping up here
-- and scrambling down naked to take her meltdown call
about my ill-fitting blue canvas shirt. (It's hard to
keep the calls separate at this distance. And soon, of
course, it'll be even harder as mnemonic cues vanish. A
strong sense right now of "History in the Making," or
maybe call it the blanking-out of true memory -- or
rather what seems to be, or seems to approach, true
memory. -- Yipe, the urge to go Profound with a capital
P, it's harder and harder to resist as the deadline
looms ever closer on Z and me going live-together Deep.)
     The ceiling looms too, just inches above my head.
In the early days I worried about sounds from up there
keeping me awake, but as it turned out the bigger issue
was sounds from down here keeping whoever was up there
awake. Also it turned out I was dead wrong to think the
low headroom here wouldn't make any difference to my
lovelife because I wouldn't have one anyway.
     Last night Z had bad dreams. The worst of them:
I'd broken up with her and then her longtime friend
Paula refused to be her new lover. "But then I woke up
and you were right there and it was okay." This morning
an hour of forbidden-fruit nookie when we should've been
devoting every minute to packing. "Why is it I just
can't get enough? Why do you make me insatiable?" We
seriously explored this mystery for the umpteenth time
(and it never ceases to intrigue). (And at the last
moment, after the usual plethora of comes for her, one
finally arrived for me, the first of the Christmas stay:
but of course not while inside her.) (And over the
weekend, two more for me, oddly enough about fifteen
minutes apart, and both following shortly upon a mini-
meltdown over her difficulties in getting me up and off.
"I can't wait until January 1st when I can let myself

have a real meltdown about this." -- Hopefully I
succeeded in dissuading her from even imagining any such
thing. A day later she called proclaiming several times
and in different ways she was finally starting to grok
it: she's happy with me, she knows I love her, why not
just accept whatever happens with us sexwise.) (But who
could blame her if she couldn't and didn't?)

     -- So I'd better stop now. Or...well, first
mention the dinner at Jess and Gwen's. They'd been
snowboarding all day and so were red-eyed and moving
stiffly. By the time we arrived they'd already guzzled
lots of wine. And probably for this reason they were
much more relaxed than I've seen them before: physically
affectionate with each other in front of us and talking
easily about themselves as "queer grrrls," "dykes on
bikes," "dykes on boards" -- dykes just about everywhere.
For hours we lolled around the dining-room table
swapping stories while nibbling away at the big meal
orchestrated by Z. Gwen became lewdly fascinated with
the bonobo book -- mainly in order to provoke Jess, I
suspect, at which she succeeded (briefly). The two of
them gave us a Feng Shui kit as a Christmas gift. A
quick browse through it confirmed our new apartment is
set up poorly in almost every conceivable way.

     Yipe yipe yipe -- gotta jump in the shower and do
some more packing too.

     Just one more jyze session this year. And maybe
just one more of this type ever, or at least for a year.
Next year jyze will be going random, or better to say
that's my thought as of this moment. A new kind of
experiment. -- And in that last entry five or six days
from now this room won't be recognizable as a lived-in
place. This is the last one for that. Cupboards,
fridge, drawers -- still full. Dirty dishes in the
sink. My trusty green armchair down below, it'll be
gone. The hardy redwood worktable too. The even
hardier hardy fuchsias. The magnificent wallful --
actually two wallfuls -- of jyze posters. All of it
will be history, including maybe even (if I'm moving
fast enough and with enough elbow power) the grease

shadows that will soon be revealing themselves on those
same walls.

    Well yeah so, of course. New life means demise of
old life, big deal. Lots of what's here now we'll still
have over at the new place, including even some detached
pieces of this loft (quite big pieces to serve as floor-
to-ceiling bookcases). Just indulging in a few moments
of nostalgia, the usual farewell thing, I'm not even
ashamed except maybe a little. (And am excited a lot
more.) (And also want to mention, I haven't worn the
blue canvas shirt a single time since Z so dramatically
panned it last spring but I'm not throwing it out either.
She hasn't seen the last of that shirt. Someday she's
gonna appreciate that shirt -- or else!)

--------·

45

--------·

    'Long about midnight, or to be exact six after, as
the final day of the year edges in. Less scoping than
expected tonight and now I'm thinking this might be my
best chance for a last jyze. Last of the year, last of
the "tripolar" era. A sappy farewell to good old B-2.
    And am appropriately situated. Kneeling on the
threefold blue gym mat where one corner of the loft used
to stand. The square indentations left in the carpet by
the four-by-four uprights are still faintly visible
through a thick layer of sawdust on all sides, like
footprints in yesterday's snow after a light new fall.
Lodged within my visual periphery down here at knee
level are a lamp, a clock, a celebratory glass of
bourbon on the rocks, a phone, a red toolbox, a hammer
and hand saw -- all made oddly vivid by being so out of
place. Also lots of empty boxes, piles of clothes, a

mound of scrap lumber, a few planks leaning against the
wall. And right here is the large wool "shawl" (more a
scarf, I'd say, muslinlike and almost transparent) which
the fabulous Z-woman kept stashed near the top of the
loft stairs so she could stay warm during her climb-
downs to pee (but to my recollection she used it only
once or twice). "Nude Descending Staircase" -- and how
grand the descents! And likewise the ascents! Together
they sum up the whole era. And also sum up, by that
same higher math, what's brought it to an end.

Tremendous good luck, that's what. I've been
thinking about it and I still can't dope out any better
explanation. Yes, it's true, along the way I came to
realize love matters more to me than art, than politics,
than having a fine place to live. I found (again) that
over the long haul solitude is damn tough to take. Yet
even so I believe I would've continued taking it this
time around had anyone but Zoelie B. been the one to
come along. If not for her I'd probably have settled
for a minimally modified loneliness. Loneliness with
occasional relief. "Renunciation lite." I'd've
convinced myself it was the best I could do. And in a
Z-less world it might well have been just that.

Or maybe I wouldn't've convinced myself. Maybe I'd
simply have remained an out-and-out isolato and every
bit as miserable if not more so. I wouldn't put it
past myself.

Instead: spectacular good fortune.

Two days ago we officially moved. As it happened
the date was gestationally perfect, humanly speaking: it
fell nine months to the day after our first meeting.
Certainly that's a respectable courtship period. Randy
the mover told me it was the fifth or sixth time he's
done the deed for Z and each time it's taken an hour
longer. This one required an extra hour beyond that, he
said, because it included some of my stuff. Since this
move took only six hours it appears Randy's math is a
little off, but he's obviously right in a larger sense:
Z is a hoarder. Our new place is stuffed to the ceiling
in every room, and mostly with her boxes -- many of

[Glennarian Rollover Jyze]

which haven't been opened since her last move two years
ago, and a few, she confessed, since the move before
that.

    Stressful week. For a couple of days there I was
afraid the loft would never come down in time. Would I
be forced to stay on in B-2 beyond the deadline and pay
a big penalty? But then I stumbled upon the "Sawzall"
(jyze-rules exception!) at a rental shop. And when
even that amazing tool proved less than a total
solution, friend Jess came through, just as Z said she
would. A former construction worker and a dynamite
hammer swinger, she dropped by the other evening and
the two of us working together were able to bring the
monster down -- or dismantle it, rather. And then she
drove off with a big load of free lumber worth several
hundred bucks. A steal -- for both of us. -- And I
credit Z with two big assists on this: for suggesting
the idea in the first place and then pushing for it
against my mulish resistance.

    I managed to salvage two large bookcases and most
of the makings for a third. I'm plenty happy.

    Meanwhile I've been going like crazy on very little
sleep and still am. Stress! For Z it's produced a few
somatic embarrassments including a little "poop-in-my-
pants" episode as well as an aggravation of an old
sacroiliac injury. Today for a while she thought she
was coming down with stomach flu. But we're still
functioning well together. I even like having the
chance to take up her part of the load at times. Be a
workhorse. Show I care. Show what a reliable dude
she's peeping up with and all that. (She confessed the
reason she held my relative youth against me early on --
in winnowing down the "callback list" of repliers to her
original ad -- was that she wanted to be a "trophy" for
the chosen candidate and therefore wanted someone older.
She thought. But she was soon convinced otherwise; she
saw she could be a trophy for me too. And now it's
become a standard part of our "origins myth": we're
mutual trophies.)

    -- And last night, our first in the new place, we

"bonoboed" most of the night despite our exhaustion and
her various injuries and illnesses, including a
possible herpes outbreak -- and thus no real copulation
could even be attempted. But what we did do we call
copulation anyway, just as before. And why not?
-- Meanwhile an article on so-called male menopause
may've persuaded her to go a little easier on me for my
continuing flunks of the peter-meter test, and therefore
maybe improved my chances of ultimately passing it.
-- But no, I haven't passed it yet. And won't in this
year's jyze, clearly, since she'll be in quarantine a
few more days. Just as predicted, it's become another
matter for next year. And I'd say it might even be
useful then, if for no other reason than to maintain a
certain degree of thematic jyze continuity, albeit
manifesting at random intervals.

   -- But I did manage to shoot off last night, and
quite impressively too, I must say, and that was right
here, as we awoke from a nap taken on this very gym mat
-- and as we were policing the area for stray gobs of G-
essence the door buzzer rang and it was Jess, come to
swing her hammer.

   Jazz playing. A long row of stacked boxes and
bundles of various makeshift sorts, looking all together
somewhat like a straggly soup-kitchen line, hugs the
hallway wall outside the door to B-2. I'll be
schlepping the whole motley queue out to the T-mobile
at two a.m. or so. The dumpster will be handily close-
by as a repository for whatever won't fit into the
wagon. Let's hope no major New Year's Eve dope deals
are going down out there. (My old portable stereo is
still here, the only piece of original furniture
remaining. Soon we'll be lugging ol' Mom's battleship-
size console over to the new place from the storage
unit and this stereo will get the heave-ho after more
than two decades of yeoman service.)

   And other lives go on. Amazing! June Q. survived
a breast cancer scare; a couple of days after the biopsy
came up benign she invited a group of us out to a
celebratory dinner (where we met her two stalwart sons,

[Glennarian Rollover Jyze]

Adam and Mike, both home from school for the holidays).
The tempestuous Aida, meanwhile, sent Z a puzzling gift
card from Djakarta ('nuff said for now). Lee M. and
Carol's separation has taken a sharply hostile turn,
causing Lee to weep copiously during a phone talk with Z
("He said what gets him most is he's not used to being
seen as the villain"). And...lots of other stuff. The
network. Things always going on. It's a done deal now:
I'm a node. And not just any node: a major one. A very
major one. In fact the most major -- nodiest -- of them
all from the point of view of the Z node (she told me so
herself). And I expect to be even more major for her
next year. And thereafter. As we romp and tumble down
that slippery Stage III slope.

        (Time to stretch. Jyzing in this doggy posture
with all fours on the mat -- as I've been doing all
along in this entry -- has its limits, as in cramps,
just as it did way back in January when I tried it for
the first time. And I'm stiff and sore anyway from all
the lifting and carrying, including a whole afternoon
of assisting Randy and Stu (his cynical No. 2 guy who's
temporarily moved in with him -- with Randy -- since
Randy's wife and kid have moved out: all day Z and I
were overhearing their surprisingly bitchy domestic
grumblings, like obscene excerpts from "The Odd Couple"
-- a one-man version of which I myself am officially
about to cease to be! -- and as they grumbled, Z and I
were glancing meaningfully at each other as if to say,
hmm, sure do hope we'll never be sounding like that).)
                          *
        Possibly I should call it quits for the year right
here. I stand up and stagger -- conclude I just might
be fading fast. But then I have every right to be doing
so. What a day! What a week! What a year! (Today
started out at six a.m. with a last quick bout of
"nooking" -- or whatever; we'll get the lingo down one
of these days -- and it's been go-go-go ever since. Z
picked up a traffic ticket for an illegal left turn just
down the hill from our new place; happily she refused to
take it as a bad omen for us. The rental guy failed to

show up on time to open the shop and we lost a crucial
hour returning the splendid sawing tool to another
outlet. Then we did breakfast at a certain cafe very
familiar to both of us from prior lives -- an event
which on any other occasion jyze would likely be
anguishing over at length. Then later, dinner at the
toney pub across the street from the B-2 building --
likening ourselves to the "eccentrically rich" in our
torn and dirty moving rags. In between, nonstop packing
and hauling. The more I think of it the more I'm
impressed. Post-peak-prime dude's still a mighty
mover!)

So this is it then? Farewell to an era? This the
very last jyze jaunt around the room? Seems likely.
I'd prefer to be addressing matters a lot more
thoughtfully but then -- it's just not in the cards
tonight. Even if I had oodles of free time it wouldn't
be. My focus is no longer here. You were a good old
isolato crib, B-2, but in the end you done broke down.
For me. For Jyzer G. For all of us Jyzer Gs cooped up
in this one deteriorating corpus. We're moving on.
WHOOO-OOO-EEE!

END